W9-BKZ-722

Praise for *The Well of Ascension*

"Sanderson's hallmark is to take traditional high-fantasy tropes and turn them upside down, and he doesn't disappoint here. Vin's a beautifully realized protagonist whose struggles are wonderfully written and, as always, the world-building is unusual and compelling." —*Romantic Times BOOKreviews*

"This entertaining read will especially please those who always wanted to know what happened after the good guys won." —*Publishers Weekly*

"Vin's struggles with love and power inject the human element into Sanderson's engaging epic." —*Booklist*

Praise for *Mistborn*

"*Mistborn* utilizes a well thought-out system of magic. It also has a great cast of believable characters, a plausible world, an intriguing political system, and a very satisfying ending. Highly recommended to anyone hungry for a good read." —Robin Hobb

"Brandon Sanderson made a sensational debut with *Elantris* as another in the recent crop of fantasy writers who use familiar epic forms to produce far-from-generic results. . . . *Mistborn* examines the makings of hero and villain, legend and myth, as seemingly different stages of what may be the same process. . . . [It's an] enjoyable, adventurous read . . . [and] along the way to the grand finale, anyone who cares to can learn a great deal about the underside of power."

—Faren Miller, *Locus*

continued . . .

Praise for Brandon Sanderson

"Brandon Sanderson is the real thing—an exciting story-teller with a unique and powerful vision."
—David Farland

"It's rare for a fiction writer to have much under-standing of how leadership works, how communities form, and how love really takes root in the human heart. Sanderson is astonishingly wise."
—Orson Scott Card

THE WELL OF ASCENSION

Tor Books by Brandon Sanderson

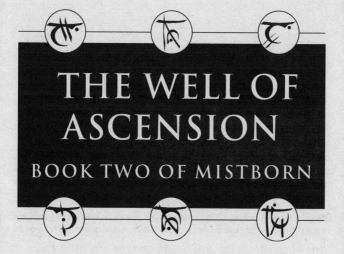

THE WELL OF ASCENSION

BOOK TWO OF MISTBORN

BRANDON SANDERSON

A TOM DOHERTY ASSOCIATES BOOK
NEW YORK

NOTE: If you purchased this book without a cover you should be aware that this book is stolen property. It was reported as "unsold and destroyed" to the publisher, and neither the author nor the publisher has received any payment for this "stripped book."

This is a work of fiction. All the characters, orgnizations, and events portrayed in this book are either products of the author's imagination or are used fictitiously.

THE WELL OF ASCENSION: BOOK TWO OF MISTBORN

Copyright © 2007 by Brandon Sanderson

All rights reserved.

Edited by Moshe Feder

Map and ornaments by Issac Stewart

A Tor Book
Published by Tom Doherty Associates, LLC
175 Fifth Avenue
New York, NY 10010

www.tor-forge.com

Tor® is a registered trademark of Tom Doherty Associates, LLC.

ISBN 978-0-7653-5613-0

First Edition: August 2007
First Mass Market Edition: June 2008

Printed in the United States of America

0 9

FOR PHYLLIS CALL,

Who may never understand my fantasy books,
yet who taught me more about life
—and therefore writing—
than she can probably ever know

(Thanks, Grandma!)

CONTENTS

ACKNOWLEDGMENTS

First off, as always, my excellent agent, Joshua Bilmes, and editor, Moshe Feder, deserve high praise for their efforts. This book in particular required some thoughtful drafting, and they were up to the task. They have my thanks, as do their assistants, Steve Mancino (an excellent agent in his own right) and Denis Wong.

There are some other fine folks at Tor who deserve my thanks. Larry Yoder (the best sales rep in the nation) did a wonderful job selling the book. Seth Lerner, Tor's mass-market art director, is a genius at matching books to artists. And, speaking of artists, I think the amazing Christian McGrath did a brilliant job with this cover. More can be seen at christianmcgrath.com. Isaac Stewart, a good friend of mine and a fellow writer, did all of the map work and the symbols for the chapter headings. Find him at nethermore.com. Shawn Boyles is the official Mistborn Llama artist, and a great guy to boot. Check my Web site for more information. Finally, I'd like to thank the Tor publicity department—specifically Dot Lin—which has been wonderful in promoting my books and taking care of me. Thank you so much, all of you!

Another round of thanks needs to go out to my alpha readers. These tireless folks provide feedback on my novels in the early stages, dealing with all of the problems, typos, and inconsistencies before I get them worked out. In no particular order, these people are:

Ben Olsen, Krista Olsen, Nathan Goodrich, Ethan Skarstedt, Eric J. Ehlers, Jillena O'Brien, C. Lee Player, Kimball Larsen, Bryce Cundick, Janci Patterson, Heather Kirby, Sally Taylor, The Almighty Pronoun, Bradley Reneer, Holly Venable, Jimmy, Alan Layton, Janette Layton, Kaylynn ZoBell, Rick Stranger, Nate Hatfield, Daniel A. Wells, Stacy Whitman, Sarah Bylund, and Benjamin R. Olsen.

A special thanks goes to the people at the Provo Walden-books for their support. Sterling, Robin, Ashley, and the terrible duo of Steve "Bookstore Guy" Diamond and Ryan McBride (who were also alpha readers). Also, I must acknowledge my brother, Jordan, for his work on my Web site (along with Jeff Creer). Jordo also is the official "keep Brandon's head on straight" guy, with his solemn duty being to make fun of me and my books.

My mother, father, and sisters are always a wonderful help as well. If I forgot any alpha readers, I'm sorry! I'll put you in twice next time. Note, Peter Ahlstrom, I didn't forget you—I just decided to stick you in late to make you sweat a bit.

Finally, my thanks go out to my wonderful wife, whom I married during the editing process of this book. Emily, I love you!

16. LAKE TYRIAN
17. LAKE LUTHADEL
18. THE BLACK LAKE
19. RIVER SEARAN

20. NORTH SEARAN
21. SOUTH SEARAN
22. THE RIVER CHANNEREL

THE FINAL EMPIRE

1. LUTHADEL
2. PITS OF HATHSIN
3. URTEAU   4. FADEX CITY
5. TREMREDARE   6. TATHINGDWEN
7. CONVENTICLE OF SEARAN
8. MOUNT DERYTATITH, HISTORIC LOCATION OF THE WELL OF ASCENSION

THE ASHMOUNTS: 9. TYRIAN
10. ZERINAH   11. FALEAST   12. DORIEL
13. MORAG   14. KALLING   15. TORINOST

LUTH

STEEL GATE

IRON GATE

THE TWIST

HOTEL DISTRICT

OLD GATE

COMMERCIAL DI

BRONZE GATE

PART ONE

HEIR OF THE
SURVIVOR

I write these words in steel, for anything not set in metal cannot be trusted.

1

THE ARMY CREPT LIKE A dark stain across the horizon.

King Elend Venture stood motionless upon the Luthadel city wall, looking out at the enemy troops. Around him, ash fell from the sky in fat, lazy flakes. It wasn't the burnt white ash that one saw in dead coals; this was a deeper, harsher black ash. The Ashmounts had been particularly active lately.

Elend felt the ash dust his face and clothing, but he ignored it. In the distance, the bloody red sun was close to setting. It backlit the army that had come to take Elend's kingdom from him.

"How many?" Elend asked quietly.

"Fifty thousand, we think," Ham said, leaning against the parapet, beefy arms folded on the stone. Like everything in the city, the wall had been stained black by countless years of ashfalls.

"Fifty thousand soldiers . . ." Elend said, trailing off. Despite heavy recruitment, Elend barely had twenty thousand men under his command—and they were peasants with less than a year of training. Maintaining even that small number was straining his resources. If they'd been able to find the Lord Ruler's atium, perhaps things would be different. As it was, Elend's rule was in serious danger of economic disaster.

"What do you think?" Elend asked.

"I don't know, El," Ham said quietly. "Kelsier was always the one with the vision."

"But you helped him plan," Elend said. "You and the others, you were his crew. You were the ones who came up with a strategy for overthrowing the empire, then made it happen."

Ham fell silent, and Elend felt as if he knew what the man was thinking. *Kelsier was central to it all. He was the one who organized, the one who took all of the wild brainstorming and turned it into a viable operation. He was the leader. The genius.*

And he'd died a year before, on the very same day that the people—as part of his secret plan—had risen up in fury to overthrow their god emperor. Elend had taken the throne in the ensuing chaos. Now it was looking more and more like he would lose everything that Kelsier and his crew had worked so hard to accomplish. Lose it to a tyrant who might be even worse than the Lord Ruler. A petty, devious bully in "noble" form. The man who had marched his army on Luthadel.

Elend's own father, Straff Venture.

"Any chance you can . . . talk him out of attacking?" Ham asked.

"Maybe," Elend said hesitantly. "Assuming the Assembly doesn't just surrender the city."

"They close?"

"I don't know, honestly. I worry that they are. That army has frightened them, Ham." *And with good reason,* he thought. "Anyway, I have a proposal for the meeting in two days. I'll try to talk them out of doing anything rash. Dockson got back today, right?"

Ham nodded. "Just before the army's advance."

"I think we should call a meeting of the crew," Elend said. "See if we can come up with a way out of this."

"We'll still be pretty shorthanded," Ham said, rubbing his chin. "Spook isn't supposed to be back for another week, and the Lord Ruler only knows where Breeze went. We haven't had a message from him in months."

Elend sighed, shaking his head. "I can't think of anything else, Ham." He turned, staring out over the ashen landscape again. The army was lighting campfires as the sun set. Soon, the mists would appear.

I need to get back to the palace and work on that proposal, Elend thought.

"Where'd Vin run off to?" Ham asked, turning back to Elend.

Elend paused. "You know," he said, "I'm not sure."

Vin landed softly on the damp cobblestones, watching as the mists began to form around her. They puffed into existence as darkness fell, growing like tangles of translucent vines, twisting and wrapping around one another.

The great city of Luthadel was still. Even now, a year after the Lord Ruler's death and the rise of Elend's new free government, the common people stayed in their homes at night. They feared the mists, a tradition that went far deeper than the Lord Ruler's laws.

Vin slipped forward quietly, senses alert. Inside herself, as always, she burned tin and pewter. Tin enhanced her senses, making it easier for her to see in the night. Pewter made her body stronger, made her lighter on her feet. These, along with copper—which had the power to hide her use of Allomancy from others who were burning bronze—were metals that she left on almost all the time.

Some called her paranoid. She thought herself prepared. Either way, the habit had saved her life on numerous occasions.

She approached a quiet street corner and paused, peeking out. She'd never really understood *how* she burned metals; she could remember doing it for as long as she'd been alive, using Allomancy instinctively even before she was formally trained by Kelsier. It didn't really matter to her. She wasn't like Elend; she didn't need a logical explanation for everything. For Vin, it was enough that when she swallowed bits of metal, she was able to draw upon their power.

Power she appreciated, for she well knew what it was like to lack it. Even now, she was not what one would likely envision as a warrior. Slight of frame and barely five feet tall, with dark hair and pale skin, she knew she had an almost frail look about her. She no longer displayed the underfed look she had during her childhood on the streets, but she certainly wasn't someone any man would find intimidating.

She liked that. It gave her an edge—and she needed every edge she could get.

She also liked the night. During the day, Luthadel was cramped and confining despite its size. But at night the mists fell like a deep cloud. They dampened, softened, shaded. Massive keeps became shadowed mountains, and crowded tenements melted together like a chandler's rejected wares.

Vin crouched beside her building, still watching the intersection. Carefully, she reached within herself and burned steel—one of the other metals she'd swallowed earlier. Immediately, a group of translucent blue lines sprang up around her. Visible only to her eyes, the lines pointed from her chest to nearby sources of metal—all metals, no matter what type. The thickness of the lines was proportionate to the size of the metal pieces they met. Some pointed to bronze door latches, others to crude iron nails holding boards together.

She waited silently. None of the lines moved. Burning steel was an easy way to tell if someone was moving nearby. If they were wearing bits of metal, they would trail telltale moving lines of blue. Of course, that wasn't the main purpose of steel. Vin reached her hand carefully into her belt pouch and pulled out one of the many coins that sat within, muffled by cloth batting. Like all other bits of metal, this coin had a blue line extending from its center to Vin's chest.

She flipped the coin into the air, then mentally grabbed its line and—burning steel—Pushed on the coin. The bit of metal shot into the air, arcing through the mists, forced away by the Push. It plinked to the ground in the middle of the street.

The mists continued to spin. They were thick and mysterious, even to Vin. More dense than a simple fog and more constant than any normal weather pattern, they churned and flowed, making rivulets around her. Her eyes could pierce them; tin made her sight more keen. The night seemed lighter to her, the mists less thick. Yet, they were still there.

A shadow moved in the city square, responding to her coin—which she had Pushed out into the square as a signal. Vin crept forward, and recognized OreSeur the kandra. He wore a different body than he had a year ago, during the days when he had acted the part of Lord Renoux. Yet, this balding, nondescript body had now become just as familiar to Vin.

OreSeur met up with her. "Did you find what you were looking for, Mistress?" he asked, tone respectful—yet somehow still a little hostile. As always.

Vin shook her head, glancing around in the darkness. "Maybe I was wrong," she said. "Maybe I *wasn't* being followed." The acknowledgment made her a bit sad. She'd been looking forward to sparring with the Watcher again tonight. She still didn't even know who he was; the first night, she'd mistaken him for an assassin. And maybe he was. Yet, he seemed to display very little interest in Elend—and a whole lot of interest in Vin.

"We should go back to the wall," Vin decided, standing up. "Elend will be wondering where I went."

OreSeur nodded. At that moment, a burst of coins shot through the mists, spraying toward Vin.

I have begun to wonder if I am the only sane man left. Can the others see? They have been waiting so long for their hero to come—the one spoken of in Terris prophecies—that they quickly jump between conclusions, presuming that each story and legend applies to this one man.

2

VIN REACTED IMMEDIATELY, SPRINGING AWAY. She moved with incredible speed, tasseled cloak swirling as she skidded across the wet cobblestones. The coins hit the ground behind her, throwing up chips of stone, then leaving trails in the mist as they ricocheted away.

"OreSeur, go!" she snapped, though he was already fleeing toward a nearby alleyway.

Vin spun into a low crouch, hands and feet on the cool stones, Allomantic metals flaring in her stomach. She burned steel, watching the translucent blue lines appear around her. She waited, tense, watching for . . .

Another group of coins shot from the dark mists, each one trailing a blue line. Vin immediately flared steel and Pushed against the coins, deflecting them out into the darkness.

The night fell still again.

The street around her was wide—for Luthadel—though tenements rose high on either side. Mist spun lazily, making the ends of the street disappear into a haze.

A group of eight men appeared from the mists and approached. Vin smiled. She *had* been right: Someone was following her. These men weren't, however, the Watcher. They didn't have his solid grace, his sense of power. These men were something far more blunt. Assassins.

It made sense. If *she* had just arrived with an army to

conquer Luthadel, the first thing she'd have done was send in a group of Allomancers to kill Elend.

She felt a sudden pressure at her side, and she cursed as she was thrown off balance, her coin pouch jerking away from her waist. She ripped its string free, letting the enemy Allomancer Push the coins away from her. The assassins had at least one Coinshot—a Misting who had the power to burn steel and Push on metals. In fact, two of the assassins trailed blue lines pointing to coin pouches of their own. Vin considered returning the favor and Pushing their pouches away, but hesitated. No need to play her hand yet. She might need those coins.

Without coins of her own, she couldn't attack from a distance. However, if this was a good team, then attacking from a distance would be pointless—their Coinshots and Lurchers would be ready to deal with shot coins. Fleeing wasn't an option either. These men hadn't come for her alone; if she fled, they'd continue on to their real goal.

Nobody sent assassins to kill bodyguards. Assassins killed important men. Men like Elend Venture, king of the Central Dominance. The man she loved.

Vin flared pewter—body growing tense, alert, dangerous. *Four Thugs at the front,* she thought, eyeing the advancing men. The pewter burners would be inhumanly strong, capable of surviving a great deal of physical punishment. Very dangerous up close. *And the one carrying the wooden shield is a Lurcher.*

She feinted forward, causing the approaching Thugs to jump backward. Eight Mistings against one Mistborn was decent odds for them—but only if they were careful. The two Coinshots moved up the sides of the street, so that they'd be able to Push at her from both directions. The last man, standing quietly beside the Lurcher, had to be a Smoker—relatively unimportant in a fight, his purpose was to hide his team from enemy Allomancers.

Eight Mistings. Kelsier could have done it; he'd killed an Inquisitor. She wasn't Kelsier, however. She had yet to decide if that was a bad or a good thing.

Vin took a deep breath, wishing she had a bit of atium to

spare, and burned iron. This let her Pull on a nearby coin—
one of those that had been shot at her—much as steel
would have let her Push on it. She caught it, dropped it,
then jumped, making as if to Push on the coin and shoot
herself into the air.

One of the Coinshots, however, Pushed against the coin,
shooting it away. Since Allomancy would only let a person
Push directly away from—or Pull directly toward—their
body, Vin was left without a decent anchor. Pushing
against the coin would only shoot her sideways.

She dropped back to the ground.

Let them think they have me trapped, she thought,
crouching in the center of the street. The Thugs approached
a little more confidently. *Yes,* Vin thought. *I know what
you're thinking. This is the Mistborn who killed the Lord
Ruler? This scrawny thing? Can it be possible?*

I wonder the same thing myself.

The first Thug ducked in to attack, and Vin burst into
motion. Obsidian daggers flashed in the night as she
ripped them free from their sheaths, and blood sprayed
black in the darkness as she ducked beneath the Thug's
staff and slashed her weapons across his thighs.

The man cried out. The night was no longer silent.

Men cursed as Vin moved through them. The Thug's
partner attacked her—blurringly fast, his muscles fueled
by pewter. His staff whipped a tassel from Vin's mistcloak
as she threw herself to the ground, then pushed herself
back up out of a third Thug's reach.

A spray of coins flew toward her. Vin reached out and
Pushed on them. The Coinshot, however, continued to
Push—and Vin's Push smashed against his.

Pushing and Pulling metals was all about weight. And—
with the coins between them—that meant Vin's weight was
slammed against the assassin's weight. Both were tossed
backward. Vin shot out of a Thug's reach; the Coinshot fell
to the ground.

A flurry of coins came at her from the other direction.
Still tumbling in the air, Vin flared steel, giving herself an
extra burst of power. Blue lines were a jumbled mess, but
she didn't need to isolate the coins to Push them all away.

This Coinshot let go of his missiles as soon as he felt Vin's touch. The bits of metal scattered out into the mists.

Vin hit the cobblestones shoulder-first. She rolled—flaring pewter to enhance her balance—and flipped to her feet. At the same time, she burned iron and Pulled hard on the disappearing coins.

They shot back toward her. As soon as they got close, Vin jumped to the side and Pushed them toward the approaching Thugs. The coins, however, immediately veered away, twisting through the mists toward the Lurcher. He was unable to Push the coins away—like all Mistings, he only had one Allomantic power, and his was to Pull with iron.

He did this effectively, protecting the Thugs. He raised his shield and grunted from the impact as the coins hit it and bounced away.

Vin was already moving again. She ran directly for the now exposed Coinshot to her left, the one who had fallen to the ground. The man yelped in surprise, and the other Coinshot tried to distract Vin, but he was too slow.

The Coinshot died with a dagger in his chest. He was no Thug; he couldn't burn pewter to enhance his body. Vin pulled out her dagger, then yanked his pouch free. He gurgled quietly and collapsed back to the stones.

One, Vin thought, spinning, sweat flying from her brow. She now faced seven men down the corridor-like street. They probably expected her to flee. Instead, she charged.

As she got close to the Thugs, she jumped—then threw down the pouch she'd taken from the dying man. The remaining Coinshot cried out, immediately Pushing it away. Vin, however, got some lift from the coins, throwing herself in a leap directly over the heads of the Thugs.

One of them—the wounded one—had unfortunately been smart enough to remain behind to protect the Coinshot. The Thug raised his cudgel as Vin landed. She ducked his first attack, raised her dagger, and—

A blue line danced into her vision. Quick. Vin reacted immediately, twisting and Pushing against a door latch to throw herself out of the way. She hit the ground on her side, then flung herself up with one hand. She landed skidding on mist-wetted feet.

A coin hit the ground behind her, bouncing against the cobbles. It hadn't come close to hitting her. In fact, it had seemed aimed at the remaining assassin Coinshot. He'd probably been forced to Push it away.

But who had fired it?

OreSeur? Vin wondered. But, that was foolish. The kandra was no Allomancer—and besides, he wouldn't have taken the initiative. OreSeur did only what he was expressly told.

The assassin Coinshot looked equally confused. Vin glanced up, flaring tin, and was rewarded with the sight of a man standing atop a nearby building. A dark silhouette. He didn't even bother to hide.

It's him, she thought. *The Watcher.*

The Watcher remained atop his perch, offering no further interference as the Thugs rushed Vin. She cursed as she found three staves coming at her at once. She ducked one, spun around the other, then planted a dagger in the chest of the man holding the third. He stumbled backward, but didn't drop. Pewter kept him on his feet.

Why did the Watcher interfere? Vin thought as she jumped away. *Why would he shoot that coin at a Coinshot who could obviously Push it away?*

Her preoccupation with the Watcher nearly cost her her life as an unnoticed Thug charged her from the side. It was the man whose legs she'd slashed. Vin reacted just in time to dodge his blow. This, however, put her into range of the other three.

All attacked at once.

She actually managed to twist out of the way of two of the strikes. One, however, crashed into her side. The powerful blow tossed her across the street, and she collided with a shop's wooden door. She heard a crack—from the door, fortunately, and not her bones—and she slumped to the ground, daggers lost. A normal person would be dead. Her pewter-strengthened body, however, was tougher than that.

She gasped for breath, forcing herself up to her feet, and flared tin. The metal enhanced her senses—including her sense of pain—and the sudden shock cleared her mind.

Her side ached where she'd been struck. But she couldn't stop. Not with a Thug charging her, swinging his staff in an overhead blow.

Crouching before the doorway, Vin flared pewter and caught the staff in both hands. She growled, pulling back her left hand, then cracking her fist against the weapon, shattering the fine hardwood in a single blow. The Thug stumbled, and Vin smashed her half of the staff across his eyes.

Though dazed, he stayed on his feet. *Can't fight the Thugs,* she thought. *I have to keep moving.*

She dashed to the side, ignoring her pain. The Thugs tried to follow, but she was lighter, thinner, and—much more important—faster. She circled them, coming back toward the Coinshot, Smoker, and Lurcher. A wounded Thug had again retreated to protect these men.

As Vin approached, the Coinshot threw a double handful of coins at her. Vin Pushed the coins away, then reached out and Pulled on the ones in the bag at the man's waist.

The Coinshot grunted as the bag whipped toward Vin. It was tied by a short tether to his waist, and the pull of her weight jerked him forward. The Thug grabbed and steadied him.

And since her anchor couldn't move, Vin was instead Pulled toward it. She flared her iron, flying through the air, raising a fist. The Coinshot cried out and he pulled a tie to free the bag.

Too late. Vin's momentum carried her forward, and she drove her fist into the Coinshot's cheek as she passed. His head spun around, neck snapping. As Vin landed, she brought her elbow up into the surprised Thug's chin, tossing him backward. Her foot followed, crashing against the Thug's neck.

Neither rose. That was three down. The discarded coin pouch fell to the ground, breaking and throwing a hundred sparkling bits of copper across the cobblestones around Vin. She ignored the throbbing in her elbow and faced down the Lurcher. He stood with his shield, looking strangely unworried.

A *crack* sounded behind her. Vin cried out, her tin-enhanced ears overreacting to the sudden sound. Pain shot through her head, and she raised hands to her ears. She'd forgotten the Smoker, who stood holding two lengths of wood, crafted to make sharp noises when pounded together.

Movements and reactions, actions and consequences— these were the essence of Allomancy. Tin made her eyes pierce the mists—giving her an edge over the assassins. However, the tin also made her ears extremely acute. The Smoker raised his sticks again. Vin growled and yanked a handful of coins off the cobblestones, then shot them at the Smoker. The Lurcher, of course, Pulled them toward him instead. They hit the shield and bounced free. And as they sprayed into the air, Vin carefully Pushed one so it fell behind him.

The man lowered his shield, unaware of the coin Vin had manipulated. Vin Pulled, whipping the single coin directly toward her—and into the back of the Lurcher's chest. He fell without a sound.

Four.

All fell still. The Thugs running toward her drew to a stop, and the Smoker lowered his sticks. They had no Coinshots and no Lurchers—nobody that could Push or Pull metal—and Vin stood amid a field of coins. If she used them, even the Thugs would fall quickly. All she had to do was—

Another coin shot through the air, fired from the Watcher's rooftop. Vin cursed, ducking. The coin, however, didn't strike her. It took the stick-holding Smoker directly in the forehead. The man toppled backward, dead.

What? Vin thought, staring at the dead man.

The Thugs charged, but Vin retreated, frowning. *Why kill the Smoker? He wasn't a threat anymore.*

Unless . . .

Vin extinguished her copper, then burned bronze, the metal that let her sense when other Allomancers were using powers nearby. She couldn't feel the Thugs burning pewter. They were still being Smoked, their Allomancy hidden.

Someone else was burning copper.

Suddenly, it all made sense. It made sense that the group

would risk attacking a full Mistborn. It made sense that the Watcher had fired at the Coinshot. It made sense that he had killed the Smoker.

Vin was in grave danger.

She only had a moment to make her decision. She did so on a hunch, but she'd grown up on the streets, a thief and a scam artist. Hunches felt more natural to her than logic ever would.

"OreSeur!" she yelled. "Go for the palace!"

It was a code, of course. Vin jumped back, momentarily ignoring the Thugs as her servant ducked out of an alleyway. He pulled something off his belt and whipped it toward Vin: a small glass vial, the kind that Allomancers used to store metal shavings. Vin quickly Pulled the vial to her hand. A short distance away, the second Coinshot—who had lain there, as if dead—now cursed and scrambled to his feet.

Vin spun, drinking the vial with a quick gulp. It contained only a single bead of metal. Atium. She couldn't risk carrying it on her own body—couldn't risk having it Pulled away from her during a fight. She'd ordered OreSeur to remain close this night, ready to give her the vial in an emergency.

The "Coinshot" pulled a hidden glass dagger from his waist, charging at Vin ahead of the Thugs, who were getting close. Vin paused for just a moment—regretting her decision, but seeing its inevitability.

The men had hidden a Mistborn among their numbers. A Mistborn like Vin, a person who could burn all ten metals. A Mistborn who had been waiting for the right moment to strike at her, to catch her unprepared.

He would have atium, and there was only one way to fight someone who had atium. It was the ultimate Allomantic metal, usable only by full Mistborn, and it could easily decide the fate of a battle. Each bead was worth a fortune—but what good was a fortune if she died?

Vin burned her atium.

The world around her seemed to change. Every moving object—swinging shutters, blowing ash, attacking Thugs, even trails of mist—shot out a translucent replica of itself.

The replicas moved just in front of their real counterparts, showing Vin exactly what would happen a few moments in the future.

Only the Mistborn was immune. Rather than shooting out a single atium shadow, he released dozens—the sign that he was burning atium. He paused just briefly. Vin's own body would have just exploded with dozens of confusing atium shadows. Now that she could see the future, she could see what he was going to do. That, in turn, changed what she was going to do. That changed what he was going to do. And so, like the reflections in two mirrors facing each other, the possibilities continued into infinity. Neither had an advantage.

Though their Mistborn paused, the four unfortunate Thugs continued to charge, having no way to know that Vin burned atium. Vin turned, standing beside the body of the fallen Smoker. With one foot, she kicked the soundsticks into the air.

A Thug arrived, swinging. His diaphanous atium shadow of a staff blow passed through her body. Vin twisted, ducking to the side, and could feel the real staff pass over her ear. The maneuver seemed easy within the aura of atium.

She snatched one of the soundsticks from the air, then slammed it up into the Thug's neck. She spun, catching the other soundstick, then twisted back and cracked it against the man's skull. He fell forward, groaning, and Vin spun again, easily dodging between two more staves.

She smashed the noise sticks against the sides of a second Thug's head. They shattered—ringing with a hollow sound like that of a musician's beat—as the Thug's skull cracked.

He fell, and did not move again. Vin kicked his staff into the air, then dropped the broken soundsticks and caught it. She spun, twisting the staff and tripping both remaining Thugs at once. In a fluid motion, she delivered two swift—yet powerful—blows to their faces.

She fell to a crouch as the men died, holding the staff in one hand, her other hand resting against the mist-wetted cobbles. The Mistborn held back, and she could see uncertainty in his eyes. Power didn't necessarily mean competence, and his two best advantages—surprise and atium—had been negated.

He turned, Pulling a group of coins up off the ground, then shot them. Not toward Vin—but toward OreSeur, who still stood in the mouth of an alleyway. The Mistborn obviously hoped that Vin's concern for her servant would draw her attention away, perhaps letting him escape.

He was wrong.

Vin ignored the coins, dashing forward. Even as Ore-Seur cried out in pain—a dozen coins piercing his skin—Vin threw her staff at the Mistborn's head. Once it left her fingers, however, its atium shadow became firm and singular.

The Mistborn assassin ducked, dodging perfectly. The move distracted him long enough for her to close the distance, however. She needed to attack quickly; the atium bead she'd swallowed had been small. It would burn out quickly. And, once it was gone, she'd be exposed. Her opponent would have total power over her. He—

Her terrified opponent raised his dagger. At that moment, his atium ran out.

Vin's predatory instincts reacted instantly, and she swung a fist. He raised an arm to block her blow, but she saw it coming, and she changed the direction of her attack. The blow took him square in the face. Then, with deft fingers, she snatched his glass dagger before it could fall and shatter. She stood and swung it through her opponent's neck.

He fell quietly.

Vin stood, breathing heavily, the group of assassins dead around her. For just a moment, she felt overwhelming power. With atium, she was invincible. She could dodge any blow, kill any enemy.

Her atium ran out.

Suddenly, everything seemed to grow dull. The pain in her side returned to her mind, and she coughed, groaning. She'd have bruises—large ones. Perhaps some cracked ribs.

But she'd won again. Barely. What would happen when she failed? When she didn't watch carefully enough, or fight skillfully enough?

Elend would die.

Vin sighed, and looked up. *He* was still there, watching her from atop a roof. Despite a half-dozen chases spread across several months, she'd never managed to catch him. Someday she would corner him in the night.

But not today. She didn't have the energy. In fact, a part of her worried that he'd strike her down. *But . . . she* thought. *He saved me. I would have died if I'd gotten too close to that hidden Mistborn. An instant of him burning atium with me unaware, and I'd have found his daggers in my chest.*

The Watcher stood for a few more moments—wreathed, as always, in the curling mists. Then he turned, jumping away into the night. Vin let him go; she had to deal with OreSeur.

She stumbled over to him, then paused. His nondescript body—in a servant's trousers and shirt—had been pelted with coins, and blood seeped from the several wounds.

He looked up at her. "What?" he asked.

"I didn't expect there to be blood."

OreSeur snorted. "You probably didn't expect me to feel pain either."

Vin opened her mouth, then paused. Actually, she hadn't ever thought about it. Then she hardened herself. *What right does this* thing *have to chastise me?*

Still, OreSeur had proven useful. "Thank you for throwing me the vial," she said.

"It was my duty, Mistress," OreSeur said, grunting as he pulled his broken body up against the side of the alleyway. "I was charged with your protection by Master Kelsier. As always, I serve the Contract."

Ah, yes. The almighty Contract. "Can you walk?"

"Only with effort, Mistress. The coins shattered several of these bones. I will need a new body. One of the assassins, perhaps?"

Vin frowned. She glanced back toward the dead men, and her stomach twisted slightly at the gruesome sight of their fallen bodies. She'd killed them, eight men, with the cruel efficiency that Kelsier had trained in her.

This is what I am, she thought. *A killer, like those men.* That was how it had to be. Someone had to protect Elend.

However, the thought of OreSeur eating one of them—digesting the corpse, letting his strange kandra senses memorize the positioning of muscles, skin, and organs, so that he could reproduce them—sickened her.

She glanced to the side, and saw the veiled scorn in Ore-Seur's eyes. They both knew what she thought of him eating human bodies. They both knew what he thought of her prejudice.

"No," Vin said. "We won't use one of these men."

"You'll have to find me another body, then," OreSeur said. "The Contract states that I cannot be forced to kill men."

Vin's stomach twisted again. *I'll think of something,* she thought. His current body was that of a murderer, taken after an execution. Vin was still worried that someone in the city would recognize the face.

"Can you get back to the palace?" Vin asked.

"With time," OreSeur said.

Vin nodded, dismissing him, then turned back toward the bodies. Somehow she suspected that this night would mark a distinct turning point in the fate of the Central Dominance.

Straff's assassins had done more damage than they would ever know. That bead of atium had been her last. The next time a Mistborn attacked her, she would be exposed.

And would likely die as easily as the Mistborn she'd slain this night.

My brethren ignore the other facts. They cannot connect the other strange things that are happening. They are deaf to my objections and blind to my discoveries.

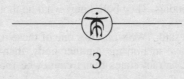

3

ELEND DROPPED HIS PEN TO his desk with a sigh, then leaned back in his chair and rubbed his forehead.

Elend figured that he knew as much about political theory as any living man. He'd certainly read more about economics, studied more about governments, and held more political debates than anyone he knew. He understood all the theories about how to make a nation stable and fair, and had tried to implement those in his new kingdom.

He just hadn't realized how incredibly frustrating a parliamentary council would be.

He stood up and walked over to get himself some chilled wine. He paused, however, as he glanced out his balcony doors. In the distance, a glowing haze shone through the mists. The campfires of his father's army.

He put down the wine. He was already exhausted, and the alcohol probably wouldn't help. *I can't afford to fall asleep until I get this done!* he thought, forcing himself to return to his seat. The Assembly would meet soon, and he needed to have the proposal finished tonight.

Elend picked up the sheet, scanning its contents. His handwriting looked cramped even to him, and the page was scattered with crossed-out lines and notations—reflections of his frustration. They'd known about the army's approach for weeks now, and the Assembly still quibbled about what to do.

Some of its members wanted to offer a peace treaty; others thought they should simply surrender the city. Still others felt they should attack without delay. Elend feared that the surrender faction was gaining strength; hence his proposal. The motion, if passed, would buy him more time. As king, he already had prime right of parlay with a foreign dictator. The proposal would forbid the Assembly from doing anything rash until he'd at least met with his father.

Elend sighed again, dropping the sheet. The Assembly was only twenty-four men, but getting them to agree on anything was almost more challenging than any of the problems they argued about. Elend turned, looking past the solitary lamp on his desk, out through the open balcony doors and toward the fires. Overhead, he heard feet scuttling on the rooftop—Vin, going about her nightly rounds.

Elend smiled fondly, but not even thinking of Vin could restore his good temper. *That group of assassins she fought tonight. Can I use that somehow?* Perhaps if he made the attack public, the Assembly would be reminded of the disdain Straff had for human life, and then be less likely to surrender the city to him. But . . . perhaps they'd also get frightened that he'd send assassins after *them,* and be more likely to surrender.

Sometimes Elend wondered if the Lord Ruler had been right. Not in oppressing the people, of course—but in retaining all of the power for himself. The Final Empire had been nothing if not stable. It had lasted a thousand years, weathering rebellions, maintaining a strong hold on the world.

The Lord Ruler was immortal, though, Elend thought. *That's an advantage I'll certainly never have.*

The Assembly was a better way. By giving the people a parliament with real legal authority, Elend would craft a stable government. The people would have a king—a man to provide continuity, a symbol of unity. A man who wouldn't be tainted by the need to get reappointed. However, they would also have an Assembly—a council made up of their peers that could voice their concerns.

It all sounded wonderful in theory. Assuming they survived the next few months.

Elend rubbed his eyes, then dipped his pen and began to scratch new sentences at the bottom of the document.

The Lord Ruler was dead.

Even a year later, Vin sometimes found that concept difficult to grasp. The Lord Ruler had been . . . everything. King and god, lawmaker and ultimate authority. He had been eternal and absolute, and now he was dead.

Vin had killed him.

Of course, the truth wasn't as impressive as the stories. It hadn't been heroic strength or mystical power that had let Vin defeat the emperor. She'd just figured out the trick that he'd been using to make himself immortal, and she'd fortunately—almost accidentally—exploited his weakness. She wasn't brave or clever. Just lucky.

Vin sighed. Her bruises still throbbed, but she had suffered far worse. She sat atop the palace—once Keep Venture—just above Elend's balcony. Her reputation might have been unearned, but it had helped keep Elend alive. Though dozens of warlords squabbled in the land that had once been the Final Empire, none of them had marched on Luthadel.

Until now.

Fires burned outside the city. Straff would soon know that his assassins had failed. What then? Assault the city? Ham and Clubs warned that Luthadel couldn't hold against a determined attack. Straff had to know that.

Still, for the moment, Elend was safe. Vin had gotten pretty good at finding and killing assassins; barely a month passed that she didn't catch someone trying to sneak into the palace. Many were just spies, and very few were Allomancers. However, a normal man's steel knife would kill Elend just as easily as an Allomancer's glass one.

She wouldn't let that occur. Whatever else happened— whatever sacrifices it required—Elend *had* to stay alive.

Suddenly apprehensive, she slipped over to the skylight to check on him. Elend sat safely at his desk below, scribbling away on some new proposal or edict. Kingship had changed the man remarkably little. About four years her senior—placing him in his early twenties—Elend was a man who put great stock in learning, but little in appearance. He only bothered to comb his hair when he attended an important function, and he somehow managed to wear even well-tailored outfits with an air of dishevelment.

He was probably the best man she had ever known. Earnest, determined, clever, and caring. And, for some reason, he loved her. At times, that fact was even more amazing to her than her part in the Lord Ruler's death.

Vin looked up, glancing back at the army lights. Then she looked to the sides. The Watcher had not returned. Often on nights like this he would tempt her, coming dangerously close to Elend's room before disappearing into the city.

Of course, if he'd wanted to kill Elend, he could just have done it while I was fighting the others. . . .

It was a disquieting thought. Vin couldn't watch Elend every moment. He was exposed a frightening amount of the time.

True, Elend had other bodyguards, and some were even Allomancers. They, however, were stretched as thin as she was. This night's assassins had been the most skilled, and most dangerous, that she had ever faced. She shivered, thinking about the Mistborn who had hid among them. He hadn't been very good, but he wouldn't have needed much skill to burn atium, then strike Vin directly in the right place.

The shifting mists continued to spin. The army's presence whispered a disturbing truth: The surrounding warlords were beginning to consolidate their domains, and were thinking about expansion. Even if Luthadel stood against Straff somehow, others would come.

Quietly, Vin closed her eyes and burned bronze, still worried that the Watcher—or some other Allomancer—might be nearby, planning to attack Elend in the supposedly safe aftermath of the assassination attempt. Most Mistborn considered bronze to be a relatively useless metal, as it was easily negated. With copper, a Mistborn could mask their Allomancy—not to mention protect themselves from emotional manipulation by zinc or brass. Most Mistborn considered it foolish not to have their copper on at all times.

And yet . . . Vin had the ability to pierce copperclouds.

A coppercloud wasn't a visible thing. It was far more vague. A pocket of deadened air where Allomancers could burn their metals and not worry that bronze burners would be able to sense them. But Vin could sense Allomancers who used metals inside of a coppercloud. She still wasn't certain why. Even Kelsier, the most powerful Allomancer she had known, hadn't been able to pierce a coppercloud.

Tonight, however, she sensed nothing.

With a sigh, she opened her eyes. Her strange power was confusing, but it wasn't unique to her. Marsh had confirmed that Steel Inquisitors could pierce copperclouds, and she was certain that the Lord Ruler had been able to do so. But . . . why her? Why could Vin—a girl who barely had two years' training as a Mistborn—do it?

There was more. She still remembered vividly the morning when she'd fought the Lord Ruler. There was something about that event that she hadn't told anyone— partially because it made her fear, just a bit, that the rumors and legends about her were true. Somehow, she'd drawn upon the mists, using *them* to fuel her Allomancy instead of metals.

It was only with that power, the power of the mists, that she had been able to beat the Lord Ruler in the end. She liked to tell herself that she had simply been lucky in fig- uring out the Lord Ruler's tricks. But . . . there *had* been something strange that night, something that she'd done. Something that she shouldn't have been able to do, and had never been able to repeat.

Vin shook her head. There was so much they didn't know, and not just about Allomancy. She and the other leaders of Elend's fledgling kingdom tried their best, but without Kelsier to guide them, Vin felt blind. Plans, successes, and even goals were like shadowy figures in the mist, formless and indistinct.

You shouldn't have left us, Kell, she thought. *You saved the world—but you should have been able to do it without dying.* Kelsier, the Survivor of Hathsin, the man who had conceived and implemented the collapse of the Final Empire. Vin had known him, worked with him, been trained by him. He was a legend and a hero. Yet, he had also been a man. Fallible. Imperfect. It was easy for the skaa to revere him, then blame Elend and the others for the dire situation that Kelsier had created.

The thought left her feeling bitter. Thinking about Kelsier often did that. Perhaps it was the sense of abandonment, or perhaps it was just the uncomfortable knowledge that Kelsier—like Vin herself—didn't fully live up to his reputation.

Vin sighed, closing her eyes, still burning bronze. The evening's fight had taken a lot out of her, and she was beginning to dread the hours she still intended to spend watching. It would be difficult to remain alert when—

She sensed something.

Vin snapped her eyes open, flaring her tin. She spun and stooped against the rooftop to obscure her profile. There was someone out there, burning metal. Bronze pulses thumped weakly, faint, almost unnoticeable—like someone playing drums very quietly. They were muffled by a coppercloud. The person—whoever it was—thought that their copper would hide them.

So far, Vin hadn't left anyone alive, save Elend and Marsh, who knew of her strange power.

Vin crept forward, fingers and toes chilled by the roof's copper sheeting. She tried to determine the direction of the pulses. Something was . . . odd about them. She had trouble distinguishing the metals her enemy was burning. Was that the quick, beating thump of pewter? Or was it the rhythm of iron? The pulses seemed indistinct, like ripples in a thick mud.

They were coming from somewhere very close. . . . On the rooftop . . .

Just in front of her.

Vin froze, crouching, the night breezes blowing a wall of mist across her. Where was he? Her senses argued with each other; her bronze said there was something right in front of her, but her eyes refused to agree.

She studied the dark mists, glanced upward just to be certain, then stood. *This is the first time my bronze has been wrong,* she thought with a frown.

Then she saw it.

Not something *in* the mists, but something *of* the mists. The figure stood a few feet away, easy to miss, for its shape was only faintly outlined by the mist. Vin gasped, stepping backward.

The figure continued to stand where it was. She couldn't tell much about it; its features were cloudy and vague, outlined by the chaotic churnings of windblown mist. If not for the form's persistence, she could have dismissed it—like the shape of an animal seen briefly in the clouds.

But it stayed. Each new curl of the mist added definition to its thin body and long head. Haphazard, yet persistent. It suggested a human, but it lacked the Watcher's solidity. It felt . . . looked . . . wrong.

The figure took a step forward.

Vin reacted instantly, throwing up a handful of coins and Pushing them through the air. The bits of metal zipped through the mist, trailing streaks, and passed right through the shadowy figure.

It stood for a moment. Then, it simply puffed away, dissipating into the mists' random curls.

Elend wrote the final line with a flair, though he knew he'd simply have a scribe rewrite the proposal. Still, he was proud. He thought that he'd been able to work out an argument that would finally convince the Assembly that they could not simply surrender to Straff.

He glanced unconsciously toward a stack of papers on his desk. On their top sat an innocent-seeming yellow letter, still folded, bloodlike smudge of wax broken at the seal. The letter had been short. Elend remembered its words easily.

Son,
I trust you've enjoyed seeing after Venture interests in Luthadel. I have secured the Northern Dominance,

and will shortly be returning to our keep in Luthadel.
You may turn over control of the city to me at that time.
                                                                    King Straff Venture

Of all the warlords and despots that had afflicted the Final Empire since the Lord Ruler's death, Straff was the most dangerous. Elend knew this firsthand. His father was a true imperial nobleman: He saw life as a competition between lords to see who could earn the greatest reputation. He had played the game well, making House Venture the most powerful of the pre-Collapse noble families.

Elend's father would not see the Lord Ruler's death as a tragedy or a victory—just as an opportunity. The fact that Straff's supposedly weak-willed fool of a son now claimed to be king of the Central Dominance probably gave him no end of mirth.

Elend shook his head, turning back to the proposal. *A few more rereads, a few tweaks, and I'll finally be able to get some sleep. I just—*

A cloaked form dropped from the skylight in the roof and landed with a quiet thump behind him.

Elend raised an eyebrow, turning toward the crouching figure. "You know, I leave the balcony open for a reason, Vin. You could come in that way, if you wanted."

"I know," Vin said. Then she darted across the room, moving with an Allomancer's unnatural litheness. She checked beneath his bed, then moved over to his closet and threw open the doors. She jumped back with the tension of an alert animal, but apparently found nothing inside that met with her disapproval, for she moved over to peek through the door leading into the rest of Elend's chambers.

Elend watched her with fondness. It had taken him some time to get used to Vin's particular . . . idiosyncrasies. He teased her about being paranoid; she just claimed she was careful. Regardless, half the time she visited his chambers she checked underneath his bed and in his closet. The other times, she held herself back—but Elend often caught her glancing distrustfully toward potential hiding places.

She was far less jumpy when she didn't have a particular reason to worry about him. However, Elend was only just beginning to understand that there was a very complex person hiding behind the face he had once known as Valette Renoux's. He had fallen in love with her courtly side without ever knowing the nervous, furtive Mistborn side. It was still a little difficult to see them as the same person.

Vin closed the door, then paused briefly, watching him with her round, dark eyes. Elend found himself smiling. Despite her oddities—or, more likely *because* of them—he loved this thin woman with the determined eyes and blunt temperament. She was like no one he had ever known—a woman of simple, yet honest, beauty and wit.

She did, however, sometimes worry him.

"Vin?" he asked, standing.

"Have you seen anything strange tonight?"

Elend paused. "Besides you?"

She frowned, striding across the room. Elend watched her small form, clothed in black trousers and a man's buttoning shirt, mistcloak tassels trailing behind her. She wore the cloak's hood down, as usual, and she stepped with a supple grace—the unconscious elegance of a person burning pewter.

Focus! he told himself. *You really* are *getting tired.* "Vin? What's wrong?"

Vin glanced toward the balcony. "That Mistborn, the Watcher, is in the city again."

"You're sure?"

Vin nodded. "But . . . I don't think he's going to come for you tonight."

Elend frowned. The balcony doors were still open, and trails of mist puffed through them, creeping along the floor until they finally evaporated. Beyond those doors was . . . darkness. Chaos.

It's just mist, he told himself. *Water vapor. Nothing to fear.* "What makes you think the Mistborn won't come for me?"

Vin shrugged. "I just feel he won't."

She often answered that way. Vin had grown up a creature of the streets, and she trusted her instincts. Oddly, so did Elend. He eyed her, reading the uncertainty in her posture. Something else had unsettled her this night. He looked into her eyes, holding them for a moment, until she glanced away.

"What?" he asked.

"I saw . . . something else," she said. "Or, I thought I did. Something in the mist, like a person formed from smoke. I could feel it, too, with Allomancy. It disappeared, though."

Elend frowned more deeply. He walked forward, putting his arms around her. "Vin, you're pushing yourself too hard. You can't keep prowling the city at night and then staying up all day. Even Allomancers need rest."

She nodded quietly. In his arms, she didn't seem to him like the powerful warrior who had slain the Lord Ruler. She felt like a woman past the edge of fatigue, a woman overwhelmed by events—a woman who probably felt a lot like Elend did.

She let him hold her. At first, there was a slight stiffness to her posture. It was as if a piece of her still expected to be hurt—a primal sliver that couldn't understand that it was possible to be touched out of love rather than anger. Then, however, she relaxed. Elend was one of the few she could do that around. When she held him—really held him—she clung with a desperation that bordered on terror. Somehow, despite her powerful skill as an Allomancer and her stubborn determination, Vin was frighteningly vulnerable. She seemed to need Elend. For that, he felt lucky.

Frustrated, at times. But lucky. Vin and he hadn't discussed his marriage proposal and her refusal, though Elend often thought of the encounter.

Women are difficult enough to understand, he thought, *and I had to go and pick the oddest one of the lot.* Still, he couldn't really complain. She loved him. He could deal with her idiosyncrasies.

Vin sighed, then looked up at him, finally relaxing as he leaned down to kiss her. He held it for a long moment, and she sighed. After the kiss, she rested her head on his shoulder. "We do have another problem," she said quietly. "I used the last of the atium tonight."

"Fighting the assassins?"

Vin nodded.

"Well, we knew it would happen eventually. Our stockpile couldn't last forever."

"Stockpile?" Vin asked. "Kelsier only left us six beads."

Elend sighed, then pulled her tight. His new government was supposed to have inherited the Lord Ruler's atium reserves—a supposed cache of the metal comprising an amazing treasure. Kelsier had counted on his new kingdom holding those riches; he had died expecting it. There was only one problem. Nobody had ever found the reserve. They had found some small bit—the atium that had made up the bracers that the Lord Ruler had used as a Feruchemical battery to store up age. However, they had spent those on supplies for the city, and they had actually contained only a very small bit of atium. Nothing like the cache was said to have. There should still be, somewhere in the city, a wealth of atium thousands of times larger than those bracers.

"We'll just have to deal with it," Elend said.

"If a Mistborn attacks you, I won't be able to kill him."

"Only if he has atium," Elend said. "It's becoming more and more rare. I doubt the other kings have much of it."

Kelsier had destroyed the Pits of Hathsin, the only place where atium could be mined. Still, if Vin *did* have to fight someone with atium . . .

Don't think about that, he told himself. *Just keep searching. Perhaps we can buy some. Or maybe we'll find the Lord Ruler's cache. If it even exists. . . .*

Vin looked up at him, reading the concern in his eyes, and he knew she had arrived at the same conclusions as he. There was little that could be accomplished at the moment; Vin had done well to conserve their atium as long as she had. Still, as Vin stepped back and let Elend return to his table, he couldn't help thinking about how they could have spent that atium. His people would need food for the winter.

But, by selling the metal, he thought, sitting, *we would have put more of the world's most dangerous Allomantic weapon into the hands of our enemies.* Better that Vin used it up.

As he began to work again, Vin poked her head over his shoulder, obscuring his lamplight. "What is it?" she asked.

"The proposal blocking the Assembly until I've had my right of parlay."

"Again?" she asked, cocking her head and squinting as she tried to make out his handwriting.

"The Assembly rejected the last version."

Vin frowned. "Why don't you just tell them that they *have* to accept it? You're the king."

"Now, see," Elend said, "that's what I'm trying to prove by all this. I'm just one man, Vin—maybe my opinion isn't better than theirs. If we all work on the proposal together, it will come out better than if one man had done it himself."

Vin shook her head. "It will be too weak. No teeth. You should trust yourself more."

"It's not about trust. It's about what's right. We spent a thousand years fighting off the Lord Ruler—if I do things the same way he did, then what will be the difference?"

Vin turned and looked him in the eyes. "The Lord Ruler was an evil man. You're a good one. *That's* the difference."

Elend smiled. "It's that easy for you, isn't it?"

Vin nodded.

Elend leaned up and kissed her again. "Well, some of us have to make things a little more complicated, so you'll have to humor us. Now, kindly remove yourself from my light so I can get back to work."

She snorted, but stood up and rounded the desk, leaving behind a faint scent of perfume. Elend frowned. *When'd she put that on?* Many of her motions were so quick that he missed them.

Perfume—just another of the apparent contradictions that made up the woman who called herself Vin. She wouldn't have been wearing it out in the mists; she usually put it on just for him. Vin liked to be unobtrusive, but she loved wearing scents—and got annoyed at him if he didn't notice when she was trying out a new one. She seemed suspicious and paranoid, yet she trusted her friends with a dogmatic loyalty. She went out at night in black and gray, trying so hard to hide—but Elend had seen her at the balls a year ago, and she had looked natural in gowns and dresses.

For some reason she had stopped wearing those. She hadn't ever explained why.

Elend shook his head, turning back to his proposal. Next to Vin, politics seemed simplistic. She rested her arms on the desktop, watching him work, yawning.

"You should get some rest," he said, dipping his pen again.

Vin paused, then nodded. She removed her mistcloak, wrapped it around herself, then curled up on the rug beside his desk.

Elend paused. "I didn't mean *here,* Vin," he said with amusement.

"There's still a Mistborn out there somewhere," she said with a tired, muffled voice. "I'm not leaving you." She twisted in the cloak, and Elend caught a brief grimace of pain on her face. She was favoring her left side.

She didn't often tell him the details of her fights. She didn't want to worry him. It didn't help.

Elend pushed down his concern and forced himself to start reading again. He was almost finished—just a bit more and—

A knock came at his door.

Elend turned with frustration, wondering at this new interruption. Ham poked his head in the doorway a second later.

"Ham?" Elend said. "You're still awake?"

"Unfortunately," Ham said, stepping into the room.

"Mardra is going to kill you for working late again," Elend said, setting down his pen. Complain though he might about some of Vin's quirks, at least she shared Elend's nocturnal habits.

Ham just rolled his eyes at the comment. He still wore his standard vest and trousers. He'd agreed to be the captain of Elend's guard on a single condition: that he would never have to wear a uniform. Vin cracked an eye as Ham wandered into the room, then relaxed again.

"Regardless," Elend said. "To what do I owe the visit?"

"I thought you might want to know that we identified those assassins who tried to kill Vin."

Elend nodded. "Probably men I know." Most Allomancers were noblemen, and he was familiar with all of those in Straff's retinue.

"Actually, I doubt it," Ham said. "They were Westerners."

Elend paused, frowning, and Vin perked up. "You're sure?"

Ham nodded. "Makes it a bit unlikely that your father sent them—unless he's done some heavy recruiting in Fadrex City. They were of Houses Gardre and Conrad, mostly."

Elend sat back. His father was based in Urteau, hereditary home of the Venture family. Fadrex was halfway across the empire from Urteau, several months' worth of travel. The chances were slim that his father would have access to a group of Western Allomancers.

"Have you heard of Ashweather Cett?" Ham asked.

Elend nodded. "One of the men who's set himself up as king in the Western Dominance. I don't know much about him."

Vin frowned, sitting. "You think he sent these?"

Ham nodded. "They must have been waiting for a chance to slip into the city, and the traffic at the gates these last few days would have provided the opportunity. That makes the arrival of Straff's army and the attack on Vin's life something of a coincidence."

Elend glanced at Vin. She met his eyes, and he could tell that she wasn't completely convinced that Straff hadn't sent the assassins. Elend, however, wasn't so skeptical. Pretty much every tyrant in the area had tried to take him out at one point or another. Why not Cett?

It's that atium, Elend thought with frustration. He'd never found the Lord Ruler's cache—but that didn't stop the despots in the empire from assuming he was hiding it somewhere.

"Well, at least your father didn't send the assassins," Ham said, ever the optimist.

Elend shook his head. "Our relationship wouldn't stop him, Ham. Trust me."

"He's your father," Ham said, looking troubled.

"Things like that don't matter to Straff. He probably hasn't sent assassins because he doesn't think I'm worth the trouble. If we last long enough, though, he will."

Ham shook his head. "I've heard of sons killing their fathers to take their place . . . but fathers killing their sons . . . I wonder what that says about old Straff's mind, that he'd be willing to kill you. You think that—"

"Ham?" Elend interrupted.

"Hum?"

"You know I'm usually good for a discussion, but I don't really have time for philosophy right now."

"Oh, right." Ham smiled wanly, turning to go. "I should get back to Mardra anyway."

Elend nodded, rubbing his forehead and picking up his pen yet again. "Make sure you gather the crew for a meeting. We need to organize our allies, Ham. If we don't come up with something incredibly clever, this kingdom may be doomed."

Ham turned back, still smiling. "You make it sound so desperate, El."

Elend looked over at him. "The Assembly is a mess, a half-dozen warlords with superior armies are breathing down my neck, barely a month passes without someone sending assassins to kill me, and the woman I love is slowly driving me insane."

Vin snorted at this last part.

"Oh, is that all?" Ham said. "See? It's not so bad after all. I mean, we *could* be facing an immortal god and his all-powerful priests instead."

Elend paused, then chuckled despite himself. "Good night, Ham," he said, turning back to his proposal.

"Good night, Your Majesty."

Perhaps they are right. Perhaps I am mad, or jealous, or simply daft. My name is Kwaan. Philosopher, scholar, traitor. I am the one who discovered Alendi, and I am the one who first proclaimed him to be the Hero of Ages. I am the one who started this all.

4

THE BODY SHOWED NO OVERT wounds. It still lay where it had fallen—the other villagers had been afraid to move it. Its arms and legs were twisted in awkward positions, the dirt around it scuffed from predeath thrashings.

Sazed reached out, running his fingers along one of the marks. Though the soil here in the Eastern Dominance held far more clay than soil did in the north, it was still more black than it was brown. Ashfalls came even this far south. Ashless soil, washed clean and fertilized, was a luxury used only for the ornamental plants of noble gardens. The rest of the world had to do what it could with untreated soil.

"You say that he was alone when he died?" Sazed asked, turning to the small cluster of villagers standing behind him.

A leather-skinned man nodded. "Like I said, Master Terrisman. He was just standing there, no one else about. He paused, then he fell and wiggled on the ground for a bit. After that, he just . . . stopped moving."

Sazed turned back to the corpse, studying the twisted muscles, the face locked in a mask of pain. Sazed had brought his medical coppermind—the metal armband wrapped around his upper right arm—and he reached into it with his mind, pulling out some of the memorized books he had stored therein. Yes, there were some diseases that killed with shakes and spasms. They rarely took a man so suddenly, but it sometimes happened. If it hadn't been for other circumstances, Sazed would have paid the death little heed.

"Please, repeat to me again what you saw," Sazed asked.

The leather-skinned man at the front of the group, Teur, paled slightly. He was in an odd position—his natural desire for notoriety would make him want to gossip about his experience. However, doing so could earn the distrust of his superstitious fellows.

"I was just passing by, Master Terrisman," Teur said. "On the path twenty yards yon. I seen old Jed working his field—a hard worker, he was. Some of us took a break when the lords left, but old Jed just kept on. Guess he knew we'd be needing food for the winter, lords or no lords."

Teur paused, then glanced to the side. "I know what people say, Master Terrisman, but I seen what I seen. It was day when I passed, but there was *mist* in the valley here. It stopped me, because I've never been out in the mist—my wife'll vouch me that. I was going to turn back, and then I seen old Jed. He was just working away, as if he hadn't seen the mist.

"I was going to call out to him, but before I could, he just . . . well, like I told you. I seen him standing there, then he froze. The mist swirled about him a bit, then he began to jerk and twist, like something really strong was holding him and shaking him. He fell. Didn't get up after that."

Still kneeling, Sazed looked back at the corpse. Teur apparently had a reputation for tall tales. Yet, the body was a chilling corroboration—not to mention Sazed's own experience several weeks before.

Mist during the day.

Sazed stood, turning toward the villagers. "Please fetch for me a shovel."

Nobody helped him dig the grave. It was slow, muggy work in the southern heat, which was strong despite the advent of autumn. The clay earth was difficult to move—but, fortunately, Sazed had a bit of extra stored-up strength inside a pewtermind, and he tapped it for help.

He needed it, for he wasn't what one would call an athletic man. Tall and long-limbed, he had the build of a scholar, and still wore the colorful robes of a Terris steward. He also still kept his head shaved, after the manner of the station he had served in for the first forty-some years of his life. He didn't wear much of his jewelry now—he didn't want to tempt highway bandits—but his earlobes were stretched out and pierced with numerous holes for earrings.

Tapping strength from his pewtermind enlarged his muscles slightly, giving him the build of a stronger man. Even with the extra strength, however, his steward's robes were stained with sweat and dirt by the time he finished digging. He rolled the body into the grave, and stood quietly for a moment. The man had been a dedicated farmer.

Sazed searched through his religions coppermind for an appropriate theology. He started with an index—one of the many that he had created. When he had located an appropriate religion, he pulled free detailed memories about its practices. The writings entered his mind as fresh as when he had just finished memorizing them. They would fade, with time, like all memories—however, he intended to place them back in the coppermind long before that happened. It was the way of the Keeper, the method by which his people retained enormous wealths of information.

This day, the memories he selected were of HaDah, a southern religion with an agricultural deity. Like most religions—which had been oppressed during the time of the Lord Ruler—the HaDah faith was a thousand years extinct.

Following the dictates of the HaDah funeral ceremony, Sazed walked over to a nearby tree—or, at least, one of the shrublike plants that passed for trees in this area. He broke off a long branch—the peasants watching him curiously—and carried it back to the grave. He stooped down and drove it into the dirt at the bottom of the hole, just beside the corpse's head. Then he stood and began to shovel dirt back into the grave.

The peasants watched him with dull eyes. *So depressed,*

Sazed thought. The Eastern Dominance was the most chaotic and unsettled of the five Inner Dominances. The only men in this crowd were well past their prime. The press gangs had done their work efficiently; the husbands and fathers of this village were likely dead on some battlefield that no longer mattered.

It was hard to believe that anything could actually be worse than the Lord Ruler's oppression. Sazed told himself that these people's pain would pass, that they would someday know prosperity because of what he and the others had done. Yet, he had seen farmers forced to slaughter each other, had seen children starve because some despot had "requisitioned" a village's entire food supply. He had seen thieves kill freely because the Lord Ruler's troops no longer patrolled the canals. He had seen chaos, death, hatred, and disorder. And he couldn't help but acknowledge that he was partially to blame.

He continued to refill the hole. He had been trained as a scholar and a domestic attendant; he was a Terrisman steward, the most useful, most expensive, and most prestigious of servants in the Final Empire. That meant almost nothing now. He'd never dug a grave, but he did his best, trying to be reverent as he piled dirt on the corpse. Surprisingly, about halfway through the process, the peasants began to help him, pushing dirt from the pile into the hole.

Perhaps there is hope for these yet, Sazed thought, thankfully letting one of the others take his shovel and finish the work. When they were done, the very tip of the HaDah branch breached the dirt at the head of the grave.

"Why'd you do that?" Teur asked, nodding to the branch.

Sazed smiled. "It is a religious ceremony, Goodman Teur. If you please, there is a prayer that should accompany it."

"A prayer? Something from the Steel Ministry?"

Sazed shook his head. "No, my friend. It is a prayer from a previous time, a time before the Lord Ruler."

The peasants eyed each other, frowning. Teur just rubbed his wrinkled chin. They all remained quiet, however, as Sazed said a short HaDah prayer. When he finished, he turned toward the peasants. "It was known as the religion of HaDah. Some of your ancestors might have followed it, I think. If any of you wish, I can teach you of its precepts."

The assembled crowd stood quietly. There weren't many of them—two dozen or so, mostly middle-aged women and a few older men. There was a single young man with a club leg; Sazed was surprised that he'd lived so long on a plantation. Most lords killed invalids to keep them from draining resources.

"When is the Lord Ruler coming back?" asked a woman.

"I do not believe that he will," Sazed said.

"Why did he abandon us?"

"It is a time of change," Sazed said. "Perhaps it is also time to learn of other truths, other ways."

The group of people shuffled quietly. Sazed sighed quietly; these people associated faith with the Steel Ministry and its obligators. Religion wasn't something that skaa worried about—save, perhaps, to avoid it when possible.

The Keepers spent a thousand years gathering and memorizing the dying religions of the world, Sazed thought. *Who would have thought that now—with the Lord Ruler gone—people wouldn't care enough to want what they'd lost?*

Yet, he found it hard to think ill of these people. They were struggling to survive, their already harsh world suddenly made unpredictable. They were tired. Was it any wonder that talk of beliefs long forgotten failed to interest them?

"Come," Sazed said, turning toward the village. "There are other things—more practical things—that I can teach you."

And I am the one who betrayed Alendi, for I now know that he must never be allowed to complete his quest.

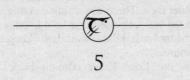

5

VIN COULD SEE SIGNS OF anxiety reflected in the city. Workers milled anxiously and markets bustled with an edge of concern—showing that same apprehension that one might see in a cornered rodent. Frightened, but not sure what to do. Doomed with nowhere to run.

Many had left the city during the last year—noblemen fleeing, merchants seeking some other place of business. Yet, at the same time, the city had swelled with an influx of skaa. They had somehow heard of Elend's proclamation of freedom, and had come with optimism—or, at least, as much optimism as an overworked, underfed, repeatedly beaten populace could manage.

And so, despite predictions that Luthadel would soon fall, despite whispers that its army was small and weak, the people had stayed. Worked. Lived. Just as they always had. The life of a skaa had never been very certain.

It was still strange for Vin to see the market so busy. She walked down Kenton Street, wearing her customary trousers and buttoned shirt, thinking about the time when she'd visited the street during the days before the Collapse. It had been the quiet home of some exclusive tailoring shops.

When Elend had abolished the restrictions on skaa merchants, Kenton Street had changed. The thoroughfare had blossomed into a wild bazaar of shops, pushcarts, and tents. In order to target the newly empowered—and newly waged—skaa workers, the shop owners had altered their selling methods. Where once they had coaxed with rich window displays, they now called and demanded, using criers, salesmen, and even jugglers to try to attract trade.

The street was so busy that Vin usually avoided it, and this day was even worse than most. The arrival of the army had sparked a last-minute flurry of buying and selling, the people trying to get ready for whatever was to come. There was a grim tone to the atmosphere. Fewer street performers, more yelling. Elend had ordered all eight city gates barred, so flight was no longer an option. Vin wondered how many of the people regretted their decision to stay.

She walked down the street with a businesslike step, hands clasped to keep the nervousness out of her posture. Even as a child—an urchin on the streets of a dozen different cities—she hadn't liked crowds. It was hard to keep track of so many people, hard to focus with so much going on. As a child, she'd stayed near the edges of crowds, hiding, venturing out to snatch the occasional fallen coin or ignored bit of food.

She was different now. She forced herself to walk with a straight back, and kept her eyes from glancing down or looking for places to hide. She was getting so much better—but seeing the crowds reminded her of what she had once been. What she would always—at least in part— still be.

As if in response to her thoughts, a pair of street urchins scampered through the throng, a large man in a baker's apron screaming at them. There were still urchins in Elend's new world. In fact, as she considered it, paying the skaa population probably made for a far better street life for urchins. There were more pockets to pick, more people to distract the shop owners, more scraps to go around, and more hands to feed beggars.

It was difficult to reconcile her childhood with such a life. To her, a child on the street was someone who learned to be quiet and hide, someone who went out at night to search through garbage. Only the most brave of urchins had dared cut purses; skaa lives had been worthless to many noblemen. During her childhood, Vin had known several urchins who been killed or maimed by passing noblemen who found them offensive.

Elend's laws might not have eliminated the poor, something he so much wanted to do, but he had improved the lives of even the street urchins. For that—among other things—she loved him.

There were still some noblemen in the crowd, men who had been persuaded by Elend or circumstances that their fortunes would be safer in the city than without. They were desperate, weak, or adventuresome. Vin watched one man pass, surrounded by a group of guards. He didn't give her a second glance; to him, her simple clothing was reason enough to ignore her. No noblewoman would dress as she did.

Is that what I am? she wondered, pausing beside a shop window, looking over the books inside—the sale of which had always been a small, but profitable, market for the idle imperial nobility. She also used the glass reflection to make certain no one snuck up behind her. *Am I a noblewoman?*

It could be argued that she was noble simply by association. The king himself loved her—had asked her to marry him—and she had been trained by the Survivor of Hathsin. Indeed, her father had been noble, even if her mother had been skaa. Vin reached up, fingering the simple bronze earring that was the only thing she had as a memento of Mother.

It wasn't much. But, then, Vin wasn't sure she wanted to think about her mother all that much. The woman had, after all, tried to kill Vin. In fact, she *had* killed Vin's full sister. Only the actions of Reen, Vin's half brother, had saved her. He had pulled Vin, bloody, from the arms of a woman who had shoved the earring into Vin's ear just moments before.

And still Vin kept it. As a reminder, of sorts. The truth was, she didn't feel like a noblewoman. At times, she thought she had more in common with her insane mother than she did with the aristocracy of Elend's world. The balls and parties she had attended before the Collapse—they had been a charade. A dreamlike memory. They had no place in this world of collapsing governments and nightly assassinations.

Plus, Vin's part in the balls—pretending to be the girl Valette Renoux—had always been a sham.

She pretended still. Pretended not to be the girl who had grown up starving on the streets, a girl who had been beaten far more often than she had been befriended. Vin sighed, turning from the window. The next shop, however, drew her attention despite herself.

It contained ball gowns.

The shop was empty of patrons; few thought of gowns on the eve of an invasion. Vin paused before the open doorway, held almost as if she were metal being Pulled. Inside, dressing dummies stood posed in majestic gowns. Vin looked up at the garments, with their tight waists and tapering, bell-like skirts. She could almost imagine she was at a ball, soft music in the background, tables draped in perfect white, Elend standing up on his balcony, leafing through a book. . . .

She almost went in. But why bother? The city was about to be attacked. Besides, the garments were expensive. It had been different when she'd spent Kelsier's money. Now she spent Elend's money—and Elend's money was the kingdom's money.

She turned from the gowns and walked back out onto the street. *Those aren't me anymore. Valette is useless to Elend—he needs a Mistborn, not an uncomfortable girl in a gown that she doesn't quite fill.* Her wounds from the night before, now firm bruises, were a reminder of her place. They were healing well—she'd been burning pewter heavily all day—but she'd be stiff for a while yet.

Vin quickened her pace, heading for the livestock pens. As she walked, however, she caught sight of someone tailing her.

Well, perhaps "tailing" was too generous a word—the man certainly wasn't doing a very good job of going unnoticed. He was balding on top, but wore the sides of his hair long. He wore a simple skaa's smock: a single-piece tan garment that was stained dark with ash.

Great, Vin thought. There was another reason she avoided the market—or any place where crowds of skaa gathered.

She sped up again, but the man hurried as well. Soon, his awkward movements gained attention—but, instead of cursing him, most people paused reverently. Soon others joined him, and Vin had a small crowd trailing her.

A part of her wanted to just slap down a coin and shoot away. *Yes,* Vin thought to herself wryly, *use Allomancy in the daylight. That'll make you inconspicuous.*

So, sighing, she turned to confront the group. None of them looked particularly threatening. The men wore trousers and dull shirts; the women wore one-piece, utilitarian dresses. Several more men wore single-piece, ash-covered smocks.

Priests of the Survivor.

"Lady Heir," one of them said, approaching and falling to his knees.

"Don't call me that," Vin said quietly.

The priest looked up at her. "Please. We need direction. We have cast off the Lord Ruler. What do we do now?"

Vin took a step backward. Had Kelsier understood what he was doing? He had built up the skaa's faith in him, then had died a martyr to turn them in rage against the Final Empire. What had he thought would happen after that? Could he have foreseen the Church of the Survivor—had he known that they would replace the Lord Ruler with Kelsier himself as God?

The problem was, Kelsier had left his followers with no doctrine. His only goal had been to defeat the Lord Ruler; partially to get his revenge, partially to seal his legacy, and partially—Vin hoped—because he had wanted to free the skaa.

But now what? These people must feel as she did. Set adrift, with no light to guide them.

Vin could not be that light. "I'm not Kelsier," she said quietly, taking another step backward.

"We know," one of the men said. "You're his heir—he passed on, and this time *you* Survived."

"Please," a woman said, stepping forward, holding a young child in her arms. "Lady Heir. If the hand that struck down the Lord Ruler could touch my child . . ."

Vin tried to back away farther, but realized she was up against another crowd of people. The woman stepped closer, and Vin finally raised an uncertain hand to the baby's forehead.

"Thank you," the woman said.

"You'll protect us, won't you, Lady Heir?" asked a young man—no older than Elend—with a dirty face but honest eyes. "The priests say that you'll stop that army out there, that its soldiers won't be able to enter the city while you're here."

That was too much for her. Vin mumbled a halfhearted response, but turned and pushed her way through the crowd. The group of believers didn't follow her, fortunately.

She was breathing deeply, though not from exertion, by the time she slowed. She moved into an alley between two shops, standing in the shade, wrapping her arms around herself. She had spent her life learning to remain unnoticed, to be quiet and unimportant. Now she could be none of those things.

What did the people expect of her? Did they really think that she could stop an army by herself? That was one lesson she'd learned very early into her training: Mistborn weren't invincible. One man, she could kill. Ten men could give her trouble. An army . . .

Vin held herself and took a few calming breaths. Eventually, she moved back out onto the busy street. She was near her destination now—a small, open-sided tent surrounded by four pens. The merchant lounged by it, a scruffy man who had hair on only half of his head—the right half. Vin stood for a moment, trying to decide if the odd hairstyle was due to disease, injury, or preference.

The man perked up when he saw her standing at the edge of his pens. He brushed himself off, throwing up a small amount of dust. Then he sauntered up to her, smiling with what teeth he still had, acting as if he hadn't heard—or didn't care—that there was an army just outside.

"Ah, young lady," he said. "Lookin' for a pup? I've got some wee scamps that any girl is sure to love. Here, let me grab one. You'll agree it's the cutest thing you ever seen."

Vin folded her arms as the man reached down to grab a puppy from one of the pens. "Actually," she said, "I was looking for a wolfhound."

The merchant looked up. "Wolfhound, miss? 'Tis no pet for a girl like yourself. Mean brutes, those. Let me find you a nice bobbie. Nice dogs, those—smart, too."

"No," Vin said, drawing him up short. "You will bring me a wolfhound."

The man paused again, looking at her, scratching himself in several undignified places. "Well, I guess I can see . . ."

He wandered toward the pen farthest from the street. Vin waited quietly, nose downturned at the smell as the merchant yelled at a few of his animals, selecting an appropriate one. Eventually, he pulled a leashed dog up to Vin. It was a wolfhound, if a small one—but it had sweet, docile eyes, and an obviously pleasant temperament.

"The runt of the litter," the merchant said. "A good animal for a young girl, I'd say. Will probably make an excellent hunter, too. These wolfhounds, they can smell better than any beast you seen."

Vin reached for her coin purse, but paused, looking down at the dog's panting face. It almost seemed to be smiling at her.

"Oh, for the Lord Ruler's sake," she snapped, pushing past the dog and master, stalking toward the back pens.

"Young lady?" the merchant asked, following uncertainly.

Vin scanned the wolfhounds. Near the back, she spotted a massive black and gray beast. It was chained to a post, and it regarded her defiantly, a low growl rising in its throat.

Vin pointed. "How much for that one in the back?"

"That?" the merchant asked. "Good lady, that's a watchbeast. It's meant to be set loose on a lord's grounds to attack anyone who enters! It's the one of the meanest things you'll ever see!"

"Perfect," Vin said, pulling out some coins.

"Good lady, I couldn't possibly sell you that beast. Not possibly at all. Why, I'll bet it weighs half again as much as you do."

Vin nodded, then pulled open the pen gate and strode in. The merchant cried out, but Vin walked right up to the wolfhound. He began to bark wildly at her, frothing.

Sorry about this, Vin thought. Then, burning pewter, she ducked in and slammed her fist into the animal's head.

The animal froze, wobbled, then fell unconscious in the dirt. The merchant stopped up short beside her, mouth open.

"Leash," Vin ordered.

He gave her one. She used it to tie the wolfhound's feet together, and then—with a flare of pewter—she threw the animal over her shoulders. She cringed only slightly at the pain in her side.

This thing better not get drool on my shirt, she thought, handing the merchant some coins and walking back toward the palace.

Vin slammed the unconscious wolfhound to the floor. The guards had given her some strange looks as she entered the palace, but she was getting used to those. She brushed off her hands.

"What is that?" OreSeur asked. He'd made it back to her rooms at the palace, but his current body was obviously unusable. He'd needed to form muscles in places that men didn't normally have them to even keep the skeleton together, and while he'd healed his wounds, his body looked unnatural. He still wore the bloodstained clothing from the night before.

"This," Vin said, pointing at the wolfhound, "is your new body."

OreSeur paused. "*That?* Mistress, that is a dog."

"Yes," Vin said.

"I am a man."

"You're a kandra," Vin said. "You can imitate flesh and muscle. What about fur?"

The kandra did not look pleased. "I cannot imitate it," he said, "but I can use the beast's own fur, like I use its bones. However, surely there is—"

"I'm not going to kill for you, kandra," Vin said. "And

even if I did kill someone, I wouldn't let you . . . eat them. Plus, this will be more inconspicuous. People will begin to talk if I keep replacing my stewards with unknown men. I've been telling people for months that I was thinking of dismissing you. Well, I'll tell them that I finally did— nobody will think to realize that my new pet hound is actually my kandra."

She turned, nodding toward the carcass. "This will be very useful. People pay less attention to hounds than they do to humans, and so you'll be able to listen in on conversations."

OreSeur's frown deepened. "I will not do this thing easily. You will need to compel me, by virtue of the Contract."

"Fine," Vin said. "You're commanded. How long will it take?"

"A regular body only takes a few hours," OreSeur said. "This could take longer. Getting that much fur to look right will be challenging."

"Get started, then," Vin said, turning toward the door. On her way, however, she noticed a small package sitting on her desk. She frowned, walking over and taking off the lid. A small note sat inside.

Lady Vin,
  Here is the next alloy you requested. Aluminum is very difficult to acquire, but when a noble family recently left the city, I was able to buy some of their diningware.
  I do not know if this one will work, but I believe it worth a try. I have mixed the aluminum with four percent copper, and found the outcome quite promising. I have read of this composition; it is called duralumin.
                                    Your servant, Terion

Vin smiled, setting aside the note and removing the rest of the box's contents: a small pouch of metal dust and a thin silvery bar, both presumably of this "duralumin" metal. Terion was a master Allomantic metallurgist. Though not an Allomancer himself, he had been mixing alloys and creating dusts for Mistborn and Mistings for most of his life.

Vin pocketed both pouch and bar, then turned toward OreSeur. The kandra regarded her with a flat expression.

"This came for me today?" Vin asked, nodding to the box.

"Yes, Mistress," OreSeur said. "A few hours ago."

"And you didn't tell me?"

"I'm sorry, Mistress," OreSeur said in his toneless way, "but you did not *command* me to tell you if packages arrived."

Vin ground her teeth. He knew how anxiously she'd been waiting for another alloy from Terion. All of the previous aluminum alloys they'd tried had turned out to be duds. It bothered her to know that there was another Allomantic metal out there somewhere, waiting to be discovered. She wouldn't be satisfied until she found it.

OreSeur just sat where he was, bland expression on his face, unconscious wolfhound on the floor in front of him.

"Just get to work on that body," Vin said, spinning and leaving the room to search for Elend.

Vin finally found Elend in his study, going over some ledgers with a familiar figure.

"Dox!" Vin said. He'd retired to his rooms soon after his arrival the day before, and she hadn't seen much of him.

Dockson looked up and smiled. Stocky without being fat, he had short dark hair and still wore his customary half beard. "Hello, Vin."

"How was Terris?" she asked.

"Cold," Dockson replied. "I'm glad to be back. Though I wish I hadn't arrived to find that army here."

"Either way, we're glad you've returned, Dockson," Elend said. "The kingdom practically fell apart without you."

"That hardly seems the case," Dockson said, closing his ledger and setting it on the stack. "All things—and armies—considered, it looks like the royal bureaucracy held together fairly well in my absence. You hardly need me anymore!"

"Nonsense!" Elend said.

Vin leaned against the door, eyeing the two men as they continued their discussion. They maintained their air of forced joviality. Both were dedicated to making the new kingdom work, even if it meant pretending that they liked each other. Dockson pointed at places in the ledgers, talking about finances and what he'd discovered in the outlying villages under Elend's control.

Vin sighed, glancing across the room. Sunlight streamed through the room's stained-glass rose window, throwing colors across the ledgers and table. Even now, Vin still wasn't accustomed to the casual richness of a noble keep. The window—red and lavender—was a thing of intricate beauty. Yet, noblemen apparently found its like so commonplace that they had put this one in the keep's back rooms, in the small chamber that Elend now used as his study.

As one might expect, the room was piled with stacks of books. Shelves lined the walls from floor to ceiling, but they were no match for the sheer volume of Elend's growing collection. She'd never cared much for Elend's taste in books. They were mostly political or historical works, things with topics as musty as their aged pages. Many of them had once been forbidden by the Steel Ministry, but somehow the old philosophers could make even salacious topics seem boring.

"Anyway," Dockson said, finally closing his ledgers. "I have some things to do before your speech tomorrow, Your Majesty. Did Ham say there's a city defense meeting that evening as well?"

Elend nodded. "Assuming I can get the Assembly to agree not to hand the city over to my father, we'll need to come up with a strategy to deal with this army. I'll send someone for you tomorrow night."

"Good," Dockson said. With that, he nodded to Elend, winked at Vin, then made his way from the cluttered room.

As Dockson shut the door, Elend sighed, then relaxed back in his oversized plush chair.

Vin walked forward. "He really is a good man, Elend."

"Oh, I realize he is. Being a good man doesn't always make one likable, however."

"He's nice, too," Vin said. "Sturdy, calm, stable. The crew relied on him." Even though Dockson wasn't an Allomancer, he had been Kelsier's right-hand man.

"He doesn't like me, Vin," Elend said. "It's . . . very hard to get along with someone who looks at me like that."

"You're not giving him a fair chance," Vin complained, stopping beside Elend's chair.

He looked up at her, smiling wanly, his vest unbuttoned, his hair an absolute mess. "Hum . . ." he said idly, taking her hand. "I really like that shirt. Red looks good on you."

Vin rolled her eyes, letting him gently pull her into the chair and kiss her. There was a passion to the kiss—a need, perhaps, for something stable. Vin responded, feeling herself relax as she pulled up against him. A few minutes later, she sighed, feeling much better snuggled into the chair beside him. He pulled her close, leaning the chair back into the window's sunlight.

He smiled and glanced at her. "That's a . . . new perfume you're wearing."

Vin snorted, putting her head against his chest. "It's not perfume, Elend. It's dog."

"Ah, good," Elend said. "I was worried that you'd departed from your senses. Now, is there any particular reason *why* you smell like dog?"

"I went to the market and bought one, then carried it back and fed it to OreSeur, so it can be his new body."

Elend paused. "Why, Vin. That's brilliant! Nobody will suspect a dog to be a spy. I wonder if anyone's ever thought of that before. . . ."

"Someone must have," Vin said. "I mean, it makes such sense. I suspect those who thought of it, however, didn't share the knowledge."

"Good point," Elend said, relaxing back. Yet, from as close as they were, she could still feel a tension in him.

Tomorrow's speech, Vin thought. *He's worried about it.*

"I must say, however," Elend said idly, "that I find it a bit disappointing that you're *not* wearing dog-scented perfume. With your social station, I could see some of the local noblewomen trying to imitate you. That could be amusing indeed."

She leaned up, looking at his smirking face. "You know, Elend—sometimes it's bloody difficult to tell when you're teasing, and when you're just being dense."

"That makes me more mysterious, right?"

"Something like that," she said, snuggling up against him again.

"Now, see, you don't understand how clever that is of me," he said. "If people can't tell when I'm being an idiot and when I'm being a genius, perhaps they'll assume my blunders are brilliant political maneuverings."

"As long as they don't mistake your actual brilliant moves for blunders."

"That shouldn't be difficult," Elend said. "I fear I have few enough of *those* for people to mistake."

Vin looked up with concern at the edge in his voice. He, however, smiled, shifting the topic. "So, OreSeur the dog. Will he still be able to go out with you at nights?"

Vin shrugged. "I guess. I wasn't really planning on bringing him for a while."

"I'd like it if you did take him," Elend said. "I worry about you out there, every night, pushing yourself so hard."

"I can handle it," Vin said. "Someone needs to watch over you."

"Yes," Elend said, "but who watches over you?"

Kelsier. Even now, that was still her immediate reaction. She'd known him for less than a year, but that year had been the first in her life that she had felt protected.

Kelsier was dead. She, like the rest of the world, had to live without him.

"I know you were hurt when you fought those Allomancers the other night," Elend said. "It would be really nice for my psyche if I knew someone was with you."

"A kandra's no bodyguard," Vin said.

"I know," Elend said. "But they're incredibly loyal—I've never heard of one breaking Contract. He'll watch out for you. I worry about you, Vin. You wonder why I stay up so late, scribbling at my proposals? I can't sleep, knowing that you might be out there fighting—or, worse, lying somewhere in a street, dying because nobody was there to help you."

"I take OreSeur with me sometimes."

"Yes," Elend said, "but I know you find excuses to leave him behind. Kelsier bought you the services of an incredibly valuable servant. I can't understand why you work so hard to avoid him."

Vin closed her eyes. "Elend. He *ate* Kelsier."

"So?" Elend asked. "Kelsier was already dead. Besides, he himself gave that order."

Vin sighed, opening her eyes. "I just . . . don't trust that thing, Elend. The creature is unnatural."

"I know," Elend said. "My father always kept a kandra. But, OreSeur is something, at least. Please. Promise me you'll take him with you."

"All right. But I don't think he's going to like the arrangement much either. He and I didn't get along very well even when he was playing Renoux, and I his niece."

Elend shrugged. "He'll hold to his Contract. That's what is important."

"He holds to the Contract," Vin said, "but only grudgingly. I swear that he enjoys frustrating me."

Elend looked down at her. "Vin, kandra are excellent servants. They don't do things like that."

"No, Elend," Vin said. "*Sazed* was an excellent servant. He enjoyed being with people, helping them. I never felt that he resented me. OreSeur may do everything I command, but he doesn't like me; he never has. I can tell."

Elend sighed, rubbing her shoulder. "Don't you think you might be a little irrational? There's no real reason to hate him so."

"Oh?" Vin asked. "Just like there's no reason you shouldn't get along with Dockson?"

Elend paused. Then he sighed. "I guess you have a point," he said. He continued to rub Vin's shoulder as he stared upward, toward the ceiling, contemplative.

"What?" Vin asked.

"I'm not doing a very good job of this, am I?"

"Don't be foolish," Vin said. "You're a wonderful king."

"I might be a passable king, Vin, but I'm not *him*."

"Who?"

"Kelsier," Elend said quietly.

"Elend, nobody expects you to be Kelsier."

"Oh?" he said. "That's why Dockson doesn't like me. He hates noblemen; it's obvious in the way that he talks, the way he acts. I don't know if I really blame him, considering the life he's known. Regardless, he doesn't think I should be king. He thinks that a skaa should be in my place—or, even better, Kelsier. They all think that."

"That's nonsense, Elend."

"Really? And if Kelsier still lived, would I be king?"

Vin paused.

"You see? They accept me—the people, the merchants, even the noblemen. But in the back of their minds, they wish they had Kelsier instead."

"I don't wish that."

"Don't you?"

Vin frowned. Then she sat up, turning so that she was kneeling over Elend in the reclined chair, their faces just inches apart. "Don't you *ever* wonder that, Elend. Kelsier was my teacher, but I didn't love him. Not like I love you."

Elend stared into her eyes, then nodded. Vin kissed him deeply, then snuggled down beside him again.

"Why not?" Elend eventually asked.

"Well, he was old, for one thing."

Elend chuckled. "I seem to recall you making fun of *my* age as well."

"That's different," Vin said. "You're only a few years older than me—Kelsier was ancient."

"Vin, thirty-eight is not ancient."

"Close enough."

Elend chuckled again, but she could tell that he wasn't satisfied. Why *had* she chosen Elend, rather than Kelsier? Kelsier had been the visionary, the hero, the Mistborn.

"Kelsier was a great man," Vin said quietly as Elend began to stroke her hair. "But . . . there were things about him, Elend. Frightening things. He was intense, reckless, even a little bit cruel. Unforgiving. He'd slaughter people without guilt or concern, just because they upheld the Final Empire or worked for the Lord Ruler.

"I could love him as a teacher and a friend. But I don't think I could ever love—not *really* love—a man like that. I don't blame him; he was of the streets, like me. When you struggle so hard for life, you grow strong—but you can grow harsh, too. His fault or not, Kelsier reminded me too much of men I . . . knew when I was younger. Kell was a far better person than they—he really could be kind, and he did sacrifice his life for the skaa. However, he was just so hard."

She closed her eyes, feeling Elend's warmth. "You, Elend Venture, are a good man. A *truly* good man."

"Good men don't become legends," he said quietly.

"Good men don't need to become legends." She opened her eyes, looking up at him. "They just do what's right anyway."

Elend smiled. Then he kissed the top of her head and leaned back. They lay there for a time, in a room warm with sunlight, relaxing.

"He saved my life, once," Elend finally said.

"Who?" Vin asked with surprise. "Kelsier?"

Elend nodded. "That day after Spook and OreSeur were captured, the day Kelsier died. There was a battle in the square when Ham and some soldiers tried to free the captives."

"I was there," Vin said. "Hiding with Breeze and Dox in one of the alleyways."

"Really?" Elend said, sounding a bit amused. "Because I came looking for you. I thought that they'd arrested you, along with OreSeur—he was pretending to be your uncle, then. I tried to get to the cages to rescue you."

"You did *what*? Elend, it was a battlefield in that square! There was an Inquisitor there, for the Lord Ruler's sake!"

"I know," Elend said, smiling faintly. "See, that Inquisitor is the one who tried to kill me. It had its axe raised and everything. And then . . . Kelsier was there. He smashed into the Inquisitor, throwing it to the ground."

"Probably just a coincidence," Vin said.

"No," Elend said softly. "He meant it, Vin. He looked at me while he struggled with the Inquisitor, and I saw it in his eyes. I've always wondered about that moment; everyone tells me that Kelsier hated the nobility even more than Dox does."

Vin paused. "He . . . started to change a little at the end, I think."

"Change enough that he'd risk himself to protect a random nobleman?"

"He knew that I loved you," Vin said, smiling faintly. "I guess, in the end, that proved stronger than his hatred."

"I didn't realize . . ." He trailed off as Vin turned, hearing something. Footsteps approaching. She sat up, and a second later, Ham poked his head into the room. He paused when he saw Vin sitting in Elend's lap, however.

"Oh," Ham said. "Sorry."

"No, wait," Vin said. Ham poked his head back in, and Vin turned to Elend. "I almost forgot why I came looking for you in the first place. I got a new package from Terion today."

"*Another* one?" Elend asked. "Vin, when are you going to give this up?"

"I can't afford to," she said.

"It can't be all that important, can it?" he asked. "I mean, if everybody's forgotten what that last metal does, then it must not be very powerful."

"Either that," Vin said, "or it was so amazingly powerful that the Ministry worked very hard to keep it a secret." She slid off of the chair to stand up, then took the pouch and thin bar out of her pocket. She handed the bar to Elend, who sat up in his plush chair.

Silvery and reflective, the metal—like the aluminum from which it was made—felt too light to be real. Any Allomancer who accidentally burned aluminum had their other metal reserves stripped away from them, leaving them powerless. Aluminum had been kept secret by the Steel Ministry; Vin had only found out about it on the night when she'd been captured by the Inquisitors, the same night she'd killed the Lord Ruler.

They had never been able to figure out the proper Allomantic alloy of aluminum. Allomantic metals always came in pairs—iron and steel, tin and pewter, copper and bronze, zinc and brass. Aluminum and . . . something. Something powerful, hopefully. Her atium was gone. She needed an edge.

Elend sighed, handing back the bar. "The last time you tried to burn one of those it left you sick for two days, Vin. I was terrified."

"It can't kill me," Vin said. "Kelsier promised that burning a bad alloy would only make me sick."

Elend shook his head. "Even Kelsier was wrong on occasion, Vin. Didn't you say that he misunderstood how bronze worked?"

Vin paused. Elend's concern was so genuine that she felt herself being persuaded. However . . .

When that army attacks, Elend is going to die. The city's skaa might survive—no ruler would be foolish enough to slaughter the people of such a productive city. The king, however, would be killed. She couldn't fight off an entire army, and she could do little to help with preparations.

She did know Allomancy, however. The better she got at it, the better she'd be able to protect the man she loved.

"I have to try it, Elend," she said quietly. "Clubs says that Straff won't attack for a few days—he'll need that long to rest his men from the march and scout the city for attack. That means I can't wait. If this metal does make me sick, I'll be better in time to help fight—but only if I try it now."

Elend's face grew grim, but he did not forbid her. He had learned better than that. Instead, he stood. "Ham, you think this is a good idea?"

Ham nodded. He was a warrior; to him, her gamble would make sense. She'd asked him to stay because she'd need someone to carry her back to her bed, should this go wrong.

"All right," Elend said, turning back to Vin, looking resigned.

Vin climbed into the chair, sat back, then took a pinch of the duralumin dust and swallowed it. She closed her eyes, and felt at her Allomantic reserves. The common eight were all there, well stocked. She didn't have any atium or gold, nor did she have either of their alloys. Even if she'd had atium, it was too precious to use except in an emergency—and the other three had only marginal usefulness.

A new reserve appeared. Just as one had the four times before. Each time she'd burned an aluminum alloy, she'd immediately felt a blinding headache. *You'd think I'd have learned . . .* she thought. Gritting her teeth, she reached inside and burned the new alloy.

Nothing happened.

"Have you tried it yet?" Elend asked apprehensively.

Vin nodded slowly. "No headache. But . . . I'm not sure if the alloy is doing anything or not."

"But it's burning?" Ham asked.

Vin nodded. She felt the familiar warmth from within, the tiny fire that told her that a metal was burning. She tried moving about a bit, but couldn't distinguish any change to her physical self. Finally she just looked up and shrugged.

Ham frowned. "If it didn't make you sick, then you've found the right alloy. Each metal only has one valid alloy."

"Or," Vin said, "that's what we've always been told."

Ham nodded. "What alloy was this?"

"Aluminum and copper," Vin said.

"Interesting," Ham said. "You don't feel anything at all?"

Vin shook her head.

"You'll have to practice some more."

"Looks like I'm lucky," Vin said, extinguishing the duralumin. "Terion came up with forty different alloys he thought we could try, once we had enough aluminum. This was only the fifth."

"Forty?" Elend asked incredulously. "I wasn't aware that there were so many metals you could make an alloy from!"

"You don't have to have two metals to make an alloy," Vin said absently. "Just one metal and something else. Look at steel—it's iron and carbon."

"Forty . . ." Elend repeated. "And you would have tried them all?"

Vin shrugged. "Seemed like a good place to start."

Elend looked concerned at that thought, but didn't say anything further. Instead, he turned to Ham. "Anyway, Ham, was there something you wanted to see us about?"

"Nothing important," Ham said. "I just wanted to see if Vin was up for some sparring. That army has me feeling antsy, and I figure Vin could still use some practice with the staff."

Vin shrugged. "Sure. Why not?"

"You want to come, El?" Ham asked. "Get in some practice?"

Elend laughed. "And face one of you two? I've got my royal dignity to think of!"

Vin frowned slightly, looking up at him. "You really should practice more, Elend. You barely know how to hold a sword, and you're *terrible* with a dueling cane."

"Now, see, why would I worry about that when I have you to protect me?"

Vin's concern deepened. "We can't always be around you, Elend. I'd worry a lot less if you were better at defending yourself."

He just smiled and pulled her to her feet. "I'll get to it eventually, I promise. But, not today—I've got too much to think about right now. How about if I just come watch you two? Perhaps I'll pick up something by observation—which is, by the way, the preferable method of weapons training, since it doesn't involve me getting beaten up by a girl."

Vin sighed, but didn't press the point further.

I write this record now, pounding it into a metal slab, because I am afraid. Afraid for myself, yes—I admit to being human. If Alendi does return from the Well of Ascension, I am certain that my death will be one of his first objectives. He is not an evil man, but he is a ruthless one. That is, I think, a product of what he has been through.

6

ELEND LEANED DOWN AGAINST THE railing, looking in at the sparring yard. Part of him did wish to go out and practice with Vin and Ham. However, the larger part of him just didn't see the point.

Any assassin likely to come after me will be an Allomancer, he thought. *I could train ten years and be no match for one of them.*

In the yard itself, Ham took a few swings with his staff, then nodded. Vin stepped up, holding her own staff, which was a good foot taller than she was. Watching the two of them, Elend couldn't help remarking on the disparity. Ham had the firm muscles and powerful build of a warrior. Vin looked even thinner than usual, wearing only a tight buttoned shirt and a pair of trousers, with no cloak to mask her size.

The inequality was enhanced by Ham's next words. "We're practicing with the staff, not practicing Pushing and Pulling. Don't use anything but pewter, all right?"

Vin nodded.

It was the way they often sparred. Ham claimed that there was no substitute for training and practice, no matter how powerful an Allomancer one was. He let Vin use pewter, however, because he said the enhanced strength and dexterity was disorienting unless one was accustomed to it.

The sparring field was like a courtyard. Situated in the palace barracks, it had an open-sided hallway built around it. Elend stood in this, roof overhead keeping the red sun out of his eyes. That was nice, for a light ashfall had begun, and occasional flakes of ash floated down from the sky. Elend crossed his arms on the railing. Soldiers passed occasionally in the hallway behind, bustling with activity. Some, however, paused to watch; Vin and Ham's sparring sessions were something of a welcome diversion to the palace guards.

I should be working on my proposal, Elend thought. *Not standing here watching Vin fight.*

But . . . the tension of the last few days had been so pressing that he was finding it difficult to get up the motivation to do yet *another* read-through of the speech. What he really needed was to just spend a few moments thinking.

So, he simply watched. Vin approached Ham warily, staff held in a firm, two-handed stance. Once, Elend probably would have found trousers and shirt on a lady to be inappropriate, but he'd been around Vin too long to still be bothered by that. Ball gowns and dresses were beautiful—but there was something *right* about Vin in simple garb. She wore it more comfortably.

Besides, he kind of liked how the tight clothing looked on her.

Vin usually let others strike first, and this day was no exception. Staves rapped as Ham engaged her, and despite her size, Vin held her own. After a quick exchange, they both backed away, circling warily.

"My money's on the girl."

Elend turned as he noticed a form limping down the hallway toward him. Clubs stepped up beside Elend, setting a ten-boxing coin down on the railing with a snap. Elend smiled to the general, and Clubs scowled back—which was generally accepted as Clubs's version of a smile. Dockson excluded, Elend had taken quickly to the other members of Vin's crew. Clubs, however, had taken a little getting used to. The stocky man had a face like a gnarled toadstool, and he always seemed to be squinting in displeasure—an expression usually matched by his tone of voice.

However, he was a gifted craftsman, not to mention an Allomancer—a Smoker, actually, though he didn't get to use his power much anymore. For the better part of a year, Clubs had acted as general of Elend's military forces. Elend didn't know where Clubs had learned to lead soldiers, but the man had a remarkable knack for it. He'd probably gotten the skill in the same place that he'd acquired the scar on his leg—a scar that produced the hobble from which Clubs drew his nickname.

"They're just sparring, Clubs," Elend said. "There won't be a 'winner.' "

"They'll end with a serious exchange," Clubs said. "They always do."

Elend paused. "You're asking me to bet against Vin, you know," he noted. "That could be unhealthy."

"So?"

Elend smiled, pulling out a coin. Clubs still kind of intimidated him, and he didn't want to risk offending the man.

"Where's that worthless nephew of mine?" Clubs asked as he watched the sparring.

"Spook?" Elend asked. "He's back? How'd he get into the city?"

Clubs shrugged. "He left something on my doorstep this morning."

"A gift?"

Clubs snorted. "It was a woodcarving from a master carpenter up in Yelva City. The note said, 'I just wanted to show you what *real* carpenters are up to, old man.' "

Elend chuckled, but trailed off as Clubs eyed him with a discomforting stare. "Whelp was never this insolent before," Clubs muttered. "I swear, you lot have corrupted the lad."

Clubs almost seemed to be smiling. Or, was he serious? Elend couldn't ever decide if the man was as crusty as he seemed, or if Elend was the butt of some elaborate joke.

"How is the army doing?" Elend finally asked.

"Terribly," Clubs said. "You want an army? Give me more than one year to train it. Right now, I'd barely trust those boys against a mob of old women with sticks."

Great, Elend thought.

"Can't do much right now, though," Clubs grumbled. "Straff is digging in some cursory fortifications, but mostly he's just resting his men. The attack will come by the end of the week."

In the courtyard, Vin and Ham continued to fight. It was slow, for the moment, Ham taking time to pause and explain principles or stances. Elend and Clubs watched for a short time as the sparring gradually became more intense, the rounds taking longer, the two participants beginning to sweat as their feet kicked up puffs of ash in the packed, sooty earth.

Vin gave Ham a good contest despite the ridiculous differences in strength, reach, and training, and Elend found himself smiling slightly despite himself. She was something special—Elend had realized that when he'd first seen her in the Venture ballroom, nearly two years before. He was only now coming to realize how much of an understatement "special" was.

A coin snapped against the wooden railing. "My money's on Vin, too."

Elend turned with surprise. The man who had spoken was a soldier who had been standing with the others watching behind. Elend frowned. "Who—"

Then, Elend cut himself off. The beard was wrong, the posture too straight, but the man standing behind him was familiar. "Spook?" Elend asked incredulously.

The teenage boy smiled behind an apparently fake beard. "Wasing the where of calling out."

Elend's head immediately began to hurt. "Lord Ruler, don't tell me you've gone back to the dialect?"

"Oh, just for the occasional nostalgic quip," Spook said with a laugh. His words bore traces of his Easterner accent; during the first few months Elend had known the boy, Spook had been utterly unintelligible. Fortunately, the boy had grown out of using his street cant, just as he'd managed to grow out of most of his clothing. Well over six feet tall, the sixteen-year-old young man hardly resembled the gangly boy Elend had met a year before.

Spook leaned against the railing beside Elend, adopting a teenage boy's lounging posture and completely destroying his image as a soldier—which, indeed, he wasn't.

"Why the costume, Spook?" Elend asked with a frown.

Spook shrugged. "I'm no Mistborn. We more mundane spies have to find ways to get information without flying up to windows and listening outside."

"How long you been standing there?" Clubs asked, glaring at his nephew.

"Since before you got here, Uncle Grumbles," Spook said. "And, in answer to your question, I got back a couple days ago. Before Dockson, actually. I just thought I'd take a bit of a break before I went back to duty."

"I don't know if you've noticed, Spook," Elend said, "but we're at war. There isn't a lot of time to take breaks."

Spook shrugged. "I just didn't want you to send me away again. If there's going to be war here, I want to be around. You know, for the excitement."

Clubs snorted. "And where did you get that uniform?"

"Uh . . . Well . . ." Spook glanced to the side, displaying just a hint of the uncertain boy Elend had known.

Clubs grumbled something about insolent boys, but Elend just laughed and clapped Spook on the shoulder. The boy looked up, smiling; though he'd been easy to ignore at first, he was proving as valuable as any of the other members of Vin's former crew. As a Tineye—a Misting who could burn tin to enhance his senses—Spook could listen to conversations from far away, not to mention notice distant details.

"Anyway, welcome back," Elend said. "What's the word from the west?"

Spook shook his head. "I hate to sound too much like Uncle Crusty over there, but the news isn't good. You know those rumors about the Lord Ruler's atium being in Luthadel? Well, they're back. Stronger this time."

"I thought we were past that!" Elend said. Breeze and

his team had spent the better part of six months spreading rumors and manipulating the warlords into believing that the atium must have been hidden in another city, since Elend hadn't found it in Luthadel.

"Guess not," Spook said. "And . . . I think someone's spreading these rumors intentionally. I've been on the street long enough to sense a planted story, and this rumor smells wrong. Someone really wants the warlords to focus on you."

Great, Elend thought. "You don't know where Breeze is, do you?"

Spook shrugged, but he no longer seemed to be paying attention to Elend. He was watching the sparring. Elend glanced back toward Vin and Ham.

As Clubs had predicted, the two had fallen into a more serious contest. There was no more instruction; there were no more quick, repetitive exchanges. They sparred in earnest, fighting in a swirling melee of staffs and dust. Ash flew around them, blown up by the wind of their attacks, and even more soldiers paused in the surrounding hallways to watch.

Elend leaned forward. There was something *intense* about a duel between two Allomancers. Vin tried an attack. Ham, however, swung simultaneously, his staff blurringly quick. Somehow, Vin got her own weapon up in time, but the power of Ham's blow threw her back in a tumble. She hit the ground on one shoulder. She gave barely a grunt of pain, however, and somehow got a hand beneath her, throwing herself up to land on her feet. She skidded for a moment, retaining her balance, holding her staff up.

Pewter, Elend thought. It made even a clumsy man dexterous. And, for a person normally graceful like Vin . . .

Vin's eyes narrowed, her innate stubbornness showing in the set of her jaw, the displeasure in her face. She didn't like being beaten—even when her opponent was obviously stronger than she was.

Elend stood up straight, intending to suggest an end to the sparring. At that moment, Vin dashed forward.

Ham brought his staff up expectantly, swinging as Vin

came within reach. She ducked to the side, passing within
inches of the attack, then brought her weapon around and
slammed it into the back of Ham's staff, throwing him off
balance. Then she ducked in for the attack.

Ham, however, recovered quickly. He let the force of
Vin's blow spin him around, and he used the momentum to
bring his staff around in a powerful blow aimed directly at
Vin's chest.

Elend cried out.

Vin jumped.

She didn't have metal to Push against, but that didn't
seem to matter. She sprang a good seven feet in the air, easily cresting Ham's staff. She flipped as the swing passed beneath her, her fingers brushing the air just above the weapon,
her own staff spinning in a one-handed grip.

Vin landed, her staff already howling in a low swing,
its tip throwing up a line of ash as it ran along the ground.
It slammed into the back of Ham's legs. The blow swept
Ham's feet out from beneath him, and he cried out as
he fell.

Vin jumped into the air again.

Ham slammed to the earth on his back, and Vin landed
on his chest. Then, she calmly rapped him on the forehead
with the end of her staff. "I win."

Ham lay, looking dazed, Vin crouching on his chest.
Dust and ash settled quietly in the courtyard.

"Damn . . ." Spook whispered, voicing a sentiment that
seemed to be shared by the dozen or so watching soldiers.

Finally, Ham chuckled. "Fine. You beat me—now, if
you would, kindly get me something to drink while I try to
massage some feeling back into my legs."

Vin smiled, hopping off his chest and scampering away
to do as requested. Ham shook his head, climbing to his
feet. Despite his words, he walked with barely a limp; he'd
probably have a bruise, but it wouldn't bother him for
long. Pewter not only enhanced one's strength, balance,
and speed, it also made one's body innately stronger. Ham
could shrug off a blow that would have shattered Elend's
legs.

Ham joined them, nodding to Clubs and punching Spook lightly on the arm. Then he leaned against the railing and rubbed his left calf, cringing slightly. "I swear, Elend— sometimes sparring with that girl is like trying to fight with a gust of wind. She's never where I think she'll be."

"How did she do that, Ham?" Elend asked. "The jump, I mean. That leap seemed inhuman, even for an Allomancer."

"Used steel, didn't she?" Spook said.

Ham shook his head. "No, I doubt it."

"Then how?" Elend asked.

"Allomancers draw strength from their metals," Ham said, sighing and putting his foot down. "Some can squeeze out more than others—but the real power comes from the metal itself, not the person's body."

Elend paused. "So?"

"So," Ham said, "an Allomancer doesn't have to be physically strong to be incredibly powerful. If Vin were a Feruchemist, it would be different—if you ever see Sazed increase *his* strength, his muscles will grow larger. But with Allomancy, all the strength comes directly from the metal.

"Now, most Thugs—myself included—figure that making their bodies strong will only add to their power. After all, a muscular man burning pewter will be that much stronger than a regular man of the same Allomantic power."

Ham rubbed his chin, eyeing the passage Vin had left through. "But . . . well, I'm beginning to think that there might be another way. Vin's a thin little thing, but when she burns pewter, she grows several times stronger than any normal warrior. She packs all that strength into a small body, and doesn't have to bother with the weight of massive muscles. She's like . . . an insect. Far stronger than her mass or her body would indicate. So, when she jumps, she can *jump*."

"But you're still stronger than she is," Spook said.

Ham nodded. "And I can make use of that—assuming I can ever hit her. That's getting harder and harder to do."

Vin finally returned, carrying a jug of chilled juice— apparently she'd decided to go all the way to the keep, rather than grabbing some of the warm ale kept on hand in the courtyard. She handed a flagon to Ham, and had thought to bring cups for Elend and Clubs.

"Hey!" Spook said as she poured. "What about me?"

"That beard looks silly on you," Vin said as she poured.

"So I don't get anything to drink?"

"No."

Spook paused. "Vin, you're a strange girl."

Vin rolled her eyes; then she glanced toward the water barrel in the corner of the courtyard. One of the tin cups lying beside it lurched into the air, shooting across the courtyard. Vin stuck her hand out, catching it with a slapping sound, then set it on the railing before Spook. "Happy?"

"I will be once you pour me something to drink," Spook said as Clubs grunted, taking a slurp from his own cup. The old general then reached over, sliding two of the coins off the railing and pocketing them.

"Hey, that's right!" Spook said. "You owe me, El. Pay up."

Elend lowered his cup. "I never agreed to the bet."

"You paid Uncle Irritable. Why not me?"

Elend paused, then sighed, pulling out a ten-boxing coin and setting it beside Spook's. The boy smiled, plucking both up in a smooth street-thief gesture. "Thanks for winning the bout, Vin," he said with a wink.

Vin frowned at Elend. "You bet against me?"

Elend laughed, leaning across the railing to kiss her. "I didn't mean it. Clubs bullied me."

Clubs snorted at that comment, downed the rest of his juice, then held out his cup for a refill. When Vin didn't respond, he turned to Spook and gave the boy a telling scowl. Finally, Spook sighed, picking up the jug to refill the cup.

Vin was still regarding Elend with dissatisfaction.

"I'd be careful, Elend," Ham said with a chuckle. "She can hit pretty hard. . . ."

Elend nodded. "I should know better than to antagonize her when there are weapons lying around, eh?"

"Tell me about it," Ham said.

Vin sniffed at that comment, rounding the railing so that she could stand next to Elend. Elend put his arm around her, and as he did, he caught a bare flash of envy in Spook's eyes. Elend suspected that the boy'd had a crush on Vin for some time—but, well, Elend couldn't really blame him for that.

Spook shook his head. "I've got to find myself a woman."

"Well, that beard isn't going to help," Vin said.

"It's just a disguise, Vin," Spook said. "El, I don't suppose you could give me a title or something?"

Elend smiled. "I don't think that will matter, Spook."

"It worked for you."

"Oh, I don't know," Elend said. "Somehow, I think Vin fell in love with me *despite* my title, rather than because of it."

"But you had others before her," Spook said. "Noble girls."

"A couple," Elend admitted.

"Though Vin has a habit of killing off her competition," Ham quipped.

Elend laughed. "Now, see, she only did that once. And I think Shan deserved it—she was, after all, trying to assassinate me at the time." He looked down fondly, eyeing Vin. "Though, I do have to admit, Vin *is* a bit hard on other women. With her around, everybody else looks bland by comparison."

Spook rolled his eyes. "It's more interesting when she kills them off."

Ham chuckled, letting Spook pour him some more juice. "Lord Ruler only knows what she'd do to you if you ever tried to leave her, Elend."

Vin stiffened immediately, pulling him a little tighter. She'd been abandoned far too many times. Even after what they'd been through, even after his proposal of marriage, Elend had to keep promising Vin that he wasn't going to leave her.

Time to change the topic, Elend thought, the joviality of the moment fading. "Well," he said, "I think I'm going to go visit the kitchens and get something to eat. You coming, Vin?"

Vin glanced at the sky—likely checking to see how soon it would grow dark. Finally, she nodded.

"I'll come," Spook said.

"No you won't," Clubs said, grabbing the boy by the back of the neck. "You're going to stay right here and explain exactly where you got one of my soldiers' uniforms."

Elend chuckled, leading Vin away. Truth be told, even with the slightly sour end of conversation, he felt better for having come to watch the sparring. It was strange how the members of Kelsier's crew could laugh and make light, even during the most terrible of situations. They had a way of making him forget about his problems. Perhaps that was a holdover from the Survivor. Kelsier had, apparently, insisted on laughing, no matter how bad the situation. It had been a form of rebellion to him.

None of that made the problems go away. They still faced an army several times larger than their own, in a city that they could barely defend. Yet, if anyone could survive such a situation, it would be Kelsier's crew.

Later that night, having filled her stomach at Elend's insistence, Vin made her way with Elend to her rooms.

There, sitting on the floor, was a perfect replica of the wolfhound she had bought earlier. It eyed her, then bowed its head. "Welcome back, Mistress," the kandra said in a growling, muffled voice.

Elend whistled appreciatively, and Vin walked in a circle around the creature. Each hair appeared to have been placed perfectly. If it hadn't spoken, one would never have been able to tell it wasn't the original dog.

"How do you manage the voice?" Elend asked curiously.

"A voice box is a construction of flesh, not bone, Your Majesty," OreSeur said. "Older kandra learn to manipulate their bodies, not just replicate them. I still need to digest a person's corpse to memorize and re-create their exact features. However, I can improvise some things."

Vin nodded. "Is that why making this body took you so much longer than you'd said?"

"No, Mistress," OreSeur said. "The hair. I'm sorry I didn't warn you—placing fur like this takes a great deal of precision and effort."

"Actually, you did mention it," Vin said, waving her hand.

"What do you think of the body, OreSeur?" Elend asked.

"Honestly, Your Majesty?"

"Of course."

"It is offensive and degrading," OreSeur said.

Vin raised an eyebrow. *That's forward of you, Renoux,* she thought. *Feeling a little belligerent today, are we?*

He glanced at her, and she tried—unsuccessfully—to read his canine expression.

"But," Elend said, "you'll wear the body anyway, right?"

"Of course, Your Majesty," OreSeur said. "I would die before breaking the Contract. It is life."

Elend nodded to Vin, as if he'd just made a major point. *Anyone can claim loyalty,* Vin thought. *If someone has a "Contract" to ensure their honor, then all the better. That makes the surprise more poignant when they do turn on you.*

Elend was obviously waiting for something. Vin sighed. "OreSeur, we'll be spending more time together in the future."

"If that is what you wish, Mistress."

"I'm not sure if it is or not," Vin said. "But it's going to happen anyway. How well can you move about in that body?"

"Well enough, Mistress."

"Come on," she said, "let's see if you can keep up."

I am also afraid, however, that all I have known—that my story—will be forgotten. I am afraid for the world that is to come. Afraid that my plans will fail.

Afraid of a doom worse, even, than the Deepness.

7

SAZED NEVER THOUGHT HE'D HAVE reason to appreciate dirt floors. However, they proved remarkably useful in writing instruction. He drew several words in the dirt with a long stick, giving his half-dozen students a model. They proceeded to scribble their own copies, rewriting the words several times.

Even after living among various groups of rural skaa for a year, Sazed was still surprised by their meager resources. There wasn't a single piece of chalk in the entire village, let alone ink or paper. Half the children ran around naked, and the only shelters were the hovels—long, one-room structures with patchy roofs. The skaa had farming tools, fortunately, but no manner of bows or slings for hunting.

Sazed had led a scavenging mission up to the plantation's abandoned manor. The leavings had been meager. He'd suggested that the village elders relocate their people to the manor itself for the winter, but he doubted they would do so. They had visited the manor with apprehension, and many hadn't been willing to leave Sazed's side. The place reminded them of lords—and lords reminded them of pain.

His students continued to scribble. He had spent quite a bit of effort explaining to the elders why writing was so important. Finally, they had chosen him some students—partially, Sazed was sure, just to appease him. He shook his head slowly as he watched them write. There was no passion in their learning. They came because they were ordered, and because "Master Terrisman" willed it, not because of any real desire for education.

During the days before the Collapse, Sazed had often imagined what the world would be like once the Lord Ruler was gone. He had pictured the Keepers emerging, bringing forgotten knowledge and truths to an excited, thankful populace. He'd imagined teaching before a warm hearth at night, telling stories to an eager audience. He'd never paused to consider a village, stripped of its working men, whose people were too exhausted at night to bother with tales from the past. He'd never imagined a people who seemed more annoyed by his presence than thankful.

You must be patient with them, Sazed told himself sternly. His dreams now seemed like hubris. The Keepers who had come before him, the hundreds who had died keeping their knowledge safe and quiet, had never expected praise or accolades. They had performed their great task with solemn anonymity.

Sazed stood up and inspected his students' writings. They were getting better—they could recognize all of the letters. It wasn't much, but it was a start. He nodded to the group, dismissing them to help prepare the evening meal.

They bowed, then scattered. Sazed followed them out, then realized how dim the sky was; he had probably kept his students too late. He shook his head as he strolled between the hill-like hovels. He again wore his steward's robes, with their colorful V-shaped patterns, and he had put in several of his earrings. He kept to the old ways because they were familiar, even though they were also a symbol of oppression. How would future Terris generations dress? Would a lifestyle forced upon them by the Lord Ruler become an innate part of their culture?

He paused at the edge of the village, glancing down the corridor of the southern valley. It was filled with blackened soil occasionally split by brown vines or shrubs. No mist, of course; mist came only during the night. The stories had to be mistakes. The thing he'd seen had to have been a fluke.

And what did it matter if it wasn't? It wasn't his duty to investigate such things. Now that the Collapse had come, he had to disperse his knowledge, not waste his time chasing after foolish stories. Keepers were no longer investigators, but instructors. He carried with him thousands of books—information about farming, about sanitation, about government, and about medicine. He needed to give these things to the skaa. That was what the Synod had decided.

And yet, a part of Sazed resisted. That made him feel deeply guilty; the villagers needed his teachings, and he wished dearly to help them. However . . . he felt that he was *missing* something. The Lord Ruler was dead, but the story did not seem finished. Was there something he had overlooked?

Something larger, even, than the Lord Ruler? Something so large, so big, that it was effectively invisible?

Or, do I just want *there to be something else?* he wondered. *I've spent most of my adult life resisting and fighting, taking risks that the other Keepers called mad. I wasn't content with feigned subservience—I had to get involved in the rebellion.*

Despite that rebellion's success, Sazed's brethren still hadn't forgiven him for his involvement. He knew that Vin and the others saw him as docile, but compared with other Keepers he was a wild man. A reckless, untrustworthy fool who threatened the entire order with his impatience. They had believed their duty was to wait, watching for the day when the Lord Ruler was gone. Feruchemists were too rare to risk in open rebellion.

Sazed had disobeyed. Now he was having trouble living the peaceful life of a teacher. Was that because some subconscious part of him knew that the people were still in danger, or was it because he simply couldn't accept being marginalized?

"Master Terrisman!"

Sazed spun. The voice was terrified. *Another death in the mists?* he thought immediately.

It was eerie how the other skaa remained inside their hovels despite the horrified voice. A few doors creaked, but nobody rushed out in alarm—or even curiosity—as the screamer dashed up to Sazed. She was one of the field-workers, a stout, middle-aged woman. Sazed checked his reserves as she approached; he had on his pewtermind for strength, of course, and a very small steel ring for speed. Suddenly, he wished he'd chosen to wear just a few more bracelets this day.

"Master Terrisman!" the woman said, out of breath. "Oh, he's come back! He's come for us!"

"Who?" Sazed asked. "The man who died in the mists?"

"No, Master Terrisman. The *Lord Ruler*."

Sazed found him standing just outside the village. It was already growing dark, and the woman who'd fetched Sazed had returned to her hovel in fear. Sazed could only imagine how the poor people felt—trapped by the onset of the night and its mist, yet huddled and worried at the danger that lurked outside.

And an ominous danger it was. The stranger waited quietly on the worn road, wearing a black robe, standing almost as tall as Sazed himself. The man was bald, and he wore no jewelry—unless, of course, you counted the massive iron spikes that had been driven point-first through his eyes.

Not the Lord Ruler. A Steel Inquisitor.

Sazed still didn't understand how the creatures continued to live. The spikes were wide enough to fill the Inquisitor's entire eye sockets; the nails had destroyed the eyes, and pointed tips jutted out the back of the skull. No blood dripped from the wounds—for some reason, that made them seem more strange.

Fortunately, Sazed knew this particular Inquisitor. "Marsh," Sazed said quietly as the mists began to form.

"You are a very difficult person to track, Terrisman," Marsh said—and the sound of his voice shocked Sazed. It had changed, somehow, becoming more grating, more gristly. It now had a grinding quality, like that of a man with a cough. Just like the other Inquisitors Sazed had heard.

"Track?" Sazed asked. "I wasn't planning on others needing to find me."

"Regardless," Marsh said, turning south. "I did. You need to come with me."

Sazed frowned. "What? Marsh, I have a work to do here."

"Unimportant," Marsh said, turning back, focusing his eyeless gaze on Sazed.

Is it me, or has he become stranger since we last met? Sazed shivered. "What is this about, Marsh?"

"The Conventical of Seran is empty."

Sazed paused. The Conventical was a Ministry stronghold to the south—a place where the Inquisitors and high obligators of the Lord Ruler's religion had retreated after the Collapse.

"Empty?" Sazed asked. "That isn't likely, I think."

"True nonetheless," Marsh said. He didn't use body language as he spoke—no gesturing, no movements of the face.

"I . . ." Sazed trailed off. *What kinds of information, wonders, secrets, the Conventical's libraries must hold.*

"You must come with me," Marsh said. "I may need help, should my brethren discover us."

My brethren. Since when are the Inquisitors Marsh's "brethren"? Marsh had infiltrated their numbers as part of Kelsier's plan to overthrow the Final Empire. He was a traitor to their numbers, not their brother.

Sazed hesitated. Marsh's profile looked . . . unnatural, even unnerving, in the dim light. Dangerous.

Don't be foolish, Sazed chastised himself. Marsh was Kelsier's brother—the Survivor's only living relative. As an Inquisitor, Marsh had authority over the Steel Ministry, and many of the obligators had listened to him despite his involvement with the rebellion. He had been an invaluable resource for Elend Venture's fledgling government.

"Go get your things," Marsh said.

My place is here, Sazed thought. *Teaching the people, not gallivanting across the countryside, chasing my own ego.*

And yet . . .

"The mists are coming during the day," Marsh said quietly.

Sazed looked up. Marsh was staring at him, the heads of his spikes shining like round disks in the last slivers of sunlight. Superstitious skaa thought that Inquisitors could read minds, though Sazed knew that was foolish. Inquisitors had the powers of Mistborn, and could therefore influence other people's emotions—but they could *not* read minds.

"Why did you say that?" Sazed asked.

"Because it is true," Marsh said. "This is not over, Sazed. It has not yet begun. The Lord Ruler . . . he was just a delay. A cog. Now that he is gone, we have little time remaining. Come with me to the Conventical—we must search it while we have the opportunity."

Sazed paused, then nodded. "Let me go explain to the villagers. We can leave tonight, I think."

Marsh nodded, but he didn't move as Sazed retreated to the village. He just remained, standing in the darkness, letting the mist gather around him.

It all comes back to poor Alendi. I feel bad for him, and for all the things he has been forced to endure. For what he has been forced to become.

8

VIN THREW HERSELF INTO THE mists. She soared in the night air, passing over darkened homes and streets. An occasional, furtive bob of light glowed in the mists— a guard patrol, or perhaps an unfortunate late-night traveler.

Vin began to descend, and she immediately flipped a coin out before herself. She Pushed against it, her weight plunging it down into the quiet depths. As soon as it hit the street below, her Push forced her upward, and she sprang back into the air. Soft Pushes were very difficult—so each coin she Pushed against, each jump she made, threw her into the air at a terrible speed. The jumping of a Mistborn wasn't like a bird's flight. It was more like the path of a ricocheting arrow.

And yet, there was a grace to it. Vin breathed deeply as she arced above the city, tasting the cool, humid air. Luthadel by day smelled of burning forges, sun-heated refuse, and fallen ash. At night, however, the mists gave the air a beautiful chill crispness—almost a cleanliness.

Vin crested her jump, and she hung for just a brief moment as her momentum changed. Then she began to plummet back toward the city. Her mistcloak tassels fluttered around her, mingling with her hair. She fell with her eyes closed, remembering her first few weeks in the mist, training beneath Kelsier's relaxed—yet watchful— tutelage. He had given her this. Freedom. Despite two years as a Mistborn, she had never lost the sense of intoxicating wonder she felt when soaring through the mists.

She burned steel with her eyes closed; the lines appeared anyway, visible as a spray of threadlike blue lines set against the blackness of her eyelids. She picked two, pointing downward behind her, and Pushed, throwing herself into another arc.

What did I ever do without this? Vin thought, opening her eyes, whipping her mistcloak behind her with a throw of the arm.

Eventually, she began to fall again, and this time she didn't toss a coin. She burned pewter to strengthen her limbs, and landed with a thump on the wall surrounding Keep Venture's grounds. Her bronze showed no signs of Allomantic activity nearby, and her steel revealed no unusual patterns of metal moving toward the keep.

Vin crouched on the dark wall for a few moments, right at the edge, toes curling over the lip of the stone. The rock was cool beneath her feet, and her tin made her skin far more sensitive than normal. She could tell that the wall needed to be cleaned; lichens were beginning to grow along its side, encouraged by the night's humidity, protected from the day's sun by a nearby tower.

Vin remained quiet, watching a slight breeze push and churn the mists. She heard the movement on the street below before she saw it. She tensed, checking her reserves, before she was able to discern a wolfhound's shape in the shadows.

She dropped a coin over the side of the wall, then leapt off. OreSeur waited as she landed quietly before him, using a quick Push on the coin to slow her descent.

"You move quickly," Vin noted appreciatively.

"All I had to do was round the palace grounds, Mistress."

"Still, you stuck closer to me this time than you ever did before. That wolfhound's body *is* faster than a human one."

OreSeur paused. "I suppose," he admitted.

"Think you can follow me through the city?"

"Probably," OreSeur said. "If you lose me, I will return to this point so you can retrieve me."

Vin turned and dashed down a side street. OreSeur then took off quietly behind her, following.

Let's see how well he does in a more demanding chase, she thought, burning pewter and increasing her speed. She sprinted along the cool cobbles, barefoot as always. A normal man could never have maintained such a speed. Even a trained runner couldn't have kept pace with her, for he would have quickly tired.

With pewter, however, Vin could run for hours at breakneck speeds. It gave her strength, lent her an unreal sense of balance, as she shot down the dark, mist-ruled street, a flurry of cloak tassels and bare feet.

OreSeur kept pace. He loped beside her in the night, breathing heavily, focused on his running.

Impressive, Vin thought, then turned down an alleyway. She easily jumped the six-foot-tall fence at the back, passing into the garden of some lesser nobleman's mansion. She spun, skidding on the wet grass, and watched.

OreSeur crested the top of the wooden fence, his dark, canine form dropping through the mists to land in the loam before Vin. He came to a stop, resting on his haunches, waiting quietly, panting. There was a look of defiance in his eyes.

All right, Vin thought, pulling out a handful of coins. *Follow this.*

She dropped a coin and threw herself backward up into the air. She spun in the mists, twisting, then Pushed herself sideways off a well spigot. She landed on a rooftop and jumped off, using another coin to Push herself over the street below.

She kept going, leaping from rooftop to rooftop, using coins when necessary. She occasionally shot a glance behind, and saw a dark form struggling to keep up. He'd rarely followed her as a human; usually, she had checked in with him at specific points. Moving out in the night, jumping through the mists . . . this was the true domain of the Mistborn. Did Elend understand what he asked when he told her to bring OreSeur with her? If she stayed down on the streets, she'd expose herself.

She landed on a rooftop, jarring to a sudden halt as she grabbed hold of the building's stone lip, leaning out over a street three stories below. She maintained her balance, mist swirling below her. All was silent.

Well, that didn't take long, she thought. *I'll just have to explain to Elend that—*

OreSeur's canine form thumped to the rooftop a short distance away. He padded over to her, then sat down on his haunches, waiting expectantly.

Vin frowned. She'd traveled for a good ten minutes, running over rooftops with the speed of a Mistborn. "How . . . how did you get up here?" she demanded.

"I jumped atop a shorter building, then used it to reach these tenements, Mistress," OreSeur said. "Then I followed you along the rooftops. They are placed so closely together that it was not difficult to jump from one to another."

Vin's confusion must have shown, for OreSeur continued. "I may have been . . . hasty in my judgment of these bones, Mistress. They certainly do have an impressive sense of smell—in fact, all of their senses are quite keen. It was surprisingly easy to track you, even in the darkness."

"I . . . see," Vin said. "Well, that's good."

"Might I ask, Mistress, the purpose of that chase?"

Vin shrugged. "I do this sort of thing every night."

"It seemed like you were particularly intent on losing me. It will be very difficult to protect you if you don't let me stay near you."

"Protect me?" Vin asked. "You can't even fight."

"The Contract forbids me from killing a human," OreSeur said. "I could, however, go for help should you need it."

Or throw me a bit of atium in a moment of danger, Vin admitted. *He's right—he could be useful. Why am I so determined to leave him behind?*

She glanced over at OreSeur, who sat patiently, his chest puffing from exertion. She hadn't realized that kandra even needed to breathe.

He ate Kelsier.

"Come on," Vin said. She jumped from the building, Pushing herself off a coin. She didn't pause to see if OreSeur followed.

As she fell, she reached for another coin, but decided not to use it. She Pushed against a passing window bracket instead. Like most Mistborn, she often used clips—the smallest denomination of coin—to jump. It was very convenient that the economy supplied a prepackaged bit of metal of an ideal size and weight for jumping and shooting. To most Mistborn, the cost of a thrown clip—or even a bag of them—was negligible.

But Vin was not most Mistborn. In her younger years, a handful of clips would have seemed an amazing treasure. That much money could have meant food for weeks, if she scrimped. It also could have meant pain—even death—if the other thieves had discovered that she'd obtained such a fortune.

It had been a long time since she'd gone hungry. Though she still kept a pack of dried foods in her quarters, she did so more out of habit than anxiety. She honestly wasn't sure what she thought of the changes within her. It was nice not to have to worry about basic necessities—and yet, those worries had been replaced by ones far more daunting. Worries involving the future of an entire nation.

The future of . . . a people. She landed on the city wall—a structure much higher, and much better fortified, than the small wall around Keep Venture. She hopped up on the battlements, fingers seeking a hold on one of the merlons as she leaned over the edge of the wall, looking out over the army's fires.

She had never met Straff Venture, but she had heard enough from Elend to be worried.

She sighed, pushing back off the battlement and hopping onto the wall walk. Then she leaned back against one of the merlons. To the side, OreSeur trotted up the wall steps and approached. Once again, he went down onto his haunches, watching patiently.

For better or for worse, Vin's simple life of starvation and beatings was gone. Elend's fledgling kingdom was in serious danger, and she'd burned away the last of his atium trying to keep herself alive. She'd left him exposed—not just to armies, but to any Mistborn assassin who tried to kill him.

An assassin like the Watcher, perhaps? The mysterious figure who had interfered in her fight against Cett's Mistborn. What did he want? Why did he watch her, rather than Elend?

Vin sighed, reaching into her coin pouch and pulling out her bar of duralumin. She still had the reserve of it within her, the bit she'd swallowed earlier.

For centuries, it had been assumed that there were only ten Allomantic metals: the four base metals and their alloys, plus atium and gold. Yet, Allomantic metals always came in pairs—a base metal and an alloy. It had always bothered Vin that atium and gold were considered a pair, when neither was an alloy of the other. In the end, it had turned out that they weren't actually paired; they each had an alloy. One of these—malatium, the so-called Eleventh Metal—had eventually given Vin the clue she'd needed to defeat the Lord Ruler.

Somehow Kelsier had found out about malatium. Sazed still hadn't been able to trace the "legends" that Kelsier had supposedly uncovered teaching of the Eleventh Metal and its power to defeat the Lord Ruler.

Vin rubbed her finger on the slick surface of the duralumin bar. When Vin had last seen Sazed, he'd seemed frustrated—or, at least, as frustrated as Sazed ever grew— that he couldn't find even hints regarding Kelsier's supposed legends. Though Sazed claimed he'd left Luthadel to teach the people of the Final Empire—as was his duty as a Keeper—Vin hadn't missed the fact that Sazed had gone south. The direction in which Kelsier claimed to have discovered the Eleventh Metal.

Are there rumors about this metal, too? Vin wondered, rubbing the duralumin. *Ones that might tell me what it does?*

Each of the other metals produced an immediate, visible effect; only copper, with its ability to create a cloud that masked an Allomancer's powers from others, didn't have an obvious sensory clue to its purpose. Perhaps duralumin was similar. Could its effect be noticed only by another Allomancer, one trying to use his or her powers on Vin? It was the opposite of aluminum, which made metals disappear. Did that mean duralumin would make other metals last longer?

Movement.

Vin just barely caught the hint of shadowed motion. At first, a primal bit of terror rose in her: Was it the misty form, the ghost in the darkness she had seen the night before?

You were just seeing things, she told herself forcefully. *You were too tired.* And, in truth, the glimmer of motion proved too dark—too *real*—to be the same ghostly image.

It was him.

He stood atop one of the watchtowers—not crouching, not even bothering to hide. Was he arrogant or foolish, this unknown Mistborn? Vin smiled, her apprehension turning to excitement. She prepared her metals, checking her reserves. Everything was ready.

Tonight I catch you, my friend.

Vin spun, throwing out a spray of coins. Either the Mistborn knew he'd been spotted, or he was ready for an attack, for he easily dodged. OreSeur hopped to his feet, spinning, and Vin whipped her belt free, dropping her metals.

"Follow if you can," she whispered to the kandra, then sprang into the darkness after her prey.

The Watcher shot away, bounding through the night. Vin had little experience chasing another Mistborn; her only real chance to practice had come during Kelsier's training sessions. She soon found herself struggling to keep up with the Watcher, and she felt a stab of guilt for what she had done to OreSeur earlier. She was learning firsthand how difficult it was to follow a determined Mistborn through the mists. And she didn't have the advantage of a dog's sense of smell.

She did, however, have tin. It made the night clearer and enhanced her hearing. With it, she managed to follow the Watcher as he moved toward the center of the city. Eventually, he let himself drop down toward one of the central fountain squares. Vin fell as well, hitting the slick cobblestones with a flare of pewter, then dodging to the side as he threw out a handful of coins.

Metal rang against stone in the quiet night, coins plinging against statues and cobblestones. Vin smiled as she landed on all fours; then she bounded forward, jumping with pewter-enhanced muscles and Pulling one of the coins up into her hand.

Her opponent leaped backward, landing on the edge of a nearby fountain. Vin landed, then dropped her coin, using it to throw herself upward over the Watcher's head. He stooped, watching warily as she passed over him.

Vin caught of one of the bronze statues at the center of the fountain itself and pulled herself to a stop atop it. She crouched on the uneven footing, looking down at her opponent. He stood balanced on one foot at the edge of the fountain, quiet and black in the churning mists. There was a . . . challenge in his posture.

Can you catch me? he seemed to ask.

Vin whipped her daggers out and jumped free of the statue. She Pushed herself directly toward the Watcher, using the cool bronze as an anchor.

The Watcher used the statue as well, Pulling himself forward. He shot just beneath Vin, throwing up a wave of water, his incredible speed letting him skid like a stone across the fountain's still surface. As he jumped clear of the water, he Pushed himself away, shooting across the square.

Vin landed on the fountain lip, chill water spraying across her. She growled, jumping after the Watcher.

As he landed, he spun and whipped out his own daggers. She rolled beneath his first attack, then brought her daggers up in a two-handed double jab. The Watcher jumped quickly out of the way, his daggers sparkling and dropping beads of fountain water. He had a lithe power about him as he came to rest in a crouch. His body looked tense and sure. Capable.

Vin smiled again, breathing quickly. She hadn't felt like this since . . . since those nights so long ago, when she'd sparred with Kelsier. She remained in a crouch, waiting, watching the mist curl between her and her opponent. He was of medium height, had a wiry build, and he wore no mistcloak.

Why no cloak? Mistcloaks were the ubiquitous mark of her kind, a symbol of pride and security.

She was too far away to distinguish his face. She thought she saw a hint of a smile, however, as he jumped backward and Pushed against another statue. The chase began again.

Vin followed him through the city, flaring steel, landing on roofs and streets, Pushing herself in great arcing leaps. The two bounded through Luthadel like children on a playground—Vin trying to cut off her opponent, he cleverly managing to stay just a little bit ahead of her.

He was good. Far better than any Mistborn she had known or faced, save perhaps for Kelsier. However, she'd grown greatly in skill since she'd sparred with the Survivor. Could this newcomer be even better? The thought thrilled her. She'd always considered Kelsier a paradigm of Allomantic ability, and it was easy to forget that he'd had his powers for only a couple of years before the Collapse.

That's the same amount of time that I've been training, Vin realized as she landed in a small, cramped street. She frowned, crouching, remaining still. She'd seen the Watcher fall toward this street.

Narrow and poorly maintained, the street was practically an alleyway, lined on both sides by three- and four-story buildings. There was no motion—either the Watcher had slipped away or he was hiding nearby. She burned iron, but the iron-lines revealed no motion.

However, there was another way. . . .

Vin pretended to still be looking around, but she turned on her bronze, flaring it, trying to pierce the coppercloud that she thought might be close.

And there he was. Hiding in a room behind the mostly closed shutters of a derelict building. Now that she knew where to look, she saw the bit of metal he'd probably used to jump up to the second story, the latch he must have Pulled on to quickly close the shutters behind him. He'd probably scouted this street beforehand, always intending to lose her here.

Clever, Vin thought.

He couldn't have anticipated her ability to pierce copperclouds. But, attacking him now might give away that ability. Vin stood quietly, thinking of him crouching above, tensely waiting for her to move off.

She smiled. Reaching inside, she examined the duralumin reserve. There was a possible way to discover if burning it created some change in the way she looked to another Mistborn. The Watcher was likely burning most of his metals, trying to determine what her next move would be.

So, thinking herself incredibly clever, Vin burned the fourteenth metal.

A massive explosion sounded in her ears. Vin gasped, dropping to her knees in shock. Everything grew bright around her, as if some crack of energy had illuminated the entire street. And she felt cold; frigidly, stunningly cold.

She moaned, trying to make sense of the sound. It . . . it wasn't an explosion, but many explosions. A rhythmic thudding, like a drum pounding just beside her. Her heartbeat. And the breeze, loud as a howling wind. The scratchings of a dog searching for food. Someone snoring in their sleep. It was as if her hearing had been magnified a hundred times.

And then . . . nothing. Vin fell backward against the cobblestones, the sudden rush of light, coldness, and sound evaporating. A form moved in the shadows nearby, but she couldn't make it out—she couldn't see in the darkness anymore. Her tin was . . .

Gone, she realized, coming to. *My entire store of tin has been burned away. I was . . . burning it, when I turned on the duralumin.*

I burned them both at once. That's the secret. The duralumin had burned away all her tin in a single, massive burst. It had made her senses amazingly acute for a very short time, but had stolen away her entire reserve. And, looking, she could see that her bronze and her pewter—the other metals she'd been burning at the time—were gone as well. The onrush of sensory information had been so vast that she hadn't noticed the effects of the other two.

Think about it later, Vin told herself, shaking her head. She felt like she should be deafened and blinded, but she wasn't. She was just a bit stunned.

The dark form moved up beside her in the mists. She didn't have time to recover; she pushed herself to her feet, stumbling. The form, it was too short to be the Watcher. It was . . .

"Mistress, do you require assistance?"

Vin paused as OreSeur padded up to her, then sat on his haunches.

"You . . . managed to follow," Vin said.

"It was not easy, Mistress," OreSeur said flatly. "Do you require assistance?"

"What? No, no assistance." Vin shook her head, clearing her mind. "I guess that's one thing I didn't think of by making you a dog. You can't carry metals for me now."

The kandra cocked his head, then padded over into an alleyway. He returned a moment later with something in his mouth. Her belt.

He dropped it by her feet, then returned to his waiting position. Vin picked up the belt, pulling off one of her extra metal vials. "Thank you," she said slowly. "That is very . . . thoughtful of you."

"I fulfill my Contract, Mistress," the kandra said. "Nothing more."

Well, this is more than you've ever done before, she thought, downing a vial and feeling her reserves return. She burned tin, restoring her night vision, releasing a veil of tension from her mind; since she'd discovered her powers, she'd never had to go out at night in complete darkness.

The shutters of the Watcher's room were open; he had apparently fled during her fit. Vin sighed.

"Mistress!" OreSeur snapped.

Vin spun. A man landed quietly behind her. He looked . . . familiar, for some reason. He had a lean face—topped with dark hair—and his head was cocked slightly in confusion. She could see the question in his eyes. Why had she fallen down?

Vin smiled. "Maybe I just did it to lure you closer," she whispered—softly, yet loud enough that she knew tin-enhanced ears would hear her.

The Mistborn smiled, then tipped his head to her as if in respect.

"Who are you?" Vin asked, stepping forward.

"An enemy," he replied, holding up a hand to ward her back.

Vin paused. Mist swirled between them on the quiet street. "Why, then, did you help me fight those assassins?"

"Because," he said. "I'm also insane."

Vin frowned, eyeing the man. She had seen insanity before in the eyes of beggars. This man was not insane. He stood proudly, eyes controlled as he regarded her in the darkness.

What kind of game is he playing? she wondered.

Her instincts—a lifetime's worth of instincts—warned her to be wary. She had only just learned to trust her friends, and she wasn't about to offer the same privilege to a man she had met in the night.

And yet, it had been over a year since she'd spoken with another Mistborn. There were conflicts within her that she couldn't explain to the others. Even Mistings, like Ham and Breeze, couldn't understand the strange dual life of a Mistborn. Part assassin, part bodyguard, part noblewoman . . . part confused, quiet girl. Did this man have similar troubles with his identity?

Perhaps she could make an ally out of him, bringing a second Mistborn to the defense of the Central Dominance. Even if she couldn't, she certainly couldn't afford to fight him. A spar in the night was one thing, but if their contest grew dangerous, atium might come into play.

If that happened, she'd lose.

The Watcher studied her with a careful eye. "Answer something for me," he said in the mists.

Vin nodded.

"Did you really kill Him?"

"Yes," Vin whispered. There was only one person he could mean.

He nodded slowly. "Why do you play their games?"

"Whose games?"

The Watcher gestured into the mists, toward Keep Venture.

"Those aren't games," Vin said. "It's no game when the people I love are in danger."

The Watcher stood quietly, then shook his head, as if . . . disappointed. Then, he pulled something from his sash.

Vin jumped back immediately. The Watcher, however, simply flipped a coin to the ground between them. It bounced a couple of times, coming to a rest on the cobbles. Then, the Watcher Pushed himself backward into the air.

Vin didn't follow. She reached up, rubbing her head; she still felt like she should have a headache.

"You're letting him go?" OreSeur asked.

Vin nodded. "We're done for tonight. He fought well."

"You sound almost respectful," the kandra said.

Vin turned, frowning at the hint of disgust in the kandra's voice. OreSeur sat patiently, displaying no further emotion.

She sighed, tying her belt around her waist. "We're going to need to come up with a harness or something for you," she said. "I want you to carry extra metal vials for me, like you did as a human."

"A harness won't be necessary, Mistress," OreSeur said.

"Oh?"

OreSeur rose, padding forward. "Please get out one of your vials."

Vin did as requested, pulling out a small glass vial. Ore-Seur stopped, then turned one shoulder toward her. As she watched, the fur parted and the flesh itself split, showing forth veins and layers of skin. Vin pulled back a bit.

"There is no need to be worried, Mistress," OreSeur said. "My flesh is not like your own. I have more . . . control over it, you might say. Place the metal vial inside my shoulder."

Vin did as asked. The flesh sealed around the vial, obscuring it from view. Experimentally, Vin burned iron. No blue lines appeared pointing toward the hidden vial. Metal inside of a person's stomach couldn't be affected by another Allomancer; indeed, metal piercing a body, like Inquisitor spikes or Vin's own earring, couldn't be Pushed or Pulled by someone else. Apparently, the same rule applied to metals hidden within a kandra.

"I will deliver this to you in an emergency," OreSeur said.

"Thank you," Vin said.

"The Contract, Mistress. Do not give me thanks. I do only what I am required."

Vin nodded slowly. "Let's go back to the palace, then," she said. "I want to check on Elend."

But, let me begin at the beginning. I met Alendi first in Khlennium; he was a young lad then, and had not yet been warped by a decade spent leading armies.

9

MARSH HAD CHANGED. THERE WAS something . . . harder about the former Seeker. Something in the way he always seemed to be staring at things Sazed couldn't see, something in his blunt responses and terse language.

Of course, Marsh had always been a straightforward man. Sazed eyed his friend as the two strode down the dusty highway. They had no horses; even if Sazed had possessed one, most beasts wouldn't go near an Inquisitor.

What did Spook say that Marsh's nickname was? Sazed thought to himself as they walked. *Before his transformation, they used to call him . . . Ironeyes.* The name that had turned out to be chillingly prophetic. Most of the others found Marsh's transformed state discomforting, and had left him isolated. Though Marsh hadn't seemed to mind the treatment, Sazed had made a special effort to befriend the man.

He still didn't know if Marsh appreciated the gesture or not. They did seem to get along well; both shared an interest in scholarship and history, and both were interested in the religious climate of the Final Empire.

And, he did come looking for me, Sazed thought. *Of course, he did claim that he wanted help in case the Inquisitors weren't all gone from the Conventical of Seran.* It was a weak excuse. Despite his powers as a Feruchemist, Sazed was no warrior.

"You should be in Luthadel," Marsh said.

Sazed looked up. Marsh had spoken bluntly, as usual, without preamble. "Why do you say that?" Sazed asked.

"They need you there."

"The rest of the Final Empire has need of me too, Marsh. I am a Keeper—one group of people should not be able to monopolize all of my time."

Marsh shook his head. "These peasants, they will forget your passing. No one will forget the things that will soon happen in the Central Dominance."

"You would be surprised, I think, at what men can forget. Wars and kingdoms may seem important now, but even the Final Empire proved mortal. Now that it has fallen, the Keepers have no business being involved in politics." *Most would say we never had any business being involved in politics at all.*

Marsh turned toward him. Those eyes, sockets filled entirely with steel. Sazed did not shiver, but he felt distinctly uncomfortable.

"And your friends?" Marsh asked.

This touched on something more personal. Sazed looked away, thinking of Vin, and of his vow to Kelsier that he would protect her. *She needs little protection now,* he thought. *She's grown more adept at Allomancy than even Kelsier was.* And yet, Sazed knew that there were modes of protection that didn't relate to fighting. These things—support, counsel, kindness—were vital to every person, and most especially to Vin. So much rested on that poor girl's shoulders.

"I have . . . sent help," Sazed said. "What help I can."

"Not good enough," Marsh said. "The things happening in Luthadel are too important to ignore."

"I am not ignoring them, Marsh," Sazed said. "I am simply performing my duty as best I can."

Marsh finally turned away. "The wrong duty. You will return to Luthadel once we are finished here."

Sazed opened his mouth to argue, but said nothing. What was there to say? Marsh was right. Though he had no proof, Sazed knew that there *were* important things happening in Luthadel—things that would require his aid to fight. Things that likely affected the future of the entire land once known as the Final Empire.

So, he closed his mouth and trudged after Marsh. He

would return to Luthadel, proving himself a rebel once again. Perhaps, in the end, he would realize that there was no ghostly threat facing the world—that he had simply returned because of his own selfish desire to be with his friends.

In fact, he hoped that proved to be the truth. The alternative made him very uncomfortable.

Alendi's height struck me the first time I saw him. Here was a man who towered over others, a man who—despite his youth and his humble clothing—demanded respect.

10

THE ASSEMBLY HALL WAS in the former Steel Ministry Canton of Finance headquarters. It was a low-ceilinged space, more of a large lecture room than an assembly hall. There were rows of benches fanning out in front of a raised stage. On the right side of the stage, Elend had constructed a tier of seats for the Assembly members. On the left of the stage, he had constructed a single lectern for speakers.

The lectern faced the Assemblymen, not the crowd. The common people were, however, encouraged to attend. Elend thought that everyone should be interested in the workings of their government; it pained him that the Assembly's weekly meetings usually had a small audience.

Vin's seat was on the stage, but at the back, directly opposite the audience. From her vantage with the other bodyguards, she would look past the lectern toward the crowd. Another row of Ham's guards—in regular clothing—sat in the first row of the audience, providing a first line of protection. Elend had balked at Vin's demands to having guards both in front of the stage and behind it—he thought that bodyguards sitting right behind the speakers would be distracting. Ham and Vin, however, had insisted. If Elend was going to stand up in front of a crowd every week, Vin wanted to be certain she could keep a close eye on him—and on those watching him.

Getting to her chair, therefore, required Vin to walk across the stage. Stares followed her. Some of the watching crowd were interested in the scandal; they assumed that she was Elend's mistress, and a king sleeping with his personal assassin made for good gossip. Others were interested in the politics; they wondered how much influence Vin had over Elend, and whether they could use her to get the king's ear. Still others were curious about the growing legends; they wondered if a girl like Vin could really have slain the Lord Ruler.

Vin hurried her pace. She passed the Assemblymen and found her seat next to Ham, who—despite the formal occasion—still wore a simple vest with no shirt. Sitting next to him in her trousers and shirt, Vin didn't feel quite so out of place.

Ham smiled, clapping her affectionately on the shoulder. She had to force herself not to jump at the touch. It wasn't that she disliked Ham—quite the opposite, actually. She loved him as she did all of the former members of Kelsier's band. It was just that . . . well, she had trouble explaining it, even to herself. Ham's innocent gesture made her want to squirm. It seemed to her that people shouldn't be so casual with the way that they touched others.

She pushed those thoughts away. She had to learn to be like other people. Elend deserved a woman who was normal.

He was already there. He nodded to Vin as he noticed her arrival, and she smiled. Then he turned back to speaking quietly with Lord Penrod, one of the noblemen in the Assembly.

"Elend will be happy," Vin whispered. "Place is packed."

"They're worried," Ham said quietly. "And worried people pay more attention to things like this. Can't say I'm happy—all these people make our job harder."

Vin nodded, scanning the audience. The crowd was a strangely mixed one—a collection of different groups who would never have met together during the days of the Final Empire. A major part were noblemen, of course. Vin frowned, thinking of how often various members of the nobility tried to manipulate Elend, and of the promises he made to them. . . .

"What's that look for?" Ham asked, nudging her.

Vin eyed the Thug. Expectant eyes twinkled in his firm, rectangular face. Ham had an almost supernatural sense when it came to arguments.

Vin sighed. "I don't know about this, Ham."

"This?"

"*This,*" Vin said quietly, waving her hand at the Assembly. "Elend tries so hard to make everyone happy. He gives so much away—his power, his money. . . ."

"He just wants to see that everyone is treated fairly."

"It's more than that, Ham," Vin said. "It's like he's determined to make everyone a nobleman."

"Would that be such a bad thing?"

"If everyone is a nobleman, then there is no such thing as a nobleman. Everyone *can't* be rich, and everyone can't be in charge. That's just not the way things work."

"Perhaps," Ham said thoughtfully. "But, doesn't Elend have a civic duty to try and make sure justice is served?"

Civic duty? Vin thought. *I should have known better than to talk to Ham about something like this. . . .*

Vin looked down. "I just think he could see that everyone was treated well without having an Assembly. All they do is argue and try to take his power away. And he lets them."

Ham let the discussion die, and Vin turned back to her study of the audience. It appeared that a large group of mill workers had arrived first and managed to get the best seats. Early in the Assembly's history—perhaps ten months before—the nobility had sent servants to reserve seats for them, or had bribed people to give up their places. As soon as Elend had discovered this, however, he had forbidden both practices.

Other than the noblemen and the mill workers, there was a large number of the "new" class. Skaa merchants and craftsmasters, now allowed to set their own prices for their services. They were the true winners in Elend's economy. Beneath the Lord Ruler's oppressive hand, only the few most extraordinarily skilled skaa had been able to rise to positions of even moderate comfort. Without those restrictions, these same people had quickly proven to have abilities and acumen far above their noble counterparts'. They represented a faction in the Assembly at least as powerful as that of the nobility.

Other skaa peppered the crowd. They looked much the same as they had before Elend's rise to power. While noblemen generally wore suits—complete with dayhats and coats—these skaa wore simple trousers. Some of them were still dirty from their day's labor, their clothing old, worn, and stained with ash.

And yet . . . there *was* something different about them. It wasn't in their clothing, but their postures. They sat a little straighter, their heads held a little higher. And they had enough free time to attend an Assembly meeting.

Elend finally stood to begin the meeting. He had let his attendants dress him this morning, and the result was attire that was almost completely free of dishevelment. His suit fit well, all the buttons were done up, and his vest was of an appropriate dark blue. His hair was even neatly styled, the short, brown curls lying flat.

Normally, Elend would begin the meeting by calling on other speakers, Assemblymen who would drone on for hours about various topics like taxation rates or city sanitation. However, this day, there were more pressing matters.

"Gentlemen," Elend said. "I beg your leave to depart from our usual agenda this afternoon, in the light of our current . . . state of city affairs."

The group of twenty-four Assemblymen nodded, a few muttering things under their breath. Elend ignored them. He was comfortable before crowds, far more comfortable than Vin would ever be. As he unrolled his speech, Vin kept one eye on the crowd, watching for reactions or problems.

"The dire nature of our situation should be quite obvious," Elend said, beginning the speech he had prepared earlier. "We face a danger that this city has never known. Invasion and siege from an outside tyrant.

"We are a new nation, a kingdom founded on principles unknown during the days of the Lord Ruler. Yet, we are already a kingdom of tradition. Freedom for the skaa. Rule by our own choice and of our own design. Noblemen who don't have to cower before the Lord Ruler's obligators and Inquisitors.

"Gentlemen, one year is not enough. We have tasted freedom, and we need time to savor it. During the last month, we have frequently discussed and argued regarding what to do should this day arrive. Obviously, we are of many minds on the issue. Therefore, I ask for a vote of solidarity. Let us promise ourselves, and these people, that we will not give this city over to a foreign power without due consideration. Let us resolve to gather more information, to seek for other avenues, and even to fight should it be deemed necessary."

The speech went on, but Vin had heard it a dozen times as Elend practiced it. As he spoke, she found herself eying the crowd. She was most worried about the obligators she saw sitting in the back. They showed little reaction to the negative light in which Elend's remarks cast them.

She'd never understood why Elend allowed the Steel Ministry to continue teaching. It was the last real remnant of the Lord Ruler's power. Most obligators obstinately refused to lend their knowledge of bureaucracy and administration to Elend's government, and they still regarded skaa with contempt.

And yet, Elend let them remain. He maintained a strict rule that they were not allowed to incite rebellion or violence. However, he also didn't eject them from the city, as Vin had suggested. Actually, if the choice had been solely hers, she probably would have executed them.

Eventually, Elend's speech drew to a close, and Vin turned her attention back to him. "Gentlemen," he said, "I make this proposal out of faith, and I make it in the names of those we represent. I ask for time. I propose that we forgo all votes regarding the future of the city until a proper royal delegation has been allowed to meet with the army outside and determine what, if any, opportunity there is for negotiations."

He lowered his sheet, looking up, waiting for comments.

"So," said Philen, one of the merchants on the Assembly. "You're asking us to give *you* the power to decide the city's fate." Philen wore his rich suit so well that an observer would never have known that he'd first put one on about a year ago.

"What?" Elend asked. "I said nothing of the sort—I'm simply asking for more time. To meet with Straff."

"He's rejected all of our earlier messages," said another Assemblyman. "What makes you think he'll listen now?"

"We're approaching this wrong!" said one of the noble representatives. "We should be resolving to *beg* Straff Venture not to attack, not resolving to meet with him and chat. We need to establish quickly that we're willing to work with him. You've all seen that army. He's planning to destroy us!"

"Please," Elend said, raising a hand. "Let us stay on topic!"

One of the other Assemblymen—one of the skaa—spoke up, as if he hadn't heard Elend. "You say that because you're noble," he said, pointing at the noble Elend had interrupted. "It's easy for you to talk about working with Straff, since you've got very little to lose!"

"Very little to lose?" the nobleman said. "I and all of my house could be executed for supporting Elend against his father!"

"Bah," said one of the merchants. "This is all pointless. We should have hired mercenaries months ago, as I'd suggested."

"And where would we have gotten the funds for that?" asked Lord Penrod, senior of the noble Assemblymen.

"Taxes," the merchant said with a wave of his hand.

"Gentlemen!" Elend said; then, louder, "Gentlemen!"

This garnered him some small measure of attention.

"We *have* to make a decision," Elend said. "Stay focused, if you please. What of my proposal?"

"It's pointless," said Philen the merchant. "Why should we wait? Let's just invite Straff into the city and be done. He's going to take it anyway."

Vin sat back as the men began to argue again. The problem was, the merchant Philen—as little as she liked him—

had a point. Fighting was looking like a very unattractive option. Straff had such a large army. Would stalling really do that much good?

"Look, see," Elend said, trying to get their attention again—and only partially succeeding. "Straff is my father. Maybe I could talk to him. Get him to listen? Luthadel was his home for years. Perhaps I can convince him not to attack it."

"Wait," said one of the skaa representatives. "What of the food issue? Have you seen what the merchants are charging for grain? Before we worry about that army, we should talk about bringing prices down."

"Always blaming us for your problems," one of the merchant Assemblymen said, pointing. And the squabbling began again. Elend slumped just slightly behind the lectern. Vin shook her head, feeling sorry for Elend as the discussion degenerated. This was what often happened at Assembly meetings; it seemed to her that they simply didn't give Elend the respect he deserved. Perhaps that was his own fault, for elevating them to his near equals.

Finally, the discussion wound down, and Elend got out a piece of paper, obviously planning to record the vote on his proposal. He did not look optimistic.

"All right," Elend said. "Let's vote. Please remember—giving me time will *not* play our hand. It will simply give me a chance to try and make my father reconsider his desire to take our city away from us."

"Elend, lad," said Lord Penrod. "We all lived here during the Lord Ruler's reign. We all know what kind of man your father is. If he wants this city, he *is* going to take it. All we can decide, then, is how to best give up. Perhaps we can find a way for the people to retain some freedom under his rule."

The group sat quietly, and for the first time nobody brought up a new squabble. A few of them turned toward Penrod, who sat with a calm, in-control expression. Vin knew little of the man. He was one of the more powerful noblemen who had remained in the city after the Collapse, and he was politically conservative. However, she had never heard him speak derogatively of the skaa, which was probably why he was so popular with the people.

"I speak bluntly," Penrod said, "for it is the truth. We are not in a position to bargain."

"I agree with Penrod," Philen said, jumping in. "If Elend wants to meet with Straff Venture, then I guess that's his right. As I understand it, kingship grants him authority to negotiate with foreign monarchs. However, we don't have to promise not to give Straff the city."

"Master Philen," Lord Penrod said. "I think you misjudged my intent. I said that giving up the city was inevitable—but that we should try to gain as much from it as possible. *That* means at least meeting with Straff to assess his disposition. Voting to give him the city now would be to play our hand too soon."

Elend looked up, looking hopeful for the first time since the discussion had first degenerated. "So, you support my proposal?" he asked.

"It is an awkward way to achieve the pause I think necessary," Penrod said. "But . . . seeing as how the army is already here, then I doubt we have time for anything else. So, yes, Your Majesty. I support your proposal."

Several other members of the Assembly nodded as Penrod spoke, as if giving the proposal consideration for the first time. *That Penrod has too much power,* Vin thought, eyes narrowing as she regarded the elderly statesman. *They listen to him more than they do Elend.*

"Should we vote, then?" one of the other Assemblymen asked.

And they did. Elend recorded votes as they moved down the line of Assemblymen. The eight noblemen—seven plus Elend—voted for the proposal, giving Penrod's opinion a great deal of weight. The eight skaa were mostly for it, and the merchants mostly against it. In the end, however, Elend got the two-thirds vote he needed.

"Proposal accepted," Elend said, making the final tally, looking a bit surprised. "The Assembly divests itself of the right to surrender the city until after the king has met with Straff Venture in official parlay."

Vin sat back in her seat, trying to decide what she thought of the vote. It was good that Elend had gotten his way, but the manner in which he'd achieved it bothered her.

Elend finally relinquished the lectern, sitting and letting a disgruntled Philen take the lead. The merchant read a proposal calling for a vote to turn control of city food stockpiles over to the merchants. However, this time Elend himself led the dissent, and the arguing began again. Vin watched with interest. Did Elend even realize how much like the others he acted while he was arguing against their proposals?

Elend and a few of the skaa Assemblymen managed to filibuster long enough that the lunch break arrived with no vote cast. The people in the audience stood, stretching, and Ham turned toward her. "Good meeting, eh?"

Vin just shrugged.

Ham chuckled. "We really have to do something about your ambivalence toward civic duty, kid."

"I already overthrew one government," Vin said. "I figure that takes care of my 'civic duty' for a while."

Ham smiled, though he kept a wary eye on the crowd— as did Vin. Now, with everyone moving about, would be the perfect time for an attempt on Elend's life. One person in particular caught her attention, and she frowned.

"Be back in a few seconds," she said to Ham, rising.

"You did the right thing, Lord Penrod," Elend said, standing beside the older nobleman, whispering quietly as break proceeded. "We need more time. You know what my father will do to this city if he takes it."

Lord Penrod shook his head. "I didn't do this for you, son. I did it because I wanted to make certain that fool Philen didn't hand the city over before the nobility extracted promises from your father about our rights to title."

"Now, see," Elend said, holding up a finger. "There has to be another way! The Survivor would never have given this city away without a fight."

Penrod frowned, and Elend paused, quietly cursing himself. The old lord was a traditionalist—quoting the Survivor at him would have little positive effect. Many of the noblemen felt threatened by Kelsier's influence with the skaa.

"Just think about it," Elend said, glancing to the side as Vin approached. She waved him away from the Assemblymen seats, and he excused himself. He crossed the stage, joining her. "What is it?" he asked quietly.

"Woman at the back," Vin said quietly, eyes suspicious. "Tall one, in the blue."

The woman in question wasn't hard to find; she wore a bright blue blouse and colorful red skirt. She was middle-aged, of lean build, and had her waist-length hair pulled back in a braid. She waited patiently as people moved about the room.

"What about her?" Elend asked.

"Terris," Vin said.

Elend paused. "You're sure?"

Vin nodded. "Those colors . . . that much jewelry. She's a Terriswoman for sure."

"So?"

"So, I've never met her," Vin said. "And she was watching you, just now."

"People watch me, Vin," Elend noted. "I *am* the king, after all. Besides, why should you have met her?"

"All of the other Terris people have come to meet me right after they enter the city," Vin said. "I killed the Lord Ruler; they see me as the one that freed their homeland. But, I don't recognize her. She hasn't ever come thank me."

Elend rolled his eyes, grabbing Vin by the shoulders and turning her away from the woman. "Vin, I feel it's my gentlemanly duty to tell you something."

Vin frowned. "What?"

"You're gorgeous."

Vin paused. "What does that have to do with anything?"

"Absolutely nothing," Elend said with a smile. "I'm just trying to distract you."

Slowly, Vin relaxed, smiling slightly.

"I don't know if anyone's ever told you this, Vin," Elend noted, "but you can be a bit paranoid at times."

She raised an eyebrow. "Oh?"

"I know it's hard to believe, but it's true. Now, I happen to find it rather charming, but do you honestly think that a *Terriswoman* would try to kill me?"

"Probably not," Vin admitted. "But, old habits . . ."

Elend smiled. Then, he glanced back at the Assembly-men, most of whom were speaking quietly in groups. They didn't mix. Noblemen spoke with noblemen, merchants with merchants, skaa workers with other skaa workers. They seemed so fragmented, so obstinate. The simplest proposals sometimes met with arguments that could take hours.

They need to give me more time! he thought. Yet, even as he thought, he realized the problem. More time for what? Penrod and Philen had accurately attacked his proposal.

The truth was, the entire city was in over its head. No-body really knew what to do about a superior invading force, least of all Elend. He just knew that they couldn't give up. Not yet. There *had* to be a way to fight.

Vin was still looking to the side, out over the audience. Elend followed her gaze. "Still watching that Terris-woman?"

Vin shook her head. "Something else . . . something odd. Is that one of Clubs's messengers?"

Elend paused, turning. Indeed, several soldiers were working their way through the crowd, approaching the stage. At the back of the room, people had begun whisper-ing and shuffling, and some were already moving quickly out of the chamber.

Elend felt Vin stiffen in anxiety, and fear stabbed him. *We're too late. The army has attacked.*

One of the soldiers finally reached the stage, and Elend rushed over. "What?" he asked. "Has Straff attacked?"

The soldier frowned, looking concerned. "No, my lord."

Elend sighed slightly. "What, then?"

"My lord, it's a second army. It just arrived outside the city."

Oddly, it was Alendi's simple ingenuousness that first led me to befriend him. I employed him as an assistant during his first months in the grand city.

11

FOR THE SECOND TIME IN two days, Elend stood atop the Luthadel city wall, studying an army that had come to invade his kingdom. Elend squinted against the red afternoon sunlight, but he was no Tineye; he couldn't make out details about the new arrival.

"Any chance they're here to help us?" Elend asked hopefully, looking toward Clubs, who stood beside him.

Clubs just scowled. "They fly Cett's banner. Remember him? Guy who sent eight Allomancer assassins to kill you two days back?"

Elend shivered in the chill autumn weather, glancing back out over the second army. It was making camp a good distance from Straff's army, close to the Luth-Davn Canal, which ran out the west side of the River Channerel. Vin stood at Elend's side, though Ham was off organizing things among the city guard. OreSeur, wearing the wolfhound's body, sat patiently on the wall walk beneath Vin.

"How did we miss their approach?" Elend asked.

"Straff," Clubs said. "This Cett came in from the same direction, and our scouts were focused on him. Straff probably knew about this other army a few days ago, but we had virtually no chance of seeing them."

Elend nodded.

"Straff is setting up a perimeter of soldiers, watching the enemy army," Vin said. "I doubt they're friendly to each other." She stood atop one of the sawtooth parapet crenels, feet positioned dangerously close to the wall's edge.

"Maybe they'll attack each other," Elend said hopefully.

Clubs snorted. "I doubt it. They're too evenly matched, though Straff might be a little stronger. I doubt Cett would take the chance by attacking him."

"Why come, then?" Elend asked.

Clubs shrugged. "Maybe he hoped he'd beat Venture to Luthadel, and get to take it first."

He spoke of the event—the capture of Luthadel—as if it were a given. Elend's stomach twisted as he leaned against the battlement, looking out through a merlon. Vin and the others were thieves and skaa Allomancers—outcasts who had been hunted for most of their lives. Perhaps they were accustomed to dealing with this pressure—this fear—but Elend was not.

How did they live with the lack of control, the sense of inevitability? Elend felt powerless. What could he do? Flee, and leave the city to fend for itself? That, of course, was not an option. But, confronted with not one, but two armies preparing to destroy his city and take his throne, Elend found it hard to keep his hands steady as he gripped the rough stone of the battlement.

Kelsier would have found a way out of this, he thought.

"There!" Vin's voice interrupted Elend's thoughts. "What's that?"

Elend turned. Vin was squinting, looking toward Cett's army, using tin to see things that were invisible to Elend's mundane eyes.

"Someone's leaving the army," Vin said. "Riding on horseback."

"Messenger?" Clubs asked.

"Maybe," Vin said. "He's riding pretty fast. . . ." She began to run from one stone tooth to the next, moving along the wall. Her kandra immediately followed, padding quietly across the wall beneath her.

Elend glanced at Clubs, who shrugged, and they began to follow. They caught up with Vin standing on the wall near one of the towers, watching the oncoming rider. Or, at least, Elend assumed that was what she watched—he still couldn't see what she had.

Allomancy, Elend thought, shaking his head. Why couldn't he have at least ended up with one power—even one of the weaker ones, like copper or iron?

Vin cursed suddenly, standing up straight. "Elend, that's *Breeze!*"

"What!" Elend said. "Are you sure?"

"Yes! He's being chased. Archers on horseback."

Clubs cursed, waving to a messenger. "Send riders! Cut off his pursuit!"

The messenger dashed away. Vin, however, shook her head. "They won't make it in time," she said, almost to herself. "The archers will catch him, or at least shoot him. Even I couldn't get there fast enough, not running. But, maybe . . ."

Elend frowned, looking up at her. "Vin, that's way too far to jump—even for you."

Vin glanced at him, smiled, then leaped off the wall.

Vin readied the fourteenth metal, duralumin. She had a reserve, but she didn't burn it—not yet. *I hope this works,* she thought, seeking an appropriate anchor. The tower beside her had a reinforced iron bulwark on the top—that would work.

She Pulled on the bulwark, yanking herself up to the top of the tower. She immediately jumped again, Pushing herself up and out, angling into the air away from the wall. She extinguished all of her metals except for steel and pewter.

Then, still Pushing against the bulwark, she burned duralumin.

A sudden force smashed against her. It was so powerful, she was certain that only an equally powerful flash of pewter held her body together. She blasted away from the keep, hurtling through the sky as if tossed by some giant, invisible god. The air rushed by so quickly that it roared, and the pressure of sudden acceleration made it difficult to think.

She floundered, trying to regain control. She had, fortunately, picked her trajectory well: she was shooting right toward Breeze and his pursuers. Whatever Breeze had done, it had been enough to make someone extremely angry—for there were a full two dozen men charging after him, arrows nocked.

Vin fell, her steel and pewter completely burned away in that single duralumin-fueled flash of power. She grabbed a metal vial off her belt, downing its contents. However, as she tossed the vial away, she suddenly felt an odd sense of vertigo. She wasn't accustomed to jumping during the day. It was strange to see the ground coming at her, strange not to have a mistcloak flapping behind her, strange not to have the mist. . . .

The lead rider lowered his bow, taking sight at Breeze. Neither appeared to have noticed Vin, swooping down like a bird of prey above.

Well, not exactly swooping. Plummeting.

Suddenly snapped back to the moment, Vin burned pewter and threw a coin toward the quickly approaching ground. She Pushed against the coin, using it to slow her momentum and to nudge her to the side. She hit right between Breeze and the archers, landing with a jarring crash, throwing up dust and dirt.

The archer released his arrow.

Even as Vin rebounded, dirt spraying around her, she reached out and Pushed herself back into the air straight at the arrow. Then she Pushed against it. The arrowhead ripped backward—throwing out shards of wood as it split its own shaft in midair—then smacked directly into the forehead of the archer who had released it.

The man toppled from his mount. Vin landed from her rebound. She reached out, Pushing against the horseshoes of the two beasts behind the leader, causing the animals to stumble. The Push threw Vin backward into the air, and cries of equine pain sounded amid the crash of bodies hitting the ground.

Vin continued to Push, flying along the road just a few feet above the ground, quickly catching up with Breeze. The portly man turned in shock, obviously stunned to find Vin hanging in the air beside his galloping horse, her clothing flapping in the wind of her passage. She winked at him, then reached out and Pulled against the armor of another rider.

She immediately lurched in the air. Her body protested the sudden shift in momentum, but she ignored the twist of pain. The man she Pulled against managed to stay in his saddle—until Vin smashed into him feet-first, throwing him backward.

She landed on the black earth, the rider tumbling to the ground beside her. A short distance away, the remaining riders finally reined in their mounts, coming to an abrupt stop a few feet away.

Kelsier probably would have attacked. There were a lot of them, true, but they were wearing armor and their horses were shod. Vin, however, was not Kelsier. She had delayed the riders long enough for Breeze to get away. That was enough.

Vin reached out and Pushed against one of the soldiers, throwing herself backward, leaving the riders to gather their wounded. The soldiers, however, promptly pulled out stone-tipped arrows and nocked their bows.

Vin hissed in frustration as the group took sight. *Well, friends,* she thought, *I suggest that you hang on tightly.*

She Pushed slightly against them all, then burned duralumin. The sudden crash of force was expected—the wrench in her chest, the massive flare in her stomach, the howling wind. What she didn't expect was the effect she'd have on her anchors. The blast of power scattered men and horses, throwing them into the air like leaves in the wind.

I'm going to have to be very careful with this, Vin thought, gritting her teeth and spinning herself in the air. Her steel and pewter were gone again, and she was forced to down her last metal vial. She'd have to start carrying more of those.

She hit the ground running, pewter keeping her from tripping despite her terrific speed. She slowed just slightly, letting the mounted Breeze catch up to her, then increased her pace to keep up with him. She dashed like a sprinter, letting pewter's strength and balance keep her upright as she paced the tiring horse. The beast eyed her as they ran, seeming to display a hint of animal frustration to see a human matching it.

They reached the city a few moments later. Breeze reined

in as the doors to Iron Gate began to open, but, rather than wait, Vin simply threw down a coin and Pushed, letting her forward momentum carry her toward the walls. As the gates swung open, she Pushed against their studs, and this second Push sent her sailing straight up. She just barely crested the battlements—passing between a pair of startled soldiers—before dropping over the other side. She landed in the courtyard, steadying herself with one hand against the cool stones, as Breeze entered through the gate.

Vin stood. Breeze patted his forehead with a handkerchief as he trotted his animal up beside her. He'd let his hair grow longer since she'd last seen him, and he kept it slicked back, its lower edges tickling his collar. It wasn't graying yet, though he was in his mid-forties. He wore no hat—it had probably blown free—but he had on one of his rich suits and silken vests. They were powdered with black ash from his hurried ride.

"Ah, Vin, my dear," Breeze said, breathing almost as deeply as his horse. "I must say, that was a timely arrival on your part. Impressively flamboyant as well. I do hate to force a rescue—but, well, if one is necessary, then it might as well happen with style."

Vin smiled as he climbed down from the horse—proving he was hardly the most adroit man in the square—and stablehands arrived to care for the beast. Breeze wiped his brow again as Elend, Clubs, and OreSeur scrambled down the steps to the courtyard. One of the aides must have finally found Ham, for he ran up through the courtyard.

"Breeze!" Elend said, approaching and clasping arms with the shorter man.

"Your Majesty," Breeze said. "You are in good health and good humor, I assume?"

"Health, yes," Elend said. "Humor . . . well, there *is* an army crouching just outside my city."

"Two armies, actually," Clubs grumbled as he hobbled up.

Breeze folded up his handkerchief. "Ah, and dear Master Cladent. Optimistic as always, I see."

Clubs snorted. To the side, OreSeur padded up to sit next to Vin.

"And Hammond," Breeze said, eyeing Ham, who was

smiling broadly. "I'd almost managed to delude myself into forgetting that *you* would be here when I returned."

"Admit it," Ham said. "You're glad to see me."

"See you, perhaps. *Hear* you, never. I had grown quite fond of my time spent away from your perpetual, pseudo-philosophical pratterings."

Ham just smiled a little broader.

"I'm glad to see you, Breeze," Elend said. "But your timing could have been a little better. I was hoping that you would be able to stop some of these armies from marching on us."

"*Stop* them?" Breeze asked. "Now, why would I want to do that, my dear man? I did, after all, just spend three months working to get Cett to march his army down here."

Elend paused, and Vin frowned to herself, standing just outside the group. Breeze looked rather pleased with himself—though that was, admittedly, rather common for him.

"So . . . Lord Cett's on our side?" Elend asked hopefully.

"Of course not," Breeze said. "He's here to ravage the city and steal your presumed atium supply."

"You," Vin said. "You're the one who has been spreading the rumors about the Lord Ruler's atium stash, aren't you?"

"Of course," Breeze said, eyeing Spook as the boy finally arrived at the gates.

Elend frowned. "But . . . why?"

"Look outside your walls, my dear man," Breeze said. "I knew that your father was going to march on Luthadel eventually—even *my* powers of persuasion wouldn't have been enough to dissuade him. So, I began spreading rumors in the Western Dominance, then made myself one of Lord Cett's advisors."

Clubs grunted. "Good plan. Crazy, but good."

"Crazy?" Breeze said. "*My* mental stability is no issue here, Clubs. The move was not crazy, but brilliant."

Elend looked confused. "Not to insult your brilliance, Breeze. But . . . how exactly is bringing a hostile army to our city a good idea?"

"It's basic negotiating strategy, my good man," Breeze

explained as a packman handed him his dueling cane, taken off the horse. Breeze used it to gesture westward, toward Lord Cett's army. "When there are only two participants in a negotiation, one is generally stronger than the other. That makes things very difficult for the weaker party—which, in this case, would have been us."

"Yes," Elend said, "but with three armies, we're still the weakest."

"Ah," Breeze said, holding up the cane, "but those other two parties are fairly even in strength. Straff is likely stronger, but Cett has a very large force. If either of those warlords risks attacking Luthadel, his army will suffer losses—enough losses that he won't be able to defend himself from the third army. To attack us is to expose oneself."

"And that makes this a standoff," Clubs said.

"Exactly," Breeze said. "Trust me, Elend my boy. In this case, two large, enemy armies are far better than a single large, enemy army. In a three-way negotiation, the weakest party actually has the most power—because his allegiance added to either of the other two will choose the eventual winner."

Elend frowned. "Breeze, we don't want to give our allegiance to *either* of these men."

"I realize that," Breeze said. "However, our opponents do not. By bringing a second army in, I've given us time to think. Both warlords thought they could get here first. Now that they've arrived at the same time, they'll have to reevaluate. I'm guessing we'll end up in an extended siege. A couple of months at least."

"That doesn't explain how we're going to get rid of them," Elend said.

Breeze shrugged. "I got them here—you get to decide what to do with them. And I'll tell you, it was no easy task to make Cett arrive on time. He was due to come in a full five days before Venture. Fortunately, a certain . . . malady spread through camp a few days ago. Apparently, someone poisoned the main water supply and gave the entire camp diarrhea."

Spook, standing behind Clubs, snickered.

"Yes," Breeze said, eyeing the boy. "I thought you might appreciate that. You still an unintelligible nuisance, boy?"

"Wassing the where of not," Spook said, smiling and slipping back into his Eastern street slang.

Breeze snorted. "You still make more sense than Hammond, half the time," he mumbled, turning to Elend. "So, isn't anyone going to send for a carriage to drive me back to the palace? I've been Soothing you ungrateful lot for the better part of five minutes—looking as tired and pathetic as I can—and not one of you has had the good graces to pity me!"

"You must be losing your touch," Vin said with a smile. Breeze was a Soother—an Allomancer who could burn brass to calm another person's emotions. A very skilled Soother—and Vin knew of none more skilled than Breeze—could dampen all of a person's emotions but a single one, effectively making them feel exactly as he wanted.

"Actually," Elend said, turning and looking back up at the wall, "I was hoping we could go back up on the wall and study the armies some more. If you spent time with Lord Cett's force, then you could probably tell us a lot about it."

"I can; I will; I am *not* going to climb those steps. Can't you see how tired I am, man?"

Ham snorted, clapping Breeze on the shoulder—and throwing up a puff of dust. "How can you be tired? Your poor horse did all the running."

"It was emotionally exhausting, Hammond," Breeze said, rapping the larger man's hand with his cane. "My departure was somewhat disagreeable."

"What happened, anyway?" Vin asked. "Did Cett find out you were a spy?"

Breeze looked embarrassed. "Let's just say that Lord Cett and I had a . . . falling-out."

"Caught you in bed with his daughter, eh?" Ham said, earning a chuckle from the group. Breeze was anything but a ladies' man. Despite his ability to play with emotions, he had expressed no interest in romance for as long as Vin had known him. Dockson had once noted that Breeze was just too focused on himself to consider such things.

Breeze simply rolled his eyes at Ham's comment. "Honestly, Hammond. I think your jokes are getting worse as you age. One too many hits on the head while sparring, I suspect."

Ham smiled, and Elend sent for a couple of carriages. While they waited, Breeze launched into a narrative of his travels. Vin glanced down at OreSeur. She still hadn't found a good opportunity to tell the rest of the crew about the body change. Perhaps now that Breeze was back, Elend would hold a conference with his inner circle. That would be a good time. She had to be quiet about it, since she wanted the palace staff to think that she'd sent OreSeur away.

Breeze continued his story, and Vin looked back at him, smiling. Not only was Breeze a natural orator, but he had a very subtle touch with Allomancy. She could barely feel his fingers on her emotions. Once, she had found his intrusions offensive, but she was growing to understand that touching people's emotions was simply part of who Breeze was. Just as a beautiful woman demanded attention by virtue of her face and figure, Breeze drew it by near unconscious use of his powers.

Of course, that didn't make him any less a scoundrel. Getting others to do as he wished was one of Breeze's main occupations. Vin just no longer resented him for using Allomancy to do it.

The carriage finally approached, and Breeze sighed in relief. As the vehicle pulled up, he eyed Vin, then nodded toward OreSeur. "What's that?"

"A dog," Vin said.

"Ah, blunt as ever, I see," Breeze said. "And, why is it that you now have a dog?"

"I gave it to her," Elend said. "She wanted one, so I bought it for her."

"And you chose a *wolfhound*?" Ham asked, amused.

"You've fought with her before, Ham," Elend said, laughing. "What would you have given her? A poodle?"

Ham chuckled. "No, I guess not. It fits, actually."

"Though it's almost as big as she is," Clubs added, regarding her with a squinty-eyed look.

Vin reached down, resting her hand on OreSeur's head.

Clubs did have a point; she'd chosen a big animal, even for a wolfhound. He stood over three feet tall at the shoulder— and Vin knew from experience how heavy that body was.

"Remarkably well-behaved for a wolfhound," Ham said, nodding. "You chose well, El."

"Regardless," Breeze said. "Can we please return to the palace? Armies and wolfhounds are all well and good, but I believe supper is more pressing at this point."

"So, why didn't we tell them about OreSeur?" Elend asked, as their carriage bumped its way back toward Keep Venture. The three of them had taken a carriage of their own, leaving the other four to follow in the other vehicle.

Vin shrugged. OreSeur sat on the seat across from her and Elend, quietly watching the conversation. "I'll tell them eventually," Vin said. "A busy city square didn't seem the right place for the revelation."

Elend smiled. "Keeping secrets is a hard habit to break, eh?"

Vin flushed. "I'm not keeping him secret, I'm just . . ." She trailed off, looking down.

"Don't feel bad, Vin," Elend said. "You lived a long time on your own, without anyone to trust. Nobody expects you to change overnight."

"It hasn't been one night, Elend," she said. "It's been two years."

Elend laid a hand on her knee. "You're getting better. The others talk about how much you've changed."

Vin nodded. *Another man would be afraid that I'm keeping secrets from him, too. Elend just tries to make me feel less guilty.* He was a better man than she deserved.

"Kandra," Elend said, "Vin says you do well at keeping up with her."

"Yes, Your Majesty," OreSeur said. "These bones, though distasteful, are well equipped for tracking and quick movement."

"And if she gets hurt?" Elend said. "Will you be able to pull her to safety?"

"Not with any speed, Your Majesty. I will, however, be

able to go for aid. These bones have many limitations, but I will do my best to fulfill the Contract."

Elend must have caught Vin's raised eyebrow, for he chuckled. "He'll do as he says, Vin."

"The Contract is everything, Mistress," OreSeur said. "It demands more than simple service. It requires diligence and devotion. It *is* the kandra. By serving it, we serve our people."

Vin shrugged. The group fell silent, Elend pulling a book from his pocket, Vin leaning against him. OreSeur lay down, filling the entire seat opposite the humans. Eventually, the carriage rolled into the Venture courtyard, and Vin found herself looking forward to a warm bath. As they were climbing from the carriage, however, a guard rushed up to Elend. Tin allowed Vin to hear what the man said, even though he spoke before she could close the distance.

"Your Majesty," the guard whispered, "our messenger reached you, then?"

"No," Elend said with a frown as Vin walked over. The soldier gave her a look, but continued speaking; the soldiers all knew that Vin was Elend's primary bodyguard and confidant. Still, the man looked oddly concerned when he saw her.

"We . . . ah, don't want to be intrusive," the soldier said. "That's why we've kept this quiet. We were just wondering if . . . everything is all right." He looked at Vin as he spoke.

"What is this about?" Elend asked.

The guard turned back toward the king. "The corpse in Lady Vin's room."

The "corpse" was actually a skeleton. One completely picked clean, without a hint of blood—or even tissue—marring its shiny white surfaces. A good number of the bones were broken, however.

"I'm sorry, Mistress," OreSeur said, speaking low enough that only she could hear. "I assumed that you were going to dispose of these."

Vin nodded. The skeleton was, of course, the one Ore-Seur had been using before she gave him the animal body.

Finding the door unlocked—Vin's usual sign that she wanted a room cleaned—the maids had entered. Vin had stashed the bones in a basket, intending to deal with them later. Apparently, the maids had decided to check and see what was in the basket, and been somewhat surprised.

"It's all right, Captain," Elend said to the young guard—Captain Demoux, second-in-command of the palace guard. Despite the fact that Ham shunned uniforms, this man seemed to take great pride in keeping his own uniform very neat and smart.

"You did well by keeping this quiet," Elend said. "We knew about these bones already. They aren't a reason for concern."

Demoux nodded. "We figured it was something intentional." He didn't look at Vin as he spoke.

Intentional, Vin thought. *Great. I wonder what this man thinks I did.* Few skaa knew what kandra were, and Demoux wouldn't know what to make of remains like these.

"Could you dispose of these quietly for me, Captain?" Elend asked, nodding to the bones.

"Of course, Your Majesty," the guard said.

He probably assumes I ate the person or something, Vin thought with a sigh. *Sucked the flesh right off his bones.*

Which, actually, wasn't that far from the truth.

"Your Majesty," Demoux said. "Would you like us to dispose of the other body as well?"

Vin froze.

"Other one?" Elend asked slowly.

The guard nodded. "When we found this skeleton, we brought in some dogs to sniff about. The dogs didn't turn up any killers, but they did find another body. Just like this one—a set of bones, completely cleaned of flesh."

Vin and Elend shared a look. "Show us," Elend said.

Demoux nodded, and led them out of the room, giving a few whispered orders to one of his men. The four of them—three humans and one kandra—traveled a short distance down the palace hallway, toward a less used section of visitors' chambers. Demoux dismissed a soldier standing at a particular door, then led them inside.

"This body wasn't in a basket, Your Majesty," Demoux

said. "It was stuffed in a back closet. We'd probably never have found it without the dogs—they picked up the scent pretty easily, though I can't see how. These corpses are completely clean of flesh."

And there it was. Another skeleton, like the first, sitting piled beside a bureau. Elend glanced at Vin, then turned to Demoux. "Would you excuse us, Captain?"

The young guard nodded, walking from the room and closing the door.

"Well?" Elend said, turning to OreSeur.

"I do not know where this came from," the kandra said.

"But it is another kandra-eaten corpse," Vin said.

"Undoubtedly, Mistress," OreSeur said. "The dogs found it because of the particular scent our digestive juices leave on recently excreted bones."

Elend and Vin shared a look.

"However," OreSeur said, "it is probably not what you think. This man was probably killed far from here."

"What do you mean?"

"They are discarded bones, Your Majesty," OreSeur said. "The bones a kandra leaves behind . . ."

"After he finds a new body," Vin finished.

"Yes, Mistress," OreSeur said.

Vin looked at Elend, who frowned. "How long ago?" he asked. "Maybe the bones were left a year before, by my father's kandra."

"Perhaps, Your Majesty," OreSeur said. But he sounded hesitant. He padded over, sniffing at the bones. Vin picked one up herself, holding it to her nose. With tin, she easily picked out a sharp scent that reminded her of bile.

"It's very strong," she said, glancing at OreSeur.

He nodded. "These bones haven't been here long, Your Majesty. A few hours at most. Perhaps even less."

"Which means we have another kandra somewhere in the palace," Elend said, looking a bit sick. "One of my staff has been . . . eaten and replaced."

"Yes, Your Majesty," OreSeur said. "There is no way to tell from these bones whom it could be, since these are the discards. The kandra would have taken the new bones, eating their flesh and wearing their clothing."

Elend nodded, standing. He met Vin's eyes, and she knew he was thinking the same thing she was. It was possible that a member of the palace staff had been replaced, which would mean a slight breach in security. There was a far more dangerous possibility, however.

Kandra were incomparable actors; OreSeur had imitated Lord Renoux so perfectly that even people who'd known him had been fooled. Such talent could have been used for the imitation of a maid or a servant. However, if an enemy had wanted to get a spy into Elend's closed meetings, he would need to replace a person far more important.

It would be someone that we haven't seen during the last few hours, Vin thought, dropping the bone. She, Elend, and OreSeur had been on the wall for most of the afternoon and evening—ever since the end of the Assembly meeting—but the city and palace had been in chaos since the second army had arrived. The messengers had had trouble finding Ham, and she still wasn't certain where Dockson was. In fact, she hadn't seen Clubs until he'd joined her and Elend on the wall just a bit before. And Spook had been the last to arrive.

Vin looked down at the pile of bones, feeling a sickening sense of unease. There was a very good chance that someone in their core team—a member of Kelsier's former band—was now an impostor.

THE END OF PART ONE

PART TWO

GHOSTS IN
THE MIST

It wasn't until years later that I became convinced that Alendi was the Hero of Ages. Hero of Ages: the one called Rabzeen in Khlennium, the Anamnesor.

   Savior.

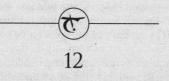

12

A FORTRESS SAT IN THE misty murk of evening.

It rested at the bottom of a large depression in the land. The steep-sided, craterlike valley was so wide that even in daylight Sazed would barely have been able to see the other side. In the oncoming darkness, obscured by mist, the far edge of the massive hole was only a deep shadow.

Sazed knew very little about tactics and strategy; though his metalminds held dozens of books on the subjects, he had forgotten their contents in order to create the stored records. The little he did know told him that this fortress—the Conventical of Seran—was not very defensible. It relinquished the high ground, and the crater sides would provide an excellent location for siege engines to pelt rocks down at the walls.

This fortress, however, had not been built to defend against enemy soldiers. It had been built to provide solitude. The crater made it difficult to find, for a slight rise in the land around the crater's lip made it practically invisible until one drew near. No roads or paths marked the way, and travelers would have great trouble getting down the sheer sides.

The Inquisitors did not want visitors.

"Well?" Marsh asked.

He and Sazed stood on the crater's northern lip, before a drop of several hundred feet. Sazed tapped his vision tin-mind, drawing forth some of the eyesight he had stored within it. The edges of his vision fuzzed, but things directly in front of him seemed to grow much closer. He tapped a little more sight, ignoring the nausea that came from compounding so much vision.

The increased eyesight let him study the Conventical as if he stood before it. He could see each notch in the dark stone walls—flat, broad, imposing. He could discern each bit of rust on the large steel plates that hung bolted into outside stones of the wall. He could see each lichen-encrusted corner and ash-stained ledge. There were no windows.

"I do not know," Sazed said slowly, releasing his vision tinmind. "It is not easy to say whether or not the fortress is inhabited. There is no motion, nor is there light. But, perhaps the Inquisitors are just hiding inside."

"No," Marsh said, his stiff voice uncomfortably loud in the evening air. "They are gone."

"Why would they leave? This is a place of great strength, I think. Poor defense against an army, but a great defense against the chaos of the times."

Marsh shook his head. "They are gone."

"How are you so certain?"

"I do not know."

"Where did they go, then?"

Marsh looked at him, then turned and glanced over his shoulder. "North."

"Toward Luthadel?" Sazed asked, frowning.

"Among other things," Marsh said. "Come. I do not know if they will return, but we should exploit this opportunity."

Sazed nodded. This was why they had come, after all. Still, a part of him hesitated. He was a man of books and genteel service. Traveling the countryside to visit villages was enough removed from his experience to be discomforting. Infiltrating the Inquisitor stronghold . . .

Marsh obviously didn't care about his companion's inner struggles. The Inquisitor turned and began to walk along the rim of the crater. Sazed threw his pack over his shoulder, then followed. They eventually arrived at a cage-like contraption, obviously meant to be lowered down to the bottom by ropes and pulleys. The cage sat locked in place at the top ledge, and Marsh stopped at its side, but did not enter.

"What?" Sazed asked.

"The pulley system," Marsh said. "The cage is meant to be lowered by men holding it from below."

Sazed nodded, realizing this was true. Marsh stepped forward and threw a lever. The cage fell. Ropes began to smoke, and pulleys squealed as the massive cage plummeted toward the chasm floor. A muted crash echoed against the rocks.

If there is anyone down there, Sazed thought, *they now know we're here.*

Marsh turned toward him, the heads of his eye-spikes glistening slightly in the failing sunlight. "Follow however you wish," he said. Then, he tied off the counterrope and began to climb down the ropes.

Sazed stepped up to the platform's edge, watching Marsh shimmy down the dangling rope into the shadowed, misty abyss. Then, Sazed knelt and opened his pack. He unhooked the large metal bracers around his upper and lower arms—his core copperminds. They contained the memories of a Keeper, the stored knowledge of centuries past. He reverently placed them to the side, then pulled a pair of much smaller bracelets—one iron, one pewter—from the pack. Metalminds for a warrior.

Did Marsh understand how unskilled Sazed was in this area? Amazing strength did not a warrior make. Regardless, Sazed snapped the two bracelets around his ankles. Next, he pulled out two rings—tin and copper. These he slipped on his fingers.

He closed the pack and threw it over his shoulder, then picked up his core copperminds. He carefully located a good hiding place—a secluded hollow between two boulders—and slid them inside. Whatever happened below, he didn't want to risk them being taken and destroyed by the Inquisitors.

In order to fill a coppermind with memories, Sazed had

listened to another Keeper recite his entire collection of histories, facts, and stories. Sazed had memorized each sentence, then shoved those memories into the copper-mind for later retrieval. Sazed remembered very little of the actual experience—but he could draw forth any of the books or essays he wished, placing them back into his mind, gaining the ability to recollect them as crisply as when he'd first memorized them. He just had to have the bracers on.

Being without his copperminds made him anxious. He shook his head, walking back over to the platform. Marsh was moving very quickly down toward the chasm floor; like all Inquisitors, he had the powers of a Mistborn. Though how he had gotten those powers—and how he managed to live despite the spikes that had been driven directly through his brain—was a mystery. Marsh had never answered Sazed's questions on the subject.

Sazed called down, drawing Marsh's attention, then held up his pack and dropped it. Marsh reached out, and the pack lurched, Pulled by its metals into Marsh's hand. The Inquisitor threw it over his shoulder before continuing his descent.

Sazed nodded thankfully, then stepped off the platform. As he began to fall, he mentally reached into his ironmind, searching for the power he had stored therein. Filling a metalmind always had a cost: in order to store up sight, Sazed had been forced to spend weeks with poor eyesight. During that time, he had worn a tin bracelet, stowing away the excess sight for later use.

Iron was a bit different from the others. It didn't store up sight, strength, endurance—or even memories. It stored something completely different: weight.

This day, Sazed didn't tap the power stored inside the ironmind; that would have made him more heavy. Instead, he began to fill the ironmind, letting it suck away his weight. He felt a familiar sense of lightness—a sense that his own body wasn't pressing upon itself as forcefully.

His fall slowed. The Terris philosophers had much to say on using an ironmind. They explained that the power didn't actually change a person's bulk or size—it just somehow changed the way that the ground pulled against them. Sazed's fall didn't slow because of his decrease in weight—it slowed because he suddenly had a relatively large amount of surface exposed to the wind of his fall, and a lighter body to go along with it.

Regardless of the scientific reasons, Sazed didn't fall as quickly. The thin metal bracelets on his legs were the heaviest things on his body, and they kept him pointed feet-downward. He held out his arms and bent his body slightly, letting the wind push against him. His descent was not terribly slow—not like that of a leaf or a feather. However, he didn't plummet either. Instead, he fell in a controlled—almost leisurely—manner. Clothing flapping, arms outspread, he passed Marsh, who watched with a curious expression.

As he approached the ground, Sazed tapped his pewtermind, drawing forth a tiny bit of strength to prepare. He hit the ground—but, because his body was so light, there was very little shock. He barely even needed to bend his knees to absorb the force of impact.

He stopped filling the ironmind, released his pewter, and waited quietly for Marsh. Beside him, the carrying cage lay in shambles. Sazed noticed several broken iron shackles with discomfort. Apparently, some of those who had visited the Conventical had not come by choice.

By the time Marsh neared the bottom, the mists were thick in the air. Sazed had lived with them all of his life, and had never before felt uncomfortable in them. Yet, now he half expected the mists to begin choking him. To kill him, as they seemed to have done to old Jed, the unfortunate farmer whose death Sazed had investigated.

Marsh dropped the last ten feet or so, landing with an Allomancer's increased agility. Even after spending so much time with Mistborn, Sazed was impressed with Allomancy's gifts. Of course, he'd never been jealous of them—not really. True, Allomancy was better in a fight; but it could not expand the mind, giving one access to the dreams, hopes, and beliefs of a thousand years of culture. It could not give the knowledge to treat a wound, or help teach a poor village to use modern fertilization techniques.

The metalminds of Feruchemy weren't flamboyant, but they had a far more lasting value to society.

Besides, Sazed knew a few tricks with Feruchemy that were bound to surprise even the most prepared warrior.

Marsh handed him the pack. "Come."

Sazed nodded, shouldering the pack and following the Inquisitor across the rocky ground. Walking next to Marsh was odd, for Sazed wasn't accustomed to being around people who were as tall as he was. Terrismen were tall by nature, and Sazed even more so: his arms and legs were a bit too long for his body, a medical condition brought on by his having been castrated as a very young boy. Though the Lord Ruler was dead, Terris culture would long feel the effects of his stewardship and breeding programs—the methods by which he had tried to breed Feruchemical powers out of the Terris people.

The Conventical of Seran loomed in the darkness, looking even more ominous now that Sazed stood within the crater. Marsh strode right up to the front doors, and Sazed followed behind. He wasn't afraid, not really. Fear had never been a strong motivator in Sazed's life. However, he did worry. There were so few Keepers left; if he died, that was one fewer person who could travel, restoring lost truths and teaching the people.

Not that I'm doing such at the moment anyway. . . .

Marsh regarded the massive steel doors. Then he threw his weight against one, obviously burning pewter to enhance his strength. Sazed joined him, pushing hard. The door did not budge.

Regretting the expenditure of power, Sazed reached into his pewtermind and tapped strength. He used far more than he had when landing, and his muscles immediately increased in size. Unlike Allomancy, Feruchemy often had direct effects on a person's body. Beneath his robes, Sazed gained the bulk and build of a lifetime warrior, easily becoming twice as strong as he had been a moment earlier. With their combined effort, the two of them managed to push the door open.

It did not creak. It slid slowly, but evenly, inward, exposing a long, dark hallway.

Sazed released his pewtermind, reverting to his normal self. Marsh strode into the Conventical, his feet kicking up the mist that had begun to pour through the open doorway.

"Marsh?" Sazed asked.

The Inquisitor turned.

"I won't be able to see inside there."

"Your Feruchemy . . ."

Sazed shook his head. "It can let me see better in darkness, but only if there's some light to begin with. In addition, tapping that much sight would drain my tinmind in a matter of minutes. I'll need a lantern."

Marsh paused, then nodded. He turned into the darkness, quickly disappearing from Sazed's view.

So, Sazed thought, *Inquisitors don't need light to see.* It was to be expected: the spikes filled Marsh's entire sockets, completely destroying the eyeballs. Whatever strange power allowed Inquisitors to see, it apparently worked just as well in pure darkness as it did in daylight.

Marsh returned a few moments later, carrying a lamp. From the chains Sazed had seen on the descent cage, Sazed suspected that the Inquisitors had kept a sizable group of slaves and servants to attend their needs. If that was the case, where had the people gone? Had they fled?

Sazed lit the lamp with a flint from his pack. The lamp's ghostly light illuminated a stark, daunting hallway. He stepped into the Conventical, holding the lamp high, and began to fill the small copper ring on his finger, the process transforming it into a coppermind.

"Large rooms," he whispered, "without adornment." He didn't really need to say the words, but he'd found that speaking helped him form distinct memories. He could then place them into the coppermind.

"The Inquisitors, obviously, had a fondness for steel," he continued. "This is not surprising, considering that their religion was often referred to as the Steel Ministry. The walls are hung with massive steel plates, which bear no rust, unlike the ones outside. Many of those here are not completely smooth, but instead crafted with some interesting patterns etched . . . almost *buffed* . . . into their surfaces."

Marsh frowned, turning toward him. "What are you doing?"

Sazed held up his right hand, showing the copper ring. "I must make an account of this visit. I will need to repeat this experience back to other Keepers when the opportunity presents itself. There is much to be learned from this place, I think."

Marsh turned away. "You should not care about the Inquisitors. They are not worthy of your record."

"It isn't a matter of worthiness, Marsh," Sazed said, holding up his lamp to study a square pillar. "Knowledge of all religions is valuable. I must make certain these things persist."

Sazed regarded the pillar for a moment, then closed his eyes and formed an image of it inside his head, which he then added to the coppermind. Visual memories, however, were less useful than spoken words. Visualizations faded very quickly once taken out of a coppermind, suffering from the mind's distortion. Plus, they could not be passed to other Keepers.

Marsh didn't respond to Sazed's comment about religion; he just turned and walked deeper into the building. Sazed followed at a slower pace, speaking to himself, recording the words in his coppermind. It was an interesting experience. As soon as he spoke, he felt the thoughts sucked from his mind, leaving behind a blank hollowness. He had difficulty remembering the specifics of what he had just been saying. However, once he was done filling his coppermind, he would be able to tap those memories later and know them with crisp clarity.

"The room is tall," he said. "There are a few pillars, and they are also wrapped in steel. They are blocky and square, rather than round. I get a sense that this place was created by a people who cared little for subtlety. They ignored small details in favor of broad lines and full geometries.

"As we move beyond the main entryway, this architectural theme continues. There are no paintings on the walls, nor are there wooden adornments or tile floors. Instead, there are only the long, broad hallways with their harsh lines and reflective surfaces. The floor is constructed of steel squares, each a few feet across. They are . . . cold to the touch.

"It is strange not to see the tapestries, stained-glass windows, and sculpted stones that are so common in Luthadel's architecture. There are no spires or vaultings here. Just squares and rectangles. Lines . . . so many lines. Nothing here is soft. No carpet, no rugs, no windows. It is a place for people who see the world differently from ordinary men.

"Marsh walked straight down this massive hallway, as if oblivious to its decor. I will follow him, then come back to record more later. He seems to be following something . . . something I cannot sense. Perhaps it is . . ."

Sazed trailed off as he stepped around a bend and saw Marsh standing in the doorway of a large chamber. The lamplight flickered unevenly as Sazed's arm quivered.

Marsh had found the servants.

They had been dead long enough that Sazed hadn't noticed the scent until he had come close. Perhaps that was what Marsh had been following; the senses of a man burning tin could be quite acute.

The Inquisitors had done their work thoroughly. These were the remnants of a slaughter. The room was large, but had only one exit, and the bodies were piled high near the back, killed by what looked like harsh sword or axe strokes. The servants had huddled up against the back wall as they died.

Sazed turned away.

Marsh, however, remained in the doorway. "There is a bad air about this place," he finally said.

"You have only just noticed that?" Sazed asked.

Marsh turned, glancing at him, demanding his gaze. "We should not spend much time here. There are stairs at the end of the hallway behind us. I will go up—that is where the Inquisitors' quarters will be. If the information I seek is here, I will find it there. You may stay, or you may descend. However, do not follow me."

Sazed frownéd. "Why?"

"I must be alone here. I cannot explain it. I do not care if you witness Inquisitor atrocities. I just . . . do not wish to be with you when you do."

Sazed lowered his lamp, turning its light away from the horrific scene. "Very well."

Marsh turned, brushing past Sazed and disappearing into the dark hallway. And Sazed was alone.

He tried not to think about that very much. He returned to the main hallway, describing the slaughter to his coppermind before giving a more detailed explanation of the architecture and the art—if, indeed, that was what the different patterns on the wall plates could be called.

As he worked—his voice echoing quietly against the rigid architecture, his lamp a weak drop of light reflected in steel—his eyes were drawn toward the back of the hallway. There was a pool of darkness there. A stairwell, leading down.

Even as he turned back to his description of one of the wall mounts, he knew that he would eventually find himself walking toward that darkness. It was the same as ever—the curiosity, the *need* to understand the unknown. This sense had driven him as a Keeper, had led him to Kelsier's company. His search for truths could never be completed, but neither could it be ignored. So, he eventually turned and approached the stairwell, his own whispering voice his only companion.

"The stairs are akin to what I saw in the hallway. They are broad and expansive, like the steps leading up to a temple or palace. Except, these go down, into darkness. They are large, likely cut from stone and then lined with steel. They are tall, meant for a determined stride.

"As I walk, I wonder what secrets the Inquisitors deemed worthy of hiding below the earth, in the basement of their stronghold. This entire building is a secret. What did they do here, in these massive hallways and open, empty rooms?

"The stairwell ends in another large, square room. I've noticed something—there are no doors in the doorways here. Each room is open, visible to those outside. As I walk, peeking into the rooms beneath the earth, I find cavernous chambers with few furnishings. No libraries, no lounges. Several contain large metal blocks that could be altars.

"There is . . . something different here in this last room, at the back of the main landing. I'm not certain what to make of it. A torture chamber, perhaps? There are tables— metal tables—set into the floor. They are bloody, though there are no corpses. Blood flakes and powders at my feet—a lot of men have died in this room, I think. There don't appear to be torture implements beyond . . .

"Spikes. Like the ones in Inquisitor eyes. Massive, heavy things—like the spikes one might pound into the ground with a very large mallet. Some are tipped with blood, though I don't think I'll handle those. These other ones . . . yes, they look indistinguishable from the ones in Marsh's eyes. Yet, some are of different metals."

Sazed set the spike down on a table, metal clinking against metal. He shivered, scanning the room again. A place to make new Inquisitors, perhaps? He had a sudden horrific vision of the creatures—once only several dozen in number—having swelled their ranks during their months sequestered in the Conventical.

But that didn't seem right. They were a secretive, exclusive bunch. Where would they have found enough men worthy of joining their ranks? Why not make Inquisitors from the servants above, rather than just killing them?

Sazed had always suspected that a man had to be an Allomancer to be changed into an Inquisitor. Marsh's own experience substantiated that premise: Marsh had been a Seeker, a man who could burn bronze, before his transformation. Sazed looked again at the blood, the spikes, and the tables, and decided he wasn't certain that he wanted to know how one made a new Inquisitor.

Sazed was about to leave the room when his lamp revealed something at the back. Another doorway.

He moved forward, trying to ignore the dried blood at his feet, and entered a chamber that didn't seem to match the rest of the Conventical's daunting architecture. It was cut directly into the stone, and it twisted down into a very small stairwell. Curious, Sazed walked down the set of worn stone steps. For the first time since entering the building, he felt cramped, and he had to stoop as he reached the bottom of the stairwell and entered a small chamber. He stood up straight, and held up his lamp to reveal . . .

A wall. The room ended abruptly, and his light sparkled off the wall. It held a steel plate, like those above. This one was a good five feet across, and nearly as tall. And it bore writing. Suddenly interested, Sazed set down his pack and stepped forward, raising his lamp to read the top words on the wall.

The text was in Terris.

It was an old dialect, certainly, but one that Sazed could make out even without his language coppermind. His hand trembled as he read the words.

> *I write these words in steel, for anything not set in metal cannot be trusted.*
>
> *I have begun to wonder if I am the only sane man remaining. Can the others not see? They have been waiting so long for their hero to come—the one spoken of in Terris prophecies—that they quickly jump between conclusions, presuming that each story and legend applies to this one man.*
>
> *My brethren ignore the other facts. They cannot connect the other strange things that are happening. They are deaf to my objections and blind to my discoveries.*
>
> *Perhaps they are right. Perhaps I am mad, or jealous, or simply daft. My name is Kwaan. Philosopher, scholar, traitor. I am the one who discovered Alendi, and I am the one who first proclaimed him to be the Hero of Ages. I am the one who started this all.*
>
> *And I am the one who betrayed him, for I now know that he must never be allowed to complete his quest.*

"Sazed."

Sazed jumped, nearly dropping the lamp. Marsh stood in the doorway behind him. Imperious, discomforting, and so dark. He fit this place, with its lines and hardness.

"The upstairs quarters are empty," Marsh said. "This trip

has been a waste—my brethren took anything of use with them."

"Not a waste, Marsh," Sazed said, turning back to the plate of text. He hadn't read all of it; he hadn't even gotten close. The script was written in a tight, cramped hand, its etchings coating the wall. The steel had preserved the words despite their obvious age. Sazed's heart beat a little faster.

This was a fragment of text from before the Lord Ruler's reign. A fragment written by a Terris philosopher—a holy man. Despite ten centuries of searching, the Keepers had never fulfilled the original goal of their creation: they had never discovered their own Terris religion.

The Lord Ruler had squelched Terris religious teachings soon after his rise to power. His persecution of the Terris people—his own people—had been the most complete of his long reign, and the Keepers had never found more than vague fragments regarding what their own people had once believed.

"I have to copy this down, Marsh," Sazed said, reaching for his pack. Taking a visual memory wouldn't work— no man could stare at a wall of so much text, then remember the words. He could, perhaps, read them into his coppermind. However, he wanted a physical record, one that perfectly preserved the structure of lines and punctuation.

Marsh shook his head. "We will not stay here. I do not think we should even have come."

Sazed paused, looking up. Then he pulled several large sheets of paper from his pack. "Very well, then," he said. "I'll take a rubbing. That will be better anyway, I think. It will let me see the text exactly as it was written."

Marsh nodded, and Sazed got out his charcoal.

This discovery . . . he thought with excitement. *This will be like Rashek's logbook. We are getting close!*

However, even as he began the rubbing—his hands moving carefully and precisely—another thought occurred to him. With a text like this in his possession, his sense of duty would no longer let him wander the villages. He had to return to the north to share what he had found, lest he die and this text be lost. He had to go to Terris.

Or . . . to Luthadel. From there he could send messages north. He had a valid excuse to get back to the center of action, to see the other crewmembers again.

Why did that make him feel even more guilty?

When I finally had the realization—finally connected all of the signs of the Anticipation to Alendi—I was so excited. Yet, when I announced my discovery to the other Worldbringers, I was met with scorn.

Oh, how I wish that I had listened to them.

13

MIST SWIRLED AND SPUN, LIKE monochrome paints running together on a canvas. Light died in the west, and night came of age.

Vin frowned. "Does it seem like the mists are coming earlier?"

"Earlier?" OreSeur asked in his muffled voice. The kandra wolfhound sat next to her on the rooftop.

Vin nodded. "Before, the mists didn't start to appear until after it grew dark, right?"

"It is dark, Mistress."

"But they're already here—they started to gather when the sun was barely beginning to set."

"I don't see that it matters, Mistress. Perhaps the mists are simply like other weather patterns—they vary, sometimes."

"Doesn't it even seem a little strange to you?"

"I will think it strange if you wish me to, Mistress," OreSeur said.

"That isn't what I meant."

"I apologize, Mistress," OreSeur said. "Tell me what you *do* mean, and I will be certain to believe as commanded."

Vin sighed, rubbing her brow. *I wish Sazed were back . . .* she thought. It was an idle wish, however. Even if Sazed were in Luthadel, he wouldn't be her steward. The Terrismen no longer called any man master. She'd have to make do with OreSeur. The kandra, at least, could provide information that Sazed could not—assuming she could get it out of him.

"We need to find the impostor," Vin said. "The one who . . . replaced someone."

"Yes, Mistress," OreSeur said.

Vin sat back in the mists, reclining on a slanted rooftop, resting her arms back on the tiles. "Then, I need to know more about you."

"Me, Mistress?"

"Kandra in general. If I'm going to find this impostor, I need to know how he thinks, need to understand his motivations."

"His motivations will be simple, Mistress," OreSeur said. "He will be following his Contract."

"What if he's acting without a Contract?"

OreSeur shook his canine head. "Kandra always have a Contract. Without one, they are not allowed to enter human society."

"Never?" Vin asked.

"Never."

"And what if this is some kind of rogue kandra?" Vin said.

"Such a thing does not exist," OreSeur said firmly.

Oh? Vin thought skeptically. However, she let the matter drop. There was little reason for a kandra to infiltrate the palace on his own; it was far more likely that one of Elend's enemies had sent the creature. One of the warlords, perhaps, or maybe the obligators. Even the other nobility in the city would have had good reason to spy on Elend.

"Okay," Vin said. "The kandra is a spy, sent to gather information for another human."

"Yes."

"But," Vin said, "if he did take the body of someone in the palace, he didn't kill them himself. Kandra can't kill humans, right?"

OreSeur nodded. "We are all bound by that rule."

"So, somebody snuck into the palace, murdered a member of the staff, then had their kandra take the body." She paused, trying to work through the problem. "The most dangerous possibilities—the crewmembers—should be considered first. Fortunately, since the killing happened yesterday, we can eliminate Breeze, who was outside the city at the time."

OreSeur nodded.

"We can eliminate Elend as well," Vin said. "He was with us on the wall yesterday."

"That still leaves the majority of the crew, Mistress."

Vin frowned, sitting back. She'd tried to establish solid alibis for Ham, Dockson, Clubs, and Spook. However, all of them had had at least a few hours unaccounted for. Long enough for a kandra to digest them and take their place.

"All right," she said. "So, how do I find the impostor? How can I tell him from other people?"

OreSeur sat quietly in the mists.

"There has to be a way," Vin said. "His imitation can't be perfect. Would cutting him work?"

OreSeur shook his head. "Kandra replicate a body perfectly, Mistress—blood, flesh, skin, and muscle. You have seen that when I split my skin."

Vin sighed, standing and stepping up on the tip of the peaked rooftop. The mists were already full, and the night was quickly becoming black. She began to walk idly back and forth on the ridge, an Allomancer's balance keeping her from falling.

"Perhaps I can just see who isn't acting oddly," she said. "Are most kandra as good at imitation as you are?"

"Among kandra, my own skill is average. Some are worse, others are better."

"But no actor is perfect," Vin said.

"Kandra don't often make mistakes, Mistress," OreSeur said. "But, this is probably your best method. Be warned, however—he could be anyone. My kind are very skilled."

Vin paused. *It's not Elend,* she told herself forcibly. *He was with me all day yesterday.* Except in the morning.

Too long, she decided. *We were on the wall for hours, and those bones were freshly expelled. Besides, I'd know if it were him . . . wouldn't I?*

She shook her head. "There has to be another way. Can I spot a kandra with Allomancy somehow?"

OreSeur didn't answer immediately. She turned toward him in the darkness, studying his canine face. "What?" she asked.

"These are not things we speak of with outsiders."

Vin sighed. "Tell me anyway."

"Do you command me to speak?"

"I don't really care to command you in anything."

"Then I may leave?" OreSeur asked. "You do not wish to command me, so our Contract is dissolved?"

"That isn't what I meant," Vin said.

OreSeur frowned—a strange expression to see on a dog's face. "It would be easier for me if you would try to say what you mean, Mistress."

Vin gritted her teeth. "Why is it you're so hostile?"

"I'm not hostile, Mistress. I am your servant, and will do as you command. That is part of the Contract."

"Sure. Are you like this with all of your masters?"

"With most, I am fulfilling a specific role," OreSeur said. "I have bones to imitate—a person to become, a personality to adopt. You have given me no direction; just the bones of this . . . animal."

So that's it, Vin thought. *Still annoyed by the dog's body.* "Look, those bones don't really change anything. You are still the same person."

"You do not understand. It is not who a kandra *is* that's important. It's who a kandra *becomes.* The bones he takes, the role he fulfills. None of my previous masters have asked me to do something like this."

"Well, I'm not like other masters," Vin said. "Anyway, I asked you a question. Is there a way I can spot a kandra with Allomancy? And yes, I command you to speak."

A flash of triumph shone in OreSeur's eyes, as if he enjoyed forcing her into her role. "Kandra cannot be affected by mental Allomancy, Mistress."

Vin frowned. "Not at all?"

"No, Mistress," OreSeur said. "You can try to Riot or Soothe our emotions, if you wish, but it will have no effect. We won't even know that you are trying to manipulate us."

Like someone who is burning copper. "That's not exactly the most useful bit of information," she said, strolling past the kandra on the roof. Allomancers couldn't read minds or emotions; when they Soothed or Rioted another person, they simply had to hope that the person reacted as intended.

She could "test" for a kandra by Soothing someone's emotions, perhaps. If they didn't react, that might mean they were a kandra—but it could also just mean that they were good at containing their emotions.

OreSeur watched her pacing. "If it were easy to detect kandra, Mistress, then we wouldn't be worth much as impostors, would we?"

"I suppose not," Vin acknowledged. However, thinking about what he'd said made her consider something else. "Can a kandra *use* Allomancy? If they eat an Allomancer, I mean?"

OreSeur shook his head.

That's another method, then, Vin thought. *If I catch a member of the crew burning metals, then I know he's not the kandra.* Wouldn't help with Dockson or the palace servants, but it would let her eliminate Ham and Spook.

"There's something else," Vin said. "Before, when we were doing the job with Kelsier, he said that we had to keep you away from the Lord Ruler and his Inquisitors. Why was that?"

OreSeur looked away. "This is not a thing we speak of."

"Then I command you to speak of it."

"Then I must refuse to answer," OreSeur said.

"Refuse to answer?" Vin asked. "You can do that?"

OreSeur nodded. "We are not required to reveal secrets about kandra nature, Mistress. It is—"

"In the Contract," Vin finished, frowning. *I really need to read that thing again.*

"Yes, Mistress. I have, perhaps, said too much already."

Vin turned away from OreSeur, looking out over the city. The mists continued to spin. Vin closed her eyes, questing out with bronze, trying to feel the telltale pulse of an Allomancer burning metals nearby.

OreSeur rose and padded over beside her, then settled down on his haunches again, sitting on the inclined roof. "Shouldn't you be at the meeting the king is having, Mistress?"

"Perhaps later," Vin said, opening her eyes. Out beyond the city, watchfires from the armies lit the horizon. Keep Venture blazed in the night to her right, and inside of it, Elend was holding council with the others. Many of the most important men in the government, sitting together in one room. Elend would call her paranoid for insisting that she be the one who watched for spies and assassins. That was fine; he could call her whatever he wanted, as long as he stayed alive.

She settled back down. She was glad Elend had decided to pick Keep Venture as his palace, rather than moving into Kredik Shaw, the Lord Ruler's home. Not only was Kredik Shaw too big to be properly defended, but it also reminded her of him. The Lord Ruler.

She thought of the Lord Ruler often, lately—or, rather, she thought of Rashek, the man who had become the Lord Ruler. A Terrisman by birth, Rashek had killed the man who should have taken the power at the Well of Ascension and . . .

And done what? They still didn't know. The Hero had been on a quest to protect the people from a danger simply known as the Deepness. So much had been lost; so much had been intentionally destroyed. Their best source of information about those days came in the form of an aged journal, written by the Hero of Ages during the days before Rashek had killed him. However, it gave precious few clues about his quest.

Why do I even worry about these things? Vin thought. *The Deepness is a thing a thousand years forgotten. Elend and the others are right to be concerned about more pressing events.*

And still, Vin found herself strangely detached from them. Perhaps that was why she found herself scouting outside. It wasn't that she didn't worry about the armies.

She just felt . . . removed from the problem. Even now, as she considered the threat to Luthadel, her mind was drawn back to the Lord Ruler.

You don't know what I do for mankind, he had said. *I was your god, even if you couldn't see it. By killing me, you have doomed yourselves.* Those were the Lord Ruler's last words, spoken as he lay dying on the floor of his own throne room. They worried her. Chilled her, even still.

She needed to distract herself. "What kinds of things do you like, kandra?" she asked, turning to the creature, who still sat on the rooftop beside her. "What are your loves, your hatreds?"

"I do not want to answer that."

Vin frowned. "Do not want to, or do not *have* to?"

OreSeur paused. "Do not want to, Mistress." The implication was obvious. *You're going to have to command me.*

She almost did. However, something gave her pause, something in those eyes—inhuman though they were. Something familiar.

She'd known resentment like that. She'd felt it often during her youth, when she'd served crewleaders who had lorded over their followers. In the crews, one did what one was commanded—especially if one was a small waif of a girl, without rank or means of intimidation.

"If you don't wish to speak of it," Vin said, turning away from the kandra, "then I won't force you."

OreSeur was silent.

Vin breathed in the mist, its cool wetness tickling her throat and lungs. "Do you know what *I* love, kandra?"

"No, Mistress."

"The mists," she said, holding out her arms. "The power, the freedom."

OreSeur nodded slowly. Nearby, Vin felt a faint pulsing with her bronze. Quiet, strange, unnerving. It was the same odd pulsing that she had felt atop Keep Venture a few nights before. She had never been brave enough to investigate it again.

It's time to do something about that, she decided. "Do you know what I hate, kandra?" she whispered, falling to a crouch, checking her knives and metals.

"No, Mistress."

She turned, meeting OreSeur's eyes. "I hate being afraid."

She knew that others thought her jumpy. Paranoid. She had lived with fear for so long that she had once seen it as something natural, like the ash, the sun, or the ground itself.

Kelsier had taken that fear away. She was careful, still, but she didn't feel a constant sense of terror. The Survivor had given her a life where the ones she loved didn't beat her, had shown her something better than fear. Trust. Now that she knew of these things, she would not quickly surrender them. Not to armies, not to assassins . . .

Not even to spirits.

"Follow if you can," she whispered, then dropped off the rooftop to the street below.

She dashed along the mist-slicked street, building momentum before she had time to lose her nerve. The source of the bronze pulses was close; it came from only one street over, in a building. Not the top, she decided. One of the darkened windows on the third floor, the shutters open.

Vin dropped a coin and jumped into the air. She shot upward, angling herself by Pushing against a latch across the street. She landed in the window's pitlike opening, arms grabbing the sides of the frame. She flared tin, letting her eyes adjust to the deep darkness within the abandoned room.

And it was there. Formed entirely of mists, it shifted and spun, its outline vague in the dark chamber. It had a vantage to see the rooftop where Vin and OreSeur had been talking.

Ghosts don't spy on people . . . do they? Skaa didn't speak of things like spirits or the dead. It smacked too much of religion, and religion was for the nobility. To worship was death for skaa. That hadn't stopped some, of course— but thieves like Vin had been too pragmatic for such things.

There was only one thing in skaa lore that this creature matched. Mistwraiths. Creatures said to steal the souls of men foolish enough to go outside at night. But, Vin now knew what mistwraiths were. They were cousins to the kandra—strange, semi-intelligent beasts who used the bones of those they ingested. They were odd, true—but hardly phantoms, and not really even that dangerous. There were no dark wraiths in the night, no haunting spirits or ghouls.

Or so Kelsier had said. The thing standing in the dark room—its insubstantial form writhing in the mists—seemed a powerful counterexample. She gripped the sides of the window, fear—her old friend—returning.

Run. Flee. Hide.

"Why have you been watching me?" she demanded.

The thing did not move. Its form seemed to draw the mists forward, and they spun slightly, as if in an air current.

I can sense it with bronze. That means it's using Allomancy—and Allomancy attracts the mist.

The thing stepped forward. Vin tensed.

And then the spirit was gone.

Vin paused, frowning. That was it? She had—

Something grabbed her arm. Something cold, something terrible, but something very real. A pain shot through her head, moving as if from her ear and into her mind. She yelled, but cut off as her voice failed. With a quiet groan—her arm quivering and shaking—she fell backward out of the window.

Her arm was still cold. She could feel it whipping in the air beside her, seeming to exude chill air. Mist passed like trailing clouds.

Vin flared tin. Pain, cold, wetness, and lucidity burst into her mind, and she threw herself into a twist and flared pewter just as she hit the ground.

"Mistress?" OreSeur said, darting from the shadows.

Vin shook her head, pushing herself up to her knees, her palms cool against the slick cobblestones. She could still feel the trailing chill in her left arm.

"Shall I go for aid?" the wolfhound asked.

Vin shook her head, forcing herself into a wobbling stand. She looked upward, through swirling mists, toward the black window above.

She shivered. Her shoulder was sore from where she

had hit the ground, and her still bruised side throbbed, but she could feel her strength returning. She stepped away from the building, still looking up. Above her, the deep mists seemed . . . ominous. Obscuring.

No, she thought forcefully. *The mists are my freedom; the night is my home! This is where I belong. I haven't needed to be afraid in the night since Kelsier taught me otherwise.*

She couldn't lose that. She wouldn't go back to the fear. Still, she couldn't help the quick urgency in her step as she waved to OreSeur and scampered away from the building. She gave no explanation for her strange actions.

He didn't ask for one.

Elend set a third pile of books onto the table, and it slumped against the other two, threatening to topple the entire lot to the floor. He steadied them, then glanced up.

Breeze, in a prim suit, regarded the table with amusement as he sipped his wine. Ham and Spook were playing a game of stones as they waited for the meeting to begin; Spook was winning. Dockson sat in the corner of the room, scribbling on a ledger, and Clubs sat in a deep plush chair, eyeing Elend with one of his stares.

Any of these men could be an impostor, Elend thought. The thought still seemed insane to him. What was he to do? Exclude them all from his confidence? No, he needed them too much.

The only option was to act normally and watch them. Vin had told him to try and spot inconsistencies in their personalities. He intended to do his best, but the reality was he wasn't sure how much he would be able to see. This was more Vin's area of expertise. He needed to worry about the armies.

Thinking of her, he glanced at the stained-glass window at the back of the study, and was surprised to see it was dark.

That late already? Elend thought.

"My dear man," Breeze noted. "When you told us you

needed to 'go and gather a few important references,' you might have warned us that you were planning to be gone for two full hours."

"Yes, well," Elend said, "I kind of lost track of time. . . ."

"For two hours?"

Elend nodded sheepishly. "There were books involved."

Breeze shook his head. "If the fate of the Central Dominance weren't at stake—and if it weren't so fantastically enjoyable to watch Hammond lose an entire month's earnings to the boy there—I'd have left an hour ago."

"Yes, well, we can get started now," Elend said.

Ham chuckled, standing up. "Actually, it's kind of like the old days. Kell always arrived late, too—and he liked to hold his meetings at night. Mistborn hours."

Spook smiled, his coin pouch bulging.

We still use boxings—Lord Ruler imperials—as our coinage, Elend thought. *We'll have to do something about that.*

"I miss the charcoal board, though," Spook said.

"I certainly don't," Breeze replied. "Kell had atrocious handwriting."

"Absolutely atrocious," Ham said with a smile, sitting. "You have to admit, though—it was distinctive."

Breeze raised an eyebrow. "It *was* that, I suppose."

Kelsier, the Survivor of Hathsin, Elend thought. *Even his handwriting is legendary.* "Regardless," he said, "I think perhaps we should get to work. We've still got two armies waiting out there. We're not leaving tonight until we have a plan to deal with them!"

The crewmembers shared looks.

"Actually, Your Majesty," Dockson said, "we've already worked on that problem for a bit."

"Oh?" Elend asked, surprised. *Well, I guess I did leave them alone for a couple of hours.* "Let me hear it, then."

Dockson stood, pulling his chair a bit closer to join the rest of the group, and Ham began to speak.

"Here's the thing, El," Ham said. "With two armies here, we don't have to worry about an immediate attack. But, we're still in serious danger. This will probably turn into an extended siege as each army tries to outlast the other."

"They'll try to starve us out," Clubs said. "Weaken us, and their enemies, before attacking."

"And," Ham continued, "that puts us in a bind—because we can't last very long. The city is already on the edge of starvation—and the enemy kings are probably aware of that fact."

"What are you saying?" Elend asked slowly.

"We have to make an alliance with one of those armies, Your Majesty," Dockson said. "They both know it. Alone, they can't reliably defeat one another. With our help, however, the balance will be tipped."

"They'll hem us in," Ham said. "Keep us blockaded until we get desperate enough to side with one of them. Eventually, we'll have to do so—either that, or let our people starve."

"The decision comes down to this," Breeze said. "We can't outlast the others, so we have to choose *which* of those men we want to take over the city. And, I would suggest making our decision quickly as opposed to waiting while our supplies run out."

Elend stood quietly. "By making a deal with one of those armies, we'll essentially be giving away our kingdom."

"True," Breeze said, tapping the side of his cup. "However, what I gained us by bringing a second army is bargaining power. You see, at least we are in a position to demand something in exchange for our kingdom."

"What good is that?" Elend asked. "We still lose."

"It's better than nothing," Breeze said. "I think that we might be able to persuade Cett to leave you as a provisional leader in Luthadel. He doesn't like the Central Dominance; he finds it barren and flat."

"Provisional leader of the city," Elend said with a frown. "That is somewhat different from king of the Central Dominance."

"True," Dockson said. "But, every emperor needs good men to administrate the cities under their rule. You wouldn't be king, but you—and our armies—would live through the next few months, and Luthadel wouldn't be pillaged."

Ham, Breeze, and Dockson all sat resolutely, looking him in the eye. Elend glanced down at his pile of books, thinking of his research and study. Worthless. How long had the crew known that there was only one course of action?

The crew seemed to take Elend's silence as assent.

"Cett really is the best choice, then?" Dockson asked. "Perhaps Straff would be more likely to make an agreement with Elend—they are, after all, family."

Oh, he'd make an agreement, Elend thought. *And he'd break it the moment it was convenient. But . . . the alternative? Give the city over to this Cett? What would happen to this land, this people, if he were in charge?*

"Cett is best, I think," Breeze said. "He is very willing to let others rule, as long as he gets his glory and his coins. The problem is going to be that atium. Cett thinks it is here, and if he doesn't find it . . ."

"We just let him search the city," Ham said.

Breeze nodded. "You'd have to persuade him that I misled him about the atium—and that shouldn't be too hard, considering what he thinks of me. Which is another small matter—you'll have to convince him that I've been dealt with. Perhaps he'd believe that I was executed as soon as Elend found out I had raised an army against him."

The others nodded.

"Breeze?" Elend asked. "How does Lord Cett treat the skaa in his lands?"

Breeze paused, then glanced away. "Not well, I'm afraid."

"Now, see," Elend said. "I think we need to consider how to best protect our people. I mean, if we give everything over to Cett, then we'd save my skin—but at the cost of the entire skaa population of the dominance!"

Dockson shook his head. "Elend, it's not a betrayal. Not if this is the only way."

"That's easy to say," Elend said. "But I'm the one who'd have to bear the guilty conscience for doing such a thing. I'm not saying that we should throw out your suggestion, but I do have a few ideas that we might talk about. . . ."

The others shared looks. As usual, Clubs and Spook remained quiet during proceedings; Clubs only spoke when he felt it absolutely necessary, and Spook tended to stay on the periphery of the conversations. Finally, Breeze, Ham, and Dockson looked back at Elend.

"This is your country, Your Majesty," Dockson said carefully. "We're simply here to give advice." *Very good advice,* his tone implied.

"Yes, well," Elend said, quickly selecting a book. In his haste, he knocked over one of the stacks, sending a clatter of books across the table and landing a volume in Breeze's lap.

"Sorry," Elend said, as Breeze rolled his eyes and sat the book back up on the table. Elend pulled open his own book. "Now, this volume had some very interesting things to say about the movement and arrangement of troop bodies—"

"Uh, El?" Ham asked, frowning. "That looks like a book on shipping grain."

"I know," Elend said. "There weren't a lot of books about warfare in the library. I guess that's what we get for a thousand years without any wars. However, this book does mention how much grain it took to keep the various garrisons in the Final Empire stocked. Do you have any idea how much food an army needs?"

"You have a point," Clubs said, nodding. "Usually, it's a blasted pain to keep soldiers fed; we often had supply problems fighting on the frontier, and we were only small bands, sent to quell the occasional rebellion."

Elend nodded. Clubs didn't often speak of his past fighting in the Lord Ruler's army—and the crew didn't often ask him about it.

"Anyway," Elend said, "I'll bet both Cett and my father are unaccustomed to moving large bodies of men. There will be supply problems, especially for Cett, since he marched so hastily."

"Maybe not," Clubs said. "Both armies have secured canal routes into Luthadel. That will make it easy for them to send for more supplies."

"Plus," Breeze added, "though much of Cett's land is

in revolt right now, he *does* still hold the city of Haverfrex, which held one of the Lord Ruler's main canneries. Cett has a remarkable amount of food a short canal trip away."

"Then, we disrupt the canals," Elend said. "We find a way to stop those supplies from coming. Canals make resupply quick, but also vulnerable, since we know exactly which route it will take. And, if we can take away their food, perhaps they'll be forced to turn around and march home."

"Either that," Breeze said, "or they'll just decide to risk attacking Luthadel."

Elend paused. "That's a possibility," he said. "But, well, I've been researching how to hold the city as well." He reached across the table, picking up a book. "Now, this is Jendellah's *City Management in the Modern Era.* He mentions how difficult Luthadel is to police because of its extreme size and large number of skaa slums. He suggests using roving bands of city watchmen. I think we could adapt his methods to use in a battle—our wall is too long to defend in detail, but if we had mobile bands of troops that could respond to—"

"Your Majesty," Dockson interrupted.

"Hum? Yes?"

"We've got a troop of boys and men who have barely a year's training, and we're facing not one overwhelming force, but *two*. We can't win this battle by force."

"Oh, yes," Elend said. "Of course. I was just saying that if we *did* have to fight, I have some strategies. . . ."

"If we fight, we lose," Clubs said. "We'll probably lose anyway."

Elend paused for a moment. "Yes, well, I just . . ."

"Attacking the canal routes is a good idea, though," Dockson said. "We can do that covertly, perhaps hire some of the bandits in the area to attack supply barges. It probably won't be enough to send Cett or Straff home, but we could make them more desperate to make alliances with us."

Breeze nodded. "Cett's already worried about instability back in his home dominance. We should send him a preliminary messenger, let him know we're interested in an alliance. That way, as soon as his supply problems begin, he'll think of us."

"We could even send him a letter explaining Breeze's execution," Dockson said, "as a sign of good faith. That—"

Elend cleared his throat. The others paused.

"I, uh, wasn't finished yet," Elend said.

"I apologize, Your Majesty," Dockson said.

Elend took a deep breath. "You're right—we can't afford to fight those armies. But, I think we need to find a way to get them to fight each other."

"A pleasant sentiment, my dear man," Breeze said. "But getting those two to attack one another isn't as simple as persuading Spook over there to refill my wine." He turned, holding out his empty cup. Spook paused, then sighed, rising to fetch the wine bottle.

"Well, yes," Elend said. "But, while there aren't a lot of books on warfare, there *are* a lot about politics. Breeze, you said the other day that being the weakest party in a three-way stalemate gives us power."

"Exactly," Breeze said. "We can tip the battle for either of the two larger sides."

"Yes," Elend said, opening a book. "Now that there are three parties involved, it's not warfare—it's politics. This is just like a contest between houses. And in house politicking, even the most powerful houses can't stand without allies. The small houses are weak individually, but they are strong when considered as a group.

"We're like one of those small houses. If we want to make any gains, we're going to have to get our enemies to forget about us—or, at least, make them think us inconsequential. If they both assume that they have the better of us—that they can use us to defeat the other army, then turn on us at their leisure—then they'll leave us alone and concentrate on each other."

Ham rubbed his chin. "You're talking about playing both sides, Elend. It's a dangerous position to put ourselves in."

Breeze nodded. "We'd have to switch our allegiance to whichever side seems weaker at the moment, keep them snapping at each other. And there's no guarantee that the winner between the two would be weakened enough for us to defeat."

"Not to mention our food problems," Dockson said. "What you propose would take time, Your Majesty. Time during which we'd be under siege, our supplies dwindling. It's autumn right now. Winter will soon be upon us."

"It will be tough," Elend agreed. "And risky. But, I think we can do it. We make them *both* think we're allied with them, but we hold back our support. We encourage them against one another, and we wear away at their supplies and morale, pushing them into a conflict. When the dust settles, the surviving army might just be weak enough for us to beat."

Breeze looked thoughtful. "It has style," he admitted. "And, it does kind of sound fun."

Dockson smiled. "You only say that because it involves making someone else do our work for us."

Breeze shrugged. "Manipulation works so well on a personal level, I don't see why it wouldn't be an equally viable national policy."

"That's actually how most rulership works," Ham mused. "What is a government but an institutionalized method of making sure somebody *else* does all the work?"

"Uh, the plan?" Elend asked.

"I don't know, El," Ham said, getting back on topic. "It sounds like one of Kell's plans—foolhardy, brave, and a little insane." He sounded as if he were surprised to hear Elend propose such a measure.

I can be as foolhardy as any man, Elend thought indignantly, then paused. Did he really want to follow that line of thought?

"We could get ourselves into some serious trouble," Dockson said. "If either side decides it's tired of our games . . ."

"They'll destroy us," Elend said. "But . . . well, gentlemen, you're gamblers. You can't tell me that this plan doesn't appeal to you more than simply bowing before Lord Cett."

Ham shared a look with Breeze, and they seemed to be considering the idea. Dockson rolled his eyes, but seemed like he was objecting simply out of habit.

No, they didn't want to take the safe way out. These were the men who had challenged the Lord Ruler, men who had made their livelihood scamming noblemen. In some ways, they were very careful; they could be precise in their attention to detail, cautious in covering their tracks and protecting their interests. But when it came time to gamble for the big prize, they were often willing.

No, not willing. Eager.

Great, Elend thought. *I've filled my inner council with a bunch of thrill-seeking masochists. Even worse, I've decided to join them.* But, what else could he do?

"We could at least consider it," Breeze said. "It does sound exciting."

"Now, see, I didn't suggest this because it was exciting, Breeze," Elend said. "I spent my youth trying to plan how I would make a better city of Luthadel once I became leader of my house. I'm not going to throw away those dreams at the first sign of opposition."

"What about the Assembly?" Ham said.

"That's the best part," Elend said. "They voted in my proposal at the meeting two days back. They can't open the city gates to any invader until I meet with my father in parlay."

The crew sat quietly for a few moments. Finally, Ham turned to Elend, shaking his head. "I really don't know, El. It sounds appealing. We actually discussed a few more daring plans like this while we were waiting for you. But . . ."

"But what?" Elend asked.

"A plan like this depends a lot on you, my dear man," Breeze said, sipping his wine. "You'd have to be the one to meet with the kings—the one to persuade them both that we're on their side. No offense, but you're new to scamming. It's difficult to agree to a daring plan that puts a newcomer in as the linchpin member of the team."

"I can do this," Elend said. "Really."

Ham glanced at Breeze, then both glanced at Clubs. The

gnarled general shrugged. "If the kid wants to try it, then let him."

Ham sighed, then looked back. "I guess I agree. As long as you're up to this, El."

"I think I am," Elend said, covering his nervousness. "I just know we can't give up, not easily. Maybe this won't work—maybe, after a couple months of being besieged, we'll just end up giving away the city anyway. However, that gives us a couple of months during which *something* could happen. It's worth the risk to wait, rather than fold. Wait, and plan."

"All right, then," Dockson said. "Give us some time to come up with some ideas and options, Your Majesty. We'll meet again in a few days to talk about specifics."

"All right," Elend said. "Sounds good. Now, if we can move on to other matters, I'd like to mention—"

A knock came at the door. At Elend's call, Captain Demoux pushed open the door, looking a little embarrassed. "Your Majesty?" he said. "I apologize, but . . . I think we caught someone listening in on your meeting."

"What?" Elend said. "Who?"

Demoux turned to the side, waving in a pair of his guards. The woman they led into the room was vaguely familiar to Elend. Tall, like most Terris, she wore a bright-colored, but utilitarian, dress. Her ears were stretched downward, the lobes elongated to accommodate numerous earrings.

"I recognize you," Elend said. "From the Assembly hall a few days ago. You were watching me."

The woman didn't answer. She looked over the room's occupants, standing stiffly—even haughtily—despite her bound wrists. Elend had never actually met a Terriswoman before; he'd only met stewards, eunuchs trained from birth to work as manservants. For some reason, Elend had expected a Terriswoman to seem a bit more servile.

"She was hiding in the next room over," Demoux said. "I'm sorry, Your Majesty. I don't know how she got past us. We found her listening against the wall, though I doubt she heard anything. I mean, those walls are made of stone."

Elend met the woman's eyes. Older—perhaps fifty—
she wasn't beautiful, but neither was she homely. She was
sturdy, with a straightforward, rectangular face. Her stare
was calm and firm, and it made Elend uncomfortable to
hold it for long.

"So, what did you expect to overhear, woman?" Elend
asked.

The Terriswoman ignored the comment. She turned to
the others, and spoke in a lightly accented voice. "I would
speak with the king alone. The rest of you are excused."

Ham smiled. "Well, at least she's got nerve."

Dockson addressed the Terriswoman. "What makes you
think that we would leave our king alone with you?"

"His Majesty and I have things to discuss," the woman
said in a businesslike manner, as if oblivious of—or unconcerned about—her status as a prisoner. "You needn't be worried about his safety; I'm certain that the young Mistborn
hiding outside the window will be more than enough to deal
with me."

Elend glanced to the side, toward the small ventilation
window beside the more massive stained-glass one. How
would the Terriswoman have known that Vin was watching? Her ears would have to be extraordinarily keen. Keen
enough, perhaps, to listen in on the meeting through a
stone wall?

Elend turned back to the newcomer. "You're a Keeper."

She nodded.

"Did Sazed send you?"

"It is because of him that I am here," she said. "But I
was not 'sent.'"

"Ham, it's all right," Elend said slowly. "You can go."

"Are you sure?" Ham asked, frowning.

"Leave me bound, if you wish," the woman said.

*If she really is a Feruchemist, that won't be much of a
hindrance,* Elend thought. *Of course, if she really is a
Feruchemist—a Keeper, like Sazed—I shouldn't have anything to fear from her. Theoretically.*

The others shuffled from the room, their postures indicating what they thought of Elend's decision. Though they
were no longer thieves by profession, Elend suspected that

they—like Vin—would always bear the effects of their up-bringing.

"We'll be just outside, El," Ham—the last one out—said, then pulled the door shut.

And yet, any who know me will realize that there was no chance I would give up so easily. Once I find something to investigate, I become dogged in my pursuit.

14

THE TERRISWOMAN SNAPPED HER BONDS, and the ropes dropped to the floor.

"Uh, Vin?" Elend said, beginning to wonder about the logic of meeting with this woman. "Perhaps it's time you came in."

"She's not actually there," the Terriswoman said offhand-edly, walking forward. "She left a few minutes ago to do her rounds. That is why I let myself be caught."

"Um, I see," Elend said. "I'll be calling for the guards now."

"Don't be a fool," the Terriswoman said. "If I wanted to kill you, I could do it before the others got back in. Now be quiet for a moment."

Elend stood uncomfortably as the tall woman walked around the table in a slow circle, studying him as a merchant might inspect a piece of furniture up for auction. Finally she stopped, placing her hands on her hips.

"Stand up straight," she commanded.

"Excuse me?"

"You're slouching," the woman said. "A king must maintain an air of dignity at all times, even when with his friends."

Elend frowned. "Now, while I appreciate advice, I don't—"

"No," the woman said. "Don't hedge. Command."

"Excuse me?" Elend said again.

The woman stepped forward, placing a hand on his shoulder and pressing his back firmly to improve his posture. She stepped back, then nodded slightly to herself.

"Now, see," Elend said. "I don't—"

"No," the woman interrupted. "You must be stronger in the way that you speak. Presentation—words, actions, postures—will determine how people judge you and react to you. If you start every sentence with softness and uncertainty, you will seem soft and uncertain. Be forceful!"

"What is going on here?" Elend demanded, exasperated.

"There," the woman said. "Finally."

"You said that you know Sazed?" Elend asked, resisting the urge to slouch back into his earlier posture.

"He is an acquaintance," the woman said. "My name is Tindwyl; I am, as you have guessed, a Keeper of Terris." She tapped her foot for a moment, then shook her head. "Sazed warned me about your slovenly appearance, but I honestly assumed that no king could have such a poor sense of self-presentation."

"Slovenly?" Elend asked. "Excuse me?"

"Stop saying that," Tindwyl snapped. "Don't ask questions; say what you mean. If you object, object—don't leave your words up to my interpretation."

"Yes, well, while this is fascinating," Elend said, walking toward the door, "I'd rather avoid further insults this evening. If you'll excuse me . . ."

"Your people think you are a fool, Elend Venture," Tindwyl said quietly.

Elend paused.

"The Assembly—a body you yourself organized—ignores your authority. The skaa are convinced that you won't be able to protect them. Even your own council of friends makes their plans in your absence, assuming your input to be no great loss."

Elend closed his eyes, taking a slow, deep breath.

"You have good ideas, Elend Venture," Tindwyl said.

"Regal ideas. However, you are not a king. A man can only lead when others accept him as their leader, and he has only as much authority as his subjects give to him. All of the brilliant ideas in the world cannot save your kingdom if no one will listen to them."

Elend turned. "This last year I've read every pertinent book on leadership and governance in the four libraries."

Tindwyl raised an eyebrow. "Then, I suspect that you spent a great deal of time in your room that you *should* have been out, being seen by your people and learning to be a ruler."

"Books have great value," Elend said.

"Actions have greater value."

"And where am I to learn the proper actions?"

"From me."

Elend paused.

"You may know that every Keeper has an area of special interest," Tindwyl said. "While we all memorize the same store of information, one person can only study and understand a limited amount of that store. Our mutual friend Sazed spends his time on religions."

"And your specialty?"

"Biographies," she said. "I have studied the lives of generals, kings, and emperors whose names you have never heard. Understanding theories of politics and leadership, Elend Venture, is not the same as understanding the lives of men who lived such principles."

"And . . . you can teach me to emulate those men?"

"Perhaps," Tindwyl said. "I haven't yet decided whether or not you're a hopeless case. But, I am here, so I will do what I can. A few months ago, I received a letter from Sazed, explaining your predicament. He did not ask me to come to train you—but, then, Sazed is perhaps another man who could learn to be more forceful."

Elend nodded slowly, meeting the Terriswoman's eyes.

"Will you accept my instruction, then?" she asked.

Elend thought for a moment. *If she's anywhere near as useful as Sazed, then . . . well, I could certainly use some help at this.* "I will," he said.

Tindwyl nodded. "Sazed also mentioned your humility. It could be an asset—assuming you don't let it get in the way. Now, I believe that your Mistborn has returned."

Elend turned toward the side window. The shutter swung open, allowing mist to begin streaming into the room and revealing a crouching, cloaked form.

"How did you know I was here?" Vin asked quietly.

Tindwyl smiled—the first such expression Elend had seen on her face. "Sazed mentioned you as well, child. You and I should speak soon in private, I think."

Vin slipped into the room, drawing mist in behind her, then closed the shutter. She didn't bother to hide her hostility or mistrust as she put herself between Elend and Tindwyl.

"Why are you here?" Vin demanded.

Tindwyl smiled again. "It took your king there several minutes to get to that question, and here you ask it after a few bare moments. You are an interesting couple, I think."

Vin's eyes narrowed.

"Regardless, I should withdraw," Tindwyl said. "We shall speak again, I assume, Your Majesty?"

"Yes, of course," Elend said. "Um . . . is there anything I should begin practicing?"

"Yes," Tindwyl said, walking to the door. "Stop saying 'um.' "

"Right."

Ham poked his head in the door as soon as Tindwyl opened it. He immediately noticed her discarded bonds. He didn't say anything, however; he likely assumed that Elend had freed her.

"I think we're done for the night, everyone," Elend said. "Ham, would you see that Mistress Tindwyl is given quarters in the palace? She's a friend of Sazed's."

Ham shrugged. "All right, then." He nodded to Vin, then withdrew. Tindwyl did not bid them good night as she left.

Vin frowned, then glanced at Elend. He seemed . . . distracted. "I don't like her," she said.

Elend smiled, stacking up the books on his table. "You don't like anyone when you first meet them, Vin."

"I liked you."

"Thereby demonstrating that you are a terrible judge of character."

Vin paused, then smiled. She walked over and began picking through the books. They weren't typical Elend fare—far more practical than the kinds of things he usually read. "How did it go tonight?" she asked. "I didn't have much time to listen."

Elend sighed. He turned, sitting down on the table, looking up at the massive rose window at the back of the room. It was dark, its colors only hinted as reflections in the black glass. "It went well, I suppose."

"I told you they'd like your plan. It's the sort of thing they'll find challenging."

"I suppose," Elend said.

Vin frowned. "All right," she said, hopping up to stand on the table. She sat down beside him. "What is it? Is it something that woman said? What did she want, anyway?"

"Just to pass on some knowledge," he said. "You know how Keepers are, always wanting an ear to listen to their lessons."

"I suppose," Vin said slowly. She hadn't ever seen Elend depressed, but he did get discouraged. He had so many ideas, so many plans and hopes, that she sometimes wondered how he kept them all straight. She would have said that he lacked focus; Reen had always said that focus kept a thief alive. Elend's dreams, however, were so much a part of who he was. She doubted he could discard them. She didn't think she would want him to, for they were part of what she loved about him.

"They agreed to the plan, Vin," Elend said, still looking up at the window. "They even seemed excited, like you said they'd be. It's just . . . I can't help thinking that their suggestion was far more rational than mine. They wanted to side with one of the armies, giving it our support in exchange for leaving me as a subjugated ruler in Luthadel."

"That would be giving up," Vin said.

"Sometimes, giving up is better than failing. I just committed my city to an extended siege. That will mean hunger, perhaps starvation, before this is over with."

Vin put a hand on his shoulder, watching him uncertainly. Usually, he was the one who reassured her. "It's still a better way," she said. "The others probably just suggested a weaker plan because they thought you wouldn't go along with something more daring."

"No," Elend said. "They weren't pandering to me, Vin. They really thought that making a strategic alliance was a good, safe plan." He paused, then looked at her. "Since when did *that* group represent the reasonable side of my government?"

"They've had to grow," Vin said. "They can't be the men they once were, not with this much responsibility."

Elend turned back toward the window. "I'll tell you what worries me, Vin. I'm worried that their plan *wasn't* reasonable—perhaps it itself was a bit foolhardy. Perhaps making an alliance would have been a difficult enough task. If that's the case, then what *I'm* proposing is just downright ludicrous."

Vin squeezed his shoulder. "We fought the Lord Ruler."

"You had Kelsier then."

"Not *that* again."

"I'm sorry," Elend said. "But, really, Vin. Maybe my plan to try and hold on to the government is just arrogance. What was it you told me about your childhood? When you were in the thieving crews, and everyone was bigger, stronger, and meaner than you, what did you do? Did you stand up to the leaders?"

Memories flashed in her mind. Memories of hiding, of keeping her eyes down, of weakness.

"That was then," she said. "You can't let others beat on you forever. That's what Kelsier taught me—that's why we fought the Lord Ruler. That's why the skaa rebellion fought the Final Empire all those years, even when there was no chance of winning. Reen taught me that the rebels were fools. But Reen is dead now—and so is the Final Empire. And . . ."

She leaned down, catching Elend's eyes. "You can't give up the city, Elend," she said quietly. "I don't think I'd like what that would do to you."

Elend paused, then smiled slowly. "You can be very wise sometimes, Vin."

"You think that?"

He nodded.

"Well," she said, "then obviously you're as poor a judge of character as I am."

Elend laughed, putting his arm around her, hugging her against his side. "So, I assume the patrol tonight was uneventful?"

The mist spirit. Her fall. The chill she could still feel—if only faintly remembered—in her forearm. "It was," she said. The last time she'd told him of the mist spirit, he'd immediately thought she'd been seeing things.

"See," Elend said, "you should have come to the meeting; I would have liked to have had you here."

She said nothing.

They sat for a few minutes, looking up at the dark window. There was an odd beauty to it; the colors weren't visible because of the lack of back light, and she could instead focus on the patterns of glass. Chips, slivers, slices, and plates woven together within a framework of metal.

"Elend?" she finally said. "I'm worried."

"I'd be concerned if you weren't," he said. "Those armies have *me* so worried that I can barely think straight."

"No," Vin said. "Not about that. I'm worried about other things."

"Like what?"

"Well . . . I've been thinking about what the Lord Ruler said, right before I killed him. Do you remember?"

Elend nodded. He hadn't been there, but she'd told him.

"He talked about what he'd done for mankind," Vin said. "He saved us, the stories say. From the Deepness."

Elend nodded.

"But," Vin said, "what *was* the Deepness? You were a nobleman—religion wasn't forbidden to you. What did the Ministry teach about the Deepness and the Lord Ruler?"

Elend shrugged. "Not much, really. Religion wasn't forbidden, but it wasn't encouraged either. There was something proprietary about the Ministry, an air that implied they would take care of religious things—that we didn't need to worry ourselves."

"But they did teach you about some things, right?"

Elend nodded. "Mostly, they talked about why the nobility were privileged and the skaa cursed. I guess they wanted us to understand how fortunate we were—though honestly, I always found the teachings a little disturbing. See, they claimed that we were noble because our ancestors supported the Lord Ruler before the Ascension. But, that means that we were privileged because of what other people had done. Not really fair, eh?"

Vin shrugged. "Fair as anything else, I guess."

"But, didn't you get angry?" Elend said. "Didn't it frustrate you that the nobility had so much while you had so little?"

"I didn't think about it," Vin said. "The nobility had a lot, so we could take it from them. Why should I care how they got it? Sometimes, when I had food, other thieves beat me and took it. What did it matter how I got my food? It was still taken from me."

Elend paused. "You know, sometimes I wonder what the political theorists I've read would say if they met you. I have a feeling they'd throw up their hands in frustration."

She poked him in the side. "Enough politics. Tell me about the Deepness."

"Well, I think it was a creature of some sort—a dark and evil thing that nearly destroyed the world. The Lord Ruler traveled to the Well of Ascension, where he was given the power to defeat the Deepness and unite mankind. There are several statues in the city depicting the event."

Vin frowned. "Yes, but they never really show what the Deepness looked like. It's depicted as a twisted lump at the Lord Ruler's feet."

"Well, the last person who actually saw the Deepness died a year ago, so I guess we'll have to make do with the statues."

"Unless it comes back," Vin said quietly.

Elend frowned, looking at her again. "Is that what this is about, Vin?" His face softened slightly. "Two armies aren't enough? You have to worry about the fate of the world as well?"

Vin glanced down sheepishly, and Elend laughed, pulling her close. "Ah, Vin. I know you're a bit paranoid—honestly, considering our situation, I'm starting to feel the same— but I think this is one problem you don't have to worry about. I haven't heard any reports of monstrous incarnations of evil rampaging across the land."

Vin nodded, and Elend leaned back a bit, obviously assuming that he'd answered her question.

The Hero of Ages traveled to the Well of Ascension to defeat the Deepness, she thought. *But the prophecies all said that the Hero shouldn't take the Well's power for himself. He was supposed to give it, trust in the power itself to destroy the Deepness.*

Rashek didn't do that—he took the power for himself. Wouldn't that mean that the Deepness was never defeated? Why, then, wasn't the world destroyed?

"The red sun and brown plants," Vin said. "Did the Deepness do that?"

"Still thinking about that?" Elend frowned. "Red sun and brown plants? What other colors would they be?"

"Kelsier said that the sun was once yellow, and plants were green."

"That's an odd image."

"Sazed agrees with Kelsier," Vin said. "The legends all say that during the early days of the Lord Ruler, the sun changed colors, and ash began to fall from the skies."

"Well," Elend said, "I guess the Deepness *could* have had something to do with it. I don't know, honestly." He sat musingly for a few moments. "Green plants? Why not purple or blue? So odd. . . ."

The Hero of Ages traveled north, to the Well of Ascension, Vin thought again. She turned slightly, her eyes drawn toward the Terris mountains so far away. Was it still up there? The Well of Ascension?

"Did you have any luck getting information out of Ore-Seur?" Elend asked. "Anything to help us find the spy?"

Vin shrugged. "He told me that kandra can't use Allomancy."

"So, you can find our impostor that way?" Elend said, perking up.

"Maybe," Vin said. "I can test Spook and Ham, at least. Regular people will be more difficult—though kandra can't be Soothed, so maybe that will let me find the spy."

"That sounds promising," Elend said.

Vin nodded. The thief in her, the paranoid girl that Elend always teased, itched to use Allomancy on him—to test him, to see if he reacted to her Pushes and Pulls. She stopped herself. This one man she would trust. The others she would test, but she would not question Elend. In a way, she'd rather trust him and be wrong than deal with the worry of mistrust.

I finally understand, she thought with a start. *Kelsier. I understand what it was like for you with Mare. I won't make your same mistake.*

Elend was looking at her.

"What?" she asked.

"You're smiling," he said. "Do I get to hear the joke?"

She hugged him. "No," she said simply.

Elend smiled. "All right then. You can test Spook and Ham, but I'm pretty sure the impostor isn't one of the crew—I talked to them all today, and they were all themselves. We need to search the palace staff."

He doesn't know how good kandra can be. The enemy kandra had probably studied his victim for months and months, learning and memorizing their every mannerism.

"I've spoken to Ham and Demoux," Elend said. "As members of the palace guard, they know about the bones—and Ham was able to guess what they were. Hopefully, they can sort through the staff with minimal disturbance and locate the impostor."

Vin's senses itched at how trusting Elend was. *No,* she thought. *Let him assume the best. He has enough to worry about. Besides, perhaps the kandra is imitating someone outside our core team. Elend can search that avenue.*

And, if the impostor is a member of the crew . . . Well,

that's the sort of situation where my paranoia comes in handy.

"Anyway," Elend said, standing. "I have a few things to check on before it gets too late."

Vin nodded. He gave her a long kiss, then left. She sat on the table for a few moments longer, not looking at the massive rose window, but at the smaller window to the side, which she'd left slightly open. It stood, a doorway into the night. Mist churned in the blackness, tentatively sending tendrils into the room, evaporating quietly in the warmth.

"I will not fear you," Vin whispered. "And I will find your secret." She climbed off the table and slipped out the window, back out to meet with OreSeur and do another check of the palace grounds.

I had determined that Alendi was the Hero of Ages, and I intended to prove it. I should have bowed before the will of the others; I shouldn't have insisted on traveling with Alendi to witness his journeys.

It was inevitable that Alendi himself would find out what I believed him to be.

15

ON THE EIGHTH DAY OUT of the Conventical, Sazed awoke to find himself alone.

He stood, pushing off his blanket and the light film of ash that had fallen during the night. Marsh's place beneath the tree's canopy was empty, though a patch of bare earth indicated where the Inquisitor had slept.

Sazed stood, following Marsh's footsteps out into the harsh red sunlight. The ash was deeper here, without the cover of trees, and there was also more wind blowing it into drifts. Sazed regarded the windswept landscape. There was no further sign of Marsh.

Sazed returned to camp. The trees here—in the middle of the Eastern Dominance—rose twisted and knotted, but they had shelflike, overlapping branches, thick with brown needles. These provided decent shelter, though the ash seemed capable of infiltrating any sanctuary.

Sazed made a simple soup for breakfast. Marsh did not return. Sazed washed his brown travel robes in a nearby stream. Marsh did not return. Sazed sewed a rent in his sleeve, oiled his walking boots, and shaved his head. Marsh did not return. Sazed got out the rubbing he'd made in the Conventical, transcribed a few words, then forced himself to put the sheet away—he worried about blurring the words by opening it too often or by getting ash on it. Better to wait until he could have a proper desk and clean room.

Marsh did not return.

Finally, Sazed left. He couldn't define the sense of urgency that he felt—part excitement to share what he had learned, part desire to see how Vin and the young king Elend Venture were handling events in Luthadel.

Marsh knew the way. He would catch up.

Sazed raised his hand, shading his eyes against the red sunlight, looking down from his hilltop vantage. There was a slight darkness on the horizon, to the east of the main road. He tapped his geography coppermind, seeking out descriptions of the Eastern Dominance.

The knowledge swelled his mind, blessing him with recollection. The darkness was a village named Urbene. He searched through one of his indexes, looking for the right gazetteer. The index was growing fuzzy, its information difficult to remember—which meant that he'd switched it from coppermind to memory and back too many times. Knowledge inside a coppermind would remain pristine, but anything inside his head—even for only a few moments— would decay. He'd have to re-memorize the index later.

He found what he was looking for, and dumped the right

memories into his head. The gazetteer listed Urbene as "picturesque," which probably meant that some important nobleman had decided to make his manor there. The listing said that the skaa of Urbene were herdsmen.

Sazed scribbled a note to himself, then redeposited the gazetteer's memories. Reading the note told him what he had just forgotten. Like the index, the gazetteer memories had inevitably decayed slightly during their stay in his head. Fortunately, he had a second set of copperminds hidden back up in Terris, and would use those to pass his knowledge on to another Keeper. His current copperminds were for everyday use. Unapplied knowledge benefited no one.

He shouldered his pack. A visit to the village would do him some good, even if it slowed him down. His stomach agreed with the decision. It was unlikely the peasants would have much in the way of food, but perhaps they would be able to provide something other than broth. Besides, they might have news of events at Luthadel.

He hiked down the short hill, taking the smaller, eastern fork in the road. Once, there had been little travel in the Final Empire. The Lord Ruler had forbidden skaa to leave their indentured lands, and only thieves and rebels had dared disobey. Still, most of the nobility had made their livings by trading, so a village such as this one might be accustomed to visitors.

Sazed began to notice the oddities immediately. Goats roamed the countryside along the road, unwatched. Sazed paused, then dug a coppermind from his pack. He searched through it as he walked. One book on husbandry claimed that herdsmen sometimes left their flocks alone to graze. Yet, the unwatched animals made him nervous. He quickened his pace.

Just to the south, the skaa starve, he thought. *Yet here, livestock is so plentiful that nobody can be spared to keep it safe from bandits or predators?*

The small village appeared in the distance. Sazed could almost convince himself that the lack of activity—the lack of movement in the streets, the derelict doors and shutters swinging in the breeze—was due to his approach. Perhaps the people were so scared that they were hiding. Or, perhaps they simply were all out. Tending flocks. . . .

Sazed stopped. A shift in the wind brought a telltale scent from the village. The skaa weren't hiding, and they hadn't fled. It was the scent of rotting bodies.

Suddenly urgent, Sazed pulled out a small ring—a scent tinmind—and slipped it on his thumb. The smell on the wind, it didn't seem like that of a slaughter. It was a mustier, dirtier smell. A smell not only of death, but of corruption, unwashed bodies, and waste. He reversed the use of the tinmind, filling it instead of tapping it, and his ability to smell grew very weak—keeping him from gagging.

He continued on, carefully entering the village proper. Like most skaa villages, Urbene was organized simply. It had a group of ten large hovels built in a loose circle with a well at the center. The buildings were wood, and for thatching they used the same needle-bearing branches from the trees he'd seen. Overseers' huts, along with a fine nobleman's manor, stood a little farther up the valley.

If it hadn't been for the smell—and the sense of haunted emptiness—Sazed might have agreed with his gazetteer's description of Urbene. For skaa residences, the hovels looked well maintained, and the village lay in a quiet hollow amid the rising landscape.

It wasn't until he got a little closer that he found the first bodies. They lay scattered around the doorway to the nearest hovel, about a half-dozen of them. Sazed approached carefully, but could quickly see that the corpses were at least several days old. He knelt beside the first one, that of a woman, and could see no visible cause of death. The others were the same.

Nervous, Sazed forced himself to reach up and pull open the door to the hovel. The stench from inside was so strong that he could smell it through his tinmind.

The hovel, like most, was only a single chamber. It was filled with bodies. Most lay wrapped in thin blankets; some sat with backs pressed up against the walls, rotting heads hanging limply from their necks. They had gaunt, nearly fleshless bodies with withered limbs and protruding ribs. Haunted, unseeing eyes sat in desiccated faces.

These people had died of starvation and dehydration.

Sazed stumbled from the hovel, head bowed. He didn't expect to find anything different in the other buildings, but he checked anyway. He saw the same scene repeated again and again. Woundless corpses on the ground outside; many more bodies huddled inside. Flies buzzing about in swarms, covering faces. In several of the buildings he found gnawed human bones at the center of the room.

He stumbled out of the final hovel, breathing deeply through his mouth. Dozens of people, over a hundred total, dead for no obvious reason. What possibly could have caused so many of them to simply sit, hidden in their houses, while they ran out of food and water? How could they have starved when there were beasts running free? And what had killed those that he'd found outside, lying in the ash? They didn't seem as emaciated as the ones inside, though from the level of decomposition, it was difficult to tell.

I must be mistaken about the starvation, Sazed told himself. *It must have been a plague of some sort, a disease. That is a much more logical explanation.* He searched through his medical coppermind. Surely there were diseases that could strike quickly, leaving their victims weakened. And the survivors must have fled. Leaving behind their loved ones. Not taking any of the animals from their pastures. . . .

Sazed frowned. At that moment, he thought he heard something.

He spun, drawing auditory power from his hearing tinmind. The sounds were there—the sound of breathing, the sound of movement, coming from one of the hovels he'd visited. He dashed forward, throwing open the door, looking again on the sorry dead. The corpses lay where they had been before. Sazed studied them very carefully, this time watching until he found the one whose chest was moving.

By the forgotten gods . . . Sazed thought. The man didn't need to work hard to feign death. His hair had fallen out, and his eyes were sunken into his face. Though he didn't look particularly starved, Sazed must have missed seeing him because of his dirty, almost corpselike body.

Sazed stepped toward the man. "I am a friend," he said quietly. The man remained motionless. Sazed frowned as he walked forward and laid a hand on the man's shoulder.

The man's eyes snapped open, and he cried out, jumping to his feet. Dazed and frenzied, he scrambled over corpses, moving to the back of the room. He huddled down, staring at Sazed.

"Please," Sazed said, setting down his pack. "You mustn't be afraid." The only food he had besides broth spices was a few handfuls of meal, but he pulled some out. "I have food."

The man shook his head. "There is no food," he whispered. "We ate it all. Except . . . the food." His eyes darted toward the center of the room. Toward the bones Sazed had noticed earlier. Uncooked, gnawed on, placed in a pile beneath a ragged cloth, as if to hide them.

"I didn't eat the food," the man whispered.

"I know," Sazed said, taking a step forward. "But, there is other food. Outside."

"Can't go outside."

"Why not?"

The man paused, then looked down. "Mist."

Sazed glanced toward the doorway. The sun was nearing the horizon, but wouldn't set for another hour or so. There was no mist. Not now, anyway.

Sazed felt a chill. He slowly turned back toward the man. "Mist . . . during the day?"

The man nodded.

"And it stayed?" Sazed asked. "It didn't go away after a few hours?"

The man shook his head. "Days. Weeks. All mist."

Lord Ruler! Sazed thought, then caught himself. It had been a long time since he'd sworn by that creature's name, even in his thoughts.

But for the mist to come during the day, then to stay—if this man were to be believed—for weeks . . . Sazed could imagine the skaa, frightened in their hovels, a thousand years of terror, tradition, and superstition keeping them from venturing outside.

But to remain inside until they starved? Even their fear of the mist, deep-seated though it was, wouldn't have been enough to make them starve themselves to death, would it?

"Why didn't you leave?" Sazed asked quietly.

"Some did," the man said, nodding as if to himself. "Jell. You know what happened to him."

Sazed frowned. "Dead?"

"Taken by the mist. Oh, how he shook. Was a bull-headed one, you know. Old Jell. Oh, how he shook. How he writhed when it took him."

Sazed closed his eyes. *The corpses I found outside the doors.*

"Some got away," the man said.

Sazed snapped his eyes open. "What?"

The crazed villager nodded again. "Some got away, you know. They called to us, after leaving the village. Said it was all right. It didn't take them. Don't know why. It killed others, though. Some, it shook to the ground, but they got up later. Some it killed."

"The mist let some survive, but it killed others?"

The man didn't answer. He'd sat down, and now he lay back, staring unfocused at the ceiling.

"Please," Sazed said. "You must answer me. Who did it kill and who did it let pass? What is the connection?"

The man turned toward him. "Time for food," he said, then rose. He wandered over to a corpse, then pulled on an arm, ripping the rotted meat free. It was easy to see why he hadn't starved to death like the others.

Sazed pushed aside nausea, striding across the room and grabbing the man's arm as he raised the near fleshless bone to his lips. The man froze, then looked up at Sazed. "It's not mine!" he yelped, dropping the bone and running to the back of the room.

Sazed stood for a moment. *I must hurry. I must get to Luthadel. There is more wrong with this world than bandits and armies.*

The wild man watched with a feral sort of terror as Sazed picked up his pack, then paused and set it down again. He pulled out his largest pewtermind. He fastened the wide metal bracer to his forearm, then turned and walked toward the villager.

"No!" the man screamed, trying to dash to the side. Sazed tapped the pewtermind, pulling out a burst of strength. He felt his muscles enlarge, his robes growing tight. He snatched the villager as the man ran passed, then held him out, far enough away that the man couldn't do either of them much harm.

Then he carried the man outside of the building.

The man stopped struggling as soon as they emerged into the sunlight. He looked up, as if seeing the sun for the first time. Sazed set him down, then released his pewtermind.

The man knelt, looking up at the sun, then turned to Sazed. "The Lord Ruler . . . why did he abandon us? Why did he go?"

"The Lord Ruler was a tyrant."

The man shook his head. "He loved us. He ruled us. Now that he's gone, the mists can kill us. They hate us."

Then, surprisingly adroit, the man leaped to his feet and scrambled down the pathway out of the village. Sazed took a step forward, but paused. What would he do? Pull the man all the way to Luthadel? There was water in the well and there were animals to eat. Sazed could only hope that the poor wretch would be able to manage.

Sighing, Sazed returned to the hovel and retrieved his pack. On his way out, he paused, then pulled out one of his steelminds. Steel held one of the very most difficult attributes to store up: physical speed. He had spent months filling this particular steelmind in preparation for the possibility that someday he might need to run somewhere very, very quickly.

He put it on now.

Yes, he was the one who fueled the rumors after that. I could never have done what he himself did, convincing and persuading the world that he was indeed the Hero. I don't know if he himself believed it, but he made others think that he must be the one.

16

VIN RARELY USED HER QUARTERS. Elend had assigned her spacious rooms—which was, perhaps, part of the problem. She'd spent her childhood sleeping in nooks, lairs, or alleys. Having three separate chambers was a bit daunting.

It didn't really matter, however. During her time awake she was with either Elend or the mists. Her rooms existed for her to sleep in. Or, in this case, for her to make a mess in.

She sat on the floor in the center of her main chamber. Elend's steward, concerned that Vin didn't have any furniture, had insisted on decorating her rooms. This morning, Vin had pushed some of this aside, bunching up rugs and chairs on one side so that she could sit on the cool stones with her book.

It was the first real book she had ever owned, though it was just a collection of pages bound loosely at one side. That suited her just fine; the simple binding had made the book that much easier to pull apart.

She sat amid stacks of paper. It was amazing how many pages there were in the book, once she had separated them. Vin sat next to one pile, looking over its contents. She shook her head, then crawled over to another pile. She leafed through the pages, eventually selecting one.

Sometimes I wonder if I'm going mad, the words read.

*Perhaps it is due to the pressure of knowing that I must
somehow bear the burden of an entire world. Perhaps it
is caused by the death I have seen, the friends I have lost.
The friends I have been forced to kill.*

*Either way, I sometimes see shadows following me.
Dark creatures that I don't understand, nor do I wish to
understand. They are, perhaps, some figment of my
overtaxed mind?*

Vin sat for a moment, rereading the paragraphs. Then
she moved the sheet over to another pile. OreSeur lay on
the side of the room, head on paws, eyeing her. "Mistress,"
he said as she set down the page, "I have been watching
you work for the last two hours, and will admit that I am
thoroughly confused. What is the point of all this?"

Vin crawled over to another stack of pages. "I thought
you didn't care how I spent my time."

"I don't," OreSeur said. "But I do get bored."

"And annoyed, apparently."

"I like to understand what is going on around me."

Vin shrugged, gesturing toward the stacks of paper.
"This is the Lord Ruler's logbook. Well, actually, it's not
the logbook of the Lord Ruler we knew, but the logbook of
the man who *should* have been the Lord Ruler."

"Should have been?" OreSeur asked. "You mean he
should have conquered the world, but didn't?"

"No," Vin said. "I mean he should have been the one
who took the power at the Well of Ascension. This man,
the man who wrote this book—we don't actually know his
name—was some kind of prophesied hero. Or . . . everyone thought he was. Anyway, the man who became the
Lord Ruler—Rashek—was this hero's packman. Don't
you remember us talking about this, back when you were
imitating Renoux?"

OreSeur nodded. "I recall you briefly mentioning it."

"Well, this is the book Kelsier and I found when we infiltrated the Lord Ruler's palace. We thought it was written by
the Lord Ruler, but it turns out it was written by the man the
Lord Ruler killed, the man whose place he took."

"Yes, Mistress," OreSeur said. "Now, why exactly are you tearing it to pieces?"

"I'm not," Vin said. "I just took off the binding so I could move the pages around. It helps me think."

"I . . . see," OreSeur said. "And, what exactly are you looking for? The Lord Ruler is dead, Mistress. Last I checked, you killed him."

What am I looking for? Vin thought, picking up another page. *Ghosts in the mist.*

She read the words on this page slowly.

> *It isn't a shadow.*
>   *This dark thing that follows me, the thing that only I can see—it isn't really a shadow. It is blackish and translucent, but it doesn't have a shadowlike solid outline. It's insubstantial—wispy and formless. Like it's made out of black fog.*
>   *Or mist, perhaps.*

Vin lowered the page. *It watched him, too,* she thought. She remembered reading the words over a year before, thinking that the Hero must have started to go mad. With all the pressures on him, who would have been surprised?

Now, however, she thought she understood the nameless logbook author better. She knew he was not the Lord Ruler, and could see him for what he might have been. Uncertain of his place in the world, but forced into important events. Determined to do the best he could. Idealistic, in a way.

And the mist spirit had chased him. What did it mean? What did seeing it imply for her?

She crawled over to another pile of pages. She'd spent the morning scanning through the logbook for clues about the mist creature. However, she was having trouble digging out much beyond these two, familiar passages.

She made piles of pages that mentioned anything strange or supernatural. She made a small pile with pages that referenced the mist spirit. She also had a special pile for references to the Deepness. This last one, ironically, was both the largest and least informative of the group.

The logbook author had a habit of mentioning the Deepness, but not saying much about it.

The Deepness was dangerous, that much was clear. It had ravaged the land, slaying thousands. The monster had sown chaos wherever it stepped, bringing destruction and fear, but the armies of mankind had been unable to defeat it. Only the Terris prophecies and the Hero of Ages had offered any hope.

If only he had been more specific! Vin thought with frustration, riffling papers. However, the tone of the logbook really was more melancholy than it was informative. It was something that the Hero had written for himself, to stay sane, to let him put his fears and hopes down on paper. Elend said he wrote for similar reasons, sometimes. To Vin, it seemed a silly method of dealing with problems.

With a sigh, she turned to the last stack of papers—the one with pages she had yet to study. She lay down on the stone floor and began to read, searching for useful information.

It took time. Not only was she a slow reader, but her mind kept wandering. She'd read the logbook before—and, oddly, hints and phrases from it reminded her of where she'd been at the time. Two years and a world away in Fellise, still recovering from her near death at the hands of a Steel Inquisitor, she'd been forced to spend her days pretending to be Valette Renoux, a young, inexperienced country noblewoman.

Back then, she still hadn't believed in Kelsier's plan to overthrow the Final Empire. She'd stayed with the crew because she valued the strange things they offered her—friendship, trust, and lessons in Allomancy—not because she accepted their goals. She would never have guessed where that would lead her. To balls and parties, to actually growing—just a bit—to become the noblewoman she had pretended to be.

But that had been a farce, a few months of make-believe. She forced her thoughts away from the frilly clothing and the dances. She needed to focus on practical matters.

And . . . is this practical? she thought idly, setting a page in one of the stacks. *Studying things I barely comprehend, fearing a threat nobody else even cares to notice?*

She sighed, folding her arms under her chin as she lay on her stomach. What was she really worried about? That the Deepness would return? All she had were a few phantom visions in the mist—things that could, as Elend implied, have easily been fabricated by her overworked mind. More important was another question. Assuming that the Deepness was real, what did she expect to do about it? She was no hero, general, or leader.

Oh, Kelsier, she thought, picking up another page. *We could use you now.* Kelsier had been a man beyond convention . . . a man who had somehow been able to defy reality. He'd thought that by giving his life to overthrow the Lord Ruler, he would secure freedom for the skaa. But, what if his sacrifice had opened the way for a greater danger, something so destructive that the Lord Ruler's oppression was a preferable alternative?

She finally finished the page, then placed it in the stack of those that contained no useful information. Then she paused. She couldn't even remember what she'd just read. She sighed, picking the page back up, looking at it again. How did Elend do it? He could study the same books over and over again. But, for Vin, it was hard to—

She paused. *I must assume that I am not mad,* the words said. *I cannot, with any rational sense of confidence, continue my quest if I do not believe this. The thing following me must, therefore, be real.*

She sat up. She only vaguely remembered this section of the logbook. The book was organized like a diary, with sequential—but dateless—entries. It had a tendency to ramble, and the Hero had been fond of droning on about his insecurities. This section had been particularly dry.

But there, in the middle of his complaining, was a tidbit of information.

I believe that it would kill me, if it could, the text continued.

There is an evil feel to the thing of shadow and fog, and my skin recoils at its touch. Yet, it seems limited in what it can do, especially to me.

It can affect this world, however. The knife it placed in

Fedik's chest proves that much. I'm still not certain which was more traumatic for him—the wound itself, or seeing the thing that did it to him.

Rashek whispers that I stabbed Fedik myself, for only Fedik and I can give witness to that night's events. However, I must make a decision. I must determine that I am not mad. The alternative is to admit that it was I who held that knife.

Somehow, knowing Rashek's opinion on the matter makes it much easier for me to believe the opposite.

The next page continued on about Rashek, and the next several entries contained no mention of the mist spirit. However, Vin found even these few paragraphs exciting.

He made a decision, she thought. *I have to make the same one.* She'd never worried that she was mad, but she had sensed some logic in Elend's words. Now she rejected them. The mist spirit was not some delusion brought on by a mixture of stress and memories of the logbook. It was real.

That didn't mean the Deepness was returning, nor did it mean that Luthadel was in any sort of supernatural danger. Both, however, were possibilities.

She set this page with the two others that contained concrete information about the mist spirit, then turned back to her studies, determined to pay closer attention to her reading.

The armies were digging in.

Elend watched from atop the wall as his plan, vague though it was, began to take form. Straff was making a defensive perimeter to the north, holding the canal route back a relatively short distance to Urteau, his home city and capital. Cett was digging in to the west of the city, holding the Luth-Davn Canal, which ran back to his cannery in Haverfrex.

A cannery. That was something Elend wished he had in the city. The technology was newer—perhaps fifty years old—but he'd read of it. The scholars had considered its main use that of providing easily carried supplies for soldiers fighting at the fringes of the empire. They hadn't considered stockpiles for sieges—particularly in Luthadel. But, then, who would have?

Even as Elend watched, patrols began to move out from the separate armies. Some moved to watch the boundaries between the two forces, but others moved to secure other canal routes, bridges across the River Channerel, and roads leading away from Luthadel. In a remarkably short time, the city felt completely surrounded. Cut off from the world, and the rest of Elend's small kingdom. No more moving in or out. The armies were counting on disease, starvation, and other weakening factors to bring Elend to his knees.

The siege of Luthadel had begun.

That's a good thing, he told himself. *For this plan to work, they have to think me desperate. They have to be so sure that I'm willing to side with them, that they don't consider that I might be working with their enemies, too.*

As Elend watched, he noticed someone climbing up the steps to the wall. Clubs. The general hobbled over to Elend, who had been standing alone. "Congratulations," Clubs said. "Looks like you now have a full-blown siege on your hands."

"Good."

"It'll give us a little breathing room, I guess," Clubs said. Then he eyed Elend with one of his gnarled looks. "You'd better be up to this, kid."

"I know," Elend whispered.

"You've made yourself the focal point," Clubs said. "The Assembly can't break this siege until you meet officially with Straff, and the kings aren't likely to meet with anyone on the crew other than yourself. This is all about you. Useful place for a king to be, I suppose. If he's a good one."

Clubs fell silent. Elend stood, looking out over the separate armies. The words spoken to him by Tindwyl the Terriswoman still bothered him. *You are a fool, Elend Venture. . . .*

So far, neither of the kings had responded to Elend's requests for a meeting—though the crew was sure that they soon would. His enemies would wait, to make Elend sweat a bit. The Assembly had just called another meeting, probably to try and bully him into releasing them from their earlier proposal. Elend had found a convenient reason to skip the meeting.

He looked at Clubs. "And am I a good king, Clubs? In your opinion."

The general glanced at him, and Elend saw a harsh wisdom in his eyes. "I've known worse leaders," he said. "But I've also known a *hell* of a lot better."

Elend nodded slowly. "I want to be good at this, Clubs. Nobody else is going to look after the skaa like they deserve. Cett, Straff. They'd just make slaves of the people again. I . . . I want to be more than my ideas, though. I want to—*need to*—be a man that others can look to."

Clubs shrugged. "My experience has been that the man is usually made by the situation. Kelsier was a selfish dandy until the Pits nearly broke him." He glanced at Elend. "Will this siege be *your* Pits of Hathsin, Elend Venture?"

"I don't know," he said honestly.

"Then we'll have to wait and see, I guess. For now, someone wants to speak with you." He turned, nodding down toward the street some forty feet below, where a tall, feminine figure stood in colorful Terris robes.

"She told me to send you down," Clubs said. He paused, then glanced at Elend. "It isn't often you meet someone who feels like they can order me around. And a Terriswoman at that. I thought those Terris were all docile and kindly."

Elend smiled. "I guess Sazed spoiled us."

Clubs snorted. "So much for a thousand years of breeding, eh?"

Elend nodded.

"You sure she's safe?" Clubs asked.

"Yes," Elend said. "Her story checks out—Vin brought in several of the Terris people from the city, and they knew and recognized Tindwyl. She's apparently a fairly important person back in her homeland."

Plus, she had performed Feruchemy for him, growing

stronger to free her hands. That meant she wasn't a kandra. All of it together meant that she was trustworthy enough; even Vin admitted that, even if she continued to dislike the Terriswoman.

Clubs nodded to him, and Elend took a deep breath. Then he walked down the stairs to meet Tindwyl for another round of lessons.

"Today, we will do something about your clothing," Tindwyl said, closing the door to Elend's study. A plump seamstress with bowl-cut white hair waited inside, standing respectfully with a group of youthful assistants.

Elend glanced down at his clothing. It actually wasn't bad. The suit coat and vest fit fairly well. The trousers weren't as stiff as those favored by imperial nobility, but he was the king now; shouldn't he be able to set the trends?

"I don't see what's wrong with it," he said. He held up a hand as Tindwyl began to speak. "I know it's not quite as formal as what other men like to wear, but it suits me."

"It's disgraceful," Tindwyl said.

"Now, I hardly see—"

"Don't argue with me."

"But, see, the other day you said that—"

"Kings don't argue, Elend Venture," Tindwyl said firmly. "They *command*. And, part of your ability to command comes from your bearing. Slovenly clothing invites other slovenly habits—such as your posture, which I've already mentioned, I believe."

Elend sighed, rolling his eyes as Tindwyl snapped her fingers. The seamstress and her assistants started unpacking a pair of large trunks.

"This isn't necessary," Elend said. "I already have some suits that fit more snugly; I wear them on formal occasions."

"You're not going to wear suits anymore," Tindwyl said.

"Excuse me?"

Tindwyl eyed him with a commanding stare, and Elend sighed.

"Explain yourself!" he said, trying to sound commanding.

Tindwyl nodded. "You have maintained the dress code preferred by the nobility sanctioned by the Final Emperor. In some respects, this was a good idea—it gave you a connection to the former government, and made you seem less of a deviant. Now, however, you are in a different position. Your people are in danger, and the time for simple diplomacy is over. You are at war. Your dress should reflect that."

The seamstress selected a particular costume, then brought it over to Elend while the assistants set up a changing screen.

Elend hesitantly accepted the costume. It was stiff and white, and the front of the jacket appeared to button all the way up to a rigid collar. All and all, it looked like . . .

"A uniform," he said, frowning.

"Indeed," Tindwyl said. "You want your people to believe that you can protect them? Well, a king isn't simply a lawmaker—he's a general. It is time you began to act like you deserve your title, Elend Venture."

"I'm no warrior," Elend said. "This uniform is a lie."

"The first point we will soon change," Tindwyl said. "The second is not true. You command the armies of the Central Dominance. That makes you a military man whether or not you know how to swing a sword. Now, go change."

Elend acceded with a shrug. He walked around the changing screen, pushed aside a stack of books to make room, then began to change. The white trousers fit snugly and fell straight around the calves. While there was a shirt, it was completely obscured by the large, stiff jacket—which had military shoulder fittings. It had an array of buttons—all of which, he noticed, were wood instead of metal—as well as a strange shieldlike design over the right breast. It seemed to have some sort of arrow, or perhaps spear, emblazoned in it.

Stiffness, cut, and design considered, Elend was surprised how well the uniform fit. "It's sized quite well," he noted, putting on the belt, then pulling down the bottom of the jacket, which came all the way to his hips.

"We got your measurements from your tailor," Tindwyl said.

Elend stepped around the changing screen, and several assistants approached. One politely motioned for him to step into a pair of shiny black boots, and the other attached a white cape to fastenings at his shoulders. The final assistant handed him a polished hardwood dueling cane and sheath. Elend hooked it onto the belt, then pulled it through a slit in the jacket so it hung outside; that much, at least, he had done before.

"Good," Tindwyl said, looking him up and down. "Once you learn to stand up straight, that will be a decent improvement. Now, sit."

Elend opened his mouth to object, but thought better of it. He sat down, and an assistant approached to attach a sheet around his shoulders. She then pulled out a pair of shears.

"Now, wait," Elend said. "I see where this is going."

"Then voice an objection," Tindwyl said. "Don't be vague!"

"All right, then," Elend said. "I like my hair."

"Short hair is easier to care for than long hair," Tindwyl said. "And you have proven that you cannot be trusted in the area of personal grooming."

"You aren't cutting my hair," Elend said firmly.

Tindwyl paused, then nodded. The apprentice backed away, and Elend stood, pulling off the sheet. The seamstress produced a large mirror, and Elend walked forward to inspect himself.

And froze.

The difference was surprising. All his life, he'd seen himself as a scholar and socialite, but also as just a bit of a fool. He was Elend—the friendly, comfortable man with the funny ideas. Easy to dismiss, perhaps, but difficult to hate.

The man he saw now was no dandy of the court. He was a serious man—a formal man. A man to be taken seriously. The uniform made him want to stand up straighter, to rest one hand on the dueling cane. His hair—slightly curled, long on the top and sides, and blown loose by the wind atop the city wall—didn't fit.

Elend turned. "All right," he said. "Cut it."

Tindwyl smiled, then nodded for him to sit. He did so, waiting quietly while the assistant worked. When he stood again, his head matched the suit. It wasn't extremely short, not like Ham's hair, but it was neat and precise. One of the assistants approached and handed him a loop of silver-painted wood. He turned to Tindwyl, frowning.

"A crown?" he asked.

"Nothing ostentatious," Tindwyl said. "This is a more subtle era than some of those gone by. The crown isn't a symbol of your wealth, but of your authority. You will wear it from now on, whether you are in private or in public."

"The Lord Ruler didn't wear a crown."

"The Lord Ruler didn't need to remind people that he was in charge," Tindwyl said.

Elend paused, then slipped on the crown. It bore no gemstones or ornamentation; it was just a simple coronet. As he might have expected, it fit perfectly.

He turned back toward Tindwyl, who waved for the seamstress to pack up and leave. "You have six uniforms like this one waiting for you in your rooms," Tindwyl said. "Until this siege is over, you will wear nothing else. If you want variety, change the color of the cape."

Elend nodded. Behind him, the seamstress and her assistants slipped out the door. "Thank you," he told Tindwyl. "I was hesitant at first, but you are right. This makes a difference."

"Enough of one to deceive people for now, at least," Tindwyl said.

"Deceive people?"

"Of course. You didn't think that this was it, did you?"

"Well . . ."

Tindwyl raised an eyebrow. "A few lessons, and you think you're through? We've barely begun. You are still a fool, Elend Venture—you just don't look like one anymore. Hopefully, our charade will begin reversing some of the damage you've done to your reputation. However, it is going to take a lot more training before I'll actually trust you to interact with people and not embarrass yourself."

Elend flushed. "What do you—" He paused. "Tell me what you plan to teach me, then."

"Well, you need to learn how to walk, for one thing."

"Something's wrong with the way I walk?"

"By the forgotten gods, yes!" Tindwyl said, sounding amused, though no smile marred her lips. "And your speech patterns still need work. Beyond that, of course, there is your inability to handle weapons."

"I've had some training," Elend said. "Ask Vin—I rescued her from the Lord Ruler's palace the night of the Collapse!"

"I know," Tindwyl said. "And, from what I've heard, it was a miracle you survived. Fortunately, the girl was there to do the actual fighting. You apparently rely on her quite a bit for that sort of thing."

"She's Mistborn."

"That is no excuse for your slovenly lack of skill," Tindwyl said. "You cannot always rely on your woman to protect you. Not only is it embarrassing, but your people—your soldiers—will expect you to be able to fight with them. I doubt you will ever be the type of leader who can lead a charge against the enemy, but you should at least be able to handle yourself if your position gets attacked."

"So, you want me to begin sparring with Vin and Ham during their training sessions?"

"Goodness, no! Can't you imagine how terrible it would be for morale if the men saw you being beaten up in public?" Tindwyl shook her head. "No, we'll have you trained discreetly by a dueling master. Given a few months, we should have you competent with the cane and the sword. Hopefully, this little siege of yours will last that long before the fighting starts."

Elend flushed again. "You keep talking down to me. It's like I'm not even king in your eyes—like you see me as some kind of placeholder."

Tindwyl didn't answer, but her eyes glinted with satisfaction. *You said it, not I,* her expression seemed to say.

Elend flushed more deeply.

"You can, perhaps, learn to be a king, Elend Venture,"

Tindwyl said. "Until then, you'll just have to learn to fake it."

Elend's angry response was cut off by a knock at the door. Elend gritted his teeth, turning. "Come in."

The door swung open. "There's news," Captain Demoux said, his youthful face excited as he entered. "I—" He froze.

Elend cocked his head. "Yes?"

"I . . . uh . . ." Demoux paused, looked Elend over again before continuing. "Ham sent me, Your Majesty. He says that a messenger from one of the kings has arrived."

"Really?" Elend said. "From Lord Cett?"

"No, Your Majesty. The messenger is from your father."

Elend frowned. "Well, tell Ham I'll be there in a moment."

"Yes, Your Majesty," Demoux said, retreating. "Uh, I like the new uniform, Your Majesty."

"Thank you, Demoux," Elend said. "Do you, by chance, know where Lady Vin is? I haven't seen her all day."

"I think she's in her quarters, Your Majesty."

Her quarters? She never stays there. Is she sick?

"Do you want me to summon her?" Demoux asked.

"No, thank you," Elend said. "I'll get her. Tell Ham to make the messenger comfortable."

Demoux nodded, then withdrew.

Elend turned to Tindwyl, who was smiling to herself with a look of satisfaction. Elend brushed by her, walking over to grab his notebook. "I'm going to learn to do more than just 'fake' being king, Tindwyl."

"We'll see."

Elend shot a glance at the middle-aged Terriswoman in her robes and jewelry.

"Practice expressions like that one," Tindwyl noted, "and you just might do it."

"Is that all it is, then?" Elend asked. "Expressions and costumes? Is that what makes a king?"

"Of course not."

Elend stopped by the door, turning back. "Then, what does? What do *you* think makes a man a good king, Tindwyl of Terris?"

"Trust," Tindwyl said, looking him in the eyes. "A good king is one who is trusted by his people—and one who deserves that trust."

Elend paused, then nodded. *Good answer,* he acknowledged, then pulled open the door and rushed out to find Vin.

If only the Terris religion, and belief in the Anticipation, hadn't spread beyond our people.

17

THE PILES OF PAPER SEEMED to multiply as Vin found more and more ideas in the logbook that she wanted to isolate and remember. What were the prophecies about the Hero of Ages? How did the logbook author know where to go, and what did he think he'd have to do when he got there?

Eventually, lying amid the mess—overlapping piles turned in odd directions to keep them separate—Vin acknowledged a distasteful fact. She was going to have to take notes.

With a sigh, she rose and crossed the room, stepping carefully over several stacks and approaching the room's desk. She'd never used it before; in fact, she'd complained about it to Elend. What need did she have of a writing desk?

So she'd thought. She selected a pen, then pulled out a little jar of ink, remembering the days when Reen had taught her to write. He'd quickly grown frustrated with her scratchings, complaining about the cost of ink and paper. He'd taught her to read so that she could decipher contracts and imitate a noblewoman, but he'd thought that writing was less useful. In general, Vin shared this opinion.

Apparently, however, writing had uses even if one wasn't a scribe. Elend was always scribbling notes and memos to himself; she'd often been impressed by how quickly he could write. How did he make the letters come so easily?

She grabbed a couple of blank sheets of paper and walked back over to her sorted piles. She sat down with crossed legs and unscrewed the top of the ink bottle.

"Mistress," OreSeur noted, still lying with his paws before him, "you do realize that you just left the writing desk behind to sit on the floor."

Vin looked up. "And?"

"The purpose of a writing desk is, well, writing."

"But my papers are all over here."

"Papers can be moved, I believe. If they prove too heavy, you could always burn pewter to give yourself more strength."

Vin eyed his amused face as she inked the nib of her pen. *Well, at least he's displaying something other than his dislike of me.* "The floor is more comfortable."

"If you say so, Mistress, I will believe it to be true."

She paused, trying to determine if he was still mocking her or not. *Blasted dog's face,* she thought. *Too hard to read.*

With a sigh, she leaned down and began to write out the first word. She had to make each line precisely so that the ink didn't smudge, and she had to pause often to sound out words and find the right letters. She'd barely written a couple of sentences before a knock came at her door. She looked up with a frown. Who was bothering her?

"Come in," she called.

She heard a door open in the other room, and Elend's voice called out. "Vin?"

"In here," she said, turning back to her writing. "Why did you knock?"

"Well, you might have been changing," he said, entering.

"So?" Vin asked.

Elend chuckled. "Two years, and privacy is still a strange concept to you."

Vin looked up. "Well, I did—"

For just the briefest flash of a moment, she thought he was someone else. Her instincts kicked in before her brain, and she reflexively dropped the pen, jumping up and flaring pewter.

Then she stopped.

"That much of a change, eh?" Elend asked, holding out his arms so she could get a better look at his costume.

Vin put a hand to her chest, so shocked that she stepped right on one of her stacks. It was Elend, but it wasn't. The brilliant white costume, with its sharp lines and firm figure, looked so different from his normal loose jacket and trousers. He seemed more commanding. More regal.

"You cut your hair," she said, walking around him slowly, studying the costume.

"Tindwyl's idea," he said. "What do you think?"

"Less for people to grab on to in a fight," Vin said.

Elend smiled. "Is that all you think about?"

"No," Vin said absently, reaching up to tug his cape. It came free easily, and she nodded approvingly. Mistcloaks were the same; Elend wouldn't have to worry about someone grabbing his cape in a fight.

She stepped back, arms folded. "Does this mean I can cut my hair, too?"

Elend paused just briefly. "You're always free to do what you want, Vin. But, I kind of think it's pretty longer."

It stays, then.

"Anyway," Elend said. "You approve?"

"Definitely," Vin said. "You look like a king." Though, she suspected a part of her would miss the tangle-haired, disheveled Elend. There had been something . . . endearing about that mixture of earnest competence and distracted inattention.

"Good," Elend said. "Because I think we're going to need the advantage. A messenger just . . ." He trailed off, looking over her stacks of paper. "Vin? Were you doing *research*?"

Vin flushed. "I was just looking through the logbook, trying to find references to the Deepness."

"You were!" Elend stepped forward excitedly. To her chagrin, he quickly located the paper with her fledgling notes on it. He held the paper up, then looked over at her. "Did you write this?"

"Yes," she said.

"Your penmanship is beautiful," he said, sounding a bit surprised. "Why didn't you tell me you could write like this?"

"Didn't you say something about a messenger?"

Elend put the sheet back down, looking oddly like a proud parent. "Right. A messenger from my father's army has arrived. I'm making him wait for a bit—it didn't seem wise to appear too eager. But, we should probably go meet with him."

Vin nodded, waving to OreSeur. The kandra rose and padded to her side, and the three of them left her quarters.

That was one nice thing about books and notes. They could always wait for another time.

They found the messenger waiting in the third-floor Venture atrium. Vin and Elend walked in, and she stopped immediately.

It was *him*. The Watcher.

Elend stepped forward to meet the man, and Vin grabbed his arm. "Wait," she hissed quietly.

Elend turned, confused.

If that man has atium, Vin thought with a stab of panic, *Elend is dead. We're all dead.*

The Watcher stood quietly. He didn't look much like a messenger or courier. He wore all black, even a pair of black gloves. He wore trousers and a silken shirt, with no cloak or cape. She remembered that face. It was him.

But . . . she thought, *if he'd wanted to kill Elend, he could have done so already.* The thought frightened her, yet she had to admit it was true.

"What?" Elend asked, standing in the doorway with her.

"Be careful," she whispered. "This is no simple messenger. That man is Mistborn."

Elend paused, frowning. He turned back toward the

Watcher, who stood quietly, clasping his hands behind his back, looking confident. Yes, he was Mistborn; only a man such as he could walk into an enemy palace, completely surrounded by guards, and not be the slightest bit unsettled.

"All right," Elend said, finally stepping into the room. "Straff's man. You bring a message for me?"

"Not just a message, Your Majesty," the Watcher said. "My name is Zane, and I am something of an . . . ambassador. Your father was very pleased to receive your invitation for an alliance. He's glad that you are finally seeing reason."

Vin studied the Watcher, this "Zane." What was his game? Why come himself? Why reveal who he was?

Elend nodded, keeping a distance from Zane. "Two armies," Elend said, "camped outside my door . . . well, that's not the kind of thing I can ignore. I'd like to meet with my father and discuss possibilities for the future."

"I think he would enjoy that," Zane said. "It has been some time since he saw you, and he has long regretted your falling-out. You are, after all, his only son."

"It's been hard on both of us," Elend said. "Perhaps we could set up a tent in which to meet outside the city?"

"I'm afraid that won't be possible," Zane said. "His Majesty rightly fears assassins. If you wish to speak with him, he'd be happy to host you at his tent in the Venture camp."

Elend frowned. "Now, I don't think that makes much sense. If he fears assassins, shouldn't I?"

"I'm certain he could protect you in his own camp, Your Majesty," Zane said. "You have nothing to fear from Cett's assassins there."

"I . . . see," Elend said.

"I'm afraid that His Majesty was quite firm on this point," Zane said. "You are the one who is eager for an alliance—if you wish a meeting, you will have to come to him."

Elend glanced at Vin. She continued to watch Zane. The man met her eyes, and spoke. "I have heard reports of the beautiful Mistborn who accompanies the Venture heir. She who slew the Lord Ruler, and was trained by the Survivor himself."

There was silence in the room for a moment.

Elend finally spoke. "Tell my father that I will consider his offer."

Zane finally turned away from Vin. "His Majesty was hoping for us to set a date and time, Your Majesty."

"I will send another message when I have made my decision," Elend said.

"Very well," Zane said, bowing slightly, though he used the move to catch Vin's eyes once again. Then he nodded once to Elend, and let the guards escort him away.

In the cold mist of early evening, Vin waited on the short wall of Keep Venture, OreSeur sitting at her side.

The mists were quiet. Her thoughts were far less serene.

Who else would he work for? she thought. *Of course he's one of Straff's men.*

That explained many things. It had been quite a while since their last encounter; Vin had begun to think that she wouldn't see the Watcher again.

Would they spar again, then? Vin tried to suppress her eagerness, tried to tell herself that she simply wanted to find this Watcher because of the threat he posed. But, the thrill of another fight in the mists—another chance to test her abilities against a Mistborn—made her tense with anticipation.

She didn't know him, and she certainly didn't trust him. That only made the prospect of a fight all the more exciting.

"Why are we waiting here, Mistress?" OreSeur asked.

"We're just on patrol," Vin said. "Watching for assassins or spies. Just like every night."

"Do you command me to believe you, Mistress?"

Vin shot him a flat stare. "Believe as you wish, kandra."

"Very well," OreSeur said. "Why did you not tell the king that you've been sparring with this Zane?"

Vin turned back toward the dark mists. "Assassins and

Allomancers are my concern, not Elend's. No need to worry him yet—he has enough troubles at the moment."

OreSeur sat back on his haunches. "I see."

"You don't believe I'm right?"

"I believe as I wish," OreSeur said. "Isn't that what you just commanded me, Mistress?"

"Whatever," Vin said. Her bronze was on, and she had to try very hard not to think about the mist spirit. She could feel it waiting in the darkness to her right. She didn't look toward it.

The logbook never did mention what became of that spirit. It nearly killed one of the Hero's companions. After that, there was barely a mention of it.

Problems for another night, she thought as another source of Allomancy appeared to her bronze senses. A stronger, more familiar source.

Zane.

Vin hopped up onto the battlements, nodded farewell to OreSeur, then jumped out into the night.

Mist twisted in the sky, different breezes forming silent streams of white, like rivers in the air. Vin skimmed them, burst through them, and rode them like a bouncing stone cast upon the waters. She quickly reached the place where she and Zane had last parted, the lonely abandoned street.

He waited in the center, still wearing black. Vin dropped to the cobbles before him in a flurry of mistcloak tassels. She stood up straight.

He never wears a cloak. Why is that?

The two stood opposite one another for a few silent moments. Zane had to know of her questions, but he offered no introduction, greeting, or explanation. Eventually, he reached into a pocket and pulled out a coin. He tossed it to the street between them, and it bounced—metal ringing against stone—and came to a stop.

He jumped into the air. Vin did likewise, both Pushing against the coin. Their separate weights nearly canceled each other out, and they shot up and back, like the two arms of a "V."

Zane spun, throwing a coin behind him. It slammed

against the side of a building and he Pushed, throwing himself toward Vin. Suddenly, she felt a force slam against her coin pouch, threatening to toss her back down to the ground.

What is the game tonight, Zane? she thought even as she yanked the tie on her pouch, dropping it free from her belt. She Pushed against it, and it shot downward, forced by her weight. When it hit the ground, Vin had the better upward force: she was Pushing against the pouch from directly above, while Zane was only pushing from the side. Vin lurched upward, streaking past Zane in the cool night air, then threw her weight against the coins in his own pocket.

Zane began to drop. However, he grabbed the coins— keeping them from ripping free—and Pushed down on her pouch. He froze in the air—Vin Pushing him from above, his own Push forcing him upward. And, because he stopped, Vin's Push suddenly threw her backward.

Vin let go of Zane and allowed herself to drop. Zane, however, didn't let himself fall. He Pushed himself back up into the air, then began to bound away, never letting his feet touch rooftops or cobblestones.

He tried to force me to the ground, Vin thought. *First one to fall loses, is that it?* Still tumbling, Vin spun herself in the air. She retrieved her coin pouch with a careful Pull, then threw it down toward the ground and Pushed herself upward.

She Pulled the pouch back into her hand even as she flew, then jumped after Zane, Pushing recklessly through the night, trying to catch up. In the darkness, Luthadel seemed cleaner than it did during the day. She couldn't see the ash-stained buildings, the dark refineries, the haze of smoke from the forges. Around her, the empty keeps of the old high nobility watched like silent monoliths. Some of the majestic buildings had been given to lesser nobles, and others had become government buildings. The rest— after being plundered at Elend's command—lay unused, their stained-glass windows dark, their vaultings, statues, and murals ignored.

Vin wasn't certain if Zane purposely headed to Keep

Hasting, or if she simply caught up to him there. Either way, the enormous structure loomed as Zane noticed her proximity and turned, throwing a handful of coins at her.

Vin Pushed against them tentatively. Sure enough, as soon as she touched them, Zane flared steel and Pushed harder. If she'd been Pushing hard, the force of his attack would have thrown her backward. As it was, she was able to deflect the coins to her sides.

Zane immediately Pushed against her coin pouch again, throwing himself upward along one of Keep Hasting's walls. Vin was ready for this move as well. Flaring pewter, she grabbed the pouch in a two-handed grip and ripped it in half.

Coins sprayed beneath her, shooting toward the ground under the force of Zane's Push. She selected one and Pushed herself, gaining lift as soon as it hit the ground. She spun, facing upward, her tin-enhanced ears hearing a shower of metal hit the stones far below. She'd still have access to the coins, but she didn't have to carry them on her body.

She shot up toward Zane, one of the keep's outer towers looming in the mists to her left. Keep Hasting was one of the finest in the city. It had a large tower at the center—tall, imposing, wide—with a ballroom at the very top. It also had six smaller towers rising equidistant around the central structure, each one connected to it by a thick wall. It was an elegant, majestic building. Somehow, she suspected that Zane had sought it out for that reason.

Vin watched him now, his Push losing power as he got too far from the coin anchor below. He spun directly above her, a dark figure against a shifting sky of mist, still well below the top of the wall. Vin yanked sharply on several coins below, Pulling them into the air in case she needed them.

Zane plummeted toward her. Vin reflexively Pushed against the coins in his pocket, then realized that was probably what he'd wanted: it gave him lift while forcing her down. She let go as she fell, and she soon passed the group of coins she'd Pulled into the air. She Pulled on one, bringing it into her hand, then Pushed on another, sending it sideways into the wall.

Vin shot to the side. Zane whooshed by her in the air, his passing churning the mists. He soon bobbed back up—probably using a coin from below—and flung a double handful of coins straight at her.

Vin spun, again deflecting the coins. They shot around her, and she heard several *pling* against something in the mists behind her. Another wall. She and Zane were sparring between a pair of the keep's outer towers; there was an angled wall to either side of them, with the central tower just a short distance in front of them. They were fighting near the tip of an open-bottomed triangle of stone walls.

Zane shot toward her. Vin reached out to throw her weight against him, but realized with a start that he was no longer carrying any coins. He was Pushing on something behind him, though—the same coin Vin had slammed against the wall with her weight. She Pushed herself upward, trying to get out of the way, but he angled upward as well.

Zane crashed into her, and they began to fall. As they spun together, Zane grabbed her by the upper arms, holding his face close to hers. He didn't seem angry, or even very forceful.

He just seemed calm.

"This is what we are, Vin," he said quietly. Wind and mist whipped around them as they fell, the tassels of Vin's mistcloak writhing in the air around Zane. "Why do you play their games? Why do you let them control you?"

Vin placed her hand lightly against Zane's chest, then Pushed on the coin that had been in her palm. The force of the Push lurched her free of his grip, flipping him up and backward. She caught herself just a few feet from the ground, Pushing against fallen coins, throwing herself upward again.

She passed Zane in the night, and saw a smile on his face as he fell. Vin reached downward, locking on to the blue lines extending toward the ground far below, then flared iron and Pulled against all of them at once. Blue lines zipped around her, the coins rising and rising shooting past the surprised Zane.

She Pulled a few choice coins into her hands. *Let's see if you can stay in the air now,* Vin thought with a smile, Pushing outward, spraying the other coins away into the night. Zane continued to fall.

Vin began to fall as well. She threw a coin to each side, then Pushed. The coins shot into the mists, flying toward the stone walls to either side. Coins slapped against stone, and Vin lurched to a halt in the air.

She Pushed hard, holding herself in place, anticipating a Pull from below. *If he pulls, I Pull, too,* she thought. *We both fall, and I keep the coins between us in the air. He'll hit the ground first.*

A coin shot past her in the air.

What! Where did he get that! She'd been sure that she'd Pushed away every coin below.

The coin arced upward, through the mists, trailing a blue line visible to her Allomancer's eyes. It crested the top of the wall to her right. Vin glanced down just in time to see Zane slow, then lurch upward—Pulling on the coin that was now held in place atop the wall by the stone railing.

He passed her with a self-satisfied look on his face.

Show-off.

Vin let go of the coin to her left while still Pushing to her right. She lurched to the left, nearly colliding with the wall before she threw another coin at it. She Pushed on this one, throwing herself upward and to the right. Another coin sent her back upward to the left, and she continued to bounce between the walls, back and forth, until she crested the top.

She smiled as she twisted in the air. Zane—hovering in the air above the wall's top—nodded appreciatively as she passed. She noticed that he'd grabbed a few of her discarded coins.

Time for a little attack myself, Vin thought.

She slammed a Push against the coins in Zane's hand, and they shot her upward. However, Zane was still Pushing against the coin on the wall top below, and so he didn't fall. Instead he hung in the air between the two forces—his own Push forcing him upward, Vin's Push forcing him downward.

Vin heard him grunt in exertion, and she Pushed harder. She was so focused, however, that she barely saw him open his other hand and Push a coin up toward her. She reached out to Push against it, but fortunately his aim was off, and the coin missed her by a few inches.

Or perhaps it didn't. Immediately, the coin zipped back downward and hit her in the back. Zane Pulled on it forcefully, and the bit of metal dug into Vin's skin. She gasped, flaring pewter to keep the coin from cutting through her.

Zane didn't relent. Vin gritted her teeth, but he weighed much more than she did. She inched down toward him in the night, her Push straining to keep the two of them apart, the coin digging painfully into her back.

Never get into a raw Pushing match, Vin, Kelsier had warned her. *You don't weigh enough—you'll lose every time.*

She stopped Pushing on the coin in Zane's hand. Immediately, she fell, Pulled by the coin on her back. She Pushed on it slightly, giving herself a little leverage, then threw her final coin to the side. It hit at the last moment, and Vin's Push scooted her out from between Zane and his coin.

Zane's coin snapped him in the chest, and he grunted: he had obviously been trying to get Vin to collide with him again. Vin smiled, then Pulled against the coin in Zane's hand.

Give him what he wants, I guess.

He turned just in time to see her slam feet-first into him. Vin spun, feeling him crumple beneath her. She exulted in the victory, spinning in the air above the wall walk. Then she noticed something: several faint lines of blue disappearing into the distance. Zane had pushed all of their coins away.

Desperately, Vin grabbed one of the coins and Pulled it back. Too late, however. She searched frantically for a closer source of metal, but all was stone or wood. Disoriented, she hit the stone wall walk, tumbling amid her mistcloak until she came to a halt beside the wall's stone railing.

She shook her head and flared tin, clearing her vision with a flash of pain and other senses. Surely Zane hadn't fared better. He must have fallen as—

Zane hung a few feet away. He'd found a coin—Vin

couldn't fathom how—and was Pushing against it below him. However, he didn't shoot away. He hovered above the wall top, just a few feet in the air, still in a half tumble from Vin's kick.

As Vin watched, Zane rotated slowly in the air, hand outstretched beneath him, twisting like a skilled acrobat on a pole. There was a look of intense concentration on his face, and his muscles—all of them, arms, face, chest— were taut. He turned in the air until he was facing her.

Vin watched with awe. It was possible to Push just slightly against a coin, regulating the amount of force with which one was thrown backward. It was incredibly difficult, however—so difficult that even Kelsier had struggled with it. Most of the time, Mistborn simply used short bursts. When Vin fell, for instance, she slowed herself by throwing a coin and Pushing against it briefly—but powerfully—to counteract her momentum.

She'd never seen an Allomancer with as much control as Zane. His ability to push slightly against that coin would be of little use in a fight; it obviously took too much concentration. Yet, there was a grace to it, a beauty to his movements that implied something Vin herself had felt.

Allomancy wasn't just about fighting and killing. It was about skill and grace. It was something beautiful.

Zane rotated until he was upright, standing in a gentleman's posture. Then he dropped to the wall walk, his feet slapping quietly against the stones. He regarded Vin—who still lay on the stones—with a look that lacked contempt.

"You are very skilled," he said. "And quite powerful."

He was tall, impressive. *Like . . . Kelsier.* "Why did you come to the palace today?" she asked, climbing to her feet.

"To see how they treated you. Tell me, Vin. What is it about Mistborn that makes us—despite our powers—so willing to act as slaves to others?"

"Slaves?" Vin said. "I'm no slave."

Zane shook his head. "They use you, Vin."

"Sometimes it's good to be useful."

"Those words are spoken of insecurity."

Vin paused; then she eyed him. "Where did you get that coin, at the end? There were none nearby."

Zane smiled, then opened his mouth and pulled out a coin. He dropped it to the stones with a *pling*. Vin opened her eyes wide. *Metal inside a person's body can't be affected by another Allomancer. . . . That's such an easy trick! Why didn't I think of it?*

Why didn't Kelsier think of it?

Zane shook his head. "We don't belong with them, Vin. We don't belong in *their* world. We belong here, in the mists."

"I belong with those who love me," Vin said.

"Love you?" Zane asked quietly. "Tell me. Do they understand you, Vin? *Can* they understand you? And, can a man love something he doesn't understand?"

He watched her for a moment. When she didn't respond, he nodded to her slightly, then Pushed against the coin he had dropped moments before, throwing himself back into the mists.

Vin let him go. His words held more weight than he probably understood. *We don't belong in their world. . . .* He couldn't know that she'd been pondering her place, wondering whether she was noblewoman, assassin, or something else.

Zane's words, then, meant something important. He felt himself to be an outsider. A little like herself. It was a weakness in him, certainly. Perhaps she could turn him against Straff—his willingness to spar with her, his willingness to reveal himself, hinted at that much.

She breathed in deeply of the cool, mist air, her heart still beating quickly from the exchange. She felt tired, yet alive, from fighting someone who might actually be better than she was. Standing in the mists atop the wall of an abandoned keep, she decided something.

She had to keep sparring with Zane.

If only the Deepness hadn't come when it did, providing a threat that drove men to desperation both in action and belief.

18

"KILL HIM," GOD WHISPERED.

Zane hung quietly in the mists, looking through Elend Venture's open balcony doors. The mists swirled around him, obscuring him from the king's view.

"You should kill him," God said again.

In a way, Zane hated Elend, though he had never met the man before today. Elend was everything that Zane should have been. Favored. Privileged. Pampered. He was Zane's enemy, a block in the road to domination, the thing that was keeping Straff—and therefore Zane—from ruling the Central Dominance.

But he was also Zane's brother.

Zane let himself drop through the mists, falling silently to the ground outside Keep Venture. He Pulled his anchors up into his hand—three small bars he had been pushing on to hold himself in place. Vin would be returning soon, and he didn't want to be near the keep when she did. She had a strange ability to know where he was; her senses were far more keen than any Allomancer he had ever known or fought. Of course, she had been trained by the Survivor himself.

I would have liked to have known him, Zane thought as he moved quietly across the courtyard. *He was a man who understood the power of being Mistborn. A man who didn't let others control him.*

A man who did what had to be done, no matter how ruthless it seemed. Or so the rumors said.

Zane paused beside the outer keep wall, below a buttress. He stooped, removing a cobblestone, and found the message left there by his spy inside Elend's palace. Zane retrieved it, replaced the cobblestone, then dropped a coin and launched himself out into the night.

Zane did not slink. Nor did he creep, skulk, or cower. In fact, he didn't even like to hide.

So, he approached the Venture army camp with a determined stride. It seemed to him that Mistborn spent too much of their existence hiding. True, anonymity offered some limited freedom. However, his experience had been that it bound them more than it freed them. It let them be controlled, and it let society pretend that they didn't exist.

Zane strode toward a guard post, where two soldiers sat beside a large fire. He shook his head; they were virtually useless, blinded by the firelight. Normal men feared the mists, and that made them less valuable. That wasn't arrogance; it was a simple fact. Allomancers were more useful, and therefore more valuable, than normal men. That was why Zane had Tineyes watching in the darkness as well. These regular soldiers were more a formality than anything else.

"Kill them," God commanded as Zane walked up to the guard post. Zane ignored the voice, though it was growing more and more difficult to do so.

"Halt!" one of the guards said, lowering a spear. "Who is that?"

Zane Pushed the spear offhandedly, flipping up the tip. "Who else would it be?" he snapped, walking into the firelight.

"Lord Zane!" the other soldier said.

"Summon the king," Zane said, passing the guard post. "Tell him to meet me in the command tent."

"But, my lord," the guard said. "The hour is late. His Majesty is probably . . ."

Zane turned, giving the guard a flat stare. The mists swirled between them. Zane didn't even have to use emotional Allomancy on the soldier; the man simply saluted, then rushed off into the night to do as commanded.

Zane strode through the camp. He wore no uniform or

mistcloak, but soldiers stopped and saluted as he passed. *This* was the way it should be. They knew him, knew what he was, knew to respect him.

And yet, a part of him acknowledged that if Straff hadn't kept his bastard son hidden, Zane might not be the powerful weapon that he was today. That secrecy had forced Zane to live a life of near squalor while his half brother, Elend, had been privileged. But it also meant that Straff had been able to keep Zane hidden for most of his life. Even still, while rumors were growing about the existence of Straff's Mistborn, few realized that Zane was Straff's son.

Plus, living a harsh life had taught Zane to survive on his own. He had become hard, and powerful. Things he suspected Elend would never understand. Unfortunately, one side effect of his childhood was that it had apparently driven him mad.

"Kill him," God whispered as Zane passed another guard. The voice spoke every time he saw a person—it was Zane's quiet, constant companion. He understood that he was insane. It hadn't really been all that hard to determine, all things considered. Normal people did not hear voices. Zane did.

He found insanity no excuse, however, for irrational behavior. Some men were blind, others had poor tempers. Still others heard voices. It was all the same, in the end. A man was defined not by his flaws, but by how he overcame them.

And so, Zane ignored the voice. He killed when he wanted to, not when it commanded. In his estimation, he was actually quite lucky. Other madmen saw visions, or couldn't distinguish their delusions from reality. Zane, at least, could control himself.

For the most part.

He Pushed on the metal clasps on the flaps of the command tent. The flaps flipped backward, opening for him as the soldiers to either side saluted. Zane ducked inside.

"My lord!" said the nightwatch officer of command.

"Kill him," God said. "He's really not that important."

"Paper," Zane ordered, walking to the room's large

table. The officer scrambled to comply, grabbing a stack of sheets. Zane Pulled on the nib of a pen, flipping it across the room to his waiting hand. The officer brought the ink.

"These are troop concentrations and night patrols," Zane said, scribbling down some numbers and diagrams on the paper. "I observed them tonight, while I was in Luthadel."

"Very good, my lord," the soldier said. "We appreciate your help."

Zane paused. Then he slowly continued to write. "Soldier, you are not my superior. You aren't even my equal. I am not 'helping' you. I am seeing to the needs of my army. Do you understand?"

"Of course, my lord."

"Good," Zane said, finishing his notes and handing the paper to the soldier. "Now, leave—or I'll do as a friend has suggested and ram this pen through your throat."

The soldier accepted the paper, then quickly withdrew. Zane waited impatiently. Straff did not arrive. Finally, Zane cursed quietly and Pushed open the tent flaps and strode out. Straff's tent was a blazing red beacon in the night, well lit by numerous lanterns. Zane passed the guards, who knew better than to bother him, and entered the king's tent.

Straff was having a late dinner. He was a tall man, brown of hair like both his sons—the two important ones, at least. He had fine nobleman's hands, which he used to eat with finesse. He didn't react as Zane entered.

"You're late," Straff said.

"Kill him," God said.

Zane clinched his fists. This command from the voice was the hardest to ignore. "Yes," he said. "I'm late."

"What happened tonight?" Straff asked.

Zane glanced at the servants. "We should do this in the command tent."

Straff continued to sip his soup, staying where he was, implying that Zane had no power to order him about. It was frustrating, but not unexpected. Zane had used virtually the same tactic on the nightwatch officer just moments before. He had learned from the best.

Finally, Zane sighed, taking a seat. He rested his arms on

the table, idly spinning a dinner knife as he watched his father eat. A servant approached to ask Zane if he wanted a meal, but he waved the man away.

"Kill Straff," God commanded. "You should be in his place. You are stronger than he is. You are more competent."

But I'm not as sane, Zane thought.

"Well?" Straff asked. "Do they have the Lord Ruler's atium or not?"

"I'm not sure," Zane said.

"Does the girl trust you?" Straff asked.

"She's beginning to," Zane said. "I did see her use atium, that once, fighting Cett's assassins."

Straff nodded thoughtfully. He really was competent; because of him, the Northern Dominance had avoided the chaos that prevailed in the rest of the Final Empire. Straff's skaa remained under control, his noblemen quelled. True, he had been forced to execute a number of people to prove that he was in charge. But, he did what needed to be done. That was one attribute in a man that Zane respected above all others.

Especially since he had trouble displaying it himself.

"*Kill him!*" God yelled. "You hate him! He kept you in squalor, forcing you to fight for your survival as a child."

He made me strong, Zane thought.

"Then use that strength to kill him!"

Zane grabbed the carving knife off the table. Straff looked up from his meal, then flinched just slightly as Zane sliced the flesh of his own arm. He cut a long gash into the top of his forearm, drawing blood. The pain helped him resist the voice.

Straff watched for a moment, then waved for a servant to bring Zane a towel so he wouldn't get blood on the rug.

"You need to get her to use atium again," Straff said. "Elend may have been able to gather one or two beads. We'll only know the truth if she runs out." He paused, turning back to his meal. "Actually, what you need to do is get her to tell you where the stash is hidden, if they even have it."

Zane sat, watching the blood seep from the gash on his forearm. "She's more capable than you think, Father."

Straff raised an eyebrow. "Don't tell me you believe those stories, Zane? The lies about her and the Lord Ruler?"

"How do you know they are lies?"

"Because of Elend," Straff said. "That boy is a fool; he only controls Luthadel because every nobleman with half a wit in his head fled the city. If that girl were powerful enough to defeat the Lord Ruler, I sincerely doubt that your brother could ever have gained her loyalty."

Zane cut another slice in his arm. He didn't cut deeply enough to do any real damage, and the pain worked as it usually did. Straff finally turned from his meal, masking a look of discomfort. A small, twisted piece of Zane took pleasure from seeing that look in his father's eyes. Perhaps it was a side effect of his insanity.

"Anyway," Straff said, "did you meet with Elend?"

Zane nodded. He turned to a serving girl. "Tea," he said, waving his uncut arm. "Elend was surprised. He wanted to meet with you, but he obviously didn't like the idea of coming into your camp. I doubt he'll come."

"Perhaps," Straff said. "But, don't underestimate the boy's foolishness. Either way, perhaps now he understands how our relationship will proceed."

So much posturing, Zane thought. By sending this message, Straff took a stand: he wouldn't be ordered about, or even inconvenienced, on Elend's behalf.

Being forced into a siege inconvenienced you, though, Zane thought with a smile. What Straff would have liked to do was attack directly, taking the city without parlay or negotiations. The arrival of the second army made that impossible. Attack now, and Straff would be defeated by Cett.

That meant waiting, waiting in a siege, until Elend saw reason and joined with his father willingly. But, waiting was something Straff disliked. Zane didn't mind as much. It would give him more time to spar with the girl. He smiled.

As the tea arrived, Zane closed his eyes, then burned tin to enhance his senses. His wounds burst to life, minor pains becoming great, shocking him to wakefulness.

There was a part of all this he wasn't telling Straff. *She is coming to trust me,* he thought. *And there's something else about her. She's like me. Perhaps . . . she could understand me.*

Perhaps she could save me.

He sighed, opening his eyes and using the towel to clean his arm. His insanity frightened him sometimes. But, it seemed weaker around Vin. That was all he had to go on for the moment. He accepted his tea from the serving girl—long braid, firm chest, homely features—and took a sip of the hot cinnamon.

Straff raised his own cup, then hesitated, sniffing delicately. He eyed Zane. "Poisoned tea, Zane?"

Zane said nothing.

"Birchbane, too," Straff noted. "That's a depressingly unoriginal move for you."

Zane said nothing.

Straff made a cutting motion. The girl looked up with terror as one of Straff's guards stepped toward her. She glanced at Zane, expecting some sort of aid, but he just looked away. She yelled pathetically as the guard pulled her off to be executed.

She wanted the chance to kill him, he thought. *I told her it probably wouldn't work.*

Straff just shook his head. Though not a full Mistborn, the king was a Tineye. Still, even for one with such an ability, sniffing birchbane amid the cinnamon was an impressive feat.

"Zane, Zane . . ." Straff said. "What would you do if you actually managed to kill me?"

If I actually wanted to kill you, Zane thought, *I'd use that knife, not poison.* But, he let Straff think what he wished. The king expected assassination attempts. So Zane provided them.

Straff held something up—a small bead of atium. "I was going to give you this, Zane. But I see that we'll have to wait. You need to get over these foolish attempts on my life. If you were ever to succeed, where would you get your atium?"

Straff didn't understand, of course. He thought that atium was like a drug, and assumed that Mistborn relished using it.

Therefore, he thought he could control Zane with it. Zane let the man continue in his misapprehension, never explaining that he had his own personal stockpile of the metal.

That, however, brought him to face the real question that dominated his life. God's whispers were returning, now that the pain was fading. And, of all the people the voice whispered about, Straff Venture was the one who most deserved to die.

"Why?" God asked. "Why won't you kill him?"

Zane looked down at his feet. *Because he's my father,* he thought, finally admitting his weakness. Other men did what they had to. They were stronger than Zane.

"You're insane, Zane," Straff said.

Zane looked up.

"Do you really think you could conquer the empire yourself, if you were to kill me? Considering your . . . particular malady, do you think you could run even a city?"

Zane looked away. "No."

Straff nodded. "I'm glad we both understand that."

"You should just attack," Zane said. "We can find the atium once we control Luthadel."

Straff smiled, then sipped the tea. The *poisoned* tea.

Despite himself, Zane started, sitting up straight.

"Don't presume to think you know what I'm planning, Zane," Straff said. "You don't understand *half* as much as you assume."

Zane sat quietly, watching his father drink the last of the tea.

"What of your spy?" Straff asked.

Zane lay the note on the table. "He's worried that they might suspect him. He has found no information about the atium."

Straff nodded, setting down the empty cup. "You'll return to the city and continue to befriend the girl."

Zane nodded slowly, then turned and left the tent.

Straff thought he could feel the birchbane already, seeping through his veins, making him tremble. He forced himself to remain in control. Waiting for a few moments.

Once he was sure Zane was distant, he called for a guard. "Bring me Amaranta!" Straff ordered. "Quickly!"

The soldier rushed to do his master's bidding. Straff sat quietly, tent rustling in the evening breeze, a puff of mist floating to the floor from the once open flap. He burned tin, enhancing his senses. Yes . . . he could feel the poison within him. Deadening his nerves. He had time, however. As long as an hour, perhaps, and so he relaxed.

For a man who claimed he didn't want to kill Straff, Zane certainly spent a lot of effort trying. Fortunately, Straff had a tool even Zane didn't know about—one that came in the form of a woman. Straff smiled as his tin-enhanced ears heard soft footsteps approaching in the night.

The soldiers sent Amaranta right in. Straff hadn't brought all of his mistresses with him on the trip—just his ten or fifteen favorites. Mixed in with the ones he was currently bedding, however, were some women that he kept for their effectiveness rather than their beauty. Amaranta was a good example. She had been quite attractive a decade before, but now she was creeping up into her late twenties. Her breasts had begun to sag from childbirth, and every time Straff looked at her, he noticed the wrinkles that were appearing on her forehead and around her eyes. He got rid of most women long before they reached her age.

This one, however, had skills that were useful. If Zane heard that Straff had sent for the woman this night, he'd assume that Straff had simply wanted to bed her. He'd be wrong.

"My lord," Amaranta said, getting down on her knees. She began to disrobe.

Well, at least she's optimistic, Straff thought. He would have thought that after four years without being called to his bed, she would understand. Didn't women realize when they were too old to be attractive?

"Keep your clothing on, woman," he snapped.

Amaranta's face fell, and she laid her hands in her lap, leaving her dress half undone, one breast exposed—as if she were trying to tempt him with her aging nudity.

"I need your antidote," he said. "Quickly."

"Which one, my lord?" she asked. She wasn't the only herbalist Straff kept; he learned scents and tastes from four different people. Amaranta, however, was the best of them.

"Birchbane," Straff said. "And . . . maybe something else. I'm not sure."

"Another general potion, then, my lord?" Amaranta asked.

Straff nodded curtly. Amaranta rose, walking to his poison cabinet. She lit the burner at the side, boiling a small pot of water as she quickly mixed powders, herbs, and liquids. The concoction was her particular specialty—a mixture of all of the basic poison antidotes, remedies, and reagents in her repertoire. Straff suspected that Zane had used the birchbane to cover something else. Whatever it was, however, Amaranta's concoction would deal with—or at least identify—it.

Straff waited uncomfortably as Amaranta worked, still half naked. The concoction needed to be prepared freshly each time, but it was worth the wait. She eventually brought him a steaming mug. Straff gulped it, forcing down the harsh liquid despite its bitterness. Immediately, he began to feel better.

He sighed—another trap avoided—as he drank the rest of the cup to be certain. Amaranta knelt expectantly again.

"Go," Straff ordered.

Amaranta nodded quietly. She put her arm back through the dress's sleeve, then retreated from the tent.

Straff sat stewing, empty cup cooling in his hand. He knew he held the edge. As long as he appeared strong before Zane, the Mistborn would continue to do as commanded.

Probably.

If only I had passed over Alendi when looking for an assistant, all those years ago.

19

SAZED UNCLASPED HIS FINAL STEELMIND. He held it up, the braceletlike band of metal glistening in the red sunlight. To another man, it might seem valuable. To Sazed, it was now just another empty husk—a simple steel bracelet. He could refill it if he wished, but for the moment he didn't consider the weight worth carrying.

With a sigh, he dropped the bracelet. It fell with a clank, tossing up a puff of ash from the ground. *Five months of storing, of spending every fifth day drained of speed, my body moving as if impeded by a thick molasses. And now it's all gone.*

The loss had purchased something valuable, however. In just six days of travel, using steelminds on occasion, he had traveled the equivalent of six weeks' worth of walking. According to his cartography coppermind, Luthadel was now a little over a week away. Sazed felt good about the expenditure. Perhaps he'd overreacted to the deaths he'd found in the little southern village. Perhaps there was no need for him to hurry. But, he'd created the steelmind to be used.

He hefted his pack, which was much lighter than it had been. Though many of his metalminds were small, they were heavy in aggregate. He'd decided to discard some of the less valuable or less full ones as he ran. Just like the steel bracelet, which he left sitting in the ash behind him as he went on.

He was definitely in the Central Dominance now. He'd passed Faleast and Tyrian, two of the northern Ashmounts. Tyrian was still just barely visible to the south—a tall, solitary peak with a cut-off, blackened top. The landscape had grown flat, the trees changing from patchy brown pines to the willowy white aspens common around Luthadel. The aspens rose like bones growing from the black soil, clumping, their ashen white bark scarred and twisted. They—

Sazed paused. He stood near the central canal, one of the main routes to Luthadel. The canal was empty of boats at the moment; travelers were rare these days, even more rare than they had been during the Final Empire, for bandits were far more common. Sazed had outrun several groups of them during his hurried flight to Luthadel.

No, solitary travelers were rare. Armies were far more common—and, judging from the several dozen trails of smoke he saw rising ahead of him, he had run afoul of one. It stood directly between him and Luthadel.

He thought quietly for a moment, flakes of ash beginning to fall lightly around him. It was midday; if that army had scouts, Sazed would have a very difficult time getting around it. In addition, his steelminds were empty. He wouldn't be able to run from pursuit.

And yet, an army within a week of Luthadel. . . . Whose was it, and what threat did it pose? His curiosity, the curiosity of a scholar, prodded him to seek a vantage from which to study the troops. Vin and the others could use any information he gathered.

Decision made, Sazed located a hill with a particularly large stand of aspens. He dropped his pack at the base of a tree, then pulled out an ironmind and began to fill it. He felt the familiar sensation of decreased weight, and he easily climbed to the top of the thin tree—his body was now light enough that it didn't take much strength to pull himself upward.

Hanging from the very tip of the tree, Sazed tapped his tinmind. The edges of his vision fuzzed, as always, but with the increased vision he could make out details about the large group settled into a hollow before him.

He was right about it being an army. He was wrong about it being made up of men.

"By the forgotten gods . . ." Sazed whispered, so shocked

that he nearly lost his grip. The army was organized in only the most simplistic and primitive way. There were no tents, no vehicles, no horses. Just hundreds of large cooking fires, each ringed with figures.

And those figures were of a deep blue. They varied greatly in size; some were just five feet tall, others were lumbering hulks of ten feet or more. They were both the same species, Sazed knew. Koloss. The creatures—though similar to men in base form—never stopped growing. They simply continued to get bigger as they aged, growing until their hearts could no longer support them. Then they died, killed by their body's own growth imperative.

Before they died, however, they got very large. And very dangerous.

Sazed dropped from the tree, making his body light enough that he hit the ground softly. He hurriedly searched through his copperminds. When he found the one he wanted, he strapped it to his upper left arm, then climbed back up the tree.

He searched an index quickly. Somewhere, he'd taken notes on a book about the koloss—he'd studied it trying to decide if the creatures had a religion. He'd had someone repeat the notes back to him, so he could store them in the coppermind. He had the book memorized, too, of course, but placing so much information directly in his mind would ruin the—

There, he thought, recovering the notes. He tapped them from the coppermind, filling his mind with knowledge.

Most koloss bodies gave out before they reached twenty years of age. The more "ancient" creatures were often a massive twelve feet in height, with stocky, powerful bodies. However, few koloss lived that long—and not just because of heart failure. Their society—if it could be called that—was extremely violent.

Excitement suddenly overcoming apprehension, Sazed tapped tin for vision again, searching through the thousands of blue humanoids, trying to get visual proof of what he'd read. It wasn't hard to find fights. Scuffles around the fires seemed common, and, interestingly, they were always between koloss of nearly the same size.

Sazed magnified his view even further—gripping the tree tightly to overcome the nausea—and got his first good look at a koloss.

It was a creature of smaller size—perhaps six feet tall. It was man-shaped, with two arms and legs, though its neck was hard to distinguish. It was completely bald. The oddest feature, however, was its blue skin, which hung loose and folded. The creature looked like a fat man might, had all his fat been drained away, leaving the stretched skin behind.

And . . . the skin didn't seem to be *connected* very well. Around the creature's red, blood-drop eyes, the skin sagged, revealing the facial muscles. The same was true around the mouth: the skin sagged a few inches below the chin, the lower teeth and jaw completely exposed.

It was a stomach-turning sight, especially for a man who was already nauseated. The creature's ears hung low, flopping down beside its jawline. Its nose was formless and loose, with no cartilage supporting it. Skin hung baggily from the creature's arms and legs, and its only clothing was a crude loincloth.

Sazed turned, selecting a larger creature—one perhaps eight feet tall—to study. The skin on this beast wasn't as loose, but it still didn't seem to fit quite right. Its nose twisted at a crooked angle, pulled flat against the face by an enlarged head that sat on a stumpy neck. The creature turned to leer at a companion, and again, the skin around its mouth didn't quite fit: the lips didn't close completely, and the holes around the eyes were too big, so they exposed the muscles beneath.

Like . . . a person wearing a mask made of skin, Sazed thought, trying to push away his disgust. *So . . . their body continues to grow, but their skin doesn't?*

His thought was confirmed as a massive, ten-foot-tall beast of a koloss wandered into the group. Smaller creatures scattered before this newcomer, who thumped up to the fire, where several horses were roasting.

This largest creature's skin was pulled so tight it was beginning to tear. The hairless blue flesh had ripped around the eyes, at the edges of the mouth, and around the massive chest muscles. Sazed could see little trails of red blood dripping from the rips. Even where the skin wasn't torn, it was pulled taut—the nose and ears were so flat they were almost indistinguishable from the flesh around them.

Suddenly, Sazed's study didn't seem so academic. Koloss had come to the Central Dominance. Creatures so violent and uncontrollable that the Lord Ruler had been forced to keep them away from civilization. Sazed extinguished his tinmind, welcoming the return to normal vision. He had to get to Luthadel and warn the others. If they—

Sazed froze. One problem with enhancing his vision was that he temporarily lost the ability to see close up—so it wasn't odd that he hadn't noticed the koloss patrol surrounding his aspens.

By the forgotten gods! He held firm to the tip of the tree, thinking quickly. Several koloss were already pushing their way into the stand. If he dropped to the ground, he'd be too slow to escape. As always, he wore a pewtermind; he could easily become as strong as ten men, and maintain it for a good amount of time. He could fight, perhaps. . . .

Yet, the koloss carried crude-looking, but massive, swords. Sazed's notes, his memory, and his lore all agreed: Koloss were very dangerous warriors. Strong as ten men or not, Sazed wouldn't have the skill to defeat them.

"Come down," called a deep, slurred voice from below. "Come down now."

Sazed looked down. A large koloss, skin just beginning to stretch, stood at the tree's base. It gave the aspen a shake.

"Come down now," the creature repeated.

The lips don't work very well, Sazed thought. *He sounds like a man trying to talk without moving his lips.* He wasn't surprised that the creature could talk; his notes mentioned that. He was, however, surprised at how calm it sounded.

I could run, he thought. He could keep to the tops of trees, perhaps cross the distance between patches of aspens by dropping his metalminds and trying to ride gusts of wind. But it would be very difficult—and very unpredictable.

And he would have to leave his copperminds—a thousand years of history—behind.

So, pewtermind ready in case he needed strength, Sazed let go of the tree. The koloss leader—Sazed could only assume that was what he was—watched Sazed fall to the ground with a red-eyed stare. The creature did not blink. Sazed wondered if it even *could* blink, its skin stretched as it was.

Sazed plunked to the ground beside the tree, then reached for his pack.

"No," the koloss snapped, grabbing the pack with an inhumanly quick swipe of the arm. It tossed the pack to another koloss.

"I need that," Sazed said. "I will be much more cooperative if—"

"Quiet!" the koloss yelled with a rage so sudden that Sazed took a step backward. Terrismen were tall—especially Terrismen eunuchs—and it was very disconcerting to be dwarfed by this beastly creature, well over nine feet in height, its skin a blackish blue, its eyes the color of the sun at dusk. It loomed over Sazed, and he cringed in spite of himself.

Apparently, that was the proper reaction, for the lead koloss nodded and turned away. "Come," it slurred, lumbering through the small aspen forest. The other koloss—about seven of them—followed.

Sazed didn't want to find out what would happen if he disobeyed. He chose a god—Duis, a god once said to watch over wearied travelers—and said a quick, silent prayer. Then he hurried forward, staying with the pack of koloss as they walked toward the camp.

At least they didn't kill me out of hand, Sazed thought. He'd half expected that, considering what he'd read. Of course, even the books didn't know much. The koloss had been kept separate from mankind for centuries; the Lord Ruler only called upon them in times of great martial need, to quell revolts, or to conquer new societies discovered on the inner islands. At those times, the koloss had caused absolute destruction and slaughter—or so the histories claimed.

Could all that have been propaganda? Sazed wondered. *Maybe the koloss aren't as violent as we assumed.*

One of the koloss beside Sazed howled in sudden anger. Sazed spun as the koloss jumped at one of its companions. The creature ignored the sword on its back, instead punching his enemy's head with a blocky fist. The others paused, turning to watch the fight, but none of them seemed alarmed.

Sazed watched with growing horror as the aggressor proceeded to repeatedly pummel his enemy. The defender tried to protect himself, getting out a dagger and managing to score a cut on the aggressor's arm. The blue skin tore, seeping bright red blood, as the aggressor got his hands around his opponent's thick head and twisted.

There was a snap. The defender stopped moving. The aggressor removed the sword from his victim's back and strapped it on beside his own weapon, then removed a small pouch that was tied beside the sword. After that, he stood, ignoring the wound on his arm, and the group began to walk again.

"Why?" Sazed asked, shocked. "What was that for?"

The wounded koloss turned around. "I hated him," he said.

"Move!" the lead koloss snapped at Sazed.

Sazed forced himself to start walking. They left the corpse lying in the road. *The pouches,* he thought, trying to find something to focus on besides the brutality. *They all carry those pouches.* The koloss kept them tied to their swords. They didn't carry the weapons in sheaths; they were simply bound on their backs with leather straps. And tied to those straps were pouches. Sometimes there was just one, though the two largest creatures in the group each had several.

They look like coin pouches, Sazed thought. *But, the koloss don't have an economy. Perhaps they keep personal possessions in them? But what would beasts like these value?*

They entered the camp. There didn't appear to be sentries at the borders—but, then, why would guards be necessary? It would be very difficult for a human to sneak into this camp.

A group of smaller koloss—the five-foot-tall ones—rushed forward as soon as the group arrived. The murderer threw his extra sword to one of them, then pointed into the distance. He kept the pouch for himself, and the small ones rushed off, following the road in the direction of the body.

Burial detail? Sazed wondered.

He walked uncomfortably behind his captors as they penetrated into the camp. Beasts of all sorts were being roasted over the firepits, though Sazed didn't think any of them had once been human. In addition, the ground around the camp had been completely stripped of plant life, as if it had been grazed by a group of particularly aggressive goats.

And, according to his coppermind, that wasn't far off the truth. Koloss could, apparently, subsist on practically anything. They preferred meat, but would eat any kind of plant—even grass, going so far as to pull it up by the roots to eat. Some reports even spoke of them eating dirt and ash, though Sazed found that a little difficult to believe.

He continued to walk. The camp smelled of smoke, grime, and a strange musk that he assumed was koloss body odor. Some of the creatures turned as he passed, watching him with steady red eyes.

It's like they only have two emotions, he thought, jumping as a fireside koloss suddenly screamed and attacked a companion. *They're either indifferent or they're enraged.*

What would it take to set them all off at once? And . . . what kind of a disaster would they cause if that happened? He nervously revised his earlier thoughts. No, the koloss had not been maligned. The stories he had heard—stories of koloss running wild in the Farmost Dominance, causing widespread destruction and death—were obviously true.

But something kept this group marginally reined in. The Lord Ruler had been able to control the koloss, though no book explained how. Most writers simply accepted this ability as part of what had made the Lord Ruler God. The man had been immortal—compared with that, other powers seemed mundane.

His immortality, however, was a trick, Sazed thought. *Simply a clever combination of Feruchemical and Allomantic powers.* The Lord Ruler had been just a normal man—albeit one with an unusual combination of abilities and opportunities.

That being the case, how had he controlled the koloss? *There* was *something different about the Lord Ruler. Something more than his powers. He did something at the Well of Ascension, something that forever changed the world. Perhaps his ability to control the koloss came from that.*

Sazed's captors ignored the occasional fights around firepits. There didn't appear to be any female koloss in the camp—or, if there were, they were indistinguishable from the males. Sazed did, however, notice a koloss corpse lying forgotten near one of the fires. It had been flayed, the blue skin ripped free.

How could any society exist like this? he thought with horror. His books said the koloss bred and aged quickly—a fortunate situation for them, considering the number of deaths he had already seen. Even so, it seemed to him that this species killed too many of its members to continue.

Yet they did continue. Unfortunately. The Keeper in him believed strongly that nothing should be lost, that every society was worth remembering. However, the brutality of the koloss camp—the wounded creatures who sat, ignoring the gashes in their skin, the flayed corpses along the path, the sudden bellows of anger and subsequent murders—tested this belief.

His captors led him around a small hillock in the land, and Sazed paused as he saw something very unexpected.

A tent.

"Go," the lead koloss said, pointing.

Sazed frowned. There were several dozen humans outside the tent, carrying spears and dressed like imperial guards. The tent was large, and behind it stood a line of boxy carts.

"Go!" the koloss yelled.

Sazed did as he was told. Behind him, one of the koloss indifferently tossed Sazed's pack toward the human guards.

The metalminds inside clinked together as they hit the ashy ground, causing Sazed to cringe. The soldiers watched the koloss retreat with a wary eye; then one picked up the pack. Another leveled his spear at Sazed.

Sazed held up his hands. "I am Sazed, a Keeper of Terris, once steward, now teacher. I am not your enemy."

"Yes, well," the guard said, still watching the retreating koloss. "You're still going to have to come with me."

"May I have my possessions back?" Sazed asked. This hollow appeared free of koloss; apparently, the human soldiers wanted to keep their distance.

The first guard turned to his companion, who was perusing Sazed's pack. The second guard looked up and shrugged. "No weapons. Some bracelets and rings, maybe worth something."

"None of them are of precious metals," Sazed said. "They are the tools of a Keeper, and are of little value to anyone but myself."

The second guard shrugged, handing the bag to the first man. Both were of standard Central Dominance coloring—dark hair, light skin, the build and height of those who'd had proper nutrition as children. The first guard was the older of the two, and was obviously in charge. He took the bag from his companion. "We'll see what His Majesty says."

Ah, Sazed thought. "Let us speak with him then."

The guard turned, pushing aside the tent door and motioning for Sazed to enter. Sazed stepped from red sunlight into a functional—if sparsely furnished—tent room. This main chamber was large, and contained several more guards. Sazed had seen perhaps two dozen so far.

The lead guard walked forward and poked his head into a room at the back. A few moments later, he waved Sazed forward and pulled back the tent door.

Sazed entered the second chamber. The man inside wore the pants and suit jacket of a Luthadel nobleman. He was balding—his hair reduced to a few struggling wisps—despite his youth. He stood, tapping the side of his leg with a nervous hand, and jumped slightly when Sazed entered.

Sazed recognized the man. "Jastes Lekal."

"*King* Lekal," Jastes snapped. "Do I know you, Terrisman?"

"We have not met, Your Majesty," Sazed said, "but I have had some dealings with a friend of yours, I think. King Elend Venture of Luthadel?"

Jastes nodded absently. "My men say the koloss brought you. They found you poking around the camp?"

"Yes, Your Majesty," Sazed said carefully, watching as Jastes began to pace. *This man isn't much more stable than the army he apparently leads,* he thought with dissatisfaction. "How is it that you have persuaded the creatures to serve you?"

"You are a prisoner, Terrisman," Jastes snapped. "No questions. Did Elend send you to spy on me?"

"I was sent by no man," Sazed said. "You happened to be in my path, Your Majesty. I meant no harm by my observations."

Jastes paused, eyeing Sazed, before beginning to pace again. "Well, never mind. I've been without a proper steward for some time now. You will serve me now."

"I apologize, Your Majesty," Sazed said, bowing slightly. "But that will not be possible."

Jastes frowned. "You're a steward—I can tell that from the robes. Is Elend so great a master that you would deny me?"

"Elend Venture is not my master, Your Majesty," Sazed said, meeting the young king's eyes. "Now that we are free, the Terrismen no longer call any man master. I cannot be your servant, for I can be no man's servant. Keep me as prisoner, if you must. But I will not serve you. I apologize."

Jastes paused again. Instead of being angry, however, he simply seemed . . . embarrassed. "I see."

"Your Majesty," Sazed said calmly, "I realize that you commanded me to ask no questions, so I will instead make observations. You appear to have placed yourself in a very poor position. I know not how you control these koloss, but I cannot help but think that your grip is tenuous. You are in danger, and you appear intent on sharing that danger with others."

Jastes flushed. "Your 'observations' are flawed, Terrisman.

I *am* in control of this army. They obey me completely. How many other noblemen have you seen gather koloss armies? None—only I have been successful."

"They do not seem very much under control, Your Majesty."

"Oh?" Jastes asked. "And did they tear you apart when they found you? Pummel you to death for sport? Ram a stick through you and roast you over one of their fires? No. They don't do these things because *I* commanded them otherwise. It may not seem like much, Terrisman, but trust me—this is a sign of great restraint and obedience for koloss."

"Civilization is no great achievement, Your Majesty."

"Do not try me, Terrisman!" Jastes snapped, running a hand through the remnants of his hair. "These are koloss we speak of—we can't expect much from them."

"And you bring them to Luthadel?" Sazed asked. "Even the Lord Ruler feared these creatures, Your Majesty. He kept them away from cities. You bring them to the most populated area in all of the Final Empire!"

"You don't understand," Jastes said. "I tried overtures of peace, but nobody listens unless you have money or an army. Well, I have one, and I'll soon have the other. I know Elend's sitting on that stash of atium—and I'm just come to . . . to make an alliance with him."

"An alliance where you take over control of the city?"

"Bah!" Jastes said with a wave of his hand. "Elend doesn't control Luthadel—he's just a placeholder waiting for someone more powerful to come along. He's a good man, but he's an innocent idealist. He's going to lose his throne to one army or another, and I'll give him a better deal than Cett or Straff will, that's certain."

Cett? Straff? What kind of trouble has young Venture gotten himself into? Sazed shook his head. "Somehow I doubt that a 'better deal' involves the use of koloss, Your Majesty."

Jastes frowned. "You certainly are smart-mouthed, Terrisman. You're a sign—your entire people are a sign—of what has gone wrong with the world. I used to respect the Terris people. There's no shame in being a good servant."

"There's often little pride in it either," Sazed said. "But, I apologize for my attitude, Your Majesty. It is not a manifestation of Terris independence. I have always been too free with my comments, I think. I never made the best of stewards." *Or the best of Keepers,* he added to himself.

"Bah," Jastes said again, resuming his pacing.

"Your Majesty," Sazed said. "I must continue to Luthadel. There are . . . events I need to deal with. Think what you will of my people, but you must know that we are honest. The work I do is beyond politics and wars, thrones and armies. It is important for all men."

"Scholars always say things like that," Jastes said. He paused. "Elend always said things like that."

"Regardless," Sazed continued, "I must be allowed to leave. In exchange for my freedom, I will deliver a message from you to His Majesty King Elend, if you wish."

"I could send a messenger of my own at any time!"

"And leave yourself with one less man to protect you from the koloss?" Sazed said.

Jastes paused just briefly.

Ah, so he does fear them. Good. At least he's not insane.

"I *will* be leaving, Your Majesty," Sazed said. "I do not mean to be arrogant, but I can see that you don't have the resources to keep prisoners. You can let me go, or you can give me to the koloss. I would be wary, however, of letting them get into a habit of killing humans."

Jastes eyed him. "Fine," he said. "Deliver this message, then. Tell Elend that I don't care if he knows I'm coming— I don't even care if you give our numbers. Be sure you're accurate, though! I have over twenty thousand koloss in this army. He can't fight me. He can't fight the others, either. But, if I had those city walls . . . well, I could hold off both other armies for him. Tell him to be logical. If he gives over the atium, I'll even let him keep Luthadel. We can be neighbors. Allies."

One bankrupt of coin, the other bankrupt of common sense, Sazed thought. "Very well, Your Majesty. I will speak with Elend. I will need the return of my possessions, however."

The king waved a hand in annoyance, and Sazed withdrew, waiting quietly as the lead guard entered the king's chambers again and received his orders. As he waited for the soldiers to prepare—his pack thankfully returned to him—Sazed thought about what Jastes had said. *Cett or Straff.* Just how many forces were working on Elend to take his city?

If Sazed had wanted a quiet place to study, he'd apparently chosen the wrong direction to run.

It wasn't until a few years later that I began to notice the signs. I knew the prophecies—I am a Terris Worldbringer, after all. And yet, not all of us are religious men; some, such as myself, are more interested in other topics. However, during my time with Alendi, I could not help but become more interested in the Anticipation. He seemed to fit the signs so well.

20

"THIS IS GOING TO BE dangerous, Your Majesty," Dockson said.

"It's our only option," Elend said. He stood behind his table; it was, as usual, stacked with books. He was backlit by the study's window, and its colors fell upon the back of his white uniform, dyeing it a brilliant maroon.

He certainly does look more commanding in that outfit, Vin thought, sitting in Elend's plush reading chair, Ore-Seur resting patiently on the floor beside her. She still wasn't sure what to think of the changes in Elend. She knew the alterations were mostly visual—new clothing, new haircut—but other things about him seemed to be changing as well. He stood up straighter when he spoke, and was more authoritative. He was even training in the sword and the cane.

Vin glanced at Tindwyl. The matronly Terriswoman sat in a stiff chair at the back of the room, watching the proceedings. She had perfect posture, and was ladylike in her colorful skirt and blouse. She didn't sit with her legs folded beneath her, as Vin currently did, and she'd never wear trousers.

What is it about her? Vin thought. *I've spent a year trying to get Elend to practice his swordsmanship. Tindwyl's been here less than a month, and she already has him sparring.*

Why did Vin feel bitter? Elend wouldn't change that much, would he? She tried to quiet the little piece of her that worried about this new confident, well-dressed warrior of a king—worried that he would turn out to be different from the man she loved.

What if he stopped needing her?

She pulled down into the chair just a little bit farther as Elend continued to speak with Ham, Dox, Clubs, and Breeze.

"El," Ham said, "you realize that if you go into the enemy camp, we won't be able to protect you."

"I'm not sure you can protect me here, Ham," Elend said. "Not with two armies camped practically against the walls."

"True," Dockson said, "but I'm worried that if you enter that camp, you'll never come out."

"Only if I fail," Elend said. "If I follow the plan—convince my father that we're his allies—he'll let me return. I didn't spend a lot of time politicking in the court when I was younger. However, one thing I *did* learn to do was manipulate my father. I know Straff Venture—and I know that I can beat him. Besides, he doesn't want me dead."

"Can we be sure of that?" Ham asked, rubbing his chin.

"Yes," Elend said. "After all, Straff hasn't sent assassins after me, while Cett has. It makes sense. What better person for Straff to leave in control of Luthadel than his own son? He thinks he can control me—he'll assume that he can make me give him Luthadel. If I play into that, I should be able to get him to attack Cett."

"He does have a point . . ." Ham said.

"Yes," Dockson said, "but what is to keep Straff from just taking you hostage and forcing his way into Luthadel?"

"He'll still have Cett at his back," Elend said. "If he fights us, he'll lose men—a lot of men—and expose himself to attack from behind."

"But he'll have you, my dear man," Breeze said. "He wouldn't have to attack Luthadel—he could force us to give in."

"You'll have orders to let me die first," Elend said. "That's why I set up the Assembly. It has the power to choose a new king."

"But why?" Ham asked. "Why take this risk, El? Let's wait a bit longer and see if we can get Straff to meet with you in a more neutral location."

Elend sighed. "You *have* to listen to me, Ham. Siege or no siege, we can't just sit here. If we do, either we'll get starved out, or one of those armies will decide to break the siege and attack us, hoping to take our walls, then turn and immediately defend against its enemies. They won't do that easily, but it could happen. It *will* happen, if we don't begin to play the kings against one another."

The room fell silent. The others slowly turned toward Clubs, who nodded. He agreed.

Good job, Elend, Vin thought.

"Someone has to meet with my father," Elend said. "And, I need to be that person. Straff thinks I am a fool, so I can convince him that I'm no threat. Then, I'll go and persuade Cett that I'm on his side. When they finally attack each other—each one thinking we're on their side— we'll withdraw instead and force them to fight it out. The winner won't have enough strength left to take the city from us!"

Ham and Breeze nodded their heads. Dockson, however, shook his. "The plan is good in theory, but going into the enemy camp unguarded? That seems foolish."

"Now, see," Elend said. "I think this is to our advantage. My father believes strongly in control and domination. If I walk into his camp, I'll essentially be telling him that I agree he has authority over me. I'll seem weak, and he'll assume that he can take me whenever he wants. It's a risk, but if I don't do this, *we die.*"

The men eyed each other.

Elend stood up a little straighter and pulled his hands into fists at his sides. He always did that when he was nervous.

"I'm afraid that this isn't a discussion," Elend said. "I've made my decision."

They're not going to accept a declaration like that, Vin thought. The crew were an independent lot.

Yet, surprisingly, none of them objected.

Dockson finally nodded his head. "All right, Your Majesty," he said. "You're going to need to walk a dangerous line—make Straff believe that he can count on our support, but also convince him that he can betray us at his leisure. You have to make him want our strength of arms while at the same time dismissing our strength of will."

"And," Breeze added, "you need to do so without him figuring out that you're playing both sides."

"Can you do it?" Ham asked. "Honestly, Elend?"

Elend nodded. "I can do it, Ham. I've gotten much better at politics this last year." He said the words with confidence, though Vin noticed that he still had his fists clenched. *He'll have to learn not to do that.*

"You may, perhaps, understand politics," Breeze said, "but *this* is scamming. Face it, my friend, you're dreadfully honest—always talking about how to defend the rights of skaa and the like."

"Now, see, you're being unfair," Elend said. "Honesty and good intentions are completely different. Why, I can be just as dishonest as—" He paused. "Why am I arguing this point? We admit what has to be done, and we know that I'm the one who has to do it. Dox, would you draft a letter to my father? Suggest that I would be happy to visit him. In fact . . ."

Elend paused, glancing at Vin. Then, he continued. "In fact, tell him that I want to discuss the future of Luthadel, and because I want to introduce him to someone special."

Ham chuckled. "Ah, nothing like bringing a girl home to meet the father."

"Especially when that girl happens to be the most dangerous Allomancer in the Central Dominance," Breeze added.

"You think he'll agree to letting her come?" Dockson said.

"If he doesn't, there's no deal," Elend said. "Make sure he knows that. Either way, I do think he'll agree. Straff has a habit of underestimating me—probably with good reason. However, I'll bet that sentiment extends to Vin as well. He'll assume she isn't as good as everyone says."

"Straff has his own Mistborn," Vin added. "To protect him. It will only be fair for Elend to be able to bring me. And, if I'm there, I can get him out should something go wrong."

Ham chuckled again. "That probably wouldn't make for a very dignified retreat—getting slung over Vin's shoulder and carried to safety."

"Better than dying," Elend said, obviously trying to act good-natured, but flushing slightly at the same time.

He loves me, but he's still a man, Vin thought. *How many times have I hurt his pride by being Mistborn while he is simply a normal person? A lesser man would never have fallen in love with me.*

But, doesn't he deserve a woman that he feels he can protect? A woman who's more like . . . a woman?

Vin pulled down in her chair again, seeking warmth within its plushness. However, it was Elend's study chair, where he read. Didn't he also deserve a woman who shared his interests, one who didn't find reading a chore? A woman with whom he could talk about his brilliant political theories?

Why am I thinking about our relationship so much lately? Vin thought.

We don't belong in their world, Zane had said. *We belong here, in the mists.*

You don't belong with them. . . .

"There is something else I wanted to mention, Your

Majesty," Dockson said. "You should meet with the Assembly. They've been growing impatient to get your ear—something about counterfeit coins being passed in Luthadel."

"I don't really have time for city business right now," Elend said. "The prime reason I set up the Assembly was so that they could deal with these kinds of issues. Go ahead and send them a message, telling them that I trust their judgment. Apologize for me, and explain that I'm seeing to the city's defense. I'll try and make the Assembly meeting next week."

Dockson nodded, scribbling a note to himself. "Though," he noted, "that is something else to consider. By meeting with Straff, you'll give up your hold on the Assembly."

"This isn't an official parlay," Elend said. "Just an informal meeting. My resolution from before will still stand."

"In all honesty, Your Majesty," Dockson said, "I highly doubt that *they* will see it that way. You know how angry they are to be left without recourse until you decide to hold the parlay."

"I know," Elend said. "But the risk is worthwhile. We *need* to meet with Straff. Once that is done, I can return with—hopefully—good news for the Assembly. At that point, I can argue that the resolution hasn't been fulfilled. For now, the meeting goes forward."

More decisive indeed, Vin thought. *He's changing. . . .*

She had to stop thinking about things like that. Instead, she focused on something else. The conversation turned to specific ways that Elend could manipulate Straff, each of the crewmembers giving him tips on how to scam effectively. Vin, however, found herself watching them, looking for discrepancies in their personalities, trying to decide if any of them might be the kandra spy.

Was Clubs being even quieter than normal? Was Spook's shift in language patterns due to growing maturity, or because the kandra had difficulty mimicking his slang? Was Ham, perhaps, too jovial? He also seemed to focus less on his little philosophical puzzles than he once had. Was that because he was more serious now, or because the kandra didn't know how to imitate him properly?

It was no good. If she thought too much, she could spot seeming discrepancies in anyone. Yet, at the same time, they all seemed like themselves. People were just too complex to reduce to simple personality traits. Plus, the kandra would be good—very good. He would have a lifetime of training in the art of imitating others, and he had probably been planning his insertion for a long time.

It came down to Allomancy, then. With all of the activities surrounding the siege and her studies about the Deepness, however, she hadn't had a chance to test her friends. As she thought about it, she admitted that the lack of time excuse was a weak one. The truth was that she was probably distracting herself because the thought of one of the crew—one of her first group of friends—being a traitor was just too upsetting.

She had to get over that. If there really were a spy in the group, that would be the end of them. If the enemy kings found out about the tricks Elend was planning . . .

This in mind, she tentatively burned bronze. Immediately, she sensed an Allomantic pulse from Breeze—dear, incorrigible Breeze. He was so good at Allomancy that even Vin couldn't detect his touch most of the time, but he was also compulsive about using his power.

He wasn't currently using it on her, however. She closed her eyes, focusing. Once, long ago, Marsh had tried to train her in the fine art of using bronze to read Allomantic pulses. She hadn't realized at the time just how large a task he'd begun.

When an Allomancer burned a metal, they gave off an invisible, drumlike beat that only another Allomancer burning bronze could sense. The rhythm of these pulses—how quickly the beats came, the way they "sounded"—told exactly what metal was being burned.

It took practice, and was difficult, but Vin was getting better at reading the pulses. She focused. Breeze was burning brass—the internal, mental Pushing metal. And . . .

Vin focused harder. She could feel a pattern washing over her, a double *dum-dum* beat with each pulse. They felt oriented to her right. The pulses were washing against something else, something that was sucking them in.

Elend. Breeze was focused on Elend. Not surprising, considering the current discussion. Breeze was always Pushing on the people he interacted with.

Satisfied, Vin sat back. But then she paused. *Marsh implied there was much more to bronze than many people thought. I wonder. . . .*

She squeezed her eyes shut—ignoring the fact that any of the others who saw her would think her actions strange—and focused again on the Allomantic pulses. She flared the bronze, concentrating so hard she felt she'd give herself a headache. There was a . . . vibration to the pulses. But what that could mean, she wasn't certain.

Focus! she told herself. However, the pulses stubbornly refused to yield any further information.

Fine, she thought. *I'll cheat.* She turned off her tin—she almost always had it on a little bit—then reached inside and burned the fourteenth metal. Duralumin.

The Allomantic pulses became so loud . . . so powerful . . . she swore she could feel their vibrations shaking her apart. They pounded like beats from a massive drum set right beside her. But she got something from them.

Anxiety, nervousness, worry, insecurity, anxiety, nervousness, worry—

It was gone, her bronze expended in one massive flare of power. Vin opened her eyes; no one in the room was looking at her except OreSeur.

She felt drained. The headache she'd predicted before now came in full force, thudding inside her head like the tiny brother of the drum she'd now banished. However, she held to the information she'd gleaned. It hadn't come in words, but feelings—and her first fear was that Breeze was making these emotions appear. Anxiety, nervousness, worry. However, she immediately realized that Breeze was a Soother. If he focused on emotions, it would be the ones he was *dampening*. The ones he was using his powers to Soothe away.

She looked from him to Elend. *Why . . . he's making Elend more confident!* If Elend stood a little taller, it was because Breeze was quietly helping, Soothing away anxiety and worry. And Breeze did this even as he argued and made his usual mocking comments.

Vin studied the plump man, ignoring her headache, feeling a newfound sense of admiration. She'd always wondered just a little at Breeze's placement in the crew. The other men were all, to an extent, idealists. Even Clubs, beneath his crotchety exterior, had always struck her as a solidly good man.

Breeze was different. Manipulative, a little selfish—he seemed like he'd joined the crew for the challenge, not because he really wanted to help the skaa. But, Kelsier had always claimed that he'd chosen his crew carefully, picking the men for their integrity, not just their skill.

Perhaps Breeze wasn't an exception after all. Vin watched him pointing his cane at Ham as he said something flippant. And yet, on the inside, he was completely different. *You're a good man, Breeze,* she thought, smiling to herself. *You just try your best to hide it.*

And he also wasn't the impostor. She'd known that before, of course; Breeze hadn't been in the city when the kandra had made the switch. However, having a second confirmation lifted a tiny bit of her burden.

Now if she could just eliminate some of the others.

Elend bid the crew farewell after the meeting. Dockson went to pen the requested letters, Ham to go over security, Clubs back to training the soldiers, and Breeze to try and placate the Assembly regarding Elend's lack of attention.

Vin trailed out of the study, shooting him a glance, then eyeing Tindwyl. *Suspicious of her still, eh?* Elend thought with amusement. He nodded reassuringly, and Vin frowned, looking just a little annoyed. He would have let her stay, but . . . well, facing Tindwyl was embarrassing enough alone.

Vin left the room, wolfhound kandra at her side. *Looks like she's growing more attached to the creature,* Elend thought with satisfaction. It was good to know that someone watched over her.

Vin shut the door behind her, and Elend sighed, rubbing his shoulder. Several weeks of training with the sword and cane were taking a lot out of him, and his body was bruised. He tried to keep the pain from showing—or, rather, from letting Tindwyl see him show the pain. *At least I proved that I'm learning,* he thought. *She had to see how well I did today.*

"Well?" he asked.

"You are an embarrassment," Tindwyl said, standing before her chair.

"So you like to say," Elend said, walking forward to begin piling up a stack of books. Tindwyl said that he needed to let servants keep his study clean, something he'd always resisted. The clutter of books and papers felt right to him, and he certainly didn't want someone else moving them around.

With her standing there looking at him, however, it was difficult not to feel self-conscious about the mess. He stacked another book on the pile.

"Surely you noticed how well I did," Elend said. "I got them to let me go into Straff's camp."

"You are king, Elend Venture," Tindwyl said, arms folded. "Nobody 'lets' you do anything. The first change in attitude has to be your own—you have to stop thinking that you need permission or agreement from those who follow you."

"A king should lead by consent of his citizens," Elend said. "I will not be another Lord Ruler."

"A king should be strong," Tindwyl said firmly. "He accepts counsel, but only when he asks for it. He makes it clear that the final decision is his, not his counselors'. You need better control over your advisors. If they don't respect you, then your enemies won't either—and the masses never will."

"Ham and the others respect me."

Tindwyl raised an eyebrow.

"They do!"

"What do they call you?"

Elend shrugged. "They're my friends. They use my name."

"Or a close approximation of it. Right, 'El'?"

Elend flushed, setting one final book on the stack. "You'd have me force my friends to address me by my title?"

"Yes," Tindwyl said. "Especially in public. You should be addressed as 'Your Majesty,' or at least as 'my lord.'"

"I doubt Ham would deal well with that," Elend said. "He has some issues with authority."

"He will get over them," Tindwyl said, wiping her finger along a bookcase. She didn't need to hold it up for Elend to know there would be dust on its tip.

"What about you?" Elend challenged.

"Me?"

"You call me 'Elend Venture,' not 'Your Majesty.'"

"I am different," Tindwyl said.

"Well, I don't see why you should be. You can call me 'Your Majesty' from now on."

Tindwyl smiled slyly. "Very well, Your Majesty. You can unclench your fists now. You're going to have to work on that—a statesman should not give visual clues of his nervousness."

Elend glanced down, relaxing his hands. "All right."

"In addition," Tindwyl continued, "you still hedge too much in your language. It makes you seem timid and hesitant."

"I'm working on that."

"Don't apologize unless you really mean it," Tindwyl said. "And don't make excuses. You don't need them. A leader is often judged by how well he bears responsibility. As king, everything that happens in your kingdom—regardless of who commits the act—is your fault. You are even responsible for unavoidable events such as earthquakes or storms."

"Or armies," Elend said.

Tindwyl nodded. "Or armies. It is your responsibility to deal with these things, and if something goes wrong, it is your fault. You simply have to accept this."

Elend nodded, picking up a book.

"Now, let's talk about guilt," Tindwyl said, seating herself. "Stop cleaning. That isn't a job for a king."

Elend sighed, setting down the book.

"Guilt," Tindwyl said, "does not become a king. You have to stop feeling sorry for yourself."

"You just told me everything that happens in the kingdom is my fault!"

"It is."

"How can I *not* feel guilty, then?"

"You have to feel confident that your actions are the best," Tindwyl explained. "You have to know that no matter how bad things get, they would be worse without you. When disaster occurs, you take responsibility, but you don't wallow or mope. You aren't allowed that luxury; guilt is for lesser men. You simply need to do what is expected."

"And that is?"

"To make everything better."

"Great," Elend said flatly. "And if I fail?"

"Then you accept responsibility, and make everything better on the second try."

Elend rolled his eyes. "And what if I can't ever make things better? What if I'm really not the best man to be king?"

"Then you remove yourself from the position," Tindwyl said. "Suicide is the preferred method—assuming, of course, that you have an heir. A good king knows not to foul up the succession."

"Of course," Elend said. "So, you're saying I should just kill myself."

"No. I'm telling you to have pride in yourself, Your Majesty."

"That's not what it sounds like. Every day you tell me how poor a king I am, and how my people will suffer because of it! Tindwyl, I'm *not* the best man for this position. He got himself killed by the Lord Ruler."

"That is enough!" Tindwyl snapped. "Believe it or not, Your Majesty, you *are* the best person for this position."

Elend snorted.

"You are best," Tindwyl said, "because you hold the throne now. If there is anything worse than a mediocre king, it is chaos—which is what this kingdom would have if *you* hadn't taken the throne. The people on both sides, noblemen and skaa, accept you. They may not believe in you, but they accept you. Step down now—or even die accidentally—and there would be confusion, collapse, and destruction. Poorly trained or not, weak of character or not, mocked or not, you are all this country has. You are *king*, Elend Venture."

Elend paused. "I'm . . . not sure if you're making me feel any better about myself, Tindwyl."

"It's—"

Elend raised a hand. "Yes, I know. It's not about how I feel."

"You have no place for guilt. Accept that you're king, accept that you can do nothing constructive to change that, and accept responsibility. Whatever you do, be confident—for if you weren't here, there would be chaos."

Elend nodded.

"Arrogance, Your Majesty," Tindwyl said. "Successful leaders all share one common trait—they believe that they can do a better job than the alternatives. Humility is fine when considering your responsibility and duty, but when it comes time to make a decision, you must not question yourself."

"I'll try."

"Good," Tindwyl said. "Now, perhaps, we can move on to another matter. Tell me, why haven't you married that young girl?"

Elend frowned. *Wasn't expecting that. . . .* "That's a very personal question, Tindwyl."

"Good."

Elend deepened his frown, but she sat expectantly, watching him with one of her unrelenting stares.

"I don't know," Elend finally said, sitting back in his chair, sighing. "Vin isn't . . . like other women."

Tindwyl raised an eyebrow, her voice softening slightly. "I think that the more women you come to know, Your Majesty, the more you'll find that statement applies to all of them."

Elend nodded ruefully.

"Either way," Tindwyl said, "things are not well as they stand. I will not pry further into your relationship, but—as we've discussed—appearances are very important to a king. It isn't appropriate for you to be seen as having a mistress. I realize that sort of thing was common for imperial nobility. The skaa, however, want to see something better in you. Perhaps because many noblemen were so frivolous with their sexual lives, the skaa have always prized monogamy. They wish desperately for you to respect their values."

"They'll just have to be patient with us," Elend said. "I actually want to marry Vin, but she won't have it."

"Do you know why?"

Elend shook his head. "She . . . doesn't seem to make sense a lot of the time."

"Perhaps she isn't right for a man in your position."

Elend looked up sharply. "What does that mean?"

"Perhaps you need someone a little more refined," Tindwyl said. "I'm certain she's a fine bodyguard, but as a lady, she—"

"Stop," Elend snapped. "Vin is fine as she is."

Tindwyl smiled.

"What?" Elend demanded.

"I've insulted you all afternoon, Your Majesty, and you barely grew sullen. I mentioned your Mistborn in a mildly disparaging way, and now you're ready to throw me out."

"So?"

"So, you do love her?"

"Of course," Elend said. "I don't understand her, but yes. I love her."

Tindwyl nodded. "I apologize, then, Your Majesty. I had to be certain."

Elend frowned, relaxing in his chair slightly. "So, this was some kind of test, then? You wanted to see how I would react to your words about Vin?"

"You will always be tested by those you meet, Your Majesty. You might as well grow accustomed to it."

"But, why do you care about my relationship with Vin?"

"Love is not easy for kings, Your Majesty," Tindwyl said in an uncharacteristically kind voice. "You will find that your affection for the girl can cause far more trouble than any of the other things we've discussed."

"And that's a reason to give her up?" Elend asked stiffly.

"No," Tindwyl said. "No, I don't think so."

Elend paused, studying the stately Terriswoman with her square features and her stiff posture. "That . . . seems odd, coming from you. What about kingly duty and appearances?"

"We must make allowances for the occasional exception," Tindwyl said.

Interesting, Elend thought. He wouldn't have considered her the type to agree to any sort of "exceptions." *Perhaps she's a little deeper than I've assumed.*

"Now," Tindwyl said. "How are your training sessions going?"

Elend rubbed his sore arm. "All right, I suppose. But—"

He was interrupted by a knock at the door. Captain Demoux entered a moment later. "Your Majesty, a visitor has arrived from Lord Cett's army."

"A messenger?" Elend said, standing.

Demoux paused, looking a little embarrassed. "Well . . . sort of. She says she's Lord Cett's daughter, and she's come looking for Breeze."

He was born of a humble family, yet married the daughter of a king.

21

THE YOUNG WOMAN'S EXPENSIVE DRESS—light red silk with a shawl and lace sleeves—might have lent her an air of dignity, had she not scampered forward as soon as Breeze entered the room. Her light Western hair bouncing, she made a squeal of happiness as she threw her arms around Breeze's neck.

She was, perhaps, eighteen years old.

Elend glanced at Ham, who stood dumbfounded.

"Well, looks like you were right about Breeze and Cett's daughter," Elend whispered.

Ham shook his head. "I didn't think . . . I mean I joked, because it was Breeze, but I didn't expect to be *right!*"

Breeze, for his part, at least had the decency to look terribly uncomfortable in the young woman's arms. They stood inside the palace atrium, the same place where Elend had met with his father's messenger. Floor-to-ceiling windows let in the afternoon light, and a group of servants stood at one side of the room to wait on Elend's orders.

Breeze met Elend's eyes, blushing deeply. *I don't think I've ever seen him do that before,* Elend thought.

"My dear," Breeze said, clearing his throat, "perhaps you should introduce yourself to the king?"

The girl finally let go of Breeze. She stepped back, curtsying to Elend with a noblewoman's grace. She was a bit plump, her hair long after pre-Collapse fashion, and her cheeks were red with excitement. She was a cute thing, obviously well trained for the court—exactly the sort of girl that Elend had spent his youth trying to avoid.

"Elend," Breeze said, "might I introduce Allrianne Cett, daughter to Lord Ashweather Cett, king of the Western Dominance?"

"Your Majesty," Allrianne said.

Elend nodded. "Lady Cett." He paused, then—with a hopeful voice—continued. "Your father sent you as an ambassador?"

Allrianne paused. "Um . . . he didn't exactly send me, Your Majesty."

"Oh, dear," Breeze said, pulling out a handkerchief to dab his brow.

Elend glanced at Ham, then back at the girl. "Perhaps you should explain," he said, gesturing toward the atrium's seats. Allrianne nodded eagerly, but stayed close to Breeze as they sat. Elend waved for some servants to bring chilled wine.

He had a feeling he was going to want something to drink.

"I seek asylum, Your Majesty," Allrianne said, speaking with a quick voice. "I had to go. I mean, Breezy must have told you how my father is!"

Breeze sat uncomfortably, and Allrianne put an affectionate hand on his knee.

"How your father is?" Elend asked.

"He is so manipulative," Allrianne said. "So *demanding*. He drove Breezy away, and I absolutely had to follow. I wouldn't spend another moment in that camp. A war camp! He brought me, a young lady, along with him to war! Why, do you know what it is like to be leered at by every passing soldier? Do you understand what it is like to live in a tent?"

"I—"

"We rarely had fresh water," Allrianne continued. "And I couldn't take a decent bath without fear of peeping soldiers! During our travels, there was dreadful nothing to do all day but sit in the carriage and bounce, bounce, bounce. Why, until Breezy came, I hadn't had a refined conversation in weeks. And then, Father drove him away. . . ."

"Because?" Ham asked eagerly.

Breeze coughed.

"I had to get away, Your Majesty," Allrianne said. "You have to give me asylum! I know things that could help you. Like, I saw my father's camp. I'll bet you don't know that he is getting supplies from the cannery in Haverfrex! What do you think of that?"

"Um . . . impressive," Elend said hesitantly.

Allrianne nodded curtly.

"And, you came to find Breeze?" Elend asked.

Allrianne flushed slightly, glancing to the side. However, when she spoke, she displayed little tact. "I had to see him again, Your Majesty. So charming, so . . . wonderful. I wouldn't have expected Father to understand a man such as he."

"I see," Elend said.

"Please, Your Majesty," Allrianne said. "You have to take me in. Now that I've left Father, I have nowhere else to go!"

"You may stay—for a time, at least," Elend said, nodding greetings to Dockson, who had entered through the atrium doors. "But, you've obviously had a difficult trip. Perhaps you would like an opportunity to refresh yourself . . . ?"

"Oh, I would much appreciate that, Your Majesty!"

Elend eyed Cadon, one of the palace stewards, who stood at the back of the room with other servants. He nodded; rooms were prepared. "Then," Elend said, standing, "Cadon will lead you to some rooms. We will take dinner this evening at seven, and can speak again then."

"Thank you, Your Majesty!" Allrianne said, jumping up from her chair. She gave Breeze another hug, then stepped forward, as if to do the same for Elend. Fortunately, she thought better of it, instead allowing the servants to lead her away.

Elend sat. Breeze sighed deeply, leaning back in a wearied posture as Dockson walked forward, taking the girl's seat.

"That was . . . unexpected," Breeze noted.

There was an awkward pause, the atrium trees shifting slightly in the breeze from the balcony. Then—with a sharp bark—Ham began to laugh. The noise sparked Elend, and—despite the danger, despite the gravity of the problem—he found himself laughing as well.

"Oh, honestly," Breeze huffed, which only prompted them further. Perhaps it was the sheer incongruity of the situation, perhaps it was because he needed to release tension, but Elend found himself laughing so hard he almost fell from the chair. Ham wasn't doing much better, and even Dockson cracked a smile.

"I fail to see the levity in this situation," Breeze said. "The daughter of Lord Cett—a man who is currently besieging our home—just demanded asylum in the city. If Cett wasn't determined to kill us before, he certainly will be now!"

"I know," Elend said, taking deep breaths. "I know. It's just . . ."

"It's the image of you," Ham said, "being hugged by that courtly fluffcake. I can't think of anything more awkward than you being confronted by an irrational young woman!"

"This throws another wrinkle into things," Dockson noted. "Although, I'm not accustomed to *you* being the one to bring us a problem of this nature, Breeze. Honestly, I thought we would be able to avoid unplanned female attachments now that Kell is gone."

"This isn't my fault," Breeze said pointedly. "The girl's affection is completely misplaced."

"That's for sure," Ham mumbled.

"All right," a new voice said. "What was that pink thing I just passed in the hallway?"

Elend turned to find Vin standing, arms folded, in the atrium doorway. *So quiet. Why does she walk stealthily even in the palace?* She never wore shoes that clicked, never wore skirts that could rustle, and never had metal on her clothing that could clink or be Pushed by Allomancers.

"That wasn't pink, my dear," Breeze said. "That was red."

"Close enough," Vin said, walking forward. "She was bubbling to the servants about how hot her bath needed to be, and making certain they wrote down her favorite foods."

Breeze sighed. "That's Allrianne. We'll probably have to get a new pastry chef—either that, or have desserts ordered in. She's rather particular about her pastries."

"Allrianne Cett is the daughter of Lord Cett," Elend explained as Vin—ignoring the chairs—sat on the edge of a planter beside his chair, laying a hand on his arm. "Apparently, she and Breeze are something of an item."

"Excuse me?" Breeze huffed.

Vin, however, wrinkled her nose. "That's disgusting, Breeze. You're old. She's young."

"There was no relationship," Breeze snapped. "Besides, I'm not *that* old—nor is she *that* young."

"She sounded like she was about twelve," Vin said.

Breeze rolled his eyes. "Allrianne was a child of the country court—a little innocent, a little spoiled—but she hardly deserves to be spoken of in that manner. She's actually quite witty, in the right circumstances."

"So, was there anything between you?" Vin pressed.

"Of course not," Breeze said. "Well, not really. Nothing

real, though it could have been taken the wrong way. *Was* taken the wrong way, actually, once her father discovered . . . Anyway, who are you to talk, Vin? I seem to remember a certain *young* girl pining for an *old* Kelsier a few years back."

Elend perked up at this.

Vin flushed. "I never pined over Kelsier."

"Not even at the beginning?" Breeze asked. "Come now, a dashing man like him? He saved you from being beaten by your old crewleader, took you in . . ."

"You're a sick man," Vin declared, folding her arms. "Kelsier was like a father to me."

"Eventually, perhaps," Breeze said, "but—"

Elend held up a hand. "Enough," he said. "This line of discussion is useless."

Breeze snorted, but fell silent. *Tindwyl is right,* Elend thought. *They will listen to me if I act like I expect them to.*

"We have to decide what to do," Elend said.

"The daughter of the man threatening us could be a very powerful bargaining chip," Dockson said.

"You mean take her hostage?" Vin said, eyes narrowing.

Dockson shrugged. "Someone has to state the obvious, Vin."

"Not really a hostage," Ham said. "She came to us, after all. Simply letting her stay could have the same effect as taking her hostage."

"That would risk antagonizing Cett," Elend said. "Our original plan was to make him think we're his ally."

"We could give her back, then," Dockson said. "That could get us a long way in the negotiations."

"And her request?" Breeze asked. "The girl wasn't happy in her father's camp. Shouldn't we at least consider her wishes?"

All eyes turned toward Elend. He paused. Just a few weeks ago, they would have kept on arguing. It seemed strange that they should so quickly begin to look to him for decisions.

Who was he? A man who had haphazardly ended up on the throne? A poor replacement for their brilliant leader? An idealist who hadn't considered the dangers his philosophies would bring? A fool? A child? An impostor?

The best they had.

"She stays," Elend said. "For now. Perhaps we'll be forced to return her eventually, but this will make a useful distraction for Cett's army. Let them sweat for a bit. It will only buy us more time."

The crewmembers nodded, and Breeze looked relieved.

I'll do what I can, make the decisions as I see they must be made, Elend thought.

Then accept the consequences.

He could trade words with the finest of philosophers, and had an impressive memory. Nearly as good, even, as my own. Yet, he was not argumentative.

22

CHAOS AND STABILITY, THE MIST was both. Upon the land there was an empire, within that empire were a dozen shattered kingdoms, within those kingdoms were cities, towns, villages, plantations. And above them all, within them all, around them all, was the mist. It was more constant than the sun, for it could not be hidden by clouds. It was more powerful than the storms, for it would outlast any weather's fury. It was always there. Changing, but eternal.

Day was an impatient sigh, awaiting the night. When the darkness did come, however, Vin found that the mists did not calm her as they once had.

Nothing seemed certain anymore. Once the night had been her refuge; now she found herself glancing behind, watching for ghostly outlines. Once Elend had been her peace, but he was changing. Once she had been able to protect the things she loved—but she was growing more and more afraid that the forces moving against Luthadel were beyond her capacity to stop.

Nothing frightened her more than her own impotence. During her childhood she had taken it for granted that she couldn't change things, but Kelsier had given her pride in herself.

If she couldn't protect Elend, what good was she?

There are still some things I can do, she thought forcefully. She crouched quietly on a ledge, mistcloak tassels hanging down, waving slightly in the wind. Just below her, torches burned fitfully at the front of Keep Venture, illuminating a pair of Ham's guards. They stood alert in the swirling mists, showing impressive diligence.

The guards wouldn't be able to see her sitting just above them; they'd barely be able to see twenty feet in the thick mists. They weren't Allomancers. Besides the core crew, Elend had access to barely half a dozen Mistings—which made him Allomantically weak compared with most of the other new kings in the Final Empire. Vin was supposed to make up the difference.

The torches flickered as the doors opened, and a figure left the palace. Ham's voice echoed quietly in the mist as he greeted his guards. One reason—perhaps the main reason—that the guards were so diligent was because of Ham. He might have been a bit of an anarchist at heart, but he could be a very good leader if he was given a small team. Though his guards weren't the most disciplined, polished soldiers Vin had seen, they were fiercely loyal.

Ham talked with the men for a time, then he waved farewell and walked out into the mists. The small courtyard between the keep and its wall contained a couple of guard posts and patrols, and Ham would visit each one in turn. He walked boldly in the night, trusting to diffused starlight to see, rather than blinding himself with a torch. A thief's habit.

Vin smiled, leaping quietly to the ground, then scampering after Ham. He walked on, ignorant of her presence.

What would it be like to have only one Allomantic power? Vin thought. *To be able to make yourself stronger, but to have ears as weak as those of any normal man?* It had been only two years, but already she had come to rely so heavily on her abilities.

Ham continued forward, Vin following discreetly, until they reached the ambush. Vin tensed, flaring her bronze.

OreSeur howled suddenly, jumping from a pile of boxes. The kandra was a dark silhouette in the night, his inhuman baying disturbing even to Vin. Ham spun, cursing quietly.

And he instinctively flared pewter. Focused on her bronze, Vin confirmed that the pulses were definitely coming from him. Ham spun around, searching in the night as OreSeur landed. Vin, however, simply smiled. Ham's Allomancy meant he wasn't the impostor. She could cross another name off her list.

"It's okay, Ham," Vin said, walking forward.

Ham paused, lowering his dueling cane. "Vin?" he asked, squinting in the mist.

"It's me," she said. "I'm sorry, you startled my hound. He can get jumpy at night."

Ham relaxed. "We all can, I guess. Anything happening tonight?"

"Not that I can tell," she said. "I'd let you know."

Ham nodded. "I'd appreciate it—though I doubt you'd need me. I'm captain of the guard, but you're the one who does all the work."

"You're more valuable than you think, Ham," Vin said. "Elend confides in you. Since Jastes and the others left him, he's needed a friend."

Ham nodded. Vin turned, glancing into the mists, where OreSeur sat waiting on his haunches. He seemed to be getting more and more comfortable with his hound's body.

Now that she knew Ham was not an impostor, there was something she needed to discuss with him. "Ham," she said, "your protection of Elend is more valuable than you know."

"You're talking about the impostor," Ham said quietly. "El has me searching through the palace staff to see who might have gone missing for a few hours on that day. It's a tough task, though."

She nodded. "There's something else, Ham. I'm out of atium."

He stood quietly in the mists for a moment, and then she heard him mutter a curse.

"I'll die the next time I fight a Mistborn," she said.

"Not unless he has atium," Ham said.

"What are the chances that someone would send a Mistborn without atium to fight me?"

He hesitated.

"Ham," she said, "I need to find a way to fight against someone who is burning atium. Tell me that you know a way."

Ham shrugged in the darkness. "There are lots of theories, Vin. I once had a long conversation with Breeze about this—though he spent most of it grumbling that I was annoying him."

"Well?" Vin asked. "What can I do?"

He rubbed his chin. "Most people agree that the best way to kill a Mistborn with atium is to surprise them."

"That doesn't help if they attack me first," Vin said.

"Well," Ham said. "Barring surprise, there isn't much. Some people think that you *might* be able to kill an atium-using Mistborn if you catch them in an unavoidable situation. It's like a game of fets—sometimes, the only way to take a piece is to corner it so that no matter which way it moves, it dies.

"Doing that to a Mistborn is pretty tough, though. The thing is, atium lets the Mistborn see the future—so he knows when a move will trap him, and so he can avoid the situation. The metal is supposed to enhance his mind somehow, too."

"It does. When I'm burning atium, I often dodge before I even register the attacks that are coming."

Ham nodded.

"So," Vin said, "what else?"

"That's it, Vin," Ham said. "Thugs talk about this topic a lot—we're all afraid of going up against a Mistborn. Those are your two options: Surprise him or overwhelm him. I'm sorry."

Vin frowned. Neither option would do her much good if she got ambushed. "Anyway, I need to keep moving. I promise to tell you about any corpses I produce."

Ham laughed. "How about you just try and avoid getting into situations where you have to produce them, eh? The Lord only knows what this kingdom would do if we lost you. . . ."

Vin nodded, though she wasn't certain how much Ham could see of her in the darkness. She waved to OreSeur, heading out toward the keep wall, leaving Ham on the cobbled path.

"Mistress," OreSeur said as they reached the top of the wall, "might I know the purpose of surprising Master Hammond like that? Are you that fond of startling your friends?"

"It was a test," Vin said, pausing beside a merlon gap, looking out over the city proper.

"A test, Mistress?"

"To see if he would use Allomancy. That way, I could know that he wasn't the impostor."

"Ah," the kandra said. "Clever, Mistress."

Vin smiled. "Thank you," she said. A guard patrol was moving toward them. Not wanting to have to deal with them, Vin nodded to the wall-top stone guardhouse. She jumped, pushing off a coin, and landed on top of it. OreSeur bounded up beside her, using his strange kandra musculature to leap the ten feet.

Vin sat down cross-legged to think, and OreSeur padded over to the roof's side and lay down, paws hanging over the edge. As they sat, Vin considered something. *OreSeur told me that a kandra didn't gain Allomantic powers if he ate an Allomancer . . . but, can a kandra be an Allomancer on his own? I never did finish that conversation.*

"This will tell me if a person isn't a kandra, won't it?" Vin asked, turning to OreSeur. "Your people don't have Allomantic powers, right?"

OreSeur didn't answer.

"OreSeur?" Vin said.

"I'm not required to answer that question, Mistress."

Yes, Vin thought with a sigh. *The Contract. How am I supposed to catch this other kandra if OreSeur won't answer any of my questions?* She leaned back in frustration, staring up into the endless mists, using her mistcloak to cushion her head.

"Your plan will work, Mistress," OreSeur said quietly.

Vin paused, rolling her head to look at him. He lay with head on forepaws, staring over the city. "If you sense Allomancy from someone, then they aren't a kandra."

Vin sensed a hesitant reluctance to his words, and he didn't look at her. It was as if he spoke grudgingly, giving up information that he'd rather have kept to himself.

So secretive, Vin thought. "Thank you," she said.

OreSeur shrugged a pair of canine shoulders.

"I know you'd rather not have to deal with me," she said. "We'd both rather keep our distance from each other. But, we'll just have to make things work this way."

OreSeur nodded again, then turned his head slightly and looked at her. "Why is it that you hate me?"

"I don't hate you," Vin said.

OreSeur raised a canine eyebrow. There was a wisdom in those eyes, an understanding that Vin was surprised to see. She'd never seen such things in him before.

"I . . ." Vin trailed off, looking away. "I just haven't ever gotten over the fact that you ate Kelsier's body."

"That isn't it," OreSeur said, turning back to look at the city. "You're too smart to be bothered by that."

Vin frowned indignantly, but the kandra wasn't looking at her. She turned, staring back up at the mists. *Why did he bring this up?* she thought. *We were just starting to get along.* She'd been willing to forget.

You really want to know? she thought. *Fine.*

"It's because you knew," she whispered.

"Excuse me, Mistress?"

"You knew," Vin said, still looking into the mists. "You were the only one on the crew who knew Kelsier was going to die. He told you that he was going to let himself be killed, and that you were to take his bones."

"Ah," OreSeur said quietly.

Vin turned accusing eyes at the creature. "Why didn't you say something? You knew how we felt about Kelsier. Did you even *consider* telling us that the idiot planned to kill himself? Did it even cross your mind that we might be able to stop him, that we might be able to find another way?"

"You are being quite harsh, Mistress."

"Well, you wanted to know," Vin said. "It was worst right after he died. When you came to be my servant, by his order. You never even spoke of what you'd done."

"The Contract, Mistress," OreSeur said. "You do not wish to hear this, perhaps, but I was bound. Kelsier did not wish you to know of his plans, so I could not tell you. Hate me if you must, but I do not regret my actions."

"I don't hate you." *I got over that.* "But, honestly, you wouldn't even break the Contract for his own good? You served Kelsier for two years. Didn't it even hurt you to know he was going to die?"

"Why should I care if one master or another dies?" Ore-Seur said. "There is always another to take their place."

"Kelsier wasn't that kind of master," Vin said.

"Wasn't he?"

"No."

"I apologize, Mistress," OreSeur said. "I will believe as commanded, then."

Vin opened her mouth to reply, then snapped it closed. If he was determined to keep thinking like a fool, then it was his right to do so. He could continue to resent masters, just as . . .

Just as she resented him. For keeping his word, for holding to his Contract.

Ever since I've known him, I've done nothing but treat him poorly, Vin thought. *First, when he was Renoux, I reacted against his haughty bearing—but that bearing wasn't his, it was part of the act he had to play. Then, as OreSeur, I avoided him. Hated him, even, for letting Kelsier die. Now I've forced him into an animal's body.*

And, in two years of knowing him, the only times I've asked about his past, I did it so that I could glean more

information about his people so that I could find the im-
postor.

Vin watched the mists. Of all the people in the crew, only OreSeur had been an outsider. He hadn't been invited to their conferences. He hadn't inherited a position in the government. He'd helped as much as any of them, playing a vital role—that of the "spirit" Kelsier, who had returned from the grave to incite the skaa to their final rebellion. Yet, while the rest of them had titles, friendships, and duties, the only thing OreSeur had gained from overthrowing the Final Empire was another master.

One who hated him.

No wonder he reacts like he does, Vin thought. Kelsier's last words to her returned to her mind: *You have a lot to learn about friendship, Vin. . . .* Kell and the others had invited her in, treated her with dignity and friendliness, even when she hadn't deserved it.

"OreSeur," she said, "what was your life like before you were recruited by Kelsier?"

"I don't see what that has to do with finding the impostor, Mistress," OreSeur said.

"It doesn't have anything to do with that," Vin said. "I just thought maybe I should get to know you better."

"My apologies, Mistress, but I don't want you to know me."

Vin sighed. *So much for that.*

But . . . well, Kelsier and the others hadn't turned away when she'd been blunt with them. There was a familiar tone to OreSeur's words. Something in them that she recognized.

"Anonymity," Vin said quietly.

"Mistress?"

"Anonymity. Hiding, even when you're with others. Being quiet, unobtrusive. Forcing yourself to stay apart—emotionally, at least. It's a way of life. A protection."

OreSeur didn't answer.

"You serve beneath masters," Vin said. "Harsh men who fear your competence. The only way to keep them from hating you is to make certain they don't pay attention to you. So, you make yourself look small and weak. Not a threat. But sometimes you say the wrong thing, or you let your rebelliousness show."

She turned toward him. He was watching her. "Yes," he finally said, turning to look back over the city.

"They hate you," Vin said quietly. "They hate you because of your powers, because they can't make you break your word, or because they worry that you are too strong to control."

"They become afraid of you," OreSeur said. "They grow paranoid—terrified, even as they use you, that you will take their place. Despite the Contract, despite knowing that no kandra would break his sacred vow, they fear you. And men hate what they fear."

"And so," Vin said, "they find excuses to beat you. Sometimes, even your efforts to remain harmless seem to provoke them. They hate your skill, they hate the fact that they don't have more reasons to beat you, so they beat you."

OreSeur turned back to her. "How do you know these things?" he demanded.

Vin shrugged. "That's not only how they treat kandra, OreSeur. That's the same way crewleaders treat a young girl—an anomaly in a thieving underground filled with men. A child who had a strange ability to make things happen—to influence people, to hear what she shouldn't, to move more quietly and quickly than others. A tool, yet a threat at the same time."

"I . . . didn't realize, Mistress. . . ."

Vin frowned. *How could he not have known about my past? He knew I was a street urchin.* Except . . . had he? For the first time, Vin realized how OreSeur must have seen her two years before, when she'd first met him. He had arrived in the area after her recruitment; he probably assumed that she'd been part of Kelsier's team for years, like the others.

"Kelsier recruited me for the first time just a few days before I met you," Vin said. "Well, actually, he didn't so much *recruit* me as *rescue* me. I spent my childhood serving in one thieving crew after another, always working for the least reputable and most dangerous men, for those were the only ones who would take in a couple of transients like my brother and me. The smart crewleaders learned that I

was a good tool. I'm not sure if they figured out that I was
an Allomancer—some probably did, others just thought I
was 'lucky.' Either way, they needed me. And that made
them hate me."

"So they beat you?"

Vin nodded. "The last one especially. That was when I
was really beginning to figure out how to use Allomancy,
even though I didn't know what it was. Camon knew,
though. And he hated me even as he used me. I think he
was afraid that I would figure out how to use my powers
fully. And on that day, he worried that I would kill him . . ."
Vin turned her head, looking at OreSeur. "Kill him and
take his place as crewleader."

OreSeur sat quietly, up on his haunches now, regarding
her.

"Kandra aren't the only ones that humans treat poorly,"
Vin said quietly. "We're pretty good at abusing each other,
too."

OreSeur snorted. "With you, at least, they had to hold
back for fear they'd kill you. Have you ever been beaten by
a master who knows that no matter how hard he hits, you
won't die? All he has to do is get you a new set of bones,
and you'll be ready to serve again the next day. We are the
ultimate servant—you can beat us to death in the morning,
then have us serve you dinner that night. All the sadism,
none of the cost."

Vin closed her eyes. "I understand. I wasn't a kandra, but
I did have pewter. I think Camon knew he could beat me far
harder than he should have been able to."

"Why didn't you run?" OreSeur asked. "You didn't have
a Contract bonding you to him."

"I . . . don't know," Vin said. "People are strange, Ore-
Seur, and loyalty is so often twisted. I stayed with Camon
because he was familiar, and I feared leaving more than I
did staying. That crew was all I had. My brother was gone,
and I was terrified of being alone. It seems kind of strange
now, thinking back."

"Sometimes a bad situation is still better than the alternative. You did what you needed to do to survive."

"Perhaps," Vin said. "But there's a better way, OreSeur. I didn't know it until Kelsier found me, but life doesn't have to be like that. You don't have to spend your years mistrusting, staying in the shadows and keeping yourself apart."

"Perhaps if you are human. I am kandra."

"You can still trust," Vin said. "You don't *have* to hate your masters."

"I don't hate them all, Mistress."

"But you don't trust them."

"It is nothing personal, Mistress."

"Yes it is," Vin said. "You don't trust us because you're afraid we'll hurt you. I understand that—I spent months with Kelsier wondering when I was going to get hurt again."

She paused. "But OreSeur, nobody betrayed us. Kelsier was *right*. It seems incredible to me even now, but the men in this crew—Ham, Dockson, Breeze—they're good people. And, even if one of them were to betray me, I'd still rather have trusted them. I can sleep at night, OreSeur. I can feel peace, I can laugh. Life is different. Better."

"You are human," OreSeur said stubbornly. "You can have friends because they don't worry that you'll eat them, or some other foolishness."

"I don't think that about you."

"Don't you? Mistress, you just admitted that you resent me because I ate Kelsier. Beyond that, you hate the fact that I followed my Contract. You, at least, have been honest.

"Human beings find us disturbing. They hate that we eat their kind, even though we only take bodies that are already dead. Your people find it unsettling that we can take their forms. Don't tell me that you haven't heard the legends of my people. Mistwraiths, they call us—creatures that steal the shapes of men who go into the mists. You think a monster like that, a legend used to frighten children, will ever find acceptance in your society?"

Vin frowned.

"This is the reason for the Contract, Mistress," OreSeur said, his muffled voice harsh as he spoke through dog's lips.

"You wonder why we don't just run away from you? Meld into your society, and become unseen? We tried that. Long ago, when the Final Empire was new. Your people found us, and they started to destroy us. They used Mistborn to hunt us down, for there were many more Allomancers in those days. Your people hated us because they feared we would replace them. We were almost completely destroyed—and then we came up with the Contract."

"But, what difference does that make?" Vin asked. "You're still doing the same things, aren't you?"

"Yes, but now we do them at *your* command," OreSeur said. "Men like power, and they love controlling something powerful. Our people offered to serve, and we devised a binding contract—one that every kandra vowed to uphold. We will not kill men. We will take bones only when we are commanded. We will serve our masters with absolute obedience. We began to do these things, and men stopped killing us. They still hated and feared us—but they also knew they could command us.

"We became your tools. As long as we remain subservient, Mistress, we survive. And that is why I obey. To break the Contract would be to betray my people. We cannot fight you, not while you have Mistborn, and so we must serve you."

Mistborn. Why are Mistborn so important? He implied that they could find kandra. . . .

She kept this tidbit to herself; she sensed that if she pointed it out, he'd close up again. So, instead, she sat up and met his eyes in the darkness. "If you wish, I will free you from your Contract."

"And what would that change?" OreSeur asked. "I'd just get another Contract. By our laws I must wait another decade before I have time for freedom—and then only two years, during which time I won't be able to leave the kandra Homeland. To do otherwise would risk exposure."

"Then, at least accept my apology," she asked. "I was foolish to resent you for following your Contract."

OreSeur paused. "That still doesn't fix things, Mistress. I still have to wear this cursed dog's body—I have no personality or bones to imitate!"

"I'd think that you would appreciate the opportunity simply to be yourself."

"I feel naked," OreSeur said. He sat quietly for a moment; then he bowed his head. "But . . . I have to admit that there are advantages to these bones. I didn't realize how unobtrusive they would make me."

Vin nodded. "There were times in my life when I would have given anything to be able to take the form of a dog and just live my life being ignored."

"But not anymore?"

Vin shook her head. "No. Not most of the time, anyway. I used to think that everyone was like you say—hateful, hurtful. But there are good people in the world, OreSeur. I wish I could prove that to you."

"You speak of this king of yours," OreSeur said, glancing toward the keep.

"Yes," Vin said. "And others."

"You?"

Vin shook her head. "No, not me. I'm not a good person or a bad person. I'm just here to kill things."

OreSeur watched her for a moment, then settled back down. "Regardless," he said, "you are not my worst master. That is, perhaps, a compliment among our people."

Vin smiled, but her own words left her a bit haunted. *Just here to kill things. . . .*

She glanced toward the light of the armies outside the city. A part—the part that had been trained by Reen, the part that still occasionally used his voice in the back of her mind—whispered that there was another way to fight these armies. Rather than rely on politics and parlays, the crew could use Vin. Send her on a quiet visit into the night that left the kings and generals of the armies dead.

But, she knew that Elend wouldn't approve of something like that. He'd argue against using fear to motivate, even on one's enemies. He'd point out that if she killed Straff or Cett, they'd just be replaced by other men, men even more hostile toward the city.

Even so, it seemed like such a brutal, logical answer. A piece of Vin itched to do it, if only to be doing something other than waiting and talking. She was not a person meant to be besieged.

No, she thought. *That's not my way. I don't have to be like Kelsier was. Hard. Unyielding. I can be something better. Something that trusts in Elend's way.*

She shoved aside that part of her that wanted to just go assassinate both Straff and Cett, then turned her attention to other things. She focused on her bronze, watching for signs of Allomancy. Though she liked to jump around and "patrol" the area, the truth was that she was just as effective staying in one place. Assassins would be likely to scout the front gates, for that was where patrols began and the largest concentration of soldiers waited.

Still, she felt her mind wandering. There were forces moving in the world, and Vin wasn't certain if she wanted to be part of them.

What is my place? she thought. She never felt that she'd discovered it—not back when she'd been playing as Valette Renoux, and not now, when she acted as the bodyguard to the man she loved. Nothing quite fit.

She closed her eyes, burning tin and bronze, feeling the touch of wind-borne mist on her skin. And, oddly, she felt something else, something very faint. In the distance she could sense Allomantic pulsings. They were so dull she almost missed them.

They were kind of like the pulses given off by the mist spirit. She could hear it, too, much closer. Atop a building out in the city. She was getting used to its presence, not that she had much choice. Still, as long as it only watched. . . .

It tried to kill one of the Hero's companions, she thought. *It knifed him, somehow.* Or so the logbook claimed.

But . . . what was that pulsing in the far distance? It was soft . . . yet powerful. Like a faraway drum. She squeezed her eyes shut, focusing.

"Mistress?" OreSeur said, suddenly perking up.

Vin snapped her eyes open. "What?"

"Didn't you hear that?"

Vin sat up. "Wha—" Then she picked it out. Footsteps outside the wall a short distance away. She leaned closer, noticing a dark figure walking down the street toward the keep. She'd been so focused on her bronze that she'd completely tuned out real sounds.

"Good job," she said, approaching the edge of the guard station's roof. Only then did she realize something important. OreSeur had taken the initiative: he'd alerted her of the danger without specifically being ordered to listen.

It was a small thing, but it seemed important.

"What do you think?" she asked quietly, watching the figure approach. He carried no torch, and he seemed very comfortable in the mists.

"Allomancer?" OreSeur asked, crouching beside her.

Vin shook her head. "There's no Allomantic pulse."

"So if he is one, he's Mistborn," OreSeur said. He still didn't know she could pierce copperclouds. "He's too tall to be your friend Zane. Be careful, Mistress."

Vin nodded, dropped a coin, then threw herself into the mists. Behind her, OreSeur jumped down from the guardhouse, then leapt off the wall and dropped some twenty feet to the ground.

He certainly does like to push the limits of those bones, she thought. Of course, if a fall couldn't kill him, then she could perhaps understand his courage.

She guided herself by Pulling on the nails in a wooden roof, landing just a short distance from the dark figure. She pulled out her knives and prepared her metals, making certain she had duralumin. Then she moved quietly across the street.

Surprise, she thought. Ham's suggestion still left her nervous. She couldn't always depend on surprise. She followed the man, studying him. He was tall—very tall. And in robes. In fact, those robes . . .

Vin stopped short. "Sazed?" she asked with shock.

The Terrisman turned, face now visible to her tin-enhanced eyes. He smiled. "Ah, Lady Vin," he said with his familiar, wise voice. "I was beginning to wonder how long it would take you to find me. You are—"

He was cut off as Vin grabbed him in an excited embrace. "I didn't think you were going to come back so soon!"

"I was not planning to return, Lady Vin," Sazed said. "But events are such that I could not avoid this place, I think. Come, we must speak with His Majesty. I have news of a rather disconcerting nature."

Vin let go, looking up at his kindly face, noting the tiredness in his eyes. Exhaustion. His robes were dirty and smelled of ash and sweat. Sazed was usually very meticulous, even when he traveled. "What is it?" she asked.

"Problems, Lady Vin," he said quietly. "Problems and troubles."

The Terris rejected him, but he came to lead them.

23

"KING LEKAL CLAIMED THAT HE had twenty thousand of the creatures in his army," Sazed said quietly.

Twenty thousand! Elend thought in shock. That was easily as dangerous as Straff's fifty thousand men. Probably more so.

The table fell silent, and Elend glanced at the others. They sat in the palace kitchen, where a couple of cooks hurriedly prepared a late-night dinner for Sazed. The white room had an alcove at the side with a modest table for servant meals. Not surprisingly, Elend had never dined in the room, but Sazed had insisted that they not wake the servants it would require to prepare the main dining hall, though he apparently hadn't eaten all day.

So, they sat on the low wooden benches, waiting while the cooks worked—far enough away that they couldn't hear the hushed conversation in the alcove. Vin sat beside Elend, arm around his waist, her wolfhound kandra on the floor beside her. Breeze sat on the other side of him, looking disheveled; he'd been rather annoyed when they'd woken him. Ham had already been up, as had Elend himself. Another proposal had needed work—a letter he would send to the Assembly explaining that he was meeting with Straff informally, rather than in official parlay.

Dockson pulled over a stool, choosing a place away from Elend, as usual. Clubs sat slumped on his side of the bench, though Elend couldn't tell if the posture was from weariness or from general Clubs grumpiness. That left only Spook, who sat on one of the serving tables a distance away, legs swinging over the side as he occasionally pilfered a tidbit of food from the annoyed cooks. He was, Elend noticed with amusement, flirting quite unsuccessfully with a drowsy kitchen girl.

And then there was Sazed. The Terrisman sat directly across from Elend with the calm sense of collectedness that only Sazed could manage. His robes were dusty, and he looked odd without his earrings—removed to not tempt thieves, Elend would guess—but his face and hands were clean. Even dirtied from travel, Sazed still gave off a sense of tidiness.

"I do apologize, Your Majesty," Sazed said. "But I do not think that Lord Lekal is trustworthy. I realize that you were friends with him before the Collapse, but his current state seems somewhat . . . unstable."

Elend nodded. "How is he controlling them, you think?"

Sazed shook his head. "I cannot guess, Your Majesty."

Ham shook his head. "I have men in the guard who came up from the South after the Collapse. They were soldiers, serving in a garrison near a koloss camp. The Lord Ruler hadn't been dead a day before the creatures went crazy. They attacked everything in the area—villages, garrisons, cities."

"The same happened in the Northwest," Breeze said. "Lord Cett's lands were being flooded with refugees running from rogue koloss. Cett tried to recruit the koloss garrison near his own lands, and they followed him for a time. But then, something set them off, and they just attacked his army. He had to slaughter the whole lot—and lost nearly two thousand soldiers killing a small garrison of five hundred koloss."

The group grew quiet again, the clacking and talking of the cooking staff sounding a short distance away. *Five hundred koloss killed two thousand men,* Elend thought. *And the Jastes force contains twenty thousand of the beasts. Lord Ruler . . .*

"How long?" said Clubs. "How far away?"

"It took me a little over a week to get here," Sazed said. "Though it looked as if King Lekal had been camped there for a time. He is obviously coming this direction, but I don't know how quickly he intends to march."

"Probably wasn't expecting to find that two other armies beat him to the city," Ham noted.

Elend nodded. "What do we do, then?"

"I don't see that we *can* do anything, Your Majesty," Dockson said, shaking his head. "Sazed's report doesn't give me much hope that we'll be able to reason with Jastes. And, with the siege we're already under, there is little we can do."

"He might just turn around and go," Ham said. "With two armies already here . . ."

Sazed looked hesitant. "He knew about the armies, Lord Hammond. He seemed to trust in his koloss over the human armies."

"With twenty thousand," Clubs said, "he could probably take *either* of those other armies."

"But he'd have trouble with both of them," Ham said. "*That* would give me pause, if I were him. By showing up with a pile of volatile koloss, he could easily worry Cett and Straff enough that they would join forces against him."

"Which would suit us just fine," Clubs said. "The more that *other* people fight, the better off we are."

Elend sat back. He felt a looming anxiety, and it was good to have Vin next to him, arm around him, even if she didn't say much. Sometimes, he felt stronger simply because of her presence. *Twenty thousand koloss.* This single threat scared him more than either of the other armies.

"This could be a good thing," Ham said. "If Jastes *were* to lose control of those beasts near Luthadel, there's a good chance they'd attack one of those other armies."

"Agreed," Breeze said tiredly. "I think we need to keep stalling, draw out this siege until the koloss army arrives. One more army in the mix means only more advantage for us."

"I don't like the idea of koloss in the area," Elend said, shivering slightly. "No matter what advantage they offer us. If they attack the city . . ."

"I say we worry about that when, and if, they arrive," Dockson said. "For now, we have to continue our plan as we intended. His Majesty meets with Straff, trying to manipulate him into a covert alliance with us. With luck, the imminent koloss presence will make him more willing to deal."

Elend nodded. Straff had agreed to meet, and they'd set a date for a few days away. The Assembly was angry that he hadn't consulted with them about the time and place, but there was little they could do about the matter.

"Anyway," Elend finally said, sighing. "You said you had other news, Saze? Better, hopefully?"

Sazed paused. A cook finally walked over, setting a plate of food before him: steamed barley with strips of steak and some spiced lagets. The scents were enough to make Elend a little hungry. He nodded thankfully to the palace chef, who had insisted on preparing the meal himself despite the late hour, and who waved to his staff and began to withdraw.

Sazed sat quietly, waiting to speak until the staff were again out of earshot. "I hesitate to mention this, Your Majesty, for your burdens already seem great."

"You might as well just tell me," Elend said.

Sazed nodded. "I fear that we may have exposed the world to something when we killed the Lord Ruler, Your Majesty. Something unanticipated."

Breeze raised a tired eyebrow. "Unanticipated? You mean other than ravaging koloss, power-hungry despots, and bandits?"

Sazed paused. "Um, yes. I speak of items a little more nebulous, I fear. There is something wrong with the mists."

Vin perked up slightly beside Elend. "What do you mean?"

"I have been following a trail of events," Sazed explained. He looked down as he spoke, as if embarrassed. "I have been performing an investigation, you might say. You see, I have heard numerous reports of the mists coming during the daytime."

Ham shrugged. "That happens sometimes. There are foggy days, especially in the fall."

"That is not what I mean, Lord Hammond," Sazed said. "There is a difference between the mist and ordinary fog. It is difficult to spot, perhaps, but it is noticeable to a careful eye. The mist is thicker, and . . . well . . ."

"It moves in larger patterns," Vin said quietly. "Like rivers in the sky. It never just hangs in one place; it floats in the breeze, almost like it makes the breeze."

"And it can't enter buildings," Clubs said. "Or tents. It evaporates soon after it does."

"Yes," Sazed said. "When I first heard these reports of day mist, I assumed that the people were just letting their superstitions get out of control. I have known many skaa who refused to go out on a foggy morning. However, I was curious about the reports, so I traced them to a village in the South. I taught there for some time, and never received confirmation of the stories. So, I made my way from that place."

He paused, frowning slightly. "Your Majesty, please do not think me mad. During those travels I passed a secluded valley, and saw what I swear was mist, not fog. It was moving across the landscape, creeping toward me. During the full light of day."

Elend glanced at Ham. He shrugged. "Don't look at me."

Breeze snorted. "He was asking your opinion, my dear man."

"Well, I don't have one."

"Some philosopher you are."

"I'm not a philosopher," Ham said. "I just like to think about things."

"Well, think about *this,* then," Breeze said.

Elend glanced at Sazed. "Have those two always been this way?"

"Honestly, I am not certain, Your Majesty," Sazed said, smiling slightly. "I have known them for only slightly longer than yourself."

"Yes, they've always been like this," Dockson said, sighing quietly. "If anything, they've gotten worse over the years."

"Aren't you hungry?" Elend asked, nodding to Sazed's plate.

"I can eat once our discussion is finished," Sazed said.

"Sazed, you're not a servant anymore," Vin said. "You don't have to worry about things like that."

"It is not a matter of serving or not, Lady Vin," Sazed said. "It is a matter of being polite."

"Sazed," Elend said.

"Yes, Your Majesty?"

He pointed at the plate. "Eat. You can be polite another time. Right now, you look famished—and you're among friends."

Sazed paused, giving Elend an odd look. "Yes, Your Majesty," he said, picking up a knife and spoon.

"Now," Elend began, "why does it matter if you saw mist during the day? We know that the things the skaa say aren't true—there's no reason to fear the mist."

"The skaa may be more wise than we credit them, Your Majesty," Sazed said, taking small, careful bites of food. "It appears that the mist has been killing people."

"What?" Vin asked, leaning forward.

"I have never seen it myself, Lady Vin," Sazed said. "But I have seen its effects, and have collected several separate reports. They all agree that the mist has been killing people."

"That's preposterous," Breeze said. "Mist is harmless."

"That is what I thought, Lord Ladrian," Sazed said. "However, several of the reports are quite detailed. The incidents always occurred during the day, and each one tells of the mist curling around some unfortunate individual, who then died—usually in a seizure. I gathered interviews with witnesses myself."

Elend frowned. From another man, he'd dismiss the news. But Sazed . . . he was not a man that one dismissed. Vin, sitting beside Elend, watched the conversation with interest, chewing slightly on her bottom lip. Oddly, she didn't object to Sazed's words—though the others seemed to be reacting as Breeze had.

"It doesn't make sense, Saze," Ham said. "Thieves, nobles, and Allomancers have gone out in the mists for centuries."

"Indeed they have, Lord Hammond," Sazed said with a nod. "The only explanation I can think of involves the Lord Ruler. I heard no substantive reports of mist deaths before the Collapse, but I have had little trouble finding them since. The reports are concentrated in the Outer Dominances, but the incidents appear to be moving inward. I found one . . . very disturbing incident several weeks to the south, where an entire village seems to have been trapped in their hovels by the mists."

"But, why would the Lord Ruler's death have anything to do with the mists?" Breeze asked.

"I am not certain, Lord Ladrian," Sazed said. "But it is the only connection I have been able to hypothesize."

Breeze frowned. "I wish you wouldn't call me that."

"I apologize, Lord Breeze," Sazed said. "I am still accustomed to calling people by their full names."

"Your name is Ladrian?" Vin asked.

"Unfortunately," Breeze said. "I've never been fond of it, and with dear Sazed putting 'Lord' before it . . . well, the alliteration makes it even more atrocious."

"Is it me," Elend said, "or are we going off on even more tangents than usual tonight?"

"We get that way when we're tired," Breeze said with a yawn. "Either way, our good Terrisman must have his facts wrong. Mist doesn't kill."

"I can only report what I have discovered," Sazed said. "I will need to do some more research."

"So, you'll be staying?" Vin asked, obviously hopeful.

Sazed nodded.

"What about teaching?" Breeze asked, waving his hand. "When you left, I recall that you said something about spending the rest of your life traveling, or some nonsense like that."

Sazed blushed slightly, glancing down again. "That duty will have to wait, I fear."

"You're welcome to stay as long as you want, Sazed," Elend said, shooting a glare at Breeze. "If what you say is true, then you'll be doing a greater service through your studies than you would by traveling."

"Perhaps," Sazed said.

"Though," Ham noted with a chuckle, "you probably could have picked a safer place to set up shop—one that isn't being pushed around by two armies and twenty thousand koloss."

Sazed smiled, and Elend gave an obligatory chuckle. *He said that the incidents involving the mist were moving inward, toward the center of the empire. Toward us.*

Something else to worry about.

"What's going on?" a voice suddenly asked. Elend turned toward the kitchen doorway, where a disheveled-looking Allrianne stood. "I heard voices. Is there a party?"

"We were just discussing matters of state interest, my dear," Breeze said quickly.

"The other girl is here," Allrianne said, pointing at Vin. "Why didn't you invite me?"

Elend frowned. *She heard voices? The guest quarters aren't anywhere near the kitchens.* And Allrianne was dressed, wearing a simple noblewoman's gown. She'd taken the time to get out of her sleeping clothing, but she'd left her hair disheveled. Perhaps to make herself look more innocent?

I'm starting to think like Vin, Elend told himself with a sigh. As if to corroborate his thoughts, he noticed Vin narrowing her eyes at the new girl.

"Go back to your rooms, dear," Breeze said soothingly. "Don't trouble His Majesty."

Allrianne sighed dramatically, but turned and did as he

asked, trailing off into the hallway. Elend turned back to Sazed, who was watching the girl with a curious expression. Elend gave him an "ask later" look, and the Terrisman turned back to his meal. A few moments later, the group began to break up. Vin hung back with Elend as the others left.

"I don't trust that girl," Vin said as a couple of servants took Sazed's pack and guided him away.

Elend smiled, turning to look down at Vin. "Do I have to say it?"

She rolled her eyes. "I know. 'You don't trust anyone, Vin.' This time I'm right. She was dressed, but her hair was disheveled. She must have done that intentionally."

"I noticed."

"You did?" She sounded impressed.

Elend nodded. "She must have heard the servants waking up Breeze and Clubs, so she got up. That means she spent a good half an hour eavesdropping. She kept her hair mussed so that we'd assume that she'd just come down."

Vin opened her mouth slightly, then frowned, studying him. "You're getting better," she eventually said.

"Either that, or Miss Allrianne just isn't very good."

Vin smiled.

"I'm still trying to figure out why you didn't hear her," Elend noted.

"The cooks," Vin said. "Too much noise. Besides, I was a little distracted by what Sazed was saying."

"And what do you think of it?"

Vin paused. "I'll tell you later."

"All right," Elend said. To Vin's side, the kandra rose and stretched its wolfhound body. *Why did she insist on bringing OreSeur to the meeting?* he wondered. *Wasn't it just a few weeks ago that she couldn't stand the thing?*

The wolfhound turned, glancing at the kitchen windows. Vin followed its gaze.

"Going back out?" Elend asked.

Vin nodded. "I don't trust this night. I'll stay near your balcony, in case there's trouble."

She kissed him; then she moved away. He watched her

go, wondering why she had been so interested in Sazed's stories, wondering what it was she wasn't telling him.

Stop it, he told himself. Perhaps he was learning her lessons a little too well—of all the people in the palace, Vin was the last one he needed to be paranoid about. However, every time he felt like he was beginning to figure Vin out, he realized just how little he understood her.

And that made everything else seem a little more depressing. With a sigh, he turned to seek out his rooms, where his half-finished letter to the Assembly waited to be completed.

Perhaps I should not have spoken of the mists, Sazed thought, following a servant up the stairs. *Now I've troubled the king about something that might just be my delusion.*

They reached the top of the stairs, and the servant asked if he wished a bath drawn. Sazed shook his head. In most other circumstances he would have welcomed the opportunity to get clean. However, running all the way to the Central Dominance, being captured by the koloss, then marching the rest of the way up to Luthadel had left him wearied to the farthest fringe of exhaustion. He'd barely had the strength to eat. Now he just wanted to sleep.

The servant nodded and led Sazed down a side corridor.

What if he was imagining connections that didn't exist? Every scholar knew that one of the greatest dangers in research was the desire to find a specific answer. He had not imagined the testimonies he had taken, but had he exaggerated their importance? What did he really have? The words of a frightened man who had seen his friend die of a seizure? The testimony of a lunatic, crazed to the point of cannibalism? The fact remained that Sazed himself had never seen the mists kill.

The servant led him to a guest chamber, and Sazed thankfully bid the man good night. He watched the man walk away, holding only a candle, his lamp left for Sazed to use. During most of Sazed's life, he had belonged to a class of servants prized for their refined sense of duty and decorum. He'd been in charge of households and manors, supervising servants just like the one who had led him to his rooms.

Another life, he thought. He had always been a little frustrated that his duties as a steward had left him little time for study. How ironic it was that he should help overthrow the Final Empire, then find himself with even less time.

He reached to push open the door, and froze almost immediately. There was already a light inside the room.

Did they leave a lamp on for me? he wondered. He slowly pushed the door open. Someone was waiting for him.

"Tindwyl," Sazed said quietly. She sat beside the room's writing desk, collected and neatly dressed, as always.

"Sazed," she replied as he stepped in, shutting the door. Suddenly, he was even more acutely aware of his dirty robes.

"You responded to my request," he said.

"And you ignored mine."

Sazed didn't meet her eyes. He walked over, setting his lamp on top of the room's bureau. "I noticed the king's new clothing, and he appears to have gained a bearing to match them. You have done well, I think."

"We are only just started," she said dismissively. "You were right about him."

"King Venture is a very good man," Sazed said, walking to the washbasin to wipe down his face. He welcomed the cold water; dealing with Tindwyl was bound to tire him even further.

"Good men can make terrible kings," Tindwyl noted.

"But bad men cannot make good kings," Sazed said. "It is better to start with a good man and work on the rest, I think."

"Perhaps," Tindwyl said. She watched him with her normal hard expression. Others thought her cold—harsh, even. But Sazed had never seen that in her. Considering what she had been through, he found it remarkable—amazing, even—that she was so confident. Where did she get it?

"Sazed, Sazed . . ." she said. "Why did you return to the Central Dominance? You know the directions the Synod gave you. You are supposed to be in the Eastern Dominance, teaching the people on the borders of the burnlands."

"That is where I was," Sazed said. "And now I am here. The South will get along for a time without me, I think."

"Oh?" Tindwyl asked. "And who will teach them irrigation techniques, so they can produce enough food to survive the cold months? Who will explain to them basic lawmaking principles so that they may govern themselves? Who will show them how to reclaim their lost faiths and beliefs? You were always so passionate about that."

Sazed set down the washcloth. "I will return to teach them when I am certain there is not a greater work I need to do."

"What greater work could there be?" Tindwyl demanded. "This is our life's duty, Sazed. This is the work of our entire *people*. I know that Luthadel is important to you, but there is nothing for you here. I will care for your king. You must go."

"I appreciate your work with King Venture," Sazed said. "My course has little to do with him, however. I have other research to do."

Tindwyl frowned, eyeing him with a cool stare. "You're still looking for this phantom connection of yours. This foolishness with the mists."

"There *is* something wrong, Tindwyl," he said.

"No," Tindwyl said, sighing. "Can't you see, Sazed? You spent ten years working to overthrow the Final Empire. Now, you can't content yourself with regular work, so you have invented some grand threat to the land. You're afraid of being irrelevant."

Sazed looked down. "Perhaps. If you are correct, then I will seek the forgiveness of the Synod. I should probably seek it anyway, I think."

"Oh, Sazed," Tindwyl said, shaking her head slightly. "I can't understand you. It makes sense when young fireheads like Vedzan and Rindel buck the Synod's advice. But you? You are the soul of what it means to be Terris—so calm, so humble, so careful and respectful. So wise. Why are you the one who consistently defies our leaders? It doesn't make sense."

"I am not so wise as you think, Tindwyl," Sazed said quietly. "I am simply a man who must do as he believes. Right now, I believe there to be a danger in the mists, and I must investigate my impressions. Perhaps it is simply arrogance and foolishness. But I would rather be known as arrogant and foolish than risk danger to the people of this land."

"You will find nothing."

"Then I will be proven wrong," Sazed said. He turned, looking into her eyes. "But kindly remember that the last time I disobeyed the Synod, the result was the collapse of the Final Empire and the freedom of our people."

Tindwyl made a tight-lipped frown. She didn't like being reminded of that fact—none of the Keepers did. They held that Sazed had been wrong to disobey, but they couldn't very well punish him for his success.

"I don't understand you," she repeated quietly. "You should be a leader among our people, Sazed. Not our greatest rebel and dissident. Everyone wants to look up to you—but they can't. Must you defy every order you are given?"

He smiled wanly, but did not answer.

Tindwyl sighed, rising. She walked toward the door, but paused, taking his hand as she passed. She looked into his eyes for a moment; then he removed the hand.

She shook her head and left.

He commanded kings, and though he sought no empire, he became greater than all who had come before.

24

SOMETHING IS GOING ON, VIN thought, sitting in the mists atop Keep Venture.

Sazed was not prone to exaggeration. He was meticulous—that much showed in his mannerisms, his cleanliness, and even the way he spoke. And, he was even more meticulous when it came to his studies. Vin was inclined to believe his discoveries.

And she'd certainly seen things in the mists. Dangerous things. Could the mist spirit explain the deaths Sazed had encountered? *But, if that's the case, why didn't Sazed speak of figures in the mist?*

She sighed, closing her eyes and burning bronze. She could hear the spirit, watching nearby. And, she could hear *it* again as well, the strange thumping in the distance. She opened her eyes, leaving her bronze on, and quietly unfolded something from her pocket: a sheet from the logbook. By the light from Elend's balcony below, and with tin, she could easily read the words.

> *I sleep but a few hours each night. We must press forward, traveling as much as we can each day—but when I finally lie down, I find sleep elusive. The same thoughts that trouble me during the day are only compounded by the stillness of night.*
>
> *And, above it all, I hear the thumping sounds from above, the pulsings from the mountains. Drawing me closer with each beat.*

She shivered. She had asked one of Elend's seekers to

burn bronze, and he had claimed to hear nothing from the north. Either he was the kandra, lying to her about his ability to burn bronze, or Vin could hear a rhythm that nobody else could. Nobody except a man a thousand years dead.

A man everyone had assumed was the Hero of Ages.

You're being silly, she told herself, refolding the paper. *Jumping to conclusions.* To her side, OreSeur rustled, lying quietly and staring out over the city.

And yet, she kept thinking of Sazed's words. Something was happening with the mists. Something was wrong.

Zane didn't find her atop Keep Hasting.

He stopped in the mists, standing quietly. He'd expected to find her waiting, for this was the place of their last fight. Even thinking of the event made him tense with anticipation.

During the months of sparring, they had always met again at the place where he'd eventually lost her. Yet, he'd returned to this location on several nights, and had never found her. He frowned, thinking of Straff's orders, and of necessity.

Eventually, he would likely be ordered to kill this girl. He wasn't certain what bothered him more—his growing reluctance to consider such an act, or his growing worry that he might not actually be able to beat her.

She could be it, he thought. *The thing that finally lets me resist. The thing that convinces me to just . . . leave.*

He couldn't explain why he needed a reason. Part of him simply ascribed it to his insanity, though the rational part of him felt that was a weak excuse. Deep down, he admitted that Straff was all he had ever known. Zane wouldn't be able to leave until he knew he had someone else to rely on.

He turned away from Keep Hasting. He'd had enough of waiting; it was time to seek her out. Zane threw a coin, bounding across the city for a time. And, sure enough, there she was: sitting atop Keep Venture, watching over his foolish brother.

Zane rounded the keep, keeping far enough away that even tin-enhanced eyes wouldn't see him. He landed on the back of the keep's roof, then walked forward quietly. He approached, watching her sit on the edge of the roof. The air was silent.

Finally, she turned around, jumping slightly. He swore that she could sense him when she shouldn't be able to.

Either way, he was discovered.

"Zane," Vin said flatly, easily identifying the silhouette. He wore his customary black on black, with no mistcloak.

"I've been waiting," he said quietly. "Atop Keep Hasting. Hoping you'd come."

She sighed, careful to keep an eye on him, but relaxing slightly. "I'm not really in the mood for sparring right now."

He watched her. "Pity," he finally said. He walked over, prompting Vin to rise cautiously to her feet. He paused beside the lip of the rooftop, looking down at Elend's lit balcony.

Vin glanced at OreSeur. He was tense, alternately watching her and Zane.

"You're so worried about him," Zane said quietly.

"Elend?" Vin asked.

Zane nodded. "Even though he uses you."

"We've had this discussion, Zane. He isn't using me."

Zane looked up at her, meeting her eyes, standing straight-backed and confident in the night.

He's so strong, she thought. *So sure of himself. So different from . . .*

She stopped herself.

Zane turned away. "Tell me, Vin," he said, "when you were younger, did you ever wish for power?"

Vin cocked her head, frowning at the strange question. "What do you mean?"

"You grew up on the streets," Zane said. "When you were younger, did you wish for power? Did you dream of having the ability to free yourself, to kill those who brutalized you?"

"Of course I did," Vin said.

"And now you have that power," Zane said. "What

would the child Vin say if she could see you? A Mistborn who is bent and bowed by the weight of another's will? Powerful, yet somehow still subservient?"

"I'm a different person now, Zane," Vin said. "I'd like to think that I've learned things since I was a child."

"I've found that a child's instincts are often the most honest," Zane said. "The most natural."

Vin didn't respond.

Zane turned quietly, looking out over the city, seemingly unconcerned that he was exposing his back to her. Vin eyed him, then dropped a coin. It plinked against the metal rooftop, and he immediately glanced back toward her.

No, she thought, *he doesn't trust me.*

He turned away again, and Vin watched him. She did understand what he meant, for she had once thought as he did. Idly, she wondered what kind of person she might have become if she'd gained full access to her powers without—at the same time—learning of friendship and trust from Kelsier's crew.

"What would you do, Vin?" Zane asked, turning back toward her. "Assuming you didn't have any constraints—assuming there were no repercussions for your actions?"

Go north. The thought was immediate. *Find out what is causing that thumping.* She didn't say it, however. "I don't know," she said instead.

He turned, eyeing her. "You aren't taking me seriously, I see. I apologize for wasting your time."

He turned to go, walking directly between her and Ore-Seur. Vin watched him, and felt a sudden stab of concern. He'd come to her, willing to talk rather than just fight—and she'd wasted the opportunity. She was never going to turn him to her side if she didn't talk to him.

"You want to know what I'd do?" she asked, her voice ringing in the silent mists.

Zane paused.

"If I could just use my power as I wanted?" Vin asked. "No repercussions? I'd protect him."

"Your king?" Zane asked, turning.

Vin nodded sharply. "These men who brought armies against him—your master, this man named Cett. I'd kill them. I'd use my power to make certain that nobody could threaten Elend."

Zane nodded quietly, and she saw respect in his eyes. "And why don't you?"

"Because . . ."

"I see the confusion in your eyes," Zane said. "You know that your instincts to kill those men are right—yet you hold back. Because of him."

"There *would* be repercussions, Zane," Vin said. "If I killed those men, their armies might just attack. Right now, diplomacy could still work."

"Perhaps," Zane said. "Until he *asks* you to go kill someone for him."

Vin snorted. "Elend doesn't work that way. He doesn't give me orders, and the only people I kill are the ones who try to kill him first."

"Oh?" Zane said. "You may not act at his order, Vin, but you certainly refrain from action at it. You are his toy. I don't say this to insult you—you see, I'm as much a toy as you are. Neither of us can break free. Not alone."

Suddenly, the coin Vin had dropped snapped into the air, flying toward Zane. She tensed, but it simply streaked into Zane's waiting hand.

"It's interesting," he said, turning the coin in his fingers. "Many Mistborn stop seeing the value in coins. To us, they simply become something to be used for jumping. It's easy to forget the value of something when you use it so often. When it becomes commonplace and convenient to you. When it becomes . . . just a tool."

He flipped the coin up, then shot it out into the night. "I must go," he said, turning.

Vin raised a hand. Seeing him use Allomancy made her realize that there was another reason she wanted to speak with him. It had been so long since she'd talked with another Mistborn, one who understood her powers. Someone like her.

But, it seemed to her that she was too desperate for him to stay. So she let him go, and returned to her vigil.

He fathered no children, yet all of the land became his progeny.

25

VIN WAS A VERY LIGHT sleeper—a heritage from her youth. Thieving crews worked together out of necessity, and any man who couldn't guard his own possessions was considered to be unworthy of them. Vin, of course, had been at the very bottom of the hierarchy—and while she hadn't had many possessions to protect, being a young girl in a primarily male environment gave her other reasons to be a light sleeper.

So it was that when she awoke to a quiet bark of warning, she reacted without thinking. She tossed off her covers, reaching immediately for the vial on her bedstand. She didn't sleep with metals inside of her; many of the Allomantic metals were, to some small extent, poisonous. It was unavoidable that she'd have to deal with some of that danger, but she had been warned to burn away excess metals at the end of each day.

She downed this vial even as she reached for the obsidian daggers hidden beneath her pillow. The door to her sleeping chamber swung open, and Tindwyl walked in. The Terriswoman froze in midstep as she saw Vin crouching on the bed's footboard a few feet away, twin daggers glistening, body tense.

Tindwyl raised an eyebrow. "So you are awake."

"Now."

The Terriswoman smiled.

"What are you doing in my rooms?" Vin demanded.

"I came to wake you. I thought we might go shopping."

"Shopping?"

"Yes, dear," Tindwyl said, walking over to pull open the curtains. It was far earlier in the day than Vin usually rose.

"From what I hear, you're going to meet with His Majesty's father on the morrow. You'll want a suitable dress for the occasion, I assume?"

"I don't wear dresses anymore." *What is your game?*

Tindwyl turned, eyeing Vin. "You sleep in your clothing?"

Vin nodded.

"You don't keep any ladies-in-waiting?"

Vin shook her head.

"Very well, then," Tindwyl said, turning to walk from the room. "Bathe and change. We'll leave when you're ready."

"I don't take commands from you."

Tindwyl paused by the door, turning. Then her face softened. "I know you don't, child. You may come with me if you wish—the choice is yours. However, do you really want to meet with Straff Venture in trousers and a shirt?"

Vin hesitated.

"At least come browse," Tindwyl said. "It will help take your mind off things."

Finally, Vin nodded. Tindwyl smiled again, then left.

Vin glanced at OreSeur, who sat beside her bed. "Thanks for the warning."

The kandra shrugged.

Once, Vin wouldn't have been able to imagine living in a place like Keep Venture. The young Vin had been accustomed to hidden lairs, skaa hovels, and the occasional alley. Now she lived in a building bespeckled with stained glass, bounded by mighty walls and grand archways.

Of course, Vin thought as she left the stairwell, *many things have happened that I didn't expect. Why think about them now?*

Her youth in the thieving crews had been much on her mind of late, and Zane's comments—ridiculous though they were—itched in her mind. Did Vin belong in a place like this keep? She had a great many skills, but few of them were beautiful hallway kinds of skills. They were more . . . ash-stained alleyway kinds of skills.

She sighed, OreSeur at her side as she made her way to the southern entryway, where Tindwyl said she'd be waiting. The hallway here grew wide and grand, and opened directly into the courtyard. Usually, coaches came right up into the entryway to pick up their occupants—that way the noblemen wouldn't be exposed to the elements.

As she approached, her tin let her hear voices. One was Tindwyl, the other . . .

"I didn't bring much," Allrianne said. "A couple hundred boxings. But I *do* so need something to wear. I can't survive on borrowed gowns forever!"

Vin paused as she turned into the last part of the hallway.

"The king's gift will surely be enough to pay for a dress, dear," Tindwyl said, noticing Vin. "Ah, here she is."

A sullen-looking Spook stood with the two women. He had on his palace guard's uniform, though he wore the jacket undone and the trousers loose. Vin walked forward slowly. "I wasn't expecting company," she said.

"Young Allrianne was trained as a courtly noblewoman," Tindwyl said. "She will know the current fashions, and will be able to advise on your purchases."

"And Spook?"

Tindwyl turned, eyeing the boy. "Packman."

Well, that explains his mood, Vin thought.

"Come," Tindwyl said, walking toward the courtyard. Allrianne followed quickly, walking with a light, graceful step. Vin glanced at Spook, who shrugged, and they followed as well.

"How did you get pulled into this?" Vin whispered to Spook.

"Was up too early, sneaking food," Spook grumbled. "Miss Imposing there noticed me, smiled like a wolfhound, and said, 'We'll be needing your services this afternoon, young man.'"

Vin nodded. "Stay alert and keep your tin burning. Remember, we're at war."

Spook obediently did what she said. Standing close to him as she was, Vin easily picked up and identified his tin's Allomantic pulses—meaning he wasn't the spy.

Another one off the list, Vin thought. *At least this trip won't be a total waste.*

A coach waited for them by the front keep gates. Spook climbed up beside the coachman, and the women piled into the back. Vin sat down inside, and OreSeur climbed in and took the seat next to her. Allrianne and Tindwyl sat across from her, and Allrianne eyed OreSeur with a frown, wrinkling her nose. "Does the animal have to sit on the seats with us?"

"Yes," Vin said as the carriage started moving.

Allrianne obviously expected more of an explanation, but Vin didn't give one. Finally, Allrianne turned to look out the window. "Are you sure we'll be safe, traveling with only one manservant, Tindwyl?"

Tindwyl eyed Vin. "Oh, I think that we'll be all right."

"Oh, that's right," Allrianne said, looking back at Vin. "You're an Allomancer! Are the things they say true?"

"What things?" Vin asked quietly.

"Well, they say you killed the Lord Ruler, for one. And that you're kind of . . . um . . . well." Allrianne bit her lip. "Well, just a little bit rickety."

"Rickety?"

"And dangerous," Allrianne said. "But, well, that can't be true. I mean, you're going shopping with us, right?"

Is she trying to provoke me on purpose?

"Do you always wear clothing like that?" Allrianne asked.

Vin was in her standard gray trousers and tan shirt. "It's easy to fight in."

"Yes, but . . . well." Allrianne smiled. "I guess that's why we're here today, right, Tindwyl?"

"Yes, dear," Tindwyl said. She'd been studying Vin through the entire conversation.

Like what you see? Vin thought. *What is it you want?*

"You have to be the strangest noblewoman I've ever met," Allrianne declared. "Did you grow up far from court? I did, but my mother was quite certain to train me well. Of course, she was just trying to make me into a good catch so Father could auction me off to make an alliance."

Allrianne smiled. It had been a while since Vin had been

forced to deal with women like her. She remembered hours spent at court, smiling, pretending to be Valette Renoux. Often when she thought of those days, she remembered the bad things. The spite she'd faced from court members, her own lack of comfort in the role.

But, there had also been good things. Elend was one. She would never have met him if she hadn't been pretending to be a noblewoman. And the balls—with their colors, their music, and their gowns—had held a certain transfixing charm. The graceful dancing, the careful interactions, the perfectly decorated rooms . . .

Those things are gone now, she told herself. *We don't have time for silly balls and gatherings, not when the dominance is on the verge of collapse.*

Tindwyl was still watching her.

"Well?" Allrianne asked.

"What?" Vin asked.

"Did you grow up far from court?"

"I'm not noble, Allrianne. I'm skaa."

Allrianne paled, then flushed, then raised her fingers to her lips. "Oh! You poor thing!" Vin's augmented ears heard something beside her—a light chuckling from Ore-Seur, soft enough that only an Allomancer could have heard him.

She resisted the urge to shoot the kandra a flat look. "It wasn't so bad," she said.

"But, well, no wonder you don't know how to dress!" Allrianne said.

"I know how to dress," Vin said. "I even own a few gowns." *Not that I've put one on in months. . . .*

Allrianne nodded, though she obviously didn't believe Vin's comment. "Breezy is skaa, too," she said quietly. "Or, half skaa. He told me. Good thing he didn't tell Father—Father never has been very nice to skaa."

Vin didn't reply.

Eventually, they reached Kenton Street, and the crowds made the carriage a liability. Vin climbed out first, OreSeur hopping down to the cobblestones beside her. The market street was busy, though not as packed as it had been the last time she'd visited. Vin glanced over the prices at some nearby shops as the others exited the coach.

Five boxings for a bin of aging apples, Vin thought with dissatisfaction. *Food is already going at a premium.* Elend had stores, fortunately. But how long would they last before the siege? Not through the approaching winter, certainly—not with so much of the dominance's grain still unharvested in the outer plantations.

Time may be our friend now, Vin thought, *but it will turn on us eventually.* They had to get those armies to fight each other. Otherwise, the city's people might die of starvation before the soldiers even tried to take the walls.

Spook hopped down from the carriage, joining them as Tindwyl surveyed the street. Vin eyed the bustling crowds. The people were obviously trying to go about their daily activities, despite the threat from outside. What else could they do? The siege had already lasted for weeks. Life had to go on.

"There," Tindwyl said, pointing to a dressmaker's shop.

Allrianne scampered forward. Tindwyl followed behind, walking with modest decorum. "Eager young thing, isn't she?" the Terriswoman asked.

Vin shrugged. The blond noblewoman had already gotten Spook's attention; he was following her with a lively step. Of course, it wasn't hard to get Spook's attention. You just had to have breasts and smell nice—and the second was sometimes optional.

Tindwyl smiled. "She probably hasn't had an opportunity to go shopping since she left with her father's army weeks ago."

"You sound like you think she went through some awful ordeal," Vin said. "Just because she couldn't go shopping."

"She obviously enjoys it," Tindwyl said. "Surely you can understand being taken from that which you love."

Vin shrugged as they reached the shop. "I have trouble feeling sympathy for a courtly puff who is tragically taken from her dresses."

Tindwyl frowned slightly as they entered the shop, Ore-Seur settling down to wait outside. "Do not be so hard on the child. She is a product of her upbringing, just as you are. If you judge her worth based on frivolities, then you are doing the same as those who judge you based on your simple clothing."

"I like it when people judge me based on my simple clothing," Vin said. "Then they don't expect too much."

"I see," Tindwyl said. "Then, you haven't missed this at all?" She nodded toward the shop's inner room.

Vin paused. The room burst with colors and fabric, lace and velvet, bodices and skirts. Everything was powdered with a light perfume. Standing before the dressing dummies in their brilliant hues, Vin was—for just a moment—again taken back to the balls. Back to when she was Valette. Back to when she had an *excuse* to be Valette.

"They say you enjoyed noble society," Tindwyl said lightly, walking forward. Allrianne was already standing near the front of the room, running her fingers across a bolt of fabric, talking to the dressmaker in a firm voice.

"Who told you that?" Vin asked.

Tindwyl turned back. "Why, your friends, dear. It's quite curious—they say you stopped wearing dresses a few months after the Collapse. They all wonder why. They say you seemed to like dressing like a woman, but I guess they were wrong."

"No," Vin said quietly. "They were right."

Tindwyl raised an eyebrow, pausing beside a dressmaker's dummy in a bright green dress, edged with lace, the bottom flaring wide with several underskirts.

Vin approached, looking up at the gorgeous costume. "I was beginning to like dressing like this. That was the problem."

"I don't see a problem in that, dear."

Vin turned away from the gown. "This isn't me. It never was—it was just an act. When wearing a dress like that, it's too easy to forget who you really are."

"And these dresses can't be part of who you really are?"

Vin shook her head. "Dresses and gowns are part of who *she* is." She nodded toward Allrianne. "I need to be something else. Something harder." *I shouldn't have come here.*

Tindwyl laid a hand on Vin's shoulder. "Why haven't you married him, child?"

Vin looked up sharply. "What kind of question is that?"

"An honest one," Tindwyl said. She seemed far less harsh than she had been the other times Vin had met her. Of course, during those times, she had mostly been addressing Elend.

"That topic is not your concern," Vin said.

"The king has asked me to help him improve his image," Tindwyl said. "And I have taken it upon myself to do more than that—I want to make a real king of him, if I can. There is some great potential in him, I think. However, he's not going to be able to realize it until he's more sure about certain things in his life. You in particular."

"I . . ." Vin closed her eyes, remembering his marriage proposal. That night, on the balcony, ash lightly falling in the night. She remembered her terror. She'd known, of course, where the relationship was going. Why had she been so frightened?

That was the day she'd stopped wearing dresses.

"He shouldn't have asked me," Vin said quietly, opening her eyes. "He can't marry me."

"He loves you, child," Tindwyl said. "In a way, that is unfortunate—this would all be much easier if he could feel otherwise. However, as things stand . . ."

Vin shook her head. "I'm wrong for him."

"Ah," Tindwyl said. "I see."

"He needs something else," Vin said. "Something better. A woman who can be a queen, not just a bodyguard. Someone . . ." Vin's stomach twisted. "Someone more like her."

Tindwyl glanced toward Allrianne, who laughed at a comment made by the elderly dressmaker as he took her measurements.

"You are the one he fell in love with, child," Tindwyl said.

"When I was pretending to be like her."

Tindwyl smiled. "Somehow, I doubt that you could be like Allrianne, no matter how hard you practiced."

"Perhaps," Vin said. "Either way, it was my courtly performance that he loved. He didn't know what I really was."

"And has he abandoned you now that he does know of it?"

"Well, no. But—"

"All people are more complex than they first appear," Tindwyl said. "Allrianne, for instance, is eager and young—perhaps a bit too outspoken. But she knows more of the court than many would expect, and she seems to know how to recognize what is good in a person. That is a talent many lack.

"Your king is a humble scholar and thinker, but he has the will of a warrior. He is a man who has the nerve to fight, and I think—perhaps—you have yet to see the best of him. The Soother Breeze is a cynical, mocking man—until he looks at young Allrianne. Then he softens, and one wonders how much of his harsh unconcern is an act."

Tindwyl paused, looking at Vin. "And you. You are so much more than you are willing to accept, child. Why look at only one side of yourself, when your Elend sees so much more?"

"Is that what this is all about?" Vin said. "You trying to turn me into a queen for Elend?"

"No, child," Tindwyl said. "I wish to help you turn into whoever you are. Now, go let the man take your measurements so you can try on some stock dresses."

Whoever I am? Vin thought, frowning. However, she let the tall Terriswoman push her forward, and the elderly dressmaker took his tape and began to measure.

A few moments and a changing room later, Vin stepped back into the room wearing a memory. Silky blue with white lace, the gown was tight at the waist and through the bust, but had a large, flowing bottom. The numerous skirts made it flare out, tapering down in a triangular shape, her feet completely covered, the bottom of the skirt flush with the floor.

It was terribly impractical. It rustled when she moved, and she had to be careful where she stepped to keep it from catching or brushing a dirty surface. But it was beautiful, and it made her feel beautiful. She almost expected a band to start playing, Sazed to stand over her shoulder like a protective sentry, and Elend to appear in the distance, lounging and watching couples dance as he flipped through a book.

Vin walked forward, letting the dressmaker watch where the garment pinched and where it bunched, and Allrianne let out an "Ooo" as she saw Vin. The old dressmaker leaned on his cane, dictating notes to a young assistant. "Move around a bit more, my lady," he requested. "Let me see how it fits when you do more than just walk in a straight line."

Vin spun slightly, turning on one foot, trying to remember the dancing moves Sazed had taught her.

I never did get to dance with Elend, she realized, stepping to the side, as if to music she could only faintly remember. *He always found an excuse to wiggle out of it.*

She twirled, getting a feel for the dress. She would have thought that her instincts would have decayed. Now that she had one on again, however, she was surprised at how easy it was to fall back into those habits—stepping lightly, turning so that the bottom of the dress flared just a bit. . . .

She paused. The dressmaker was no longer dictating. He watched her quietly, smiling.

"What?" Vin asked, flushing.

"I'm sorry, my lady," he said, turning to tap on his assistant's notebook, sending the boy away with a point of his finger. "But I don't rightly think I've ever seen someone move so gracefully. Like a . . . passing breath."

"You flatter me," Vin said.

"No, child," Tindwyl said, standing to the side. "He's right. You move with a grace that most women can only envy."

The dressmaker smiled again, turning as his assistant approached with a group of square cloth color samples. The old man began to sort through them with a wizened hand, and Vin stepped over to Tindwyl, holding her hands at the sides, trying not to let the traitorous dress take control of her again.

"Why are you being so nice to me?" Vin demanded quietly.

"Why shouldn't I be?" Tindwyl asked.

"Because you're mean to Elend," Vin said. "Don't deny it—I've listened in on your lessons. You spend the time insulting and disparaging him. But now you're pretending to be nice."

Tindwyl smiled. "I am not pretending, child."

"Then why are you so mean to Elend?"

"The lad grew up as a pampered son of a great lord," Tindwyl said. "Now that he's king, he needs a little harsh truth, I think." She paused, glancing down at Vin. "I sense that you've had quite enough of that in your life."

The dressmaker approached with his swatches, spreading them out on a low table. "Now, my lady," he said, tapping one group with a bent finger. "I think your coloring would look particularly good with dark cloth. A nice maroon, perhaps?"

"What about a black?" Vin asked.

"Heavens, no," Tindwyl said. "Absolutely no more black or gray for you, child."

"What about this one, then?" Vin asked, pulling out a royal blue swatch. It was nearly the shade she'd worn the first night she'd met Elend, so long ago.

"Ah, yes," the dressmaker said. "That would look wonderful against that light skin and dark hair. Hum, yes. Now, we'll have to pick a style. You need this by tomorrow evening, the Terriswoman said?"

Vin nodded.

"Ah, then. We'll have to modify one of the stock dresses, but I think I have one in this color. We'll have to take it in quite a bit, but we can work through the night for a beauty like yourself, can't we, lad? Now, as for the style . . ."

"This is fine, I guess," Vin said, looking down. The gown was the standard cut of those she'd worn at previous balls.

"Well, we're not looking for 'fine,' now, are we?" the dressmaker said with a smile.

"What if we removed some of the pettiskirts?" Tindwyl said, pulling at the sides of Vin's dress. "And perhaps raised the hem just a bit, so that she could move more freely?"

Vin paused. "You could do that?"

"Of course," the dressmaker said. "The lad says thinner skirts are more popular to the south, though they tend to lag in fashion a bit behind Luthadel." He paused. "Though, I don't know that Luthadel even really *has* a fashion anymore. . . ."

"Make cuffs of the sleeves wide," Tindwyl said. "And sew a couple of pockets into them for certain personal items."

The old man nodded as his quiet assistant scribbled down the suggestion.

"The chest and waist can be tight," Tindwyl continued, "but not restrictive. Lady Vin needs to be able to move freely."

The old man paused. "Lady Vin?" he asked. He looked a little closer at Vin, squinting, then turned to his assistant. The boy nodded quietly.

"I see . . ." the man said, paling, hand shaking just a little bit more. He placed it on the top of his cane, as if to give himself a little more stability. "I'm . . . I'm sorry if I offended you, my lady. I didn't know."

Vin flushed again. *Another reason why I shouldn't go shopping.* "No," she said, reassuring the man. "It's all right. You haven't offended me."

He relaxed slightly, and Vin noticed Spook strolling over.

"Looks like we've been found," Spook said, nodding to the front windows.

Vin glanced past dressing dummies and bales of cloth to see a crowd gathering outside. Tindwyl watched Vin with curiosity.

Spook shook his head. "Why do you get to be so popular?"

"I killed their god," Vin said quietly, ducking around a dressing dummy, hiding from the dozens of peeking eyes.

"I helped too," Spook said. "I even got my nickname from Kelsier himself! But nobody cares about poor little Spook."

Vin scanned the room for windows. *There's got to be a back door. Of course, there might be people in the alley.*

"What are you doing?" Tindwyl asked.

"I have to go," Vin said. "Get away from them."

"Why don't you go out and talk to them?" Tindwyl asked. "They're obviously very interested in seeing you."

Allrianne emerged from a dressing room—wearing a gown of yellow and blue—and twirled dramatically. She was obviously put out when she didn't even get Spook's attention.

"I'm not going out there," Vin said. "Why would I want to do something like that?"

"They need hope," Tindwyl said. "Hope you can give them."

"A false hope," Vin said. "I'd only encourage them to think of me as some object of worship."

"That's not true," Allrianne said suddenly, walking forward, looking out the windows without the least bit of embarrassment. "Hiding in corners, wearing strange clothing, and being mysterious—*that's* what has gotten you this amazing reputation. If people knew how ordinary you were, they wouldn't be so crazy to get a look at you." She paused, then looked back. "I . . . uh, didn't mean that like I think it sounded."

Vin flushed. "I'm not Kelsier, Tindwyl. I don't want people to worship me. I just want to be left alone."

"Some people don't have that choice, child," Tindwyl said. "You struck down the Lord Ruler. You were trained by the Survivor, and you are the king's consort."

"I'm not his consort," Vin said, flushing. "We're just . . ." *Lord, even I don't understand our relationship. How am I supposed to explain it?*

Tindwyl raised an eyebrow.

"All right," Vin said, sighing and walking forward.

"I'll go with you," Allrianne said, grabbing Vin's arm as if they had been friends since childhood. Vin resisted, but couldn't figure a way to pry her off without making a scene.

They stepped out of the shop. The crowd was already large, and the periphery was filling as more and more people came to investigate. Most were skaa in brown, ash-stained work coats or simple gray dresses. The ones in the front backed away as Vin stepped out, giving her a little ring of empty space, and a murmur of awed excitement moved through the crowd.

"Wow," Allrianne said quietly. "There sure are a lot of them. . . ."

Vin nodded. OreSeur sat where he had before, near the door, and he watched her with a curious canine expression.

Allrianne smiled at the crowd, waving with a sudden hesitance. "You can, you know, fight them off or something if this turns messy, right?"

"That won't be necessary," Vin said, finally slipping her arm free of Allrianne's grasp and giving the crowd a bit of a Soothing to calm them. After that, she stepped forward, trying to push down her sense of itching nervousness. She'd grown to no longer feel she needed to hide when she went out in public, but standing before a crowd like this . . . well, she almost turned and slinked back into the dressmaker's shop.

A voice, however, stopped her. The speaker was a middle-aged man with an ash-stained beard and a dirty black cap held nervously in his hands. He was a strong man, probably a mill worker. His quiet voice seemed a contrast to his powerful build. "Lady Heir. What will become of us?"

The terror—the uncertainty—in the large man's voice was so piteous that Vin hesitated. He regarded her with hopeful eyes, as did most of the others.

So many, Vin thought. *I thought the Church of the Survivor was small.* She looked at the man, who stood wringing his cap. She opened her mouth, but then . . . couldn't do it. She couldn't tell him that she didn't know what would happen; she couldn't explain to those eyes that she wasn't the savior that he needed.

"Everything will be all right," Vin heard herself say, increasing her Soothing, trying to take away some of their fear.

"But the armies, Lady Heir!" one of the women said.

"They're trying to intimidate us," Vin said. "But the king won't let them. Our walls are strong, as are our soldiers. We can outlast this siege."

The crowd was silent.

"One of those armies is led by Elend's father, Straff Venture," Vin said. "Elend and I are going to go meet with Straff tomorrow. We will persuade him to be our ally."

"The king is going to surrender!" a voice said. "I heard it. He's going to trade the city for his life."

"No," Vin said. "He would never do that!!"

"He won't fight for us!" a voice called. "He's not a soldier. He's a politician!"

Other voices called out in agreement. Reverence disappeared as people began to yell out concerns, while others began to demand help. The dissidents continued to rail against Elend, yelling that there was no way he could protect them.

Vin raised her hands to her ears. Trying to ward off the crowd, the chaos. *"Stop!"* she yelled, Pushing out with steel and brass. Several people stumbled back away from her, and she could see a wave in the crowd as buttons, coins, and buckles suddenly pressed backward.

The people grew suddenly quiet.

"I will suffer no ill words spoken of our king!" Vin said, flaring her brass and increasing her Soothing. "He is a good man, and a good leader. He has sacrificed much for you—your freedom comes because of his long hours spent drafting laws, and your livelihoods come because of his work securing trade routes and agreements with merchants."

Many members of the crowd looked down. The bearded man at the front continued to twist his cap, however, looking at Vin. "They're just right frightened, Lady Heir. Right frightened."

"We'll protect you," Vin said. *What am I saying?* "Elend and I, we'll find a way. We stopped the Lord Ruler. We can stop these armies . . ." She trailed off, feeling foolish.

Yet, the crowd responded. Some were obviously still unsatisfied, but many seemed calmed. The crowd began to break up, though some of its members came forward, leading or carrying small children. Vin paused nervously. Kelsier had often met with and held the children of the skaa, as if giving them his blessing. She bid the group a hasty farewell and ducked back into the shop, pulling Allrianne after her.

Tindwyl waited inside, nodding with satisfaction.

"I lied," Vin said, pushing the door closed.

"No you didn't," Tindwyl said. "You were optimistic. The truth or fiction of what you said has yet to be proven."

"It won't happen," Vin said. "Elend can't defeat three armies, not even with my help."

Tindwyl raised an eyebrow. "Then you should leave. Run away, leave the people to deal with the armies themselves."

"I didn't mean that," Vin said.

"Well, make a decision then," Tindwyl said. "Either give up on the city or believe in it. Honestly, the pair of you. . . ." She shook her head.

"I thought you weren't going to be harsh with me," Vin noted.

"I have trouble with that sometimes," Tindwyl said. "Come, Allrianne. Let's finish your fitting."

They moved to do so. However, at that moment—as if to belie Vin's assurances of safety—several warning drums began to beat atop the city wall.

Vin froze, glancing through the window, out over the anxious crowd.

One of the armies was attacking. Cursing the delay, she rushed into the back of the shop to change out of the bulky dress.

Elend scrambled up the steps to the city wall, nearly tripping on his dueling cane in his haste. He stumbled out of the stairwell, moving onto the wall top, rearranging the cane at his side with a curse.

The wall top was in chaos. Men scrambled about, calling to each other. Some had forgotten their armor, others their bows. So many tried to get up after Elend that the stairwell got clogged, and he watched hopelessly as men crowded around the openings below, creating an even larger jam of bodies in the courtyard.

Elend spun, watching a large group of Straff's men—thousands of them—rush toward the wall. Elend stood near Tin Gate, at the north of the city, nearest Straff's army. He could see a separate group of soldiers rushing toward Pewter Gate, a little to the east.

"Archers!" Elend yelled. "Men, where are your bows?"

His voice, however, was lost in the shouting. Captains moved about, trying to organize the men, but apparently too many footmen had come to the wall, leaving a lot of the archers trapped in the courtyard below.

Why? Elend thought desperately, turning back toward the charging army. *Why is he attacking? We had an a agreement to meet!*

Had he, perhaps, gotten wind of Elend's plan to play both sides of the conflict? Perhaps there really *was* a spy in the inner crew.

Either way, Elend could only watch hopelessly as the army approached his wall. One captain managed to get off a pathetic volley of arrows, but it didn't do much good. As the army approached, arrows began to zip up toward the wall, mixed with flying coins. Straff had Allomancers in the group.

Elend cursed, ducking down below a merlon as coins bounced against the stonework. A few soldiers fell. Elend's soldiers. Killed because he'd been too proud to surrender the city.

He peeked carefully over the wall. A group of men carrying a battering ram were approaching, their bodies carefully protected by men with shields. The care probably meant that the rammers were Thugs, a suspicion confirmed by the sound the ram made when it smashed into the gate. That was not the blow of ordinary men.

Hooks followed next. Shot up toward the wall by Coinshots below, falling far more accurately than if they'd been thrown. Soldiers moved to pull them off, but coins shot up, taking the men almost as quickly as they made the attempt. The gate continued to thump beneath him, and he doubted it would last for long.

And so we fall, Elend thought. *With barely a hint of resistance.*

And there was nothing he could do. He felt impotent, forced to keep ducking down lest his white uniform make him a target. All of his politicking, all of his preparations, all of his dreams and his plans. Gone.

And then Vin was there. She landed atop the wall, breathing hard, amid a group of wounded men. Coins and arrows that came near to her deflected back out into the air. Men rallied around her, moving to remove hooks and pull the wounded to safety. Her knives cut ropes, dropping them back down below. She met Elend's eyes, looking determined, then moved as if to leap over the side of the wall and confront the Thugs with their battering ram.

Elend raised a hand, but someone else spoke.

"Vin, wait!" Clubs bellowed, bursting out of the stairwell.

She paused. Elend had never heard such a forceful command from the gnarled general.

Arrows stopped flying. The booming calmed. Elend stood hesitantly, watching with a frown as the army retreated back across the ash-strewn fields toward their camp. They left a couple of corpses behind; Elend's men had actually managed to hit a few with their arrows. His own army had taken far heavier casualties: some two dozen men appeared to be wounded.

"What . . . ?" Elend asked, turning to Clubs.

"They weren't putting up scaling ladders," Clubs said, eyeing the retreating force. "This wasn't an actual attack."

"What was it then?" Vin asked, frowning.

"A test," Clubs said. "It's common in warfare—a quick skirmish to see how your enemy responds, to feel out their tactics and preparations."

Elend turned, watching the disorganized soldiers make way for healers to care for the wounded. "A test," he said, glancing at Clubs. "My guess is that we didn't do very well."

Clubs shrugged. "Far worse than we should have. Maybe this will scare the lads into paying better attention during drills." He paused, and Elend could see something he wasn't expressing. Worry.

Elend glanced out over the wall, watching the retreating

army. Suddenly, it made sense. It was exactly the kind of move that his father liked to make.

The meeting with Straff would take place as planned. However, before it happened, Straff wanted Elend to know something.

I can take this city any time, the attack seemed to say. *It's mine, no matter what you do. Remember that.*

He was forced into war by a misunderstanding—and always claimed he was no warrior—yet he came to fight as well as any man.

26

"THIS IS NOT A GOOD idea, Mistress." OreSeur sat on his haunches, watching Vin unpack a large, flat box.

"Elend thinks it's the only way," she said, pulling off the top of the box. The luxurious blue dress lay wrapped within. She pulled it out, noting its comparatively light weight. She walked over to the changing screen and began to disrobe.

"And the assault on the walls yesterday?" OreSeur asked.

"That was a warning," she said, continuing to unbutton her shirt. "Not a serious attack." Though, apparently, it had really unsettled the Assembly. Perhaps that had been the point. Clubs could say all he wished about strategy and testing the walls, but from Vin's standpoint, the thing Straff had gained most was even more fear and chaos inside Luthadel.

Only a few weeks of being besieged, and the city was already strained near to breaking. Food was terribly expensive, and Elend had been forced to open the city stockpiles. The people were on edge. Some few thought the attack had been a victory for Luthadel, taking it as a good sign that the army had been "repelled." Most, however, were simply even more scared than they had been before.

But, again, Vin was left with a conundrum. How to react, facing such an overpowering force? Cower, or try to continue with life? Straff had tested the walls, true—but he had maintained the larger part of his army back and in position, should Cett have tried to make an opportunistic attack at that time. He'd wanted information, and he'd wanted to intimidate the city.

"I still don't know if this meeting is a good idea," Ore-Seur said. "The attack aside, Straff is not a man to be trusted. Kelsier had me study all of the major noblemen in the city when I was preparing to become Lord Renoux. Straff is deceitful and harsh, even for a human."

Vin sighed, removing her trousers, then pulled on the dress's slip. It wasn't as tight as some, and gave her a lot of room to move through the thigh and legs. *Good so far.*

OreSeur's objection was logical. One of the first things she had learned on the street was to avoid situations where it was difficult to flee. Her every instinct rebelled at the idea of walking into Straff's camp.

Elend had made his decision, however. And, Vin understood that she needed to support him. In fact, she was even coming to agree with the move. Straff wanted to intimidate the entire city—but he really wasn't as threatening as he thought. Not as long as he had to worry about Cett.

Vin had had enough of intimidation in her life. In a way, Straff's attack on the walls left her feeling even more determined to manipulate him to their own ends. Going into his camp seemed a bit crazy on first impression, but the more she thought about it, the more she realized that it was the only way they were going to get to Straff. He had to see them as weak, had to feel that his bullying tactics had worked. That was the only way they would win.

That meant doing something she didn't like. It meant being surrounded, entering the enemy's den. However, if

Elend did manage to get out of the camp safely, it would provide a large morale boost for the city. Beyond that, it would make Ham and the rest of the crew more confident in Elend. Nobody would even have questioned the idea of Kelsier entering an enemy camp to negotiate; in fact, they probably would have expected him to come back from the negotiations somehow having convinced Straff to surrender.

I just need to make sure he comes back out safely, Vin thought, pulling on the dress. *Straff can display all the muscle he wants—none of it will matter if we're the ones directing his attacks.*

She nodded to herself, smoothing her dress. Then she walked out from behind the changing screen, studying herself in her mirror. Though the dressmaker had obviously sewn it to retain a traditional form, it didn't have a completely triangular bell shape, but instead fell a bit straighter down along her thighs. It was cut open near the shoulders—though it had tight sleeves and open cuffs—and the waist bent with her and gave her a good range of motion.

Vin stretched a bit, jumping, twisting. She was surprised at how light the dress felt, and how well she moved in it. Of course, any skirt would hardly be ideal for fighting—but this one would be an enormous improvement over the bulky creations she had worn to the parties a year before.

"Well?" she asked, spinning.

OreSeur raised a canine eyebrow. "What?"

"What do you think?"

OreSeur cocked his head. "Why ask me?"

"Because I care what you think," Vin said.

"The dress is very nice, Mistress. Though, to be honest, I have always found the garments to be a little ridiculous. All of that cloth and color, it doesn't seem very practical."

"Yes, I know," Vin said, using a pair of sapphire barrettes to pin the sides of her hair back a bit from her face. "But . . . well, I'd forgotten how much fun these things could be to wear."

"I fail to see why that would be, Mistress."

"That's because you're a man."

"Actually, I'm a kandra."

"But you're a boy kandra."

"How do you know that?" OreSeur asked. "Gender is not easy to tell in my people, since our forms are fluid."

Vin looked at him, raising an eyebrow. "I can tell." Then she turned back to her jewelry cabinet. She didn't have much; though the crew had outfitted her with a good sampling of jewelry during her days as Valette, she had given most of it to Elend to help fund various projects. She had, however, kept a few of her favorites—as if she'd known that she'd someday find her way back into a dress.

I'm just wearing it this once, she thought. *This still isn't me.*

She snapped on a sapphire bracelet. Like her barrettes, it contained no metal; the gemstones were set into a thick hardwood that closed with a wooden twist-clasp. The only metal on her body, then, would be her coins, her metal vial, and the single earring. Kept, by Kelsier's suggestion, as a bit of metal she could Push on in an emergency.

"Mistress," OreSeur said, pulling something out from under her bed with his paw. A sheet of paper. "This fell from the box as you were opening it." He grabbed it between two of his surprisingly dexterous paw fingers and held it up for her.

Vin accepted the paper. *Lady Heir,* it read.

> *I made the chest and bodice extra tight to give support— and cut the skirts so they would resist flaring—in case you need to jump. There are slits for metal vials in each of the cuffs, as well as a ripple in the cloth cut to obscure a dagger strapped around each forearm. I hope you find the alterations suitable.*
>   *Feldeu, Dressmaker.*

She glanced down, noting the cuffs. They were thick and wide, and the way they pointed at the sides made perfect hiding places. Though the sleeves were tight around the upper arms, the forearms were looser, and she could see where the daggers could be strapped.

"It seems that he has made dresses for Mistborn before," OreSeur noted.

"Probably," Vin said. She moved over to her dressing mirror to apply a little makeup, and found that several of her makeup pads had dried out. *Guess I haven't done this for a while either. . . .*

"What time are we leaving, Mistress?" OreSeur asked.

Vin paused. "Actually, OreSeur, I wasn't planning to bring you. I still intend to keep your cover with the other people in the palace, and I think it would look very suspicious of me to bring my pet dog on this particular trip."

OreSeur was silent for a moment. "Oh," he said. "Of course. Good luck, then, Mistress."

Vin felt only a tiny stab of disappointment; she'd expected him to object more. She pushed the emotion aside. Why should she fault him? He'd been the one to rightly point out the dangers of going into the camp.

OreSeur simply lay down, resting head on paws as he watched her continue applying her makeup.

"But, El," Ham said, "you should at least let us send you in our own carriage."

Elend shook his head, straightening his jacket as he looked in the mirror. "That would require sending in a coachman, Ham."

"Right," Ham said. "Who would be me."

"One man won't make a difference in getting us out of that camp. And, the fewer people I take with me, the fewer people Vin and I have to worry about."

Ham shook his head. "El, I . . ."

Elend laid a hand on Ham's shoulder. "I appreciate the concern, Ham. But, I can do this. If there's one man in this world I can manipulate, it's my father. I'll come out of this with him feeling assured that he has the city in his pocket."

Ham sighed. "All right."

"Oh, one other thing," Elend said hesitantly.

"Yes?"

"Would you mind calling me 'Elend' instead of just 'El'?"

Ham chuckled. "I suppose that one's easy enough to do."

Elend smiled thankfully. *It's not what Tindwyl wanted, but it's a start. We'll worry about the "Your Majesty"s later.*

The door opened, and Dockson walked in. "Elend," he said. "This just arrived for you." He held up a sheet of paper.

"From the Assembly?" Elend asked.

Dockson nodded. "They're not happy about you missing the meeting this evening."

"Well, I can't change the appointment with Straff just because they want to meet a day early," Elend said. "Tell them I'll try and visit when I get back."

Dockson nodded, then turned as a rustling sounded from behind him. He stepped to the side, a strange look on his face, as Vin walked up to the doorway.

And she was wearing a dress—a beautiful blue gown that was sleeker than the common courtly fare. Her black hair sparkled with a pair of sapphire barrettes, and she seemed . . . different. More feminine—or, rather, more confident in her femininity.

How much she's changed since I first met her, Elend thought, smiling. Almost two years had passed. Then she had been a youth, albeit one with the life experiences of someone far older. Now she was a woman—a very dangerous woman, but one who still looked up at him with eyes that were just a bit uncertain, just a bit insecure.

"Beautiful," Elend whispered. She smiled.

"Vin!" Ham said, turning. "You're wearing a dress!"

Vin flushed. "What did you expect, Ham? That I would meet with the king of the Northern Dominance in trousers?"

"Well . . ." Ham said. "Actually, yes."

Elend chuckled. "Just because *you* insist on going about everywhere in casual clothing, Ham, doesn't mean that everyone does. Honestly, don't you get tired of those vests?"

Ham shrugged. "They're easy. And simple."

"And cold," Vin said, rubbing her arms. "I'm glad I asked for something with sleeves."

"Be thankful for the weather," Ham said. "Every chill you suffer will seem far worse to the men out in those armies."

Elend nodded. Winter had, technically, started. The weather probably wouldn't get bad enough to be more than a mild discomfort—they rarely got snow in the Central Dominance—but the chill nights certainly wouldn't improve morale.

"Well, let's go," Vin said. "The sooner we get this over with, the better."

Elend stepped forward, smiling, taking Vin's hands. "I appreciate this, Vin," he said quietly. "And you really do look gorgeous. If we weren't marching off to near certain doom, I'd be tempted to command a ball be held tonight just for the opportunity to show you off."

Vin smiled. "Near certain doom is that compelling?"

"Guess I've been spending too much time with the crew." He leaned down to kiss her, but she yelped and jumped back.

"It took me the better part of an hour to get this makeup on right," she snapped. "No kissing!"

Elend chuckled as Captain Demoux poked his head in the door. "Your Majesty, the carriage has arrived."

Elend looked at Vin. She nodded.

"Let's go," he said.

Sitting inside the carriage Straff had sent for them, Elend could see a solemn group standing on the wall, watching them roll away. The sun was near to setting.

He commands us to come in the evening; we'll have to leave when the mists are out, Elend thought. *A crafty way of pointing out how much power he has over us.*

It was his father's way—a move, in a way, that was similar to the attack on the walls a day before. To Straff, everything was about posturing. Elend had watched his father at court, and had seen him manipulate even obligators. By holding the contract to oversee the Lord Ruler's atium mine, Straff Venture had played a game even more dangerous than his fellow noblemen. And he had played that game very well. He hadn't factored in Kelsier throwing chaos into the mix, but who had?

Since the Collapse, Straff had secured the most stable,

and most powerful, kingdom in the Final Empire. He was a crafty, careful man who knew how to plan for years to get what he wanted. And this was the man Elend had to manipulate.

"You look worried," Vin said. She was across from him in the carriage, sitting in a prim, ladylike posture. It was as if donning a dress somehow granted her new habits and mannerisms. Or just a return to old ones—she'd once been able to act like a noblewoman well enough to fool Elend.

"We'll be all right," she said. "Straff won't hurt you—even if things go bad, he won't dare make a martyr of you."

"Oh, I'm not worried about my safety," Elend said.

Vin raised an eyebrow. "Because?"

"Because I have you," Elend said with a smile. "You're worth an army, Vin."

This, however, didn't seem to console her.

"Come here," he said, scooting over and waving her to the seat beside him.

She rose and moved across the carriage—but paused, eyeing him. "Makeup."

"I'll be careful," Elend promised.

She nodded, sitting and letting him put an arm around her. "Be careful of the hair, too," she said. "And your suit coat—don't get anything on it."

"When did you get so fashion-conscious?" he asked.

"It's the dress," Vin said with a sigh. "As soon as I put it on, all of Sazed's lessons started coming back to me."

"I really do like the dress on you," Elend said.

Vin shook her head.

"What?" Elend asked as the carriage bumped, pushing her a bit closer to him. *Another new perfume,* he thought. *At least that's one habit she never got out of.*

"This isn't me, Elend," she said quietly. "This dress, these mannerisms. They're a lie."

Elend sat quietly for a moment.

"No objections?" Vin said. "Everyone else thinks I'm speaking nonsense."

"I don't know," Elend said honestly. "Changing into my new clothes made *me* feel different, so what you say makes sense. If wearing dresses feels wrong to you, then you don't have to wear them. I want you to be happy, Vin."

Vin smiled, looking up at him. Then she leaned up and kissed him.

"I thought you said none of that," he said.

"From you," she said. "I'm Mistborn—we're more precise."

Elend smiled, though he couldn't quite feel jovial. Conversation, however, did keep him from fretting. "I feel uncomfortable in these clothes, sometimes. Everyone expects so much more from me when I wear them. They expect a king."

"When I wear a dress," Vin said, "they expect a lady. Then they're disappointed when they find me instead."

"Anyone who would feel disappointed to find *you* is too dense to be of any relevance," Elend said. "I don't want you to be like them, Vin. They're not honest. They don't care. I like you as you are."

"Tindwyl thinks that I can be both," Vin said. "A woman and a Mistborn."

"Tindwyl is wise," Elend said. "A bit brutal, but wise. You should listen to her."

"You just told me you liked me how I am."

"I do," Elend said. "But I'd like you *however* you were, Vin. I love you. The question is, how do you like yourself?"

That gave her pause.

"Clothing doesn't really change a man," Elend said. "But it changes how others react to him. Tindwyl's words. I think . . . I think the trick is convincing yourself that you *deserve* the reactions you get. You can wear the court's dresses, Vin, but make them your own. Don't worry that you aren't giving people what they want. Give them who you are, and let that be enough." He paused, smiling. "It was for me."

She smiled back, then carefully leaned against him. "All right," she said. "Enough insecurity for the moment. Let's review. Tell me more about your father's disposition."

"He's a perfect imperial nobleman. Ruthless, clever, and infatuated with power. You remember my . . . experience when I was thirteen?"

Vin nodded.

"Well, Father was very fond of skaa brothels. I think that he liked how strong he felt by taking a girl while knowing that she would be killed for his passion. He keeps several dozen mistresses, and if they don't please him, they get removed."

Vin muttered something quietly in response to this.

"He's the same way with political allies. One didn't ally with House Venture—one agreed to be dominated by House Venture. If you weren't willing to be our slave, then you didn't get to contract with us."

Vin nodded. "I've known crewleaders like that."

"And how did you survive when they turned an eye toward you?"

"By acting unimportant," Vin said. "By crawling on the ground when they passed and by never giving them reason to challenge me. Exactly what you're planning to do tonight."

Elend nodded.

"Be careful," Vin said. "Don't let Straff think that you're mocking him."

"All right."

"And don't promise too much," Vin said. "Act like you're trying to seem tough. Let him think he's bullying you into doing what he wants—he'll enjoy that."

"You've had experience with this before, I see."

"Too much of it," Vin said. "But, you've heard this before."

Elend nodded. They'd planned and replanned this meeting. Now he simply had to do what the crew had taught him. *Make Straff think we're weak, imply we'll give him the city—but only if he helps us against Cett first.*

Outside the window, Elend could see that they were approaching Straff's army. *So big!* he thought. *Where did Father learn to administrate a force like this?*

Elend had hoped, perhaps, that his father's lack of military experience would translate to a poorly run army. Yet, the tents were arranged in a careful pattern, and the soldiers wore neat uniforms. Vin moved over to her window, looking out with avid eyes, showing far more interest than an imperial noblewoman would have dared. "Look," she said, pointing.

"What?" Elend asked, leaning over.

"Obligator," Vin said.

Elend looked over her shoulder, spotting the former imperial priest—the skin around his eyes tattooed in a wide pattern—directing a line of soldiers outside a tent. "So that's it. He's using obligators to administrate."

Vin shrugged. "It makes sense. They'd know how to manage large groups of people."

"And how to supply them," Elend said. "Yes, it's a good idea—but it's still surprising. It implies that he still needs obligators—and that he's still subject to the Lord Ruler's authority. Most of the other kings threw off the obligators as soon as they could."

Vin frowned. "I thought you said your father likes being in power."

"He does," Elend said. "But also likes powerful tools. He always keeps a kandra, and he has a history of associating with dangerous Allomancers. He believes that he can control them—and he probably believes the same thing about the obligators."

The carriage slowed, then stopped beside a large tent. Straff Venture emerged a moment later.

Elend's father had always been a large man, firm of figure with a commanding posture. The new beard only heightened the effect. He wore a sharp, well-cut suit, just like the suits he had tried to get Elend to wear as a boy. That was when Elend had begun wearing his clothing disheveled—the buttons undone, the jackets too large. Anything to separate him from his father.

Elend's defiance had never been meaningful, however. He had annoyed Straff, pulling small stunts and acting foolish when he knew he could get away with it. None of it had mattered.

Not until that final night. Luthadel in flames, the skaa rebellion running out of control, threatening to bring down the entire city. A night of chaos and destruction, with Vin trapped somewhere within it.

Then Elend had stood up to Straff Venture.

I'm not the same boy you pushed around, Father. Vin squeezed his arm, and Elend climbed out of the carriage as the coachman opened the door. Straff waited quietly, a strange look on his face as Elend raised a hand to help Vin down.

"You came," Straff said.

"You seem surprised, Father."

Straff shook his head. "I see that you're just as big an idiot as ever, boy. You're in my power now—I could have you killed with a bare wave of my hand." He raised his arm, as if to do just that.

Now's the moment, Elend thought, heart thumping. "I've *always* been in your power, Father," he said. "You could have had me killed months ago, could have taken my city away at a bare whim. I don't see how my coming here changes anything."

Straff hesitated.

"We came for dinner," Elend said. "I had hoped to give you a chance to meet Vin, and had hoped that we might discuss certain . . . issues of particular import to you."

Straff frowned.

That's right, Elend thought. *Wonder if I have some offer yet to make. You know that the first man to play his hand usually loses.*

Straff wouldn't pass up an opportunity for gain—even a slim opportunity, like the one Elend represented. He probably figured there was nothing Elend could say that was of real importance. But could he be sure? What did he have to lose?

"Go and confirm with my chef that there will be three for dinner," Straff said to a servant.

Elend let out a lightly held breath.

"That girl's your Mistborn, then?" Straff asked.

Elend nodded.

"Cute little thing," Straff said. "Tell her to stop Soothing my emotions."

Vin flushed.

Straff nodded toward the tent. Elend led Vin forward, though she glanced over her shoulder, obviously not liking the idea of exposing her back to Straff.

Little bit late for that . . . Elend thought.

The tent chamber was what Elend would have expected of his father: stuffed with pillows and rich furniture, very little of which Straff would actually use. Straff furnished to suggest his power. Like the massive keeps of Luthadel, a nobleman's surroundings were an expression of how important he was.

Vin waited quietly, tensely, at Elend's side in the center of the room. "He's good," she whispered. "I was as subtle as I can manage, and he still noticed my touch."

Elend nodded. "He's also a Tineye," he said in a normal voice. "So he's probably listening to us right now."

Elend looked toward the door. Straff walked in a few moments later, giving no indication as to whether he had heard Vin or not. A group of servants entered a few moments later, carrying a large dining table.

Vin inhaled sharply. The servants were skaa—imperial skaa, after the old tradition. They were ragged, their clothing made of torn smocks, and showed bruises from a recent beating. They carried their loads with lowered eyes.

"Why the reaction, girl?" Straff asked. "Oh, that's right. You're skaa, aren't you—pretty dress notwithstanding? Elend is very kind; I wouldn't let you wear something like that." *Or much at all,* his tone implied.

Vin shot Straff a look, but pulled a little closer to Elend, grabbing his arm. Again, Straff's words were only about posturing; Straff was cruel, but only insofar as it served him. He wanted to make Vin uncomfortable.

Which he seemed to be doing. Elend frowned, glancing down, and caught just a hint of a sly smile on her lips.

Breeze has told me that Vin is more subtle with her Allomancy than most Soothers, he recalled. *Father's good, but for him to pick out her touch . . .*

She let him, of course.

Elend looked back at Straff, who hit one of the skaa servants on their way out. "I hope none of them are relatives of yours," Straff said to Vin. "They haven't been very diligent lately. I might have to execute a few."

"I'm not skaa anymore," Vin said quietly. "I'm a noble-woman."

Straff just laughed. He had already dismissed Vin as a threat. He knew she was Mistborn, he must have heard that she was dangerous, and yet he now assumed that she was weak and inconsequential.

She is good at this, Elend thought with wonder. Servants began to bring in a feast that was impressive considering the circumstances. As they waited, Straff turned to an aide. "Send in Hoselle," he ordered. "And tell her to be quick."

He seems less reserved than I remember, Elend thought. In the Lord Emperor's day, a good nobleman had been stiff and inhibited when in public, though many had turned to extravagant indulgence when in private. They would dance and have quiet dinner conversation at the ball, for instance, but enjoy whores and drunkenness in the small hours of night.

"Why the beard, Father?" Elend asked. "Last I knew, those weren't in fashion."

"I set the fashion now, boy," Straff said. "Sit." Vin waited respectfully, Elend noticed, until Elend was seated before taking her place. She managed to maintain an air of half jumpiness: she'd look Straff in the eyes, but always gave a reflexive twitch, as if part of her wanted to glance away.

"Now," Straff said, "tell me why you're here."

"I thought it was obvious, Father," Elend said. "I'm here to discuss our alliance."

Straff raised an eyebrow. "Alliance? We both just agreed that your life is mine. I don't see a need to ally with you."

"Perhaps," Elend said. "But, there are other factors at play here. I assume that you weren't expecting Cett's arrival?"

"Cett is of little concern," Straff said, turning his attention to the meal: big slabs of barely cooked beef. Vin wrinkled her nose, though Elend couldn't tell if that was part of her act or not.

Elend cut his steak. "A man with an army nearly as large as your own is hardly of 'little' concern, Father."

Straff shrugged. "He'll be of no trouble to me once I have the city walls. You'll turn those over to me as part of our alliance, I assume?"

"And invite Cett to attack the city?" Elend said. "Yes, together you and I could hold against him, but why go on the defensive? Why let him weaken our fortifications, and possibly just continue this siege until both of our armies are starving? We need to *attack* him, Father."

Straff snorted. "You think I need your help to do so?"

"You do if you want to beat him with any measure of assured success," Elend said. "We can take him easily together—but never alone. We need each other. Let's attack, you leading your armies, me leading mine."

"Why are you so eager?" Straff asked, narrowing his eyes.

"Because I want to prove something," Elend said. "Look, we both know you're going to take Luthadel from me. But, if we ride together against Cett first, it will look like I *wanted* to ally with you all along. I'll be able to give you the city without looking like a complete buffoon. I can spin it that I brought in my father to help us against the army I knew was coming. I turn the city over to you, and then become your heir again. We both get what we want. But *only* once Cett is dead."

Straff paused, and Elend could see that his words were having an effect. *Yes,* he thought. *Think that I'm just the same boy you left behind—eccentric, eager to resist you for silly reasons. And, saving face is a very Venture thing to do.*

"No," Straff said.

Elend started.

"No," Straff said again, turning to his meal. "That's not how we're going to do this, boy. I'll decide when—or even *if*—I attack Cett."

That should have worked! Elend thought. He studied Straff, trying to judge what was wrong. There was a faint hesitance about his father.

I need more information, he thought. He glanced to his side, to where Vin sat, spinning something lightly in her hand. Her fork. She met his eyes, then tapped it lightly.

Metal, Elend thought. *Good idea.* He looked over at Straff. "You came for the atium," he said. "You don't have to conquer my city to get it."

Straff leaned forward. "Why haven't you spent it?"

"Nothing brings sharks faster than fresh blood, Father," Elend said. "Spending large amounts of atium would only have indicated for certain that I had it—a bad idea, considering the trouble we took to squelch those rumors."

There was a sudden motion at the front of the tent, and soon a flustered young girl entered. She wore a ball gown—red—and had her black hair pulled back into a long, flowing tail. She was, perhaps, fifteen.

"Hoselle," Straff said, pointing to the chair next to him.

The girl nodded obediently, scurrying forward to sit beside Straff. She was done up in makeup, and the dress was low-cut. Elend had little doubt as to her relationship with Straff.

Straff smiled and chewed his food, calm and gentlemanly. The girl looked a little bit like Vin—same almond face, similar dark hair, same fine features and thin build. It was a statement. *I can get one just like yours—only younger and prettier.* More posturing.

It was that moment—that smirk in Straff's eyes—which reminded Elend more than ever why he hated his father.

"Perhaps we *can* make a deal, boy," Straff said. "Deliver the atium to me, and I'll deal with Cett."

"Getting it to you will take time," Elend said.

"Why?" Straff asked. "Atium is light."

"There's a lot of it."

"Not so much you couldn't pack it on a cart and send it out," Straff said.

"It's more complicated than that," Elend said.

"I don't think it is," Straff said, smiling. "You just don't want to give it to me."

Elend frowned.

"We don't have it," Vin whispered.

Straff turned.

"We never found it," she said. "Kelsier overthrew the Lord Ruler just so he could get that atium. But we never could find out where the metal was. It probably wasn't ever in the city."

Wasn't expecting that . . . Elend thought. Of course, Vin tended to do things by instinct, much as Kelsier was said to have done. All the planning in the world could go out the window with Vin around—but what she did instead was usually better.

Straff sat for a moment. He seemed to believe Vin. "So you really have nothing at all to offer me."

I need to act weak, Elend remembered. *Need him to think he can take the city any time, but also think it isn't worth taking right now.* He began to tap the table quietly with his index finger, trying to look nervous. *If Straff thinks we don't have the atium . . . then he'll be a lot less likely to risk attacking the city. Less gain. That's why Vin said what she did.*

"Vin doesn't know what she's talking about," Elend said. "I've kept the atium hidden, even from her. I'm sure we can arrange something, Father."

"No," Straff said, now sounding amused. "You really *don't* have it. Zane said . . . but, well, I didn't believe . . ."

Straff shook his head, turning back toward his meal. The girl at his side didn't eat; she sat quietly, like the ornament she was expected to be. Straff took a long drink of his wine, then let out a satisfied sigh. He looked at his child mistress. "Leave us," he said.

She immediately did as commanded.

"You, too," Straff said to Vin.

Vin stiffened slightly. She looked toward Elend.

"It's all right," he said slowly.

She paused, then nodded. Straff himself was little danger to Elend, and she was a Mistborn. If something went wrong, she could get to Elend quickly. And, if she left, it would do what they wanted—make Elend look less powerful. In a better position to deal with Straff.

Hopefully.

"I'll wait just outside," Vin said quietly, withdrawing.

He was no simple soldier. He was a force of leadership—a man that fate itself seemed to support.

27

"ALL RIGHT," STRAFF SAID, setting down his fork. "Let's be honest, boy. I'm this close to simply having you killed."

"You'd execute your only son?" Elend asked.

Straff shrugged.

"You need me," Elend said. "To help you fight Cett. You can kill me, but you'd gain nothing. You'd still have to take Luthadel by force, and Cett would still be able to attack—and defeat you—in your weakened state."

Straff smiled, folding his arms, leaning forward so he loomed over the table. "You are wrong on both counts, boy. First, I think that if I killed you, the next leader of Luthadel would be more accommodating. I have certain interests in the city who indicate that is true. Second, I don't need your help to fight Cett. He and I already have a treaty."

Elend paused. "What?"

"What do you think I've been doing these last few weeks? Sitting and waiting on your whims? Cett and I have exchanged pleasantries. He's not interested in the city—he just wants the atium. We agreed to split what we discover in Luthadel, then work together to take the rest of the Final Empire. He conquers to the west and north, I head east and south. Very accommodating man, Cett."

He's bluffing, Elend thought with reasonable certainty. That wasn't Straff's way; he wouldn't make an alliance with someone so near to him in strength. Straff feared betrayal too much.

"You think I would believe that?" Elend said.

"Believe what you wish," Straff said.

"And the koloss army marching this way?" Elend asked, playing one of their trump cards.

This made Straff pause.

"If you want to take Luthadel before those koloss get here, Father," Elend said, "then I think you might want to be a little more accommodating toward the man who's come, offering you everything you want. I only ask one thing—let me have a victory. Let me fight Cett, secure my legacy. *Then* you can have the city."

Straff thought about it, thought about it long enough that Elend dared to hope he might just have won. Then, however, Straff shook his head. "No, I think not. I'll take my chances with Cett. I don't know why he is willing to let me have Luthadel, but he doesn't seem to care much about it."

"And you do?" Elend said. "You know we don't have the atium. What does the city matter to you now?"

Straff leaned forward a bit farther. Elend could smell his breath, odorous from the dinner spices. "That's where you are wrong about me, boy. That's why—even if you'd been able to promise me that atium—you would never have left this camp tonight. I made a mistake a year ago. If I'd stayed in Luthadel, I would have been the one on that throne. Instead, it was you. I can't imagine why—I guess a weak Venture was still better than the other alternatives."

Straff was everything Elend had hated about the old empire. Presumptuous. Cruel. Arrogant.

Weakness, Elend thought, calming himself. *I can't be threatening.* He shrugged. "It's only a city, Father. From my position, it doesn't matter half as much as your army."

"It's more than a city," Straff said. "It's the Lord Ruler's city—and it has my home in it. My keep. I understand that you're using it as your palace."

"I didn't really have any other place to go."

Straff turned back to his meal. "All right," he said in between cutting chunks of steak, "at first, I thought you were an idiot for coming tonight, but now I'm not so certain. You must have seen the inevitable."

"You're stronger," Elend said. "I can't stand up to you."

Straff nodded. "You've impressed me, boy. Wearing

proper clothing, getting yourself a Mistborn mistress, maintaining control of the city. I'm going to let you live."

"Thank you," Elend said.

"And, in exchange, you're going to give me Luthadel."

"As soon as Cett is dealt with."

Straff laughed. "No, that's not the way these things work, boy. We're not negotiating. You're listening to my orders. Tomorrow, we'll ride to the city together, and you'll order the gates opened. I'll march my army in and take command, and Luthadel will become the new capital of my kingdom. If you stay in line and do as I say, I'll name you heir again."

"We can't do that," Elend said. "I left orders that the gates weren't to be opened to you, no matter what."

Straff paused.

"My advisors thought you might try and use Vin as a hostage, forcing me to relinquish the city," Elend said. "If we go together, they'll assume you're threatening me."

Straff's mood darkened. "You'd better hope that they don't."

"They will," Elend said. "I know these men, Father. They'd be eager for an excuse to take the city away from me."

"Then, why come here?"

"To do as I said," Elend said. "To negotiate an alliance against Cett. I can deliver Luthadel to you—but I still need time. Let's take down Cett first."

Straff grabbed his dinner knife by the hilt and slammed it down into the table. "I said this wasn't a negotiation! You don't make demands, boy. I could have you killed!"

"I'm just stating facts, Father," Elend said quickly. "I don't want to—"

"You've gotten smooth," Straff said, eyes narrowing. "What did you hope to accomplish with this game? Coming to my camp? Bringing nothing to offer . . ." He paused, then continued. "Nothing to offer except for that girl. Pretty little thing, she is."

Elend flushed. "That won't get you into the city. Remember, my advisors thought you might try threatening her."

"Fine," Straff snapped. "You die; I take the city by force."

"And Cett attacks you from behind," Elend said. "Pinning you against our wall and forcing you to fight surrounded."

"He'd take heavy losses," Straff said. "He wouldn't be able to take and hold the city after that."

"Even with diminished forces, he'd have a better chance of taking it from us than he would if he waited and then tried to take it from you."

Straff stood. "I'll have to take that chance. I left you behind before. I'm not going to let you loose again, boy. Those cursed skaa were supposed to kill you and leave me free of you."

Elend stood as well. However, he could see the resolve in Straff's eyes.

It isn't working, Elend thought, panic beginning to set in. This plan had been a gamble, but he hadn't ever really thought that he'd fail. Indeed, he'd played his cards well. But, something was wrong—something he hadn't anticipated, and still didn't understand. Why was Straff resisting so much?

I'm too new to this, Elend thought. Ironically, if he had let his father train him better as a child, he might have known what he'd done wrong. As it was, he suddenly realized the gravity of his situation. Surrounded by a hostile army. Separated from Vin.

He was going to die.

"Wait!" Elend said desperately.

"Ah," Straff said smiling. "Finally realized what you've gotten yourself into?" There was pleasure in Straff's smile. Eagerness. There had always been something inside Straff that had enjoyed hurting others, though Elend had rarely seen it applied to him. Propriety had always been there to stop Straff.

Propriety enforced by the Lord Ruler. At that moment, Elend saw murder in his father's eyes.

"You never intended to let me live," Elend said. "Even if I'd given you the atium, even if I'd gone with you to the city."

"You were dead the moment I decided to march here," Straff said. "Idiot boy. I do thank you for bringing me that girl, though. I'll take her tonight. We'll see if she cries my name or yours while I'm—"

Elend laughed.

It was a desperate laugh, a laugh at the ridiculous situation he'd gotten himself into, a laugh at his sudden worry and fear—but most of all, it was a laugh at the idea of Straff trying to force himself upon Vin. "You have no idea how foolish you sound," Elend said.

Straff flushed. "For that, boy, I'll be extra rough with her."

"You are a pig, Father," Elend said. "A sick, disgusting man. You thought you were a brilliant leader, but you were barely competent. You nearly got our house destroyed—only the Lord Ruler's own death saved you!"

Straff called for his guards.

"You may take Luthadel," Elend said, "but you'll lose it! I may have been a bad king, but you'll be a terrible one. The Lord Ruler was a tyrant, but he was also a genius. You're neither. You're just a selfish man who'll use up his resources, then end up dead from a knife in the back."

Straff pointed at Elend as soldiers rushed in. Elend didn't cringe. He'd grown up with this man, been raised by him, been tortured by him. And, despite it all, Elend had never spoken his mind. He'd rebelled with the petty timidity of a teenage boy, but he'd never spoken the truth.

It felt good. It felt right.

Perhaps playing the weak hand was a mistake against Straff. He always was fond of crushing things.

And suddenly Elend knew what he had to do. He smiled, looking Straff in the eyes.

"Kill me, Father," he said, "and you'll die, too."

"Kill me, Father," Elend said, "and you'll die, too."

Vin paused. She stood outside the tent, in the darkness of early night. She'd been standing with Straff's soldiers, but they'd rushed in at his command. She'd moved into the darkness, and now stood on the north side of the tent, watching the shadowed forms move within.

She'd been about to burst in. Elend hadn't been doing very well—not that he was a bad negotiator. He was just too honest by nature. It wasn't difficult to tell when he was bluffing, especially if you knew him well.

But, this new proclamation was different. It wasn't a sign of Elend attempting to be clever, nor was it an angry outburst like the one he'd made moments before. Suddenly, he seemed calm and forceful.

Vin waited quietly, her daggers out, tense in the mists before the glowing tent. Something told her she had to give Elend just a few more moments.

Straff laughed at Elend's threat.

"You are a fool, Father," Elend said. "You think I came here to negotiate? You think I would willingly deal with one such as you? No. You know me better than that. You know that I'd never submit to you."

"Then why?" Straff asked.

She could almost hear Elend's smile. "I came to get near you, Father . . . and to bring my Mistborn to the very heart of your camp."

Silence.

Finally, Straff laughed. "You threaten me with that wisp of a girl? If that's the great Mistborn of Luthadel I've been hearing of, then I'm sorely disappointed."

"That's because she wants you to feel that way," Elend said. "Think, Father. You were suspicious, and the girl confirmed those suspicions. But, if she's as good as the rumors say—and I know you've heard the rumors—then how would you have spotted her touch on your emotions?

"You caught her Soothing you, and you called her on it. Then, you didn't feel the touch anymore, so you assumed that she was cowed. But, after that, you began to feel confident. Comfortable. You dismissed Vin as a threat—but would any rational man dismiss a Mistborn, no matter how small or quiet? In fact, you'd think that the small, quiet ones would be the assassins you'd want to pay the *most* attention to."

Vin smiled. *Clever,* she thought. She reached out, Rioting Straff's emotions, flaring her metal and stoking his sense of anger. He gasped in sudden shock. *Take the clue, Elend.*

"Fear," Elend said.

She Soothed away Straff's anger and exchanged it for fear.

"Passion."

She complied.

"Calmness."

She soothed everything away. Inside the tent, she saw Straff's shadow standing stiffly. An Allomancer couldn't force a person to do anything—and usually, strong Pushes or Pulls on an emotion were less effective, since they alerted the target that something was wrong. In this case, however, Vin wanted Straff to know for certain she was watching.

She smiled, extinguishing her tin. Then she burned duralumin and Soothed Straff's emotions with explosive pressure, wiping away all capacity for feeling within him. His shadow stumbled beneath the attack.

Her brass was gone a moment later, and she turned on her tin again, watching the black patterns on the canvas.

"She's powerful, Father," Elend said. "She's more powerful than any Allomancer you've known. She killed the Lord Ruler. She was trained by the Survivor of Hathsin. And if you kill me, *she'll kill you.*"

Straff righted himself, and the tent fell silent again.

A footstep sounded. Vin spun, ducking, raising her dagger.

A familiar figure stood in the night mists. "Why is it I can never sneak up on you?" Zane asked quietly.

Vin shrugged and turned back to the tent—but moved herself so she could keep an eye on Zane, too. He walked over and crouched beside her, watching the shadows.

"That's hardly a useful threat," Straff finally said from within. "You'll be dead, even if your Mistborn does get to me."

"Ah, Father," Elend said. "I was wrong about your interest in Luthadel. However, you're also wrong about me— you've *always* been wrong about me. I don't care if I die, not if it brings safety to my people."

"Cett will take the city if I'm gone," Straff said.

"I think my people might be able to hold against him," Elend said. "After all, he has the smaller army."

"This is idiocy!" Straff snapped. He didn't, however, order his soldiers forward any farther.

"Kill me, and you die, too," Elend said. "And not just you. Your generals. Your captains. Even your obligators. She has orders to slaughter you all."

Zane took a step closer to Vin, his feet crunching slightly on the packed-down weeds that made up the floor of the camp. "Ah," he whispered, "clever. No matter how strong your opponent is, he can't attack if you've got a knife at his throat."

Zane leaned even closer, and Vin looked up at him, their faces just inches from each other. He shook his head in the soft mists. "But tell me—why is it that people like you and me always have to be the knives?"

Inside the tent, Straff was growing concerned. "No one is that powerful, boy," he said, "not even a Mistborn. She might be able to kill some of my generals, but she'd never get to me. I have my own Mistborn."

"Oh?" Elend said. "And why hasn't he killed her? Because he's afraid to attack? If you kill me, Father—if you even make so much as a *move* toward my city—then she'll begin the slaughter. Men will die like prisoners before the fountains on a day of execution."

"I thought you said he was above this kind of thing," Zane whispered. "You claimed you weren't his tool. You said he wouldn't use you as an assassin. . . ."

Vin shuffled uncomfortably. "He's bluffing, Zane," she said. "He'd never actually do anything like that."

"She is an Allomancer like you've never seen, Father," Elend said, voice muffled by the tent. "I've seen her fight other Allomancers—none of them can even touch her."

"Is that true?" Zane asked.

Vin paused. Elend hadn't actually ever seen her attack other Allomancers. "He saw me attack some soldiers once, and I've told him about my fights with other Allomancers."

"Ah," Zane said softly. "So it's only a small lie, then. Those are fine when one is king. Many things are. Exploiting one person to save an entire kingdom? What leader wouldn't pay such a cheap price? Your freedom in exchange for his victory."

"He's not using me," Vin said.

Zane stood. Vin turned slightly, watching carefully as he walked into the mists, away from tents, torches, and soldiers. He paused, standing a short distance away, looking up. Even with the light of tent and fires, this camp was claimed by the mists. It spun all around them. From within it, the torchlight and campfires seemed insignificant. Like dying coals.

"What is this to *him*," Zane said quietly, sweeping a hand around him. "Can he ever understand the mists? Can he ever understand you?"

"He loves me," Vin said, glancing back at the shadowed forms. They had fallen quiet for a moment, Straff obviously considering Elend's threats.

"He loves *you*?" Zane asked. "Or he loves *having you*?"

"Elend isn't like that," Vin said. "He's a good man."

"Good or not, you aren't like him," Zane said, voice echoing in the night to her tin-enhanced ears. "Can he understand what it is like to be one of us? Can he know the things we know, care about the things we love? Has he ever seen those?" Zane gestured upward, toward the sky. Far beyond the mists, lights shone in the sky, like tiny freckles. Stars, invisible to the normal eye. Only a person burning tin could penetrate the mists and see them shining.

She remembered the first time Kelsier had shown them to her. She remembered how stunned she had been that the stars had been there all along, invisible beyond the mists. . . .

Zane continued to point upward. "Lord Ruler!" Vin whispered, taking a small step away from the tent. Through the swirling mists, in the reflected light of the tent, she could see something on Zane's arm.

The skin was covered with thin white streaks. Scars.

Zane immediately lowered his arm, hiding the scarred flesh with his sleeve.

"You were in the Pits of Hathsin," Vin said quietly. "Like Kelsier."

Zane looked away.

"I'm sorry," Vin said.

Zane turned back, smiling in the night. It was a firm,

confident smile. He stepped forward. "I understand you, Vin."

Then he bowed slightly to her and jumped away, disappearing into the mists. Inside the room, Straff spoke to Elend.

"Go. Leave here."

The carriage rolled away. Straff stood outside his tent, heedless of the mists, still feeling a bit stunned.

I let him go. Why did I let him go?

Yet—even now—he could feel her touch slamming against him. One emotion after another, like a treasonous maelstrom within him, and then . . . nothing. Like a massive hand, grabbing his soul and squeezing it into painful submission. It had felt the way he thought death might.

No Allomancer could be that powerful.

Zane respects her, Straff thought. *And everyone says she killed the Lord Ruler. That little thing. It couldn't be.*

It seemed impossible. And apparently, that was just the way she wanted it to seem.

Everything had been going so well. The information provided by Zane's kandra spy had been accurate: Elend *did* try to make an alliance. The frightening thing about it was that Straff might have gone along with it, assuming Elend to be of no consequence, if the spy hadn't sent warning.

Even so, Elend had bested him. Straff had even been *prepared* for their feint of weakness, and he had still fallen.

She's so powerful. . . .

A figure in black stepped out of the mists and walked up to Straff. "You look like you've seen a ghost, Father," Zane said with a smile. "Your own, perhaps?"

"Was there anyone else out there, Zane?" Straff asked, too shaken for repartee at the moment. "Another couple of Mistborn, perhaps, helping her?"

Zane shook his head. "No. She really is that strong." He turned to walk back out into the mists.

"Zane!" Straff snapped, making the man pause. "We're going to change plans. I want you to kill her."

Zane turned. "But—"

"She's too dangerous. Plus, we now have the information we wanted to get from her. They don't have the atium."

"You believe them?" Zane asked.

Straff paused. After how thoroughly he'd been manipulated this evening, he wasn't going to trust anything he thought he'd learned. "No," he decided. "But we'll find it another way. I want that girl *dead,* Zane."

"Are we attacking the city for real, then?"

Straff almost gave the order right then, commanding his armies to prepare for a morning assault. The preliminary attack had gone well, showing that the defenses were hardly impressive. Straff could take that wall, then use it against Cett.

However, Elend's final words before departing this evening made him stop. *Send your armies against my city, Father,* the boy had said, *and die. You've felt her power—you know what she can do. You can try and hide, you can even conquer my city.*

But she will find you. And she will kill you.

Your only option is to wait. I'll contact you when my armies are prepared to attack Cett. We'll strike together, as I said earlier.

Straff couldn't depend on that. The boy had changed—had become strong, somehow. If Straff and Elend attacked together, Straff had no illusions as to how quickly he'd be betrayed. But Straff couldn't attack Luthadel while that girl was alive. Not knowing her strength, having felt her touch on his emotions.

"No," he finally said to Zane's question. "We won't attack. Not until you kill her."

"That might be harder than you make it sound, Father," Zane said. "I'll need some help."

"What kind of help?"

"A strike team. Allomancers that can't be traced."

Zane was speaking of a particular group. Most Allomancers were easy to identify because of their noble lineages. Straff, however, had access to some special resources. There was a reason that he had so many mistresses—dozens and dozens of them. Some thought it was just because he was lustful.

That wasn't it at all. More mistresses meant more children. And more children, born from a high noble line like his, meant more Allomancers. He'd only spawned one Mistborn, but there were many Mistings.

"It will be done," Straff said.

"They might not survive the encounter, Father," Zane warned, still standing in the mists.

That awful sensation returned. The sense of nothingness, the horrible knowledge that someone else had complete and total control over his emotions. Nobody should have that much power over him. Especially not Elend.

He should be dead. He came right to me. And I let him go.

"Get rid of her," Straff said. "Do anything you need to, Zane. Anything."

Zane nodded, then walked away with a self-satisfied stroll.

Straff returned to his tent and sent for Hoselle again. She looked enough like Elend's girl. It would do him good to remind himself that most of the time, he really was in control.

Elend sat back in the carriage, a little stunned. *I'm still alive!* he thought with growing excitement. *I did it! I convinced Straff to leave the city alone.*

For a time, at least. Luthadel's safety depended on Straff remaining frightened of Vin. But . . . well, any victory was an enormous one for Elend. He hadn't failed his people. He was their king, and his plan—crazy though it might have seemed—had worked. The small crown on his head suddenly didn't seem as heavy as it had before.

Vin sat across from him. She didn't look nearly as pleased as she could have.

"We did it, Vin!" Elend said. "It wasn't what we planned, but it worked. Straff won't dare attack the city now."

She nodded quietly.

Elend frowned. "Um, it's because of you that the city

will be safe. You know that, right? If you hadn't been there . . . well, of course, if it hadn't been for you, the entire Final Empire would still be enslaved."

"Because I killed the Lord Ruler," she said quietly.

Elend nodded.

"But it was *Kelsier's* plan—the crew's skills, the people's strength of will—that freed the empire. I just held the knife."

"You make it sound like a trivial thing, Vin," he said. "It's not! You're a fantastic Allomancer. Ham says he can't beat you even in an *unfair* fight anymore, and you've kept the palace free of assassins. There's nobody like you in all of the Final Empire!"

Strangely, his words made her huddle into the corner just a little farther. She turned, watching out the window, eyes staring into the mists. "Thank you," she said softly.

Elend wrinkled his brow. *Every time I begin to think I've figured out what's going on in her head . . .* He moved over, putting an arm around her. "Vin, what's wrong?"

She was silent, then finally shook her head, forcing a smile. "It's nothing, Elend. You're right to be excited. You were brilliant in there—I doubt even Kelsier could have manipulated Straff so neatly."

Elend smiled, and pulled her close, impatient as the carriage rolled up to the dark city. The doors of Tin Gate opened hesitantly, and Elend saw a group of men standing just inside of the courtyard. Ham held aloft a lantern in the mists.

Elend didn't wait for the carriage to stop on its own. He opened the door and hopped down as it was rolling to a halt. His friends began to smile eagerly. The gates thumped closed.

"It worked?" Ham asked hesitantly as Elend approached. "You did it?"

"Kind of," Elend said with a smile, clasping hands with Ham, Breeze, Dockson, and finally Spook. Even the kandra, OreSeur, was there. He padded over to the carriage, waiting for Vin. "The initial feint didn't go so well—my father didn't bite on an alliance. But then I told him I'd kill him!"

"Wait. How was that a good idea?" Ham asked.

"We overlooked one of our greatest resources, my friends," Elend said as Vin climbed down from the carriage. Elend turned, waving his hand toward her. "We have a weapon like nothing they can match! Straff expected me to come begging, and he was ready to control that situation. However, when I mentioned what would happen to him and his army if Vin's anger was roused . . ."

"My dear man," Breeze said. "You went into the camp of the strongest king in the Final Empire, and you *threatened* him?"

"Yes I did!"

"Brilliant!"

"I know!" Elend said. "I told my Father that he *was* going to let me leave his camp and that he *was* going to leave Luthadel alone, otherwise I'd have Vin kill him and every general in his army." He put his arm around Vin. She smiled at the group, but he could tell that something was still troubling her.

She doesn't think I did a good job, Elend realized. *She saw a better way to manipulate Straff, but she doesn't want to spoil my enthusiasm.*

"Well, guess we won't need a new king," Spook said with a smile. "I was kind of looking forward to taking the job. . . ."

Elend laughed. "I don't intend to vacate the position for quite some time yet. We'll let the people know that Straff has been cowed, if temporarily. That should boost morale a bit. Then, we deal with the Assembly. Hopefully, they'll pass a resolution to wait for me to meet with Cett like I just did with Straff."

"Shall we have a celebration back at the palace?" Breeze asked. "As fond as I am of the mists, I doubt the courtyard is an appropriate place to be discussing these issues."

Elend patted him on the back and nodded. Ham and Dockson joined him and Vin, while the others took the carriage they'd come in. Elend glanced oddly at Dockson as he climbed into the carriage. Ordinarily, the man would have chosen the other vehicle—the one Elend wasn't in.

"Honestly, Elend," Ham said as he settled into his seat.

"I'm impressed. I half thought we were going to have to raid that camp to get you back."

Elend smiled, eyeing Dockson, who sat down as the carriage began moving. He pulled open his satchel and took out a sealed envelope. He looked up and met Elend's eyes. "This came from the Assembly members for you a short time ago, Your Majesty."

Elend paused. Then he took it and broke the seal. "What is it?"

"I'm not sure," Dockson said. "But . . . I've already started hearing rumors."

Vin leaned in, reading over Elend's arm as he scanned the sheet inside. *Your Majesty,* it read.

> *This note is to inform you that by majority vote, the Assembly has decided to invoke the charter's no-confidence clause. We appreciate your efforts on behalf of the city, but the current situation calls for a different kind of leadership than Your Majesty can provide. We take this step with no hostility, but only resignation. We see no other alternative, and must act for the good of Luthadel.*
>
> *We regret to have to inform you of this by letter.*

It was signed by all twenty-three members of the Assembly.

Elend lowered the paper, shocked.

"What?" Ham asked.

"I've just been deposed," Elend said quietly.

THE END OF PART TWO

PART THREE

KING

He left ruin in his wake, but it was forgotten. He created kingdoms, and then destroyed them as he made the world anew.

28

"LET ME SEE IF I understand this correctly," Tindwyl said, calm and polite, yet somehow still stern and disapproving. "There is a clause in the kingdom's legal code that lets the Assembly overthrow their king?"

Elend wilted slightly. "Yes."

"And you wrote the law yourself?" Tindwyl demanded.

"Most of it," Elend admitted.

"You wrote into your own law a way that you could be deposed?" Tindwyl repeated. Their group—expanded from those who had met in the carriages to include Clubs, Tindwyl, and Captain Demoux—sat in Elend's study. The group's size was such that they'd run out of chairs, and Vin sat quietly at the side, on a stack of Elend's books, having quickly changed to trousers and shirt. Tindwyl and Elend were standing, but the rest were seated—Breeze prim, Ham relaxed, and Spook trying to balance his chair as he leaned back on two legs.

"I put in that clause intentionally," Elend said. He stood at the front of the room, leaning with one arm against the glass of his massive stained-glass window, looking up at its dark shards. "This land wilted beneath the hand of an oppressive ruler for a thousand years. During that time, philosophers and thinkers dreamed of a government where a bad ruler could be ousted without bloodshed. I took this throne through an unpredictable and unique series of events, and I didn't think it right to unilaterally impose my will—or the will of my descendants—upon the people. I wanted to start a government whose monarchs would be responsible to their subjects."

Sometimes, he talks like those books he reads, Vin thought. *Not like a normal man at all . . . but like words on a page.*

Zane's words came back to her, seeming to whisper in her mind. *You aren't like him.* She pushed the thought out.

"With respect, Your Majesty," Tindwyl said, "this has to be one of the most foolish things I've ever seen a leader do."

"It was for the good of the kingdom," Elend said.

"It was sheer idiocy," Tindwyl snapped. "A king doesn't subject himself to the whims of another ruling body. He is valuable to his people because he is an absolute authority!"

Vin had rarely seen Elend so sorrowful, and she cringed a bit at the sadness in his eyes. However, a different piece of her was rebelliously happy. He wasn't king anymore. Now maybe people wouldn't work so hard to kill him. Maybe he could just be Elend again, and they could leave. Go somewhere. A place where things weren't so complicated.

"Regardless," Dockson said to the quiet room, "something must be done. Discussing the prudence of decisions already past has little current relevance."

"Agreed," Ham said. "So, the Assembly tried to kick you out. What are we going to do about it?"

"We obviously can't let them have their way," Breeze said. "Why, the people overthrew a government just last year! This is a bad habit to be getting into, I should think."

"We need to prepare a response, Your Majesty," Dockson said. "Something decrying this deceitful maneuver, performed while you were negotiating for the very safety of the city. Now that I look back, it's obvious that they arranged this meeting so that you *couldn't* be present and defend yourself."

Elend nodded, still staring up at the dark glass. "There's probably no need to call me Your Majesty anymore, Dox."

"Nonsense," Tindwyl said, arms folded as she stood beside a bookcase. "You are still king."

"I've lost the mandate of the people," Elend said.

"Yes," Clubs said, "but you've still got the mandate of my armies. That makes you king no matter what the Assembly says."

"Exactly," Tindwyl said. "Foolish laws aside, you're still in a position of power. We need to tighten martial law, restrict movement within the city. Seize control of key points, and sequester the members of the Assembly so that your enemies can't raise a resistance against you."

"I'll have my men on the streets before light," Clubs said.

"No," Elend said quietly.

There was a pause.

"Your Majesty?" Dockson asked. "It really is the best move. We can't let this faction against you gain momentum."

"It's not a faction, Dox," Elend said. "It's the elected representatives of the Assembly."

"An Assembly you formed, my dear man," Breeze said. "They have power because *you* gave it to them."

"The law gives them their power, Breeze," Elend said. "And we are all subject to it."

"Nonsense," Tindwyl said. "As king, you are the law. Once we secure the city, you can call in the Assembly and explain to its members that you need their support. Those who disagree can be held until the crisis is over."

"No," Elend said, a little more firm. "We will do none of that."

"That's it, then?" Ham asked. "You're giving up?"

"I'm not giving up, Ham," Elend said, finally turning to regard the group. "But I'm not going to use the city's armies to pressure the Assembly."

"You'll lose your throne," Breeze said.

"See reason, Elend," Ham said with a nod.

"I will *not* be an exception to my own laws!" Elend said.

"Don't be a fool," Tindwyl said. "You should—"

"Tindwyl," Elend said, "respond to my ideas as you wish, but do not call me a fool again. I will not be belittled because I express my opinion!"

Tindwyl paused, mouth partially open. Then she pressed her lips together and took her seat. Vin felt a quiet surge of satisfaction. *You trained him, Tindwyl,* she thought with a smile. *Can you really complain if he stands up to you?*

Elend walked forward, placing his hands on the table as he regarded the group. "Yes, we will respond. Dox, you write a letter informing the Assembly of our disappointment and feelings of betrayal—inform them of our success with Straff, and lay on the guilt as thickly as possible.

"The rest of us will begin planning. We'll get the throne back. As has been stated, I know the law. I wrote it. There are ways to deal with this. Those ways do *not,* however, include sending our armies to secure the city. I will not be like the tyrants who would take Luthadel from us! I will not force the people to do my will, even if I know it is best for them."

"Your Majesty," Tindwyl said carefully, "there is nothing immoral about securing your power during a time of chaos. People react irrationally during such times. That is one of the reasons why they need strong leadership. They need you."

"Only if they want me, Tindwyl," Elend said.

"Forgive me, Your Majesty," Tindwyl said, "but that statement seems somewhat naive to me."

Elend smiled. "Perhaps it is. You can change my clothing and my bearing, but you can't change the soul of who I am. I'll do what I think is right—and that includes letting the Assembly depose me, if that is their choice."

Tindwyl frowned. "And if you can't get your throne back through lawful means?"

"Then I accept that fact," Elend said. "And do my best to help the kingdom anyway."

So much for running away, Vin thought. However, she couldn't help smiling. Part of what she loved about Elend was his sincerity. His simple love for the people of Luthadel—his determination to do what was right for them—was what separated him from Kelsier. Even in martyrdom, Kelsier had displayed a hint of arrogance. He'd made certain that he would be remembered like few men who had ever lived.

But Elend—to him, ruling the Central Dominance wasn't about fame or glory. For the first time, completely and honestly, she decided something. Elend was a far better king than Kelsier would ever have been.

"I'm . . . not certain what I think of this experience, Mistress," a voice whispered beside her. Vin paused, looking down as she realized that she had begun idly scratching OreSeur's ears.

She pulled her hand back with a start. "Sorry," she said.

OreSeur shrugged, resting his head back on his paws.

"So, you said there's a legal way to get the throne back," Ham said. "How do we go about it?"

"The Assembly has one month to choose a new king," Elend said. "Nothing in the law says that the new king can't be the same as the old one. And, if they can't come up with a majority decision by that deadline, the throne reverts to me for a minimum of one year."

"Complicated," Ham said, rubbing his chin.

"What did you expect?" Breeze said. "It's the law."

"I didn't mean the law itself," Ham said. "I meant getting the Assembly to either choose Elend or not choose anyone. They wouldn't have deposed him in the first place unless they had another person in mind for the throne."

"Not necessarily," Dockson said. "Perhaps they simply meant this as a warning."

"Perhaps," Elend said. "Gentlemen, I think this is a sign. I've been ignoring the Assembly—we thought that they were taken care of, since I got them to sign that proposal giving me right of parlay. However, we never realized that an easy way for them to get around that proposal was to choose a new king, then have *him* do as they wished."

He sighed, shaking his head. "I have to admit, I've never been very good at handling the Assembly. They don't see me as a king, but as a colleague—and because of that, they can easily see themselves taking my place. I'll bet one of the Assemblymen has convinced the others to-put him on the throne instead."

"So, we just make him disappear," Ham said. "I'm sure Vin could . . ."

Elend frowned.

"I'm joking, El," Ham said.

"You know, Ham," Breeze noted. "The only funny thing about your jokes is how often they lack any humor whatsoever."

"You're only saying that because they usually involve you in the punch line."

Breeze rolled his eyes.

"You know," OreSeur muttered quietly, obviously counting on her tin to let Vin hear him, "it seems that these meetings would be more productive if someone forgot to invite those two."

Vin smiled. "They're not *that* bad," she whispered.

OreSeur raised an eyebrow.

"Okay," Vin said. "They do distract us a little bit."

"I could always eat one of them, if you wish," OreSeur said. "That might speed things up."

Vin paused.

OreSeur, however, had a strange little smile on his lips. "Kandra humor, Mistress. I apologize. We can be a bit grim."

Vin smiled. "They probably wouldn't taste very good anyway. Ham's far too stringy, and you don't want to know the kinds of things that Breeze spends his time eating. . . ."

"I'm not sure," OreSeur said. "One is, after all, named 'Ham.' As for the other . . ." He nodded to the cup of wine in Breeze's hand. "He does seem quite fond of marinating himself."

Elend was picking through his stacks of books, pulling out several relevant volumes on law—including the book of Luthadel law that he himself had written.

"Your Majesty," Tindwyl said, emphasizing the term. "You have two armies on your doorstep, and a group of koloss making their way into the Central Dominance. Do you honestly think that you have time for a protracted legal battle now?"

Elend set down the books and pulled his chair to the table. "Tindwyl," he said. "I have two armies on my doorstep, koloss coming to pressure them, and I myself am the main obstacle keeping the leaders of this city from handing the kingdom over to one of the invaders. Do you honestly think that it's a coincidence that I get deposed *now*?"

Several members of the crew perked up at this, and Vin cocked her head.

"You think one of the invaders might be behind this?" Ham asked, rubbing his chin.

"What would you do, if you were them?" Elend said, opening a book. "You can't attack the city, because it will cost you too many troops. The siege has already lasted weeks, your troops are getting cold, and the men Dockson hired have been attacking your canal supply barges, threatening your food supply. Add on top of that, you know that a large force of koloss are marching this way . . . and, well, it makes sense. If Straff and Cett's spies are any good, they'll know that the Assembly just about capitulated and gave the city away when that army first arrived. Assassins have failed to kill me, but if there were another way to remove me . . ."

"Yes," Breeze said. "This does sound like something Cett would do. Turn the Assembly against you, put a sympathizer on the throne, then get him to open the gates."

Elend nodded. "And my father seemed hesitant to side with me this evening, as if he felt he had some other way to get the city. I can't be certain if either monarch is behind this move, Tindwyl, but we certainly can't ignore the possibility. This isn't a distraction—this is very much part of the same siege tactics we've been fighting since those armies arrived. If I can put myself back on the throne, then Straff and Cett will know that I'm the only one they can work with—and that will, hopefully, make them more likely to side with me in desperation, particularly as those koloss draw near."

With that, Elend began riffling through a stack of books. His depression seemed to be abating in face of this new academic problem. "There might be a few other clauses of relevance in the law," he half mumbled. "I need to do some studying. Spook, did you invite Sazed to this meeting?"

Spook shrugged. "I couldn't get him to wake up."

"He's recovering from his trip here," Tindwyl said, turning away from her study of Elend and his books. "It's an issue of the Keepers."

"Needs to refill one of his metalminds?" Ham asked.

Tindwyl paused, her expression darkening. "He explained that to you, then?"

Ham and Breeze nodded.

"I see," Tindwyl said. "Regardless, he could not help with this problem, Your Majesty. I give you some small aid in the area of government because it is my duty to train leaders in knowledge of the past. However, traveling Keepers such as Sazed do not take sides in political matters."

"Political matters?" Breeze asked lightly. "You mean, perhaps, like overthrowing the Final Empire?"

Tindwyl closed her mouth, lips growing thin. "You should not encourage him to break his vows," she finally said. "If you were his friends, you would see that to be true, I think."

"Oh?" Breeze asked, pointing at her with his cup of wine. "Personally, I think you're just embarrassed that he disobeyed you all, but then actually ended up freeing your people."

Tindwyl gave Breeze a flat stare, her eyes narrow, her posture stiff. They sat that way for a long moment. "Push on my emotions all you wish, Soother," Tindwyl said. "My feelings are my own. You will have no success here."

Breeze finally turned back to his drink, muttering something about "damn Terrismen."

Elend, however, wasn't paying attention to the argument. He already had four books open on the table before him, and was flipping through a fifth. Vin smiled, remembering the days—not so long ago—when his courtship of her had often involved him plopping himself down in a nearby chair and opening a book.

He is the same man, she thought. *And that soul, that man, is the one who loved me before he knew I was Mistborn. He loved me even after he discovered I was a thief, and thought I was trying to rob him. I need to remember that.*

"Come on," she whispered to OreSeur, standing as Breeze

and Ham got into another argument. She needed time to think, and the mists were still fresh.

This would be a lot easier if I weren't so skilled, Elend thought with amusement, poking through his books. *I set up the law too well.*

He followed a particular passage with his finger, rereading it as the crew slowly trailed away. He couldn't remember if he'd dismissed them or not. Tindwyl would probably chastise him for that.

Here, he thought, tapping the page. *I might have grounds to argue for a revote if any of the members of the Assembly arrived late to the meeting, or made their votes in absentia.* The vote to depose had to be unanimous—save, of course, for the king being deposed.

He paused, noticing movement. Tindwyl was the only one still in the room with him. He looked up from his books with resignation. *I probably have this coming. . . .*

"I apologize for treating you with disrespect, Your Majesty," she said.

Elend frowned. *Wasn't expecting that.*

"I have a habit of treating people like children," Tindwyl said. "It is not something that I should be proud of, I think."

"It's—" Elend paused. Tindwyl had taught him never to excuse people's failings. He could accept people with failings—even forgive them—but if he glossed over the problems, then they would never change. "I accept your apology," he said.

"You've learned quickly, Your Majesty."

"I haven't had much choice," Elend said with a smile. "Of course, I didn't change fast enough for the Assembly."

"How did you let this happen?" she asked quietly. "Even considering our disagreement over how a government should be run, I should think that these Assemblymen would be supporters of yours. You gave them their power."

"I ignored them, Tindwyl. Powerful men, friends or not, never like being ignored."

She nodded. "Though, perhaps we should pause to take

note of your successes, rather than simply focusing on your failings. Vin tells me that your meeting with your father went well."

Elend smiled. "We scared him into submission. It felt very good to do something like that to Straff. But, I think I might have offended Vin somehow."

Tindwyl raised an eyebrow.

Elend set down his book, leaning forward with his arms on the desk. "She was in an odd mood on the way back. I could barely get her to talk to me. I'm not sure what it was."

"Perhaps she was just tired."

"I'm not convinced that Vin *gets* tired," Elend said. "She's always moving, always doing something. Sometimes, I worry that she thinks I'm lazy. Maybe that's why . . ." He trailed off, then shook his head.

"She doesn't think that you are lazy, Your Majesty," Tindwyl said. "She refused to marry you because she doesn't think that she is worthy of you."

"Nonsense," Elend said. "Vin's Mistborn, Tindwyl. She knows she's worth ten men like me."

Tindwyl raised an eyebrow. "You understand very little about women, Elend Venture—especially young women. To them, their competence has a surprisingly small amount to do with how they feel about themselves. Vin is insecure. She doesn't believe that she deserves to be with you—it is less that she doesn't think she deserves you personally, and more that she isn't convinced that she deserves to be happy at all. She has led a very confusing, difficult life."

"How sure are you about this?"

"I've raised a number of daughters, Your Majesty," Tindwyl said. "I understand the things of which I speak."

"Daughters?" Elend asked. "You have children?"

"Of course."

"I just . . ." The Terrismen he'd known were eunuchs, like Sazed. The same couldn't be true for a woman like Tindwyl, of course, but he'd assumed that the Lord Ruler's breeding programs would have affected her somehow.

"Regardless," Tindwyl said curtly, "you must make some decisions, Your Majesty. Your relationship with Vin is going to be difficult. She has certain issues that will provide more problems than you would find in a more conventional woman."

"We've already discussed this," Elend said. "I'm not looking for a more 'conventional' woman. I love Vin."

"I'm not implying that you shouldn't," Tindwyl said calmly. "I am simply giving you instruction, as I have been asked to do. You need to decide how much you're going to let the girl, and your relationship with her, distract you."

"What makes you think I'm distracted?"

Tindwyl raised an eyebrow. "I asked you about your success with Lord Venture this evening, and all you wanted to talk about was how Vin felt during the ride home."

Elend hesitated.

"Which is more important to you, Your Majesty?" Tindwyl asked. "This girl's love, or the good of your people?"

"I'm not going to answer a question like that," Elend said.

"Eventually, you may not have a choice," Tindwyl said. "It is a question most kings face eventually, I fear."

"No," Elend said. "There's no reason that I can't both love Vin and protect my people. I've studied too many hypothetical dilemmas to be caught in a trap like that."

Tindwyl shrugged, standing. "Believe as you wish, Your Majesty. However, I already see a dilemma, and I find it not at all hypothetical." She bowed her head slightly in deference, then withdrew from the room, leaving him with his books.

There were other proofs to connect Alendi to the Hero of Ages.
Smaller things, things that only one trained in the lore of the
Anticipation would have noticed. The birthmark on his arm.
The way his hair turned gray when he was barely twenty and
five years of age. The way he spoke, the way he treated people,
the way he ruled.

He simply seemed to fit.

29

"TELL ME, MISTRESS," ORESEUR SAID, lying lazily,
head on paws. "I have been around humans for a goodly
number of years. I was under the impression that they
needed regular sleep. I guess I was mistaken."

Vin sat on a wall-top stone ledge, one leg up against her
chest, the other dangling over the side of the wall. Keep
Hasting's towers were dark shadows in the mists to her
right and to her left. "I sleep," she said.

"Occasionally." OreSeur yawned a deep, tongue-stretching
yawn. Was he adopting more canine mannerisms?

Vin turned away from the kandra, looking east, over the
slumbering city of Luthadel. There was a fire in the distance, a growing light that was too large to be of man's
touch. Dawn had arrived. Another night had passed, making it nearly a week since she and Elend had visited
Straff's army. Zane had yet to appear.

"You're burning pewter, aren't you?" OreSeur asked.
"To stay awake?"

Vin nodded. Beneath a light burn of pewter, her fatigue
was only a mild annoyance. She could feel it deep within
her, if she looked hard, but it had no power over her. Her
senses were keen, her body strong. Even the night's cold
wasn't as bothersome. The moment she extinguished her
pewter, however, she'd feel the exhaustion in force.

"That cannot be healthy, Mistress," OreSeur said. "You sleep barely three or four hours a day. Nobody—Mistborn, man, or kandra—can survive on a schedule like that for long."

Vin looked down. How could she explain her strange insomnia? She should be over that; she no longer had to be frightened of the other crewmembers around her. And yet, no matter how exhausted she grew, she was finding sleep more and more difficult to claim. How could she sleep, with that quiet thumping in the distance?

It seemed to be getting closer, for some reason. Or simply stronger? *I hear the thumping sounds from above, the pulsings from the mountains. . . .* Words from the logbook.

How could she sleep, knowing that the spirit watched her from the mist, ominous and hateful? How could she sleep when armies threatened to slaughter her friends, when Elend's kingdom had been taken from him, when everything she thought she'd known and loved was getting muddled and obscure?

. . . when I finally lie down, I find sleep elusive. The same thoughts that trouble me during the day are only compounded by the stillness of night. . . .

OreSeur yawned again. "He's not coming, Mistress."

Vin turned, frowning. "What do you mean?"

"This is the last place you sparred with Zane," OreSeur said. "You're waiting for him to come."

Vin paused. "I could use a spar," she finally said.

Light continued to grow in the east, slowly brightening the mists. The mists persisted, however, reticent to give way before the sun.

"You shouldn't let that man influence you so, Mistress," OreSeur said. "I do not think he is the person you believe him to be."

Vin frowned. "He's my enemy. What else would I believe?"

"You do not treat him like an enemy, Mistress."

"Well, he hasn't attacked Elend," Vin said. "Maybe Zane isn't fully under Straff's control."

OreSeur sat quietly, head on paws. Then he turned away.

"What?" Vin asked.

"Nothing, Mistress. I will believe as I'm told."

"Oh, no," Vin said, turning on the ledge to look at him. "You're not going back to that excuse. What were you thinking?"

OreSeur sighed. "I was thinking, Mistress, that your fixation with Zane is disconcerting."

"Fixation?" Vin said. "I'm just keeping an eye on him. I don't like having another Mistborn—enemy or not—running around in my city. Who knows what he could be up to?"

OreSeur frowned, but said nothing.

"OreSeur," Vin said, "if you have things to say, speak!"

"I apologize, Mistress," OreSeur said. "I'm not accustomed to chatting with my masters—especially not candidly."

"It's all right. Just speak your mind."

"Well, Mistress," OreSeur said, raising his head off his paws, "I do not like this Zane."

"What do you know of him?"

"Nothing more than you," OreSeur admitted. "However, most kandra are very good judges of character. When you practice imitation for as long as I have, you learn to see to the hearts of men. I do not like what I have seen of Zane. He seems too pleased with himself. He seems too deliberate in the way he has befriended you. He makes me uncomfortable."

Vin sat on the ledge, legs parted, hands before her with palms down, resting on the cool stone. *He might be right.*

But, OreSeur hadn't flown with Zane, hadn't sparred in the mists. Through no fault of his own, OreSeur was like Elend. Not an Allomancer. Neither of them could understand what it was to soar on a Push of steel, to flare tin and experience the sudden shock of five heightened senses. They couldn't know. They couldn't understand.

Vin leaned back. Then, she regarded the wolfhound in the growing light. There was something she'd been meaning to mention, and now seemed as good a time as any. "OreSeur, you can switch bodies, if you want."

The wolfhound raised an eyebrow.

"We have those bones that we found in the palace," Vin said. "You can use those, if you're tired of being a dog."

"I couldn't use them," OreSeur said. "I haven't digested their body—I wouldn't know the proper arrangement of muscles and organs to make the person look correct."

"Well, then," Vin said. "We could get you a criminal."

"I thought you liked these bones on me," OreSeur said.

"I do," Vin said. "But, I don't want you to stay in a body that makes you unhappy."

OreSeur snorted. "My happiness is not an issue."

"It is to me," Vin said. "We could—"

"Mistress," OreSeur interrupted.

"Yes?"

"I shall keep these bones. I've grown accustomed to them. It is very frustrating to change forms often."

Vin hesitated. "All right," she finally said.

OreSeur nodded. "Though," he continued, "speaking of bodies, Mistress, are we ever planning to return to the palace? Not all of us have the constitution of a Mistborn—some people need sleep and food on occasion."

He certainly complains a lot more now, Vin thought. However, she found the attitude to be a good sign; it meant OreSeur was growing more comfortable with her. Comfortable enough to tell her when he thought she was being stupid.

Why do I even bother with Zane? she thought, rising and turning eyes northward. The mist was still moderately strong, and she could barely make out Straff's army, still holding the northern canal, maintaining the siege. It sat like a spider, waiting for the right time to spring.

Elend, she thought. *I should be more focused on Elend.* His motions to dismiss the Assembly's decision, or to force a revote, had all failed. And, stubbornly lawful as always, Elend continued to accept his failures. He still thought he had a chance to persuade the Assembly to choose him as king—or at least not vote anybody else to the position.

So he worked on speeches and planned with Breeze and Dockson. This left him little time for Vin, and rightly so. The last thing he needed was her distracting him. This was something she couldn't help him with—something she couldn't fight or scare away.

His world is of papers, books, laws, and philosophies, she thought. *He rides the words of his theories like I ride the mists. I always worry that he can't understand me . . . but can I really even understand him?*

OreSeur stood, stretched, and placed his forepaws on the wall's railing to raise himself and look north, like Vin.

Vin shook her head. "Sometimes, I wish Elend weren't so . . . well, noble. The city doesn't need this confusion right now."

"He did the right thing, Mistress."

"You think so?"

"Of course," OreSeur said. "He made a contract. It is his duty to keep that contract, no matter what. He must serve his master—in his case, that would be the city—even if that master makes him do something very distasteful."

"That's a very kandralike way of seeing things," Vin said.

OreSeur looked up at her, raising a canine eyebrow, as if to ask *Well, what did you expect?* She smiled; she had to suppress a chuckle every time she saw that expression on his dog face.

"Come on," Vin said. "Let's get back to the palace."

"Excellent," OreSeur said, dropping down to all fours. "That meat I set out should be perfect by now."

"Unless the maids found it again," Vin said with a smile.

OreSeur's expression darkened. "I thought you were going to warn them."

"What would I say?" Vin asked with amusement. "Please don't throw away this rancid meat—my dog likes to eat it?"

"Why not?" OreSeur asked. "When I imitate a human, I almost never get to have a good meal, but dogs eat aged meat sometimes, don't they?"

"I honestly don't know," Vin said.

"Aged meat is delicious."

"You mean 'rotten' meat."

"Aged," OreSeur said insistently as she picked him up, preparing to carry him down from the wall. The top of Keep Hasting was a good hundred feet tall—far too high up for OreSeur to jump, and the only path down would be through the inside of the abandoned keep. Better to carry him.

"Aged meat is like aged wine or aged cheese," OreSeur continued. "It tastes better when it's a few weeks old."

I suppose that's one of the side effects of being related to scavengers, Vin thought. She hopped up on the lip of the wall, dropping a few coins. However, as she prepared to jump—OreSeur a large bulk in her arms—she hesitated. She turned one last time, looking out at Straff's army. It was fully visible now; the sun had risen completely above the horizon. Yet, a few insistent swirls of mist wavered in the air, as if trying to defy the sun, to continue to cloak the city, to stave off the light of day. . . .

Lord Ruler! Vin thought, struck by a sudden insight. She'd been working on this problem so long, it had begun to frustrate her. And now, when she'd been ignoring it, the answer had come to her. As if her subconscious had still been picking it apart.

"Mistress?" OreSeur asked. "Is everything all right?"

Vin opened her mouth slightly, cocking her head. "I think I just realized what the Deepness was."

But, I must continue with the sparsest of detail. Space is limited. The other Worldbringers must have thought themselves humble when they came to me, admitting that they had been wrong. Even then, I was beginning to doubt my original declaration.

But, I was prideful.

30

I write this record now, Sazed read, *pounding it into a metal slab, because I am afraid. Afraid for myself, yes— I admit to being human. If Alendi does return from the Well of Ascension, I am certain that my death will be one of his first objectives. He is not an evil man, but he is a ruthless one. That is, I think, a product of what he has been through.*

I am also afraid, however, that all I have known—that my story—will be forgotten. I am afraid for the world that is to come. Afraid that Alendi will fail. Afraid of a doom brought by the Deepness.

It all comes back to poor Alendi. I feel bad for him, and for all the things he has been forced to endure. For what he has been forced to become.

But, let me begin at the beginning. I met Alendi first in Khlennium; he was a young lad then, and had not yet been warped by a decade spent leading armies.

Alendi's height struck me the first time I saw him. Here was a man who was small of stature, but who seemed to tower over others, a man who demanded respect.

Oddly, it was Alendi's simple ingenuousness that first led me to befriend him. I employed him as an assistant during his first months in the grand city.

It wasn't until years later that I became convinced that Alendi was the Hero of Ages. Hero of Ages: the one called Rabzeen in Khlennium, the Anamnesor.

Savior.

When I finally had the realization—finally connected all of the signs of the Anticipation to him—I was so excited. Yet, when I announced my discovery to the other Worldbringers, I was met with scorn. Oh, how I wish that I had listened to them.

And yet, any who know me will realize that there was no chance I would give up so easily. Once I find something to investigate, I become dogged in my pursuit. I had determined that Alendi was the Hero of Ages, and I intended to prove it. I should have bowed before the will of the others; I shouldn't have insisted on traveling with Alendi to witness his journeys. It was inevitable that Alendi himself would find out what I believed him to be.

Yes, he was the one who fueled the rumors after that. I could never have done what he himself did, convincing and persuading the world that he was indeed the Hero. I don't know if he himself believed it, but he made others think that he must be the one.

If only the Terris religion, and belief in the Anticipation, hadn't spread beyond our people. If only the Deepness hadn't come, providing a threat that drove men to desperation both in action and belief. If only I had passed over Alendi when looking for an assistant, all those years ago.

Sazed sat back from his work of transcribing the rubbing. There was still a great deal to do—it was amazing how much writing this Kwaan had managed to cram onto the relatively small sheet of steel.

Sazed looked over his work. He'd spent his entire trip north anticipating the time when he could finally begin work on the rubbing. A part of him had been worried. Would the dead man's words seem as important sitting in a well-lit room as they had when in the dungeons of the Conventical of Seran?

He scanned to another part of the document, reading a few choice paragraphs. Ones of particular importance to him.

As the one who found Alendi, however, I became some-one important. Foremost amongst the Worldbringers.

There was a place for me, in the lore of the Anticipation—I thought myself the Announcer, the prophet foretold to discover the Hero of Ages. Renouncing Alendi then would have been to renounce my new position, my acceptance, by the others.

And so I did not.

But I do so now. Let it be known that I, Kwaan, Worldbringer of Terris, am a fraud.

Sazed closed his eyes. *Worldbringer.* The term was known to him; the order of the Keepers had been founded upon memories and hopes from Terris legends. The Worldbringers had been teachers, Feruchemists who had traveled the lands bearing knowledge. They had been a prime inspiration for the secret order of Keepers.

And now he had a document made by a Worldbringer's own hand.

Tindwyl is going to be very annoyed with me, Sazed thought, opening his eyes. He'd read the entire rubbing, but he would need to spend time studying it. Memorizing it. Cross-referencing it with other documents. This one bit of writing—perhaps twenty pages total—could easily keep him busy for months, even years.

His window shutters rattled. Sazed looked up. He was in his quarters at the palace—a tasteful collection of well-decorated rooms that were far too lavish for one who had spent his life as a servant. He rose, walked over to the window, undid the latch, and pulled open the shutters. He smiled as he found Vin crouching on the ledge outside.

"Um . . . hi," Vin said. She wore her mistcloak over gray shirt and black trousers. Despite the onset of morning, she obviously hadn't yet gone to bed after her nightly prowling. "You should leave your window unlatched. I can't get in if it's locked. Elend got mad at me for breaking too many latches."

"I shall try to remember that, Lady Vin," Sazed said, and gesturing for her to enter.

Vin hopped spryly through the window, mistcloak rustling. "*Try* to remember?" she asked. "You never forget anything. Not even the things you don't have stuck in a metalmind."

She's grown so much more bold, he thought as she walked over to his writing desk, peering over his work. *Even in the months I've been away.*

"What's this?" Vin asked, still looking at the desk.

"I found it at the Conventical of Seran, Lady Vin," Sazed said, walking forward. It felt so good to be wearing clean robes again, to have a quiet and comfortable place in which to study. Was he a bad man for preferring this to travel?

One month, he thought. *I will give myself one month of study. Then I will turn the project over to someone else.*

"What is it?" Vin asked, holding up the rubbing.

"If you please, Lady Vin," Sazed said apprehensively. "That is quite fragile. The rubbing could be smudged. . . ."

Vin nodded, putting it down and scanning his transcription. There had been a time when she would have avoided anything that smelled of stuffy writing, but now she looked intrigued. "This mentions the Deepness!" she said with excitement.

"Among other things," Sazed said, joining her at the desk. He sat down, and Vin walked over to one of the room's low-backed, plush chairs. However, she didn't sit on it as an ordinary person would; instead, she hopped up and sat down on the top of the chair's back, her feet resting on the seat cushion.

"What?" she asked, apparently noticing Sazed's smile.

"Just amused at a proclivity of Mistborn, Lady Vin," he said. "Your kind has trouble simply sitting—it seems you always want to perch instead. That is what comes from having such an incredible sense of balance, I think."

Vin frowned, but passed over the comment. "Sazed," she said, "what was the Deepness?"

He laced his fingers before himself, regarding the young woman as he mused. "The Deepness, Lady Vin? That is a subject of much debate, I think. It was supposedly something great and powerful, though some scholars have dismissed the entire legend as a fabrication concocted by the Lord Ruler. There is some reason to believe this theory, I think, for the only real records of those times are the ones sanctioned by the Steel Ministry."

"But, the logbook mentions the Deepness," Vin said. "And so does that thing you're translating now."

"Indeed, Lady Vin," Sazed said. "But, even among those who assume the Deepness was real, there is a great deal of debate. Some hold to the Lord Ruler's official story, that the Deepness was a horrible, supernatural beast—a dark god, if you will. Others disagree with this extreme interpretation. They think the Deepness was more mundane— an army of some sort, perhaps invaders from another land. The Farmost Dominance, during pre-Ascension times, was apparently populated with several breeds of men who were quite primitive and warlike."

Vin was smiling. He looked at her questioningly, and

she just shrugged. "I asked Elend this same question," she explained, "and I got barely a sentence-long response."

"His Majesty has different areas of scholarship; pre-Ascension history may be too stuffy a topic even for him. Besides, anyone who asks a Keeper about the past should be prepared for an extended conversation, I think."

"I'm not complaining," Vin said. "Continue."

"There isn't much more to say—or, rather, there is a great deal more to say, but I doubt much of it has relevance. Was the Deepness an army? Was it, perhaps, the first attack from koloss, as some theorize? That would explain much—most stories agree that the Lord Ruler gained some power to defeat the Deepness at the Well of Ascension. Perhaps he gained the support of the koloss, and then used them as his armies."

"Sazed," Vin said. "I don't think the Deepness was the koloss."

"Oh?"

"I think it was the mist."

"That theory has been proposed," Sazed said with a nod.

"It has?" Vin asked, sounding a bit disappointed.

"Of course, Lady Vin. During the thousand-year reign of the Final Empire, there are few possibilities that *haven't* been discussed, I think. The mist theory has been advanced before, but there are several large problems with it."

"Such as?"

"Well," Sazed said, "for one thing, the Lord Ruler is said to have defeated the Deepness. However, the mist is obviously still here. Also, if the Deepness was simply mist, why call it by such an obscure name? Of course, others point out that much of what we know or have heard of the Deepness comes from oral lore, and something very common can take on mystical properties when transferred verbally through generations. The 'Deepness' therefore could mean not just the mist, but the event of its coming or alteration.

"The larger problem with the mist theory, however, is one of malignance. If we trust the accounts—and we have little else to go on—the Deepness was terrible and destructive. The mist seems to display none of this danger."

"But it kills people now."

Sazed paused. "Yes, Lady Vin. It apparently does."

"And what if it did so before, but the Lord Ruler stopped it somehow? You yourself said that you think we did something—something that changed the mist—when we killed the Lord Ruler."

Sazed nodded. "The problems I have been investigating are quite terrible, to be certain. However, I do not see that they could be a threat on the same level as the Deepness. Certain people have been killed by the mists, but many are elderly or otherwise lacking in constitution. It leaves many people alone."

He paused, tapping his thumbs together. "But, I would be remiss if I didn't admit some merit to the suggestion, Lady Vin. Perhaps even a few deaths would be enough to cause a panic. The danger could have been exaggerated by retelling—and, perhaps the killings were more widespread before. I haven't been able to collect enough information to be certain of anything yet."

Vin didn't respond. *Oh, dear,* Sazed thought, sighing to himself. *I've bored her. I really do need to be more careful, watching my vocabulary and my language. One would think that after all my travels among the skaa, I would have learned—*

"Sazed?" Vin said, sounding thoughtful. "What if we're looking at it wrong? What if these random deaths in the mists aren't the problem at all?"

"What do you mean, Lady Vin?"

She sat quietly for a moment, one foot tapping back idly against the chair's back cushion. She finally looked up, meeting his eyes. "What would happen if the mists came during the day permanently?"

Sazed mused on that for a moment.

"There would be no light," Vin continued. "Plants would die, people would starve. There would be death . . . chaos."

"I suppose," Sazed said. "Perhaps that theory has merit."

"It's not a theory," Vin said, hopping down from her chair. "It's what happened."

"You're so certain, already?" Sazed asked with amusement.

Vin nodded curtly, joining him at the desk. "I'm right," she said with her characteristic bluntness. "I know it." She pulled something out of a trouser pocket, then drew over a stool to sit beside him. She unfolded the wrinkled sheet and flattened it on the desk.

"These are quotes from the logbook," Vin said. She pointed at a paragraph. "Here the Lord Ruler talks about how armies were useless against the Deepness. At first, I thought this meant that the armies hadn't been able to defeat it—but look at the wording. He says 'The swords of my armies are useless.' What's more useless than trying to swing a sword at mist?"

She pointed at another paragraph. "It left destruction in its wake, right? Countless thousands died because of it. But, he never says that the Deepness actually attacked them. He says that they 'died because of it.' Maybe we've just been looking at this the wrong way all along. Those people weren't crushed or eaten. They starved to death because their land was slowly being swallowed by the mists."

Sazed studied her paper. She seemed so certain. Did she know nothing of proper research techniques? Of questioning, of studying, of postulating and devising answers?

Of course she doesn't, Sazed chastised himself. *She grew up on the streets—she doesn't use research techniques.*

She just uses instinct. And she's usually right.

He smoothed the paper again, reading its passages. "Lady Vin? Did you write this yourself?"

She flushed. "Why is everybody so surprised about that?"

"It just doesn't seem in your nature, Lady Vin."

"You people have corrupted me," she said. "Look, there isn't a single comment on this sheet that contradicts the idea that the Deepness was mist."

"Not contradicting a point and proving it are different things, Lady Vin."

She waved indifferently. "I'm right, Sazed. I *know* I am."

"What about this point, then?" Sazed asked, pointing to

a line. "The Hero implies that he can sense a sentience to the Deepness. The mist isn't alive."

"Well, it does swirl around someone using Allomancy."

"That isn't the same thing, I think," Sazed said. "He says that the Deepness was mad . . . destructively insane. Evil."

Vin paused. "There is something, Sazed," she admitted.

He frowned.

She pointed at another section of notes. "Do you recognize these paragraphs?" *It isn't a shadow,* the words read.

> *This dark thing that follows me, the thing that only I can see—it isn't really a shadow. It is blackish and translucent, but it doesn't have a shadowlike solid outline. It's insubstantial—wispy and formless. Like it's made out of a dark fog.*
>
> *Or mist, perhaps.*

"Yes, Lady Vin," Sazed said. "The Hero saw a creature following him. It attacked one of his companions, I think."

Vin looked in his eyes. "I've seen it, Sazed."

He felt a chill.

"It's out there," she said. "Every night, in the mists. Watching me. I can *feel* it, with Allomancy. And, if I get close enough, I can see it. As if formed from the mist itself. Insubstantial, yet somehow still there."

Sazed sat quietly for a moment, not certain what to think.

"You think me mad," Vin accused.

"No, Lady Vin," he said quietly. "I don't think any of us are in a position to call such things madness, not considering what is happening. Just . . . are you certain?"

She nodded firmly.

"But," Sazed said. "Even if this is true, it does not answer my question. The logbook author saw that same creature, and he didn't refer to it as the Deepness. It was not the Deepness, then. The Deepness was something else—something dangerous, something he could feel as evil."

"That's the secret, then," Vin said. "We have to figure out why he spoke of the mists that way. Then we'll know . . ."

"Know what, Lady Vin?" Sazed asked.

Vin paused, then looked away. She didn't answer, instead turning to a different topic. "Sazed, the Hero never did what he was supposed to. Rashek killed him. And, when Rashek took the power at the Well, he didn't give it up like he was supposed to—he kept it for himself."

"True," Sazed said.

Vin paused again. "And the mists have started killing people. They've started coming during the day. It's . . . like things are repeating again. So . . . maybe that means that the Hero of Ages will have to come again."

She glanced back at him, looking a bit . . . embarrassed? *Ah* . . . Sazed thought, sensing her implication. She saw things in the mists. The previous Hero had seen the same things. "I am not certain that is a valid statement, Lady Vin."

She snorted. "Why can't you just come out and say 'you're wrong,' like regular people?"

"I apologize, Lady Vin. I have had much training as a servant, and we are taught to be nonconfrontational. Nevertheless, I do not think that you are wrong. However, I also think that, perhaps, you haven't fully considered your position."

Vin shrugged.

"What makes you think that the Hero of Ages will return?"

"I don't know. Things that happen; things I feel. The mists are coming again, and someone needs to stop them."

Sazed ran his fingers across his translated section of the rubbing, looking over its words.

"You don't believe me," Vin said.

"It isn't that, Lady Vin," Sazed said. "It's just that I am not prone to rushing to decisions."

"But, you've thought about the Hero of Ages, haven't you?" Vin said. "He was part of your religion—the lost religion of Terris, the thing you Keepers were founded to try and discover."

"That is true," Sazed admitted. "However, we do not know much about the prophecies that our ancestors used to find their Hero. Besides, the reading I've been doing lately suggests that there was something wrong with their interpretations. If the greatest theologians of pre-Ascension Terris were unable to properly identify their Hero, how are we supposed to do so?"

Vin sat quietly. "I shouldn't have brought it up," she finally said.

"No, Lady Vin, please don't think that. I apologize—your theories have great merit. I simply have a scholar's mind, and must question and consider information when I am given it. I am far too fond of arguing, I think."

Vin looked up, smiling slightly. "Another reason you never made a good Terris steward?"

"Undoubtedly," he said with a sigh. "My attitude also tends to cause conflicts with the others of my order."

"Like Tindwyl?" Vin asked. "She didn't sound happy when she heard that you'd told us about Feruchemy."

Sazed nodded. "For a group dedicated to knowledge, the Keepers can be rather stingy with information about their powers. When the Lord Ruler still lived—when Keepers were hunted—the caution was warranted, I think. But, now that we are free from that, my brethren and sisters seem to have found the habit of secrecy a difficult one to break."

Vin nodded. "Tindwyl doesn't seem to like you very much. She says that she came because of your suggestion, but every time someone mentions you, she seems to get . . . cold."

Sazed sighed. Did Tindwyl dislike him? He thought, perhaps, that her inability to do so was a large part of the problem. "She is simply disappointed in me, Lady Vin. I'm not sure how much you know of my history, but I had been working against the Lord Ruler for some ten years before Kelsier recruited me. The other Keepers thought that I endangered my copperminds, and the very order itself. They believed that the Keepers should remain quiet—waiting for the day when the Lord Ruler fell, but not seeking to make it happen."

"Seems a bit cowardly to me," Vin said.

"Ah, but it was a very prudent course. You see, Lady Vin, had I been captured, there are many things I could have revealed. The names of other Keepers, the location of our safe houses, the means by which we managed to hide ourselves in Terris culture. My brethren worked for many decades to make the Lord Ruler think that Feruchemy had finally been exterminated. By revealing myself, I could have undone all of that."

"That would only have been bad had we failed," Vin said. "We didn't."

"We could have."

"We didn't."

Sazed paused, then smiled. Sometimes, in a world of debate, questions, and self-doubt, Vin's simple bluntness was refreshing. "Regardless," he continued, "Tindwyl is a member of the Synod—a group of Keeper elders who guide our sect. I have been in rebellion against the Synod a number of times during my past. And, by returning to Luthadel, I am defying them once again. She has good reason to be displeased with me."

"Well, *I* think you're doing the right thing," Vin said. "We need you."

"Thank you, Lady Vin."

"I don't think you have to listen to Tindwyl," she said. "She's the type who acts like she knows more than she does."

"She is very wise."

"She's hard on Elend."

"Then she probably does so because it is best for him," Sazed said. "Do not judge her too harshly, child. If she seems off-putting, it is only because she has lived a very hard life."

"Hard life?" Vin asked, tucking her notes back into her pocket.

"Yes, Lady Vin," Sazed said. "You see, Tindwyl spent most of her life as a Terris mother."

Vin hesitated, hand in pocket, looking surprised. "You mean . . . she was a Breeder?"

Sazed nodded. The Lord Ruler's breeding program included selecting a few, special individuals to use for birthing new children—with the goal being to breed Feruchemy out of the population.

"Tindwyl had, at last count, birthed over twenty children," he said. "Each with a different father. Tindwyl had her first child when she was fourteen, and spent her entire life being taken repeatedly by strange men until she became pregnant. And, because of the fertility drugs the Breeding masters forced upon her, she often bore twins or triplets."

"I . . . see," Vin said softly.

"You are not the only one who knew a terrible childhood, Lady Vin. Tindwyl is perhaps the strongest woman I know."

"How did she bear it?" Vin asked quietly. "I think . . . I think I would probably have just killed myself."

"She is a Keeper," Sazed said. "She suffered the indignity because she knew that she did a great service for her people. You see, Feruchemy is hereditary. Tindwyl's position as a mother ensured future generations of Feruchemists among our people. Ironically, she is exactly the sort of person that the Breeding masters were supposed to avoid letting reproduce."

"But, how did such a thing happen?"

"The breeders assumed they'd already cut Feruchemy out of the population," Sazed said. "They started looking to create other traits in the Terris—docility, temperance. They bred us like fine horses, and it was a great stroke when the Synod managed to get Tindwyl chosen for their program.

"Of course, Tindwyl has very little training in Feruchemy. She did, fortunately, receive some of the copperminds that we Keepers carry. So, during her many years locked away, she was able to study and read biographies. It was only during the last decade—her childbearing years through—that she was able to join and gain fellowship with the other Keepers."

Sazed paused, then shook his head. "By comparison, the rest of us have known a life of freedom, I think."

"Great," Vin mumbled, standing and yawning. "Another reason for you to feel guilty."

"You should sleep, Lady Vin," Sazed noted.

"For a few hours," Vin said, walking toward the door, leaving him alone again with his studies.

In the end, my pride may have doomed us all.

31

PHILEN FRANDEU WAS NOT SKAA. He had *never* been skaa. Skaa made things or grew things. Philen sold things. There was an enormous difference between the two.

Oh, some people had called him skaa. Even now, he could see that word in the eyes of some of the other Assemblymen. They regarded Philen and his fellow merchants with the same disdain that they gave the eight skaa workers on the Assembly. Couldn't they see that the two groups were completely different?

Philen shifted a bit on the bench. Shouldn't the Assembly hall at least have comfortable seating? They were waiting on just a few members; the tall clock in the corner said that fifteen minutes still remained until the meeting began. Oddly, one of those who had yet to arrive was Venture himself. King Elend was usually early.

Not king anymore, Philen thought with a smile. *Just plain old Elend Venture.* It was a poor name—not as good as Philen's own. Of course, he had been just "Lin" until a year and a half ago. Philen Frandeu was what he had dubbed himself after the Collapse. It delighted him to no end that the others had taken to calling him the name without pause. But, why shouldn't he have a grand name? A lord's name? Was Philen not as good as any of the "noble-men" sitting aloofly in their places?

Oh, he was just as good. Better, even. Yes, they had called him skaa—but during those years, they had come to him out of need, and so their arrogant sneers had lacked power. He'd seen their insecurity. They'd needed him. A man they called skaa. But he'd also been a merchant. A merchant who wasn't noble. Something that wasn't supposed to have ex-isted in the Lord Ruler's perfect little empire.

But, noblemen merchants had to work with the obliga-tors. And, where there had been obligators, nothing illegal could occur. Hence Philen. He'd been . . . an intermediary, of sorts. A man capable of arranging deals between inter-ested parties who, for various reasons, wanted to avoid the watchful eyes of the Lord Ruler's obligators. Philen hadn't been part of a thieving crew—no, that was far too danger-ous. And far too mundane.

He had been born with an eye for finances and trades. Give him two rocks, and he'd have a quarry by the end of the week. Give him a spoke, and he'd change it to a fine horse-drawn carriage. Two bits of corn, and he'd eventu-ally have a massive shipment of grain sailing to the Far-most Dominance markets. Actual noblemen had done the trades, of course, but Philen had been behind it all. A vast empire of his own.

And still, they couldn't see. He wore a suit as fine as theirs; now that he could trade openly, he had become one of the wealthiest men in Luthadel. Yet, the noblemen ig-nored him, just because he lacked a valid pedigree.

Well, they would see. After today's meeting . . . yes, they would see. Philen looked out into the crowd, looking anx-iously for the person he had hidden there. Reassured, he looked toward the noblemen of the Assembly, who sat chat-ting a short distance away. One of their last members—Lord Ferson Penrod—had just arrived. The older man walked up onto the Assembly's dais, passing by the mem-bers, greeting each in turn.

"Philen," Penrod said, noticing him. "A new suit, I see. The red vest suits you."

"Lord Penrod! Why, you're looking well. You got over the other night's ailment, then?"

"Yes, it passed quickly," the lord said, nodding a head topped with silver hair. "Just a touch of stomach ills."

Pity, Philen thought, smiling. "Well, we'd best be seated. I see that young Venture isn't here, though. . . ."

"Yes," Penrod said, frowning. He'd been most difficult to convince to vote against Venture; he had something of a fondness for the boy. He had come around in the end. They all had.

Penrod moved on, joining the other noblemen. The old fool probably thought he was going to end up as king. Well, Philen had other plans for that throne. It wasn't Philen's own posterior that would sit in it, of course; he had no interest in running a country. Seemed like a terrible way to make money. Selling things. That was a much better way. More stable, less likely to lose one his head.

Oh, but Philen had plans. He'd always had those. He had to keep himself from glancing at the audience again.

Philen turned, instead, to study the Assembly. They had all arrived except Venture. Seven noblemen, eight merchants, and eight skaa workers: twenty-four men, with Venture. The three-way division was supposed to give the commoners the most power, since they ostensibly outnumbered the noblemen. Even Venture hadn't understood that merchants weren't skaa.

Philen wrinkled his nose. Even though the skaa Assemblymen usually cleaned up before coming to the meetings, he could smell the stink of forges, mills, and shops on them. Men who made things. Philen would have to be certain they were put back in their place, once this was over. An Assembly was an interesting idea, but it should be filled only with those who deserved the station. Men like Philen.

Lord Philen, he thought. *Not long now.*

Hopefully, Elend would be late. Then, maybe they could avoid his speech. Philen could imagine how it would go anyway.

Um . . . now, see, this wasn't fair. I should be king. Here, let me read you a book about why. Now, um, can you all please give some more money to the skaa?

Philen smiled.

The man next to him, Getrue, nudged him. "You think he's going to show up?" he whispered.

"Probably not. He must know that we don't want him. We kicked him out, didn't we?"

Getrue shrugged. He'd gained weight since the Collapse—a lot of it. "I don't know, Lin. I mean . . . we didn't mean. He was just . . . the armies . . . We have to have a strong king, right? Someone who will keep the city from falling?"

"Of course," Philen said. "And my name isn't Lin."

Getrue flushed. "Sorry."

"We did the right thing," Philen continued. "Venture is a weak man. A fool."

"I wouldn't say that," Getrue said. "He has good ideas. . . ." Getrue glanced downward uncomfortably.

Philen snorted, glancing at the clock. It was time, though he couldn't hear the chimes over the crowd. The Assembly meetings had become busy since Venture's fall. Benches fanned out before the stage, benches crowded with people, mostly skaa. Philen wasn't sure why they were allowed to attend. They couldn't vote or anything.

More Venture foolishness, he thought, shaking his head. At the very back of the room—behind the crowd, opposite the stage—sat two large, broad doors letting in the red sunlight. Philen nodded toward some men, and they pushed the doors shut. The crowds hushed.

Philen stood to address the Assembly. "Well, since—"

The Assembly hall doors burst back open. A man in white stood with a small crowd of people, backlit by red sunlight. Elend Venture. Philen cocked his head, frowning.

The former king strode forward, white cape fluttering behind him. His Mistborn was at his side, as usual, but she was wearing a dress. From the few times Philen had spoken with her, he would have expected her to look awkward in a noblewoman's gown. And yet, she seemed to wear it well, walking gracefully. She actually looked rather fetching.

At least, until Philen met her eyes. She did not have a warm look for the Assembly members, and Philen glanced away. Venture had brought all of his Allomancers with him—the former thugs of the Survivor's crew. Elend apparently wanted to remind everyone who his friends were. Powerful men. Frightening men.

Men who killed gods.

And Elend had not one, but two Terrismen with him. One was only a woman—Philen had never seen a Terriswoman before—but still, it was impressive. Everyone had heard how the stewards had left their masters after the Collapse; they refused to work as servants anymore. Where had Venture found not one, but two of the colorful-robed stewards to serve him?

The crowd sat quietly, watching Venture. Some seemed uncomfortable. How were they to treat this man? Others seemed . . . awed? Was that right? Who would be awed by Elend Venture—even if the Elend Venture in question was clean-shaven, had styled hair, wore new clothing and . . . ? Philen frowned. Was that a dueling cane the king was wearing? And a wolfhound at his side?

He's not king anymore! Philen reminded himself again.

Venture strode up onto the Assembly stage. He turned, waving for his people—all eight of them—to sit with the guards. Venture then turned and glanced at Philen. "Philen, did you want to say something?"

Philen realized he was still standing. "I . . . was just—"

"Are you Assembly chancellor?" Elend asked.

Philen paused. "Chancellor?"

"The king presides at Assembly meetings," Elend said. "We now have no king—and so, by law, the Assembly should have elected a chancellor to call speakers, adjudicate time allotments, and break tie votes." He paused, eyeing Philen. "Someone needs to lead. Otherwise there is chaos."

Despite himself, Philen grew nervous. Did Venture know that Philen had organized the vote against him? No, no he didn't, he couldn't. He was looking at each of the Assembly members in turn, meeting their eyes. There was none of the jovial, dismissible boy that had attended these meetings before. Standing in the militaristic suit, firm instead of hesitant . . . he almost seemed like a different person.

You found a coach, it appears, Philen thought. *A little too late. Just wait. . . .*

Philen sat down. "Actually, we didn't get a chance to choose a chancellor," he said. "We were just getting to that."

Elend nodded, a dozen different instructions rattling in his head. Keep eye contact. Use subtle, but firm, expressions. Never appear hurried, but don't seem hesitant. Sit down without wiggling, don't shuffle, use a straight posture, don't form your hands into fists when you're nervous. . . .

He shot a quick glance at Tindwyl. She gave him a nod.

Get back to it, El, he told himself. *Let them sense the differences in you.*

He walked over to take his seat, nodding to the other seven noblemen on the Assembly. "Very well," he said, taking the lead. "Then, might I nominate a chancellor?"

"Yourself?" asked Dridel, one of the noblemen; his sneer seemed permanent, as far as Elend could tell. It was a passably appropriate expression for one with such a sharp face and dark hair.

"No," Elend said. "I'm hardly an unbiased party in today's proceedings. Therefore, I nominate Lord Penrod. He's as honorable a man as we're likely to find, and I believe he can be trusted to mediate our discussions."

The group was quiet for a moment.

"That seems logical," Hettel, a forge worker, finally said.

"All in favor?" Elend said, raising his hand. He got a good sixteen hands—all of the skaa, most of the nobility, only one of the merchants. It was a majority, however.

Elend turned to Lord Penrod. "I believe that means that you are in charge, Ferson."

The stately man nodded appreciatively, then rose to formally open the meeting, something Elend had once done. Penrod's mannerisms were polished, his posture strong as he stood in his well-cut suit. Elend couldn't help but feel a little jealous, watching Penrod act so naturally in the things that Elend was struggling to learn.

Maybe he would make a better king than I, Elend thought. *Perhaps . . .*

No, he thought firmly. *I have to be confident. Penrod is a decent man and an impeccable noble, but those things do not make a leader. He hasn't read what I've read, and doesn't understand legislative theory as I do. He's a good man, but he's still a product of his society—he doesn't consider skaa animals, but he'll never be able to think of them as equals.*

Penrod finished the introductions, then turned to Elend. "Lord Venture, you called this meeting. I believe that the law grants you first opportunity to address the Assembly."

Elend nodded thankfully, rising.

"Will twenty minutes be enough time?" Penrod asked.

"It should be," Elend said, passing Penrod as they traded places. Elend stood up at the lectern. To his right, the floor of the hall was packed with shuffling, coughing, whispering people. There was a tension to the room—this was the first time Elend had confronted the group that had betrayed him.

"As many of you know," Elend said to the twenty-three Assembly members, "I recently returned from a meeting with Straff Venture—the warlord who is, unfortunately, my father. I would like to give a report of this encounter. Realize that because this is an open meeting, I will adjust my report to avoid mentioning sensitive matters of national security."

He paused just slightly, and saw the looks of confusion he had expected. Finally, Philen the merchant cleared his throat.

"Yes, Philen?" Elend asked.

"This is all well and good, Elend," Philen said. "But aren't you going to address the matter that brought us here?"

"The reason we meet together, Philen," Elend said, "is so that we can discuss how to keep Luthadel safe and prosperous. I think the people are most worried about the armies—and we should, primarily, seek to address their concerns. Matters of leadership in the Assembly can wait."

"I . . . see," Philen said, obviously confused.

"The time is yours, Lord Venture," Penrod said. "Proceed as you wish."

"Thank you, Chancellor," Elend said. "I wish to make it very clear that my father is *not* going to attack this city. I can understand why people would be concerned, particularly because of last week's preliminary assault on our walls. That, however, was simply a test—Straff fears attacking too much to commit all of his resources.

"During our meeting, Straff told me that he had made an alliance with Cett. However, I believe this to have been a bluff—if, unfortunately, a bluff with teeth. I suspect that he was, indeed, planning to risk attacking us, despite Cett's presence. That attack has been halted."

"Why?" asked one of the worker representatives. "Because you're his son?"

"No, actually," Elend said. "Straff is not one to let familial relationships hamper his determination." Elend paused, glancing at Vin. He was beginning to realize that she didn't like being the one who held the knife at Straff's throat, but she had given him permission to speak of her in his speech.

Still . . .

She said it was all right, he told himself. *I'm not choosing duty over her!*

"Come now, Elend," Philen said. "Stop with the theatrics. What did you promise Straff to keep his armies out of the city?"

"I threatened him," Elend said. "My fellow Assemblymen, when facing down my father in parlay, I realized that we—as a group—have generally ignored one of our greatest resources. We think of ourselves as an honorable body, created by the mandate of the people. However, we are not here because of anything we ourselves did. There is only one reason we have the positions we do—and that reason is the Survivor of Hathsin."

Elend looked the members of the Assembly in the eyes as he continued. "I have, at times, felt as I suspect that many of you do. The Survivor is a legend already, one we cannot hope to emulate. He has power over this people—a power stronger than our own, even though he is dead. We're jealous. Insecure, even. These are natural, human feelings. Leaders feel them just as acutely as other people—perhaps even more so.

"Gentlemen, we cannot afford to continue thinking like this. The Survivor's legacy doesn't belong to one group, or even to this city alone. He is our progenitor—the father of everyone who is free in this land. Whether or not you accept his religious authority, you must admit that without his bravery and sacrifice, we would not now enjoy our current freedom."

"What does this have to do with Straff?" Philen snapped.

"Everything," Elend said. "For, though the Survivor is gone, his legacy remains. Specifically, in the form of his apprentice." Elend nodded toward Vin. "She is the most powerful Mistborn alive—something Straff now knows for himself. Gentlemen, I know my father's temperament. He will not attack this city while he fears retribution from a source he cannot stop. He now realizes that if he attacks, he will incur the wrath of the Survivor's heir—a wrath not even the Lord Ruler himself could withstand."

Elend fell silent, listening to the whispered conversations move through the crowd. News of what he'd just said would reach the populace, and bring them strength. Perhaps, even, news would reach Straff's army through the spies Elend knew must be in the audience. He'd noticed his father's Allomancer sitting in the crowd, the one named Zane.

And when news reached Straff's army, the men there might think twice about obeying any orders to attack. Who would want to face the very force that had destroyed the Lord Ruler? It was a weak hope—the men of Straff's army probably didn't believe all of the stories out of Luthadel—but every little bit of weakened morale would help.

It also wouldn't hurt for Elend to associate himself a little more strongly with the Survivor. He was just going to have to get over his insecurity; Kelsier had been a great man, but he was gone. Elend would just have to do his best to see that the Survivor's legacy lived on.

For that was what would be best for his people.

Vin sat with a twisted stomach, listening to Elend's speech.

"You okay with this?" Ham whispered, leaning over to her as Elend gave a more detailed account of his visit with Straff.

Vin shrugged. "Whatever helps the kingdom."

"You were never comfortable with the way that Kell set himself up with the skaa—none of us were."

"It's what Elend needs," Vin said.

Tindwyl, who sat just before them, turned and gave her a flat look. Vin expected some recrimination for whispering during the Assembly proceedings, but apparently the Terriswoman had a different kind of castigation in mind.

"The king—" She still referred to Elend that way. "—needs this link with the Survivor. Elend has very little of his own authority to rely upon, and Kelsier is currently the most well loved, most celebrated man in the Central Dominance. By implying that the government was founded by the Survivor, the king will make the people think twice about meddling with it."

Ham nodded thoughtfully. Vin glanced downward, however. *What's the problem? Just earlier, I was beginning to wonder if I were the Hero of Ages, and now I'm worried about the notoriety Elend is giving me?*

She sat uncomfortably, burning bronze, feeling the pulsing from far away. It was growing even louder. . . .

Stop it! she told herself. *Sazed doesn't think the Hero would return, and he knows the histories better than anyone. It was foolish, anyway. I need to focus on what's happening here.*

After all, Zane was in the audience.

Vin sought out his face near the back of the room, a light burn of tin—not enough to blind her—letting her study his features. He wasn't looking at her, but watching the Assembly. Was he working at Straff's command, or was this visit his own? Straff and Cett both undoubtedly had spies in the audience—and, of course, Ham had guards mixed with the people as well. Zane unnerved her, however. Why didn't he turn toward her? Wasn't—

Zane met her eyes. He smiled slightly, then turned back to his study of Elend.

Vin felt a shiver despite herself. So, did this mean he wasn't avoiding her? *Focus!* She told herself. *You need to pay attention to what Elend is saying.*

He was almost done, however. He wrapped up his speech with a few comments on how he thought they could keep Straff off-balance. Again, he couldn't be too detailed—not without giving away secrets. He glanced at the large clock in the corner; done three minutes early, he moved to leave the lectern.

Lord Penrod cleared his throat. "Elend, aren't you forgetting something?"

Elend hesitated, then looked back at the Assembly. "What is it that you all want me to say?"

"Don't you have a reaction?" one of the skaa workers said. "About . . . what happened at the last meeting?"

"You received my missive," Elend said. "You know how I feel about the matter. However, this public forum is not a place for accusations or denunciations. The Assembly is too noble a body for that kind of thing. I wish that a time of danger were not when the Assembly had chosen to voice its concerns, but we cannot alter what has happened."

He moved to sit again.

"That's it?" asked one of the skaa. "You're not even going to argue for yourself, try and persuade us to reinstate you?"

Elend paused again. "No," he said. "No, I don't think that I will. You have made your opinions known to me, and I am disappointed. However, you are the representatives chosen by the people. I believe in the power that you have been given.

"If you have questions, or challenges, I will be happy to defend myself. However, I am not going to stand and preach my virtues. You all know me. You know what I can do, and what I intend to do, for this city and the surrounding populace. Let that stand as my argument."

He returned to his seat. Vin could see hints of a frown on Tindwyl's face. Elend hadn't given the speech that she and he had prepared, a speech giving the very arguments the Assembly was obviously expecting.

Why the change? Vin wondered. Tindwyl obviously didn't think it was a good idea. And yet, oddly, Vin found herself trusting Elend's instincts more than she did Tindwyl's.

"Well," Lord Penrod said, approaching the lectern again. "Thank you for that report, Lord Venture. I'm not certain if we have other items of business. . . ."

"Lord Penrod?" Elend asked.

"Yes?"

"Perhaps you should hold the nominations?"

Lord Penrod frowned.

"The nominations for king, Penrod," Philen snapped.

Vin paused, eyeing the merchant. *He certainly seems up on things,* she noted.

"Yes," Elend said, eyeing Philen as well. "In order for the Assembly to choose a new king, nominations must be held at least three days before the actual voting. I suggest we hold the nominations now, so that we can hold the vote as soon as possible. The city suffers each day it is without a leader."

Elend paused, then smiled. "Unless, of course, you intend to let the month lapse without choosing a new king. . . ."

Good to confirm that he still wants the crown, Vin thought.

"Thank you, Lord Venture," Penrod said. "We'll do that now, then. . . . And, how exactly do we proceed?"

"Each member of the Assembly may make one nomination, if he wishes," Elend said. "So that we don't become overburdened with options, I would recommend that we all exercise restraint—only choose someone that you honestly and sincerely think would make the finest king. If you have a nomination to make, you may stand and announce it to the rest of the group."

Penrod nodded, returning to his seat. Almost as soon as he sat, however, one of the skaa stood. "I nominate Lord Penrod."

Elend had to expect that, Vin thought. *After nominating Penrod to be chancellor. Why give such authority to the man that he knew would be his greatest contender for the throne?*

The answer was simple. Because Elend knew that Lord Penrod was the best choice for chancellor. *Sometimes, he's a little* too *honorable,* Vin thought, not for the first time. She turned to study the skaa Assemblyman who had nominated Penrod. Why were the skaa so quick to unify behind a nobleman?

She suspected that it was still too soon. The skaa were accustomed to being led by noblemen, and even with their freedom, they were traditional beings—more traditional, even, than the noblemen. A lord like Penrod—calm, commanding—seemed inherently better suited to the title of king than a skaa.

They'll have to get over that, eventually, Vin thought. *At least, they will if they're ever going to be the people that Elend wants them to be.*

The room remained quiet, no other nominations being made. A few people coughed in the audience, even the whispers now dead. Finally, Lord Penrod himself stood.

"I nominate Elend Venture," he said.

"Ah . . ." someone whispered behind her.

Vin turned, glancing at Breeze. "What?" she whispered.

"Brilliant," Breeze said. "Don't you see? Penrod is an honorable man. Or, at least, as honorable as noblemen get—which means that he insists on being *seen* as honorable. Elend nominated Penrod for chancellor. . . ."

Hoping, in turn, that Penrod would feel obligated to nominate Elend for king, Vin realized. She glanced at Elend, noting a slight smile on his lips. Had he really crafted the exchange? It seemed a move subtle enough for Breeze himself.

Breeze shook his head appreciatively. "Not only did Elend not have to nominate himself—which would have made him look desperate—but now everyone on the Assembly thinks that the man they respect, the man they would probably choose as king, would rather have Elend hold the title. Brilliant."

Penrod sat, and the room remained quiet. Vin suspected that he also had made the nomination so that he wouldn't go uncontested to the throne. The entire Assembly probably thought that Elend deserved a chance to reclaim his place; Penrod was just the one who was honorable enough to voice the feeling.

But, what about the merchants? Vin thought. *They've got to have their own plan.* Elend thought that it was probably Philen who had organized the vote against him. They'd want to put one of their own on the throne, one who could open the city gates to whichever of the kings was manipulating them—or whichever one paid the best.

She studied the group of eight men, in their suits that seemed—somehow—even more fine than those of the noblemen. They all seemed to be waiting on the whims of a single man. What was Philen planning?

One of the merchants moved as if to stand, but Philen shot him a harsh glance. The merchant did not rise. Philen sat quietly, a nobleman's dueling cane across his lap. Finally, when most of the room had noticed the merchant's focus on him, he slowly rose to his feet.

"I have a nomination of my own," he said.

There was a snort from the skaa section. "Now who's being melodramatic, Philen?" one of the Assemblymen there said. "Just go ahead and do it—nominate yourself."

Philen raised an eyebrow. "Actually, I'm *not* going to nominate myself."

Vin frowned, and she saw confusion in Elend's eyes.

"Though I appreciate the sentiment," Philen continued, "I am but a simple merchant. No, I think that the title of king should go to someone whose skills are a little more specialized. Tell me, Lord Venture, must our nominations be for people on the Assembly?"

"No," Elend said. "The king doesn't have to be an Assemblyman—I accepted this position after the fact. The king's primary duty is that of creating, then enforcing, the law. The Assembly is only an advisory council with some measure of counterbalancing power. The king himself can be anyone—actually, the title was intended to be hereditary. I didn't expect . . . certain clauses to be invoked quite so quickly."

"Ah, yes," Philen said. "Well, then. I think the title should go to someone who has a little practice with it. Someone who has shown skill with leadership. Therefore, I nominate Lord Ashweather Cett to be our king!"

What? Vin thought with shock as Philen turned, gesturing toward the audience. A man sitting there removed his skaa cloak, pulling down the hood, revealing a suit and a face with a bristling beard.

"Oh dear . . ." Breeze said.

"It's actually him?" Vin asked incredulously as the whispers began in the audience.

Breeze nodded. "Oh, that's him. Lord Cett himself." He paused, then eyed her. "I think we might be in trouble."

I had never received much attention from my brethren; they thought that my work and my interests were unsuitable to a Worldbringer. They couldn't see how my work, studying nature instead of religion, benefited the people of the fourteen lands.

32

VIN SAT QUIETLY, TENSELY, SCANNING the crowd. *Cett wouldn't have come alone,* she thought.

And then she saw them, now that she knew what she was looking for. Soldiers in the crowd, dressed like skaa, forming a small protective buffer around Cett's seat. The king did not rise, though a young man at his side did.

Maybe thirty guards, Vin thought. *He may not be foolish enough to come alone . . . but entering the very city you're besieging?* It was a bold move—one that bordered on stupidity. Of course, many had said the same about Elend's visit to Straff's army.

But Cett wasn't in the same position as Elend. He wasn't desperate, wasn't in danger of losing everything. Except . . . he had a smaller army than Straff, and the koloss were coming. And if Straff did secure the supposed atium supply, Cett's days as leader in the West would certainly be numbered. Coming into Luthadel might not have been an act of desperation, but it also wasn't the act of a man who held the upper hand. Cett was gambling.

And he seemed to be enjoying it.

Cett smiled as the room waited in silence, Assemblymen and audience alike too shocked to speak. Finally, Cett waved to a few of his disguised soldiers, and the men picked up Cett's chair and carried it to the stage. Assemblymen whispered and commented, turning to aides or companions, seeking confirmation of Cett's identity. Most of the noblemen sat quietly—which should have been enough of a confirmation, in Vin's mind.

"He's not what I expected," Vin whispered to Breeze as the soldiers climbed up on the dais.

"Nobody told you he was crippled?" Breeze asked.

"Not just that," Vin said. "He's not wearing a suit." He had on a pair of trousers and a shirt, but instead of a nobleman's suit coat, he was wearing a worn black jacket. "Plus, that beard. He couldn't have grown a beast like that in one year—he must have had it before the Collapse."

"You only knew noblemen in Luthadel, Vin," Ham said. "The Final Empire was a big place, with a lot of different societies. Not everybody dresses like they do here."

Breeze nodded. "Cett was the most powerful nobleman in his area, so he needn't worry about tradition and propriety. He did what he wished, and the local nobility pandered. There were a hundred different courts with a hundred different little 'Lord Rulers' in the empire, each region having its own political dynamic."

Vin turned back to the stage front. Cett sat in his chair, having yet to speak. Finally, Lord Penrod stood. "This is most unexpected, Lord Cett."

"Good!" Cett said. "That was, after all, the point!"

"Do you wish to address the Assembly?"

"I thought I already was."

Penrod cleared his throat, and Vin's tin-enhanced ears heard a disparaging mutter from the noblemen's section regarding "Western noblemen."

"You have ten minutes, Lord Cett," Penrod said, sitting.

"Good," Cett said. "Because—unlike the boy over there—I intend to tell you exactly *why* you should make me king."

"And that is?" one of the merchant Assemblymen asked.

"Because I've got an army on your damn doorstep!" Cett said with a laugh.

The Assembly looked taken aback.

"A threat, Cett?" Elend asked calmly.

"No, Venture," Cett replied. "Just honesty—something you Central noblemen seem to avoid at all cost. A threat is only a promise turned around. What was it you told these people? That your mistress had her knife at Straff's throat? So, were you implying that if you *weren't* elected, you'd have your Mistborn withdraw, and let the city be destroyed?"

Elend flushed. "Of course not."

"Of course not," Cett repeated. He had a loud voice—unapologetic, forceful. "Well, I don't pretend, and I don't hide. My army is here, and my intention is to take this city. However, I'd much rather that you just give it to me."

"You, sir, are a tyrant," Penrod said flatly.

"So?" Cett asked. "I'm a tyrant with forty thousand soldiers. That's *twice* what you've got guarding these walls."

"What's to stop us from simply taking you hostage?" asked one of the other noblemen. "You seem to have delivered yourself to us quite neatly."

Cett bellowed a laugh. "If I don't return to my camp this evening, my army has orders to attack and raze the city immediately—no matter what! They'll probably get destroyed by Venture afterward—but it won't matter to me, or to you, at that point! We'll all be dead."

The room fell silent.

"See, Venture?" Cett asked. "Threats work wonderfully."

"You honestly expect us to make you our king?" Elend asked.

"Actually, I do," Cett said. "Look, with your twenty thousand added to my forty, we could easily hold these walls against Straff—we could even stop that army of koloss."

Whispers began immediately, and Cett raised a bushy eyebrow, turning to Elend. "You didn't tell them about the koloss, did you?"

Elend didn't respond.

"Well, they'll know soon enough," Cett said. "Regardless, I don't see that you have any other option but to elect me."

"You're not an honorable man," Elend said simply. "The people expect more from their leaders."

"I'm not an honorable man?" Cett asked with amusement. "And you *are*? Let me ask you a direct question, Venture. During the proceedings of this meeting, have any of your Allomancers over there been Soothing members of the Assembly?"

Elend paused. His eyes glanced to the side, finding Breeze. Vin closed her eyes. *No, Elend, don't—*

"Yes, they have," Elend admitted.

Vin heard Tindwyl groan quietly.

"And," Cett continued, "can you honestly say that you've never doubted yourself? Never wondered if you were a good king?"

"I think every leader wonders these things," Elend said.

"Well, I haven't," Cett said. "I've always known I was meant to be in charge—and I've always done the best job of making certain that I stayed in power. I know how to make myself strong, and that means I know how to make those who associate with me strong as well.

"Here's the deal. You give me the crown, and I'll take charge here. You all get to keep your titles—and those of the Assembly who don't have titles will *get* them. In addition, you'll get to keep your heads—which is a far better deal than Straff would offer, I assure you.

"The people get to keep working, and I'll make certain

that they're fed this winter. Everything goes back to normal, the way it was before this insanity began a year back. The skaa work, the nobility administrates."

"You think they'd go back to that?" Elend asked. "After all we fought for, you think I will simply let you force the people back into slavery?"

Cett smiled beneath his large beard. "I wasn't under the impression that the decision was yours, Elend Venture."

Elend fell silent.

"I want to meet with each of you," Cett said to the Assemblymen. "If you'll allow, I wish to move into Luthadel with some of my men. Say, a force of five thousand—enough to make me feel safe, but not to be of any real danger to you. I'll take up residence in one of the abandoned keeps, and wait until your decision next week. During that time, I'll meet with each of you in turn and explain the . . . benefits that would come from choosing me as your king."

"Bribes," Elend spat.

"Of course," Cett said. "Bribes for all of the people of this city—the foremost bribe being that of peace! You're so fond of name-calling, Venture. 'Slaves,' 'threats,' 'honorable.' 'Bribe' is just a word. Looked at another way, a bribe is just a promise, turned on *its* head." Cett smiled.

The group of Assemblymen was silent. "Shall we vote, then, on whether to let him enter the city?" Penrod asked.

"Five thousand is way too many," one of the skaa Assemblymen said.

"Agreed," Elend said. "There's no way we can let that many foreign troops into Luthadel."

"I don't like it at all," another said.

"What?" said Philen. "A monarch inside our city will be less dangerous than one outside, wouldn't you say? And besides, Cett has promised us all titles."

This gave the group something to think about.

"Why not just give me the crown now?" Cett said. "Open your gates to my army."

"You can't," Elend said immediately. "Not until there is a king—or unless you can get a unanimous vote right now."

Vin smiled. Unanimous wouldn't happen in that case as long as Elend was on the Assembly.

"Bah," Cett said, but he obviously was smooth enough not to insult the legislative body further. "Let me take up residence in the city, then."

Penrod nodded. "All in favor of allowing Lord Cett to take up residence inside with . . . say . . . a thousand troops?"

A full nineteen of the Assemblymen raised their hands. Elend was not one of them.

"It is done, then," Penrod said. "We adjourn for two weeks."

This can't be happening, Elend thought. *I thought maybe Penrod would provide a challenge, Philen a lesser one. But . . . one of the very tyrants who is threatening the city? How could they? How could they even consider his suggestion?*

Elend stood, catching Penrod's arm as he turned to walk off the dais. "Ferson," Elend said quietly, "this is insanity."

"We have to consider the option, Elend."

"Consider selling out the people of this city to a tyrant?"

Penrod's face grew cold, and he shook Elend's arm free. "Listen, lad," he said quietly. "You are a good man, but you've always been an idealist. You've spent time in books and philosophy—I've spent my life fighting politics with the members of the court. You know theories; I know people."

He turned, nodding to the audience. "Look at them, lad. They're *terrified.* What good do your dreams do them when they're starving? You talk of freedom and justice when two armies are preparing to slaughter their families."

Penrod turned back to Elend, staring him in the eyes. "The Lord Ruler's system wasn't perfect, but it kept these people safe. We don't even have that anymore. Your ideals can't face down armies. Cett might be a tyrant, but given the choice between him and Straff, I'd have to choose Cett. We'd probably have given him the city weeks ago, if you hadn't stopped us."

Penrod nodded to Elend, then turned and joined a few

of the noblemen who were leaving. Elend stood quietly for a moment.

We have seen a curious phenomenon associated with rebel groups that break off of the Final Empire and attempt to seek autonomy, he thought, recalling a passage from Ytves's book *Studies in Revolution. In almost all cases, the Lord Ruler didn't need to send his armies to reconquer the rebels. By the time his agents arrived, the groups had overthrown themselves.*

It seems that the rebels found the chaos of transition more difficult to accept than the tyranny they had known before. They joyfully welcomed back authority—even oppressive authority—for it was less painful for them than uncertainty.

Vin and the others joined him on the stage, and he put his arm around her shoulders, standing quietly as he watched people trail from the building. Cett sat surrounded by a small group of Assemblymen, arranging meetings with them.

"Well," Vin said quietly. "We know *he's* Mistborn."

Elend turned toward her. "You sensed Allomancy from him?"

Vin shook her head. "No."

"Then, how do you know?" Elend asked.

"Well, look at him," Vin said with a wave of her hand. "He acts like he can't walk—that *has* to be covering up something. What would be more innocent than a cripple? Can you think of a better way to hide the fact that you're a Mistborn?"

"Vin, my dear," Breeze said, "Cett has been crippled since childhood, when a disease rendered his legs useless. He's not Mistborn."

Vin raised an eyebrow. "That has to be one of the best cover stories I've ever heard."

Breeze rolled his eyes, but Elend just smiled.

"What now, Elend?" Ham asked. "We obviously can't deal with things the same way now that Cett has entered the city."

Elend nodded. "We have to plan. Let's . . ." He trailed off as a young man left Cett's group, walking toward Elend. It was the same man who had been sitting next to Cett.

"Cett's son," Breeze whispered. "Gneorndin."

"Lord Venture," Gneorndin said, bowing slightly. He was, perhaps, about Spook's age. "My father wishes to know when you would like to meet with him."

Elend raised an eyebrow. "I have no intention of joining the line of Assemblymen waiting upon Cett's bribes, lad. Tell your father that he and I have nothing to discuss."

"You don't?" Gneorndin asked. "And what about my sister? The one you kidnapped?"

Elend frowned. "You know that isn't true."

"My father would still like to discuss the event," Gneorndin said, shooting a hostile glance at Breeze. "Besides, he thinks that a conversation between you two might be in the city's best interests. You met with Straff in his camp—don't tell me that you aren't willing to do the same for Cett inside your own city?"

Elend paused. *Forget your biases,* he told himself. *You need to talk to this man, if only for the information the meeting might provide.*

"All right," Elend said. "I'll meet with him."

"Dinner, in one week?" Gneorndin asked.

Elend nodded curtly.

As the one who found Alendi, however, I became someone important. Foremost among the Worldbringers.

33

VIN LAY ON HER STOMACH, arms folded, head resting on them as she studied a sheet of paper on the floor in front of her. Considering the last few days of chaos, it was surprising to her that she found returning to her studies to be a relief.

A small one, however, for her studies held their own problems. *The Deepness has returned,* she thought. *Even if the mists only kill infrequently, they've begun to turn hostile again. That means the Hero of Ages needs to come again too, doesn't it?*

Did she honestly think that might be her? It sounded ridiculous, when she considered it. Yet, she heard the thumping in her head, saw the spirit in the mists. . . .

And what of that night, over a year gone, when she'd confronted the Lord Ruler? That night when somehow, she'd drawn the mists into herself, burning them as if they were metal?

That's not enough, she told herself. *One freak event—one I've never been able to replicate—doesn't mean I'm some mythological savior.* She didn't even really know most of the prophecies about the Hero. The logbook mentioned that he was supposed to come from humble origins—but that pretty much described every skaa in the Final Empire. He was supposed to have hidden royal bloodlines, but that made every half-breed in the city a candidate. In fact, she'd be willing to bet that most skaa had one or another hidden nobleman progenitor.

She sighed, shaking her head.

"Mistress?" OreSeur asked, turning. He stood on a chair, his forepaws up against the window as he looked out at the city.

"Prophecies, legends, foretellings," Vin said, slapping her hand down on her sheet of notes. "What's the point? Why did the Terris even believe in these things? Shouldn't a religion teach something practical?"

OreSeur settled down on his haunches upon the chair. "What would be more practical than gaining knowledge of the future?"

"If these actually said something useful, I'd agree. But even the logbook acknowledges that the Terris prophecies could be understood many different ways. What good are promises that could be interpreted so liberally?"

"Do not dismiss someone's beliefs because you do not understand them, Mistress."

Vin snorted. "You sound like Sazed. A part of me is

tempted to think that all these prophecies and legends were devised by priests who wanted to make a living."

"Only a part of you?" OreSeur asked, sounding amused.

Vin paused, then nodded. "The part that grew up on the streets, the part that always expects a scam." That part didn't want to acknowledge the other things she felt.

The thumpings were getting stronger and stronger.

"Prophecies do not have to be a scam, Mistress," Ore-Seur said. "Or even, really, a promise for the future. They can simply be an expression of hope."

"What do you know of such things?" Vin said dismissively, setting aside her sheet.

There was a moment of silence. "Nothing, of course, Mistress," OreSeur eventually said.

Vin turned toward the dog. "I'm sorry, OreSeur. I didn't mean . . . Well, I've just been feeling distracted lately."

Thump. Thump. Thump. . . .

"You need not apologize to me, Mistress," OreSeur said. "I am only kandra."

"Still a person," Vin said. "If one with dog breath."

OreSeur smiled. "You chose these bones for me, Mistress. You must deal with the consequences."

"The bones might have something to do with it," Vin said, rising. "But I don't think that carrion you eat is helping. Honestly, we have to get you some mint leaves to chew."

OreSeur raised a canine eyebrow. "And you don't think a dog with sweet breath would attract attention?"

"Only from anyone you happen to kiss in the near future," Vin said, returning her stacks of paper to her desk.

OreSeur chuckled softly in his canine way, turning back to study the city.

"Is the procession finished yet?" Vin asked.

"Yes, Mistress," OreSeur said. "It is difficult to see, even from a height. But, it does look like Lord Cett has finished moving in. He certainly did bring a lot of carts."

"He's Allrianne's father," Vin said. "Despite how much that girl complains about accommodations in the army, I'd bet that Cett likes to travel in comfort."

OreSeur nodded. Vin turned, leaning against the desk,

watching him and thinking of what he'd said earlier. *Expression of hope. . . .*

"The kandra have a religion, don't they?" Vin guessed.

OreSeur turned sharply. That was enough of a confirmation.

"Do the Keepers know of it?" Vin asked.

OreSeur stood on his hind legs, paws against the windowsill. "I should not have spoken."

"You needn't be afraid," Vin said. "I won't give away your secret. But, I don't see why it has to be secret anymore."

"It is a kandra thing, Mistress," OreSeur said. "It wouldn't be of any interest to anyone else."

"Of course it would," Vin said. "Don't you see, OreSeur? The Keepers believe that the last independent religion was destroyed by the Lord Ruler centuries ago. If the kandra managed to keep one, that suggests that the Lord Ruler's theological control of the Final Empire *wasn't* absolute. That has to mean something."

OreSeur paused, cocking his head, as if he hadn't considered such things.

His theological control wasn't absolute? Vin thought, a bit surprised at the words. *Lord Ruler—I'm starting to sound like Sazed and Elend. I've been studying too much lately.*

"Regardless, Mistress," OreSeur said. "I'd rather you didn't mention this to your Keeper friends. They would probably begin asking discomforting questions."

"They're like that," Vin said with a nod. "What is it your people have prophecies about, anyway?"

"I don't think you want to know, Mistress."

Vin smiled. "They talk about overthrowing us, don't they?"

OreSeur sat down, and she could almost see a flush on his canine face. "My . . . people have dealt with the Contract for a great long time, Mistress. I know it is difficult for you to understand why we would live under this burden, but we find it necessary. Yet, we do dream of a day when it may not be."

"When all the humans are subject to you?" Vin asked.

OreSeur looked away. "When they're all dead, actually."

"Wow."

"The prophecies are not literal, Mistress," OreSeur said. "They're metaphors—expressions of hope. Or, at least, that is how I have always seen them. Perhaps your Terris prophecies are the same? Expressions of a belief that if the people were in danger, their gods would send a Hero to protect them? In this case, the vagueness would be intentional—and rational. The prophecies were never meant to mean someone specific, but more to speak of a general feeling. A general hope."

If the prophecies weren't specific, why could only she sense the drumming beats?

Stop it, she told herself. *You're jumping to conclusions.* "All the humans dead," she said. "How do we die off? The kandra kill us?"

"Of course not," OreSeur said. "We honor our Contract, even in religion. The stories say that you'll kill yourselves off. You're of Ruin, after all, while the kandra are of Preservation. You're . . . actually supposed to destroy the world, I believe. Using the koloss as your pawns."

"You actually sound sorry for them," Vin noted with amusement.

"The kandra actually tend to think well of the koloss, Mistress," OreSeur said. "There is a bond between us; we both understand what it is to be slaves, we both are outsiders to the culture of the Final Empire, we both—"

He paused.

"What?" Vin asked.

"Might I speak no further?" OreSeur asked. "I have said too much already. You put me off balance, Mistress."

Vin shrugged. "We all need secrets." She glanced toward the door. "Though there's one I still need to figure out."

OreSeur hopped down from his chair, joining her as she strode out the door.

There was still a spy somewhere in the palace. She'd been forced to ignore that fact for far too long.

Elend looked deeply into the well. The dark pit—wide-mouthed to accommodate the comings and goings of numerous skaa—seemed a large mouth opening up, stone lips spread and preparing to swallow him down. Elend glanced to the side, where Ham stood speaking with a group of healers.

"We first noticed when so many people came to us complaining of diarrhea and abdominal pains," the healer said. "The symptoms were unusually strong, my lord. We've . . . already lost several to the malady."

Ham glanced at Elend, frowning.

"Everyone who grew sick lived in this area," the healer continued. "And drew their water from this well or another in the next square."

"Have you brought this to the attention of Lord Penrod and the Assembly?" Elend asked.

"Um, no, my lord. We figured that you . . ."

I'm not king anymore, Elend thought. However, he couldn't say the words. Not to this man, looking for help.

"I'll take care of it," Elend said, sighing. "You may return to your patients."

"They are filling our clinic, my lord," he said.

"Then appropriate one of the empty noble mansions," Elend said. "There are plenty of those. Ham, send him with some of my guard to help move the sick and prepare the building."

Ham nodded, waving over a soldier, telling him to gather twenty on-duty men from the palace to meet with the healer. The healer smiled, looking relieved, and bowed to Elend as he left.

Ham walked up, joining Elend beside the well. "Coincidence?"

"Hardly," Elend said, gripping the edge if the well with frustrated fingers. "The question is, which one poisoned it?"

"Cett just came into the city," Ham said, rubbing his chin. "Would have been easy to send out some soldiers to covertly drop in the poison."

"Seems more like something my father would do," Elend said. "Something to increase our tension, to get back at us for playing him for a fool in his camp. Plus, he's got that Mistborn who could have easily placed the poison."

Of course, Cett had had this same thing happen to him—Breeze poisoning his water supply back before he reached the city. Elend ground his teeth. There was really no way to know which one was behind the attack.

Either way, the poisoned wells meant trouble. There were others in the city, of course, but they were just as vulnerable. The people might have to start relying on the river for their water, and it was far less healthy, its waters muddy and polluted by waste from both the army camps and the city itself.

"Set guards around these wells," Elend said, waving a hand. "Board them up, post warnings, and then tell the healers to watch with particular care for other outbreaks."

We just keep getting wound tighter and tighter, he thought as Ham nodded. *At this rate, we'll snap long before winter ends.*

After a detour for a late dinner—where some talk about servants getting sick left her concerned—Vin went in and checked on Elend, who had just returned from walking the city with Ham. After that, Vin and OreSeur continued their original quest: that of finding Dockson.

They located him in the palace library. The room had once been Straff's personal study; Elend seemed to find the room's new purpose amusing for some reason.

Personally, Vin didn't find the library's location nearly as amusing as its contents. Or, rather, lack thereof. Though the room was lined with shelves, nearly all of them showed signs of having been pillaged by Elend. The rows of books lay pocked by forlorn empty spots, their companions taken away one by one, as if Elend were a predator, slowly whittling down a herd.

Vin smiled. It probably wouldn't be too long before Elend had stolen every book in the small library, carrying the tomes up to his study, then forgetfully placing them in one of his piles—ostensibly for return. Still, there were a large number of volumes left—ledgers, books of figures, and notebooks on finances; things that Elend usually found of little interest.

Dockson sat at the library's desk now, writing in a ledger. He noticed her arrival, and glanced over with a smile, but then turned back to his notations—apparently not wanting to lose his place. Vin waited for him to finish, OreSeur at her side.

Of all the members of the crew, Dockson seemed to have changed the most during the last year. She remembered her first impressions of him, back in Camon's lair. Dockson had been Kelsier's right-hand man, and the more "realistic" of the pair. And yet, there had always been an edge of humor to Dockson—a sense that he enjoyed his role as the straight man. He hadn't foiled Kelsier so much as complemented him.

Kelsier was dead. Where did that leave Dockson? He wore a nobleman's suit, as he always had—and of all the crewmembers, the suits seemed to fit him the best. If he shaved off the half beard, he could pass for a nobleman— not a rich high courtier, but a lord in early middle age who had lived his entire life trading goods beneath a great house master.

He wrote in his ledgers, but he had always done that. He still played the role of the responsible one in the crew. So, what was different? He was the same person, did the same things. He just *felt* different. The laughter was gone; the quiet enjoyment of the eccentricity in those around him. Without Kelsier, Dockson had somehow changed from temperate to . . . boring.

And that was what made her suspicious.

This has to be done, she thought, smiling at Dockson as he set down his pen and waved her to take a seat.

Vin sat down, OreSeur padding over to stand beside her chair. Dockson eyed the dog, shaking his head slightly. "That's such a remarkably well-trained beast, Vin," he said. "I don't think I've ever seen one quite like it. . . ."

Does he know? Vin wondered with alarm. *Would one kandra be able to recognize another in a dog's body?* No, that couldn't be. Otherwise OreSeur could find the impostor for her. So, she simply smiled again, patting OreSeur's head. "There is a trainer in the market. He teaches wolfhounds to be protective—to stay with young children and keep them out of danger."

Dockson nodded. "So, any purpose to this visit?"

Vin shrugged. "We never chat anymore, Dox."

Dockson sat back in his chair. "This might not be the best time for chatting. I have to prepare the royal finances to be taken over by someone else, should the vote go against Elend."

Would a kandra be able to do the ledgers? Vin wondered. *Yes. They'd have known—they'd have been prepared.*

"I'm sorry," Vin said. "I don't mean to bother you, but Elend has been so busy lately, and Sazed has his project. . . ."

"It's all right," Dockson said. "I can spare a few minutes. What's on your mind?"

"Well, do you remember that conversation we had, back before the Collapse?"

Dockson frowned. "Which one?"

"You know. . . . The one about your childhood."

"Oh," Dockson said, nodding. "Yes, what about it?"

"Well, do you still think the same way?"

Dockson paused thoughtfully, fingers slowly tapping on the desktop. Vin waited, trying not to show her tension. The conversation in question had been between the two of them, and during it, Dockson had first spoken to her of how much he'd hated the nobility.

"I suppose I don't," Dockson said. "Not anymore. Kell always said that you gave the nobility too much credit, Vin. But you started to change even him there at the end. No, I don't think that noble society needs to be completely destroyed. They aren't all monsters as once presumed."

Vin relaxed. He not only knew the conversation, he knew the details of the tangents they'd discussed. She had been the only one there with him. That had to mean that he wasn't the kandra, right?

"This is about Elend, isn't it?" Dockson asked.

Vin shrugged. "I suppose."

"I know that you wish he and I could get along better,

Vin. But, all things considered, I think we're doing pretty well. He is a decent man; I can acknowledge that. He has some faults as a leader: he lacks boldness, lacks presence."

Not like Kelsier.

"But," Dockson continued, "I don't want to see him lose his throne. He has treated the skaa fairly, for a nobleman."

"He's a good person, Dox," Vin said quietly.

Dockson looked away. "I know that. But . . . well, every time I talk to him, I see Kelsier standing over his shoulder, shaking his head at me. Do you know how long Kell and I dreamed of toppling the Lord Ruler? The other crewmembers, they thought Kelsier's plan was a newfound passion—something that came to him in the Pits. But it was older than that, Vin. Far older.

"We always hated the nobility, Kell and I. When we were youths, planning our first jobs, we wanted to be rich—but we also wanted to hurt them. Hurt them for taking from us things they had no right to. My love . . . Kelsier's mother. . . . Every coin we stole, every nobleman we left dead in an alleyway—this was our way of waging war. Our way of punishing them."

Vin sat quietly. It was these kinds of stories, these memories of a haunted past, that had always made her just a little uncomfortable with Kelsier—and with the person he had been training her to become. It was this sentiment that gave her pause, even when her instincts whispered that she should go and exact retribution on Straff and Cett with knives in the night.

Dockson held some of that same hardness. Kell and Dox weren't evil men, but there was an edge of vengefulness to them. Oppression had changed them in ways that no amount of peace, reformation, or recompense could redeem.

Dockson shook his head. "And we put one of them on the throne. I can't help but think that Kell would be angry with me for letting Elend rule, no matter how good a man he is."

"Kelsier changed at the end," Vin said quietly. "You said it yourself, Dox. Did you know that he saved Elend's life?"

Dockson turned, frowning. "When?"

"On that last day," Vin said. "During the fight with the Inquisitor. Kell protected Elend, who came looking for me."

"Must have thought he was one of the prisoners."

Vin shook her head. "He knew who Elend was, and knew that I loved him. In the end, Kelsier was willing to admit that a good man was worth protecting, no matter who his parents were."

"I find that hard to accept, Vin."

"Why?"

Dockson met her eyes. "Because if I accept that Elend bears no guilt for what his people did to mine, then I must admit to being a monster for the things that I did to them."

Vin shivered. In those eyes, she saw the truth behind Dockson's transformation. She saw the death of his laughter. She saw the guilt. The murders.

This man is no impostor.

"I can find little joy in this government, Vin," Dockson said quietly. "Because I know what we did to create it. The thing is, I'd do it all again. I tell myself it's because I believe in skaa freedom. I still lie awake at nights, however, quietly satisfied for what we've done to our former rulers. Their society undermined, their god dead. Now they know."

Vin nodded. Dockson looked down, as if ashamed, an emotion she'd rarely seen in him. There didn't seem to be anything else to say. Dockson sat quietly as she withdrew, his pen and ledger forgotten on the desktop.

"It's not him," Vin said, walking down an empty palace hallway, trying to shake the haunting sound of Dockson's voice from her mind.

"You are certain, Mistress?" OreSeur asked.

Vin nodded. "He knew about a private conversation that Dockson and I had before the Collapse."

OreSeur was silent for a moment. "Mistress," he finally said, "my brethren can be *very* thorough."

"Yes, but how could he have known about such an event?"

"We often interview people before we take their bones, Mistress," OreSeur explained. "We'll meet them several times, in different settings, and find ways to talk about their lives. We'll also talk to their friends and acquaintances. Did you ever tell anyone about this conversation you had with Dockson?"

Vin stopped to lean against the side of the stone hallway. "Maybe Elend," she admitted. "I think I mentioned it to Sazed too, just after it happened. That was almost two years ago."

"That could have been enough, Mistress," OreSeur said. "We cannot learn everything about a person, but we try our best to discover items like this—private conversations, secrets, confidential information—so that we can mention them at appropriate times and reinforce our illusion."

Vin frowned.

"There are . . . other things as well, Mistress," OreSeur said. "I hesitate because I do not wish you to imagine your friends in pain. However, it is common for our master—the one who actually does the killing—to torture their victim for information."

Vin closed her eyes. Dockson felt so real . . . his guilt, his reactions . . . that couldn't be faked, could it?

"Damn," she whispered quietly, opening her eyes. She turned, sighing as she pushed open the shutters of a hallway window. It was dark out, and the mists curled before her as she leaned against the stone windowsill and looked out at the courtyard two stories below.

"Dox isn't an Allomancer," she said. "How can I find out for certain if he's the impostor or not?"

"I do not know, Mistress," OreSeur said. "This is never an easy task."

Vin stood quietly. Absently, she pulled out her bronze earring—her mother's earring—and worked it between her fingers, watching it reflect light. It had once been gilded with silver, but that had worn off in most places.

"I hate this," she finally whispered.

"What, Mistress?"

"This . . . distrust," she said. "I hate being suspicious of my friends. I thought I was through mistrusting those around me. I feel like a knife is twisting inside of me, and it cuts deeper every time I confront one of the crew."

OreSeur sat on his haunches beside her, and he cocked his head. "But, Mistress. You've managed to eliminate several of them as impostors."

"Yes," Vin said. "But that only narrows the field—brings me one step closer to knowing which one of them is dead."

"And that knowledge isn't a good thing?"

Vin shook her head. "I don't want it to be any of them, OreSeur. I don't want to distrust them, don't want to find out that we're right. . . ."

OreSeur didn't respond at first, leaving her to stare out the window, mists slowly streaming to the floor around her.

"You are sincere," OreSeur finally said.

She turned. "Of course I am."

"I'm sorry, Mistress," OreSeur said. "I did not wish to be insulting. I just . . . Well, I have been kandra to many masters. So many of them are suspicious and hateful of everyone around them, I had begun to think that your kind lacked the capacity for trust."

"That's silly," Vin said, turning back to the window.

"I know it is," OreSeur said. "But people often believe silly things, if given enough proof. Either way, I apologize. I do not know which of your friends is dead, but I am sorry that one of my kind brought you this pain."

"Whoever he is, he's just following his Contract."

"Yes, Mistress," OreSeur said. "The Contract."

Vin frowned. "Is there a way that you could find out which kandra has a Contract in Luthadel?"

"I'm sorry, Mistress," OreSeur said. "That is not possible."

"I figured as much," she said. "Are you likely to know him, whoever he is?"

"The kandra are a close-knit group, Mistress," OreSeur said. "And our numbers are small. There is a good chance that I know him quite well."

Vin tapped her finger against the windowsill, frowning as she tried to decide if the information was useful.

"I still don't think it's Dockson," she finally said, replacing the earring. "We'll ignore him for now. If I can't get any other leads, we'll come back . . ." She trailed off as something caught her attention. A figure walking in the courtyard, bearing no light.

Ham, she thought. But the walk wasn't right.

She Pushed on the shield of the lamp hanging on the wall a short distance away. It snapped closed, the lamp shaking as the hallway fell into darkness.

"Mistress?" OreSeur asked as Vin climbed up into the window, flaring her tin as she squinted into the night.

Definitely not Ham, she thought.

Her first thought was of Elend—a sudden terror that assassins had come while she was talking to Dockson. But, it was early in the night, and Elend would still be speaking with his counselors. It was an unlikely time for an assassination.

And only one man? Not Zane, not judging from the height.

Probably just a guard, Vin thought. *Why do I have to be so paranoid all the time?*

And yet . . . she watched the figure walking into the courtyard, and her instincts kicked in. He seemed to be moving suspiciously, as if he were uncomfortable—as if he didn't want to be seen.

"In my arms," she said to OreSeur, tossing a padded coin out the window.

He hopped up obligingly, and she leaped out the window, fell twenty-five feet, and landed with the coin. She released OreSeur and nodded into the mists. He followed closely as she moved into the darkness, stooping and hiding, trying to get a good look at the lone figure. The man walked briskly, moving toward the side of the palace, where the servants' entrances were. As he passed, she finally saw his face.

Captain Demoux? she thought.

She sat back, crouching with OreSeur beside a small stack of wooden supply boxes. What did she really know of Demoux? He was one of the skaa rebels recruited by Kelsier almost two years before. He'd taken to command,

and had been promoted quickly. He was one of the loyal men who had stayed behind when the rest of the army had followed Yeden to their doom.

After the Collapse, he'd stayed in with the crew, eventually becoming Ham's second. He had received no small amount of training from Ham—which might explain why he'd go out at night without a torch or lantern. But, even so. . . .

If I were going to replace someone on the crew, Vin thought, *I wouldn't pick an Allomancer—that would make the impostor too easy to spot. I'd pick someone ordinary, someone who wouldn't have to make decisions or attract notice.*

Someone close to the crew, but not necessarily on it. Someone who is always near important meetings, but someone that others don't really know that well. . . .

She felt a small thrill. If the impostor were Demoux, it would mean that one of her good friends *hadn't* been killed. And it would mean that the kandra's master was even smarter than she'd given him credit for being.

He rounded the keep, and she followed quietly. However, whatever he'd been doing this night, it was already completed—for he moved in through one of the entrances on the side of the building, greeting the guards posted there to watch.

Vin sat back in the shadows. He'd spoken to the guards, so he hadn't snuck out of the palace. And yet . . . she recognized the stooped posture, the nervous movements. He'd been nervous about something.

That's him, she thought. *The spy.*

But now, what should she do about it?

There was a place for me, in the lore of the Anticipation—I thought myself the Announcer, the prophet foretold to discover the Hero of Ages. Renouncing Alendi then would have been to renounce my new position, my acceptance, by the others.

And so I did not.

34

"THAT WON'T WORK," ELEND SAID, shaking his head. "We need a unanimous decision—minus the person being ousted, of course—in order to depose a member of the Assembly. We'd never manage to vote out all eight merchants."

Ham looked a bit deflated. Elend knew that Ham liked to consider himself a philosopher; indeed, Ham had a good mind for abstract thinking. However, he wasn't a scholar. He liked to think up questions and answers, but he didn't have experience studying a text in detail, searching out its meaning and implications.

Elend glanced at Sazed, who sat with a book open on the table before him. The Keeper had at least a dozen volumes stacked around him—though, amusingly, his stacks were neatly arranged, spines pointing the same direction, covers flush. Elend's own stacks were characteristically haphazard, pages of notes sticking out at odd angles.

It was amazing how many books one could fit into a room, assuming one didn't want to move around very much. Ham sat on the floor, a small pile of books beside him, though he spent most of his time voicing one random idea or another. Tindwyl had a chair, and did not study. The Terriswoman found it perfectly acceptable to train Elend as a king; however, she refused to research and give suggestions about keeping his throne. This seemed, in her eyes, to cross some unseen line between being an educator and a political force.

Good thing Sazed isn't like that, Elend thought. *If he were, the Lord Ruler might still be in charge. In fact, Vin and I would probably both be dead—Sazed was the one who actually rescued her when she was imprisoned by the Inquisitors. It wasn't me.*

He didn't like to think about that event. His bungled attempt at rescuing Vin now seemed a metaphor for all he had done wrong in his life. He'd always been well-intentioned, but he'd rarely been able to deliver. That was going to change.

"What about this, Your Majesty?" The one who spoke was the only other person in the room, a scholar named Noorden. Elend tried to ignore the intricate tattoos around the man's eyes, indications of Noorden's former life as an obligator. He wore large spectacles to try to hide the tattoos, but he had once been relatively well placed in the Steel Ministry. He could renounce his beliefs, but the tattoos would always remain.

"What have you found?" Elend asked.

"Some information on Lord Cett, Your Majesty," Noorden said. "I found it in one of the ledgers you took from the Lord Ruler's palace. It seems Cett isn't as indifferent to Luthadel politics as he'd like us to think." Noorden chuckled to himself at the thought.

Elend had never met a cheerful obligator before. Perhaps that was why Noorden hadn't left the city like most of his kind; he certainly didn't seem to fit into their ranks. He was only one of several men that Elend had been able to find to act as scribes and bureaucrats in his new kingdom.

Elend scanned Noorden's page. Though the page was filled with numbers rather than words, his scholar's mind easily parsed the information. Cett had done a lot of trading with Luthadel. Most of his work had been done using lesser houses as fronts. That might have fooled noblemen, but not the obligators, who had to be informed of the terms of any deal.

Noorden passed the ledger over to Sazed, who scanned the numbers.

"So," Noorden said, "Lord Cett wanted to appear un-connected to Luthadel—the beard and the attitude only serving to reinforce that impression. Yet, he always had a very quiet hand in things here."

Elend nodded. "Maybe he realized that you can't avoid politics by pretending you're not part of them. There's no way he would have been able to grab as much power as he did without some solid political connections."

"So, what does this tell us?" Sazed asked.

"That Cett is far more accomplished at the game than he wants people to believe," Elend said, standing, then step-ping over a pile of books as he made his way back to his chair. "But, I think that much was obvious by the way he manipulated me and the Assembly yesterday."

Noorden chuckled. "You should have seen the way you all looked, Your Majesty. When Cett revealed himself, a few of the noble Assemblymen actually jumped in their seats! I think the rest of you were too shocked to—"

"Noorden?" Elend said.

"Yes, Your Majesty?"

"Please focus on the task at hand."

"Um, yes, Your Majesty."

"Sazed?" Elend asked. "What do you think?"

Sazed looked up from his book—a codified and anno-tated version of the city's charter, as written by Elend him-self. The Terrisman shook his head. "You did a very good job with this, I think. I can see very few methods of pre-venting Lord Cett's appointment, should the Assembly choose him."

"Too competent for your own good?" Noorden said.

"A problem which, unfortunately, I've rarely had," Elend said, sitting and rubbing his eyes.

Is this how Vin feels all the time? he wondered. She got less sleep than he, and she was always moving about, run-ning, fighting, spying. Yet, she always seemed fresh. Elend was beginning to droop after just a couple of days of hard study.

Focus, he told himself. *You have to know your enemies so that you can fight them. There has to be a way out of this.*

Dockson was still composing letters to the other Assemblymen. Elend wanted to meet with those who were willing. Unfortunately, he had a feeling that number would be small. They had voted him out, and now they had been presented with an option that seemed an easy way out of their problems.

"Your Majesty . . ." Noorden said slowly. "Do you think, maybe, that we should just let Cett take the throne? I mean, how bad could he be?"

Elend stopped. One of the reasons he employed the former obligator was because of Noorden's different viewpoint. He wasn't a skaa, nor was he a high nobleman. He wasn't a thief. He was just a scholarly little man who had joined the Ministry because it had offered an option other than becoming a merchant.

To him, the Lord Ruler's death had been a catastrophe that had destroyed his entire way of life. He wasn't a bad man, but he had no real understanding of the plight of the skaa.

"What do you think of the laws I've made, Noorden?" Elend asked.

"They're brilliant, Your Majesty," Noorden said. "Keen representations of the ideals spoken of by old philosophers, along with a strong element of modern realism."

"Will Cett respect these laws?" Elend asked.

"I don't know. I haven't ever really met the man."

"What do your instincts tell you?"

Noorden hesitated. "No," he finally said. "He isn't the type of man who rules by law. He just does what he wants."

"He would bring only chaos," Elend said. "Look at the information we have from his homeland and the places he's conquered. They are in turmoil. He's left a patchwork of half alliances and promises—threats of invasion acting as the thread that—barely—holds it all together. Giving him rule of Luthadel would just set us up for another collapse."

Noorden scratched his cheek, then nodded thoughtfully and turned back to his reading.

I can convince him, Elend thought. *If only I could do the same for the Assemblymen.*

But Noorden was a scholar; he thought the way Elend did. Logical facts were enough for him, and a promise of stability was more powerful than one of wealth. The Assembly was a different beast entirely. The noblemen wanted a return to what they'd known before; the merchants saw an opportunity to grab the titles they'd always envied; and the skaa were simply worried about a brutal slaughter.

And yet, even those were generalizations. Lord Penrod saw himself as the city's patriarch—the ranking nobleman, the one who needed to bring a measure of conservative temperance to their problems. Kinaler, one of the steelworkers, was worried that the Central Dominance needed a kinship with the kingdoms around it, and saw an alliance with Cett as the best way to protect Luthadel in the long run.

Each of the twenty-three Assemblymen had their own thoughts, goals, and problems. That was what Elend had intended; ideas proliferated in such an environment. He just hadn't expected so many of their ideas to contradict his own.

"You were right, Ham," Elend said, turning.

Ham looked up, raising an eyebrow.

"At the beginning of this all, you and the others wanted to make an alliance with one of the armies—give them the city in exchange for keeping it safe from the other armies."

"I remember," Ham said.

"Well, that's what the people want," Elend said. "With or without my consent, it appears they're going to give the city to Cett. We should have just gone with your plan."

"Your Majesty?" Sazed asked quietly.

"Yes?"

"My apologies, but it is not your duty to do what the people want."

Elend blinked. "You sound like Tindwyl."

"I have known few people as wise as she, Your Majesty," Sazed said, glancing at her.

"Well, I disagree with both of you," Elend said. "A ruler should only lead by the consent of the people he rules."

"I do not disagree with that, Your Majesty," Sazed said. "Or, at least, I do believe in the theory of it. Regardless, I still do not believe that your duty is to do as the people wish. Your duty is to lead as best you can, following the dictates of your conscience. You must be true, Your Majesty, to the man you wish to become. If that man is not whom the people wish to have lead them, then they will choose someone else."

Elend paused. *Well, of course. If I shouldn't be an exception to my own laws, I shouldn't be an exception to my own ethics, either.* Sazed's words were really just a rephrasing of things Tindwyl had said about trusting oneself, but Sazed's explanation seemed a better one. A more honest one.

"Trying to guess what people wish of you will only lead to chaos, I think," Sazed said. "You cannot please them all, Elend Venture."

The study's small ventilation window bumped open, and Vin squeezed through, pulling in a puff of mist behind her. She closed the window, then surveyed the room.

"More?" she asked incredulously. "You found more books?"

"Of course," Elend said.

"How many of those things have people written?" she asked with exasperation.

Elend opened his mouth, then paused as he saw the twinkle in her eye. Finally, he just sighed. "You're hopeless," he said, turning back to his letters.

He heard rustling from behind, and a moment later Vin landed on one of his stacks of books, somehow managing to balance atop it. Her mistcloak tassels hung down around her, smudging the ink on his letter.

Elend sighed.

"Oops," Vin said, pulling back the mistcloak. "Sorry."

"Is it really necessary to leap around like that all the time, Vin?" Elend asked.

Vin jumped down. "Sorry," she repeated, biting her lip. "Sazed says it's because Mistborn like to be up high, so we can see everything that's going on."

Elend nodded, continuing the letter. He preferred them to be in his own hand, but he'd need to have a scribe rewrite this one. He shook his head. *So much to do.* . . .

Vin watched Elend scribble. Sazed sat reading, as did one of Elend's scribes—the obligator. She eyed the man, and he shrank down a little in his seat. He knew that she'd never trusted him. Priests shouldn't be cheerful.

She was excited to tell Elend what she'd discovered about Demoux, but she hesitated. There were too many people around, and she didn't really have any evidence— just her instincts. So, she held herself back, looking over the stacks of books.

There was a dull quiet in the room. Tindwyl sat with her eyes slightly glazed; she was probably studying some ancient biography in her mind. Even Ham was reading, though he flipped from book to book, hopping topics. Vin felt as if she should be studying something, too. She thought of the notes she'd been making about the Deepness and the Hero of Ages, but couldn't bring herself to get them out.

She couldn't tell him about Demoux, yet, but there *was* something else she'd discovered.

"Elend," she said quietly. "I have something to tell you."

"Humm?"

"I heard the servants talking when OreSeur and I got dinner earlier," Vin said. "Some people they know have been sick lately—a lot of them. I think that someone might be fiddling with our supplies."

"Yes," Elend said, still writing. "I know. Several wells in the city have been poisoned."

"They have?"

He nodded. "Didn't I tell you when you checked on me earlier? That's where Ham and I were."

"You didn't tell me."

"I thought I did," Elend said, frowning.

Vin shook her head.

"I apologize," he said, leaned up and kissed her, then turned back to his scribbling.

And a kiss is supposed to make it all right? she thought sullenly, sitting back on a stack of books.

It was a silly thing; there was really no reason that Elend *should* have told her so quickly. And yet, the exchange left her feeling odd. Before, he would have asked her to do something about the problem. Now, he'd apparently handled it all on his own.

Sazed sighed, closing his tome. "Your Majesty, I can find no holes. I have read your laws over six times now."

Elend nodded. "I feared as much. The only advantage we could gain from the law is to misinterpret it intentionally—which I will not do."

"You are a good man, Your Majesty," Sazed said. "If you had seen a hole in the law, you would have fixed it. Even if you hadn't caught the flaws, one of us would have, when you asked for our opinions."

He lets them call him "Your Majesty," Vin thought. *He tried to get them to stop that. Why let them use it now?*

Odd, that Elend would finally start to think of himself as king after the throne had been taken from him.

"Wait," Tindwyl said, eyes unglazing. "You read over this law before it was ratified, Sazed?"

Sazed flushed.

"He did," Elend said. "In fact, Sazed's suggestions and ideas were instrumental in helping me craft the current code."

"I see," Tindwyl said through tight lips.

Elend frowned. "Tindwyl, you were not invited to this meeting. You are suffered at it. Your advice has been well appreciated, but I will not allow you to insult a friend and guest of my household, even if those insults are indirect."

"I apologize, Your Majesty."

"You will not apologize to me," Elend said. "You will apologize to Sazed, or you will leave this conference."

Tindwyl sat for a moment; then she stood and left the room. Elend didn't appear offended. He simply turned back to writing his letters.

"You didn't need to do that, Your Majesty," Sazed said. "Tindwyl's opinions of me are well founded, I think."

"I will do as I see fit, Sazed," Elend said, still writing.

"No offense, my friend, but you have a history of letting people treat you poorly. I won't stand for it in my house— by insulting your help with my laws, she insulted me as well."

Sazed nodded, then reached over to pick up a new volume.

Vin sat quietly. *He's changing so quickly. How long has it been since Tindwyl arrived? Two months?* None of the things Elend said were that different from what he would have said before—but the way he said them was completely different. He was firm, demanding in a way that implied he expected respect.

It's the collapse of his throne, the danger of the armies, Vin thought. *The pressures are forcing him to change, to either step up and lead or get crushed.* He'd known about the wells. What other things had he discovered, and not told her?

"Elend?" Vin asked. "I've thought more about the Deepness."

"That's wonderful, Vin," Elend said, smiling at her. "But, I really don't have time right now. . . ."

Vin nodded, and smiled at him. However, her thoughts were more troubled. *He's not uncertain, like he once was. He doesn't have to rely on people as much for support.*

He doesn't need me anymore.

It was a foolish thought. Elend loved her; she knew that. His aptitude wouldn't make her less valuable to him. And yet, she couldn't stamp out her worries. He'd left her once before, when he'd been trying to juggle the needs of his house with his love for her, and the action had nearly crushed her.

What would happen if he abandoned her now?

He won't, she told herself. *He's a better man than that.*

But, good men had failed relationships, didn't they? People grew apart—particularly people who were so different to begin with. Despite herself—despite her self-assurances—she heard a small voice pop up in the back of her mind.

It was a voice she'd thought banished, a voice she hadn't ever expected to hear again.

Leave him first, Reen, her brother, seemed to whisper in her head. *It will hurt less.*

Vin heard a rustling outside. She perked up slightly, but it had been too soft for the others to hear. She stood, walking over to the ventilation window.

"Going back on patrol?" Elend asked.

She turned, then nodded.

"You might want to scout out Cett's defenses at Keep Hasting," Elend said.

Vin nodded again. Elend smiled at her, then turned back to his letters. Vin pulled open the window and stepped out into the night. Zane stood in the mists, feet barely resting against the stone lip running beneath the window. He stood at a skewed angle, feet against the wall, body jutting out into the night.

Vin glanced to the side, noting the bit of metal that Zane was Pulling against to hold himself stationary. Another feat of prowess. He smiled at her in the night.

"Zane?" she whispered.

Zane glanced upward, and Vin nodded. A second later, they both landed atop Keep Venture's metal roof.

Vin turned to Zane. "Where have you been?"

He attacked.

Vin jumped back in surprise as Zane spun forward, a swirling form in black, knives twinkling. She came down with her feet half off the rooftop, tense. *A spar, then?* she thought.

Zane struck, his knife coming dangerously close to her neck as she dodged to the side. There was something different about his attacks this time. Something more dangerous.

Vin cursed and pulled out her own daggers, jumping back from another attack. As she moved, Zane sliced through the air, cutting the tip off one of her mistcloak tassels.

She turned to face him. He walked forward, but held no combat posture. He seemed confident, yet unconcerned, as if he were strolling up to an old friend, not entering a fight.

All right then, she thought, jumping forward, swiping with her daggers.

Zane stepped forward casually, turning just slightly to the side, easily dodging one knife. He reached out, grabbing her other hand with an effortless motion, stopping its blow.

Vin froze. Nobody was that good. Zane looked down at her, eyes dark. Unconcerned. Unworried.

He was burning atium.

Vin pulled free of his grip, jumping backward. He let her go, watching as she fell into a crouch, sweat beading on her brow. She felt a sudden, sharp stab of terror—a guttural, primal feeling. She had feared this day from the moment she'd learned of atium. It was the terror of knowing she was powerless, despite all of her skills and abilities.

It was the terror of knowing she was going to die.

She turned to jump away, but Zane leaped forward before she even began to move. He knew what she would do before she did herself. He grabbed her shoulder from behind, pulling her backward, throwing her down to the rooftop.

Vin slammed against the metal roofing, gasping in pain. Zane stood above her, looking down, as if waiting.

I won't be beaten this way! Vin thought with desperation. *I won't be killed like a trapped rat!*

She reached and swung a knife at his leg, but it was useless. He pulled the leg back slightly—just enough—so that her swing didn't even nick the cloth of his trousers. She was like a child, being held at a distance by a much larger, more powerful foe. This was what it must be like, being a normal person, trying to fight her.

Zane stood in the darkness.

"What?" she finally demanded.

"You really don't have it," he said quietly. "The Lord Ruler's atium stash."

"No," she said.

"You don't have any at all," he said flatly.

"I used the last bead the day I fought Cett's assassins."

He stood for a moment; then he turned, stepping away from her. Vin sat up, heart thumping, hands shaking just a bit. She forced herself to her feet, then stooped and retrieved her fallen daggers. One had cracked against the roof's copper top.

Zane turned back toward her, quiet in the mists.

Zane watched her in the darkness, saw her fear—yet also her determination.

"My father wants me to kill you," Zane said.

She stood, watching him, eyes still afraid. She was strong, and she repressed the fear well. The news from their spy, the words Vin had spoken while visiting Straff's tent, were all true. There was no atium to be had in this city.

"Is that why you stayed away?" she asked.

He nodded, turning away from her.

"So?" she asked. "Why let me live?"

"I'm not sure," he admitted. "I may still kill you. But . . . I don't have to. Not to fulfill his order. I could just take you away—that would have the same effect."

He turned back toward her. She was frowning, a small, quiet figure in the mists.

"Come with me," he said. "Both of us could leave— Straff would lose his Mistborn, and Elend would lose his. We could deny them *both* their tools. And we could be free."

She didn't respond immediately. Finally, she shook her head. "This . . . thing between us, Zane. It isn't what you think."

"What do you mean?" he said, stepping forward.

She looked up at him. "I love Elend, Zane. I really do."

And you think that means you can't feel anything for me? Zane thought. *What of that look I've seen in your eyes, that longing? No, it isn't as easy as you imply, is it?*

It never is.

And yet, what else had he expected? He turned away. "It makes sense. That's the way it has always been."

"What is that supposed to mean?" she demanded.

Elend. . . .

"Kill him," God whispered.

Zane squeezed his eyes shut. She would not be fooled; not a woman who had grown up on the streets, a woman who was friends with thieves and scammers. This was the difficult part. She would need to see things that terrified Zane.

She would need truth.

"Zane?" Vin asked. She still seemed a bit shaken by his attack, but she was the type who recovered quickly.

"Can't you see the resemblance?" Zane asked, turning. "The same nose, the same slant of the face? I cut my hair shorter than he, but it has the same curl. Is it so hard to see?"

Her breath caught in her throat.

"Who else would Straff Venture trust as his Mistborn?" Zane asked. "Why else would he let me get so close, why else would he feel so comfortable letting me in on his plans?"

"You're his son," Vin whispered. "Elend's brother."

Zane nodded.

"Elend . . ."

"Doesn't know of me," Zane said. "Ask him about our father's sexual habits sometime."

"He's told me," Vin said. "Straff likes mistresses."

"For more than one reason," Zane said. "More women means more children. More children means more Allomancers. More Allomancers means more chances at having a Mistborn son to be your assassin."

Breeze-blown mist washed over them. In the distance, a soldier's armor clinked as he patrolled.

"While the Lord Ruler lived, I could never inherit," Zane said. "You know how strict the obligators were. I grew up in the shadows, ignored. You lived on the streets—I assume that was terrible. But, think of what it would be like to be a scavenger in your own home, unacknowledged by your father, treated like a beggar. Think of watching your brother, a boy your same age, growing up privileged. Think of watching his disdain for the things you longed to have. Comfort, idleness, love . . ."

"You must hate him," Vin whispered.

"Hate?" Zane asked. "No. Why hate a man for what he is? Elend has done nothing to me, not directly. Besides, Straff found a reason to need me, eventually—after I

Snapped, and he finally got what he'd been gambling to get for the last twenty years No, I don't hate Elend. Sometimes, however, I do envy him. He has everything. And still . . . it seems to me like he doesn't appreciate it."

Vin stood quietly. "I'm sorry."

Zane shook his head sharply. "Don't pity me, woman. If I were Elend, I wouldn't be Mistborn. I wouldn't understand the mists, nor would I know what it was like to grow up alone and hated." He turned, looking into her eyes. "Don't you think a man better appreciates love when he has been forced for so long to go without?"

"I . . ."

Zane turned away. "Anyway," he said, "I didn't come here tonight to lament my childhood. I came with a warning."

Vin grew tense.

"A short time ago," Zane said, "my father let several hundred refugees through his barricade to approach the city. You know of the koloss army?"

Vin nodded.

"It attacked and pillaged the city of Suisna earlier."

Vin felt a start of fright. Suisna was only a day away from Luthadel. The koloss were close.

"The refugees came to my father for help," Zane said. "He sent them on to you."

"To make the people of the city more afraid," Vin said. "And to provide a further drain on our resources."

Zane nodded. "I wanted to give you warning. Both of the refugees, and of my orders. Think about my offer, Vin. Think about this man who claims to love you. You know he doesn't understand you. If you leave, it will be better for both of you."

Vin frowned. Zane bowed his head slightly to her, then jumped into the night, Pushing against the metal rooftop. She still didn't believe him about Elend. He could see that in her eyes.

Well, proof was coming. She'd soon see. She'd soon understand what Elend Venture truly thought of her.

But I do so now. Let it be known that I, Kwaan, Worldbringer of Terris, am a fraud.

35

IT FELT LIKE SHE WAS going to a ball again.

The beautiful maroon gown would have fit in perfectly at one of the parties she had attended during the months before the Collapse. The dress was untraditional, but not unfashionable. The changes simply made the dress seem distinctive.

The alterations left her freer to move; let her walk more gracefully, turn more naturally. That, in turn, made her feel even more beautiful. Standing before her mirror, Vin thought of what it might have been like to wear the dress to a real ball. To be herself—not Valette, the uncomfortable country noblewoman. Not even Vin, the skaa thief. To be herself.

Or, at least, as she could imagine herself. Confident because she accepted her place as a Mistborn. Confident because she accepted her place as the one who had struck down the Lord Ruler. Confident because she knew that the king loved her.

Maybe I could *be both,* Vin thought, running her hands down the sides of the dress, feeling the soft satin.

"You look beautiful, child," Tindwyl said.

Vin turned, smiling hesitantly. "I don't have any jewelry. I gave the last of it to Elend to help feed the refugees. It was the wrong color to go with this dress anyway."

"Many women use jewelry to try and hide their own plainness," Tindwyl said. "You don't have that need."

The Terriswoman stood with her usual posture, hands clasped before her, rings and earrings sparkling. None of her jewelry, however, had gemstones; in fact, most of it

THE WELL OF ASCENSION

was made from simple materials. Iron, copper, pewter. Feruchemical metals.

"You haven't been in to see Elend lately," Vin said, turning back to the mirror and using a few wooden barrettes to hold her hair back.

"The king is quickly approaching the point where he no longer needs my instruction."

"He's that close then?" Vin asked. "To being like the men from your biographies?"

Tindwyl laughed. "Goodness, no, child. He's quite far from that."

"But—"

"I said he would no longer need my instruction," Tindwyl said. "He is learning that he can rely only so much upon the words of others, and has reached the point where he will have to learn more for himself. You would be surprised, child, how much about being a good leader simply comes from experience."

"He seems very different to me," Vin said quietly.

"He is," Tindwyl said, walking forward to lay a hand on Vin's shoulder. "He is becoming the man that he always knew he would have to be—he just didn't know the path. Though I am hard on him, I think he would have found his way, even if I hadn't come. A man can only stumble for so long before he either falls or stands up straight."

Vin looked at her mirror self, pretty in its maroon dressings. "This is what *I* have to become. For him."

"For him," Tindwyl agreed. "And for yourself. This is where *you* were heading, before you got distracted."

Vin turned. "Are you going to come with us tonight?"

Tindwyl shook her head. "That is not my place. Now, go meet your king."

This time, Elend did not intend to enter his enemy's lair without a proper escort. Two hundred soldiers stood in the courtyard, waiting to accompany him to Cett's dinner, and Ham—fully armed—was playing personal bodyguard. Spook would act as Elend's coachman. That only left

Breeze, who—understandably—was a bit nervous about the idea of going to the dinner.

"You don't have to come," Elend told the portly man as they assembled in the Venture courtyard.

"I don't?" Breeze said. "Well then, I shall remain here. Enjoy the dinner!"

Elend paused, frowning.

Ham clapped Elend on the shoulder. "You should know better than to give that one any wiggle room, Elend!"

"Well, I meant my words," Elend said. "We could really use a Soother, but he doesn't have to come if he doesn't want to."

Breeze looked relieved.

"You don't even feel a bit guilty, do you?" Ham asked.

"Guilty?" Breeze asked, hand resting on his cane. "My dear Hammond, have you *ever* known me to express such a dreary and uninspired emotion? Besides, I have a feeling Cett will be more amiable without me around."

He's probably right, Elend thought as his coach pulled up.

"Elend," Ham said. "Don't you think bringing two hundred soldiers with us is . . . well, a little obvious?"

"Cett is the one who said we should be honest with our threats," Elend said. "Well, I'd say two hundred men is on the conservative side of how well I trust the man. He'll still have us outnumbered five to one."

"But you'll have a Mistborn sitting a few seats from him," a soft voice said from behind.

Elend turned, smiling at Vin. "How can you possibly move so quietly in a dress like that?"

"I've been practicing," she said, taking his arm.

Thing is, she probably has, he thought, inhaling her perfume, imagining Vin creeping through the palace hallways in a massive ball gown.

"Well, we should get moving," Ham said. He gestured for Vin and Elend to enter the carriage, and they left Breeze behind on the palace steps.

After a year of passing Keep Hasting in the night, its windows darkened, it felt right to see them glowing again.

"You know," Elend said from beside her, "we never did get to attend a ball together."

Vin turned from her contemplation of the approaching keep. Around her, the carriage bounced along to the sound of several hundred tromping feet, the evening just beginning to grow dark.

"We met up several times at the balls," Elend continued, "but we never officially attended one together. I never got the chance to pick you up in my carriage."

"Is that really so important?" Vin asked.

Elend shrugged. "It's all part of the experience. Or, it was. There was a comfortable formality to it all; the gentleman arriving to accompany the lady, then everyone watching you enter and evaluating how you look together. I did it dozens of times with dozens of women, but never with the one that would have made the experience special."

Vin smiled. "Do you think we'll ever have balls again?"

"I don't know, Vin. Even if we survive all of this . . . well, could you dance while so many people starved?" He was probably thinking about the hundreds of refugees, wearied from their travels, stripped of all food and equipment by Straff's soldiers, huddled together in the warehouse Elend had found for them.

You danced before, she thought. *People starved then, too.* But that was a different time; Elend hadn't been king then. In fact, as she thought about it, he had never actually danced at those balls. He had studied and met with his friends, planning how he could make a better place out of the Final Empire.

"There has to be a way to have both," Vin said. "Maybe we could throw balls, and ask the nobility who came to donate money to help feed the people."

Elend smiled. "We'd probably spend twice as much on the party as we got in donations."

"And the money we spent would go to skaa merchants."

Elend paused thoughtfully, and Vin smirked to herself. *Odd that I would end up with the only frugal nobleman in the city.* What a pair they were—a Mistborn who felt guilty wasting coins to jump and a nobleman who thought balls were too expensive. It was a wonder that Dockson could pry enough money out of them to keep the city running.

"We'll worry about that later," Elend said as the Hasting gates opened, revealing a field of soldiers at attention.

You can bring your soldiers if you want, the display seemed to say. *I've got more.* In reality, they were entering a strange allegory of Luthadel itself. Elend's two hundred were now surrounded by Cett's thousand—which, in turn, were surrounded by Luthadel's twenty thousand. The city, of course, was then surrounded by nearly a hundred thousand troops on the outside. Layer upon layer of soldiers, all tensely waiting for a fight. Thoughts of balls and parties fled her mind.

Cett did not greet them at the door. That duty was performed by a soldier in a simple uniform.

"Your soldiers can remain here," the man said as they entered the main entryway. Once, the large, pillared room had been draped in fine rugs and wall hangings, but Elend had taken those to fund his government. Cett, obviously, hadn't brought replacements, and that left the inside of the keep feeling austere. Like a battlefront fortress, rather than a mansion.

Elend turned, waving to Demoux, and the captain ordered his men to wait indoors. Vin stood for a moment, consciously keeping herself from shooting a glare at Demoux. If he *was* the kandra, as her instincts warned, then it was dangerous to have him too close. Part of her itched to simply throw him in a dungeon.

And yet, a kandra couldn't hurt humans, so he wasn't a direct threat. He was simply there to relay information. Plus, he'd already know their most sensitive secrets; there was little point in striking now, playing her hand so quickly. If she waited, saw where he went when he slipped out of the city, then maybe she could find out which army—or sect in the city—he was reporting to. Learn what information he had betrayed.

And so, she stayed her hand, waiting. The time to strike would come.

Ham and Demoux arranged their men, and then a smaller honor guard—including Ham, Spook, and Demoux—gathered to stay with Vin and Elend. Elend nodded to Cett's man, and the soldier led them down a side passageway.

We're not heading toward the lifts, Vin thought. The Hasting ballroom was at the very top of the keep's central tower; the times she had attended balls in the structure, she had been taken to the top on one of four human-drawn lifts. Either Cett didn't want to waste the manpower, or . . .

He picked the tallest keep in the city, Vin thought. *The one with the fewest windows as well.* If Cett pulled all the lifts to the top, it would be very difficult for an invading force to claim the keep.

Fortunately, it didn't appear that they would have to go all the way to the top this evening. After they climbed two flights in a twisting stone stairwell—Vin having to pull her dress in at the sides to keep from brushing against the stones—their guide led them out into a large, circular room with stained-glass windows running around the entire perimeter, broken only by columns to support the ceiling. The single room was nearly as wide around as the tower itself.

A secondary ballroom, perhaps? Vin wondered, taking in the beauty. The glass wasn't lit, though she suspected that there were clefts for limelights on the outside. Cett didn't appear to care about such things. He had set up a large table in the very center of the room, and sat at its head. He was already eating.

"You're late," he called out to Elend, "so I started without you."

Elend frowned. To this, Cett laughed a full bellow, holding up a drumstick. "You seem more aghast at my breach of etiquette than you do about the fact that I brought an army to conquer you, boy! But, I suppose that's Luthadel. Sit down before I eat this all myself."

Elend held out an arm for Vin, leading her to the table. Spook took up position near the stairwell, his Tineye's ears listening for danger. Ham led their ten men to a position from which they could watch the only entrances to the room—the entry from the stairs and the door the serving staff used.

Cett ignored the soldiers. He had a group of his own bodyguards standing near the wall on the other side of the room, but he seemed unconcerned that Ham's troop had them slightly outnumbered. His son—the young man who had attended him at the Assembly meeting—stood at his side, waiting quietly.

One of the two has to be Mistborn, Vin thought. *And I still think it is Cett.*

Elend seated her, then took a chair next to her, both of them sitting directly across from Cett. He barely paused in his eating as the servers brought Vin's and Elend's dishes.

Drumsticks, Vin thought, *and vegetables in gravy. He wants this to be a messy meal—he wants to make Elend uncomfortable.*

Elend didn't start on his food immediately. He sat, watching Cett, his expression thoughtful.

"Damn," Cett said. "This is good food. You have no idea how hard it is to get proper meals when traveling!"

"Why did you want to speak with me?" Elend asked. "You know I won't be convinced to vote for you."

Cett shrugged. "I thought it might be interesting."

"Is this about your daughter?" Elend asked.

"Lord Ruler, no!" Cett said with a laugh. "Keep the silly thing, if you want. The day she ran off was one of the few joys I've had this last month."

"And if I threaten to harm her?" Elend asked.

"You won't," Cett said.

"You're certain?"

Cett smiled through his thick beard, leaning toward Elend. "I know you, Venture. I'd been watching you, studying you, for months. And then, you were kind enough to send one of your friends to spy on me. I learned a lot about you from him!"

Elend looked troubled.

Cett laughed. "Honestly, you didn't think I'd recognize one of the Survivor's own crewmembers? You Luthadel noblemen must assume that everyone outside the city is a damn fool!"

"And yet, you listened to Breeze," Elend said. "You let him join you, listened to his advice. And then, you only chased him away when you found him being intimate with your daughter—the one you claim to have no affection for."

"Is *that* why he told you he left the camp?" Cett asked, laughing. "Because I caught him with Allrianne? Goodness, what do I care if the girl seduced him?"

"You think *she* seduced *him*?" Vin asked.

"Of course," Cett said. "Honestly, I only spent a few weeks with him, and even *I* know how useless he is with women."

Elend was taking all this in stride. He watched Cett with narrow, discerning eyes. "So why *did* you chase him away?"

Cett leaned back. "I tried to turn him. He refused. I figured killing him would be preferable to letting him return to you. But, he's remarkably agile for a man his size."

If Cett really is Mistborn, there's no way Breeze got away without Cett letting him, Vin thought.

"So you see, Venture," Cett said. "I know you. I know you better, perhaps, than you know yourself—for I know what your friends think of you. It takes a pretty extraordinary man to earn the loyalty of a weasel like Breeze."

"So you think I won't harm your daughter," Elend said.

"I *know* you won't," Cett said. "You're honest—I happen to like that about you. Unfortunately, honesty is very easy to exploit—I knew, for instance, that you'd admit Breeze was Soothing that crowd." Cett shook his head. "Honest men weren't meant to be kings, lad. It's a damn shame, but it's true. That's why I have to take the throne from you."

Elend was silent for a moment. Finally, he looked to Vin. She took his plate, sniffing it with an Allomancer's senses.

Cett laughed. "Think I'd poison you?"

"No, actually," Elend said as Vin set the plate down. She wasn't as good as some, but she'd leaned the obvious scents.

"You wouldn't use poison," Elend said. "That isn't your way. You seem to be a rather honest man yourself."

"I'm just blunt," Cett said. "There's a difference."

"I haven't heard you tell a lie yet."

"That's because you don't know me well enough to discern the lies," Cett said. He held up several grease-stained fingers. "I've already told you three lies tonight, lad. Good luck guessing which ones they were."

Elend paused, studying Cett. "You're playing with me."

"Of course I am!" Cett said. "Don't you see, boy? This is why you shouldn't be king. Leave the job to men who understand their own corruption; don't let it destroy you."

"Why do you care?" Elend asked.

"Because I'd rather not kill you," Cett said.

"Then don't."

Cett shook his head. "That isn't how all this works, lad. If there is an opportunity to stabilize your power, or to get more power, you'd damn well better take it. And I will."

The table fell silent again. Cett eyed Vin. "No comments from the Mistborn?"

"You swear a lot," Vin said. "You're not supposed to do that in front of ladies."

Cett laughed. "That's the funny thing about Luthadel, lass. They're all so concerned about doing what is 'proper' when people can see them—but, at the same time, they find nothing wrong with going and raping a couple skaa women when the party is through. At least *I* swear to your face."

Elend still hadn't touched his food. "What will happen if you win the vote for the throne?"

Cett shrugged. "Honest answer?"

"Always."

"First thing, I'd have you assassinated," Cett said. "Can't have old kings sticking around."

"And if I step down?" Elend said. "Withdraw from the vote?"

"Step down," Cett said, "vote for me, and then leave town, and I'll let you live."

"And the Assembly?" Elend asked.

"Dissolved," Cett said. "They're a liability. Any time you give a committee power, you just end up with confusion."

"The Assembly gives the people power," Elend said. "That's what a government should provide."

Surprisingly, Cett didn't laugh at that comment. Instead,

he leaned in again, setting one arm on the table, discarding a half-eaten drumstick. "That's the thing, boy. Letting the people rule themselves is fine when everything is bright and happy, but what about when you have two armies facing you? What about when there's a band of insane koloss destroying villages on your frontier? Those aren't the times when you can afford to have an Assembly around to depose you." Cett shook his head. "The price is too high. When you can't have both freedom and safety, boy, which do you choose?"

Elend was silent. "I make my own choice," he finally said. "And I leave the others to make their own as well."

Cett smiled, as if he'd expected such a reply. He started in on another drumstick.

"Let's say I leave," Elend said. "And let's say you do get the throne, protect the city, and dissolve the Assembly. What then? What of the people?"

"Why do you care?"

"You need ask?" Elend said. "I thought you 'understood' me."

Cett smiled. "I put the skaa back to work, in the way the Lord Ruler did. No pay, no emancipated peasant class."

"I can't accept that," Elend said.

"Why not?" Cett said. "It's what they want. You gave them a choice—and they chose to throw you out. Now they're going to choose to put me on the throne. They know that the Lord Ruler's way was the best. One group must rule, and another must serve. Someone has to grow the food and work the forges, boy."

"Perhaps," Elend said. "But you're wrong about one thing."

"And what is that?"

"They're not going to vote for you," Elend said, standing. "They're going to choose me. Faced with the choice between freedom and slavery, they will choose freedom. The men of the Assembly are the finest of this city, and they will make the best choice for its people."

Cett paused, then he laughed. "The best thing about you, lad, is that you can say that and sound serious!"

"I'm leaving, Cett," Elend said, nodding to Vin.

"Oh, sit down, Venture," Cett said, waving toward Elend's chair. "Don't act indignant because I'm being honest with you. We still have things to discuss."

"Such as?" Elend asked.

"Atium," Cett said.

Elend stood for a moment, apparently forcing down his annoyance. When Cett didn't speak immediately, Elend finally sat and began to eat. Vin just picked quietly at her food. As she did, however, she studied the faces of Cett's soldiers and servants. There were bound to be Allomancers mixed among them—finding out how many could give Elend an advantage.

"Your people are starving," Cett said. "And, if my spies are worth their coin, you just got another influx of mouths. You can't last much longer under this siege."

"And?" Elend asked.

"I have food," Cett said. "A lot of it—more than my army needs. Canned goods, packed with the new method the Lord Ruler developed. Long-lasting, no spoilage. Really a marvel of technology. I'd be willing to trade you some of them. . . ."

Elend paused, fork halfway to his lips. Then he lowered it and laughed. "You still think I have the Lord Ruler's atium?"

"Of course you have it," Cett said, frowning. "Where else would it be?"

Elend shook his head, taking a bite of gravy-drenched potato. "Not here, for certain."

"But . . . the rumors . . ." Cett said.

"Breeze spread those rumors," Elend said. "I thought you'd figured out why he joined your group. He wanted you to come to Luthadel so that you'd stop Straff from taking the city."

"But, Breeze did everything he could to *keep* me from coming here," Cett said. "He downplayed the rumors, he tried to distract me, he . . ." Cett trailed off, then he bellowed a laugh. "I thought he was just there to spy! It seems we both underestimated each other."

"My people could still use that food," Elend said.

"And they'll have it—assuming I become king."

"They're starving now," Elend said.

"And their suffering will be your burden," Cett said, his face growing hard. "I can see that you have judged me, Elend Venture. You think me a good man. You're wrong. Honesty does not make a man less of a tyrant. I slaughtered thousands to secure my rule. I put burdens on the skaa that make even the Lord Ruler's hand seem pleasant. I made certain that I stayed in power. I will do the same here."

The men fell silent. Elend ate, but Vin only mixed her food around. If she had missed a poison, she wanted one of them to remain alert. She still wanted to find those Allomancers, and there was only one way to be certain. She turned off her copper, then burned bronze.

There was no Coppercloud burning; Cett apparently didn't care if someone recognized his men as Allomancers. Two of his men were burning pewter. Neither, however, were soldiers; both were pretending to be members of the serving staff who were bringing meals. There was also a Tineye pulsing in the other room, listening.

Why hide Thugs as servants, then use no copper to hide their pulses? In addition, there were no Soothers or Rioters. Nobody was trying to influence Elend's emotions. Neither Cett nor his youthful attendant were burning any metals. Either they weren't actually Allomancers, or they feared exposing themselves. Just to be certain, Vin flared her bronze, seeking to pierce any hidden copperclouds that might be nearby. She could see Cett putting out some obvious Allomancers as a distraction, then hiding the others inside a cloud.

She found nothing. Finally satisfied, she returned to picking at her meal. *How many times has this ability of mine—the ability to pierce copperclouds—proven useful?* She'd forgotten what it was like to be blocked from sensing Allomantic pulses. This one little ability—simple though it seemed—provided an enormous advantage. And the Lord Ruler and his Inquisitors had probably been able to do it from the beginning. What other tricks was she missing, what other secrets had died with the Lord Ruler?

He knew the truth about the Deepness, Vin thought. *He must have. He tried to warn us, at the end. . . .*

Elend and Cett were talking again. Why couldn't she focus on the problems of the city?

"So you don't have any atium at all?" Cett said.

"None that we're willing to sell," Elend said.

"You've searched the city?" Cett asked.

"A dozen times."

"The statues," Cett said. "Perhaps the Lord Ruler hid the metal by melting it down, then building things out of it."

Elend shook his head. "We thought of that. The statues aren't atium, and they aren't hollow either—that would have been a good place to hide metal from Allomancer eyes. We thought maybe that it would be hidden in the palace somewhere, but even the spires are simple iron."

"Caves, tunnels. . . ."

"None that we can find," Elend said. "We've had Allomancers patrol, searching for large sources of metals. We've done everything we can think of, Cett, short of tearing holes in the ground. Trust me. We've been working on this problem for a while."

Cett nodded, sighing. "So, I suppose holding you for ransom would be pointless?"

Elend smiled. "I'm not even king, Cett. The only thing you'd do is make the Assembly less likely to vote for you."

Cett laughed. "Suppose I'll have to let you go, then."

Alendi was never the Hero of Ages. At best, I have amplified his virtues, creating a Hero where there was none. At worst, I fear that all we believe may have been corrupted.

36

ONCE THIS WAREHOUSE HAD HELD swords and armor, scattered across its floor in heaps, like some mythical treasure. Sazed remembered walking through it, marveling at the preparations Kelsier had made without alerting any of his crewmembers. Those weapons had armed the rebellion on the eve of the Survivor's own death, letting it take the city.

Those weapons were now stored in lockers and armories. In their place, a desperate, beaten people huddled in what blankets they could find. There were very few men, none of fighting quality; Straff had pressed those into his army. These others—the weak, the sickly, the wounded—he had allowed to Luthadel, knowing that Elend wouldn't turn them away.

Sazed moved among them, offering what comfort he could. They had no furniture, and even changes of clothing were becoming scarce in the city. The merchants, realizing that warmth would be a premium for the upcoming winter, had begun raising prices on all their wares, not just foodstuffs.

Sazed knelt beside a crying woman. "Peace, Genedere," he said, his coppermind reminding him of her name.

She shook her head. She had lost three children in the koloss attack, two more in the flight to Luthadel. Now the final one—the babe she had carried the entire way—was sick. Sazed took the child from her arms, carefully studying his symptoms. Little had changed from the day before.

"Is there hope, Master Terrisman?" Genedere asked.

Sazed glanced down at the thin, glassy-eyed baby. The chances were not good. How could he tell her such a thing?

"As long as he breathes, there is hope, dear woman," Sazed said. "I will ask the king to increase your portion of food—you need strength to give suck. You *must* keep him warm. Stay near the fires, and use a damp cloth to drip water in his mouth even when he is not eating. He has great need of liquids."

Genedere nodded dully, taking back the baby. How Sazed wished he could give her more. A dozen different religions passed through his mind. He had spent his entire life trying to encourage people to believe in something other than the Lord Ruler. Yet, for some reason, at this moment he found it difficult to preach one of them to Genedere.

It had been different before the Collapse. Each time he'd spoken of a religion, Sazed had felt a subtle sense of rebellion. Even if people hadn't accepted the things he taught— and they rarely had—his words had reminded them that there had once been beliefs other than the doctrines of the Steel Ministry.

Now there was nothing to rebel against. In the face of the terrible grief he saw in Genedere's eyes, he found it difficult to speak of religions long dead, gods long forgotten. Esoterica would not ease this woman's pain.

Sazed stood, moving on to the next group of people.

"Sazed?"

Sazed turned. He hadn't noticed Tindwyl entering the warehouse. The doors of the large structure were closed against approaching night, and the firepits gave an inconsistent light. Holes had been knocked in the roof to let out the smoke; if one looked up, trails of mist could be seen creeping into the room, though they evaporated before they reached halfway to the floor.

The refugees didn't often look up.

"You've been here nearly all day," Tindwyl said. The room was remarkably quiet, considering its occupancy. Fires crackled, and people lay silent in their pain or numbness.

"There are many wounded here," Sazed said. "I am the

best one to look after them, I think. I am not alone—the king has sent others and Lord Breeze is here, Soothing the people's despair."

Sazed nodded to the side, where Breeze sat in a chair, ostensibly reading a book. He looked terribly out of place in the room, wearing his fine three-piece suit. Yet, his mere presence said something remarkable, in Sazed's estimation.

These poor people, Sazed thought. *Their lives were terrible under the Lord Ruler. Now even what little they had has been taken from them.* And they were only a tiny number—four hundred compared with the hundreds of thousands who still lived in Luthadel.

What would happen when the final stores of food ran out? Rumors were already abroad regarding the poisoned wells, and Sazed had just heard that some of their stored food had been sabotaged as well. What would happen to these people? How long could the siege continue?

In fact, what would happen when the siege ended? What would happen when the armies finally began to attack and pillage? What destruction, what grief, would the soldiers cause in searching for hidden atium?

"You do care for them," Tindwyl said quietly, stepping up.

Sazed turned toward her. Then he looked down. "Not as much as I should, perhaps."

"No," Tindwyl said. "I can see it. You confuse me, Sazed."

"I seem to have a talent in that area."

"You look tired. Where is your bronzemind?"

Suddenly, Sazed felt the fatigue. He'd been ignoring it, but her words seemed to bring it in like a wave, rolling over him.

He sighed. "I used most of my wakefulness in my run to Luthadel. I was so eager to get here. . . ." His studies had languished recently. With the problems in the city, and the arrival of the refugees, he hadn't had much time. Besides, he had already transcribed the rubbing. Further work would require detailed cross-referencing to other works, searching for clues. He probably wouldn't even have time to . . .

He frowned, noting the odd look in Tindwyl's eyes.

"All right," she said, sighing. "Show me."

"Show you?"

"Whatever it was you found," she said. "The discovery that prompted you to run across two dominances. Show it to me."

Suddenly, everything seemed to lighten. His fatigue, his worry, even his sorrow. "I would love to," he said quietly.

Another job well done, Breeze thought, congratulating himself as he watched the two Terrismen leave the warehouse.

Most people, even noblemen, misunderstood Soothing. They thought of it as some kind of mind control, and even those who knew more presumed that Soothing was an invasive, terrible thing.

Breeze had never seen it that way. Soothing wasn't invasive. If it was, then ordinary interaction with another person was comparably invasive. Soothing, when done right, was no more a violation of another person than it was for a woman to wear a low-cut gown or speak in a commanding voice. All three produced common, understandable, and— most important—natural reactions in people.

Take Sazed, for example. Was it "invasive" to make the man less fatigued, so he could better go about his ministrations? Was it wrong to Soothe away his pain—just a bit— thereby making him better able to cope with the suffering?

Tindwyl was an even better example. Perhaps some would call Breeze a meddler for Soothing her sense of responsibility, and her disappointment, when she saw Sazed. But, Breeze had not created the emotions that the disappointment had been overshadowing. Emotions like curiosity. Respect. Love.

No, if Soothing were simple "mind control," Tindwyl would have turned away from Sazed as soon as the two left Breeze's area of influence. But Breeze knew that she wouldn't. A crucial decision had been made, and Breeze had not made that decision for her. The moment had been building for weeks; it would have occurred with or without Breeze.

He had just helped it happen sooner.

Smiling to himself, Breeze checked his pocket watch. He still had a few more minutes, and he settled back in his chair, sending out a general Soothing wave, lessening people's grief and pain. Focusing on so many at once, he couldn't be very specific; some would find themselves made a little emotionally numb as he Pushed too strongly against them. But, it would be good for the group as a whole.

He didn't read his book; in truth, he couldn't understand how Elend and the rest spent so much time with them. Dreadfully boring things. Breeze could only see himself reading if there were no people around. Instead, he went back to what he'd been doing before Sazed had drawn his attention. He studied the refugees, trying to decide what each one was feeling.

This was the other great misunderstanding about Soothing. Allomancy wasn't nearly as important as observational talent. True, having a subtle touch certainly helped. However, Soothing didn't give an Allomancer the ability to know someone's feelings. Those, Breeze had to guess on his own.

It all came back to what was natural. Even the most inexperienced skaa would realize they were being Soothed if unexpected emotions began bouncing around inside of them. True subtlety in Soothing was about encouraging natural emotions, all done by carefully making the right other emotions less powerful. People were a patchwork of feelings; usually, what they thought they were "feeling" at the moment only related to which emotions were currently most dominant within them.

The careful Soother saw what was beneath the surface. He understood what a man was feeling, even when that man himself didn't understand—or acknowledge—those emotions. Such was the case with Sazed and Tindwyl.

Odd pair, that one, Breeze thought to himself, idly Soothing one of the skaa to make him more relaxed as he tried to sleep. *The rest of the crew is convinced that those two are enemies. But, hatred rarely creates that measure of bitterness and frustration. No, those two emotions come from an entirely different set of problems.*

Of course, isn't Sazed supposed to be a eunuch? I wonder how this all came about. . . .

His speculations trailed off as the warehouse doors opened. Elend walked in—Ham, unfortunately, accompanying him. Elend was wearing one of his white uniforms, complete with white gloves and a sword. The white was an important symbol; with all of the ash and soot in the city, a man in white was quite striking. Elend's uniforms had to been crafted of special fabrics designed to be resistant to ash, and they still had to be scrubbed every day. The effect was worth the effort.

Breeze immediately picked at Elend's emotions, making the man less tired, less uncertain—though the second was becoming almost unnecessary. That was partially the Terriswoman's doing; Breeze had been impressed with her ability to change how people felt, considering her lack of Allomancy.

Breeze left Elend's emotions of disgust and pity; both were appropriate considering the environment. He did, however, give Ham a nudge to make him less argumentative; Breeze wasn't in a mood to deal with the man's prattlings at the moment.

He stood as the two men approached. People perked up as they saw Elend, his presence somehow bringing them a hope that Breeze couldn't emulate with Allomancy. They whispered, calling Elend King.

"Breeze," Elend said, nodding. "Is Sazed here?"

"He just left, I'm afraid," Breeze said.

Elend seemed distracted. "Ah, well," he said. "I'll find him later." Elend looked around the room, lips downturned. "Ham, tomorrow, I want you to round up the clothing merchants on Kenton Street and bring them here to see this."

"They might not like that, Elend," Ham said.

"I hope they don't," Elend said. "But we'll see how they feel about their prices once they visit this room. I can understand food's expense, considering its scarcity. However, there is no reason but greed to deny the people clothing."

Ham nodded, but Breeze could see the reticence in his posture. Did the others realize how strangely nonconfrontational Ham was? He liked to argue with friends, but he rarely actually came to any conclusions in his philosophizing. Plus, he absolutely hated fighting with strangers; Breeze had always found that an odd attribute in one who was hired, essentially, to hit people. He gave Ham a bit of a Soothing to make him less worried about confronting the merchants.

"You aren't going to stay here all night, are you, Breeze?" Elend asked.

"Lord Ruler, no!" Breeze said. "My dear man, you're lucky you managed to get me to come at all. Honestly, this is no place for a gentleman. The dirt, the depressing atmosphere—and that's not even making mention of the smell!"

Ham frowned. "Breeze, someday you're going to have to learn to think about other people."

"As long as I can think about them from a distance, Hammond, I shall be happy to engage in the activity."

Ham shook his head. "You're hopeless."

"Are you heading back to the palace then?" Elend asked.

"Yes, actually," Breeze said, checking his pocket watch. "Do you need a ride?"

"I brought my own carriage," Breeze said.

Elend nodded, then turned to Ham, and the two retreated the way they had come, talking about Elend's next meeting with one of the other Assemblymen.

Breeze wandered into the palace a short time later. He nodded to the door guards, Soothing away their mental fatigue. They perked up in response, watching the mists with renewed vigilance. It wouldn't last long, but little touches like that were second nature to Breeze.

It was getting late, and few people were in the hallways. He made his way through the kitchens, Nudging the scullery maids to make them more chatty. It would make their cleaning pass more quickly. Beyond the kitchens he found a small stone room, lit by a couple of plain lamps, set with a small table. It was one of the palace's boothlike, solitary dining rooms.

Clubs sat in one corner of the booth, gimped leg stretched out on the bench. He eyed Breeze with a scowl. "You're late."

"You're early," Breeze said, sliding into the bench across from Clubs.

"Same thing," Clubs grumbled.

There was a second cup on the table, along with a bottle of wine. Breeze unbuttoned his vest, sighed quietly, and poured himself a cup as he leaned back with his legs up on his bench.

Clubs sipped his wine.

"You have your cloud up?" Breeze asked.

"Around you?" Clubs said. "Always."

Breeze smiled, taking a sip, and relaxed. Though he rarely had opportunities to use his powers anymore, Clubs was a Smoker. When he was burning copper, every Allomancer's abilities were invisible to those burning bronze. But more important—at least to Breeze—burning copper made Clubs immune to any form of emotional Allomancy.

"Don't see why that makes you so happy," Clubs said. "I thought you liked playing with emotions."

"I do," Breeze said.

"Then why come drink with me every night?" Clubs asked.

"You mind the company?"

Clubs didn't answer. That was pretty much his way of saying he didn't mind. Breeze eyed the grumpy general. Most of the other crewmembers stayed away from Clubs; Kelsier had brought him in at the last moment, since the Coppercloud they usually used had died.

"Do you know what it's like, Clubs?" Breeze asked. "Being a Soother?"

"No."

"It gives you remarkable control. It's a wonderful feeling, being able to influence those around you, always feeling like you have a handle on how people will react."

"Sounds delightful," Clubs said flatly.

"And yet, it does things to you. I spend most of my time watching people—tweaking, Nudging, and Soothing. That's changed me. I don't . . . look at people the same way. It's hard to just be friends with someone when you see them as something to be influenced and changed."

Clubs grunted. "So that's why we never used to see you with women."

Breeze nodded. "I can't help it anymore. I always touch the emotions of everyone around me. And so, when a woman comes to love me . . ." He liked to think he wasn't invasive. Yet, how could he trust anyone who said they loved him? Was it he, or his Allomancy, that they responded to?

Clubs filled his cup. "You're a lot sillier than you act."

Breeze smiled. Clubs was one of the few people who was completely immune to his touch. Emotional Allomancy wouldn't work on him, and he was always completely forthcoming with his emotions: everything made him grumpy. Manipulating him through non-Allomantic means had proven to be a fruitless waste of time.

Breeze regarded his wine. "The amusing thing is, you almost didn't join the crew because of me."

"Damn Soothers," Clubs muttered.

"But you're immune to us."

"To your Allomancy, maybe," Clubs said. "But that isn't the only way you people do things. A man always has to watch himself around Soothers."

"Then why let me join you every evening for wine?"

Clubs was silent for a moment, and Breeze almost thought he wasn't going to respond. Finally, Clubs muttered, "You're not as bad as most."

Breeze took a gulp of wine. "That is as honest a compliment as I think I've ever received."

"Don't let it ruin you," Clubs said.

"Oh, I think I'm too late for ruining," Breeze said, topping off his cup. "This crew . . . Kell's plan . . . has already done a thorough job of that."

Clubs nodded in agreement.

"What happened to us, Clubs?" Breeze asked. "I joined Kell for the challenge. I never did know why you joined."

"Money."

Breeze nodded. "His plan fell apart, his army got destroyed, and we stayed. Then he died, and we *still* stayed. This blasted kingdom of Elend's is doomed, you know."

"We won't last another month," Clubs said. It wasn't idle pessimism; Breeze knew people well enough to tell when they were serious.

"And yet, here we are," Breeze said. "I spent all day making skaa feel better about the fact that their families had been slaughtered. You spent all day training soldiers that—with or without your help—will barely last a few heartbeats against a determined foe. We follow a boy of a king who doesn't seem to have a shade of a clue just how bad his predicament is. Why?"

Clubs shook his head. "Kelsier. Gave us a city, made us think we were responsible for protecting it."

"But we aren't that kind of people," Breeze said. "We're thieves and scammers. We shouldn't care. I mean . . . I've gotten so bad that I Soothe scullery maids so that they'll have a happier time at work! I might as well start dressing in pink and carrying around flowers. I could probably make quite a bundle at weddings."

Clubs snorted. Then he raised his cup. "To the Survivor," he said. "May he be damned for knowing us better than we knew ourselves."

Breeze raised his own cup. "Damn him," he agreed quietly.

The two fell silent. Talking to Clubs tended to turn into . . . well, not talking. However, Breeze felt a simple contentment. Soothing was wonderful; it made him who he was. But it was also work. Even birds couldn't fly all the time.

"*There* you are."

Breeze snapped his eyes open. Allrianne stood at the entrance to the room, just at the edge of the table. She wore light blue; where had she gotten so many dresses? Her makeup was, of course, immaculate—and there was a bow in her hair. That long blond hair—common in the West but almost unheard of in the Central Dominance—and that perky, inviting figure.

Desire immediately blossomed inside of him. *No!* Breeze thought. *She's half your age. You're a dirty old man. Dirty!* "Allrianne," he said uncomfortably, "shouldn't you be in bed or something?"

She rolled her eyes, shooing his legs out of the way so she could sit on the bench beside him. "It's only nine o'clock, Breeze. I'm eighteen, not ten."

You might as well be, he thought, looking away from her, trying to focus on something else. He knew that he should be stronger, shouldn't let the girl get near him, but he did nothing as she slid up to him and took a drink from his cup.

He sighed, putting his arm around her shoulders. Clubs just shook his head, the hint of a smile on his lips.

"Well," Vin said quietly, "that answers one question."

"Mistress?" OreSeur said, sitting across the table from her in the dark room. With her Allomancer's ears, she could hear exactly what was going on in the next boothlike room over.

"Allrianne is an Allomancer," Vin said.

"Really?"

Vin nodded. "She's been Rioting Breeze's emotions ever since she arrived, making him more attracted to her."

"One would think that he'd notice," OreSeur said.

"You'd think," Vin said. She probably shouldn't feel as amused as she did. The girl could be a Mistborn—though the idea of that puff flying through the mists seemed ridiculous.

Which is probably exactly how she wants me to think, Vin thought. *I have to remember Kliss and Shan—neither one of them turned out to be the person I thought they were.*

"Breeze probably just doesn't think his emotions are unnatural," Vin said. "He must be attracted to her already."

OreSeur closed his mouth and cocked his head—his dog's version of a frown.

"I know," Vin agreed. "But, at least we know he isn't the one using Allomancy to seduce *her.* Either way, that's irrelevant. Clubs isn't the kandra."

"How could you possibly know that, Mistress?"

Vin paused. Clubs always turned his copper on around Breeze; it was one of the few times he used it. However, it was difficult to tell if someone was burning copper. After all, if they turned on their metal, they hid themselves by default.

But Vin could pierce copperclouds. She could sense Allrianne's Rioting; she could even sense a faint thumping coming from Clubs himself, copper's own Allomantic pulse, something that Vin suspected few people beyond herself and the Lord Ruler had ever heard.

"I just know," Vin said.

"If you say so, Mistress," OreSeur said. "But . . . didn't you already decide the spy was Demoux?"

"I wanted to check Clubs anyway," she said. "Before I did anything drastic."

"Drastic?"

Vin sat quietly for a moment. She didn't have much proof, but she did have her instincts—and those instincts told her Demoux was the spy. That sneaking way he'd gone out the other night . . . the obvious logic of choosing him . . . it all fit.

She stood. Things were getting too dangerous, too sensitive. She couldn't ignore it any longer. "Come on," she said, leaving the booth behind. "It's time to put Demoux in prison."

"What do you mean you *lost* him?" Vin asked, standing outside the door to Demoux's room.

The servant flushed. "My lady, I'm sorry. I watched him, like you told me—but he went out on patrol. Should I have followed? I mean, don't you think that would have looked suspicious?"

Vin cursed quietly to herself. She knew that she didn't have much right to be angry, however. *I should have told Ham straight off,* she thought with frustration.

"My lady, he only left a few minutes ago," the servant said.

Vin glanced at OreSeur, then took off down the corridor. As soon as they reached a window, Vin leaped out into the dark night, OreSeur following behind her, dropping the short distance to the courtyard.

Last time, I saw him come back in through the gates to

the palace grounds, she thought, running through the mist. She found a couple of soldiers there, guarding.

"Did Captain Demoux come this way?" she demanded, bursting into their ring of torchlight.

They perked up, at first shocked, then confused.

"Lady Heir?" one of them said. "Yes, he just went out, on patrol just a minute or two ago."

"By himself?" Vin asked.

They nodded.

"Isn't that a little odd?"

They shrugged. "He goes by himself sometimes," one said. "We don't question. He's our superior, after all."

"Which way?" Vin demanded.

One pointed, and Vin took off, OreSeur at her side. *I should have watched better. I should have hired real spies to keep an eye on him. I should have—*

She froze. Up ahead, walking down a quite street in the mists, was a figure, walking into the city. Demoux.

Vin dropped a coin and threw herself into the air, passing far over his head, landing on top of a building. He continued, oblivious. Demoux or kandra, neither would have Allomantic powers.

Vin paused, daggers out, ready to spring. But . . . she still didn't have any real proof. The part of her that Kelsier had transformed, the part that had come to trust, thought of the Demoux she knew.

Do I really believe he's the kandra? she thought. *Or do I just* want *him to be the kandra, so that I don't have to suspect my real friends?*

He continued to walk below, her tin-enhanced ears easily picking out his footfalls. Behind, OreSeur scrambled up onto the top of the roof, then padded over and sat down beside her.

I can't just attack, she thought. *I need to at least watch, see where he's going. Get proof.* Perhaps learn something in the process.

She waved to OreSeur, and they quietly followed along the rooftops, trailing Demoux. Soon, Vin noticed something odd—a flicker of firelight illuminating the mists a few streets over, making haunted shadows of buildings.

Vin glanced at Demoux, trailing him with her eyes as he wandered down an alleyway, moving toward the illumination.

What . . . ?

Vin threw herself off the roof. It took only three bounds for her to reach the source of the light. A modest bonfire crackled in the center of a small square. Skaa huddled around it for warmth, looking a little frightened in the mists. Vin was surprised to see them. She hadn't seen skaa go out in the mists since the night of the Collapse.

Demoux approached down a side street, greeting several of the others. In the firelight she could confirm for certain that it was him—or, at least, a kandra with his face.

There were, perhaps, two hundred people in the square. Demoux moved as if to sit on the cobblestones, but someone quickly approached with a chair. A young woman brought him a mug of something steaming, which he received gratefully.

Vin leaped to a rooftop, staying low to keep from being exposed by the firelight. More skaa arrived, mostly in groups, but some brave individuals came alone.

A sound came from behind her, and Vin turned as OreSeur—apparently having barely made the jump—scrambled the last few feet over the edge onto the roof. He glanced down at the street below, shook his head, then padded over to join her. She raised a finger to her lips, nodding down at the growing group of people. OreSeur cocked his head at the sight, but said nothing.

Finally, Demoux stood, holding the still steaming cup in his hands. People gathered around, sitting on the cold cobblestones, huddled beneath blankets or cloaks.

"We shouldn't fear the mists, my friends," Demoux said. His wasn't the voice of a strong leader or forceful battle commander—it was the voice of hardened youth, a little hesitant, but compelling nonetheless.

"The Survivor taught us of this," he continued. "I know it's very hard to think of the mists without remembering stories of mistwraiths or other horrors. But, the Survivor gave the mists to us. We should try and remember him, through them."

Lord Ruler . . . Vin thought with shock. *He's one of them—a member of the Church of the Survivor!* She wavered, uncertain what to think. Was he the kandra or wasn't he? Why would the kandra meet with a group of people like this? But . . . why would Demoux himself do it?

"I know it's hard," Demoux said below, "without the Survivor. I know you're afraid of the armies. Trust me, I know. I see them too. I know you suffer beneath this siege. I . . . don't know if I can even tell you not to worry. The Survivor himself knew great hardship—the death of his wife, his imprisonment in the Pits of Hathsin. But he survived. That's the point, isn't it? We have to live on, no matter how hard this all gets. We'll win, in the end. Just like he did."

He stood with his mug in his hands, looking nothing like the skaa preachers Vin had seen. Kelsier had chosen a passionate man to found his religion—or, more precisely, to found the revolution the religion had come from. Kelsier had needed leaders who could enflame supporters, whip them up into a destructive upheaval.

Demoux was something different. He didn't shout, but spoke calmly. Yet, people paid attention. They sat on the stones around him, looking up with hopeful—even worshipful—eyes.

"The Lady Heir," one of them whispered. "What of her?"

"Lady Vin bears a great responsibility," Demoux said. "You can see the weight bowing her down, and how frustrated she is with the problems in the city. She is a straightforward woman, and I don't think she likes the Assembly's politicking."

"But, she'll protect us, right?" one asked.

"Yes," Demoux said. "Yes, I believe she will. Sometimes, I think that she's even more powerful than the Survivor was. You know that he only had two years to practice as a Mistborn? She's barely had that much time herself."

Vin turned away. *It comes back to that,* she thought. *They sound rational until they talk about me, and then . . .*

"She'll bring us peace, someday," Demoux said. "The heir will bring back the sun, stop the ash from falling. But we have to survive until then. And we have to fight. The Survivor's entire work was to see the Lord Ruler dead and make us free. What gratitude do we show if we run now that armies have come?

"Go and tell your Assemblymen that you don't want Lord Cett, or even Lord Penrod, to be your king. The vote happens in one day, and we *need* to make certain the right man is made king. The Survivor chose Elend Venture, and that is whom we must follow."

That's new, Vin thought.

"Lord Elend is weak," one of the people said. "He won't defend us."

"Lady Vin loves him," Demoux said. "She wouldn't love a weak man. Penrod and Cett treat you like the skaa *used* to be treated, and that's why you think they're strong. But that's not strength—it's oppression. We have to be better than that! We have to trust the Survivor's judgment!"

Vin relaxed against the lip of the roof, tension melting a bit. If Demoux really was the spy, then he wasn't going to give her any evidence this night. So, she put her knives away, then rested with her arms folded on the rooftop's edge. The fire crackled in the cool winter evening, sending billows of smoke to mix with the mists, and Demoux continued to speak in his quiet, reassuring voice, teaching the people about Kelsier.

It's not even really a religion, Vin thought as she listened. *The theology is so simple—not at all like the complex beliefs that Sazed speaks about.*

Demoux taught basic concepts. He held up Kelsier as a model, talking about survival, and about enduring hardships. Vin could see why the direct words would appeal to the skaa. The people really only had two choices: to struggle on, or to give up. Demoux's teachings gave them an excuse to keep living.

The skaa didn't need rituals, prayers, or codes. Not yet. They were too inexperienced with religion in general, too frightened of it, to want such things. But, the more she listened, the more Vin understood the Church of the Survivor. It was what they needed; it took what the skaa already knew—a life filled with hardship—and elevated it to a higher, more optimistic plane.

And the teachings were still evolving. The deification of Kelsier she had expected; even the reverence for her was understandable. But, where did Demoux get the promises that Vin would stop the ash and bring back the sun? How did he know to preach of green grasses and blue skies, describing the world as it was known only in some of the world's most obscure texts?

He described a strange world of colors and beauty—a place foreign and difficult to conceive, but somehow wonderful all the same. Flowers and green plants were strange, alien things to these people; even Vin had trouble visualizing them, and she had heard Sazed's descriptions.

Demoux was giving the skaa a paradise. It had to be something completely removed from normal experience, for the mundane world was not a place of hope. Not with a foodless winter approaching, not with armies threatening and the government in turmoil.

Vin pulled back as Demoux finally ended the meeting. She lay for a moment, trying to decide how she felt. She'd been near certain about Demoux, but now her suspicions seemed unfounded. He'd gone out at night, true, but she saw now what he was doing. Plus, he'd acted so suspiciously when sneaking out. It seemed to her, as she reflected, that a kandra would know how to go about things in a much more natural way.

It's not him, she thought. *Or, if it is, he's not going to be as easy to unmask as I thought.* She frowned in frustration. Finally, she just sighed, rising, and walked to the other side of the roof. OreSeur followed, and Vin glanced at him. "When Kelsier told you to take his body," she said, "what did he want you to preach to these people?"

"Mistress?" OreSeur asked.

"He had you appear, as if you were him returned from the grave."

"Yes."

"Well, what did he have you say?"

OreSeur shrugged. "Very simple things, Mistress. I told them that the time for rebellion had arrived. I told them that I—Kelsier—had returned to give them hope for victory."

I represent that thing you've never been able to kill, no matter how hard you try. They had been Kelsier's final words, spoken face-to-face with the Lord Ruler. *I am hope.*

I am hope.

Was it any wonder that this concept would become central to the church that sprang up around him? "Did he have you teach things like we just heard Demoux say?" Vin asked. "About the ash no longer falling, and the sun turning yellow?"

"No, Mistress."

"That's what I thought," Vin said as she heard rustling on the stones below. She glanced over the side of the building, and saw Demoux returning to the palace.

Vin dropped to the alleyway floor behind him. To the man's credit, he heard her, and he spun, hand on dueling cane.

"Peace, Captain," she said, rising.

"Lady Vin?" he asked with surprise.

She nodded, approaching closer so that he'd be able to see her better in the night. Fading torchlight still lit the air from behind, swirls of mist playing with shadows.

"I didn't know you were a member of the Church of the Survivor," she said softly.

He looked down. Though he was easily two hands taller than she, he seemed to shrink a bit before her. "I . . . I know it makes you uncomfortable. I'm sorry."

"It's all right," she said. "You do a good thing for the people. Elend will appreciate hearing of your loyalty."

Demoux looked up. "Do you have to tell him?"

"He needs to know what the people believe, Captain. Why would you want me to keep it quiet?"

Demoux sighed. "I just . . . I don't want the crew to think I'm out here pandering to the people. Ham thinks preaching about the Survivor is silly, and Lord Breeze says the only reason to encourage the church is to make people more pliant."

Vin regarded him in the darkness. "You really believe, don't you?"

"Yes, my lady."

"But you knew Kelsier," she said. "You were with us from near the beginning. You know he's no god."

Demoux looked up, a bit of a challenge in his eyes. "He died to overthrow the Lord Ruler."

"That doesn't make him divine."

"He taught us how to survive, to have hope."

"You survived before," Vin said. "People had hope before Kelsier got thrown in those pits."

"Not like we do now," Demoux said. "Besides . . . he had power, my lady. I felt it."

Vin paused. She knew the story; Kelsier had used Demoux as an example to the rest of the army in a fight with a skeptic, directing his blows with Allomancy, making Demoux seem as if he had supernatural powers.

"Oh, I know about Allomancy now," Demoux said. "But . . . I felt him Pushing on my sword that day. I felt him use me, making me more than I was. I think I can still feel him, sometimes. Strengthening my arm, guiding my blade. . . ."

Vin frowned. "Do you remember the first time we met?"

Demoux nodded. "Yes. You came to the caverns where we were hiding on the day when the army was destroyed. I was on guard duty. You know, my lady—even then, I knew that Kelsier would come for us. I knew that he'd come and get those of us who had been faithful and guide us back to Luthadel."

He went to those caves because I forced him to. He wanted to get himself killed fighting an army on his own.

"The destruction of the army was a test," Demoux said, looking up into the mists. "These armies . . . the siege . . . they're just tests. To see if we will survive or not."

"And the ash?" Vin asked. "Where did you hear that it would stop falling?"

Demoux turned back to her. "The Survivor taught that, didn't he?"

Vin shook her head.

"A lot of the people are saying it," Demoux said. "It must be true. It fits with everything else—the yellow sun, the blue sky, the plants. . . ."

"Yes, but where did you first hear those things?"

"I'm not sure, my lady."

Where did you hear that I would be the one to bring them about? she thought, but she somehow couldn't bring herself to voice the question. Regardless, she knew the answer: Demoux wouldn't know. Rumors were propagating. It would be difficult indeed to trace them back to their source now.

"Go back to the palace," Vin said. "I have to tell Elend what I saw, but I'll ask him not to tell the rest of the crew."

"Thank you, my lady," Demoux said, bowing. He turned and hurried away. A second later, Vin heard a thump from behind: OreSeur, jumping down to the street.

She turned. "I was sure it was him."

"Mistress?"

"The kandra," Vin said, turning back toward the disappearing Demoux. "I thought I'd discovered him."

"And?"

She shook her head. "It's like Dockson—I think Demoux knows too much to be faking. He feels . . . real to me."

"My brethren—"

"Are quite skilled," Vin said with a sigh. "Yes, I know. But we're not going to arrest him. Not tonight, at least. We'll keep an eye on him, but I just don't think it's him anymore."

OreSeur nodded.

"Come on," she said. "I want to check on Elend."

And so, I come to the focus of my argument. I apologize. Even forcing my words into steel, sitting and scratching in this frozen cave, I am prone to ramble.

37

SAZED GLANCED AT THE WINDOW SHUTTERS, noting the hesitant beams of light that were beginning to shine through the cracks. *Morning already?* he thought. *We studied all night?* It hardly seemed possible. He had tapped no wakefulness, yet he felt more alert—more alive—than he had in days.

Tindwyl sat in the chair beside him. Sazed's desk was filled with loose papers, two sets of ink and pen waiting to be used. There were no books; Keepers had no need of such.

"Ah!" Tindwyl said, grabbing a pen and beginning to write. She didn't look tired either, but she had likely dipped into her bronzemind, tapping the wakefulness stored within.

Sazed watched her write. She almost looked young again; he hadn't seen such overt excitement in her since she had been abandoned by the Breeders some ten years before. On that day, her grand work finished, she had finally joined her fellow Keepers. Sazed had been the one to present her with the collected knowledge that had been discovered during her thirty years of cloistered childbirth.

It hadn't taken her long to achieve a place in the Synod. By then, however, Sazed had been ousted from their ranks.

Tindwyl finished writing. "The passage is from a biography of King Wednegon," she said. "He was one of the last leaders who resisted the Lord Ruler in any sort of meaningful combat."

"I know who he was," Sazed said, smiling.

She paused. "Of course." She obviously wasn't accustomed to studying with someone who had access to as much information as she did. She pushed the written passage over to Sazed; even with his mental indexes and self-notes, it would be faster for her to write out the passage than it would be for him to try and find it within his own copperminds.

I spent a great deal of time with the king during his final weeks, the text read.

> *He seemed frustrated, as one might imagine. His soldiers could not stand against the Conqueror's koloss, and his men had been beaten back repeatedly ever since FellSpire. However, the king didn't blame his soldiers. He thought that his problems came from another source: food.*
>
> *He mentioned this idea several times during those last days. He thought that if he'd had more food, he could have held out. In this, Wednegon blamed the Deepness. For, though the Deepness had been defeated—or at least weakened—its touch had depleted Darrelnai's food stores.*
>
> *His people could not both raise food and resist the Conqueror's demon armies. In the end, that was why they fell.*

Sazed nodded slowly. "How much of this text do we have?"

"Not much," Tindwyl said. "Six or seven pages. This is the only section that mentions the Deepness."

Sazed sat quietly for a moment, rereading the passage. Finally, he looked up at Tindwyl. "You think Lady Vin is right, don't you? You think the Deepness was mist."

Tindwyl nodded.

"I agree," Sazed said. "At the very least, what we now call 'the Deepness' was some sort of change in the mist."

"And your arguments from before?"

"Proven wrong," Sazed said, setting down the paper. "By your words and my own studies. I did not wish this to be true, Tindwyl."

Tindwyl raised an eyebrow. "You defied the Synod again to seek after something you didn't even want to believe?"

He looked into her eyes. "There is a difference between fearing something and desiring it. The return of the Deepness could destroy us. I did not want this information—but neither could I pass by the opportunity to discover it."

Tindwyl looked away. "I do not believe that this will destroy us, Sazed. You have made a grand discovery, that I will admit. The writings of the man Kwaan tell us much. Indeed, if the Deepness was the mists, then our understanding of the Lord Ruler's Ascension has been enhanced greatly."

"And if the mists are growing stronger?" Sazed asked. "If, by killing the Lord Ruler, we also destroyed whatever force was keeping the mists chained?"

"We have no proof that the mists are coming by day," Tindwyl said. "And on the possibility of them killing people, we have only your hesitant theories."

Sazed glanced away. On the table, his fingers had smudged Tindwyl's hurriedly written words. "That is true," he said.

Tindwyl sighed softly in the dim room. "Why do you never defend yourself, Sazed?"

"What defense is there?"

"There must be some. You apologize and ask forgiveness, but your apparent guilt never seems to change your behavior! Do you never think that, perhaps, if you had been more outspoken, you might be leading the Synod? They cast you out because you refused to offer arguments on your own behalf. You're the most contrite rebel I've ever known."

Sazed didn't respond. He glanced to the side, seeing her concerned eyes. Beautiful eyes. *Foolish thoughts,* he told himself, looking away. *You've always known that. Some things were meant for others, but never for you.*

"You were right about the Lord Ruler, Sazed," Tindwyl said. "Perhaps the others would have followed you if you had been just a little more . . . insistent."

Sazed shook his head. "I am not a man from one of your biographies, Tindwyl. I am not even, really, a man."

"You are a better man than they, Sazed," Tindwyl said quietly. "The frustrating part is, I've never been able to figure out why."

They fell silent. Sazed rose and walked to the window, opening the shutters, letting in the light. Then he extinguished the room's lamp.

"I will leave today," Tindwyl said.

"Leave?" Sazed asked. "The armies might not let you pass."

"I wasn't going to pass them, Sazed. I plan to visit them. I have given knowledge to young Lord Venture; I need to offer the same aid to his opponents."

"Ah," Sazed said. "I see. I should have realized this."

"I doubt they will listen as he has," Tindwyl said, a hint of fondness slipping into her voice. "Venture is a fine man."

"A fine king," Sazed said.

Tindwyl didn't respond. She looked at the table, with its scattered notations, each drawn from one or another of their copperminds, scribbled in haste, then shown and reread.

What was this night, then? This night of study, this night sharing thoughts and discoveries?

She was still beautiful. Auburn hair graying, but kept long and straight. Face marked by a lifetime of hardship that had not broken her. And eyes . . . keen eyes, with the knowledge and love of learning that only a Keeper could claim.

I should not consider these things, Sazed thought again. *There is no purpose to them. There never was.* "You must go, then," he said, turning.

"Again, you refuse to argue," she said.

"What would be the point of argument? You are a wise and determined person. You must be guided by your own conscience."

"Sometimes, people only seem determined upon one course because they have been offered no other options."

Sazed turned toward her. The room was quiet, the only sounds coming from the courtyard below. Tindwyl sat half in sunlight, her bright robes slowly growing more illuminated as the shadows fell away. She seemed to be implying something, something he had not expected to ever hear from her.

"I am confused," he said, sitting back down in a slow motion. "What of your duty as a Keeper?"

"It is important," she admitted. "But . . . certain, occasional exceptions must be allowed. This rubbing you found . . . well, perhaps it merits further study before I depart."

Sazed watched her, trying to read her eyes. *What is it I feel?* he wondered. Confused? Dumbfounded?

Afraid?

"I cannot be what you wish, Tindwyl," he said. "I am not a man."

She waved her hand indifferently. "I have had more than enough of 'men' and childbearing over the years, Sazed. I have done my duty to the Terris people. I should like to stay away from them for a time, I think. A part of me resents them, for what was done to me."

He opened his mouth to speak, but she held up a hand. "I know, Sazed. I took that duty upon myself, and am glad for my service. But . . . during the years spent alone, meeting with the Keepers only on occasion, I found it frustrating that all their planning seemed to be directed at maintaining their status as a conquered people.

"I only ever saw one man pushing the Synod toward active measures. While they planned how to keep themselves hidden, one man wanted to attack. While they decided the best ways to foil the Breeders, one man wanted to plot the downfall of the Final Empire. When I rejoined my people, I found that man still fighting. Alone. Condemned for fraternizing with thieves and rebels, he quietly accepted his punishment."

She smiled. "That man went on to free us all."

She took his hand. Sazed sat, astonished.

"The men I read about, Sazed," Tindwyl said quietly, "these were not men who sat and planned the best ways to hide. They fought; they sought victory. Sometimes, they were reckless—and other men called them fools. Yet, when the dice were cast and the bodies counted, they were men who *changed* things."

Sunlight entered the room in full, and she sat, cupping his hand in hers. She seemed . . . anxious. Had he ever seen that emotion in her? She was strong, the strongest woman he knew. That couldn't possibly be apprehension he saw in her eyes.

"Give me an excuse, Sazed," she whispered.

"I should . . . very much like it if you stayed," Sazed said, one hand in hers, the other resting on the tabletop, fingers trembling slightly.

Tindwyl raised an eyebrow.

"Stay," Sazed said. "Please."

Tindwyl smiled. "Very well—you have persuaded me. Let us return to our studies, then."

Elend walked the top of the city wall in the morning light, sword at his hip clicking against the side of the stonework with each step.

"You almost look like a king," a voice noted.

Elend turned as Ham climbed the last few steps up to the wall walk. The air was brisk, frost still crystalline in shadows on the stone. Winter was approaching. Perhaps it had arrived. Yet, Ham wore no cloak—only his usual vest, trousers, and sandals.

I wonder if he even knows what it is like to be cold, Elend thought. *Pewter. Such an amazing talent.*

"You say I nearly look like a king," Elend said, turning to continue walking along the wall as Ham joined him. "I guess Tindwyl's clothing has done wonders for my image."

"I didn't mean the clothing," Ham said. "I was talking about that look on your face. How long have you been up here?"

"Hours," Elend said. "How did you find me?"

"The soldiers," Ham said. "They're starting to see you as a commander, Elend. They watch where you are; they stand a little straighter when you're around, polish their weapons if they know you'll be stopping by."

"I thought you didn't spend much time with them," Elend said.

"Oh, I never said that," Ham said. "I spend lots of time with the soldiers—I just can't be intimidating enough to be their commander. Kelsier always wanted me to be a general—I think, deep down, he thought that befriending people was inferior to leading them. Perhaps he was right; men need leaders. I just don't want to be one of them."

"I do," Elend said, surprised to hear himself say so.

Ham shrugged. "That's probably a good thing. You are, after all, king."

"Kind of," Elend said.

"You're still wearing the crown."

Elend nodded. "It felt wrong to go without it. It sounds silly, I know—I only wore it for a short time. But, people need to know that someone is still in charge. For a few more days at least."

They continued to walk. In the distance, Elend could see a shadow upon the land: the third army had finally arrived in the wake of the refugees it had sent. Their scouts weren't certain why the koloss force had taken so long to get to Luthadel. The villagers' sad tale, however, gave some clue.

The koloss had not attacked Straff or Cett. They lay waiting. Apparently, Jastes had enough control over them to keep them in check. And so they joined the siege, another beast waiting for the opportunity to spring on Luthadel.

When you can't have both freedom and safety, which do you choose . . . ?

"You seem surprised to realize that you want to be in charge," Ham said.

"I just haven't ever voiced the desire before," Elend said. "It sounds so arrogant, when I actually say it. I want to be king. I don't want another man to take my place. Not Penrod, not Cett . . . not anyone. The position is mine. This city is mine."

"I don't know if 'arrogant' is the right word, El," Ham said. "Why do you want to be king?"

"To protect this people," Elend said. "To guard their safety—and their rights. But, also to make certain that the noblemen don't end up on the wrong end of another rebellion."

"That's not arrogance."

"It is, Ham," Elend said. "But it's an understandable arrogance. I don't think a man could lead without it. Actually, I think it's what I've been missing through most of my reign. Arrogance."

"Self-confidence."

"A nicer word for the same concept," Elend said. "I can do a better job for this people than another man could. I just have to find a way to prove that fact to them."

"You will."

"You're an optimist, Ham," Elend said.

"So are you," Ham noted.

Elend smiled. "True. But this job is changing me."

"Well, if you want to keep the job, we should probably get back to studying. We only have one day left."

Elend shook his head. "I've read all I can, Ham. I will not take advantage of the law, so there's no reason to search for loopholes, and studying other books looking for inspiration just isn't working. I need time to think. Time to walk. . . ."

They continued to do so. As they did, Elend noticed something out in the distance. A group of enemy soldiers doing something he couldn't distinguish. He waved over one of his men.

"What is that?" he asked.

The soldier shaded his eyes, looking. "Looks like another skirmish between Cett's men and Straff's, Your Majesty."

Elend raised an eyebrow. "That happens often?"

The soldier shrugged. "More and more often, lately. Usually the scouting patrols run afoul of each other and get into a conflict. Leave a few bodies behind when they retreat. Nothing big, Your Majesty."

Elend nodded, dismissing the man. *Big enough,* he thought to himself. *Those armies must be as tense as we are. The soldiers can't enjoy remaining so long in a siege, particularly with the winter weather.*

They were close. The arrival of the koloss would only cause more chaos. If he shoved right, Straff and Cett would be pushed into a head-on battle. *I just need a little more time!* he thought, continuing to walk, Ham at his side.

Yet, first he needed to get his throne back. Without that authority, he was nothing—and could do nothing.

The problem gnawed at his mind. As the walk continued, however, something distracted him—this time, something inside the walls rather than outside of them. Ham was right—the soldiers *did* stand a little taller when Elend approached their posts. They saluted him, and he nodded to them, walking with hand on pommel, as Tindwyl had instructed.

If I do keep my throne, I owe it to that woman, he thought. Of course, she'd chastise him for that thought. She would tell him that he kept his throne because he deserved to—because he was king. In changing himself, he had simply used the resources at hand to overcome his challenges.

He wasn't certain if he'd ever be able to see things that way. But, her final lesson to him the day before—he somehow knew that it was her last—had taught him only one new concept: that there was no one mold for kingship. He would not be like the kings of the past, any more than he would be like Kelsier.

He would be Elend Venture. His roots were in philosophy, so he would be remembered as a scholar. He'd best use that to his advantage, or he wouldn't be remembered at all. No kings could admit their weaknesses, but they were certainly wise to admit their strengths.

And what are my strengths? he thought. *Why should I be the one who rules this city, and those around it?*

Yes, he was a scholar—and an optimist, as Ham had noted. He was no master duelist, though he was improving. He wasn't an excellent diplomat, though his meetings with Straff and Cett proved that he could hold his own.

What was he?

A nobleman who loved the skaa. They'd always fascinated him, even before the Collapse—before he'd met Vin and the others. It had been one of his pet philosophical puzzles to try and prove them no different from men of noble birth. It sounded idealistic, even a little prim, when he thought about it—and, if he was truthful, much of his interest in the skaa before the Collapse had been academic. They had been unknown, and so they had seemed exotic and interesting.

He smiled. *I wonder what the plantation workers would have thought, had anyone told them they were "exotic."*

But then the Collapse had come—the rebellion predicted in his books and theories coming to life. His beliefs hadn't been able to continue as mere academic abstractions. And he'd come to know the skaa—not just Vin and the crew, but the workers and the servants. He'd seen the hope beginning to grow within them. He'd seen the awakening of self-respect, and of self-worth, in the people of the city, and it excited him.

He would not abandon them.

That's what I am, Elend thought, pausing as he walked the wall. *An idealist. A melodramatic idealist who, despite his books and learning, never did make a very good nobleman.*

"What?" Ham asked, stopping next to him.

Elend turned toward him. "I've got an idea," he said.

This is the problem. Though I believed in Alendi at first, I later became suspicious. It seemed that he fit the signs, true. But, well, how can I explain this?

Could it be that he fit them too well?

38

HOW CAN HE POSSIBLY LOOK so *confident when I feel so nervous?* Vin thought, standing beside Elend as the Assembly Hall began to fill. They had arrived early; this time, Elend said he wanted to appear in control by being the one who greeted each Assemblyman as he arrived.

Today, the vote for king would occur.

Vin and Elend stood on the stage, nodding to the Assemblymen as they entered through the room's side door. On the floor of the room, the benches were already growing crowded. The first few rows, as always, were seeded with guards.

"You look beautiful today," Elend said, looking at Vin.

Vin shrugged. She had worn her white gown, a flowing garment with a few diaphanous layers on the top. Like the others, it was designed for mobility, and it matched Elend's new outfits—especially with the dark embroidery on the sleeves. Her jewelry was gone, but she did have a few white wooden barrettes for her hair.

"It's odd," she said, "how quickly wearing these gowns became natural for me again."

"I'm glad you made the switch," Elend said. "The trousers and shirt are you . . . but this is you, too. The part of you I remember from the balls, when we barely knew each other."

Vin smiled wistfully, looking up at him, the gathering crowd growing a bit more distant. "You never did dance with me."

"I'm sorry," he said, holding her arm with a light touch. "We haven't had much time for each other lately, have we?"

Vin shook her head.

"I'll fix that," Elend said. "Once this confusion is all through, once the throne is secure, we can get back to us."

Vin nodded, then turned sharply as she noticed movement behind her. An Assemblyman walking across the stage.

"You're jumpy," Elend said, frowning slightly. "Even more than usual. What am I missing?"

Vin shook her head. "I don't know."

Elend greeted the Assemblyman—one of the skaa representatives—with a firm handshake. Vin stood at his side, her earlier wistfulness evaporating like mist as her mind returned to the moment. *What* is *bothering me?*

The room was packed—everyone wanted to witness the events of the day. Elend had been forced to post guards at the doors to maintain order. But, it wasn't just the number of people that made her edgy. It was a sense of . . . wrongness to the event. People were gathering like carrion feeders to a rotting carcass.

"This isn't right," Vin said, holding Elend's arm as the Assemblyman moved off. "Governments shouldn't change hands based on arguments made from a lectern."

"Just because it hasn't happened that way in the past doesn't mean it *shouldn't* happen," Elend said.

Vin shook her head. "Something is going to go wrong, Elend. Cett will surprise you, and maybe Penrod will, too. Men like them won't sit still and let a vote decide their future."

"I know," Elend said. "But they aren't the only ones who can offer up surprises."

Vin looked at him quizzically. "You're planning something?"

He paused, then glanced at her. "I . . . well, Ham and I came up with something last night. A ploy. I've been trying to find a way to talk to you about it, but there just hasn't been time. We had to move quickly."

Vin frowned, sensing his apprehension. She started to say something, but then stopped, studying his eyes. He seemed a little embarrassed. "What?" she asked.

"Well . . . it kind of involves you, and your reputation. I was going to ask permission, but . . ."

. Vin felt a slight chill. Behind them, the last Assemblyman took his seat, and Penrod stood up to conduct the meeting. He glanced toward Elend, clearing his throat.

Elend cursed quietly. "Look, I don't have time to explain," he said. "But, it's really not a big deal—it might not even get me that many votes. But, well, I had to try. And it doesn't change anything. Between us, I mean."

"What?"

"Lord Venture?" Penrod said. "Are you ready for this meeting to begin?"

The hall grew quiet. Vin and Elend still stood in the center of the stage, between the lectern and the seats of the Assembly members. She looked at him, torn between a sense of dread, a sense of confusion, and a slight sense of betrayal.

Why didn't you tell me? she thought. *How can I be ready if you don't tell me what you're planning? And . . . why are you looking at me like that?*

"I'm sorry," Elend said, moving over to take his seat.

Vin remained standing alone before the audience. Once, so much attention would have terrified her. It still made her uncomfortable. She ducked her head slightly, walking toward the back benches and her empty spot.

Ham wasn't there. Vin frowned, turning as Penrod opened the proceedings. *There,* she thought, finding Ham in the audience, sitting calmly with a group of skaa. The group was obviously conversing quietly, but even with tin, Vin would never be able to pick out their voices in the large crowd. Breeze stood with some of Ham's soldiers at the back of the room. It didn't matter if they knew about Elend's plan—they were too far away for her to interrogate them.

Annoyed, she arranged her skirts, then sat. She hadn't felt so blind since . . .

Since that night a year ago, she thought, *that moment just before we figured out Kelsier's true plan, that moment when I thought everything was collapsing around me.*

Perhaps that was a good sign. Had Elend cooked up some last-minute flash of political brilliance? It didn't really matter that he hadn't shared it with her; she probably wouldn't understand the legal basis for it anyway.

But . . . he always shared his plans with me before.

Penrod continued to drone on, likely maximizing his time in front of the Assembly. Cett was on the front bench of the audience, surrounded by a good twenty soldiers, sitting with a look of self-satisfaction. As well he should. From the accounts she'd heard, Cett stood to take the vote with ease.

But what was Elend planning?

Penrod will vote for himself, Vin thought. *So will Elend. That leaves twenty-two votes. The merchants are behind Cett, and so are the skaa. They're too afraid of that army to vote for anyone else.*

That only leaves the nobility. Some of them will vote for Penrod—he's the strongest nobleman in the city; many of the members of the Assembly are longtime political allies of his. But, even if he takes half of the nobility—which he probably won't—Cett will win. Cett only needs a two-thirds majority to get the throne.

Eight merchants, eight skaa. Sixteen men on Cett's side. He was going to win. What could Elend possibly do?

Penrod finally finished his opening announcements. "But, before we vote," he said, "I would like to offer time to the candidates to make any final addresses they wish. Lord Cett, would you care to go first?"

In the audience, Cett shook his head. "I've made my offers and my threats, Penrod. You all know you have to vote for me."

Vin frowned. He seemed certain of himself, and yet . . . She scanned the crowd, eyes falling on Ham. He was talking to Captain Demoux. And seated next to them was one of the men who had followed her in the market. A priest of the Survivor.

Vin turned, studying the Assembly. The skaa representatives looked uncomfortable. She glanced at Elend, who stood up to take his turn at the front of the lectern. His earlier confidence had returned, and he looked regal in his sharp white uniform. He still wore his crown.

It doesn't change things, he'd said. *Between us. . . .*

I'm sorry.

Something that would use her reputation to gain him votes. Her reputation was Kelsier's reputation, and only the skaa really cared about that. And there was one easy way to gain influence with them. . . .

"You joined the Church of the Survivor, didn't you?" she whispered.

The reactions of the skaa Assemblymen, the logic of the moment, Elend's words to her before, all of them suddenly made sense. If Elend joined the Church, the skaa Assemblymen might be afraid to vote against him. And, Elend didn't need sixteen votes to gain the throne; if the Assembly deadlocked, he won. With the eight skaa and his own vote, the others would never be able to oust him.

"Very clever," she whispered.

The ploy might not work. It would depend on how much hold the Church of the Survivor had on the skaa Assemblymen. Yet, even if some skaa voted against Elend, there were still the noblemen who would probably vote for Penrod. If enough did, Elend would still deadlock the Assembly and keep his throne.

All it would cost was his integrity.

That's unfair, Vin told herself. If Elend had joined with the Church of the Survivor, he would hold to whatever promises he had made. And, if the Church of the Survivor gained official backing, it could become as powerful in Luthadel as the Steel Ministry had once been. And . . . how would that change the way Elend saw her?

This doesn't change anything, he had promised.

She dully heard him begin to speak, and his references to Kelsier now seemed obvious to her. Yet, the only thing she could feel was a slight sense of anxiety. It was as Zane had said. She was the knife—a different kind of knife, but still a tool. The means by which Elend would protect the city.

She should be furious, or at least sick. Why did her eyes keep darting toward the crowd? Why couldn't she focus on what Elend was saying, on how he was elevating her? Why was she suddenly so on edge?

Why were those men subtly moving their way around the edges of the room?

"So," Elend said, "by the blessing of the Survivor himself, I ask you to vote for me."

He waited quietly. It was a drastic move; joining the Church of the Survivor put Elend under the spiritual authority of an external group. But, Ham and Demoux both had thought it a good idea. Elend had spent the better part of the previous day getting the word out to the skaa citizens about his decision.

It felt like a good move. The only thing he worried about was Vin. He glanced at her. She didn't like her place in the Church of the Survivor, and having Elend join it meant that he—technically—accepted her part in the mythology. He tried to catch her eye and smile, but she wasn't watching him. She was looking out into the audience.

Elend frowned. Vin stood up.

A man from the audience suddenly shoved aside two soldiers in the front row, then leaped supernaturally far to land up on the dais. The man pulled out a dueling cane.

What? Elend thought in shock. Fortunately, months spent sparring at Tindwyl's command had given him instincts he didn't know he had. As the Thug charged, Elend tucked and rolled. He hit the ground, scrambling, and turned to see the beefy man bearing down on him, dueling cane raised.

A flurry of white lace and skirts fluttered through the air over Elend. Vin slammed feet-first into the Thug, throwing him backward as she spun, skirts flaring.

The man grunted. Vin landed with a thump directly in front of Elend. The Assembly Hall echoed with sudden screaming and shouts.

Vin kicked the lectern out of the way. "Stay behind me," she whispered, an obsidian dagger glittering in her right hand.

Elend nodded hesitantly, unbuckling the sword at his waist as he climbed to his feet. The Thug wasn't alone; three small groups of armed men were moving through the room. One attacked the front row, distracting the guards there. Another group was climbing onto the dais. The third group seemed occupied by something in the crowd. Cett's soldiers.

The Thug had regained his feet. He didn't look like he had suffered much from Vin's kick.

Assassins, Elend thought. *But who sent them?*

The man smiled as he was joined by a group of five friends. Chaos filled the room, Assemblymen scattering, their bodyguards rushing to surround them. Yet, the fighting in front of the stage kept anyone from escaping in that direction. The Assemblymen clogged around the stage's side exit. The attackers, however, didn't seem concerned with them.

Only with Elend.

Vin remained in her crouch, waiting for the men to attack first, her posture threatening despite the frilly dress. Elend thought he actually heard her growl quietly.

The men attacked.

Vin snapped forward, swiping at the lead Thug with a dagger. His reach was too great, however, and he easily fended her off with a swipe of his staff. There were six men in total; three who were obviously Thugs, leaving the other three to likely be Coinshots or Lurchers. A strong component of metal-controllers. Someone didn't want her ending this fight quickly with coins.

They didn't understand that she would never use coins in this situation. Not with Elend standing so close and with so many people in the room. Coins couldn't be deflected safely. If she shot a handful at her enemies, random people would die.

She had to kill these men fast. They were already fanning out, surrounding her and Elend. They moved in pairs—one Thug and one Coinshot in each team. They would attack from the sides, trying to get past her to Elend.

Vin reached behind herself with iron, Pulling Elend's sword from its sheath with a ringing squeal. She caught it by the hilt, throwing it at one of the teams. The Coinshot Pushed it back at her, and she in turn Pushed it to the side, spinning it toward a second pair of Allomancers.

One of them Pushed it back at her again. Vin Pulled from behind, whipping Elend's metal-tipped sheath out of his hands and shooting it through the air by its clasp. Sheath passed sword in the air. This time, the enemy Coinshots Pushed both items out of the way, deflecting them toward the fleeing audience.

Men shouted in desperation as they trampled and tried to force their way out of the room. Vin gritted her teeth. She needed a better weapon.

She flung a stone dagger at one assassin pair, then jumped toward another, spinning beneath the attacking Thug's weapon. The Coinshot didn't have any metal on him that she could sense; he was just there to keep her from killing the Thug with coins. They probably assumed that Vin would be easy to defeat, as she was deprived of the ability to shoot coins.

The Thug brought his staff back around, trying to catch her with the end. She caught the weapon, yanking it forward and jumping up as she Pushed against the Assembly bleachers behind her. Her feet hit the Thug in the chest, and she kicked hard with flared pewter. As he grunted, Vin Pulled herself back toward the nails in the bleachers as hard as she could.

The Thug managed to stay on his feet. He seemed completely surprised, however, to find Vin streaking away from him, holding his staff in her hands.

She landed and spun toward Elend. He'd found himself a weapon—a dueling cane—and had the good sense to back himself against a wall. To her right, some of the Assemblymen stood in a huddle, surrounded by their guards. The room was too full, the exits too small and cramped, for them all to escape.

The Assemblymen made no moves to help Elend.

One of the assassins cried out, pointing as Vin Pushed against the bleachers and shot toward them, moving herself in front of Elend. Two Thugs raised their weapons as Vin turned in the air, lightly Pulling against a door's hinges to spin herself. Her gown fluttered as she landed.

I really have to thank that dressmaker, she thought as she raised the staff. She briefly considered ripping the dress free anyway, but the Thugs were upon her too quickly. She blocked both blows at once, then threw herself between the men, flaring pewter, moving faster than even they.

One of them cursed, trying to bring his staff around. Vin broke his leg before he could. He dropped with a howl, and Vin leaped onto his back, forcing him to the ground as she swung an overhand blow at the second Thug. He blocked, then shoved his weapon against hers to throw her back off his companion.

Elend attacked. The king's actions, however, seemed sluggish compared with the movements of men burning pewter. The Thug turned almost nonchalantly, smashing Elend's weapon with an easy blow.

Vin cursed as she fell. She hurled her staff at the Thug, forcing him to turn away from Elend. He barely ducked out of the way as Vin hit the ground, bounced to her feet, and whipped out a second dagger. She dashed forward before the Thug could turn back to Elend.

A spray of coins flew toward her. She couldn't Push them back, not toward the crowd. She cried out—throwing herself between the coins and Elend—then Pushed to the sides, dividing them as best she could so they sprayed against the wall. Even so, she felt a flash of pain from her shoulder.

Where did he get the coins? she thought with frustration. However, as she glanced to the side, she saw the Coinshot standing beside a cowering Assemblyman, who had been forced to give up his coin pouch.

Vin gritted her teeth. Her arm still worked. That was all that mattered. She yelled and threw herself at the closest Thug. However, the third Thug had regained his weapon— the one Vin had thrown—and was now circling with his Coinshot to try and get behind Vin.

One at a time, Vin thought.

The Thug nearest her swung his weapon. She needed to surprise him. So, she didn't dodge or block. She simply took his blow in the side, burning duralumin and pewter to resist. Something cracked within her as she was hit, but with duralumin, she was strong enough to stay up. Wood shattered, and she continued forward, slamming her dagger into the Thug's neck.

He dropped, revealing a surprised Coinshot behind him. Vin's pewter evaporated with the duralumin, and pain blossomed like a sunrise in her side. Even so, she yanked her dagger free as the Thug fell, still moving quickly enough to drop the Coinshot with a dagger in the chest.

Then she stumbled, gasping quietly, holding her side as two men died at her feet.

One Thug left, she thought desperately. *And two Coinshots.*

Elend needs me. To the side, she saw one of the Coinshots fire a spray of stolen coins at Elend. She cried out, Pushing them away, and she heard the Coinshot cursing.

She turned—counting on the blue lines from her steel to warn her if the Coinshots tried shooting anything else at Elend—and ripped her backup vial of metal from her sleeve, where it had been tied tightly to keep it from being Pulled away. However, even as she yanked the stopper open, the vial lurched from her now undexterous hand. The second Coinshot grinned as he Pushed the vial away, tipping it and spraying its contents across the floor.

Vin growled, but her mind was growing fuzzy. She needed pewter. Without it, the large coin wound in her shoulder—its blood turning her lacy sleeve red—and the crushing pain in her side were too much. She almost couldn't think.

A staff swung toward her head. She jerked to the side, rolling. However, she no longer had the grace or speed of pewter. A normal man's blow she could have dodged, but the attack of an Allomancer was another thing.

I shouldn't have burned duralumin! she thought. It had been a gamble, letting her kill two assassins, but it had left her too exposed. The staff descended toward her.

Something large slammed into the Thug, bearing him to the ground in a growling flurry of claws. Vin came out of her dodge as the Thug punched OreSeur in the head, cracking his skull. Yet, the Thug was bleeding and cursing, and his staff had rolled free. Vin snatched it up, scrambling to her feet and gritting her teeth as she drove the butt of the staff down into the man's face. He took the blow with a curse, swiping her feet out from under her with a kick.

She fell beside OreSeur. The wolfhound, oddly, was smiling. There was a wound in his shoulder.

No, not a wound. An opening in the flesh—and a vial of metal hidden inside. Vin snatched it, rolling, keeping it hidden as the Thug regained his feet. She downed the liquid, and the flakes of metal it contained. On the floor before her, she could see the shadow of the Thug raising his weapon in a mighty overhand blow.

Pewter flared to life inside of her, and her wounds became

mere annoying buzzes. She jerked to the side as the blow fell, hitting the floor, throwing up bits of wood. Vin flipped to her feet, slamming her fist into the arm of her surprised opponent.

It wasn't enough to break the bones, but it obviously hurt. The Thug—now missing two teeth—grunted in pain. To the side, Vin saw OreSeur on his feet, his dog's jaw hanging unnaturally. He nodded to her; the Thug would think him dead from the cracked skull.

More coins flew at Elend. She Pushed them away without even looking. In front of her, OreSeur struck the Thug from behind, making him spin in surprise just as Vin attacked. The Thug's staff passed within a finger's width of her head as it smashed into OreSeur's back, but her own hand took the man in the face. She didn't punch, however; that wouldn't do much against a Thug.

She had one finger out, and she had incredible aim. The Thug's eye popped as she rammed her finger into the socket.

She hopped back as he cried out, raising a hand to his face. She smashed her fists into his chest, throwing him to the ground, then jumped over OreSeur's crumpled form and grabbed her dagger off the ground.

The Thug died, clutching his face in agony, her dagger in his chest.

Vin spun, searching desperately for Elend. He'd taken one of the fallen Thugs' weapons and was fending off the two remaining Coinshots, who had apparently grown frustrated by her Pushing away all of their coin attacks. Instead, they had pulled out dueling canes to attack him directly. Elend's training had apparently been enough to keep him alive—but only because his opponents had to keep an eye on Vin to make certain she didn't try using coins herself.

Vin kicked up the staff of the man she'd just killed, catching it. A Coinshot cried out as she growled and dashed toward them, spinning her weapon. One had the presence of mind to Push off the bleachers and launch himself away. Vin's weapon still caught him in midair, throwing him to the side. The next swing took down his companion, who had tried to dash away.

Elend stood breathing heavily, his costume disheveled.

He did better than I thought he would, Vin admitted, flexing, trying to judge the damage to her side. She needed to get a bandage on that shoulder. The coin hadn't hit bone, but the bleeding would—

"Vin!" Elend cried out.

Something very strong suddenly grabbed her from behind. Vin choked as she was jerked backward and thrown to the ground.

The first Thug. She'd broken his leg, then forgotten—

He got his hands around her neck, squeezing as he knelt above her, his legs pressing against her chest, his face wild with rage. His eyes bulged, adrenaline mixing with pewter.

Vin gasped for breath. She was taken back to years before, to beatings performed by men looming above her. Camon, and Reen, and a dozen others.

No! she thought, flaring her pewter, struggling. He had her pinned, however, and he was much larger then she was. Much stronger. Elend slammed his staff against the man's back, but the Thug barely even flinched.

Vin couldn't breathe. She felt her throat being crushed. She tried to pry the Thug's hands apart, but it was as Ham had always said. Her small size was a great advantage to her in most situations—but when it came down to brute strength, she was no match for a man of bulk and muscle. She tried Pulling herself to the side, but the man's grip was too strong, her weight too small compared with his.

She struggled in vain. She had duralumin still—burning it only made other metals vanish, not the duralumin itself— but last time that had nearly gotten her killed. If she didn't take the Thug down quickly, she'd be left without pewter once again.

Elend pounded, yelling for help, but his voice sounded distant. The Thug pressed his face almost up against Vin's, and she could see his fury. At that moment, incredibly, a thought occurred to her.

Where have I seen this man before?

Her vision darkened. However, as the Thug constricted his grip, he leaned closer, closer, closer. . . .

She didn't have a choice. Vin burned duralumin and

flared her pewter. She flung her opponent's hands aside and smashed her head upward into his face.

The man's head exploded as easily as the eyeball had earlier.

Vin gasped for breath and pushed the headless corpse off her. Elend stumbled back, his suit and face sprayed red. Vin stumbled to her feet. Her vision swam as her pewter dissipated—but even through that, she could see an emotion on Elend's face, stark as the blood on his brilliant white uniform.

Horror.

No, she thought, her mind fading. *Please, Elend, not that. . . .*

She fell forward, unable to maintain consciousness.

Elend sat in his ruined suit, hands against forehead, the wreckage of the Assembly Hall hauntingly empty around him.

"She'll live," Ham said. "She actually isn't hurt that badly. Or . . . well, not that badly for Vin. She just needs plenty of pewter and some of Sazed's care. He says the ribs aren't even broken, just cracked."

Elend nodded absently. Some soldiers were clearing away the corpses, among them the six men that Vin had killed, including the one at the end. . . .

Elend squeezed his eyes shut.

"What?" Ham asked.

Elend opened his eyes, forming his hand into a fist to keep it from shaking. "I know you've seen a lot of battles, Ham," he said. "But, I'm not used to them. I'm not used to . . ." He turned away as the soldiers dragged away the headless body.

Ham watched the corpse go.

"I've only actually seen her fight once before, you know," Elend said quietly. "In the palace, a year ago. She only threw a few men against the walls. It was nothing like this."

Ham took a seat beside Elend on the benches. "She's Mistborn, El. What did you expect? A single Thug can easily take down ten men—dozens, if he has a Coinshot to support him. A Mistborn . . . well, they're like an army in one person."

Elend nodded. "I know, Ham. I know she killed the Lord Ruler—she's even told me how she faced several Steel Inquisitors. But . . . I've just never seen . . ."

He closed his eyes again. The image of Vin stumbling toward him at the end, her beautiful white ball gown covered in the gore of a man she'd just killed with her forehead . . .

She did it to protect me, he thought. *But that doesn't make it any less disturbing.*

Maybe that even makes it a little more disturbing.

He forced his eyes open. He couldn't afford to be distracted; he had to be strong. He was king.

"You think Straff sent them?" Elend asked.

Ham nodded. "Who else? They targeted you and Cett. I guess your threat to kill Straff wasn't as binding as we assumed."

"How is Cett?"

"He barely escaped alive. As it is, they slaughtered half of his soldiers. In the fray, Demoux and I couldn't even see what was happening up on the stage with you and Vin."

Elend nodded. By the time Ham had arrived, Vin had already dealt with the assassins. It had taken her only a few minutes to wipe out all six of them.

Ham was silent for a moment. Finally, he turned to Elend. "I'll admit, El," he said quietly. "I'm impressed. I didn't see the fight, but I saw the aftermath. It's one thing to fight six Allomancers, but it's another to do that while trying to protect a regular person, and to keep any bystanders from harm. And that last man . . ."

"Do you remember when she saved Breeze?" Elend asked. "It was so far away, but I swear I saw her throw horses into the air with her Allomancy. Have you ever heard of anything like that?"

Ham shook his head.

Elend sat quietly for a moment. "I think we need to do some planning. What with today's events, we can't . . ."

Ham looked up as Elend trailed off. "What?"

"Messenger," Elend said, nodding toward the doorway.

Sure enough, the man presented himself to the soldiers, then was escorted up to the stage. Elend stood, walking over to meet the short man, who wore Penrod's heraldry on his coat.

"My lord," the man said, bowing. "I've been sent to inform you that the voting will proceed at Lord Penrod's mansion."

"The voting?" Ham asked. "What nonsense is this? His Majesty was nearly killed today!"

"I'm sorry, my lord," the aide said. "I was simply told to deliver the message."

Elend sighed. He'd hoped that, in the confusion, Penrod wouldn't remember the deadline. "If they don't choose a new leader today, Ham, then I get to retain the crown. They've already wasted their grace period."

Ham sighed. "And if there are more assassins?" he asked quietly. "Vin will be laid up for a few days, at least."

"I can't rely on her to protect me all the time," Elend said. "Let's go."

"I vote for myself," Lord Penrod said.

Not unexpected, Elend thought. He sat in Penrod's comfortable lounge, accompanied by a group of shaken Assemblymen—none of whom, thankfully, had been hurt in the attack. Several held drinks, and there was a veritable army of guards waiting around the perimeter, eyeing each other warily. The crowded room also held Noorden and three other scribes, who were there to witness the voting, according to the law.

"I vote for Lord Penrod as well," said Lord Dukaler.

Also not unexpected, Elend thought. *I wonder how much that cost Penrod.*

Mansion Penrod was not a keep, but it was lavishly decorated. The plushness of Elend's chair was welcome as a relief from the tensions of the day. Yet, Elend feared that it was too soothing. It would be very easy to drift off. . . .

"I vote for Cett," said Lord Habren.

Elend perked up. It was the second for Cett, which put him behind Penrod by three.

Everyone turned to Elend. "I vote for myself," he said, trying to project a firmness that was hard to maintain after everything that had happened. The merchants were next. Elend settled back, prepared for the expected run of votes for Cett.

"I vote for Penrod," Philen said.

Elend sat upright, alert. *What!*

The next merchant voted for Penrod as well. As did the next, and the next. Elend sat stunned, listening. *What did I miss?* he thought. He glanced at Ham, who shrugged in confusion.

Philen glanced at Elend, smiling pleasantly. Elend couldn't tell if there was bitterness or satisfaction in that look, however. *They switched allegiances? That quickly?* Philen had been the one to sneak Cett into the city in the first place.

Elend looked down the row of merchants, trying with little success to gauge their reactions. Cett himself wasn't in the meeting; he had retreated to Keep Hasting to nurse his wound.

"I vote for Lord Venture," said Haws, foremost of the skaa faction. This also managed to get a stir out of the room. Haws met Elend's eye, and nodded. He was a firm believer in the Church of the Survivor, and while the different preachers of the religion were beginning to disagree on how to organize their followers, they all agreed that a believer on the throne would be better for them than handing the city over to Cett.

There will be a price to pay for this allegiance, Elend thought as the skaa voted. They knew Elend's reputation for honesty, and he would not betray their trust.

He had told them he would become an open member of their sect. He hadn't promised them belief, but he had promised them devotion. He still wasn't certain what he had given away, but both of them knew they would need each other.

"I vote for Penrod," said Jasten, a canal worker.

"As do I," said Thurts, his brother.

Elend gritted his teeth. He'd known they would be trouble; they never had liked the Church of the Survivor. But, four of the skaa had already given him their votes. With only two remaining, he had a very good shot at a deadlock.

"I vote for Venture," said the next man.

"I do, too," said the final skaa. Elend gave the man, Vet, a smile of appreciation.

That left fifteen votes for Penrod, two for Cett, and seven for Elend. Deadlock. Elend reclined slightly, head resting against the chair's pillowed back, sighing softly.

You did your job, Vin, he thought. *I did mine. Now we just need to keep this country in one piece.*

"Um," a voice asked, "am I allowed to change my vote?"

Elend opened his eyes. It was Lord Habren, one of the votes for Cett.

"I mean, it's obvious now that Cett isn't going to win," Habren said, flushing slightly. The young man was a distant cousin of the Elariel family, which was probably how he'd gotten his seat. Names still meant power in Luthadel.

"I'm not sure if you can change or not," Lord Penrod said.

"Well, I'd rather my vote meant something," Habren said. "There are only two votes for Cett, after all."

The room fell silent. One by one, the members of the Assembly turned to Elend. Noorden the scribe met Elend's eyes. There was a clause allowing for men to change their votes, assuming that the chancellor hadn't officially closed the voting—which, indeed, he hadn't.

The clause was a rather oblique; Noorden was probably the only other one in the room who knew the law well enough to interpret it. He nodded slightly, still meeting Elend's eyes. He would hold his tongue.

Elend sat still in a room full of men who trusted him, even as they rejected him. He could do as Noorden did. He could say nothing, or could say that he didn't know.

"Yes," Elend said softly. "The law allows for you to change your vote, Lord Habren. You may only do so once, and must do so before the winner is declared. Everyone else has the same opportunity."

"Then I vote for Lord Penrod," Habren said.

"As do I," said Lord Hue, the other who had voted for Cett.

Elend closed his eyes.

"Are there any other alterations?" Lord Penrod asked.

No one spoke.

"Then," Penrod said, "I see seventeen votes for myself, seven votes for Lord Venture. I officially close the voting and humbly accept your appointment as king. I shall serve as best I can in this capacity."

Elend stood, then slowly removed his crown. "Here," he said, setting it on the mantle. "You'll need this."

He nodded to Ham, then left without looking back at the men who had discarded him.

THE END OF PART THREE

PART FOUR

KNIVES

I know your argument. We speak of the Anticipation, of things foretold, of promises made by our greatest prophets of old. Of course the Hero of Ages will fit the prophecies. He will fit them perfectly. That's the idea.

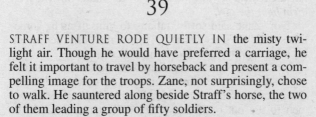

39

STRAFF VENTURE RODE QUIETLY IN the misty twilight air. Though he would have preferred a carriage, he felt it important to travel by horseback and present a compelling image for the troops. Zane, not surprisingly, chose to walk. He sauntered along beside Straff's horse, the two of them leading a group of fifty soldiers.

Even with the troops, Straff felt exposed. It wasn't just the mists, and it wasn't just the darkness. He could still remember her touch on his emotions.

"You've failed me, Zane," Straff said.

The Mistborn looked up, and—burning tin—Straff could see a frown on his face. "Failed?"

"Venture and Cett still live. Beyond that, you sent a batch of my best Allomancers to their deaths."

"I warned you that they might die," Zane said.

"For a purpose, Zane," Straff said sternly. "Why did you need a group of secret Allomancers if you were just going to send them on a suicide mission in the middle of a public gathering? You may assume our resources to be unlimited, but let me assure you—those six men can*not* be replaced."

It had taken Straff decades of work with his mistresses to gather so many hidden Allomancers. It had been pleasurable work, but work all the same. In one reckless gambit, Zane had destroyed a good third of Straff's Allomancer children.

My children dead, our hand exposed, and that . . . creature of Elend's still lives!

"I'm sorry, Father," Zane said. "I thought that the chaos and crowded quarters would keep the girl isolated, and force her not to use coins. I really thought this would work."

Straff frowned. He well knew that Zane thought himself more competent than his father; what Mistborn wouldn't think such a thing? Only a delicate mixture of bribery, threats, and manipulation kept Zane under control.

Yet, no matter what Zane thought, Straff was no fool. He knew, at that moment, that Zane was hiding something. *Why send those men to die?* Straff thought. *He must have intended them to fail—otherwise he would have helped them fight the girl.*

"No," Zane said softly, talking to himself as he sometimes did. "He's my father . . ." He trailed off, then shook his head sharply. "No. Not them either."

Lord Ruler, Straff thought, looking down at the muttering madman beside him. *What have I gotten myself into?* Zane was growing more unpredictable. Had he sent those men to die out of jealousy, out of lust for violence, or had he simply been bored? Straff didn't *think* that Zane had turned on him, but it was difficult to tell. Either way, Straff didn't like having to rely on Zane for his plans to work. He didn't really like having to rely on Zane for *anything.*

Zane looked up at Straff, and stopped talking. He did a good job of hiding his insanity, most of the time. A good enough job that Straff sometimes forgot about it. Yet, it still lurked there, beneath the surface. Zane was as dangerous a tool as Straff had ever used. The protection provided by a Mistborn outweighed the danger of Zane's insanity.

Barely.

"You needn't worry, Father," Zane said. "The city will still be yours."

"It will never be mine as long as that woman lives," Straff said. He shivered. *Perhaps that's what this was all about. Zane's attack was so obvious that everyone in the city knows I was behind it, and when that Mistborn demon wakes, she will come after me in retribution.*

But, if that were Zane's goal, then why not just kill me himself? Zane didn't make sense. He didn't have to. That was, perhaps, one of the advantages of being insane.

Zane shook his head. "I think you will be surprised, Father. One way or another, you will soon have nothing to fear from Vin."

"She thinks I tried to have her beloved king assassinated."

Zane smiled. "No, I don't think that she does. She's far too clever for that."

Too clever to see the truth? Straff thought. However, his tin-enhanced ears heard shuffling in the mists. He held up a hand, halting his procession. In the distance, he could just barely pick out the flickering blobs of wall-top torches. They were close to the city—uncomfortably close.

Straff's procession waited quietly. Then, from the mists before them, a man on horseback appeared, accompanied by fifty soldiers of his own. Ferson Penrod.

"Straff," Penrod said, nodding.

"Ferson."

"Your men did well," Penrod said. "I'm glad your son didn't have to die. He's a good lad. A bad king, but an earnest man."

A lot of my sons died today, Ferson, Straff thought. *The fact that Elend still lives isn't fortunate—it's irony.*

"You are ready to deliver the city?" Straff asked.

Penrod nodded. "Philen and his merchants want assurances that they will have titles to match those Cett promised them."

Straff waved a dismissive hand. "You know me, Ferson." *You used to practically grovel before me at parties every week.* "I always honor business agreements. I'd be an idiot not to appease those merchants—they're the ones who will bring me tax revenue from this dominance."

Penrod nodded. "I'm glad we could come to an understanding, Straff. I don't trust Cett."

"I doubt you trust me," Straff said.

Penrod smiled. "But I do know you, Straff. You're one of us—a Luthadel nobleman. Besides, you have produced the most stable kingdom in the dominances. That's all we're looking for right now. A little stability for this people."

"You almost sound like that fool son of mine."

Penrod paused, then shook his head. "Your boy isn't a fool, Straff. He's just an idealist. In truth, I'm sad to see his little utopia fall."

"If you are sad for him, Ferson, then you are an idiot, too."

Penrod stiffened. Straff caught the man's proud eyes, holding them with his stare, until Penrod looked down. The exchange was a simple one, mostly meaningless—but it did serve as a very important reminder.

Straff chuckled. "You're going to have to get used to being a small fish again, Ferson."

"I know."

"Be cheerful," Straff said. "Assuming this turnover of power happens as you promised, no one will have to end up dead. Who knows, maybe I'll let you keep that crown of yours."

Penrod looked up.

"For a long time, this land didn't have kings," Straff said quietly. "It had something greater. Well, I'm not the Lord Ruler—but I can be an emperor. You want to keep your crown and rule as a subject king under me?"

"That depends on the cost, Straff," Penrod said carefully.

Not completely quelled, then. Penrod had always been clever; he'd been the most important nobleman to stay behind in Luthadel, and his gamble had certainly worked.

"The cost is exorbitant," Straff said. "Ridiculously so."

"The atium," Penrod guessed.

Straff nodded. "Elend hasn't found it, but it's here, somewhere. I was the one who mined those geodes—my men spent decades harvesting them and bringing them to Luthadel. I know how much of it we harvested, and I know that nowhere near the same amount came back out in dis-

bursements to the nobility. The rest is in that city, somewhere."

Penrod nodded. "I'll see what I can find, Straff."

Straff raised an eyebrow. "You need to get back into
practice, Ferson."

Penrod paused, then bowed his head. "I'll see what I can
find, *my lord.*"

"Good. Now, what news did you bring of Elend's mistress?"

"She collapsed after the fight," Penrod said. "I employ a
spy on the cooking staff, and she said she delivered a bowl
of broth to Lady Vin's room. It returned cold."

Straff frowned. "Could this woman of yours slip the
Mistborn something?"

Penrod paled slightly. "I . . . don't think that would be
wise, my lord. Besides, you know Mistborn constitutions."

Perhaps she really is incapacitated, Straff thought. *If we
moved in . . .* The chill of her touch on his emotions returned. Numbness. Nothingness.

"You needn't fear her so, my lord," Penrod said.

Straff raised an eyebrow. "I'm not afraid, I'm wary. I
will not move into that city until my safety is assured—and
until I move in, your city is in danger from Cett. Or, worse.
What would happen if those koloss decide to attack the
city, Ferson? I'm in negotiations with their leader, and he
seems to be able to control them. For now. Have you ever
seen the aftermath of a koloss slaughter?"

He probably hadn't; Straff hadn't until just recently.
Penrod just shook his head. "Vin won't attack you. Not if
the Assembly votes to put you in command of the city. The
transfer will be perfectly legal."

"I doubt she cares about legality."

"Perhaps," Penrod said. "But Elend *does.* And, where he
commands, the girl follows."

*Unless he has as little control over her as I have over
Zane,* Straff thought, shivering. No matter what Penrod
said, Straff wasn't going to take the city until that horrible
creature was dealt with. In this, he could rely only on Zane.

And that thought frightened him almost as much as
Vin did.

Without further discussion, Straff waved to Penrod, dismissing him. Penrod turned and retreated into the mists with his entourage. Even with his tin, Straff barely heard Zane land on the ground beside him. Straff turned, looking at the Mistborn.

"You really think he'd turn the atium over to you if he found it?" Zane asked quietly.

"Perhaps," Straff said. "He has to know that he'd never be able to hold on to it—he doesn't have the military might to protect a treasure like that. And, if he doesn't give it to me . . . well, it would probably be easier to take the atium from him than it would be to find it on my own."

Zane seemed to find the answer satisfactory. He waited for a few moments, staring into the mists. Then he looked at Straff, a curious expression on his face. "What time is it?"

Straff checked his pocket watch, something no Mistborn would carry. Too much metal. "Eleven seventeen," he said.

Zane nodded, turning back to look at the city. "It should have taken effect by now."

Straff frowned. Then he began to sweat. He flared tin, clamping his eyes shut. *There!* he thought, noticing a weakness inside of him. "More poison?" he asked, keeping the fear from his voice, forcing himself to be calm.

"How do you do it, Father?" Zane asked. "I thought for certain you'd missed this one. Yet, here you are, just fine."

Straff was beginning to feel weak. "One doesn't need to be Mistborn to be capable, Zane," he snapped.

Zane shrugged, smiling in the haunting way only he could—keenly intelligent, yet eerily unstable. Then he just shook his head. "You win again," he said, then shot upward into the sky, churning mists with his passing.

Straff immediately turned his horse, trying to maintain his decorum as he urged it back toward the camp. He could feel the poison. Feel it stealing his life. Feel it threatening him, overcoming him. . . .

He went, perhaps, too quickly. It was difficult to maintain an air of strength when you were dying. Finally, he broke into a gallop. He left his startled guards behind, and they called in surprise, breaking into a jog to try and keep up.

Straff ignored their complaints. He kicked the horse faster. Could he feel the poison slowing his reactions? Which one had Zane used? Gurwraith? No, it required injection. Tompher, perhaps? Or . . . perhaps he had found one that Straff didn't even know about.

He could only hope that wasn't the case. For, if Straff didn't know of the poison, then Amaranta probably wouldn't know of it either, and wouldn't be able to put the antidote into her catch-all healing potion.

The lights of camp illuminated the mists. Soldiers cried out as Straff approached, and he was nearly run through as one of his own men leveled a spear at the charging horse. Fortunately, the man recognized him in time. Straff rode the man down even as he turned aside his spear.

Straff charged right up to his tent. By now, his men were scattering, preparing as if for an invasion, or some other attack. There was no way he could hide this from Zane.

I wouldn't be able to hide my death either.

"My lord!" a captain said, dashing up to him.

"Send for Amaranta," Straff said, stumbling off his horse.

The soldier paused. "Your mistress, lord?" the man said, frowning. "Why—"

"Now!" Straff commanded, throwing back his tent flap, walking inside. He paused, legs trembling as the tent flap closed. He wiped his brow with a hesitant hand. Too much sweat.

Damn him! he thought with frustration. *I have to kill him, contain him . . . I have to do something. I can't rule like this!*

But what? He'd sat up nights, he'd wasted days, trying to decide what to do about Zane. The atium he used to bribe the man no longer seemed a good motivator. Zane's actions this day—slaughtering Straff's children in an obviously hopeless attempt to kill Elend's mistress—proved that he could no longer be trusted, even in a small way.

Amaranta arrived with surprising speed, and she immediately began mixing her antidote. Eventually, as Straff slurped down the horrid-tasting concoction—feeling its healing effects immediately—he came to an uneasy conclusion.

Zane had to die.

And yet . . . something about all this seemed so convenient. It felt almost as if we constructed a hero to fit our prophecies, rather than allowing one to arise naturally. This was the worry I had, the thing that should have given me pause when my brethren came to me, finally willing to believe.

40

ELEND SAT BESIDE HER BED.

That comforted her. Though she slept fitfully, a piece of her knew that he was there, watching over her. It felt odd to be beneath his protective care, for she was the one who usually did the guarding.

So, when she finally woke, she wasn't surprised to find him in the chair beside her bed, reading quietly by soft candlelight. As she came fully awake, she didn't jump up, or search the room with apprehension. Instead, she sat up slowly, pulling the blanket up under her arms, then took a sip of the water that had been left for her beside the bed.

Elend closed the book and turned toward her, smiling. Vin searched those soft eyes, delving for hints of the horror she had seen before. The disgust, the terror, the shock.

He knew her for a monster. How could he smile so kindly?

"Why?" she asked quietly.

"Why what?" he asked.

"Why wait here?" she said. "I'm not dying—I remember that much."

Elend shrugged. "I just wanted to be near you."

She said nothing. A coal stove burned in the corner, though it needed more fuel. Winter was close, and it was looking to be a cold one. She wore only a nightgown; she'd asked the maids not to put one on her, but by then Sazed's draught—to help her sleep—had already begun taking effect, and she hadn't had the energy to argue.

She pulled the blanket closer. Only then did she realize something she should have noticed earlier. "Elend! You're not wearing your uniform."

He looked down at his clothing—a nobleman's suit from his old wardrobe, with an unbuttoned maroon vest. The jacket was too big for him. He shrugged. "No need to continue the charade anymore, Vin."

"Cett is king?" she asked with a sinking feeling.

Elend shook his head. "Penrod."

"That doesn't make sense."

"I know," he said. "We aren't sure why the merchants betrayed Cett—but it doesn't really matter anymore. Penrod is a far better choice anyway. Than either Cett, or me."

"You know that's not true."

Elend sat back contemplatively. "I don't know, Vin. I thought I was the better man. Yet, while I thought up all kinds of schemes to keep the throne from Cett, I never really considered the one plan that would have been certain to defeat him—that of giving my support to Penrod, combining our votes. What if my arrogance had landed us with Cett? I wasn't thinking of the people."

"Elend . . ." she said, laying a hand on his arm.

And he flinched.

It was slight, almost unnoticeable, and he covered it quickly. But the damage was done. Damage she had caused, damage within him. He had finally seen—really seen—what she was. He'd fallen in love with a lie.

"What?" he said, looking into her face.

"Nothing," Vin said. She withdrew her hand. Inside, something cracked. *I love him so much. Why? Why did I let him see? If only I'd had a choice!*

He's betraying you, Reen's voice whispered in the back of her mind. *Everyone will leave you eventually, Vin.*

Elend sighed, glancing toward the shutters to her room. They were closed, keeping the mists out, though Vin could see the darkness beyond.

"The thing is, Vin," he said quietly, "I never really thought it would end this way. I trusted them, right to the end. The people—the Assemblymen they chose—I trusted that they would do the right thing. When they didn't choose me, I was actually surprised. I shouldn't have been. We *knew* that I was the long shot. I mean, they had already voted me out once. But, I'd convinced myself that was just a warning. Inside, in my heart, I thought that they would reinstate me."

He shook his head. "Now, I either have to admit that my faith in them was wrong, or I have to trust in their decision."

That was what she loved: his goodness, his simple honesty. Things as odd and exotic to a skaa urchin as her own Mistborn nature must be to most people. Even among all the good men of Kelsier's crew, even amid the best of the nobility, she had never found another man like Elend Venture. A man who would rather believe that the people who had dethroned him were just trying to do the right thing.

At times, she had felt a fool for falling in love with the first nobleman whom she grew to know. But now she realized that her love of Elend had not come about because of simple convenience or proximity. It had come because of who Elend was. The fact that she had found him first was an event of incredible fortune.

And now . . . it was over. At least, in the form it had once had. But, she'd known all along that it would turn out this way. That was why she'd refused his marriage proposal, now over a year old. She couldn't marry him. Or, rather, she couldn't let him marry her.

"I know that sorrow in your eyes, Vin," Elend said softly. She looked at him with shock.

"We can get past this," he said. "The throne wasn't everything. We might be better off this way, actually. We did our best. Now it's someone else's turn to try."

She smiled wanly. *He doesn't know. He must never know how much this hurts. He's a good man—he'd try to force himself to keep loving me.*

"But," he said, "you should get some more rest."

"I feel fine," Vin said, stretching slightly. Her side hurt, and her neck ached, but pewter burned within her, and none of her wounds were debilitating. "I need to—"

She cut herself off as a realization hit her. She sat upright, the sudden motion making her rigid with pain. The day before was a blur, but . . .

"*OreSeur!*" she said, pushing aside the blanket.

"He's fine, Vin," Elend said. "He's a kandra. Broken bones mean nothing to him."

She paused, half out of bed, suddenly feeling foolish. "Where is he?"

"Digesting a new body," Elend said, smiling.

"Why the smile?" she asked.

"I've just never heard someone express that much concern for a kandra before."

"Well, I don't see why not," Vin said, climbing back in bed. "OreSeur risked his life for me."

"He's a kandra, Vin," Elend repeated. "I don't think those men could have killed him; I doubt even a Mistborn could."

Vin paused. *Not even a Mistborn could.* . . . What bothered her about that statement? "Regardless," she said. "He feels pain. He took two serious blows on my behalf."

"Just fulfilling his Contract."

His Contract. . . . OreSeur had attacked a human. He had *broken* his Contract. For her.

"What?" Elend asked.

"Nothing," Vin said quickly. "Tell me about the armies."

Elend eyed her, but allowed the conversation to change directions. "Cett is still holed up in Keep Hasting. We're not sure what his reaction will be. The Assembly didn't choose him, which can't be good. And yet, he hasn't protested—he has to realize that he's trapped in here now."

"He must have really believed that we'd choose him," Vin said, frowning. "Why else would he come into the city?"

Elend shook his head. "It was an odd move in the first place. Anyway, I have advised the Assembly to try and make a deal with him. I think he believes that the atium isn't in the city, so there's really no reason for him to want Luthadel."

"Except for the prestige."

"Which wouldn't be worth losing his army," Elend's said. "Or his life."

Vin nodded. "And your father?"

"Silent," Elend said. "It's strange, Vin. This isn't like him—those assassins were so blatant. I'm not sure what to make of them."

"The assassins," Vin said, sitting back in the bed. "You've identified them?"

Elend shook his head. "Nobody recognizes them."

Vin frowned.

"Maybe we aren't as familiar with the noblemen out in the Northern Dominance as we thought we were."

No, Vin thought. *No, if they were from a city as close as Urteau—Straff's home—some of them would be known, wouldn't they?* "I thought I recognized one of them," Vin finally said.

"Which one?"

"The . . . last one."

Elend paused. "Ah. Well, I guess we won't be able to identify him now."

"Elend, I'm sorry you had to see that."

"What?" Elend asked. "Vin, I've seen death before. I was forced to attend the Lord Ruler's executions, remember?" He paused. "Not that what you did was like that, of course."

Of course.

"You were amazing," Elend said. "I'd be dead right now if you hadn't stopped those Allomancers—and it's likely that Penrod and the other Assemblymen would have fared the same. You saved the Central Dominance."

We always have to be the knives. . . .

Elend smiled, standing. "Here," he said, walking to the side of the room. "This is cold, but Sazed said you should eat it when you awoke." He returned with a bowl of broth.

"Sazed sent it?" Vin asked skeptically. "Drugged, then?"

Elend smiled. "He warned me not to taste it myself—he

said it was filled with enough sedatives to knock me out for a month. It takes a lot to affect you pewter burners."

He set the bowl on the bedstand. Vin eyed it through narrowed eyes. Sazed was probably worried that, despite her wounds, she'd go out and prowl the city if she were left on her own. He was probably right. With a sigh, Vin accepted the bowl and began to sip at it.

Elend smiled. "I'll send someone to bring you more coal for the stove," he said. "There are some things I need to do."

Vin nodded, and he left, pulling the door shut behind him.

When Vin next awoke, she saw that Elend was still there. He stood in the shadows, watching her. It was still dark outside. The shutters to her window were open, and mist coated the floor of the room.

The shutters were *open*.

Vin sat upright and turned toward the figure in the corner. It wasn't Elend. "Zane," she said flatly.

He stepped forward. It was so easy to see the similarities between him and Elend, now that she knew what to look for. They had the same jaw, the same wavy dark hair. They even had similar builds, now that Elend had been exercising.

"You sleep too soundly," Zane said.

"Even a Mistborn's body needs sleep to heal."

"You shouldn't have been hurt in the first place," Zane said. "You should have been able to kill those men with ease, but you were distracted by my brother, and by trying to keep the people of the room from harm. *This* is what he's done to you—he's changed you, so that you no longer see what needs to be done, you just see what he wants you to do."

Vin raised an eyebrow, quietly feeling beneath her pillow. Her dagger was there, fortunately. *He didn't kill me in my sleep,* she thought. *That has to be a good sign.*

He took another step forward. She tensed. "What is your game, Zane?" she said. "First, you tell me that you've decided not to kill me—then you send a group of assassins. What now? Have you come to finish the job?"

"We didn't send those assassins, Vin," Zane said quietly.

Vin snorted.

"Believe as you wish," Zane said, taking another step forward so that he stood right beside her bed, a tall figure of blackness and solemnity. "But, my father is still terrified of you. Why would he risk retribution by trying to kill Elend?"

"It was a gamble," Vin said. "He hoped those assassins would kill me."

"Why use them?" Zane asked. "He has me—why use a bunch of Mistings to attack you in the middle of a crowded room, when he could just have me use atium in the night and kill you?"

Vin hesitated.

"Vin," he said, "I watched the corpses being carried away from the Assembly Hall, and I recognized some of them from Cett's entourage."

That's it! Vin thought. *That's where I saw that Thug whose face I smashed! He was at Keep Hasting, peeking out from the kitchen while we ate with Cett, pretending to be a servant.*

"But, the assassins attacked Cett too . . ." Vin trailed off. It was basic thieving strategy: if you had a front that you wanted to escape suspicion as you burgled the shops around it, you made certain to "steal" from yourself as well.

"The assassins who attacked Cett were all normal men," Vin said. "No Allomancers. I wonder what he told them— that they'd be allowed to 'surrender' once the battle turned? But why fake an attack in the first place? He was favored for the throne."

Zane shook his head. "Penrod made a deal with my father, Vin. Straff offered the Assembly wealth beyond anything Cett could provide. That's why the merchants changed their votes. Cett must have gotten wind of their betrayal. He has spies enough in the city."

Vin sat, dumbfounded. *Of course!* "And the only way that Cett could see to win . . ."

"Was to send the assassins," Zane said with a nod.

"They were to attack all three candidates, killing Penrod and Elend, but leaving Cett alive. The Assembly would assume that they'd been betrayed by Straff, and Cett would become king."

Vin gripped her knife with a shaking hand. She was growing tired of games. Elend had almost died. She had almost failed.

Part of her, a burning part, wanted to do what she'd first been inclined to. To go out and kill Cett and Straff, to remove the danger the most efficient way possible.

No, she told herself forcefully. *No, that was Kelsier's way. It's not my way. It's not . . . Elend's way.*

Zane turned away, facing toward her window, staring at the small waterfall-like flow of mist spilling through. "I should have arrived sooner to the fight. I was outside, with the crowds that came too late to get a seat. I didn't even know what was happening until the people started piling out."

Vin raised an eyebrow. "You almost sound sincere, Zane."

"I have no wish to see you dead," he said, turning. "And I certainly don't want to see harm befall Elend."

"Oh?" Vin asked. "Even though he's the one who had all the privileges, while you were despised and kept locked away?"

Zane shook his head. "It isn't like that. Elend is . . . pure. Sometimes—when I hear him speak—I wonder if I would have become like him, if my childhood had been different."

He met her eyes in the dark room. "I'm . . . broken, Vin. Maddened. I can never be like Elend. But, killing him wouldn't change me. It's probably best that he and I were raised apart—it's far better that he doesn't know about me. Better that he remain as he is. Untainted."

"I . . ." Vin floundered. What could she say? She could see actual sincerity in Zane's eyes.

"I'm not Elend," Zane said. "I never will be—I'm not a part of his world. But, I don't think that I *should* be. Neither should you. After the fighting was done, I finally got into the Assembly Hall. I saw Elend standing over you, at the end. I saw the look in his eyes."

She turned away.

"It's not his fault that he is what he is," Zane said. "As I said, he's pure. But, that makes him different from us. I've tried to explain it to you. I wish you could have seen that look in his eyes. . . ."

I saw it, Vin thought. She didn't want to remember it, but she *had* seen it. That awful look of horror, a reaction to something terrible and alien, something beyond understanding.

"I can't be Elend," Zane said quietly, "but you don't want me to be." He reached over and dropped something on her bedstand. "Next time, be prepared."

Vin snatched the object as Zane began to walk toward the window. The ball of metal rolled in her palm. The shape was bumpy, but the texture was smooth—like a nugget of gold. She knew it without having to swallow it. *"Atium?"*

"Cett may send other assassins," Zane said, hopping up onto the windowsill.

"You're *giving* it to me?" she asked. "There's enough here for a good two minutes of burning!" It was a small fortune, easily worth twenty thousand boxings before the Collapse. Now, with the scarcity of atium . . .

Zane turned back toward her. "Just keep yourself safe," he said, then launched himself out into the mists.

Vin did not like being injured. Logically, she knew that other people probably felt the same way; after all, who would enjoy pain and debilitation? Yet, when the others got sick, she sensed frustration from them. Not terror.

When sick, Elend would spend the day in bed, reading books. Clubs had taken a bad blow during practice several months before, and he had grumbled about the pain, but had stayed off his leg for a few days without much prodding.

Vin was growing to be more like them. She could lie in bed as she did now, knowing that nobody would try to slit her throat while she was too weak to call for help. Still, she itched to rise, to show that she wasn't very badly wounded. Lest someone think otherwise, and try to take advantage.

It isn't like that anymore! she told herself. It was light outside, and though Elend had been back to visit several times, he was currently away. Sazed had come to check on her wounds, and had begged her to stay in bed for "at least one more day." Then he'd gone back to his studies. With Tindwyl.

What ever happened to those two hating each other? she thought with annoyance. *I barely get to see him.*

Her door opened. Vin was pleased that her instincts were still keen enough that she immediately grew tense, reaching for her daggers. Her pained side protested the sudden motion.

Nobody entered.

Vin frowned, still tense, until a canine head popped up over the top of her footboard. "Mistress?" said a familiar, half growl of a voice.

"OreSeur?" Vin said. "You're wearing another dog's body!"

"Of course, Mistress," OreSeur said, hopping up onto the bed. "What else would I have?"

"I don't know," Vin said, putting away her daggers. "When Elend said you'd had him get you a body, I just assumed that you'd asked for a human. I mean, everyone saw my 'dog' die."

"Yes," OreSeur said, "but it will be simple to explain that you got a new animal. You are expected to have a dog with you now, and so *not* having one would provoke notice."

Vin sat quietly. She'd changed back to trousers and shirt, despite Sazed's protests. Her dresses hung in the other room, one noticeably absent. At times, when she looked at them, she thought she saw the gorgeous white gown hanging there, sprayed with blood. Tindwyl had been wrong: Vin couldn't be both Mistborn and lady. The horror she had seen in the eyes of the Assemblymen was enough proof for her.

"You didn't need to take a dog's body, OreSeur," Vin said quietly. "I'd rather that you were happy."

"It is all right, Mistress," OreSeur said. "I have grown . . . fond of these kinds of bones. I should like to explore their advantages a little more before I return to human ones."

Vin smiled. He'd chosen another wolfhound—a big brute of a beast. The colorings were different: more black than gray, without any patches of white. She approved.

"OreSeur . . ." Vin said, looking away. "Thank you for what you did for me."

"I fulfill my Contract."

"I've been in other fights," Vin said. "You never intervened in those."

OreSeur didn't answer immediately. "No, I didn't."

"Why this time?"

"I did what felt right, Mistress," OreSeur said.

"Even if it contradicted the Contract?"

OreSeur sat up proudly on his haunches. "I did *not* break my Contract," he said firmly.

"But you attacked a human."

"I didn't kill him," OreSeur said. "We are cautioned to stay out of combat, lest we accidentally cause a human death. Indeed, most of my brethren think that helping someone kill is the same as killing, and feel it is a breach of the Contract. The words are distinct, however. I did nothing wrong."

"And if that man you tackled had broken his neck?"

"Then I would have returned to my kind for execution," OreSeur said.

Vin smiled. "Then you *did* risk your life for me."

"In a small way, I suppose," OreSeur said. "The chances of my actions directly causing that man's death were slim."

"Thank you anyway."

OreSeur bowed his head in acceptance.

"Executed," Vin said. "So you can be killed?"

"Of course, Mistress," OreSeur said. "We aren't immortal."

Vin eyed him.

"I will say nothing specific, Mistress," OreSeur said. "As you might imagine, I would rather not reveal the weaknesses of my kind. Please suffice it to say that they exist."

Vin nodded, but frowned in thought, bringing her knees up to her chest. Something was still bothering her, something about what Elend had said earlier, something about Ore-Seur's actions. . . .

"But," she said slowly, "you couldn't have been killed by swords or staves, right?"

"Correct," OreSeur said. "Though our flesh looks like yours, and though we feel pain, beating us has no permanent effect."

"Then why are you afraid?" Vin said, finally lighting upon what was bothering her.

"Mistress?"

"Why did your people make the Contract?" Vin asked. "Why subjugate yourselves to mankind? If our soldiers couldn't hurt you, then why even worry about us?"

"You have Allomancy," OreSeur said.

"So, Allomancy can kill you?"

"No," OreSeur said, shaking his canine head. "It cannot. But, perhaps we should change the topic. I'm sorry, Mistress. This is very dangerous ground for me."

"I understand," Vin said, sighing. "It's just so frustrating. There's so much I don't know—about the Deepness, about the legal politics . . . even about my own friends!" She sat back, looking up at the ceiling. *And there's still a spy in the palace. Demoux or Dockson, likely. Maybe I should just order them both taken and held for a time? Would Elend even do such a thing?*

OreSeur was watching her, apparently noting her frustration. Finally, he sighed. "Perhaps there are some things I can speak of, Mistress, if I am careful. What do you know of the origin of the kandra?"

Vin perked up. "Nothing."

"We did not exist before the Ascension," he said.

"You mean to say that the Lord Ruler created you?"

"That is what our lore teaches," OreSeur said. "We are not certain of our purpose. Perhaps we were to be Father's spies."

"Father?" Vin said. "It seems strange to hear him spoken of that way."

"The Lord Ruler created us, Mistress," OreSeur said. "We are his children."

"And I killed him," Vin said. "I . . . feel like I should apologize."

"Just because he is our Father does not mean we accepted everything he did, Mistress," OreSeur said. "Cannot a human man love his father, yet not believe he is a good person?"

"I suppose."

"Kandra theology about Father is complex," OreSeur said. "Even for us, it is difficult to sort through it sometimes."

Vin frowned. "OreSeur? How old are you?"

"Old," he said simply.

"Older than Kelsier?"

"Much," OreSeur said. "But not as old as you are thinking. I do not remember the Ascension."

Vin nodded. "Why tell me all of this?"

"Because of your original question, Mistress. Why do we serve the Contract? Well, tell me—if you were the Lord Ruler, and had his power, would you have created servants without building into them a way that you could control them?"

Vin nodded slowly in understanding.

"Father took little thought of the kandra from about the second century after his Ascension," OreSeur said. "We tried to be independent for a time, but it was as I explained, humankind resented us. Feared us. And, some of them knew of our weaknesses. When my ancestors considered their options, they eventually chose voluntary servitude as opposed to forced slavery."

He created them, Vin thought. She had always shared a bit of Kelsier's view regarding the Lord Ruler—that he was more man than deity. But, if he'd truly created a completely new species, then there had to have been some divinity in him.

The power of the Well of Ascension, she thought. *He took it for himself—but it didn't last. It must have run out, and quickly. Otherwise, why would he have needed armies to conquer?*

An initial burst of power, the ability to create, to change—perhaps to save. He'd pushed back the mists, and in the process he'd somehow made the ash begin to fall and the sky turn red. He'd created the kandra to serve him—and probably the koloss, too. He might even have created Allomancers themselves.

And after that, he had returned to being a normal man. Mostly. The Lord Ruler had still held an inordinate amount of power for an Allomancer, and had managed to keep control of his creations—and he had somehow kept the mists from killing.

Until Vin had slain him. Then the koloss had begun to rampage, and the mists had returned. The kandra hadn't been beneath his control at that time, so they remained as they were. But, he built into them a method of control, should he need it. A way to make the kandra serve him. . . .

Vin closed her eyes, and quested out lightly with her Allomantic senses. OreSeur had said that kandra couldn't be affected by Allomancy—but she knew something else about the Lord Ruler, something that had distinguished him from other Allomancers. His inordinate power had allowed him to do things he shouldn't have been able to.

Things like pierce copperclouds, and affect metals inside of a person's body. Maybe *that* was how he controlled the kandra, the thing that OreSeur was speaking of. The reason they feared Mistborn.

Not because Mistborn could kill them, but because Mistborn could do something else. Enslave them, somehow. Tentatively, testing what he'd said earlier, Vin reached out with a Soothing and touched OreSeur's emotions. Nothing happened.

I can do some of the same things as the Lord Ruler, she thought. *I can pierce copperclouds. Perhaps, if I just Push harder . . .*

She focused, and *Pushed* on his emotions with a powerful Soothing. Again, nothing happened. Just as he'd told her. She sat for a moment. And then, impulsively, she burned duralumin and tried one final, massive Push.

OreSeur immediately let out a howl so bestial and unexpected that Vin jumped to her feet in shock, flaring pewter.

OreSeur fell to the bed, shaking.

"OreSeur!" she said, dropping to her knees, grabbing his head. "I'm sorry!"

"Said too much . . ." he muttered, still shaking. "I knew I'd said too much."

"I didn't mean to hurt you," Vin said.

The shaking subsided, and OreSeur fell still for a moment, breathing quietly. Finally, he pulled his head out of her arms. "What you meant is immaterial, Mistress," he said flatly. "The mistake was mine. Please, never do that again."

"I promise," she said. "I'm sorry."

He shook his head, crawling off the bed. "You shouldn't even have been able to do it. There are strange things about you, Mistress—you are like the Allomancers of old, before the passage of generations dulled their powers."

"I'm sorry," Vin said again, feeling helpless. *He saved my life, nearly broke his Contract, and I do this to him. . . .*

OreSeur shrugged. "It is done. I need to rest. I suggest that you do the same."

After that, I began to see other problems.

41

" 'I WRITE THIS RECORD NOW,' " Sazed read out loud, " 'pounding it into a metal slab, because I am afraid. Afraid for myself, yes—I admit to being human. If Alendi does return from the Well of Ascension, I am certain that my death will be one of his first objectives. He is not an evil man, but he is a ruthless one. That is, I think, a product of what he has been through.' "

"That fits what we know of Alendi from the logbook," Tindwyl said. "Assuming that Alendi is that book's author."

Sazed glanced at his pile of notes, running over the basics in his mind. Kwaan had been an ancient Terris scholar. He had discovered Alendi, a man he began to think—through his studies—might be the Hero of Ages, a figure from Terris prophecy. Alendi had listened to him, and had become a political leader. He had conquered much of the world, then traveled north to the Well of Ascension. By then, however, Kwaan had apparently changed his mind about Alendi—and had tried to stop him from getting to the Well.

It fit together. Even though the logbook author never mentioned his own name, it was obvious that he was Alendi. "It is a very safe assumption, I think," Sazed said. "The logbook even speaks of Kwaan, and the falling-out they had."

They sat beside each other in Sazed's rooms. He had requested, and received, a larger desk to hold their multitudinous notes and scribbled theories. Beside the door sat the remnants of their afternoon meal, a soup they had hurriedly gulped down. Sazed itched to take the dishes down to the kitchens, but he hadn't been able to pull himself away yet.

"Continue," Tindwyl requested, sitting back in her chair, looking more relaxed than Sazed had ever seen her. The rings running down the sides of her ears alternated in color—a gold or copper followed by a tin or iron. It was such a simple thing, but there was a beauty to it.

"Sazed?"

Sazed started. "I apologize," he said, then turned back to his reading. " 'I am also afraid, however, that all I have known—that my story—will be forgotten. I am afraid for the world that may come. Afraid because my plans failed. Afraid of a doom brought by the Deepness.' "

"Wait," Tindwyl said. "Why did he fear that?"

"Why would he not?" Sazed asked. "The Deepness—which we assume is the mist—was killing his people. Without sunlight, their crops would not grow, and their animals could not graze."

"But, if Kwaan feared the Deepness, then he should not have opposed Alendi," Tindwyl said. "He was climbing to the Well of Ascension to *defeat* the Deepness."

"Yes," Sazed said. "But by then, Kwaan was convinced that Alendi wasn't the Hero of Ages."

"But why would that matter?" Tindwyl said. "It didn't take a specific person to stop the mists—Rashek's success proves that. Here, skip to the end. Read that passage about Rashek."

" 'I have a young nephew, one Rashek,' " Sazed read. " 'He hates all of Khlennium with the passion of envious youth. He hates Alendi even more acutely—though the two have never met—for Rashek feels betrayed that one of our oppressors should have been chosen as the Hero of Ages.

" 'Alendi will need guides through the Terris mountains. I have charged Rashek with making certain that he and his trusted friends are chosen as those guides. Rashek is to try and lead Alendi in the wrong direction, to discourage him or otherwise foil his quest. Alendi won't know that he has been deceived.

" 'If Rashek fails to lead Alendi astray, then I have instructed the lad to kill my former friend. It is a distant hope. Alendi has survived assassins, wars, and catastrophes. And yet, I hope that in the frozen mountains of Terris, he may finally be exposed. I hope for a miracle.

" 'Alendi must not reach the Well of Ascension. He must not take the power for himself.' "

Tindwyl sat back, frowning.

"What?"

"Something is wrong there, I think," she said. "But I cannot tell you precisely what."

Sazed scanned the text again. "Let us break it down to simple statements, then. Rashek—the man who became the Lord Ruler—was Kwaan's nephew."

"Yes," Tindwyl said.

"Kwaan sent Rashek to mislead, or even kill, his once-friend Alendi the Conqueror—a man climbing the mountains of Terris to seek the Well of Ascension."

Tindwyl nodded.

"Kwaan did this because he feared what would happen if Alendi took the Well's power for himself."

Tindwyl raised a finger. "Why did he fear that?"

"It seems a rational fear, I think," Sazed said.

"Too rational," Tindwyl replied. "Or, rather, perfectly rational. But, tell me, Sazed. When you read Alendi's logbook, did you get the impression that he was the type who would take that power for himself?"

Sazed shook his head. "Actually, the opposite. That is part of what made the logbook so confusing—we couldn't figure out why the man represented within would have done as we assumed he must have. I think that is part of what eventually led Vin to guess that the Lord Ruler wasn't Alendi at all, but Rashek, his packman."

"And Kwaan says that he knew Alendi well," Tindwyl said. "In fact, in this very rubbing, he compliments the man on several occasions. Calls him a good person, I believe."

"Yes," Sazed said, finding the passage. " 'He is a good man—despite it all, he is a good man. A sacrificing man. In truth, all of his actions—all of the deaths, destructions, and pains that he has caused—have hurt him deeply.' "

"So, Kwaan knew Alendi well," Tindwyl said. "And thought highly of him. He also, presumably, knew his nephew Rashek well. Do you see my problem?"

Sazed nodded slowly. "Why send a man of wild temperament, one whose motivations are based on envy and hatred, to kill a man you thought to be good and of worthy temperament? It does seem an odd choice."

"Exactly," Tindwyl said, resting her arms on the table.

"But," Sazed said, "Kwaan says right here that he 'doubts that if Alendi reaches the Well of Ascension, he will take the power and then—in the name of the greater good—give it up.' "

Tindwyl shook her head. "It doesn't make sense, Sazed. Kwaan wrote several times about how he feared the Deepness, but then he tried to foil the hope of stopping it by sending a hateful youth to kill a respected, and presumably wise, leader. Kwaan practically *set up* Rashek to take the power—if letting Alendi take the power was such a concern, wouldn't he have feared that Rashek might do the same?"

"Perhaps we simply see things with the clarity of those regarding events that have already occurred," Sazed said.

Tindwyl shook her head. "We're missing something, Sazed. Kwaan is a very rational, even deliberate, man—one can tell that from his narrative. He was the one who discovered Alendi, and was the first to tout him as the Hero of Ages. Why would he turn against him as he did?"

Sazed nodded, flipping through his translation of the rubbing. Kwaan had gained much notoriety by discovering the Hero. He found the place he was looking for.

There was a place for me in the lore of the Anticipation, the text read. *I thought myself the Announcer, the prophet foretold to discover the Hero of Ages. Renouncing Alendi then would have been to renounce my new position, my acceptance, by the others.*

"Something dramatic must have happened," Tindwyl said. "Something that would make him turn against his friend, the source of his own fame. Something that pricked his conscience so sharply that he was willing to risk opposing the most powerful monarch in the land. Something so frightening that he took a ridiculous chance by sending this Rashek on an assassination mission."

Sazed leafed through his notes. "He fears both the Deepness and what would happen if Alendi took the power. Yet, he cannot seem to decide which one is the greater threat, and neither seems more present in the narrative than the other. Yes, I can see the problem here. Do you think, perhaps, Kwaan was trying to imply something by the inconsistency in his own arguments?"

"Perhaps," Tindwyl said. "The information is just so slim. I cannot judge a man without knowing the context of his life!"

Sazed looked up, eyeing her. "Perhaps we have been studying too hard," he said. "Shall we take a break?"

Tindwyl shook her head. "We don't have the time, Sazed."

He met her eyes. She was right on that point.

"You sense it too, don't you?" she asked.

He nodded. "This city will soon fall. The forces pressing upon it . . . the armies, the koloss, the civil confusion . . ."

"I fear it will be more violent than your friends hope, Sazed," Tindwyl said quietly. "They seem to believe that they can just continue to juggle their problems."

"They are an optimistic group," he said with a smile. "Unaccustomed to being defeated."

"This will be worse than the revolution," Tindwyl said. "I have studied these things, Sazed. I know what happens when a conqueror takes a city. People will die. Many people."

Sazed felt a chill at her words. There was a tension to Luthadel; war was coming to the city. Perhaps one army or another would enter by the blessing of the Assembly, but the other would still strike. The walls of Luthadel would run red when the siege finally ended.

And he feared that end was coming very, very soon.

"You are right," he said, turning back to the notes on his desktop. "We must continue to study. We should collect more of what we can find about the land before the Ascension, so that you may have the context you seek."

She nodded, showing a fatalistic resolve. This was not a task they could complete in the time they had. Deciphering the meaning of the rubbing, comparing it to the logbook, and relating it to the context of the period was a scholarly undertaking that would require the determined work of years.

Keepers had much knowledge—but in this case, it was almost too much. They had been gathering and transmitting records, stories, myths, and legends for so long that it took years for one Keeper to recite the collected works to a new initiate.

Fortunately, included with the mass of information were indexes and summaries created by the Keepers. On top of this came the notes and personal indexes each individual Keeper made. And yet, these only helped the Keeper understand just how much information he had. Sazed himself had spent his life reading, memorizing, and indexing religions. Each night, before he slept, he read some portion of a note or story. He was probably the world's foremost scholar on pre-Ascension religions, and yet he felt as if he knew so little.

Compounding all of that was the inherent unreliability of their information. A great deal of it came from the mouths of simple people, doing their best to remember what their lives had once been like—or, more often, what the lives of their grandparents had once been like. The Keepers hadn't been founded until late in the second century of the Lord Ruler's reign. By then, many religions had already been wiped out in their pure forms.

Sazed closed his eyes, dumped another index from a coppermind into his head, then began to search it. There wasn't much time, true, but Tindwyl and he were Keepers. They were accustomed to beginning tasks that others would have to finish.

Elend Venture, once king of the Central Dominance, stood on the balcony of his keep, overlooking the vast city of Luthadel. Though the first snows had yet to fall, the weather had grown cold. He wore an overcloak, tied at the front, but it didn't protect his face. A chill tingled his cheeks as a wind blew across him, whipping at his cloak. Smoke rose from chimneys, gathering like an ominous shadow above the city before rising up to meld with the ashen red sky.

For every house that produced smoke, there were two that did not. Many of those were probably deserted; the city held nowhere near the population it once had. However, he knew that many of those smokeless houses were still inhabited. Inhabited, and freezing.

I should have been able to do more for them, Elend thought, eyes open to the piercing cold wind. *I should have found a way to get more coal; I should have managed to provide for them all.*

It was humbling, even depressing, to admit that the Lord Ruler had done better than Elend himself. Despite being a heartless tyrant, the Lord Ruler had at least kept a significant portion of the population from starving or freezing. He had kept armies in check, and had kept crime at a manageable level.

To the northeast, the koloss army waited. It had sent no

emissaries to the city, but it was more frightening than either Cett's or Straff's armies. The cold wouldn't scare away its occupants; despite their bare skin, they apparently took little notice of weather changes. This final army was the most disturbing of the three—more dangerous, more unpredictable, and impossible to deal with. Koloss did not bargain.

We haven't been paying enough attention to that threat, he thought as he stood on the balcony. *There's just been so much to do, so much to worry about, that we couldn't focus on an army that might be as dangerous to our enemies as it is to us.*

It was looking less and less likely that the koloss would attack Cett or Straff. Apparently, Jastes was enough in control to keep them waiting to take a shot at Luthadel itself.

"My lord," said a voice from behind. "Please, come back in. That's a fell wind. No use killing yourself from a chill."

Elend turned back. Captain Demoux stood dutifully in the room, along with another bodyguard. In the aftermath of the assassination attempt, Ham had insisted that Elend go about guarded. Elend hadn't complained, though he knew there was little reason for caution anymore. Straff wouldn't want to kill him now that he wasn't king.

So earnest, Elend thought, studying Demoux's face. *Why do I find him youthful? We're nearly the same age.*

"Very well," Elend said, turning and striding into the room. As Demoux closed the balcony doors, Elend removed his cloak. The suit below felt wrong on him. Sloppy, even though he had ordered it cleaned and pressed. The vest was too tight—his practice with the sword was slowly modifying his body—while the coat hung loosely.

"Demoux," Elend said. "When is your next Survivor rally?"

"Tonight, my lord."

Elend nodded. He'd feared that; it would be a cold night.

"My lord," Demoux said, "do you still intend to come?"

"Of course," Elend said. "I gave my word that I would join with your cause."

"That was before you lost the vote, my lord."

"That is immaterial," Elend said. "I am joining your movement because it is important to the skaa, Demoux, and I want to understand the will of my . . . of the people. I promised you dedication—and you shall have it."

Demoux seemed a bit confused, but spoke no further. Elend eyed his desk, considering some studying, but found it hard to motivate himself in the chill room. Instead, he pushed open the door and strode out into the hallway. His guards followed.

He stopped himself from turning toward Vin's rooms. She needed her rest, and it didn't do her much good to have him peeking in every half hour to check on her. So instead he turned to wander down a different passageway.

The back hallways of Keep Venture were tight, dark, stone constructions of labyrinthine complexity. Perhaps it was because he'd grown up in these passages, but he felt at home in their dark, secluded confines. They had been the perfect place for a young man who didn't really care to be found. Now he used them for another reason; the corridors provided a perfect place for extended walking. He didn't point himself in any particular direction, he just moved, working out his frustration to the beating of his own footsteps.

I can't fix the city's problems, he told himself. *I have to let Penrod handle that—he's the one the people want.*

That should have made things easier for Elend. It let him focus on his own survival, not to mention let him spend time revitalizing his relationship with Vin. She, however, seemed different lately. Elend tried to tell himself it was just her injury, but he sensed something deeper. Something in the way she looked at him, something in the way she reacted to his affection. And, despite himself, he could think of only one thing that had changed.

He was no longer king.

Vin was not shallow. She had shown him nothing but devotion and love during their two years together. And yet, how could she not react—even if unconsciously—to his colossal failure? During the assassination attempt, he had watched her fight. *Really* watched her fight, for the first time. Until that day, he hadn't realized just how amazing she was. She wasn't just a warrior, and she wasn't just an Allomancer. She was a force, like thunder or wind. The way she had killed that last man, smashing his head with her own . . .

How could she love a man like me? he thought. *I couldn't even hold my throne. I wrote the very laws that deposed me.*

He sighed, continuing to walk. He felt like he should be scrambling, trying to figure out a way to convince Vin that he was worthy of her. But that would just make him seem more incompetent. There was no correcting past mistakes, especially since he could see no real "mistakes" he had made. He had done the best he could, and that had proven insufficient.

He paused at an intersection. Once, a relaxing dip into a book would have been enough to calm him. Now he felt nervous. Tense. A little . . . like he assumed Vin usually felt.

Maybe I could learn from her, he thought. *What would Vin do in my situation?* She certainly wouldn't just wander around, brooding and feeling sorry for herself. Elend frowned, looking down a hallway lighted by flickering oil lamps, only half of them lit. Then he took off, walking with a determined stride toward a particular set of rooms.

He knocked quietly, and got no response. Finally, he poked his head in. Sazed and Tindwyl sat quietly before a desk piled high with scraps of paper and ledgers. They both sat staring, as if at nothing, their eyes bearing the glazed-over look of someone who had been stunned. Sazed's hand rested on the table. Tindwyl's rested on top of it.

Sazed shook himself alert suddenly, turning to regard Elend. "Lord Venture! I am sorry. I did not hear you enter."

"It's all right, Saze," Elend said, walking into the room. As he did, Tindwyl shook awake as well, and she removed her hand from Sazed's. Elend nodded to Demoux and his companion—who were still following—indicating that they should remain outside, then closed the door.

"Elend," Tindwyl said, her voice laced with its typical

undercurrent of displeasure. "What is your purpose in bothering us? You have already proven your incompetence quite soundly—I see no need for further discussion."

"This is still my home, Tindwyl," Elend replied. "Insult me again, and you will find yourself ejected from the premises."

Tindwyl raised an eyebrow.

Sazed paled. "Lord Venture," he said quickly, "I don't think that Tindwyl meant to—"

"It's all right, Sazed," Elend said, raising a hand. "She was just testing to see if I had reverted back to my previous state of insultability."

Tindwyl shrugged. "I have heard reports of your moping through the palace hallways like a lost child."

"Those reports are true," Elend said. "But that doesn't mean that my pride is completely gone."

"Good," Tindwyl said, nodding to a chair. "Seat yourself, if you wish."

Elend nodded, pulling the chair over before the two and sitting. "I need advice."

"I've given you what I can already," Tindwyl said. "In fact, I've perhaps given you too much. My continued presence here makes it seem that I'm taking sides."

"I'm not king anymore," Elend said. "Therefore, I have no side. I'm just a man seeking truth."

Tindwyl smiled. "Ask your questions, then."

Sazed watched the exchange with obvious interest.

I know, Elend thought, *I'm not sure I understand our relationship either.* "Here is my problem," he said. "I lost the throne, essentially, because I wasn't willing to lie."

"Explain," Tindwyl said.

"I had a chance to obscure a piece of the law," Elend said. "At the last moment, I could have made the Assembly take me as king. Instead, I gave them a bit of information that was true, but which ended up costing me the throne."

"I'm not surprised," Tindwyl said.

"I doubted that you would be," Elend said. "Now, do you think I was foolish to do as I did?"

"Yes."

Elend nodded.

"But," Tindwyl said, "that moment isn't what cost you the throne, Elend Venture. That moment was a small thing, far too simple to credit with your large-scale failure. You lost the throne because you wouldn't command your armies to secure the city, because you insisted on giving the Assembly too much freedom, and because you don't employ assassins or other forms of pressure. In short, Elend Venture, you lost the throne because you are a good man."

Elend shook his head. "Can you not be both a man who follows his conscience *and* a good king, then?"

Tindwyl frowned in thought.

"You ask an age-old question, Lord Venture," Sazed said quietly. "A question that monarchs, priests, and humble men of destiny have always asked. I do not know that there is an answer."

"Should I have told the lie, Sazed?" Elend asked.

"No," Sazed said, smiling. "Perhaps another man should have, in your same position. But, a man must be cohesive with himself. You have made your decisions in life, and changing yourself at the last moment—telling this lie—would have been against who you are. It is better for you to have done as you did and lost the throne, I think."

Tindwyl frowned. "His ideals are nice, Sazed. But what of the people? What if they die because Elend wasn't capable of controlling his own conscience?"

"I do not wish to argue with you, Tindwyl," Sazed said. "It is simply my opinion that he chose well. It is his right to follow his conscience, then trust in providence to fill in the holes caused by the conflict between morality and logic."

Providence. "You mean God," Elend said.

"I do."

Elend shook his head. "What is God, Sazed, but a device used by obligators?"

"Why do you make the choices that you do, Elend Venture?"

"Because they're right," Elend said.

"And why are these things right?"

"I don't know," Elend said with a sigh, leaning back. He caught a disapproving glance from Tindwyl at his posture, but he ignored her. He wasn't king; he could slouch if he wanted to. "You talk of God, Sazed, but don't you preach of a hundred different religions?"

"Three hundred, actually," Sazed said.

"Well, which one do *you* believe?" Elend asked.

"I believe them all."

Elend shook his head. "That doesn't make sense. You've only pitched a half-dozen to me, but I can already see that they're incompatible."

"It is not my position to judge truth, Lord Venture," Sazed said, smiling. "I simply carry it."

Elend sighed. *Priests . . .* he thought. *Sometimes, talking to Sazed is like talking to an obligator.*

"Elend," Tindwyl said, her tone softening. "I think you handled this situation in the wrong way. However, Sazed does have a point. You were true to your own convictions, and that is a regal attribute, I think."

"And what should I do now?" he asked.

"Whatever you wish," Tindwyl said. "It was never my place to tell you what to do. I simply gave you knowledge of what men in your place did in the past."

"And what would they have done?" Elend asked. "These great leaders of yours, how would they have reacted to my situation?"

"It is a meaningless question," she said. "They would not have found themselves in this situation, for they would not have lost their titles in the first place."

"Is that what it's about, then?" Elend asked. "The title?"

"Isn't that what we were discussing?" Tindwyl asked.

Elend didn't answer. *What do you think makes a man a good king?* he had once asked of Tindwyl. *Trust,* she had replied. *A good king is one who is trusted by his people— and one who deserves that trust.*

Elend stood up. "Thank you, Tindwyl," he said.

Tindwyl frowned in confusion, then turned to Sazed. He looked up and met Elend's eyes, cocking his head slightly. Then he smiled. "Come, Tindwyl," he said. "We should return to our studies. His Majesty has work to do, I think."

Tindwyl continued to frown as Elend left the room. His

guards followed behind as he quickly strode down the hallway.

I won't go back to the way I was, Elend thought. *I won't continue to fret and worry. Tindwyl taught me better than that, even if she never really understood me.*

Elend arrived at his rooms a few moments later. He stalked directly in, then opened his closet. The clothing Tindwyl had chosen for him—the clothing of a king—waited inside.

Some of you may know of my fabled memory. It is true; I need not a Feruchemist's metalmind to memorize a sheet of words in an instant.

42

"GOOD," ELEND SAID, USING A charcoal stick to circle another section on the city map before him. "What about here?"

Demoux scratched his chin. "Grainfield? That's a nobleman's neighborhood, my lord."

"It used to be," Elend said. "Grainfield was filled with cousin houses to the Ventures. When my father pulled out of the city, so did most of them."

"Then we'll probably find the homes filled with skaa transients, I'd guess."

Elend nodded. "Move them out."

"Excuse me, my lord?" Demoux said. The two stood in Keep Venture's large carriage landing. Soldiers moved in a bustle through the spacious room. Many of them didn't wear uniforms; they weren't on official city business. Elend was no longer king, but they had still come at his request.

That said something, at least.

"We need to move the skaa out of those homes," Elend continued. "Noblemen's houses are mostly stone mansions with a lot of small rooms. They're extremely hard to heat, requiring a separate hearth or a stove for every room. The skaa tenements are depressing, but they have massive hearths and open rooms."

Demoux nodded slowly.

"The Lord Ruler couldn't have his workers freezing," Elend said. "Those tenements are the best way to efficiently look after a large population of people with limited resources."

"I understand, my lord," Demoux said.

"Don't force them, Demoux," Elend said. "My personal guard—even augmented with army volunteers—has no official authority in the city. If a family wants to stay in their pilfered aristocratic house, let them. Just make certain that they know there's an alternative to freezing."

Demoux nodded, then moved over to pass on the commands. Elend turned as a messenger arrived. The man had to weave his way through an organized jumble of soldiers receiving orders and making plans.

Elend nodded to the newcomer. "You're on the demolitions scout group, correct?"

The man nodded as he bowed. He wasn't in uniform; he was a soldier, not one of Elend's guards. He was a younger man, with a square jaw, balding head, and honest smile.

"Don't I know you?" Elend said.

"I helped you a year ago, my lord," the man said. "I led you into the Lord Ruler's palace to help rescue Lady Vin. . . ."

"Goradel," Elend said, remembering. "You used to be in the Lord Ruler's personal guard."

The man nodded. "I joined up in your army after that day. Seemed like the thing to do."

Elend smiled. "Not my army anymore, Goradel, but I do appreciate you coming to help us today. What's your report?"

"You were right, my lord," Goradel said, "the skaa have already robbed the empty homes for furniture. But, not many thought of the walls. A good half of the abandoned mansions have wooden walls on the inside, and a lot of the tenements were made of wood. Most all of them have wooden roofs."

"Good," Elend said. He surveyed the gathering mass of men. He hadn't told them his plans; he'd simply asked for volunteers to help him with some manual labor. He hadn't expected the response to number in the hundreds.

"It looks like we're gathering quite a group, my lord," Demoux said, rejoining Elend.

Elend nodded, giving leave for Goradel to withdraw. "We'll be able to try an even more ambitious project than I'd planned."

"My lord," Demoux said. "Are you certain you want to start tearing the city down around ourselves?"

"We either lose buildings or we lose people, Demoux," Elend said. "The buildings go."

"And if the king tries to stop us?"

"Then we obey," Elend said. "But I don't think Lord Penrod will object. He's too busy trying to get a bill through the Assembly that hands the city over to my father. Besides, it's probably better for him to have these men here, working, than it is to have them sitting and worrying in the barracks."

Demoux fell silent. Elend did as well; both knew how precarious their position was. Only a short time had passed since the assassination attempt and the transfer of power, and the city was in shock. Cett was still holed up inside of Keep Hasting, and his armies had moved into position to attack the city. Luthadel was like a man with a knife pressed very closely to his throat. Each breath cut the skin.

I can't do much about that now, Elend thought. *I have to make certain the people don't freeze these next few nights.* He could feel the bitter cold, despite the daylight, his cloak, and the shelter. There were a lot of people in Luthadel, but if he could get enough men tearing down enough buildings, he just might be able to do some good.

"My lord!"

Elend turned as a short man with a drooping mustache approached. "Ah, Felt," he said. "You have news?" The man was working on the poisoned-food problem—specifically how the city was being breached.

The scout nodded. "I do indeed, my lord. We interrogated the refugees with a Rioter, and we came up dry. Then, however, I started thinking. The refugees seemed too obvious to me. Strangers in the city? Of course they'd be the first ones we'd suspect. I figured, with how much has been going wrong with the wells and the food and the like, someone *has* to be sneaking in and out of the city."

Elend nodded. They'd been watching Cett's soldiers inside Keep Hasting very carefully, and none of them was responsible. Straff's Mistborn was still a possibility, but Vin had never believed that he was behind the poisoning. Elend hoped that the trail—if it could be found—would lead back to someone in his own palace, hopefully revealing who on his serving staff had been replaced by a kandra.

"Well?" Elend asked.

"I interrogated the people who run passwalls," Felt continued. "I don't think they're to blame."

"Passwalls?"

Felt nodded. "Covert passages out of the city. Tunnels or the like."

"Such things exist?" Elend asked with surprise.

"Of course, my lord," Felt said. "Moving between cities was very difficult for skaa thieves during the Lord Ruler's reign. Everyone who entered Luthadel was subject to interview and interrogation. So, ways to get into the city covertly were very prevalent. Most of those have shut down—the ones who used to lower people up and down by ropes over the walls. A few are still running, but I don't think they are letting the spies in. Once that first well was poisoned, the passwalls all got paranoid that you'd come after them. Since then, they've only been letting people *out* of the city—ones who want to run from the besieged city and the like."

Elend frowned. He wasn't certain what he thought of the fact that people were disobeying his order that the gates be shut, with no passage out.

"Next," Felt said, "I tried the river."

"We thought of that," Elend said. "The grates covering the water are all secure."

Felt smiled. "That they are. I sent some men down under the water to search about, and we found several locks down below, keeping the river grates in place."

"What?"

"Someone pried the grates free, my lord," Felt said, "then locked them back into place so it wouldn't look suspicious. That way, they could swim in and out at their leisure."

Elend raised an eyebrow.

"You want us to replace the grates?" Felt asked.

"No," Elend said. "No, just replace those locks with new ones, then post men to watch. Next time those poisoners try and get into the city, I want them to find themselves trapped."

Felt nodded, retreating with a happy smile on his face. His talents as a spy hadn't been put to much good use lately, and he seemed to be enjoying the tasks Elend was giving him. Elend made a mental note to think about putting Felt to work on locating the kandra spy—assuming, of course, that Felt himself wasn't the spy.

"My lord," Demoux said, approaching. "I think I might be able to offer a second opinion on how the poisonings are occurring."

Elend turned. "Oh?"

Demoux nodded, waving for a man to approach from the side of the room. He was younger, perhaps eighteen, and had the dirty face and clothing of a skaa worker.

"This is Larn," Demoux said. "A member of my congregation."

The young man bowed to Elend, posture nervous.

"You may speak, Larn," Demoux said. "Tell Lord Venture what you saw."

"Well, my lord," the young man said. "I tried to go tell this to the king. The new king, I mean." He flushed, embarrassed.

"It's all right," Elend said. "Continue."

"Well, the men there turned me away. Said the king didn't

have time for me. So, I came to Lord Demoux. I figured he might believe me."

"About what?" Elend asked.

"Inquisitor, my lord," the man said quietly. "I saw one in the city."

Elend felt a chill. "You're sure?"

The young man nodded. "I've lived in Luthadel all my life, my lord. Watched executions a number of times. I'd recognize one of those monsters, sure I would. I saw him. Spikes through the eyes, tall and robed, slinking about at night. Near the center squares of the city. I promise you."

Elend shared a look with Demoux.

"He's not the only one, my lord," Demoux said quietly. "Some other members of my congregation claimed to have seen an Inquisitor hanging around Kredik Shaw. I dismissed the first few, but Larn, he's trustworthy. If he said he saw something, he did. Eyes nearly as good as a Tineye, that one."

Elend nodded slowly, and ordered a patrol from his personal guard to keep watch in the area indicated. After that, he turned his attention back to the wood-gathering effort. He gave the orders, organizing the men into teams, sending some to begin working, others to gather recruits. Without fuel, many of the city's forges had shut down, and the workers were idle. They could use something to occupy their time.

Elend saw energy in the men's eyes as they began to split up. Elend knew that determination, that firmness of eye and arm. It came from the satisfaction of doing something, of not just sitting around and waiting for fate—or kings—to act.

Elend turned back to the map, making a few notations. From the corner of his eye, he saw Ham saunter in. "So this is where they all went!" Ham said. "The sparring grounds are empty."

Elend looked up, smiling.

"You're back to the uniform, then?" Ham asked.

Elend glanced down at his white outfit. Designed to stand out, to set him apart from a city stained by ash. "Yes."

"Too bad," Ham said with a sigh. "Nobody should have to wear a uniform."

Elend raised an eyebrow. In the face of undeniable winter, Ham had finally taken to wearing a shirt beneath his vest. He wore no cloak or coat, however.

Elend turned back to the map. "The clothing suits me," he said. "It just feels right. Anyway, that vest of yours is as much a uniform as this is."

"No it's not."

"Oh?" Elend asked. "Nothing screams Thug like a man who goes about in the winter without a coat, Ham. You've used your clothing to change how people react to you, to let them know who you are and what you represent—which is essentially what a uniform does."

Ham paused. "That's an interesting way of looking at it."

"What?" Elend said. "You never argued about something like this with Breeze?"

Ham shook his head as he turned to look over the groups of men, listening to the men Elend had appointed to give orders.

He's changed, Elend thought. *Running this city, dealing with all of this, it's even changed him.* The Thug was more solemn, now—more focused. Of course, he had even more stake in the city's safety than the rest of the crew. It was sometimes hard to remember that the free-spirited Thug was a family man. Ham tended to not talk much about Mardra or his two children. Elend suspected it was habit; Ham had spent much of his marriage living apart from his family in order to keep them safe.

This whole city is my family, Elend thought, watching the soldiers leave to do their work. Some might have thought something as simple as gathering firewood to be a mundane task, of little relevance in a city threatened by three armies. However, Elend knew that the freezing skaa people would receive the fuel with as much appreciation as they would salvation from the armies.

The truth was that Elend felt a little like his soldiers did. He felt a satisfaction—a thrill even—from doing something, *anything,* to help.

"What if Cett's attack comes?" Ham said, still looking over the soldiers. "A good portion of the army will be out scattered through the city."

"Even if we have a thousand men in my teams, that's not much of a dent in our forces. Besides, Clubs thinks there will be plenty of time to gather them. We've got messengers set up."

Elend looked back at his map. "Anyway, I don't think Cett's going to attack just yet. He's pretty safe in that keep, there. We'll never take him—we'd have to pull too many men away from the city defenses, leaving ourselves exposed. The only thing he really has to worry about is my father . . ."

Elend trailed off.

"What?" Ham said.

"That's why Cett is here," Elend said, blinking in surprise. "Don't you see? He intentionally left himself without options. If Straff attacks, Cett's armies will end up fighting alongside our own. He's locked in his fate with ours."

Ham frowned. "Seems like a pretty desperate move."

Elend nodded, thinking back to his meeting with Cett. " 'Desperate,' " he said. "That's a good word. Cett is desperate for some reason—one I haven't been able to figure out. Anyway, by putting himself in here, he sides with us against Straff—whether we want the alliance or not."

"But, what if the Assembly gives the city to Straff? If our men join with him and attack Cett?"

"That's the gamble he took," Elend said. *Cett never intended to be able to walk away from the confrontation here in Luthadel. He intends to take the city or be destroyed.*

He is waiting, hoping Straff will attack, worrying that we'll just give into him. But neither can happen as long as Straff is afraid of Vin. A three-way standoff. With the koloss as a fourth element that nobody can predict.

Someone needed to do something to tip the scales. "Demoux," Elend said. "Are you ready to take over here?"

Captain Demoux looked over, nodding.

Elend turned to Ham. "I have a question for you, Ham."

Ham raised an eyebrow.

"How insane are you feeling at the moment?

Elend led his horse out of the tunnel into the scraggly land-scape outside of Luthadel. He turned, craning to look up at the wall. Hopefully, the soldiers there had gotten his message, and wouldn't mistake him for a spy or a scout of one of the enemy armies. He'd rather not end up in Tindwyl's histories as the ex-king who'd died by an arrow from one of his own men.

Ham led a small, grizzled woman from the tunnel. As Elend had guessed, Ham had easily found a suitable pass-wall to get them out of the city.

"Well, there you go," said the elderly woman, resting on her cane.

"Thank you, good woman," Elend said. "You have served your dominance well this day."

The woman snorted, raising an eyebrow—though, from what Elend could tell, she was quite nearly blind. Elend smiled, pulling out a pouch and handing it to her. She reached into it with gnarled, but surprisingly dexterous, fingers and counted out the contents. "Three extra?"

"To pay you to leave a scout here," Elend said. "To watch for our return."

"Return?" the woman asked. "You aren't running?"

"No," Elend said. "I just have some business with one of the armies."

The woman raised the eyebrow again. "Well, none of Granny's business," she muttered, turning back down the hole with a tapping cane. "For three clips, I can find a grandson to sit out here for a few hours. Lord Ruler knows, I have enough of them."

Ham watched her go, a spark of fondness in his eyes.

"How long have you known about this place?" Elend asked, watching as a couple of burly men pulled closed the hidden section of stone. Half burrowed, half cut from the wall's stones themselves, the tunnel was a remarkable feat. Even after hearing about the existence of such things from

Felt earlier, it was still a shock to travel through one hidden not a few minutes' ride from Keep Venture itself.

Ham turned back to him as the false wall snapped shut. "Oh, I've known of this for years and years," he said. "Granny Hilde used to give me sweets when I was a kid. Of course, that was really just a cheap way of getting some quiet—yet well-targeted—publicity for her passwall. When I was grown, I used to use this to sneak Mardra and the kids in and out of the city when they came to visit."

"Wait," Elend said. "You grew up in Luthadel?"

"Of course."

"On the streets, like Vin?"

Ham shook his head. "Not really like Vin," he said in a subdued voice, scanning the wall. "I don't really think anyone grew up like Vin. I had skaa parents—my grandfather was the nobleman. I was involved with the underground, but I had my parents for a good portion of my childhood. Besides, I was a boy—and a large one." He turned toward Elend. "I suspect that makes a big difference."

Elend nodded.

"You're not going to shut this place down, are you?" Ham asked.

Elend turned with shock. "Why would I?"

Ham shrugged. "It doesn't exactly seem like the kind of honest enterprise that you would approve of. There are probably people fleeing from the city nightly through this hole. Granny Hilde is known to take coin and not ask questions—even if she does grumble at you a bit."

Ham did have a point. *Probably why he didn't tell me about the place until I specifically asked.* His friends walked a fine line, close to their old ties with the underground, yet working hard to build up the government they'd sacrificed so much to create.

"I'm not king," Elend said, leading his horse away from the city. "What Granny Hilde does isn't any of my business."

Ham moved up beside him, looking relieved. Elend could see that relief dissipate, however, as the reality of what they were doing settled in. "I don't like this, El."

They stopped walking as Elend mounted. "Neither do I."

Ham took a deep breath, then nodded.

My old nobleman friends would have tried to talk me out of this, Elend thought with amusement. *Why did I surround myself with people who had been loyal to the Survivor? They* expect *their leaders to take irrational risks.*

"I'll go with you," Ham said.

"No," Elend said. "It won't make a difference. Stay here, wait to see if I get back. If I don't, tell Vin what happened."

"Sure, I'll tell her," Ham said wryly. "Then I'll proceed to remove her daggers from my chest. Just make sure you come back, all right?"

Elend nodded, barely paying attention. His eyes were focused on the army in the distance. An army without tents, carriages, food carts, or servants. An army who had eaten the foliage to the ground in a wide swath around them. Koloss.

Sweat made the reins slick in Elend's hands. This was different from before, when he'd gone into Straff's army and Cett's keep. This time he was alone. Vin couldn't get him out if things went bad; she was still recovering from her wounds, and nobody knew what Elend was doing but Ham.

What do I owe the people of this city? Elend thought. *They rejected me. Why do I still insist on trying to protect them?*

"I recognize that look, El," Ham said. "Let's go back."

Elend closed his eyes, letting out a quiet sigh. Then he snapped his eyes open and kicked his horse into a gallop.

It had been years since he'd seen koloss, and that experience had come only at his father's insistence. Straff hadn't trusted the creatures, and had never liked having garrisons of them in the Northern Dominance, one just a few days' march from his home city of Urteau. Those koloss had been a reminder, a warning, from the Lord Ruler.

Elend rode his horse hard, as if using its momentum to bolster his own will. Aside from one brief visit to the Urteau koloss garrison, everything he knew of the creatures came from books—but Tindwyl's instruction had weakened his once absolute, and slightly naive, trust in his learning.

It will have to be enough, Elend thought as he approached the camp. He gritted his teeth, slowing his animal as he approached a wandering squad of Koloss.

It was as he remembered. One large creature—its skin revoltingly split and cracked by stretch marks—led a few medium-sized beasts, whose bleeding rips were only beginning to appear at the corners of their mouths and the edges of their eyes. A smattering of smaller creatures—their baggy skin loose and sagging beneath their eyes and arms—accompanied their betters.

Elend reined in his horse, trotting it over to the largest beast. "Take me to Jastes."

"Get off your horse," the koloss said.

Elend looked the creature directly in the eyes. Atop his horse, he was nearly the same height. "Take me to Jastes."

The koloss regarded him with a set of beady, unreadable eyes. It bore a rip from one eye to the other, above the nose, a secondary rip curving down to one of the nostrils. The nose itself was pulled so tight it was twisted and flattened, held to the bone a few inches off-center.

This was the moment. The books said the creature would either do as commanded or simply attack him. Elend sat tensely.

"Come," the koloss snapped, turning to walk back toward the camp. The rest of the creatures surrounded Elend's horse, and the beast shuffled nervously. Elend kept a tight hold on his reins and nudged the animal forward. It responded skittishly.

He should have felt good at his small victory, but his tension only increased. They moved forward into the koloss camp. It was like being swallowed. Like letting a rockslide collapse around you. Koloss looked up as he passed, watching him with their red, emotionless eyes. Many others just stood silently around their cooking fires, unresponsive, like men who had been born dull-minded and witless.

Others fought. They killed each other, wrestling on the ground before their uncaring companions. No philosopher, scientist, or scholar had been able to determine exactly what set off a koloss. Greed seemed a good motivation. Yet, they would sometimes attack when there was plenty of food, killing a companion for *his* hunk of beef. Pain was another good motivator, apparently, as was a challenge to authority. Carnal, visceral reasons. And yet, there seemed to be times when they attacked without any cause or reason.

And after fighting, they would explain themselves in calm tones, as if their actions were perfectly rational. Elend shivered as he heard yells, telling himself that he would probably be all right until he reached Jastes. Koloss usually just attacked each other.

Unless they got into a blood frenzy.

He pushed that thought away, instead focusing on the things that Sazed had mentioned about his trip into the koloss camp. The creatures wore the wide, brutish iron swords that Sazed had described. The bigger the koloss, the bigger the weapon. When a koloss reached a size where he thought he needed a larger sword, he had only two choices: find one that had been discarded, or kill someone and take theirs. A koloss population could often be crudely controlled by increasing or decreasing the number of swords available to the group.

None of the scholars knew how the creatures bred.

As Sazed had explained, these koloss also had strange little pouches tied to their sword straps. *What are they?* Elend thought. *Sazed said he saw the largest koloss carrying three or four. But that one leading my group has almost twenty.* Even the small koloss in Elend's group had three pouches.

That's the difference, he thought. *Whatever is in those pouches, could it be the way Jastes controls the creatures?*

There was no way to know, save begging one of the pouches off a koloss—and he doubted they would let them go.

As he walked, he noticed another oddity: some of the koloss were wearing clothing. Before, he'd seen them only in loincloths, as Sazed had reported. Yet, many of these koloss had pants, shirts, or skirts pulled onto their bodies. They wore the clothing without regard for size, and most pieces were so tight they had torn. Others were so loose they had to be tied on. Elend saw a few of the larger koloss wearing garments like bandanas tied around their arms or heads.

"We are not koloss," the lead koloss suddenly said, turning to Elend as they walked.

Elend frowned. "Explain."

"You think we are koloss," it said through lips that were stretched too tightly to work properly. "We are humans. We will live in your city. We will kill you, and we will take it."

Elend shivered, realizing the source of the mismatched garments. They had come from the village that the koloss had attacked, the one whose refugees had trickled into Luthadel. This appeared to be a new development in koloss thinking. Or, had it always been there, repressed by the Lord Ruler? The scholar in Elend was fascinated. The rest of him was simply horrified.

His koloss guide paused before a small group of tents, the only such structures in the camp. Then the lead koloss turned and yelled, startling Elend's horse. Elend fought to keep his mount from throwing him as the koloss jumped and attacked one of its companions, proceeding to pummel it with a massive fist.

Elend won his struggle. The lead koloss, however, did not.

Elend climbed off his horse, patting the beast on the neck as the victimized koloss pulled his sword from the chest of his former leader. The survivor—who now bore several cuts in his skin that hadn't come from stretching— bent down to harvest the pouches tied to the corpse's back. Elend watched with a muted fascination as the koloss stood and spoke.

"He was never a good leader," it said in a slurred voice.

I can't let these monsters attack my city, Elend thought. *I have to do something.* He pulled his horse forward, turning his back on the koloss as he entered the secluded section of camp, watched over by a group of nervous young men in uniforms. Elend handed his reins to one of them.

"Take care of this for me," Elend said, striding forward.

"Wait!" one of the soldiers said. "Halt!"

Elend turned sharply, facing the shorter man, who was trying to both level his spear at Elend and keep an eye on the koloss. Elend didn't try to be harsh; he just wanted to keep his own anxiety under control and keep moving. Either way, the resulting glare probably would have impressed even Tindwyl.

The soldier jerked to a halt.

"I am Elend Venture," Elend said. "You know that name?"

The man nodded.

"You may announce me to Lord Lekal," Elend said. "Just get to the tent before I do."

The young man took off at a dash. Elend followed, striding up to the tent, where other soldiers stood hesitantly.

What must it have done to them, Elend wondered, *living surrounded by koloss, so terribly outnumbered?* Feeling a stab of pity, he didn't try to bully his way in. He stood with faux patience until a voice called from inside. "Let him in."

Elend brushed past the guards and threw open the tent flap.

The months had not been kind to Jastes Lekal. Somehow, the few wisps of hair on his head looked far more pathetic than complete baldness would have. His suit was sloppy and stained, his eyes underlined by a pair of deep bags. He was pacing, and jumped slightly when Elend entered.

Then he froze for a moment, eyes wide. Finally, he raised a quivering hand to push back hair he didn't have. "Elend?" he asked. "What in the Lord Ruler's name happened to you?"

"Responsibility, Jastes," Elend said quietly. "It appears that neither of us were ready for it."

"Out," Jastes said, waving to his guards. They shuffled past Elend, closing the tent flap behind them.

"It's been a while, Elend," Jastes said, chuckling weakly.

Elend nodded.

"I remember those days," Jastes said, "sitting in your den

or mine, sharing a drink with Telden. We were so innocent, weren't we?"

"Innocent," Elend said, "but hopeful."

"Want something to drink?" Jastes said, turning toward the room's desk. Elend eyed the bottles and flasks lying in the corner of the room. They were all empty. Jastes removed a full bottle from the desk and poured Elend a small cup, the size and clear color an indication that this was no simple dinner wine.

Elend accepted the small cup, but did not drink. "What happened, Jastes? How did the clever, thoughtful philosopher I knew turn into a tyrant?"

"Tyrant?" Jastes snapped, downing his cup in a single shot. "I'm no tyrant. Your father's the tyrant. I'm just a realist."

"Sitting at the center of a koloss army doesn't seem to be a very realistic position to me."

"I can control them."

"And Suisna?" Elend asked. "The village they slaughtered?"

Jastes wavered. "That was an unfortunate accident."

Elend looked down at the drink in his hand, then threw it aside, the liquor splashing on the dusty tent floor. "This isn't my father's den, and we are not friends any longer. I will call no man friend who leads something like *this* against my city. What happened to your honor, Jastes Lekal?"

Jastes snorted, glancing at the spilled liquor. "That's always been the problem with you, Elend. So certain, so optimistic, so self-righteous."

"It was *our* optimism," Elend said, stepping forward. "We wanted to change things, Jastes, not destroy them!"

"Is that so?" Jastes countered, showing a temper Elend had never seen in his friend. "You want to know why I'm here, Elend? Did you even *pay attention* to what was happening in the Southern Dominance while you played in Luthadel?"

"I'm sorry about what happened to your family, Jastes."

"Sorry?" Jastes said, snatching the bottle off his desk. "You're *sorry*? I implemented your plans, Elend. I did everything we talked about—freedom, political honesty. I trusted my allies rather than crushing them into submission. And you know what happened?"

Elend closed his eyes.

"They killed everyone, Elend," Jastes said. "That's what you do when you take over. You kill your rivals and their families—even the young girls, even the babies. And you leave their bodies, as a warning. That's good politics. That's how you stay in power!"

"It's easy to believe in something when you win all the time, Jastes," Elend said, opening his eyes. "The losses are what define a man's faith."

"Losses?" Jastes demanded. "My sister was a *loss*?"

"No, I mean—"

"Enough!" Jastes snapped, slamming the bottle down on his desk. "Guards!"

Two men threw back the tent flap and moved into the room.

"Take His Majesty captive," Jastes said, with an unsteady wave of his hand. "Send a messenger to the city, tell them that we want to negotiate."

"I'm not king anymore, Jastes," Elend said.

Jastes stopped.

"Do you think I'd come here and let myself get captured if I were king?" Elend asked. "They deposed me. The Assembly invoked a no-confidence clause and chose a new king."

"You bloody idiot," Jastes said.

"Losses, Jastes," Elend said. "It hasn't been as hard for me as it was for you, but I do think I understand."

"So," Jastes said, running a hand through his "hair," "that fancy suit and haircut didn't save you, eh?"

"Take your koloss and go, Jastes."

"That sounded like a threat, Elend," Jastes said. "You aren't king, you don't have an army, and I don't see your Mistborn around. What grounds do you have for threats?"

"They're *koloss*," Elend said. "Do you really want them getting into the city? It's your home, Jastes—or, it was once. There are thousands of people inside!"

"I can . . . control my army," Jastes said.

"No, I doubt you can," Elend said. "What happened, Jastes? Did they decide they needed a king? They decided that's the way that 'humans' did it, so they should do it, too? What is it that they carry in those pouches?"

Jastes didn't answer.

Elend sighed. "What happens when one of them just snaps and attacks you?"

Jastes shook his head. "I'm sorry, Elend," he said quietly. "I can't let Straff get that atium."

"And my people?"

Jastes paused only briefly, then lowered his eyes and motioned to the guards. One laid a hand on Elend's shoulder.

Elend's reaction surprised even himself. He slammed his elbow up into the man's face, shattering his nose, then took the other man down with a kick to the leg. Before Jastes could do more than cry out, Elend jumped forward.

Elend ripped an obsidian knife—given to him by Vin— from his boot and caught Jastes by the shoulder. Elend slammed the whimpering man around, pushing him backward onto the desk and—barely thinking to consider his actions—rammed the knife into his old friend's shoulder.

Jastes emitted a loud, pathetic scream.

"If killing you would do anything useful, Jastes," Elend growled, "I'd do it right now. But I don't know how you control these things, and I don't want to set them loose."

Soldiers piled into the room. Elend didn't look up. He slapped Jastes, stopping his cries of pain.

"You listen," Elend said. "I don't care if you've been hurt, I don't care if you don't believe in the philosophies anymore, and I don't really care if you get yourself killed playing politics with Straff and Cett.

"But I *do* care if you threaten my people. I want you to march your army out of my dominance—go attack Straff's homeland, or maybe Cett's. They're both undefended. I promise I won't let your enemies get the atium.

"And, as a friend, I'll give you a bit of counsel. Think about that wound in your arm for a little while, Jastes. I was your best friend, and I nearly killed you. What the *hell* are you doing sitting in the middle of an entire army of de-ranged koloss?"

Soldiers surrounded him. Elend stood, ripping the knife from Jastes's body and spinning the man around, pressing the weapon against his throat.

The guards froze.

"I'm leaving," Elend said, pushing the confused Jastes ahead of him, moving out of the tent. He noticed with some concern that there were barely a dozen human guards. Sazed had counted more. Where had Jastes lost them?

There was no sign of Elend's horse. So he kept a wary eye on the soldiers, pulling Jastes toward the invisible line between the human camp and the koloss one. Elend turned as he reached the perimeter, then pushed Jastes back to-ward his men. They caught him, one pulling out a bandage for the arm. Others made moves as if to chase Elend, but they paused, hesitant.

Elend had crossed the line into the koloss camp. He stood quietly, watching the pathetic group of young sol-diers, Jastes at their center. Even as they ministered to him, Elend could see the look in Jastes's eyes. Hatred. He wouldn't retreat. The man Elend had known was dead, re-placed by this product of a new world that didn't kindly re-gard philosophers and idealists.

Elend turned away, walking among the koloss. A group of them quickly approached. The same one as before? He couldn't tell for certain.

"Take me out," Elend commanded, meeting the eyes of the largest koloss in the team. Either Elend seemed more commanding now, or this koloss was more easily cowed, for there was no argument. The creature simply nodded and began to shuffle out of the camp, his team surrounding Elend.

This trip was a waste, Elend thought with frustration. *All I did was antagonize Jastes. I risked my life for nothing.*

If only I could find out what was in those pouches!

He eyed the group of koloss around him. It was a typi-cal group, ranging in size from five feet to one ten-foot monstrosity. They walked along with slumped, unengaged postures. . . .

Elend still had his knife out.

This is stupid, he thought. For some reason, that didn't stop him from choosing the smallest koloss in the group, taking a deep breath, and attacking.

The rest of the koloss paused to watch. The creature Elend had chosen spun—but in the wrong direction. It turned to face its companion koloss, the one nearest to it in size, as Elend tackled it, ramming the knife into its back.

Even at five feet with a small build, the koloss was incredibly strong. It tossed Elend off, bellowing in pain. Elend, however, managed to keep hold of his dagger.

Can't let it get out that sword, he thought, scrambling to his feet and ramming his knife into the creature's thigh. The koloss dropped again, punching at Elend with one arm, fingers reaching for its sword with the other. Elend took the punch to the chest, and fell back to the sooty ground.

He groaned, gasping. The koloss pulled out its sword, but had trouble standing. Both knife wounds bled stark red blood; the liquid seemed brighter, more reflective, than that of a human, but that might have just been a contrast with the deep blue skin.

The koloss finally managed to gain its feet, and Elend realized his mistake. He'd let the adrenaline of his confrontation with Jastes—his frustration at his inability to stop the armies—drive him. He'd sparred a lot lately, but he was in no position to take a koloss.

But it was far too late to worry about that now.

Elend rolled out of the way as a thick, clublike sword smashed to the ground beside him. Instincts overrode terror, and he mostly managed to avoid the backswing. It took him a bit in the side, spraying a patch of blood across his once white uniform, but he barely even felt the cut.

Only one way to win a knife fight against a guy with a sword . . . Elend thought, gripping his knife. The thought, oddly, hadn't come from one of his trainers, or even from Vin. He wasn't sure where it came from, but he trusted it.

Close in tight as fast as possible, and kill quickly.

And Elend attacked. The koloss swung as well. Elend

could see the attack, but couldn't do anything about it. He could only throw himself forward, knife raised, teeth clenched.

He rammed his knife into the koloss's eye, barely managing to get inside the creature's reach. Even so, the hilt of the sword hit him in the stomach.

Both dropped.

Elend groaned quietly, slowly becoming aware of the hard, ash-packed earth and weeds eaten down to their roots. A fallen twig was scratching his cheek. Odd that he would notice that, considering the pain in his chest. He stumbled to his feet. The koloss he'd attacked did not rise. Its companions stood, looking unconcerned, though their eyes were focused on him. They seemed to want something.

"He ate my horse," Elend said, saying the first thing that came to his clouded mind.

The group of koloss nodded. Elend stumbled forward, wiping the ash from his cheek with a dazed hand as he knelt beside the dead creature. He ripped his knife out, then slid it back in his boot. Next he unfastened the pouches; this koloss had two.

Finally, not certain why, he grabbed the creature's large sword and rested it up on his shoulder. It was so weighty that he could barely carry it, and certainly wouldn't be able to swing it. *How does a creature so small use something like this?*

The koloss watched him work without comment; then they led him out of the camp. Once they had retreated, Elend pulled open one of the pouches and looked inside.

He shouldn't have been surprised by what he found inside. Jastes had decided to control his army the old-fashioned way.

He was paying them.

The others call me mad. As I have said, that may be true.

43

MIST POURED INTO THE DARK room, collapsing around Vin like a waterfall as she stood in the open balcony doorway. Elend was a motionless lump sleeping in his bed a short distance away.

Apparently, Mistress, OreSeur had explained, *he went into the koloss camp alone. You were asleep, and none of us knew what he was doing. I don't think he managed to persuade the creatures not to attack, but he did come back with some very useful information.*

OreSeur sat on his haunches beside her. He had not asked why Vin had come to Elend's rooms, nor why she stood, quietly watching the former king in the night.

She couldn't protect him. She tried so hard, but the impossibility of keeping even *one person* safe suddenly seemed so real—so tangible—to her that she felt sick.

Elend had been right to go out. He was his own man, competent, kingly. What he had done would only put him in more danger, however. Fear had been a companion of hers for such a long time that she had grown accustomed to it, and it rarely caused a physical reaction in her. Yet, watching him sleep quietly, she found her hands traitorously unsteady.

I saved him from the assassins. I protected him. I'm a powerful Allomancer. Why, then, do I feel so helpless?

So alone.

She walked forward, bare feet silent as she stepped up to Elend's bed. He did not wake. She stood for a long moment, just looking at him peaceful in his slumber.

OreSeur growled quietly.

Vin spun. A figure stood on the balcony, straight-backed and black, a near silhouette even to her tin-enhanced eyes. Mist fell before him, pooling on the floor, spreading out like an ethereal moss.

"Zane," she whispered.

"He is not safe, Vin," he said, stepping slowly into the room, pushing a wave of mist before him.

She looked back at Elend. "He never will be."

"I came to tell you that there is a traitor in your midst."

Vin looked up. "Who?" she asked.

"The man, Demoux," Zane said. "He contacted my father a short time before the assassination attempt, offering to open the gates and give up the city."

Vin frowned. *That makes no sense.*

Zane stepped forward. "Cett's work, Vin. He is a snake, even among high lords. I don't know how he bribed away one of your own men, but I do know that Demoux tried to provoke my father to attack the city during the voting."

Vin paused. If Straff had attacked at that moment, it would have reinforced the impression that he had sent the assassins in the first place.

"Elend and Penrod were supposed to die," Zane said. "With the Assembly in chaos, Cett could have taken charge. He could have led his forces—along with your own—against Straff's attacking army. He would have become the savior who protected Luthadel against the tyranny of an invader. . . ."

Vin stood quietly. Just because Zane said it didn't mean it was true. Yet, her investigations whispered that Demoux was the traitor.

She'd recognized the assassin at the assembly, and he *had* been from Cett's retinue, so she knew that Zane was telling the truth about at least one thing. Plus, Cett had precedent for sending Allomancer assassins: he had sent the ones months ago, when Vin had used the last of her atium. Zane had saved her life during that fight.

She clenched her fists, frustration biting at her chest. *If he's right, then Demoux is dead, and an enemy kandra has been in the palace, spending his days just steps away from*

Elend. Even if Zane lies, we still have a tyrant inside the city, another without. A force of koloss salivating over the people. And Elend doesn't need me.

Because there's nothing I can do.

"I see your frustration," Zane whispered, stepping up beside Elend's bed, looking down at his sleeping brother. "You keep listening to him. You want to protect him, but he won't let you." Zane looked up, meeting her eyes. She saw an implication in them.

There *was* something she could do—the thing a part of her had wanted to do from the beginning. The thing she'd been trained to do.

"Cett almost killed the man you love," Zane said. "Your Elend does as he wishes. Well, let us do as *you* wish." He looked into her eyes. "We have been someone else's knives for too long. Let's show Cett why he should fear us."

Her fury, her frustration at the siege, yearned to do as Zane suggested. Yet, she wavered, her thoughts in chaos. She had killed—killed well—just a short time before, and it had terrified her. Yet . . . Elend could take risks—insane risks, traveling into an army of koloss on his own. It almost felt like a betrayal. She had worked so hard to protect him, straining herself, exposing herself. Then, just a few days later, he wandered alone into a camp full of monsters.

She gritted her teeth. Part of her whispered that if Elend wouldn't be reasonable and stay out of danger, she'd just have to go and make *sure* the threats against him were removed.

"Let's go," she whispered.

Zane nodded. "Realize this," he said. "We can't just assassinate him. Another warlord will take his place, and take his armies. We have to attack *hard*. We have to hit that army so soundly that whoever takes over for Cett is so frightened that he withdraws."

Vin paused, looking away from him, nails biting into her own palms.

"Tell me," he said, stepping closer to her. "What would your Kelsier tell you to do?"

The answer was simple. Kelsier would never have gotten into this situation. He had been a hard man, a man with little tolerance for any who threatened those he loved. Cett and Straff wouldn't have lasted a single night at Luthadel without feeling Kelsier's knife.

There was a part of her that had always been awed by his powerful, utilitarian brutality.

There are two ways to stay safe, Reen's voice whispered to her. *Either be so quiet and harmless that people ignore you, or be so dangerous that they're terrified of you.*

She met Zane's eyes and nodded. He smiled, then moved over and jumped out the window.

"OreSeur," she whispered once he was gone. "My atium."

The dog paused, then padded up to her, his shoulder splitting. "Mistress . . ." he said slowly. "Do not do this."

She glanced at Elend. She couldn't protect him from everything. But she could do something.

She took the atium from OreSeur. Her hands no longer shook. She felt cold.

"Cett has threatened all that I love," she whispered. "He will soon know that there is something in this world more deadly than his assassins. Something more powerful than his army. Something more terrifying than the Lord Ruler himself.

"And I am coming for him."

Mist duty, they called it.

Every soldier had to take his turn, standing in the dark with a sputtering torch. Someone had to watch. Had to stare into those shifting, deceitful mists and wonder if anything was out there. Watching.

Wellen knew there was.

He knew it, but he never spoke. Soldiers laughed at such superstitions. They had to go out in the mists. They were used to it. They knew better than to fear it.

Supposedly.

"Hey," Jarloux said, stepping up to the edge of the wall. "Wells, do you see something out there?"

Of course he didn't. They stood with several dozen others on the perimeter of Keep Hasting, watching from the outer keep wall—a low fortification, perhaps fifteen feet tall, that surrounded the grounds. Their job was to look for anything suspicious in the mists.

"Suspicious." That was the word they used. It was *all* suspicious. It was mist. That shifting darkness, that void made of chaos and hatred. Wellen had never trusted it. They were out there. He knew.

Something moved in the darkness. Wellen stepped back, staring into the void, his heart beginning to flutter, hands beginning to sweat as he raised his spear.

"Yeah," Jarloux said, squinting. "I swear, I see . . ."

It came, as Wellen had always known it would. Like a thousand gnats on a hot day, like a hail of arrows shot by an entire army. Coins sprayed across the battlements. A wall of shimmering death, hundreds of trails zipping through the mists. Metal rang against stone, and men cried out in pain.

Wellen stepped back, raising his spear, as Jarloux yelled the alarm. Jarloux died halfway through the call, a coin snapping through his mouth, throwing out a chip of tooth as it proceeded out the back of his head. Jarloux collapsed, and Wellen stumbled away from the corpse, knowing that it was too late to run.

The coins stopped. Silence in the air. Men lay dying or groaning at his feet.

Then they came. Two dark shadows of death in the night. Ravens in the mist. They flew over Wellen with a rustle of black cloth.

And they left him behind, alone amid the corpses of what had once been a squad of forty men.

Vin landed in a crouch, bare feet on the cool stone cobbles of the Hasting courtyard. Zane landed upright, standing— as always—with his towering air of self-confidence.

Pewter blazed within her, giving her muscles the taut energy of a thousand excited moments. She easily ignored the pain of her wounded side. Her sole bead of atium rested in her stomach, but she didn't use it. Not yet. Not unless she was right, and Cett proved to be Mistborn.

"We'll go from the bottom up," Zane said.

Vin nodded. The central tower of Keep Hasting was many stories high, and they couldn't know which one Cett was on. If they started low, he wouldn't be able to escape.

Besides. Going up would be more difficult. The energy in Vin's limbs cried for release. She'd waited, remained coiled, for far too long. She was tired of weakness, tired of being restrained. She had spent months as a knife, held immobile at someone's throat.

It was time to cut.

The two dashed forward. Torches began to light around them as Cett's men—those who camped in the courtyard—awakened to the alarm. Tents unfurled and collapsed, men yelling in surprise, looking for the army that assailed them. They could only wish that they were so lucky.

Vin jumped straight up into the air, and Zane spun, throwing a bag of coins around him. Hundreds of bits of copper sparkled in the air beneath her—a peasant's fortune. Vin landed with a rustle, and they both Pushed, their power throwing the coins outward. The torch-sparkled missiles ripped through the camp, dropping surprised, drowsy men.

Vin and Zane continued toward the central tower. A squad of soldiers had formed up at the tower's front. They still seemed disoriented, confused, and sleepy, but they were armed. Armed with metal armor and steel weapons— a choice that, had they actually been facing an enemy army, would have been wise.

Zane and Vin slid into the midst of the soldiers. Zane tossed a single coin into the air between them. Vin reached out and Pushed against it, feeling Zane's weight as he also Pushed against it.

Braced against each other, they both Pushed in opposite directions, throwing their weight against the breastplates of the soldiers to either side. With flared pewter—holding each other steady—their Pushes scattered the soldiers as if they had been slapped by enormous hands. Spears and swords twisted in the night, clattering to the cobbles. Breastplates towed bodies away.

Vin extinguished her steel as she felt Zane's weight come off the coin. The sparkling bit of metal bounced to the ground between them, and Zane turned, throwing up his hand toward the single soldier who remained standing directly between Zane and the keep doors.

A squad of soldiers raced up behind Zane, but they suddenly halted as he Pushed against them—then sent the transfer of weight directly into the lone soldier. The unfortunate man crashed backward into the keep doors.

Bones crunched. The doors flung open as the soldier burst into the room beyond. Zane ducked through the open doorway, and Vin moved smoothly behind him, her bare feet leaving rough cobbles and falling on smooth marble instead.

Soldiers waited inside. These didn't wear armor, and they carried large wooden shields to block coins. They were armed with staves or obsidian swords. Hazekillers—men trained specifically to fight Allomancers. There were, perhaps, fifty of them.

Now it begins in earnest, Vin thought, leaping into the air and Pushing off the door's hinges.

Zane led by Pushing on the same man he'd used to break open the doors, throwing the corpse toward a group of hazekillers. As the soldier crashed into them, Vin landed amid a second group. She spun on the floor, whipping out her legs and flaring pewter, tripping a good four men. As the others tried to strike, she Pushed downward against a coin in her pouch, ripping it free and throwing herself upward. She spun in the air, catching a falling staff discarded by a tripped soldier.

Obsidian cracked against the white marble where she had been. Vin came down with her own weapon and struck, attacking faster than anyone should be able to, hitting ears, chins, and throats. Skulls cracked. Bones broke. She was barely breathing hard when she found all ten of her opponents down.

Ten men . . . didn't Kelsier once tell me he had trouble with half a dozen hazekillers?

No time to think. A large group of soldiers charged her. She yelled and jumped toward them, throwing her staff into the face of the first man she met. The others raised their shields, surprised, but Vin whipped out a pair of obsidian daggers as she landed. She rammed them into the thighs of two men before her, then spun past them, attacking flesh where she saw it.

An attack flickered from the corner of her eye, and she snapped up an arm, blocking the wooden staff as it came for her head. The wood cracked, and she took the man down with a wide sweep of the dagger, nearly beheading him. She jumped backward as the others moved in, braced herself, then yanked on the armored corpse Zane had used before, Pulling it toward her.

Shields did little good against a missile so large. Vin smashed the corpse into her opponents, sweeping them before her. To the side, she could see the remnants of the hazekillers who had attacked Zane. Zane stood among them, a black pillar before the fallen, arms outstretched. He met her eyes, then nodded toward the rear of the chamber.

Vin ignored the few remaining hazekillers. She Pushed against the corpse and sent herself sliding across the floor. Zane jumped up, Pushing back, shattering his way through a window and into the mists. Vin quickly did a check of the back rooms: no Cett. She turned and took down a straggling hazekiller as she ducked into the lift shaft.

She needed no elevator. She shot straight up on a Pushed coin, bursting out onto the third floor. Zane would take the second.

Vin landed quietly on the marble floor, hearing footsteps come down a stairwell beside her. She recognized this large, open room: it was the chamber where she and Elend had met Cett for dinner. It was now empty, even the table removed, but she recognized the circular perimeter of stained-glass windows.

Hazekillers burst from the kitchen room. Dozens. *There must be another stairwell back there,* Vin thought as she darted toward the stairwell beside her. Dozens more were coming out there, however, and the two groups moved to surround her.

Fifty-to-one must have seemed like good odds for the

men, and they charged confidently. She glanced at the open kitchen doors, and saw no Cett beyond. This floor was clear.

Cett certainly brought a lot of hazekillers, she thought, backing quietly to the center of the room. Save for the stairwell, kitchens, and pillars, the room was mostly surrounded in arched stained-glass windows.

He planned for my attack. Or, he tried to.

Vin ducked down as the waves of men surrounded her. She turned her head up, eyes closed, and burned duralumin.

Then she Pulled.

Stained-glass windows—set in metal frames inside their arches—exploded around the room. She felt the metal frames burst inward, twisting on themselves before her awesome power. She imagined twinkling slivers of multicolored glass in the air. She heard men scream as glass and metal hit them, embedding in their flesh.

Only the outer layer of men would die from the blast. Vin opened her eyes and jumped as a dozen dueling canes fell around her. She passed through a hail of attacks. Some hit. It didn't matter. She couldn't feel pain at the moment.

She Pushed against a broken metal frame, throwing herself over the heads of soldiers, landing outside the large circle of attackers. The outer line of men was down, impaled by glass shards and twisted metal frames. Vin raised a hand and bowed her head.

Duralumin and steel. She Pushed. The world lurched.

Vin shot out into the mists through a broken window as she Pushed against the line of corpses impaled by metal frames. The bodies were thrown away from her, smashing into the men who were still alive in the center.

Dead, dying, and unharmed were swept from the room, Pushed out the window opposite Vin. Bodies twisted in the mists, fifty men thrown into the night, leaving the room empty save for trails of blood and discarded bits of glass.

Vin downed a vial of metals as the mists rushed around her; then she Pulled herself back toward the keep, using a window on the fourth floor. As she approached, a corpse crashed through the window, falling out into the night. She caught a glimpse of Zane disappearing out another window on the opposite side. This level was clear.

Lights burned on the fifth floor. They probably could have come here first, but that wasn't the plan. Zane was right. They didn't just need to kill Cett. They needed to terrify his entire army.

Vin Pushed against the same corpse that Zane had thrown out the window, using its metal armor as an anchor. It shot down at an angle, passing just inside a broken window, and Vin soared upward in an angle away from the building. A quick Pull directed her back to the building once she reached the elevation she needed. She landed at a window on the fifth floor.

Vin grasped the stone sill, heart thumping, breaths coming in deep gasps. Sweat made her face cold in the winter breeze, despite the heat burning within her. She gulped, eyes wide, and flared her pewter.

Mistborn.

She shattered the window with a slap. The soldiers that waited beyond jumped backward, spinning. One wore a metal belt buckle. He died first. The other twenty barely knew how to react as the buckle buzzed through their ranks, twisting between Vin's Pushes and Pulls. They had been trained, instructed, and perhaps even tested against Allomancers.

But they had never fought Vin.

Men screamed and fell, Vin ripping through their ranks with only the buckle as a weapon. Before the force of her pewter, tin, steel, and iron, the possible use of atium seemed an incredible waste. Even without it, she was a terrible weapon—one that, until this moment, even she hadn't understood.

Mistborn.

The last man fell. Vin stood among them, feeling a numbing sense of satisfaction. She let the belt buckle slip from her fingers. It hit carpet. She stood in a room that wasn't unadorned as the rest of the building had been; there was furniture here, and there were some minor decorations. Perhaps Elend's clearing crews hadn't gotten this far before Cett's arrival, or perhaps he'd simply brought some of his own comforts.

Behind her was the stairwell. In front of her was a fine wooden wall set with a door—the inner apartments. Vin stepped forward quietly, mistcloak rustling as she Pulled four lamps off the brackets behind her. They whipped forward, and she sidestepped, letting them crash into the wall. Fire blossomed across splattered oil, billowing across the wall, the force of the lamps breaking the door on its hinges. She raised a hand, Pushing it fully open.

Fire dripped around her as she stepped into the room beyond. The richly decorated chamber was quiet, and eerily empty save for two figures. Cett sat in a simple wooden chair, bearded, sloppily dressed, and looking very, very tired. Cett's young son stepped in between Cett and Vin. The boy held a dueling cane.

So, which one is Mistborn?

The boy swung. Vin caught the weapon, then shoved the boy to the side. He crashed into the wooden wall, then slumped to the ground. Vin eyed him.

"Leave Gneorndin alone, woman," Cett said. "Do what you came to do."

Vin turned toward the nobleman. She remembered her frustration, her rage, her cool, icy anger. She stepped forward and grabbed Cett by the front of his suit. "Fight me," she said, and tossed him backward.

He slammed against the back wall, then slumped to the ground. Vin prepared her atium, but he did not rise. He simply rolled to the side, coughing.

Vin walked over, pulling him up by one arm. He balled a fist, trying to strike her, but he was pathetically weak. She let the blows bounce off her side.

"Fight me," she commanded, tossing him to the side. He tumbled across the floor—head hitting hard—and came to rest against the burning wall, a trickle of blood running from his brow. He didn't rise.

Vin gritted her teeth, striding forward.

"Leave him alone!" The boy, Gneorndin, stumbled in front of Cett, raising his dueling cane in a wavering hand.

Vin paused, cocking her head. The boy's brow was

streaked with sweat, and he was unsteady on his feet. She looked into his eyes, and saw absolute terror therein. This boy was no Mistborn. Yet, he held his ground. Pathetically, hopelessly, he stood before the body of the fallen Cett.

"Step aside, son," Cett said in a tired voice. "There is nothing you can do here."

The boy started to shake, then began to weep.

Tears, Vin thought, feeling an oddly surreal feeling cloud her mind. She reached up, surprised to find wet streaks on her own cheeks.

"You have no Mistborn," she whispered.

Cett had struggled to a half-reclining position, and he looked into her eyes.

"No Allomancers faced us this night," she said. "You used them all on the assassination attempt in the Assembly Hall?"

"The only Allomancers I had, I sent against you months ago," Cett said with a sigh. "They were all I ever had, my only hope of killing you. Even they weren't from my family. My whole line has been corrupted by skaa blood— Allrianne is the only Allomancer to be born to us for centuries."

"You came to Luthadel . . ."

"Because Straff would have come for me eventually," Cett said. "My best chance, lass, was to kill *you* early on. That's why I sent them all against you. Failing that, I knew I had to try and take this damn city and its atium so I could buy myself some Allomancers. Didn't work."

"You could have just offered us an alliance."

Cett chuckled, pulling himself up to a sitting position. "It doesn't work that way in real politics. You take, or you get taken. Besides, I've always been a gambling man." He looked up at her, meeting her eyes. "Do what you came to," he repeated.

Vin shivered. She couldn't feel her tears. She could barely feel anything.

Why? Why can't I make sense of anything anymore?

The room began to shake. Vin spun, looking toward the back wall. The wood there quivered and spasmed like a dying animal. Nails began to pop, ripping backward through the paneling; then the entire wall burst away from Vin. Burning boards, splinters, nails, and shingles sprayed in the air, flying around a man in black. Zane stood sideways in the room beyond, death strewn at his feet, hands at his sides.

Red streamed from the tips of his fingers, running in a steady drip. He looked up through the burning remnants of the wall, smiling. Then he stepped toward Cett's room.

"No!" Vin said, dashing at him.

Zane paused, surprised. He stepped to the side, easily dodging Vin, walking toward Cett and the boy.

"Zane, leave them!" Vin said, turning toward him, Pushing herself in a skid across the room. She reached for his arm. The black fabric glistened wet with blood that was only his own.

Zane dodged. He turned toward her, curious. She reached for him, but he moved out of the way with supernatural ease, outstepping her like a master swordsman facing a young boy.

Atium, Vin thought. *He probably burned it this entire time. But, he didn't need it to fight those men . . . they didn't have a chance against us anyway.*

"Please," she asked. "Leave them."

Zane turned toward Cett, who sat expectant. The boy was at his side, trying to pull his father away.

Zane looked back at her, head cocked.

"Please," Vin repeated.

Zane frowned. "He still controls you, then," he said, sounding disappointed. "I thought, maybe, if you could fight and see just how powerful you were, you'd shake yourself free of Elend's grip. I guess I was wrong."

Then he turned his back on Cett and walked out through the hole he had made. Vin followed quietly, feet crunching splinters of wood as she slowly withdrew, leaving a broken keep, shattered army, and humiliated lord behind.

But must not even a madman rely on his own mind, his own experience, rather than that of others?

44

IN THE COLD CALM OF morning, Breeze watched a very disheartening sight: Cett's army withdrawing.

Breeze shivered, breath puffing as he turned toward Clubs. Most people wouldn't have been able to read beyond the sneer on the squat general's face. But Breeze saw more: he saw the tension in the taut skin around Clubs's eyes, he noticed the way that Clubs tapped his finger against the frosty stone wall. Clubs was not a nervous man. The motions meant something.

"This is it, then?" Breeze asked quietly.

Clubs nodded.

Breeze couldn't see it. There were still two armies out there; it was still a standoff. Yet, he trusted Clubs's assessment. Or, rather, he trusted his own knowledge of people enough to trust his assessment of Clubs.

The general knew something he didn't.

"Kindly explain," Breeze said.

"This'll end when Straff figures it out," Clubs said.

"Figures what out?"

"That those koloss will do his job for him, if he lets them."

Breeze paused. *Straff doesn't really care about the people in the city—he just wants to take it for the atium. And for the symbolic victory.*

"If Straff pulls back . . ." Breeze said.

"Those koloss will attack," Clubs said with a nod. "They'll slaughter everyone they find and generally make rubble out of the city. Then Straff can come back and find his atium once the koloss are done."

"Assuming they leave, my dear man."

Clubs shrugged. "Either way, he's better off. Straff will face one weakened enemy instead of two strong ones."

Breeze felt a chill, and pulled his cloak closer. "You say that all so . . . straightforwardly."

"We were dead the moment that first army got here, Breeze," Clubs said. "We're just good at stalling."

Why in the name of the Lord Ruler do I spend my time with this man? Breeze thought. *He's nothing more than a pessimistic doomsayer.* And yet, Breeze knew people. This time, Clubs wasn't exaggerating.

"Bloody hell," Breeze muttered.

Clubs just nodded, leaning against the wall and looking out at the disappearing army.

"Three hundred men," Ham said, standing in Elend's study. "Or, at least, that's what our scouts say."

"That's not as bad as I'd feared," Elend said. They stood in Elend's study, the only other occupant being Spook, who sat lounging beside the table.

"El," Ham said, "Cett only had a thousand men with him here in Luthadel. That means that during Vin's attack, Cett took thirty percent casualties in *less than ten minutes.* Even on a battlefield, most armies will break if they take thirty or forty percent casualties in the course of an *entire day's* fighting."

"Oh," Elend said, frowning.

Ham shook his head, sitting down, pouring himself something to drink. "I don't get it, El. Why'd she attack him?"

"She's loony," Spook said.

Elend opened his mouth to counter that comment, but found it difficult to explain his feelings. "I'm not sure why she did it," he finally admitted. "She did mention that she didn't believe those assassins at the Assembly came from my father."

Ham shrugged. He looked . . . haggard. This wasn't his element, dealing with armies and worrying about the fate of kingdoms. He preferred to concern himself with smaller spheres.

Of course, Elend thought, *I'd just prefer to be in my chair, reading quietly. We do what we must.*

"Any news of her yet?" Elend asked.

Spook shook his head. "Uncle Grumpy has the scouts searching the city, but so far nothing."

"If Vin doesn't want to be found . . ." Ham said.

Elend began to pace. He couldn't keep still; he was beginning to think he must look like Jastes, wandering in circles, running his hand through his hair.

Be firm, he told himself. *You can afford to seem worried, but you mustn't ever seem uncertain.*

He continued to pace, though he slowed his step, and he didn't voice his concerns to Ham or Spook. What if Vin was wounded? What if Cett had killed her? Their scouts had seen very little of the attack the night before. Vin had definitely been involved, and there were conflicting reports that said she'd been fighting another Mistborn. She had left the keep with one of the top floors in flames—and, for some reason, she had left Cett alive.

Since then, nobody had seen her.

Elend closed his eyes, pausing as he leaned a hand against the stone wall. *I've been ignoring her lately. I've helped the city . . . but what good will it do to save Luthadel if I lose her? It's almost like I don't know her anymore.*

Or did I ever know her in the first place?

It felt wrong to not have her with him. He had come to rely on her simple bluntness. He needed her genuine realism—her sheer sense of concreteness—to keep him grounded. He needed to hold her, so that he could know that there was something more important than theories and concepts.

He loved her.

"I don't know, El," Ham finally said. "I never thought that Vin would be a liability, but she had a hard youth. I remember once she exploded at the crew for little reason, yelling and screaming about her childhood. I . . . don't know that she's completely stable."

Elend opened his eyes. "She's stable, Ham," he said firmly. "And she's more capable than any of us."

Ham frowned. "But—"

"She had a good reason for attacking Cett," Elend said. "I trust her."

Ham and Spook exchanged glances, and Spook just shrugged.

"It's more than last night, El," Ham said. "Something's not right with that girl—not just mentally, either. . . ."

"What do you mean?" Elend asked.

"Remember the attack on the Assembly?" Ham said. "You told me you saw her get hit square-on by a Thug's staff."

"And?" Elend asked. "It laid her out for three full days."

Ham shook his head. "Her complete collection of wounds—getting hit in the side, the shoulder wound, nearly being choked to death—those all together laid her out for a couple of days. But, if she'd really gotten hit that hard by a Thug, she shouldn't have been out for days, Elend. She should have been out for weeks. Maybe longer. She certainly shouldn't have escaped without broken ribs."

"She was burning pewter," Elend said.

"Presumably, so was the Thug."

Elend paused.

"You see?" Ham said. "If both were flaring pewter, then they should have balanced each other out. That leaves Vin—a girl who can't weigh more than a hundred pounds—getting clobbered full-on by a trained soldier with three times her weight. She shrugged it off with barely a few days' rest."

"Vin's special," Elend finally said.

"I won't argue with that," Ham said. "But she's also hiding things from us. Who was that other Mistborn? Some of the reports make it sound like they were working together."

She said there was another Mistborn in the city, Elend thought. *Zane—Straff's messenger. She hasn't mentioned him in a very long while.*

Ham rubbed his forehead. "This is all falling apart around us, El."

"Kelsier could have kept it together," Spook mumbled.

"When he was here, even our failures were part of his plan."

"The Survivor is dead," Elend said. "I never knew him, but I've listened to enough about him to learn one thing. He didn't give in to despair."

Ham smiled. "That much is true. He was laughing and joking the day after we lost our entire army to a miscalculation. Arrogant bastard."

"Callous," Spook said.

"No," Ham said, reaching for his cup. "I used to think that. Now . . . I just think he was determined. Kell always looked toward tomorrow, no matter what the consequences."

"Well, we have to do the same," Elend said. "Cett is gone—Penrod let him leave. We can't change that fact. But, we do have information on the koloss army."

"Oh, about that," Spook said, reaching into his pouch. He tossed something to the table. "You're right—they're the same."

The coin rolled to a stop, and Elend picked it up. He could see where Spook had scraped it with a knife, peeling off the gold paint to reveal the dense hardwood beneath. It was a poor representation of a boxing; it was little wonder that the fakes had been so easy to pick out. Only a fool would try to pass them off as real. A fool, or a koloss.

Nobody was certain how some of Jastes's fake boxings had worked their way up to Luthadel; perhaps he had tried giving them to peasants or beggars in his home dominance. Either way, it was fairly apparent what he was doing. He'd needed an army, and had needed cash. He'd fabricated the one to get the other. Only koloss would have fallen for such a ploy.

"I don't get it," Ham said as Elend passed him the coin. "How come the koloss have suddenly decided to take money? The Lord Ruler never paid them."

Elend paused, thinking back to his experience with the camp. *We are humans. We will live in your city. . . .*

"The koloss are changing, Ham," Elend said. "Or maybe we never really understood them in the first place. Either way, we need to be strong. This isn't over yet."

"It would be easier to be strong if I knew our Mistborn wasn't insane. She didn't even discuss this with us!"

"I know," Elend said.

Ham rose, shaking his head. "There's a reason the Great Houses were always so reluctant to use their Mistborn against each other. Things just got a whole lot more dangerous. If Cett does have a Mistborn, and he decides to retaliate . . ."

"I know," Elend said again, bidding the two farewell.

Ham waved to Spook, and the two of them left, off to check with Breeze and Clubs.

They all act so glum, Elend thought, leaving his rooms to find something to eat. *It's like they think we're doomed because of one setback. But, Cett's withdrawal is a good thing. One of our enemies is leaving—and there are still two armies out there. Jastes won't attack if doing so exposes him to Straff, and Straff himself is too scared of Vin to do anything. In fact, her attack on Cett will only make my father more frightened. Maybe that's why she did it.*

"Your Majesty?" a voice whispered.

Elend spun, searching the hallway.

"Your Majesty," said a short figure in the shadows. Ore-Seur. "I think I've found her."

Elend didn't bring anyone with him save for a few guards. He didn't want to explain to Ham and the others how he'd gotten his information; Vin still insisted on keeping Ore-Seur secret.

Ham's right about one thing, Elend thought as his carriage pulled to a stop. *She is hiding things. She does it all the time.*

But that didn't stop him from trusting her. He nodded to OreSeur, and they left the carriage. Elend waved his guards back as he approached a dilapidated building. It had probably once been a poor merchant's shop—a place run by extremely low nobility, selling meager necessities to skaa workers in exchange for food tokens, which could in turn be exchanged for money from the Lord Ruler.

The building was in a sector that Elend's fuel-collection crews hadn't reached yet. It was obvious, however, that it hadn't seen a lot of use lately. It had been ransacked long ago, and the ash coating the floor was a good four inches deep. A small trail of footprints led toward a back stairwell.

"What is this place?" Elend asked with a frown.

OreSeur shrugged a pair of dog's shoulders.

"Then how did you know she was here?"

"I followed her last night, Your Majesty," OreSeur said. "I saw the general direction she went. After that, it was simply a process of careful searching."

Elend frowned. "That still must have taken some pretty mean tracking abilities, kandra."

"These bones have unusually keen senses."

Elend nodded. The stairwell led up into a long hallway with several rooms at the ends. Elend began to walk down the hallway, then paused. To one side, a panel on the wall had been slid back, revealing a small cubby. He could hear movement within.

"Vin?" he asked, poking his head into the cubby.

There was a small room hidden behind the wall, and Vin sat on the far side. The room—more of a nook—was only a few feet across, and even Vin wouldn't have been able to stand up in it. She didn't respond to him. She simply sat, leaning against the far wall, head turned away from him.

Elend crawled inside the small chamber, getting ash on his knees. It was barely large enough for him to enter without bumping into her. "Vin? Are you all right?"

She sat, twisting something between her fingers. And she was looking at the wall—looking through a narrow hole. Elend could see sunlight shining through.

It's a peephole, he realized. *To watch the street below. This isn't a shop—it's a thieving hideout. Or, it was.*

"I used to think Camon was a terrible man," Vin said quietly.

Elend paused, on hands and knees. Finally, he settled back into a cramped seated position. At least Vin didn't look hurt. "Camon?" he asked. "Your old crewleader, before Kelsier?"

Vin nodded. She turned away from the slit, sitting with her arms around her knees. "He beat people, he killed those who disagreed with him. Even among street thugs, he was brutal."

Elend frowned.

"But," Vin said quietly, "I doubt he killed as many people during his entire life as I killed last night."

Elend closed his eyes. Then he opened them and shuffled a little closer, laying a hand on Vin's shoulder. "Those were enemy soldiers, Vin."

"I was like a child in a room full of bugs," Vin whispered. He could finally see what was in her fingers. It was her earring, the simple bronze stud that she always wore. She looked down at it, twisting it between her fingers.

"Did I ever tell you how I got this?" she asked. He shook his head. "My mother gave it to me," she said. "I don't remember it happening—Reen told me about it. My mother . . . she heard voices sometimes. She killed my baby sister, slaughtered her. And that same day she gave me this, one of her own earrings. As if . . . as if choosing me over my sister. A punishment for one, a twisted present for another."

Vin shook her head. "My entire life has been death, Elend. Death of my sister, the death of Reen. Crewmembers dead around me, Kelsier falling to the Lord Ruler, then my own spear in the Lord Ruler's chest. I try to protect, and tell myself that I'm escaping it all. And then . . . I do something like I did last night."

Not certain what else to do, Elend pulled her close. She was stiff, however. "You had a good reason for what you did," he said.

"No I didn't," Vin said. "I just wanted to hurt them. I wanted to scare them and make them leave you alone. It sounds childish, but that's how I felt."

"It's not childish, Vin," Elend said. "It was good strategy. You gave our enemies a show of force. You frightened away one of our major opponents, and now my father will be even more afraid to attack. You've bought us more time!"

"Bought it with the lives of hundreds of men."

"Enemy soldiers who marched into our city," Elend said. "Men who were protecting a tyrant who oppresses his people."

"That's the same rationale Kelsier used," Vin said quietly, "when he killed noblemen and their guards. He said they were upholding the Final Empire, so they deserved to die. He frightened me."

Elend didn't know what to say to that.

"It was like he thought himself a god," Vin whispered. "Taking life, giving life, where he saw fit. I don't want to be like him, Elend. But, everything seems to be pushing me in that direction."

"I . . ." *You're not like him,* he wanted to say. It was true, but the words wouldn't come out. They rang hollow to him.

Instead, he pulled Vin close, her shoulder up against his chest, head beneath his chin. "I wish I knew the right things to say, Vin," he whispered. "Seeing you like this makes every protective instinct inside of me twist. I want to make it better—I want to fix everything—but I don't know how. Tell me what to do. Just tell me how I can help!"

She resisted his embrace a little at first, but then sighed quietly and slid her arms around him, holding him tightly. "You can't help with this," she said softly. "I have to do it alone. There are . . . decisions I have to make."

He nodded. "You'll make the right ones, Vin."

"You don't even know what I'm deciding."

"It doesn't matter," he said. "I know I can't help—I couldn't even hold on to my own throne. You're ten times as capable as I am."

She squeezed his arm. "Don't say things like that. Please?"

He frowned at the tension in her voice, then nodded. "All right. But, either way, I trust you, Vin. Make your decisions—I'll support you."

She nodded, relaxing a bit beneath his arms. "I think . . ." she said. "I think I have to leave Luthadel."

"Leave? And go where?"

"North," she said. "To Terris."

Elend sat back, resting against the wooden wall. *Leave?*

he thought with a twisting feeling. *Is this what I've earned by being so distracted lately?*

Have I lost her?

And yet, he'd just told her that he'd support her decisions. "If you feel you have to go, Vin," he found himself saying, "then you should do so."

"If I were to leave, would you go with me?"

"Now?"

Vin nodded, head rubbing his chest.

"No," he finally said. "I couldn't leave Luthadel, not with those armies still out there."

"But the city rejected you."

"I know," he said, sighing. "But . . . I can't leave them, Vin. They rejected me, but I won't abandon them."

Vin nodded again, and something told him this was the answer she had expected.

Elend smiled. "We're a mess, aren't we?"

"Hopeless," she said softly, sighing as she finally pulled away from him. She seemed so tired. Outside the room, Elend could hear footsteps. OreSeur appeared a moment later, poking his head into the hidden chamber.

"Your guards are growing restless, Your Majesty," he said to Elend. "They will soon come looking for you."

Elend nodded, shuffling over to the exit. Once in the hallway, he offered a hand to help Vin out. She took the hand, crawling out, then stood and dusted off her clothing—her typical shirt and trousers.

Will she ever go back to dresses now? he wondered.

"Elend," she said, fishing in a pocket. "Here, you can spend this, if you want."

She opened up her hand, dropping a bead into his hand.

"Atium?" he asked incredulously. "Where did you get it?"

"From a friend," she said.

"And you didn't burn it last night?" Elend asked. "When you were fighting all those soldiers?"

"No," Vin said. "I swallowed it, but I didn't end up needing it, so I forced it back up."

Lord Ruler! Elend thought. *I didn't even consider that she didn't have atium. What could she have done if she'd burned that bit?* He looked up at her. "Some reports say that there's another Mistborn in the city."

"There is. Zane."

Elend dropped the bead back into her hand. "Then keep this. You might need it to fight him."

"I doubt that," Vin said quietly.

"Keep it anyway," Elend said. "This is worth a small fortune—but we'd need a very *large* fortune to make any difference now. Besides, who would buy it? If I used it to bribe Straff or Cett, they'd only become more certain I'm holding atium against them."

Vin nodded, then glanced at OreSeur. "Keep this," she said, handing the bead toward him. "It's big enough that another Allomancer could pull it off me if he wanted."

"I will guard it with my life, Mistress," OreSeur said, his shoulder splitting open to make room for the bit of metal.

Vin turned to join Elend as they walked down the steps, moving to meet with the guards below.

I know what I have memorized. I know what is now repeated by the other Worldbringers.

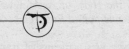

45

"THE HERO OF AGES WON'T be Terris," Tindwyl said, scribbling a note at the bottom of their list.

"We knew that already," Sazed said. "From the log-book."

"Yes," Tindwyl said, "but Alendi's account was only a reference—a thirdhand mention of the effects of a prophecy. I found someone quoting the prophecy itself."

"Truly?" Sazed asked, excited. "Where?"

"The biography of Helenntion," Tindwyl said. "One of the last survivors of the Council of Khlennium."

"Write it for me," Sazed said, scooting his chair a bit closer to hers. He had to blink a few times as she wrote, his head clouding for a moment from fatigue.

Stay alert! he told himself. *There isn't much time left. Not much at all. . . .*

Tindwyl was doing a little better than he, but her wakefulness was obviously beginning to run out, for she was starting to droop. He'd taken a quick nap during the night, rolled up on her floor, but she had carried on. As far as he could tell, she'd been awake for over a week straight.

There was much talk of the Rabzeen, during those days, Tindwyl wrote. *Some said he would come to fight the Conqueror. Others said he was the Conqueror. Helenntion didn't make his thoughts on the matter known to me. The Rabzeen is said to be "He who is not of his people, yet fulfills all of their wishes." If this is the case, then perhaps the Conqueror is the one. He is said to have been of Khlennium.*

She stopped there. Sazed frowned, reading the words again. Kwaan's last testimony—the rubbing Sazed had taken at the Conventical of Seran—had proven useful in more than one way. It had provided a key.

It wasn't until years later that I became convinced that he was the Hero of Ages, Kwaan had written. *Hero of Ages: the one called Rabzeen in Khlennium, the Anamnesor. . . .*

The rubbing was a means of translation—not between languages, but between synonyms. It made sense that there would be other names for the Hero of Ages; a figure so important, so surrounded by lore, would have many titles. Yet, so much had been lost from those days. The Rabzeen and the Anamnesor were both mythological figures vaguely familiar to Sazed—but they were only two among hosts. Until the discovery of the rubbing, there had been no way to connect their names to the Hero of Ages.

Now Tindwyl and he could search their metalminds with open eyes. Perhaps, in the past, Sazed had read this very passage from Helenntion's biography; he had at least skimmed many of the older records, searching for religious references. Yet, he would never have been able to realize that the passage was referring to the Hero of Ages, a figure from Terris lore that the Khlenni people had renamed into their own tongue.

"Yes . . ." he said slowly. "This is good, Tindwyl. Very good." He reached over, laying his hand on hers.

"Perhaps," she said, "though it tells us nothing new."

"Ah, but the wording might be important, I think," Sazed said. "Religions are often very careful with their writings."

"Especially prophecies," Tindwyl said, frowning just a bit. She was not fond of anything that smacked of superstition or soothsaying.

"I would have thought," Sazed noted, "that you would no longer have this prejudice, considering our current enterprise."

"I gather information, Sazed," she said. "Because of what it says of people, and because of what the past can teach us. However, there is a reason I took to studying history as opposed to theology. I don't approve of perpetuating lies."

"Is that what you think I do when I teach of religions?" he asked in amusement.

Tindwyl looked toward him. "A bit," she admitted. "How can you teach the people to look toward the gods of the dead, Sazed? Those religions did their people little good, and their prophecies are now dust."

"Religions are an expression of hope," Sazed said. "That hope gives people strength."

"Then you don't believe?" Tindwyl asked. "You just give the people something to trust, something to delude themselves?"

"I would not call it so."

"Then you think the gods you teach of *do* exist?"

"I . . . think that they deserved to be remembered."

"And their prophecies?" Tindwyl said. "I see scholarly value in what we do—the bringing to light of facts from the past could give us information about our current problems. Yet, this soothsaying for the future is, at its core, foolishness."

"I would not say that," Sazed said. "Religions are promises—promises that there is something watching over us, guiding us. Prophecies, therefore, are natural extensions of the hopes and desires of the people. Not foolishness at all."

"So, your interest is purely academic?" Tindwyl said.

"I wouldn't say that."

Tindwyl studied him, watching his eyes. She frowned slowly. "You believe it, don't you?" she asked. "You believe that this girl is the Hero of Ages."

"I have not yet decided," Sazed said.

"How can you even consider such a thing, Sazed?" Tindwyl asked. "Don't you see? Hope is a good thing—a wonderful thing—but you must have hope in something appropriate. If you perpetuate the dreams of the past, then you stifle your own dreams of the future."

"What if the past dreams are worthy of being remembered?"

Tindwyl shook her head. "Look at the odds, Sazed. What are the chances we would end up where we are, studying this rubbing, in the very same household as the Hero of Ages?"

"Odds are irrelevant when a foretelling is involved."

Tindwyl closed her eyes. "Sazed . . . I think religion is a good thing, and belief is a good thing, but it is foolishness to look for guidance in a few vague phrases. Look at what happened last time someone assumed they had found this Hero. The Lord Ruler, the Final Empire, was the result."

"Still, I will hope. If you did not believe the prophecies, then why work so hard to discover information about the Deepness and the Hero?"

"It's simple," Tindwyl said. "We are obviously facing a danger that has come before—a recurring problem, like a plague that plays itself out, only to return again centuries later. The ancient people knew of this danger, and had information about it. That information, naturally, broke down and became legends, prophecies, and even religions. There will be, then, clues to our situation hidden in the past. This is not a matter of soothsaying, but of research."

Sazed lay his hand on hers. "I think, perhaps, that this is something we cannot agree upon. Come, let us return to our studies. We must use the time we have left."

"We should be all right," Tindwyl said, sighing and reaching to tuck a bit of hair back into her bun. "Apparently, your Hero scared off Lord Cett last night. The maid who brought breakfast was speaking of it."

"I know of the event," Sazed said.

"Then things are growing better for Luthadel."

"Yes," Sazed said. "Perhaps."

She frowned. "You seem hesitant."

"I do not know," he said, glancing down. "I do not feel that Cett's departure is a good thing, Tindwyl. Something is very wrong. We need to be finished with these studies."

Tindwyl cocked her head. "How soon?"

"We should try to be done tonight, I think," Sazed said, glancing toward the pile of unbound sheets they had stacked on the table. That stack contained all the notes, ideas, and connections that they'd made during their furious bout of study. It was a book, of sorts—a guidebook that told of the Hero of Ages and the Deepness. It was a good document—incredible, even, considering the time they'd been given. It was not comprehensive. It was, however, probably the most important thing he'd ever written.

Even if he wasn't certain why.

"Sazed?" Tindwyl asked, frowning. "What is this?" She reached to the stack of papers, pulling out a sheet that was slightly askew. As she held it up, Sazed was shocked to see that a chunk from the bottom right corner had been torn off.

"Did you do this?" she asked.

"No," Sazed said. He accepted the paper. It was one of the transcriptions of the rubbing; the tear had removed the last sentence or so. There was no sign of the missing piece.

Sazed looked up, meeting Tindwyl's confused gaze. She turned, shuffling through a stack of papers to the side. She pulled out another copy of the transcription and held it up.

Sazed felt a chill. The corner was missing.

"I referenced this yesterday," Tindwyl said quietly. "I

haven't left the room save for a few minutes since then, and you were always here."

"Did you leave last night?" Sazed asked. "To visit the privy while I slept?"

"Perhaps. I don't remember."

Sazed sat for a moment, staring at the page. The tear was eerily similar in shape to the one from their main stack. Tindwyl, apparently thinking the same thing, laid it over its companion. It matched perfectly; even the smallest ridges in the tears were identical. Even if they'd been torn lying right on top of one another, the duplication wouldn't have been so perfect.

Both of them sat, staring. Then they burst into motion, riffling through their stacks of pages. Sazed had four copies of the transcription. All were missing the same exact chunk.

"Sazed . . ." Tindwyl said, her voice shaking just a bit. She held up a sheet of paper—one that had only half of the transcription on it, ending near the middle of the page. A hole had been torn directly in the middle of the page, removing the exact same sentence.

"The rubbing!" Tindwyl said, but Sazed was already moving. He left his chair, rushing to the trunk where he stored his metalminds. He fumbled with the key at his neck, pulling it off and unlocking the trunk. He threw it open, removed the rubbing, then unfolded it delicately on the ground. He withdrew his fingers suddenly, feeling almost as if he'd been bitten, as he saw the tear at the bottom. The same sentence, removed.

"How is this possible?" Tindwyl whispered. "How could someone know so much of our work—so much of us?"

"And yet," Sazed said, "how could they know so little of our abilities? I have the entire transcription stored in my metalmind. I can remember it right now."

"What does the missing sentence say?"

" 'Alendi must not reach the Well of Ascension; he must not be allowed to take the power for himself.' "

"Why remove this sentence?" Tindwyl asked.

Sazed stared at the rubbing. *This seems impossible. . . .*

A noise sounded at the window. Sazed spun, reaching

reflexively into his pewtermind and increasing his strength. His muscles swelled, his robe growing tight.

The shutters swung open. Vin crouched on the sill. She paused as she saw Sazed and Tindwyl—who had also apparently tapped strength, growing to have almost masculine bulk.

"Did I do something wrong?" Vin asked.

Sazed smiled, releasing his pewtermind. "No, child," he said. "You simply startled us." He met Tindwyl's eye, and she began to gather up the ripped pieces of paper. Sazed folded up the rubbing; they would discuss it further later.

"Have you seen anyone spending too much time around my room, Lady Vin?" Sazed asked as he replaced the rubbing. "Any strangers—or even any particular guards?"

"No," Vin said, climbing into the room. She walked barefoot, as usual, and she didn't wear her mistcloak; she rarely did in the daytime. If she had fought the night before, she had changed clothing, for there were no stains of blood—or even sweat—on this outfit. "Do you want me to watch for anyone suspicious?" she asked.

"Yes, please," Sazed said, locking the chest. "We fear that someone has been riffling through our work, though why they would wish to do so is confusing."

Vin nodded, remaining where she was as Sazed returned to his seat. She regarded him and Tindwyl for a moment.

"I need to talk to you, Sazed," Vin said.

"I can spare a few moments, I think," Sazed said. "But, I must warn you that my studies are very pressing."

Vin nodded, then glanced at Tindwyl. Finally, she sighed, rising. "I guess I will go and see about lunch, then."

Vin relaxed slightly as the door closed; then she moved over to the table, sitting down in Tindwyl's chair, pulling her legs up before her on the wooden seat.

"Sazed," she asked, "how do you know if you're in love?"

Sazed blinked. "I . . . I do not think *I* am one to speak on this topic, Lady Vin. I know very little about it."

"You always say things like that," Vin said. "But really, you're an expert on just about everything."

Sazed chuckled. "In this case, I assure you that my insecurity is heartfelt, Lady Vin."

"Still, you've got to know something."

"A bit, perhaps," Sazed said. "Tell me, how do you feel when you are with young Lord Venture?"

"I want him to hold me," Vin said quietly, turning to the side, looking out the window. "I want him to talk to me, even if I don't understand what he's saying. Anything to keep him there, with me. I want to be better because of him."

"That seems like a very good sign, Lady Vin."

"But . . ." Vin glanced down. "I'm not good for him, Sazed. He's scared of me."

"Scared?"

"Well, he's at least uncomfortable with me. I saw the look in his eyes when he saw me fighting on the day of the Assembly attack. He stumbled away from me, Sazed, horrified."

"He'd just seen a man slain," Sazed said. "Lord Venture is somewhat innocent in these matters, Lady Vin. It wasn't you, I think—it was simply a natural reaction to the horror of death."

"Either way," Vin said, glancing back out the window. "I don't want him to see me that way. I want to be the girl he needs—the girl who can support his political plans. The girl who can be pretty when he needs her on his arm, and who can comfort him when he's frustrated. Except, that's not me. You're the one who trained me to act like a courtly woman, Saze, but we both know that I wasn't all that good at it."

"And Lord Venture fell in love with you," Sazed said, "because you *didn't* act like the other women. Despite Lord Kelsier's interference, despite your knowledge that all noblemen were our enemies, Elend fell in love with you."

"I shouldn't have let him," Vin said quietly. "I need to stay away from him, Saze—for his own good. That way, he can fall in love with someone else. Someone who is a better match for him. Someone who doesn't go kill a hundred people when she gets frustrated. Someone who deserves his love."

Sazed rose, robes swishing as he stepped to Vin's chair. He stooped down, placing his head even with hers, laying a hand on her shoulder. "Oh, child. When will you stop worrying and simply let yourself be loved?"

Vin shook her head. "It's not that easy."

"Few things are. Yet, I tell you this, Lady Vin. Love must be allowed to flow both ways—if it is not, then it is not truly love, I think. It is something else. Infatuation, perhaps? Either way, there are some of us who are far too quick to make martyrs of ourselves. We stand at the side, watching, thinking that we do the right thing by inaction. We fear pain—our own, or that of another."

He squeezed her shoulder. "But . . . is that love? Is it love to assume for Elend that he has no place with you? Or, is it love to let him make his own decision in the matter?"

"And if I'm wrong for him?" Vin asked.

"You must love him enough to trust his wishes, even if you disagree with them. You must respect him—no matter how wrong you think he may be, no matter how poor you think his decisions, you must respect his desire to make them. Even if one of them includes loving you."

Vin smiled slightly, but she still seemed troubled. "And . . ." she said very slowly, "if there is someone else? For me?"

Ah. . . .

She tensed immediately. "You mustn't tell Elend I said that."

"I won't," Sazed promised. "Who is this other man?"

Vin shrugged. "Just . . . someone more like myself. The kind of man I *should* be with."

"Do you love him?"

"He's strong," Vin said. "He makes me think of Kelsier."

So there is *another Mistborn,* Sazed thought. In this matter, he knew he should remain unbiased. He didn't know enough about this second man to make a judgment—and Keepers were supposed to give information, but avoid specific advice.

Sazed, however, had never been very good at following that rule. He didn't know this other Mistborn, true, but he *did* know Elend Venture. "Child," he said, "Elend is the best of men, and you have been so much happier since you've been with him."

"But, he's really the first man I loved," Vin said quietly. "How do I know it's right? Shouldn't I pay more attention to the man who is a better match for me?"

"I don't know, Lady Vin. I honestly don't know. I warned you of my ignorance in this area. But, can you really hope to find a better person than Lord Elend?"

She sighed. "It's all so frustrating. I should be worrying about the city and the Deepness, not which man to spend my evenings with!"

"It is hard to defend others when our own lives are in turmoil," Sazed said.

"I just have to decide," Vin said, standing, walking over toward the window. "Thank you, Sazed. Thank you for listening . . . thank you for coming back to the city."

Sazed nodded, smiling. Vin shot backward out the open window, shoving herself against some bit of metal. Sazed sighed, rubbing his eyes as he walked over to the room's door and pulled it open.

Tindwyl stood outside, arms crossed. "I think I would feel more comfortable in this city," she said, "if I didn't know that our Mistborn had the volatile emotions of a teenage girl."

"Lady Vin is more stable than you think," Sazed said.

"Sazed, I've raised some fifteen daughters," Tindwyl said, entering the room. "*No* teenage girl is stable. Some are just better at hiding it than others."

"Then, be glad she didn't hear you eavesdropping," Sazed said. "She is usually rather paranoid about such things."

"Vin has a weak spot regarding Terris people," Tindwyl said with a wave of her hand. "We can likely thank you for that. She seems to give great value to your advice."

"Such as it is."

"I thought what you said was very wise, Sazed," Tindwyl said, sitting. "You would have made an excellent father."

Sazed bowed his head in embarrassment, then moved over to sit down. "We should—"

A knock came at the door.

"Now what?" Tindwyl asked.

"Did you not order us lunch?"

Tindwyl shook her head. "I never even left the hallway."

A second later, Elend poked his head into the room. "Sazed? Could I talk to you for a bit?"

"Of course, Lord Elend," Sazed said, rising.

"Great," Elend said, striding into the room. "Tindwyl, you are excused."

She rolled her eyes, shooting an exasperated glance at Sazed, but stood and walked from the room.

"Thank you," Elend said as she shut the door. "Please, sit," he said, waving to Sazed.

Sazed did so, and Elend took a deep breath, standing with hands clasped behind his back. He had gone back to his white uniforms, and stood with a commanding posture despite his obvious frustration.

Someone stole my friend the scholar away, Sazed thought, *and left a king in his place.* "I assume this is about Lady Vin, Lord Elend?"

"Yes," Elend said, beginning to pace, gesturing with one hand as he spoke. "She doesn't make any sense, Sazed. I expect that—hell, I count on it. She's not just female, she's *Vin*. But, I'm left unsure how to react. One minute she seems warm to me—like we were before this mess hit the city—and the next minute she's distant and stiff."

"Perhaps she's just confused herself."

"Perhaps," Elend agreed. "But shouldn't at least *one* of us know what is going on in our relationship? Honestly, Saze, sometimes I just think we're too different to be together."

Sazed smiled. "Oh, I don't know about that, Lord Elend. You may be surprised at how similarly the two of you think."

"I doubt that," Elend said, continuing to pace. "She's Mistborn; I'm just a regular man. She grew up on the streets; I grew up in a mansion. She is wily and clever; I'm book-learned."

"She is extremely competent, and so are you," Sazed said. "She was oppressed by her brother, you by your father. Both of you hated the Final Empire, and fought it. And both of you think far too much about what *should* be, rather than what is."

Elend paused, looking at Sazed. "What does that mean?"

"It means that I think you two are right for each other," Sazed said. "I am not supposed to make such judgments, and truly, this is just the opinion of a man who hasn't seen much of you two in the last few months. But, I believe it to be true."

"And our differences?" Elend asked.

"At first glance, the key and the lock it fits may seem very different," Sazed said. "Different in shape, different in function, different in design. The man who looks at them without knowledge of their true nature might think them opposites, for one is meant to open, and the other to keep closed. Yet, upon closer examination, he might see that without one, the other becomes useless. The wise man then sees that both lock and key were created for the same purpose."

Elend smiled. "You need to write a book sometime, Sazed. That's as profound as anything I've read."

Sazed flushed, but glanced at the stack of papers on the desktop. Would they be his legacy? He wasn't certain if they were profound, but they did represent the most cohesive attempt that he'd ever made at writing something original. True, most of the sheets contained quotes or references, but a great deal of the text also included his thoughts and annotations.

"So," Elend said, "what should I do?"

"About Lady Vin?" Sazed asked. "I would suggest simply giving her—and yourself—a little more time."

"Time is at a premium these days, Saze."

"When is it not?"

"When your city isn't besieged by two armies," Elend said, "one of them led by a megalomaniac tyrant, the other by a reckless fool."

"Yes," Sazed said slowly. "Yes, I think you may be right. I should return to my studies."

Elend frowned. "What are you working on, anyway?"

"Something that has little relevance to your current problem, I fear," Sazed said. "Tindwyl and I are collecting and compiling references about the Deepness and the Hero of Ages."

"The Deepness . . . Vin mentioned it, too. You really think it might return?"

"I think it has returned, Lord Elend," Sazed said. "It never left, really. I believe the Deepness was—*is*—the mists."

"But, why . . ." Elend said, then held up a hand. "I'll read your conclusions when you have finished. I can't afford to get sidetracked right now. Thank you, Sazed, for your advice."

Yes, a king indeed, Sazed thought.

"Tindwyl," Elend said, "you may come back in now. Sazed, good day." Elend turned toward the door, and it cracked open slowly. Tindwyl strode in, hiding her embarrassment.

"How did you know I was out there?" she asked.

"I guessed," Elend said. "You're as bad as Vin. Anyway, good day, both of you."

Tindwyl frowned as he left; then she glanced at Sazed.

"You really did do a fine job with him," Sazed said.

"Too fine a job," Tindwyl said, sitting. "I actually think that if the people had let him remain in command, he might have found a way to save the city. Come, we must return to work—this time, I actually did send someone for lunch, so we should get as much done as possible before it arrives."

Sazed nodded, seating himself and picking up his pen. Yet, he found it difficult to focus on his work. His mind kept returning to Vin and Elend. He wasn't certain why it was so important to him that they make their relationship work. Perhaps it was simply because they were both friends of his, and he wished to see them happy.

Or perhaps there was something else. Those two were the best Luthadel had to offer. The most powerful Mistborn of the skaa underground, and the most noble leader of the aristocratic culture. They needed each other, and the Final Empire needed them both.

Plus, there was the work he was doing. The specific pronoun used in much of the Terris prophetic language was gender neutral. The actual word meant "it," though it was commonly translated into modern tongues as "he." Yet each "he" in his book could also have been written as "she." If Vin really was the Hero of Ages . . .

I need to find a way to get them out of the city, Sazed thought, a sudden realization washing over him. *Those two must not be here when Luthadel falls.*

He put aside his notes and immediately began writing a quick series of letters.

The two are not the same.

46

BREEZE COULD SMELL INTRIGUE FROM two streets away. Unlike many of his fellow thieves, he hadn't grown up impoverished, nor had he been forced to live in the underground. He'd grown up in a place far more cutthroat: an aristocratic court. Fortunately, the other crewmembers didn't treat him differently because of his full-blooded noble origin.

That was, of course, because they didn't know about it.

His upbringing afforded him certain understandings. Things that he doubted any skaa thief, no matter how competent, knew. Skaa intrigue made a brutal kind of sense; it was a matter of naked life and death. You betrayed your allies for money, for power, or to protect yourself.

In the noble courts, intrigue was more abstract. Betrayals wouldn't often end with either party dead, but the ramifications could span generations. It was a game—so much of one, in fact, that the young Breeze had found the open brutality of the skaa underground to be refreshing.

He sipped his warm mug of mulled wine, eyeing the note in his fingers. He'd come to believe that he wouldn't have to worry about intracrew conspiracies anymore: Kelsier's crew was an almost sickeningly tight group, and Breeze did everything within his Allomantic powers to keep it that way. He'd seen what infighting could do to a family.

That was why he was so surprised to receive this letter. Despite its mock innocence, he could easily pick out the signs. The hurried pace of the writing, smudged in places but not rewritten. Phrases like "No need to tell others of this" and "do not wish to cause alarm." The extra drops of sealing wax, spread gratuitously on the lip of the letter, as if to give extra protection against prying eyes.

There was no mistaking the tone of the missive. Breeze had been invited to a conspiratorial conference. But, why in the Lord Ruler's name would *Sazed,* of all people, want to meet in secret?

Breeze sighed, pulling out his dueling cane and using it to steady himself. He grew light-headed sometimes when he stood; it was a minor malady he'd always had, though it seemed to have grown worse during the last few years. He glanced over his shoulder as his vision cleared, toward where Allrianne slept in his bed.

I should probably feel more guilty about her, he thought, smiling despite himself and reaching to put his vest and jacket on over his trousers and shirt. *But . . . well, we're all going to be dead in a few days anyway.* An afternoon spent speaking with Clubs could certainly put one's life in perspective.

Breeze wandered out into the hallway, making his way though the gloomy, inadequately lit Venture passageways. *Honestly,* he thought, *I understand the value in saving lamp oil, but things are depressing enough right now without the dark corridors.*

The meeting place was only a few short twists away. Breeze located it easily because of the two soldiers standing watch outside the door. Demoux's men—soldiers who reported to the captain religiously, as well as vocationally.

Interesting, Breeze thought, remaining hidden in the side hallway. He quested out with his Allomantic powers and Soothed the men, taking away their relaxation and certainty, leaving behind anxiety and nervousness. The guards began to grow restless, shuffling. Finally, one turned and opened the door, checking on the room inside. The motion gave Breeze a full view of the room's contents. Only one man sat within. Sazed.

Breeze stood quietly, trying to decide his next course of action. There was nothing incriminating in the letter; this couldn't all simply be a trap on Elend's part, could it? An obscure attempt at finding out which crewmembers would betray him and which wouldn't? Seemed like too distrustful a move for the good-natured boy. Besides, if that were the case, Sazed would have to try and get Breeze to do more than simply meet in a clandestine location.

The door swung closed, the soldier returning to his place. *I can trust Sazed, can't I?* Breeze thought. But, if that was the case, why the quiet meeting? Was Breeze overreacting?

No, the guards proved that Sazed worried about this meeting being discovered. It was suspicious. If it were anyone else, Breeze would have gone straight to Elend. But Sazed . . .

Breeze sighed, then wandered into the hallway, dueling cane clicking against the floor. *Might as well see what he has to say. Besides, if he* is *planning something devious, it'd almost be worth the danger to see it.* Despite the letter, despite the strange circumstances, Breeze had trouble imagining a Terrisman being involved in something that wasn't completely honest.

Perhaps the Lord Ruler had had the same problem.

Breeze nodded to the soldiers, Soothing away their anxiety and restoring them to a more temperate humor. There was another reason why he was willing to chance the meeting. Breeze was only just beginning to realize how dangerous his predicament was. Luthadel would soon fall. Every instinct he'd nurtured during thirty years in the underground was telling him to run.

That feeling made him more likely to take risks. The Breeze of a few years earlier would already have abandoned the city. *Damn you, Kelsier,* he thought as he pushed open the door.

Sazed looked up with surprise from his table. The room was sparse, with several chairs and only two lamps. "You're early, Lord Breeze," Sazed said, standing quickly.

"Of course I am," Breeze snapped. "I had to make certain this wasn't a trap of some sort." He paused. "This isn't a trap of some sort, right?"

"Trap?" Sazed asked. "What are you talking about?"

"Oh, don't sound so shocked," Breeze said. "This is no simple meeting."

Sazed wilted slightly. "It's . . . that obvious, is it?"

Breeze sat, laying his cane across his lap, and eyed Sazed tellingly, Soothing the man to make him feel a little more self-conscious. "You may have helped us overthrow the Lord Ruler, my dear man—but you have a lot to learn about being sneaky."

"I apologize," Sazed said, sitting. "I simply wanted to meet quickly, to discuss certain . . . sensitive issues."

"Well, I'd recommend getting rid of those guards," Breeze said. "They make the room stand out. Then, light a few more lamps and get us something to eat or drink. If Elend walks in—I assume it's Elend we're hiding from?"

"Yes."

"Well, if he comes and sees us sitting here in the dark, eyeing each other insidiously, he'll know something is up. The less natural the occasion, the more natural you want to appear."

"Ah, I see," Sazed said. "Thank you."

The door opened and Clubs hobbled in. He eyed Breeze, then Sazed, then wandered over toward a chair. Breeze glanced at Sazed—no surprise there. Clubs was obviously invited as well.

"Lose those guards," Clubs snapped.

"Immediately, Lord Cladent," Sazed said, standing and shuffling over to the door. He spoke briefly with the guards, then returned. As Sazed was sitting, Ham poked his head into the room, looking suspicious.

"Wait a minute," Breeze said. "How many people are coming to this secret meeting?"

Sazed gestured for Ham to sit. "All of the more . . . experienced members of the crew."

"You mean everyone but Elend and Vin," Breeze said.

"I did not invite Lord Lestibournes either," Sazed said. *Yes, but Spook isn't the one we're hiding from.*

Ham sat down hesitantly, shooting a questioning glance at Breeze. "So . . . why exactly are we meeting behind the backs of our Mistborn and our king?"

"King no longer," a voice noted from the door. Dockson walked in. "In fact, it could be argued that Elend isn't leader of this crew anymore. He fell into that position by happenstance—just like he fell into the throne."

Ham flushed. "I know you don't like him, Dox, but I'm not here to talk treason."

"There's no treason if there's no throne to betray," Dockson said, sitting. "What are we going to do—stay here and be servants in his house? Elend doesn't need us. Perhaps it's time to transfer our services to Lord Penrod."

"Penrod is a nobleman, too," Ham said. "You can't tell me you like him any better than you do Elend."

Dockson thumped the table quietly with his fist. "It's not about who I *like,* Ham. It's about seeing that this damn kingdom Kelsier threw at us remains standing! We've spent a year and a half cleaning up his mess. Do you want to see that work wasted?"

"Please, gentlemen," Sazed said, trying—without success—to break into the conversation.

"Work, Dox?" Ham said, flushed. "What work have you done? I haven't seen you do much of anything besides sit and complain every time someone offers a plan."

"Complain?" Dockson snapped. "Do you have any idea how much administrative work it has taken to keep this city from falling upon itself? What have you done, Ham? You refused to take command of the army. All you do is drink and spar with your friends!"

That's enough of that, Breeze thought, Soothing the men. *At this rate, we'll strangle each other before Straff can have us executed.*

Dockson settled back in his chair, waving a dismissive hand at Ham, who still sat red-faced. Sazed waited, obviously chagrined by the outbreak. Breeze Soothed away his insecurity. *You're in charge here, Sazed. Tell us what is going on.*

"Please," Sazed said. "I did not bring us together so that we could argue. I understand that you are all tense—that is understandable, considering the circumstances."

"Penrod is going to give our city to Straff," Ham said.

"That's better than letting him slaughter us," Dockson countered.

"Actually," Breeze said, "I don't think we have to worry about Straff slaughtering us."

"No?" Dockson asked, frowning. "Do you have some information you haven't been sharing with us, Breeze?"

"Oh, get over yourself, Dox," Ham snapped. "You've never been happy that you didn't end up in charge when Kell died. That's the real reason you never liked Elend, isn't it?"

Dockson flushed, and Breeze sighed, slapping both of them with a powerful blanket Soothing. They both jumped slightly, as if they'd been stung—though the sensation would be quite the opposite. Their emotions, once volatile, would suddenly have become numb and unresponsive.

Both looked at Breeze.

"Yes," he said, "of course I'm Soothing you. Honestly, I know Hammond is a bit immature—but you, Dockson?"

Dockson sat back, rubbing his forehead. "You can let go, Breeze," he said after a moment. "I'll keep my tongue."

Ham just grumbled, settling one hand on the table. Sazed watched the exchange with a little bit of shock.

This is what cornered men are like, my dear Terrisman, Breeze thought. *This is what happens when they lose hope. They might be able to keep up appearances in front of the soldiers, but put them alone with their friends . . .*

Sazed was a Terrisman; his entire life had been one of oppression and loss. But these men, Breeze himself included, were accustomed to success. Even against overwhelming odds, they were confident. They were the type of men who could go up against a god, and expect to win. They wouldn't deal well with losing. Of course, when losing meant death, who would?

"Straff's armies are getting ready to break camp," Clubs finally said. "He's doing it subtly, but the signs are there."

"So, he's coming for the city," Dockson said. "My men in Penrod's palace say the Assembly has been sending missive after missive to Straff, all but begging him to come take up occupation of Luthadel."

"He's not going to take the city," Clubs said. "At least, not if he's smart."

"Vin is still a threat," Breeze said. "And it doesn't look like Straff has a Mistborn to protect him. If he came into Luthadel, I doubt there is a single thing he could do to keep her from slitting his throat. So, he'll do something else."

Dockson frowned, and glanced at Ham, who shrugged.

"It's really quite simple," Breeze said, tapping the table with his dueling cane. "Why, even I figured it out." Clubs snorted at this. "If Straff makes it look like he's withdrawing, the koloss will probably attack Luthadel for him. They're too literal to understand the threat of a hidden army."

"If Straff withdraws," Clubs said, "Jastes won't be able to keep them from the city."

Dockson blinked. "But they'd . . ."

"Slaughter?" Clubs asked. "Yes. They'd pillage the richest sectors of the town—probably end up killing most of the noblemen in the city."

"Eliminating the men that Straff has been forced—against his will, knowing that man's pride—to work with," Breeze added. "In fact, there's a good chance the creatures will kill Vin. Can you imagine her not joining the fight if koloss broke in?"

The room fell silent.

"But, that doesn't really help Straff get the city," Dockson said. "He'll still have to fight the koloss."

"Yes," Clubs said, scowling. "But, they'll probably take down some of the city gates, not to mention level a lot of the homes. That will leave Straff with a clear field to attack a weakened foe. Plus, koloss don't strategize—for them, city walls won't be much help. Straff couldn't ask for a better setup."

"He'd be seen as a liberator," Breeze said quietly. "If he returns at the right time—after the koloss have broken into the city and fought the soldiers, but before they've done serious damage to the skaa quarter—he could free the people and establish himself as their protector, not their conqueror. Knowing how the people feel, I think they'd welcome him. Right now, a strong leader would mean more to them than coins in their pockets and rights in the Assembly."

As the group thought on this, Breeze eyed Sazed, who still sat quietly. He'd said so little; what was his game? Why gather the crew? Was he subtle enough to know that they'd simply needed to have an honest discussion like this, without Elend's morals to clutter things up?

"We could just let Straff have it," Dockson finally said. "The city, I mean. We could promise to call Vin off. If that is where this is heading anyway . . ."

"Dox," Ham said quietly, "what would Kell think, to hear you talk like that?"

"We could give the city to Jastes Lekal," Breeze said. "Perhaps he can be persuaded to treat the skaa with dignity."

"And let twenty thousand koloss into the city?" Ham asked. "Breeze, have you ever *seen* what those things can do?"

Dockson pounded the table. "I'm just giving options, Ham. What else are we going to do?"

"Fight," Clubs said. "And die."

The room fell silent again.

"You sure know how to kill a conversation, my friend," Breeze finally said.

"It needed to be said," Clubs muttered. "No use fooling yourselves anymore. We can't win a fight, and a fight is where this was always going. The city is going to get attacked. We're going to defend it. And we'll lose.

"You wonder if we should just give up. Well, we're not going to do that. Kell wouldn't let us, and so we won't let ourselves. We'll fight, and we'll die with dignity. Then, the city will burn—but we'll have said something. The Lord Ruler pushed us around for a thousand years, but now we skaa have pride. We fight. We resist. And we die."

"What was this all worth, then?" Ham said with frustration. "Why overthrow the Final Empire? Why kill the Lord Ruler? Why do anything, if it was just going to end like this? Tyrants ruling every dominance, Luthadel smashed to rubble, our crew dead?"

"Because," Sazed said softly, "someone had to begin it. While the Lord Ruler ruled, society could not progress. He kept a stabilizing hand on the empire, but it was an oppressive hand as well. Fashion stayed remarkably unchanged for a thousand years, the noblemen always trying to fit the Lord Ruler's ideals. Architecture and science did not progress, for the Lord Ruler frowned on change and invention.

"And the skaa could not be free, for he would not let them. However, killing him did not free our peoples, my friends. Only time will do that. It will take centuries, perhaps—centuries of fighting, learning, and growth. At the beginning, unfortunately and unavoidably, things will be very difficult. Worse even than they were beneath the Lord Ruler."

"And we die for nothing," Ham said with a scowl.

"No," Sazed said. "Not nothing, Lord Hammond. We will die to show that there are skaa who will not be bullied, who will not back down. This is a very important precedent, I think. In the histories and legends, this is the kind of event that inspires. If the skaa are ever to take rule of themselves, there will need to be sacrifices they can look to for motivation. Sacrifices like that of the Survivor himself."

The men sat in silence.

"Breeze," Ham said, "I could use a little more confidence right now."

"Of course," Breeze said, carefully Soothing away the man's anxiety and fear. His face lost some of its pallor, and he sat up a little straighter. Just for good measure, Breeze gave the rest of the crew a little of the same treatment.

"How long have you known?" Dockson asked Sazed.

"For some time now, Lord Dockson," Sazed said.

"But, you couldn't have known that Straff would pull back and give us to the koloss. Only Clubs figured that out."

"My knowledge was general, Lord Breeze," Sazed said in his even voice. "It did not relate to the koloss specifically. I have thought for some time that this city would fall. In all honesty, I am deeply impressed with your efforts. This people should long since have been defeated, I think. You have done something grand—something that will be remembered for centuries."

"Assuming anyone survives to tell the story," Clubs noted.

Sazed nodded. "That, actually, is why I called this gathering. There is little chance of those of us who remain in the city surviving—we will be needed to help with defenses, and if we do survive the koloss attack, Straff will try to execute us. However, it is not necessary for us *all* to remain in Luthadel for its fall—someone, perhaps, should be sent out to organize further resistance against the warlords."

"I won't leave my men," Clubs grumbled.

"Nor I," Ham said. "Though I *did* send my family to ground yesterday." The simple phrase meant that he'd had them leave, perhaps to hide in the city's underground, perhaps to escape through one of the passwalls. Ham wouldn't know—and that way he couldn't betray their location. Old habits died hard.

"If this city falls," Dockson said, "I'll be here with it. That's what Kell would expect. I'm not leaving."

"I'll go," Breeze said, looking at Sazed. "Is it too early to volunteer?"

"Um, actually, Lord Breeze," Sazed said, "I wasn't—"

Breeze held up a hand. "It's all right, Sazed. I believe it's obvious whom you think should be sent away. You didn't invite them to the meeting."

Dockson frowned. "We're going to defend Luthadel to the death, and you want to send away our only Mistborn?"

Sazed nodded his head. "My lords," he said softly, "the

men of this city will need our leadership. We gave them this city and put them in this predicament. We cannot abandon them now. But . . . there are great things at work in this world. Greater things than us, I think. I am convinced that Mistress Vin is part of them.

"Even if these matters are delusions on my part, then Lady Vin still *must* not be allowed to die in this city. She is the people's most personal and powerful link to the Survivor. She has become a symbol to them, and her skills as a Mistborn give her the best chance of being able to get away, then survive the attacks Straff will undoubtedly send. She will be a great value in the fight to come—she can move quickly and stealthily, and can fight alone, doing much damage, as she proved last night."

Sazed bowed his head. "My lords, I called you here today so that we could decide how to convince her to run, when the rest of us stay to fight. It will not be an easy task, I think."

"She won't leave Elend," Ham said. "He'll have to go, too."

"My thoughts as well, Lord Hammond," Sazed said.

Clubs chewed his lip in thought. "That boy won't be easily convinced to flee. He still thinks we can win this fight."

"And we may yet," Sazed said. "My lords, my purpose is not to leave you without any hope at all. But, the dire circumstances, the likelihood of success . . ."

"We know, Sazed," Breeze said. "We understand."

"There have to be others of the crew who can go," Ham said, looking down. "More than just the two."

"I would send Tindwyl with them," Sazed said. "She will carry to my people many discoveries of great importance. I also plan to send Lord Lestibournes. He would do little good in the battle, and his abilities as a spy could be of help to Lady Vin and Lord Elend as they try to rally resistance among the skaa.

"However, those four will not be the only ones who survive. Most of the skaa should be safe—Jastes Lekal seems to be able to control his koloss somehow. Even if he cannot, then Straff should arrive in time to protect the city's people."

"Assuming Straff is planning what Clubs thinks he is," Ham said. "He could actually be withdrawing, cutting his losses and leaving Luthadel behind."

"Either way," Clubs said. "Not many can get out. Neither Straff nor Jastes are likely to allow large groups of people to flee the city. Right now, confusion and fear in the streets will serve their purposes far better than depopulation. We might be able to get a few riders on horseback out—especially if one of those riders is Vin. The rest of the people will have to take their chances with the koloss."

Breeze felt his stomach turn. Clubs spoke so bluntly . . . so callously. But that was Clubs. He wasn't even really a pessimist; he just said the things that he didn't think others wanted to acknowledge.

Some of the skaa will survive to become slaves for Straff Venture, Breeze thought. *But those who fight—and those who have led the city this last year—are doomed. That includes me.*

It's true. This time there really is no way out.

"Well?" Sazed asked, hands spread before him. "Are we in agreement that these four should go?"

The members of the group nodded.

"Let us discuss, then," Sazed said, "and devise a plan for sending them away."

"We could just make Elend think that the danger isn't that great," Dockson said. "If he believes that the city is in for a long siege, he might be willing to go with Vin on a mission somewhere. They wouldn't realize what was happening back here until it was too late."

"A good suggestion, Lord Dockson," Sazed said. "I think, also, that we could work with Vin's concept of the Well of Ascension."

The discussion continued, and Breeze sat back, satisfied. *Vin, Elend, and Spook will survive,* he thought. *I'll have to convince Sazed to let Allrianne go with them.* He glanced around the room, noticing a release of tension in the postures of the others. Dockson and Ham seemed at peace, and even Clubs was nodding quietly to himself, looking satisfied as they talked through suggestions.

The disaster was still coming. But, somehow, the possibility that some would escape—the youngest crewmembers, the ones still inexperienced enough to hope—made everything else a little easier to accept.

Vin stood quietly in the mists, looking up at the dark spires, columns, and towers of Kredik Shaw. In her head, two sounds thumped. The mist spirit and the larger, vaster sound.

It was growing more and more demanding.

She continued forward, ignoring the thumps as she approached Kredik Shaw. The Hill of a Thousand Spires, once home of the Lord Ruler. It had been abandoned for well over a year, but no vagrants had made their home here. It was too ominous. Too terrible. Too much a reminder of *him*.

The Lord Ruler had been a monster. Vin remembered well the night, over a year before, when she had come to this palace intending to kill him. To do the job that Kelsier had unwittingly trained her to do. She had walked through this very courtyard, had passed guards at the doors before her.

And she had let them live. Kelsier would have just fought his way in. But Vin had talked them into leaving, into joining the rebellion. That act had saved her life when one of those very men, Goradel, had led Elend to the palace dungeons to help rescue Vin.

In a way, the Final Empire had been overthrown because she *hadn't* acted like Kelsier.

And yet, could she base future decisions upon a coincidence like that? Looking back, it seemed too perfectly allegorical. Like a neat little tale told to children, intended to teach a lesson.

Vin had never heard those tales as a child. And, she had survived when so many others had died. For every lesson like the one with Goradel, it seemed that there were a dozen that ended in tragedy.

And then there was Kelsier. He'd been right, in the end. His lesson was very different from the ones taught by the children's tales. Kelsier had been bold, even excited, when he executed those who stood in his path. Ruthless. He had looked toward the greater good; he'd always had his eyes focused on the fall of the empire, and the eventual rise of a kingdom like Elend's.

He had succeeded. Why couldn't she kill as he had, knowing she was doing her duty, never feeling guilt? She'd always been frightened by the edge of danger Kelsier had displayed. Yet, wasn't that very edge the thing that had let him succeed?

She passed into the tunnel-like corridors of the palace, feet and mistcloak tassels trailing marks in the dust. The mists, as always, remained behind. They didn't enter buildings—or, if they did, they usually didn't remain for long. With them, she left behind the mist spirit.

She had to make a decision. She didn't like the decision, but she was accustomed to doing things she didn't like. That was life. She hadn't wanted to fight the Lord Ruler, but she had.

It soon became too dark even for Mistborn eyes, and she had to light a lantern. When she did, she was surprised to see that her footsteps weren't the only ones in the dust. Apparently, someone else had been haunting the corridors. However, whoever it was, she didn't encounter them as she walked through the hallways.

She entered the chamber a few moments later. She wasn't sure what had drawn her to Kredik Shaw, let alone the hidden chamber at its center. It seemed, however, that she had been feeling a kinship with the Lord Ruler lately. Her walkings had brought her here, to a place she hadn't visited since that night when she'd slain the only God she'd ever known.

He had spent a lot of time in this hidden chamber, a place he had apparently built to remind him of his homeland. The chamber had a domed roof that arced overhead. The walls were filled with silvery murals and the floor was filled with metallic inlays. She ignored these, walking forward toward the room's central feature—a small stone building that had been built within the larger chamber.

It was here that Kelsier and his wife had been captured many years before, during Kelsier's first attempt to rob the

Lord Ruler. Mare had been murdered at the Pits. But Kelsier had survived.

It was here, in this same chamber, that Vin had first faced an Inquisitor, and had nearly been killed herself. It was also here that she had come months later in her first attempt to kill the Lord Ruler. She had been defeated that time, too.

She stepped into the small building-within-a-building. It had only one room. The floor had been torn up by Elend's crews, searching for the atium. The walls were still hung, however, with the trappings the Lord Ruler had left behind. She raised her lantern, looking at them.

Rugs. Furs. A small wooden flute. The things of his people, the Terris people, from a thousand years before. Why had he built his new city of Luthadel here, to the south, when his homeland—and the Well of Ascension itself— had been to the north? Vin had never really understood that.

Perhaps it came down to decision. Rashek, the Lord Ruler, had been forced to make a decision, too. He could have continued as he was, the pastoral villager. He would probably have had a happy life with his people.

But he had decided to become something more. In doing so, he had committed terrible atrocities. Yet, could she blame him for the decision itself? He had become what he'd thought he needed to be.

Her decision seemed more mundane, but she knew that other things—the Well of Ascension, the protection of Luthadel—could not be considered until she was certain what she wanted and who she was. And yet, standing in that room where Rashek had spent much of his time, thinking about the Well, the demanding thumps in her head sounded louder than they ever had before.

She had to decide. Elend was the one she wanted to be with. He represented peace. Happiness. Zane, however, represented what she felt she had to become. For the good of everyone involved.

The Lord Ruler's palace held no clues or answers for her. A few moments later, frustrated and baffled at why she had even come, she left it behind, walking back out into the mists.

Zane awoke to the sound of a tent spike being pounded in a specific rhythm. His reaction was immediate.

He burned steel and pewter. He always swallowed a new bit of each before sleeping. He knew the habit would probably kill him someday; metals were poisonous if allowed to linger.

Dying someday was better, in Zane's opinion, than dying today.

He flipped out of his cot, tossing his blanket toward the opening tent flap. He could barely see in the darkness of night. Even as he jumped, he heard something ripping. The tent walls being slit.

"Kill them!" God screamed.

Zane thumped to the ground and grabbed a handful of coins from the bowl beside his bed. He heard cries of surprise as he spun, throwing coins in a spinning spray around him.

He Pushed. Tiny plunks of sound thumped around him as coins met canvas, then continued on.

And men began to scream.

Zane fell to a crouch, waiting silently as the tent collapsed around him. Someone was thrashing the cloth to his right. He shot a few coins, and heard a satisfying grunt of pain. In the stillness, canvas resting atop him like a blanket, he heard footsteps running away.

He sighed, relaxing, and used a dagger to slice away the top of his tent. He emerged to a misty night. He'd gone to sleep later today than he usually did; it was probably near midnight. Time to be up anyway.

He strode across the fallen top of his tent—moving over to the now cloaked form of his cot—and cut a hole so he could reach through and pluck out the vial of metal he'd stored in a pocket beneath it. He downed the metals, and tin brought near light to his surroundings. Four men lay dying or dead around his tent. They were soldiers, of course—Straff's soldiers. The attack had come later than Zane had expected.

Straff trusts me more than I assumed. Zane stepped over the dead form of an assassin and cut his way into a storage chest, then pulled out his clothing. He changed quietly, then removed a small bag of coins from the chest. *It must have been the attack on Cett's keep,* he thought. *It finally convinced Straff that I was too dangerous to let live.*

Zane found his man working quietly beside a tent a short distance away, ostensibly testing the strength of a tent cord. He watched every night, paid to pound on a tent spike should anyone approach Zane's tent. Zane tossed the man a bag of coins, then moved off into the darkness, passing the canal waters with their supply barges on his way to Straff's tent.

His father had some few limitations. Straff was fine at large-scale planning, but the details—the subtleties—often got away from him. He could organize an army and crush his enemies. He, however, liked to play with dangerous tools. Like the atium mines at the Pits of Hathsin. Like Zane.

Those tools often ended up burning him.

Zane walked up to the side of Straff's tent, then ripped a hole in the canvas and strode in. Straff waited for him. Zane gave the man credit: Straff watched his death coming with defiance in his eyes. Zane stopped in the middle of the room, in front of Straff, who sat in his hard wooden chair.

"Kill him," God commanded.

Lamps burned in the corners, illuminating the canvas. The cushions and blankets in the corner were rumpled; Straff had taken one last romp with his favorite mistresses before sending his assassins. The king displayed his characteristic air of strong defiance, but Zane saw more. He saw a face too slick with sweat, and he saw hands trembling, as if from a disease.

"I have atium for you," Straff said. "Buried in a place only I know."

Zane stood quietly, staring at his father.

"I will proclaim you openly," Straff said. "Name you my heir. Tomorrow, if you wish."

Zane didn't respond. Straff continued to sweat.

"The city is yours," Zane finally said, turning away.

He was rewarded with a startled gasp from behind.

Zane glanced back. He'd never seen such a look of shock on his father's face. That alone was almost worth everything.

"Pull your men back, as you are planning," Zane said, "but don't return to the Northern Dominance. Wait for those koloss to invade the city, let them take down the defenses and kill the defenders. Then, you can sweep in and rescue Luthadel."

"But, Elend's Mistborn . . ."

"Will be gone," Zane said. "She's leaving with me, tonight. Farewell, Father." He turned and left through the slit he'd made.

"Zane?" Straff called from inside the tent.

Zane paused again.

"Why?" Straff asked, looking out through the slit. "I sent assassins to kill you. Why are you letting me live?"

"Because you're my father," Zane said. He turned away, looking into the mists. "A man shouldn't kill his father."

With that, Zane bid a final farewell to the man who had created him. A man whom Zane—despite his insanity, despite the abuse he'd known over the years—loved.

In the dark mists he threw down a coin and shot out over the camp. Outside its confines, he landed and easily located the bend in the canal he used as a marker. From the hollow of a small tree there, he pulled a bundle of cloth. A mistcloak, the first gift Straff had given him, years before when Zane had first Snapped. To him, it was too precious to wear around, to soil and use.

He knew himself a fool. However, he could not help how he felt. One could not use emotional Allomancy on one's self.

He unwrapped the mistcloak and withdrew the things it protected—several vials of metal and a pouch filled with beads. Atium.

He knelt there for a long moment. Then, he reached up

to his chest, feeling the space just above his rib cages. Where his heart thumped.

There was a large bump there. There always had been. He didn't think about it often; his mind seemed to get distracted when he did. It, however, was the real reason he never wore cloaks.

He didn't like the way that cloaks rubbed against the small point of the spike that stuck out of his back just between the shoulder blades. The head was against his sternum, and couldn't be seen beneath clothing.

"It is time to go," God said.

Zane stood, leaving the mistcloak behind. He turned from his father's camp, leaving behind that which he had known, instead seeking the woman who would save him.

Alendi believes as they do.

47

A PART OF VIN WASN'T EVEN bothered by how many people she had killed. That very indifference, however, terrified her.

She sat on her balcony a short time after her visit to the palace, the city of Luthadel lost in darkness before her. She sat in the mists—but knew better, now, than to think she'd find solace in their swirling patterns. Nothing was that simple anymore.

The mist spirit watched her, as always. It was too distant to see, but she could feel it. And, even stronger than the mist spirit, she could feel something else. That powerful thumping, growing louder and louder. It had once seemed distant, but no longer.

The Well of Ascension.

That was what it had to be. She could *feel* its power returning, flowing back into the world, demanding to be taken up and used. She kept finding herself glancing north, toward Terris, expecting to see something on the horizon. A burst of light, a blazing fire, a tempest of winds. Something. But there was just mist.

It seemed that she couldn't succeed at anything, lately. Love, protection, duty. *I've let myself get stretched too thin,* she thought.

There were so many things that demanded her attention, and she'd tried to give heed to them all. As a result, she had accomplished nothing. Her research about the Deepness and the Hero of Ages lay untouched for days, still arranged in piles scattered across her floor. She knew next to nothing about the mist spirit—only that it watched her, and that the logbook author had thought it dangerous. She hadn't dealt with the spy in her crew; she didn't know if Zane's claims regarding Demoux were true.

And Cett still lived. She couldn't even perform a proper massacre without stumbling halfway through. It was Kelsier's fault. He had trained her to take his place, but could anyone ever really do that?

Why do we always have to be someone else's knives? Zane's voice whispered in her head.

His words had seemed to make sense sometimes, but they had a flaw. Elend. Vin wasn't his knife—not really. He didn't want her to assassinate or kill. But, his ideals had left him without a throne, and had left his city surrounded by enemies. If she really loved Elend—if she really loved the people of Luthadel—wouldn't she have done more?

The pulsings thumped against her, like the beats of a drum the size of the sun. She burned bronze almost constantly now, listening to the rhythm, letting it pull her away. . . .

"Mistress?" OreSeur asked from behind. "What are you thinking about?"

"The end," Vin said quietly, staring outward.

Silence.

"The end of what, Mistress?"

"I don't know."

OreSeur padded over to the balcony, walking into the mists and sitting down beside her. She was getting to know him well enough that she could see concern in his canine eyes.

She sighed, shaking her head. "I just have decisions to make. And, no matter which choice I make, it will mean an end."

OreSeur sat for a moment, head cocked. "Mistress," he finally said, "that seems excessively dramatic to me."

Vin shrugged. "No advice for me, then?"

"Just make the decision," OreSeur said.

Vin sat for a moment, then smiled. "Sazed would have said something wise and comforting."

OreSeur frowned. "I fail to see why he should be part of this conversation, Mistress."

"He was my steward," Vin said. "Before he left, and before Kelsier switched your Contract to me."

"Ah," OreSeur said. "Well, I never did much like Terrismen, Mistress. Their self-important sense of subservience is very difficult to imitate—not to mention the fact that their muscles are far too stringy to taste good."

Vin raised an eyebrow. "You've imitated Terrismen? I didn't think there would be much cause for that—they weren't a very influential people during the days of the Lord Ruler."

"Ah," OreSeur said. "But they were always *around* influential people."

Vin nodded, standing. She walked back into her empty room and lit a lamp, extinguishing her tin. Mist carpeted the room, flowing over her stacks of paper, her feet throwing up puffs as she walked toward the bedroom.

She paused. That was a bit strange. Mist rarely remained long when it came indoors. Elend said it had to do with heat and enclosed spaces. Vin had always ascribed to it something more mystical. She frowned, watching it.

Even without tin, she heard the creak.

Vin spun. Zane stood on the balcony, his figure a black silhouette in the mists. He stepped forward, the mist following around him, as it did around anyone burning metals. And yet . . . it also seemed to be pushing *away* from him slightly.

OreSeur growled quietly.

"It's time," Zane said.

"Time for what?" Vin asked, setting the lamp down.

"To go," Zane said. "To leave these men and their armies. To leave the squabbling. To be free."

Free.

"I . . . don't know, Zane," Vin said, looking away.

She heard him step forward. "What do you owe him, Vin? He doesn't know you. He fears you. The truth is, he was never worthy of you."

"No," Vin said, shaking her head. "That's not it at all, Zane. You don't understand. I was never worthy of him. Elend deserves someone better. He deserves . . . someone who shares his ideals. Someone who thinks he was right to give up his throne. Someone who sees more honor—and less foolishness—in that."

"Either way," Zane said, stopping a short distance from her. "He cannot understand you. Us."

Vin didn't reply.

"Where would you go, Vin?" Zane asked. "If you weren't bound to this place, bound to him? If you were free, and could do whatever you wished, where would you go?"

The thumpings seemed louder. She glanced toward Ore-Seur, who sat quietly by the side wall, mostly in the dark. Why feel guilty? What did she have to prove to him?

She turned back to Zane. "North," she said. "To Terris."

"We can go there. Wherever you want. Location is irrelevant to me, as long as it is not this place."

"I can't abandon them," Vin said.

"Even if by doing so, you steal away Straff's only Mistborn?" Zane asked. "The trade is a good one. My father will know that I have disappeared, but he will not realize that you aren't still in Luthadel. He'll be even more afraid to attack. By giving yourself freedom, you'll also be leaving your allies with a precious gift."

Zane took her hand, forcing her to look at him. He did

look like Elend—like a hard version of Elend. Zane had been broken by life, just as she had been, but both had put themselves back together. Had the re-forming made them stronger, or more fragile?

"Come," Zane whispered. "You can save me, Vin."

A war is coming to the city, Vin thought with a chill. *If I stay, I will have to kill again.*

And slowly, she let him draw her away from her desk, toward the mists and the comforting darkness beyond. She reached up, pulling out a metal vial for the journey, and the motion caused Zane to spin suspiciously.

He has good instincts, Vin thought. *Instincts like my own. Instincts that won't let him trust, but that keep him alive.*

He relaxed as he saw what she was doing, and smiled and turned away again. Vin followed him, walking again, but she felt a sudden stab of fear. *This is it,* she thought. *After this, everything changes. The time for decisions has passed.*

And I made the wrong choice.

Elend wouldn't have jumped like that when I took out the vial.

She froze. Zane tugged on her wrist, but she didn't move. He turned toward her in the mists, frowning as he stood at the edge of her balcony.

"I'm sorry," Vin whispered, slipping her hand free. "I can't go with you."

"What?" Zane asked. "Why not?"

Vin shook her head, turning and walking back into the room.

"Tell me what it is!" Zane said, tone rising. "What is it about him that draws you? He isn't a great leader. He's not a warrior. He's no Allomancer or general. *What is it about him?*"

The answer came to her simply and easily. *Make your decisions—I'll support you in them.* "He trusts me," she whispered.

"What?" Zane asked incredulously.

"When I attacked Cett," Vin said, "the others thought I was acting irrationally—and they were right. But Elend told them I had a good reason, even if he didn't know what it was."

"So he's a fool," Zane said.

"When we spoke later," Vin continued, not looking at Zane, "I was cold to him. I think he knew that I was trying to decide whether to stay with him or not. And . . . he told me that he trusted my judgment. He'd support me if I chose to leave him."

"So he's also unappreciative," Zane said.

Vin shook her head. "No. He just loves me."

"I love you."

Vin paused, looking at Zane. He looked angry. Desperate, even. "I believe you. I still can't go with you."

"But *why*?"

"Because it would require leaving Elend," she said. "Even if I can't share his ideals, I can respect them. Even if I don't deserve him, I can be near him. I'm staying, Zane."

Zane stood quietly for a moment, mist falling around his shoulders. "I've failed, then."

Vin turned away from him. "No. It isn't that you've failed. You aren't flawed simply because I—"

He slammed into her, throwing her toward the mist-covered floor. Vin turned her head, shocked, as she crashed into the wooden floor, the breath going out of her.

Zane loomed above her, his face dark. "You were supposed to save me," he hissed.

Vin flared every metal she had in a sudden jolt. She shoved Zane backward and Pulled herself against the door hinges. She flew backward and hit the door hard, the wood cracking slightly, but she was too tense—too shocked—to feel anything but the thud.

Zane rose quietly, standing tall, dark. Vin rolled forward into a crouch. Zane was attacking her. Attacking her for real.

But . . . he . . .

"OreSeur!" Vin said, ignoring her mind's objections, whipping out her daggers. "Run away!"

The code given, she charged, trying to distract Zane's attention from the wolfhound. Zane sidestepped her attacks with a casual grace. Vin whipped a dagger toward his neck. It barely missed as Zane tipped his head backward. She struck at his side, at his arm, at his chest. Each strike missed.

She'd known he'd burn atium. She'd expected that. She skidded to a stop, looking at him. He hadn't even bothered to pull out his own weapons. He stood before her, face dark, mist a growing lake at his feet. "Why didn't you listen to me, Vin?" he asked. "Why force me to keep being Straff's tool? We both know where that must lead."

Vin ignored him. Gritting her teeth, she launched into an attack. Zane backhanded her indifferently, and she Pushed slightly against the deskmounts behind him—tossing herself backward, as if thrown by the force of his blow. She slammed into the wall, then slumped to the ground.

Directly beside the startled OreSeur.

He hadn't ôpened his shoulder to give her the atium. Hadn't he understood the code? "The atium I gave you," Vin hissed. "I need it. *Now*."

"Kandra," Zane said. "Come to me."

OreSeur met her eyes, and she saw something within them. Shame. He glanced away, then padded across the floor, mist up to his knees, as he joined Zane in the center of the room.

"No . . ." Vin whispered. "OreSeur—"

"You will no longer obey her commands, TenSoon," Zane said.

OreSeur bowed his head.

"The Contract, OreSeur!" Vin said, climbing to her knees. "You *must* obey my orders!"

"My servant, Vin," Zane said. "My Contract. *My* orders."

My servant. . . .

And suddenly, it clicked. She'd suspected everyone—Dockson, Breeze, even Elend—but she'd never connected the spy to the one person that made the most sense. There *had* been a kandra in the palace all along. And he had been at her side.

"I'm sorry, Mistress," OreSeur whispered.

"How long?" Vin asked, bowing her head.

"Since you gave my predecessor—the real OreSeur—the dog's body," the kandra said. "I killed him that day and took his place, wearing the body of a dog. You never saw him as a wolfhound."

What easier way to mask the transformation? Vin thought. "But, the bones we discovered in the palace," she said. "You were with me on the wall when they appeared. They—"

She'd taken his word on how fresh those bones had been; she'd taken his word on when they had been produced. She'd assumed all along that the switch must have happened that day, when she was with Elend on the city wall—but she'd done so primarily because of what Ore-Seur had said.

Idiot! she thought. OreSeur—or, TenSoon, as Zane had called him—had led her to suspect everyone but himself. What was wrong with her? She was usually so good at sniffing out traitors, at noticing insincerity. How had she missed spotting her own kandra?

Zane walked forward. Vin waited, on her knees. *Weak,* she told herself. *Look weak. Make him leave you alone. Try to—*

"Soothing me will do no good," Zane said quietly, grabbing her by the front of her shirt, picking her up, then throwing her back down. Mist sprayed beneath her, puffing up in a splash as she slammed to the floor. Vin stifled her cry of pain.

I have to stay quiet. If guards come, he'll kill them. If Elend comes . . .

She had to stay quiet, quiet even as Zane kicked her in her wounded side. She grunted, eyes watering.

"You could have saved me," Zane said, peering down at her. "I was willing to go with you. Now, what is left? Nothing. Nothing, but Straff's orders." He punctuated that sentence with a kick.

Stay small, she told herself through the pain. *He'll leave you alone eventually. . . .*

But it had been years since she'd had to bow before anyone. Her days of cringing before Camon and Reen were almost misty shadows, forgotten before the light offered by

Elend and Kelsier. As Zane kicked again, Vin found herself growing angry.

He brought his foot back, angling it toward her face, and Vin moved. As his foot arced down, she threw herself backward, Pushing against the window latches to scoot herself through the mists. She flared pewter, throwing herself up to her feet, trailing mist from the floor. It was up past her knees now.

She glared at Zane, who looked back with a dark expression. Vin ducked forward, but Zane moved faster—moved *first*—stepping between her and the balcony. Not that getting to it would do her any good; with atium, he could chase her down easily.

It was like before, when he'd attacked her with atium. Only this time it was worse. Before, she'd been able to believe—if just a little—that they were still sparring. Still not enemies, even if they weren't friends. She hadn't really believed that he wanted to kill her.

She had no such illusions this time. Zane's eyes were dark, his expression flat—just like that night a few days before, when slaughtering Cett's men.

Vin was going to die.

She hadn't felt such fear in a long time. But now she saw it, felt it, smelled it on herself as she shied away from the approaching Zane. She felt what it was like to face a Mistborn—what it must have been like for those soldiers she'd killed. There was no fighting. There was no chance.

No, she told herself forcefully, holding her side. *Elend didn't back down against Straff. He doesn't have Allomancy, but he marched into the center of the koloss camp.*

I can beat this.

With a cry, Vin dashed toward TenSoon. The dog backed away in shock, but he needn't have worried. Zane was there again. He slammed a shoulder into Vin, then whipped his dagger around and slashed a wound across her cheek as she fell backward. The cut was precise. Perfect. Matching the wound on her other cheek, one given to her during her first fight with a Mistborn, nearly two years before.

Vin gritted her teeth, burning iron as she fell. She Pulled on a pouch on her desk, whipping the coins into her hand.

She hit the ground on her side, other hand down, and threw herself back to her feet. She dumped a shower of coins from the pouch into her hand, then raised them at Zane.

Blood dripped from her chin. She threw the coins out. Zane moved to Push them away.

Vin smiled, then burned duralumin as she Pushed. The coins snapped forward, and the wind of their sudden passing parted the mist on the ground, revealing the floor beneath.

The room shook.

And in an eyeblink, Vin found herself slammed back against the wall. She gasped in surprise, breath knocked from her lungs, her vision swimming. She looked up, disoriented, surprised to find herself on the ground again.

"Duralumin," Zane said, still standing with a hand up before him. "TenSoon told me about it. We deduced you must have a new metal from the way you can sense me when my copper is on. After that, a little searching, and he found that note from your metallurgist, which handily had the instructions for making duralumin."

Her addled mind struggled to connect ideas. Zane had duralumin. He'd used the metal, and had Pushed against one of the coins she'd shot at him. He must have Pushed behind himself as well, to keep from being forced backward as his weight met hers.

And her own duralumin-enhanced Push had slammed her against the wall. She had trouble thinking. Zane walked forward. She looked up, dazed, then scrambled away on hands and knees, crawling in the mists. It was at face level, and her nostrils tickled as she inhaled the cool, quiet chaos.

Atium. She needed atium. But, the bead was in TenSoon's shoulder; she couldn't Pull it to herself. The reason he carried it there was that the flesh protected it from being affected by Allomancers. Just like the spikes piercing an Inquisitor's body, just like her own earring. Metal inside— or even piercing—a person's body could not be Pulled or Pushed except with the most extreme of Allomantic forces.

But she'd done it once. When fighting the Lord Ruler. It hadn't been her own power, or even duralumin, that had let her accomplish it. It had been something else. The mists.

She'd drawn upon them.

Something hit her on her back, pushing her down. She rolled over, kicking upward, but her foot missed Zane's face by a few atium-aided inches. Zane slapped her foot aside, then reached down, slamming her against the floor by her shoulders.

Mists churned around him as he looked down at her. Through her terror, she reached out for the mists, as she had over a year before when fighting the Lord Ruler. That day, they had fueled her Allomancy, giving her a strength that she shouldn't have had. She reached out for them, begging for their help.

And nothing happened.

Please. . . .

Zane slammed her down again. The mists continued to ignore her pleas.

She twisted, Pulling against the window frame to get leverage, and pushed Zane to the side. They rolled, Vin coming around on top.

Suddenly, both of them lurched off the floor, bursting out of the mists and flying toward the ceiling, thrown upward as Zane Pushed against coins on the floor. They slammed against the ceiling, Zane's body pushing against hers, pinning her to the wooden planks. He was on top again—or, rather, he was on the bottom, but that was now the point of leverage.

Vin gasped. He was so strong. Stronger than she. His fingers bit into the flesh of her arms despite her pewter, and her side ached from her earlier wounds. She was in no condition to fight—not against another Mistborn.

Especially not one with atium.

Zane continued to Push them against the ceiling. Vin's hair fell toward him, and mists churned the floor below, like a whirlpool vortex that was slowly rising.

Zane released his Push, and they fell. Yet, he was still in control. He spun her, throwing her down below him as they entered the mists again. They hit the ground, the blow knocking the wind from Vin's lungs yet again. Zane loomed above her, speaking through gritted teeth.

"All that effort, wasted," he hissed. "Hiding an Allomancer in Cett's hirelings so that you would suspect him of attacking you at the Assembly. Forcing you to fight in front of Elend so that he'd be intimidated by you. Pushing you to explore your powers and kill so that you'd realize just how powerful you truly are. All wasted!"

He leaned down. "You. Were. Supposed. To. *Save me!*" he said, his face just inches from hers, breathing heavily. He pinned one of her struggling arms to the floor with his knee, and then, in a strangely surreal moment, he kissed her.

And at the same time, he rammed his dagger into the side of one of her breasts. Vin tried to cry out, but his mouth held hers as the dagger cut her flesh.

"Be careful, Master!" OreSeur—TenSoon—suddenly yelled. "She knows much about kandra!"

Zane looked up, his hand stilled. The voice, the pain, brought lucidity to Vin. She flared tin, using the pain to shock herself awake, clearing her mind.

"What?" Zane asked, looking down toward the kandra.

"She knows, Master," TenSoon said. "She knows our secret. The reason why we served the Lord Ruler. The reason why we serve the Contract. She knows *why we fear Allomancers so much.*"

"Be silent," Zane commanded. "And speak no more."

TenSoon fell silent.

Our secret . . . Vin thought, glancing over at the wolfhound, sensing the anxiety in his canine expression. *He's trying to tell me something. Trying to help me.*

Secret. The secret of the kandra. The last time she'd tried Soothing him, he'd howled with pain. Yet, she saw permission in his expression. It was enough.

She slammed TenSoon with a Soothing. He cried out, howling, but she Pushed harder. Nothing happened. Gritting her teeth, she burned duralumin.

Something broke. She was in two places at once. She could feel TenSoon standing by the wall, and she could feel her own body in Zane's grip. TenSoon was hers, totally and completely. Somehow, not quite knowing how, she ordered him forward, controlling his body.

The massive wolfhound's body slammed into Zane, throwing him off Vin. The dagger flipped to the ground, and Vin stumbled to her knees, grabbing her chest, feeling warm blood there. Zane rolled, obviously shocked, but he came to his feet and kicked TenSoon.

Bones broke. The wolfhound tumbled across the floor—right toward Vin. She snatched the dagger off the ground as he rolled to her feet, then plunged it into his shoulder, cutting the shoulder, her fingers feeling in the muscle and sinew. She came up with bloodied hands and a single bead of atium. She swallowed it with a gulp, spinning toward Zane.

"Now let's see how you fare," she hissed, burning atium. Dozens of atium shadows burst from Zane, showing her possible actions he could take—all of them ambiguous. She would be giving off the same confusing mess to his eyes. They were even.

Zane turned, looking into her eyes, and his atium shadows disappeared.

Impossible! she thought. TenSoon groaned at her feet as she realized that her atium reserve was gone. Burned away. But the bead had been so large. . . .

"Did you think I'd give you the very weapon you needed to fight me?" Zane asked quietly. "Did you think I'd really give up atium?"

"But—"

"A lump of lead," Zane said, walking forward. "Plated with a thin layer of atium around it. Oh, Vin. You really need to be more careful whom you trust."

Vin stumbled backward, feeling her confidence wilt. *Make him talk!* she thought. *Try to get his atium to run out.*

"My brother said that I shouldn't trust anyone . . ." she mumbled. "He said . . . anyone would betray me."

"He was a wise man," Zane said quietly, standing chest-deep in mists.

"He was a paranoid fool," Vin said. "He kept me alive, but he left me broken."

"Then he did you a favor."

Vin glanced toward TenSoon's mangled, bleeding form. He was in pain; she could see it in his eyes. In the distance she could hear . . . thumping. She'd turned her bronze back on. She looked up slowly. Zane was walking toward her. Confident.

"You've been playing with me," she said. "You drove a

wedge between me and Elend. You made me think he feared me, made me think he was using me."

"He was," Zane said.

"Yes," Vin said. "But it doesn't matter—not the way you made it seem. Elend uses me. Kelsier used me. We use each other, for love, for support, for trust."

"Trust will kill you," he said.

"Then it is better to die."

"I trusted you," he said, stopping before her. "And you betrayed me."

"No," Vin said, raising her dagger. "I'm going to save you. Just like you want." She snapped forward and struck, but her hope—that he'd run out of atium—was in vain. He sidestepped indifferently; he let her dagger come within an inch of striking, but he was never really in danger.

Vin spun to attack, but her blade cut only air, skimming along the top of the rising mists.

Zane moved before her next attack came, dodging even before she knew what she was going to do. Her dagger stabbed the place where he had been standing.

He's too fast, she thought, side burning, mind thumping. Or was that the Well of Ascension thumping. . . .

Zane stopped just in front of her.

I can't hit him, she thought with frustration. *Not when he knows where I'll strike before I do!*

Vin paused.

Before I do. . . .

Zane stepped away to a place near the center of the room, then kicked her fallen dagger into the air and caught it. He turned back toward her, mist trailing from the weapon in his hand, jaw set and eyes dark.

He knows where I'll strike before I do.

Vin raised her dagger, blood trickling down face and side, thunderous drumbeats booming in her mind. The mist was nearly up to her chin.

She cleared her mind. She didn't plan an attack. She didn't react to Zane as he ran toward her, dagger raised. She loosened her muscles and closed her eyes, listening to his footsteps. She felt the mist rise around her, churned by Zane's advent.

She snapped her eyes open. He had the dagger raised; it glittered as it swung. Vin prepared to attack, but didn't think about the strike; she simply let her body react.

And she watched Zane very, very carefully.

He flinched just slightly to the left, open hand moving upward, as if to grab something.

There! Vin thought, immediately wrenching herself to the side, forcing her instinctive attack out of its natural trajectory. She twisted her arm—and dagger—midswing. She had been about to attack left, as Zane's atium had anticipated.

But, by reacting, Zane had shown her what she was going to do. Let her see the future. And if she could see it, she could change it.

They met. Zane's weapon took her in the shoulder. But Vin's knife took him in the neck. His left hand closed on empty air, snatching at a shadow that should have told him where her arm would be.

Zane tried to gasp, but her knife had pierced his windpipe. Air sucked through blood around the blade, and Zane stumbled back, eyes wide with shock. He met her eyes, then collapsed into the mists, his body thumping against the wooden floor.

Zane looked up through the mists, looked up at her. *I'm dying,* he thought.

Her atium shadow had *split* at the last moment. Two shadows, two possibilities. He'd counteracted the wrong one. She'd tricked him, defeated him somehow. And now he was dying.

Finally.

"You know why I thought you'd save me?" he tried to whisper to her, though he somehow knew that his lips weren't properly forming the words. "The voice. You were the first person I ever met that it didn't tell me to kill. The only person."

"Of course I didn't tell you to kill *her*," God said.

Zane felt his life seeping away.

"You know the really funny thing, Zane?" God asked. "The most amusing part of this all? You're not insane.

"You never were."

Vin watched quietly as Zane sputtered, blood coming from his lips. She watched cautiously; a knife to the throat should have been enough to kill even a Mistborn, but sometimes pewter could let one do awesome things.

Zane died. She checked his pulse, then retrieved her dagger. After that, she stood for a moment, feeling . . . numb, in both mind and body. She raised a hand to her wounded shoulder—and in doing so, she brushed her wounded breast. She was bleeding too much, and her mind was growing fuzzy again.

I killed him.

She flared pewter, forcing herself to keep moving. She stumbled over to TenSoon, kneeling beside him.

"Mistress," he said. "I'm sorry. . . ."

"I know," she said, staring at the terrible wound she'd made. His legs no longer worked, and his body lay in an unnatural twist. "How can I help?"

"Help?" TenSoon said. "Mistress, I nearly got you killed!"

"I know," she said again. "How can I make the pain go away? Do you need another body?"

TenSoon was quiet for a moment. "Yes."

"Take Zane's," Vin said. "For the moment, at least."

"He is dead?" TenSoon asked with surprise.

He couldn't see, she realized. *His neck is broken.*

"Yes," she whispered.

"How, Mistress?" TenSoon asked. "He ran out of atium?"

"No," Vin said.

"Then, how?"

"Atium has a weakness," she said. "It lets you see the future."

"That . . . doesn't sound like a weakness, Mistress."

Vin sighed, wobbling slightly. *Focus!* she thought. "When you burn atium, you see a few moments into the future—and you can change what will happen in that future. You can grab an arrow that should have kept flying. You can dodge a blow that should have killed you. And you can move to block an attack before it even happens."

TenSoon was quiet, obviously confused.

"He showed me what *I* was going to do," Vin said. "I couldn't change the future, but Zane could. By reacting to my attack before I even knew what I was going to do, he inadvertently showed me the future. I reacted against him, and he tried to block a blow that never came. That let me kill him."

"Mistress . . ." TenSoon whispered. "That is brilliant."

"I'm sure I'm not the first to think of it," Vin said wearily. "But it isn't the sort of secret that you share. Anyway, take his body."

"I . . . would rather not wear the bones of that creature," TenSoon said. "You don't know how broken he was, Mistress."

Vin nodded tiredly. "I could just find you another dog body, if you want."

"That won't be necessary, Mistress," TenSoon said quietly. "I still have the bones of the other wolfhound you gave me, and most of them are still good. If I replace a few of them with the good bones from this body, I should be able to form a complete skeleton to use."

"Do it, then. We're going to need to plan what to do next."

TenSoon was quiet for a moment. Finally, he spoke. "Mistress, my Contract is void, now that my master is dead. I . . . need to return to my people for reassignment."

"Ah," Vin said, feeling a wrench of sadness. "Of course."

"I do not want to go," TenSoon said. "But, I must at least report to my people. Please, forgive me."

"There is nothing to forgive," Vin said. "And thank you for that timely hint at the end."

TenSoon lay quietly. She could see guilt in his canine eyes. *He shouldn't have helped me against his current master.*

"Mistress," TenSoon said. "You know our secret now. Mistborn can control a kandra's body with Allomancy. I don't know what you will do with it—but realize that I have entrusted you with a secret that my people have kept sacred for a thousand years. The way that Allomancers could take control of our bodies and make slaves of us."

"I . . . don't even understand what happened."

"Perhaps it is better that way," TenSoon said. "Please, leave me. I have the other dog's bones in the closet. When you return, I will be gone."

Vin rose, nodding. She left, then, pushing through the mists and seeking the hallway outside. Her wounds needed tending. She knew that she should go to Sazed, but somehow she couldn't force herself in that direction. She walked faster, feet taking her down the hallway, until she was running.

Everything was collapsing around her. She couldn't manage it all, couldn't keep things straight. But she did know what she wanted.

And so she ran to him.

He is a good man—despite it all, he is a good man. A sacrificing man. In truth, all of his actions—all of the deaths, destructions, and pains that he has caused—have hurt him deeply. All of these things were, in truth, a kind of sacrifice for him.

48

ELEND YAWNED, LOOKING OVER THE letter he'd penned to Jastes. Perhaps he could persuade his former friend to see reason.

If he couldn't . . . well, a duplicate of the wooden coin Jastes had been using to "pay" the koloss sat on Elend's desk. It was a perfect copy, whittled by Clubs himself.

Elend was pretty certain that he had access to more wood than Jastes did. If he could help Penrod stall for a few more weeks, they might be able to make enough "money" to bribe the koloss away.

He set down his pen, rubbing his eyes. It was late. Time to—

His door slammed open. Elend spun, and caught sight of a flustered Vin dashing across the room and into his arms. She was crying.

And she was bloody.

"Vin!" he said. "What happened?"

"I killed him," she said, head buried in Elend's chest.

"Who?"

"Your brother," she said. "Zane. Straff's Mistborn. I killed him."

"Wait. What? My *brother*?"

Vin nodded. "I'm sorry."

"Forget about that, Vin!" Elend said, gently prying her back and pushing her into his chair. She had a gash on her cheek, and her shirt was slick with blood. "Lord Ruler! I'm going to get Sazed right now."

"Don't leave me," she said, holding his arm.

Elend paused. Something had changed. She seemed to need him again. "Come with me, then. We'll both go see him."

Vin nodded, standing. She teetered just a bit, and Elend felt a spike of fear, but the determined look in her eyes wasn't something he wanted to challenge. He put his arm around her, letting her lean on him as they walked to Sazed's quarters. Elend paused to knock, but Vin simply pushed her way into the dark room, then wobbled and sat down on the floor just inside.

"I'll . . . sit here," she said.

Elend paused worriedly by her side, then raised his lamp and called toward the bedchamber. "Sazed!"

The Terrisman appeared a moment later, looking exhausted and wearing a white sleeping robe. He noticed Vin, blinked a few times, then disappeared into his chambers. He returned a moment later with a metalmind bracer strapped to his forearm and a bag of medical equipment.

"Now, Lady Vin," Sazed said, setting the bag down.

"What would Master Kelsier think, seeing you in this condition? You ruin more clothing in this manner, I think. . . ."

"This isn't a time for levity, Sazed," Elend said.

"I apologize, Your Majesty," Sazed said, carefully cutting the clothing away from Vin's shoulder. "However, if she is still conscious, then she isn't in serious danger." He peered closer at the wound, absently lifting clean cloths from his bag.

"You see?" Sazed asked. "This gash is deep, but the blade was deflected by the bone, and missed hitting any major vessels. Hold this here." He pressed a cloth to the wound, and Elend put his hand on it. Vin sat with her eyes closed, resting back against the wall, blood dripping slowly from her chin. She seemed more exhausted than in pain.

Sazed took his knife and cut away the front of Vin's shirt, exposing her wounded chest.

Elend paused. "Perhaps I should . . ."

"Stay," Vin said. It wasn't a plea, but a command. She raised her head, opening her eyes as Sazed tisked quietly at the wound, then got out a numbing agent and some needle and thread.

"Elend," she said, "I need to tell you something."

He paused. "All right."

"I've realized something about Kelsier," she said quietly. "I always focus on the wrong things, when it comes to him. It's hard to forget the hours he spent training me to be an Allomancer. Yet, it wasn't his ability to fight that made him great—it wasn't his harshness or his brutality, or even his strength or his instincts."

Elend frowned.

"Do you know what it was?" she asked.

He shook his head, still pressing the cloth against her shoulder.

"It was his ability to trust," she said. "It was the way that he made good people into *better* people, the way that he inspired them. His crew worked because he had confidence in them—because he respected them. And, in return, they respected each other. Men like Breeze and Clubs became heroes because Kelsier had faith in them."

She looked up at him, blinking tired eyes. "And you are far better at that than Kelsier ever was, Elend. He had to work at it. You do it instinctively, treating even weasels like Philen as if they were good and honorable men. It's not naiveté, as some think. It's what Kelsier had, only greater. He could have learned from you."

"You give me too much credit," he said.

She shook a tired head. Then she turned to Sazed.

"Sazed?" she asked.

"Yes, child?"

"Do you know any wedding ceremonies?"

Elend nearly dropped the cloth in shock.

"I know several," Sazed said as he tended the wound. "Some two hundred, actually."

"Which one is the shortest?" Vin asked.

Sazed pulled a stitch tight. "The people of Larsta only required a profession of love before a local priest. Simplicity was a tenet of their belief structure—a reaction, perhaps, to the traditions of the land they were banished from, which was known for its complex system of bureaucratic rules. It is a good religion, one that focused on simple beauty found in nature."

Vin looked at Elend. Her face was bloody, her hair a mess.

"Now, see," he said. "Vin, don't you think that maybe this should wait until, you know—"

"Elend?" she interrupted. "I love you."

He froze.

"Do you love me?" she asked.

This is insane. "Yes," he said quietly.

Vin turned to Sazed, who was still working. "Well?"

Sazed looked up, fingers bloodied. "This is a very strange time for such an event, I think."

Elend nodded in agreement.

"It's just a little bit of blood," Vin said tiredly. "I'm really all right, now that I've sat down."

"Yes," Sazed said, "but you seem somewhat distraught, Lady Vin. This isn't a decision to be made lightly, under the influence of strong emotions."

Vin smiled. "The decision to get married shouldn't be made because of strong emotions?"

Sazed floundered. "That isn't exactly what I meant. I'm simply not certain that you are fully in control of your faculties, Lady Vin."

Vin shook her head. "I'm more in control than I have been for months. It's time for me to stop hesitating, Sazed—time to stop worrying, time to accept my place in this crew. I know what I want, now. I love Elend. I don't know what kind of time we'll have together, but I want some, at least."

Sazed sat for a moment, then returned to his sewing. "And you, Lord Elend? What are your thoughts?"

What *were* his thoughts? He remembered just the day before, when Vin had spoken of leaving, and the wrenching he had felt. He thought of how much he depended on her wisdom, and her bluntness, and her simple—but not simplistic—devotion to him. Yes, he did love her.

The world had gone chaotic recently. He had made mistakes. Yet, despite everything that had happened, and despite his frustrations, he still felt strongly that he wanted to be with Vin. It wasn't the idyllic infatuation he'd felt a year and a half ago, at the parties. But it felt more solid.

"Yes, Sazed," he said. "I do want to marry her. I have wanted it for some time. I . . . I don't know what's going to happen to the city, or my kingdom, but I want to be with Vin when it comes."

Sazed continued to work. "Very well, then," he finally said. "If it is my witness you require, then you have it."

Elend knelt, still pressing the cloth on Vin's shoulder, feeling a little bit stunned. "That's it then?"

Sazed nodded. "It is as valid as any witness the obligators could give you, I think. Be warned, the Larsta love oath is binding. They knew no form of divorce in their culture. Do you accept my witness of this event?"

Vin nodded. Elend felt himself doing the same.

"Then you are married," Sazed said, tying off his thread, then draping a cloth across Vin's chest. "Hold this for a bit, Lady Vin, and stanch the rest of the bleeding." Then he moved on to her cheek.

"I feel like there should be a ceremony or something," Elend said.

"I could give one, if you wish," Sazed said, "but I do not think you need one. I have known you both for some time, and am willing to give my blessing to this union. I simply offer counsel. Those who take lightly promises they make to those they love are people who find little lasting satisfaction in life. This is not an easy time in which to live. That does not mean that it has to be a difficult time to love, but it does mean that you will find unusual stresses upon your lives and your relationship.

"Do not forget the love oath you made to each other this evening. It will give you much strength in the days to come, I think." With that, he pulled the last stitch tight on Vin's face, then finally moved to the shoulder. The bleeding there had mostly stopped, and Sazed studied the wound for a moment before beginning work on it.

Vin looked up at Elend, smiling, looking a bit drowsy. He stood and walked over to the room's washbasin, and returned with a damp cloth to wipe off her face and cheek.

"I'm sorry," she said quietly as Sazed moved around and took the place Elend had been kneeling in.

"Sorry?" Elend said. "About my father's Mistborn?"

Vin shook her head. "No. For taking so long."

Elend smiled. "You're worth the wait. Besides, I think I had to figure a few things out as well."

"Like how to be a king?"

"And how to stop being one."

Vin shook her head. "You never stopped being one, Elend. They can take your crown, but they can't take your honor."

Elend smiled. "Thank you. However, I don't know how much good I've done the city. By even being here, I divided the people, and now Straff will end up in control."

"I'll kill Straff if he puts one foot in this city."

Elend gritted his teeth. *Back to the same problems again.* They could only hold Vin's knife against his neck for so long. He'd figure out a way to wiggle around, and there was always Jastes and those koloss. . . .

"Your Majesty," Sazed said as he worked, "perhaps I can offer a solution."

Elend glanced down at the Terrisman, raising an eyebrow.

"The Well of Ascension," Sazed said.

Vin opened her eyes immediately.

"Tindwyl and I have been researching the Hero of Ages," Sazed continued. "We are convinced that Rashek never did what the Hero was supposed to. In fact, we aren't even convinced that this Alendi of a thousand years ago *was* the Hero. There are too many discrepancies, too many problems and contradictions. In addition, the mists—the Deepness—are still here. And now they are killing people."

Elend frowned. "What are you saying?"

Sazed pulled a stitch tight. "Something still needs to be done, Your Majesty. Something important. Looking at it from a smaller perspective, it might seem that the events at Luthadel and the rise of the Well of Ascension are unrelated. However, from a larger view, they may be solutions to one another."

Elend smiled. "Like the lock and the key."

"Yes, Your Majesty," Sazed said, smiling. "Precisely like that."

"It thumps," Vin whispered, eyes closing. "In my head. I can *feel* it."

Sazed paused, then wrapped a bandage around Vin's arm. "Can you feel where it is?"

Vin shook her head. "I . . . There doesn't seem to be a direction to the pulses. I thought they were distant, but they're getting louder."

"That must be the Well returning to power," Sazed said. "It is fortunate that I know where to find it."

Elend turned, and Vin opened her eyes again.

"My research has revealed the location, Lady Vin," Sazed said. "I can draw you a map, from my metalminds."

"Where?" Vin whispered.

"North," Sazed said. "In the mountains of Terris. Atop one of the lower peaks, known as Derytatith. Travel there will be difficult this time of year. . . ."

"I can do it," Vin said firmly as Sazed turned to working

on her chest wound. Elend flushed again, then paused as he turned away.

I'm . . . married. "You're going to leave?" Elend asked, looking to Vin. "Now?"

"I have to," Vin whispered. "I *have* to go to it, Elend."

"You should go with her, Your Majesty," Sazed said.

"What?"

Sazed sighed, looking up. "We have to face facts, Your Majesty. As you said earlier, Straff will soon take this city. If you are here, you will be executed. However, Lady Vin will undoubtedly need help securing the Well."

"It's supposed to hold great power," Elend said, rubbing his chin. "Could we, you think, destroy those armies?"

Vin shook her head. "We couldn't use it," she whispered. "The power is a temptation. That's what went wrong last time. Rashek took the power instead of giving it up."

"Giving it up?" Elend asked. "What does that mean?"

"Letting it go, Your Majesty," Sazed said. "Letting *it* defeat the Deepness on its own."

"Trust," Vin whispered. "It's about trust."

"However," Sazed said, "I think that releasing this power could do great things for the land. Change things, and undo much of the damage the Lord Ruler did. I have a strong suspicion that it would destroy the koloss, since they were created by the Lord Ruler's misuse of the power."

"But Straff would hold the city," Elend said.

"Yes," Sazed said, "but if you leave, the transition will be peaceful. The Assembly has all but decided to accept him as their emperor, and it appears that he'll let Penrod rule as a subject king. There will be no bloodshed, and you will be able to organize resistance from outside. Besides, who knows what releasing the power will do? Lady Vin could be left changed, much as the Lord Ruler was. With the crew in hiding within the city, it should not be so difficult to oust your father—particularly when he grows complacent in a year or so."

Elend gritted his teeth. *Another revolution.* Yet, what Sazed said made sense. *For so long, we've been worrying about the small-scale.* He glanced at Vin, feeling a surge of warmth and love. *Maybe it's time I started listening to the things she's been trying to tell me.*

"Sazed," Elend said, a sudden thought occurring to him, "do you think that I could convince the Terris people to help us?"

"Perhaps, Your Majesty," Sazed said. "My prohibition against interfering—the one I have been ignoring—comes because I was given a different assignment by the Synod, not because we believe in avoiding all action. If you could convince the Synod that the future of the Terris people will be benefited by having a strong ally in Luthadel, you may just be able to get yourself military aid from Terris."

Elend nodded, thoughtful.

"Remember the lock and the key, Your Majesty," Sazed said, finishing off Vin's second wound. "In this case, leaving seems like the opposite of what you should do. However, if you look at the larger picture, you will see that it's precisely what you *need* to do."

Vin opened her eyes, looking up at him, smiling. "We can do this, Elend. Come with me."

Elend stood for a moment. *Lock and key. . . .* "All right," he said. "We'll leave as soon as Vin is able."

"She should be able to ride tomorrow," Sazed said. "You know what pewter can do for a body."

Elend nodded. "All right. I should have listened to you earlier, Vin. Besides, I've always wanted to see your homeland, Sazed. You can show it to us."

"I will need to stay here, I fear," Sazed said. "I should soon leave for the South to continue my work there. Tindwyl, however, can go with you—she has important information that needs to be passed on to my brethren the Keepers."

"It will need to be a small group," Vin said. "We'll have to outrun—or perhaps sneak past—Straff's men."

"Just you three, I think," Sazed said. "Or, perhaps one other person to help with watches while you sleep, someone skilled in hunting and scouting. Lord Lestibournes, perhaps?"

"Spook would be perfect," Elend said, nodding. "You're sure the other crewmembers will be safe in the city?"

"Of course they won't," Vin said, smiling. "But they're experts. They hid from the Lord Ruler—they'll be able to hide from Straff. Particularly if they don't have to worry about keeping you safe."

"Then it is decided," Sazed said, standing. "You two should try to rest well tonight, despite the recent change in your relationship. Can you walk, Lady Vin?"

"No need," Elend said, leaning down and picking her up. She wrapped her arms around him, though her grip was not tight, and he could see that her eyes were already drooping again.

He smiled. Suddenly, the world seemed a much simpler place. He would take some time and spend it on what was really important; then, once he and Vin had sought help from the North, they could return. He actually looked forward to coming back and tackling their problems with renewed vigor.

He held Vin tight, nodding good night to Sazed, then walking out toward his rooms. It seemed that everything had worked out fine in the end.

Sazed stood slowly, watching the two leave. He wondered what they would think of him, when they heard of Luthadel's fall. At least they would have each other for support.

His wedding blessing was the last gift he could give them—that, and their lives. *How will history judge me for my lies?* he wondered. *What will it think of the Terrisman who took such a hand in politics, the Terrisman who would fabricate mythology to save the lives of his friends?* The things he'd said about the Well were, of course, falsehoods. If there was such a power, he had no idea where it was, nor what it would do.

How history judged him would probably depend on what Elend and Vin did with their lives. Sazed could only hope that he had done the right thing. Watching them go, knowing that their youthful love would be spared, he couldn't help but smile at his decision.

With a sigh, he stooped down and gathered up his medical items; then he retreated to his rooms to fabricate the map he had promised Vin and Elend.

THE END OF PART FOUR

PART FIVE

SNOW AND ASH

He is accustomed to giving up his own will before the greater good, as he sees it.

49

"YOU ARE A FOOL, ELEND Venture," Tindwyl snapped, arms folded, eyes wide with displeasure.

Elend pulled a strap tight on his saddle. Part of the wardrobe Tindwyl had made for him included a black and silver riding uniform, and he wore this now, fingers snug within the leather gloves, and a dark cloak to keep off the ash.

"Are you listening to me?" Tindwyl demanded. "You can't leave. Not now! Not when your people are in such danger!"

"I'll protect them in another way," he said, checking on the packhorses.

They were in the keep's covered way, used for arrivals and departures. Vin sat on her own horse, enveloped almost completely in her cloak, hands holding her reins tensely. She had very little experience riding, but Elend refused to let her run. Pewter or no pewter, the wounds from her fight at the Assembly still hadn't healed completely, not to mention the damage she'd taken the night before.

"Another way?" Tindwyl asked. "You should be with them. You're their king!"

"No, I'm *not*," Elend snapped, turning toward the Terriswoman. "They rejected me, Tindwyl. Now I have to worry about more important events on a larger stage. They wanted a traditional king? Well, let them have my father. When I return from Terris, perhaps they will have realized what they lost."

Tindwyl shook her head and stepped forward, speaking in a quiet voice. "Terris, Elend? You go north. For her. You know why she wants to go there, don't you?"

He paused.

"Ah, so you do know," Tindwyl said. "What do you think of it, Elend? Don't tell me you believe these delusions. She thinks she's the Hero of Ages. She supposes that she'll find something in the mountains up there— some power, or perhaps some revelation, that will transform her into a divinity."

Elend glanced at Vin. She looked down at the ground, hood down, still sitting quietly on her horse.

"She's trying to follow her master, Elend," Tindwyl whispered. "The Survivor became a god to these people, so she thinks she has to do the same."

Elend turned to Tindwyl. "If that is what she truly believes, then I support her."

"You support her madness?" Tindwyl demanded.

"Do not speak of my wife in that manner," Elend said, his commanding tone causing Tindwyl to flinch. He swung up into his saddle. "I trust her, Tindwyl. Part of trust is belief."

Tindwyl snorted. "You can't possibly believe that she is some prophesied messiah, Elend. I know you—you're a scholar. You may have professed allegiance to the Church of the Survivor, but you don't believe in the supernatural any more than I do."

"I believe," he said firmly, "that Vin is my wife, and that I love her. Anything important to her is important to me— and anything she believes has at least that much weight of truth to me. We are going north. We will return once we've released the power there."

"Fine," Tindwyl said. "Then you will be remembered as a coward who abandoned his people."

"Leave us!" Elend ordered, raising his finger and pointing toward the keep.

Tindwyl spun, stalking toward the doorway. As she

passed it, she pointed at the supply table, where she had previously placed a book-sized package, wrapped in brown paper, tied with a thick string. "Sazed wishes you to deliver this to the Keeper Synod. You'll find them in the city of Tathingdwen. Enjoy your exile, Elend Venture." Then, she left.

Elend sighed, moving his horse over beside Vin's.

"Thank you," she said quietly.

"For what?"

"For what you said."

"I meant it, Vin," Elend said, reaching over to lay a hand on her shoulder.

"Tindwyl might be right, you know," she said. "Despite what Sazed said, I could be mad. Do you remember when I told you that I'd seen a spirit in the mists?"

Elend nodded slowly.

"Well, I've seen it again," Vin said. "It's like a ghost, formed from the patterns in mist. I see it all the time, watching me, following me. And I hear those rhythms in my head—majestic, powerful thumpings, like Allomantic pulses. Only, I don't need bronze anymore to hear them."

Elend squeezed her shoulder. "I believe you, Vin."

She looked up, reserved. "Do you, Elend? Do you really?"

"I'm not sure," he admitted. "But I'm trying very hard to. Either way, I think going north is the right thing to do."

She nodded slowly. "That's enough, I think."

He smiled, turning back to the doorway. "Where is Spook?"

Vin shrugged beneath her cloak. "I assume Tindwyl won't be coming with us, then."

"Probably not," Elend said, smiling.

"How will we find our way to Terris?"

"It won't be hard," Elend said. "We'll just follow the imperial canal to Tathingdwen." He paused, thinking of the map Sazed had given them. It led straight into the Terris Mountains. They'd have to get supplies in Tathingdwen, and the snows would be high, but . . . well, that was a problem for another time.

Vin smiled, and Elend walked over to pick up the package

Tindwyl had left. It appeared to be a book of some sort. A few moments later, Spook arrived. He wore his soldier's uniform, and had saddlebags slung over his shoulder. He nodded to Elend, handed Vin a large bag, then moved to his own horse.

He looks nervous, Elend thought as the boy slung his bags over his horse. "What's in the bag?" he asked, turning to Vin.

"Pewter dust," she said. "I think we might need it."

"Are we ready?" Spook asked, looking over at them.

Elend glanced at Vin, who nodded. "I guess we—"

"Not quite yet," a new voice said. "I'm not ready at *all*."

Elend turned as Allrianne swept into the passage. She wore a rich brown and red riding skirt, and had her hair tied up beneath a scarf. *Where'd she get that outfit?* Elend wondered. Two servants followed her, bearing bundles.

Allrianne paused, tapping her lip with a thoughtful expression. "I think I'm going to need a packhorse."

"What are you doing?" Vin demanded.

"Going with you," Allrianne said. "Breezy says I have to leave the city. He's a very silly man, sometimes, but he can be quite stubborn. He spent the entire conversation Soothing me—as if I couldn't recognize his touch by now!"

Allrianne waved to one of the servants, who ran to get a stablehand.

"We're going to be riding very hard," Elend said. "I'm not sure if you'll be able to keep up."

Allrianne rolled her eyes. "I rode all the way out here from the Western Dominance! I think I can manage. Besides, Vin is hurt, so you probably won't be going *that* fast."

"We don't want you along," Vin said. "We don't trust you—and we don't like you."

Elend closed his eyes. *Dear, blunt Vin.*

Allrianne just twittered a laugh as the servant returned with two horses, then began to load one. "Silly Vin," she said. "How can you say that after all we've shared?"

"Shared?" Vin asked. "Allrianne, we went shopping together *one time*."

"And I felt we bonded quite well," Allrianne said. "Why, we're practically sisters!"

Vin gave the girl a flat stare.

"Yes," Allrianne said, "and you're *definitely* the older, boring sister." She smiled sweetly, then swung easily up into her saddle, suggesting considerable horsemanship. One of the servants led her packhorse over, then tied the reins into place behind Allrianne's saddle.

"All right, Elend dear," she said. "I'm ready. Let's go."

Elend glanced at Vin, who shook her head with a dark look.

"You can leave me behind if you wish," Allrianne said, "but I'll just follow and get into trouble, and then you'll have to come save me. And don't even try and pretend that you wouldn't!"

Elend sighed. "Very well," he said. "Let's go."

They made their way slowly through the city, Elend and Vin at the lead, Spook bringing their packhorses, Allrianne riding to the side. Elend kept his head up, but that only let him see the faces that poked out of windows and doorways as he passed. Soon, a small crowd was trailing them—and while he couldn't hear their whispers, he could imagine what they were saying.

The king. The king is abandoning us. . . .

He knew that many of them still couldn't understand that Lord Penrod held the throne. Elend glanced away from an alleyway, where he saw many eyes watching him. There was a haunted fear in those eyes. He had expected to see accusations, but somehow their despondent acceptance was even more disheartening. They expected him to flee. They expected to be abandoned. He was one of the few rich enough, and powerful enough, to get away. Of course he'd run.

He squeezed his own eyes shut, trying to force down his guilt. He wished that they could have left at night, sneaking out the passwall as Ham's family had. However, it was important that Straff saw Elend and Vin leaving, so that he understood he could take the city without attacking.

I'll be back, Elend promised the people. *I'll save you. For now, it's better if I leave.*

The broad doors of Tin Gate appeared ahead of them. Elend kicked his horse forward, speeding ahead of his silent wave of followers. The guards at the gate already had their orders. Elend gave them a nod, reining in his horse, and the men swung the doors open. Vin and the others joined him before the opening portal.

"Lady Heir," one of the guards asked quietly. "Are you leaving, too?"

Vin looked to the side. "Peace," she said. "We're not abandoning you. We're going for help."

The soldier smiled.

How can he trust her so easily? Elend thought. *Or, is hope all he has left?*

Vin turned her horse around, facing the crowd of people, and she lowered her hood. "We will return," she promised. She didn't seem as nervous as she had before when dealing with people who revered her.

Ever since last night, something has changed in her, Elend thought.

As a group, the soldiers saluted them. Elend saluted back; then he nodded to Vin. He led the way as they galloped out the gates, angling toward the northern highway—a path that would allow them to skirt just west of Straff's army.

They hadn't gone far before a group of horsemen moved to intercept them. Elend rode low on his horse, sparing a glance for Spook and the packhorses. What caught Elend's attention, however, was Allrianne: she rode with amazing proficiency, a look of determination on her face. She didn't seem the least bit nervous.

To the side, Vin whipped her cloak back, bringing out a handful of coins. She flung them into the air, and they shot forward with a speed Elend had never seen, even from other Allomancers. *Lord Ruler!* he thought with shock as the coins zipped away, disappearing faster than he could track.

Soldiers fell, and Elend barely heard the *pling*ing of metal against metal over the sound of wind and hoofbeats. He rode directly through the center of the chaotic group of men, many of them down and dying.

Arrows began to fall, but Vin scattered these without

even waving a hand. She had opened the bag of pewter, he noticed, and was releasing the dust in a shower behind her as she rode, Pushing some of it to the sides.

The next arrows won't have metal heads, Elend thought nervously. Soldiers were forming up behind, shouting.

"I'll catch up," Vin said, then jumped off her horse.

"Vin!" Elend yelled, turning his beast. Allrianne and Spook shot past him, riding hard. Vin landed and, amazingly, didn't even stumble as she began to run. She downed a vial of metal, then looked toward the archers.

Arrows flew. Elend cursed, but kicked his horse into motion. There was little he could do now. He rode low, galloping as the arrows fell around him. One passed within inches of his head, falling to stick into the road.

And then they stopped falling. He glanced backward, teeth gritted. Vin stood before a rising cloud of dust. *The pewter dust,* he thought. *She's Pushing on it—Pushing the flakes along the ground, stirring up the dust and ash.*

A massive wave of dust, metal, and ash slammed into the archers, washing over them. It blew around the soldiers, making them curse and shield their eyes, and some fell to the ground, holding their faces.

Vin swung back onto her horse, then galloped away from the billowing mass of wind-borne particles. Elend slowed his horse, letting her catch up. The army was in chaos behind them, men giving orders, people scattering.

"Speed up!" Vin said as she approached. "We're almost out of bowshot!"

Soon they joined Allrianne and Spook. *We aren't out of danger—my father could still decide to send pursuit.*

But, the soldiers couldn't have mistaken Vin. If Elend's instincts were right, Straff would let them run. His prime target was Luthadel. He could go after Elend later; for now, he would simply be happy to see Vin leaving.

"Thank you kindly for the help getting out," Allrianne suddenly said, watching the army. "I'll be going now."

With that, she veered her two horses away, angling toward a group of low hills to the west.

"What?" Elend asked with surprise, pulling up next to Spook.

"Leave her," Vin said. "We don't have time."

Well, that solves one problem, Elend thought, turning his horse to the northern highway. *Farewell, Luthadel. I'll be back for you later.*

"Well, that solves one problem," Breeze noted, standing atop the city wall and watching Elend's group disappear around a hillside. To the east, a large—and still unexplained—pillar of smoke rose from the koloss camp. To the west, Straff's army was buzzing about, stirred by the escape.

At first, Breeze had worried about Allrianne's safety—but then he'd realized that, enemy army notwithstanding, there was no safer place for her than beside Vin. As long as Allrianne didn't get too far away from the others, she would be safe.

It was a quiet group that stood atop the wall with him, and for once, Breeze barely touched their emotions. Their solemnity seemed appropriate. The young Captain Demoux stood beside the aging Clubs, and the peaceful Sazed stood with Ham the warrior. Together, they watched the seed of hope they'd cast to the winds.

"Wait," Breeze said, frowning as he noticed something. "Wasn't Tindwyl supposed to be with them?"

Sazed shook his head. "She decided to stay."

"Why would she do that?" Breeze asked. "Didn't I hear her babbling something about not interfering in local disputes?"

Sazed shook his head. "I do not know, Lord Breeze. She is a difficult woman to read."

"They all are," Clubs muttered.

Sazed smiled. "Either way, it appears our friends have escaped."

"May the Survivor protect them," Demoux said quietly.

"Yes," Sazed said. "May he indeed."

Clubs snorted. Resting one arm on the battlements, he turned to eye Sazed with a gnarled face. "Don't encourage him."

Demoux flushed, then turned and walked away.

"What was that about?" Breeze asked curiously.

"The boy has been preaching to my soldiers," Clubs said. "Told him I didn't want his nonsense cluttering their minds."

"It is not nonsense, Lord Cladent," Sazed said, "it's faith."

"Do you honestly think," Clubs said, "that *Kelsier* is going to protect these people?"

Sazed wavered. "They believe it, and that is—"

"No," Clubs interrupted, scowling. "That *isn't* enough, Terrisman. These people fool themselves by believing in the Survivor."

"You believed in him," Sazed said. Breeze was tempted to Soothe him, make the argument less tense, but Sazed already seemed completely calm. "You followed him. You believed in the Survivor enough to overthrow the Final Empire."

Clubs scowled. "I don't like your ethics, Terrisman—I never have. Our crew—Kelsier's crew—fought to free this people because it was *right*."

"Because you believed it to be right," Sazed said.

"And what do you believe to be right, Terrisman?"

"That depends," Sazed said. "There are many different systems with many different worthy values."

Clubs nodded, then turned, as if the argument were over.

"Wait, Clubs," Ham said. "Aren't you going to respond to that?"

"He said enough," Clubs said. "His belief is situational. To him, even the Lord Ruler was a deity because people worshipped him—or were forced to worship him. Aren't I right, Terrisman?"

"In a way, Lord Cladent," Sazed said. "Though, the Lord Ruler might have been something of an exception."

"But you still keep records and memories of the Steel Ministry's practices, don't you?" Ham asked.

"Yes," Sazed admitted.

"Situational," Clubs spat. "At least that fool Demoux had the sense to choose *one* thing to believe in."

"Do not deride someone's faith simply because you do not share it, Lord Cladent," Sazed said quietly.

Clubs snorted again. "It's all very easy for you, isn't it?" he asked. "Believing everything, never having to choose?"

"I would say," Sazed replied, "that it is more difficult to believe as I do, for one must learn to be inclusionary and accepting."

Clubs waved a dismissive hand, turning to hobble toward the stairs. "Suit yourself. I have to go prepare my boys to die."

Sazed watched him go, frowning. Breeze gave him a Soothing—taking away his self-consciousness—for good measure.

"Don't mind him, Saze," Ham said. "We're all a little on edge, lately."

Sazed nodded. "Still, he makes good points—ones I have never before had to face. Until this year, my duty was to collect, study, and remember. It is still very hard for me to consider setting one belief beneath another, even if that belief is based on a man that I know to have been quite mortal."

Ham shrugged. "Who knows? Maybe Kell *is* out there somewhere, watching over us."

No, Breeze thought. *If he were, we wouldn't have ended up here—waiting to die, locked in a city we were supposed to save.*

"Anyway," Ham said, "I still want to know where that smoke is coming from."

Breeze glanced at the koloss camp. The dark pillar was too centralized to be coming from cooking fires. "The tents?"

Ham shook his head. "El said there were only a couple of tents—far too few to make that much smoke. That fire has been burning for some time."

Breeze shook his head. *Doesn't really matter now, I guess.*

Straff Venture coughed again, curling over in his chair. His arms were slick with sweat, his hands trembling.

He wasn't getting better.

At first, he'd assumed that the chills were a side effect of his nervousness. He'd had a hard evening, sending assassins after Zane, then somehow escaping death at the insane Mistborn's hands. Yet, during the night, Straff's shakes hadn't gotten better. They'd grown worse. They weren't just from nervousness; he must have a disease of some sort.

"Your Majesty!" a voice called from outside.

Straff straightened himself, trying to look as presentable as possible. Even so, the messenger paused as he entered the tent, apparently noting Straff's wan skin and tired eyes.

"My . . . lord," the messenger said.

"Speak, man," Straff said curtly, trying to project a regality he didn't feel. "Out with it."

"Riders, my lord," the man said. "They left the city!"

"What!" Straff said, throwing off his blanket and standing. He managed to stand upright despite a bout of dizziness. "Why wasn't I informed?"

"They passed quickly, my lord," the messenger said. "We barely had time to send the interception crew."

"You caught them, I assume," Straff said, steadying himself on his chair.

"Actually, they escaped, my lord," the messenger said slowly.

"*What?*" Straff said, spinning in rage. The motion was too much. The dizziness returned, blackness creeping across his field of vision. He stumbled, catching himself on the chair, managing to collapse into it rather than onto the floor.

"Send for the healer!" he heard the messenger shout. "The king is sick!"

No, Straff thought groggily. *No, this came too quickly. It can't be a disease.*

Zane's last words. What had they been? *A man shouldn't kill his father. . . .*

Liar.

"Amaranta," Straff croaked.

"My lord?" a voice asked. Good. Someone was with him.

"Amaranta," he said again. "Send for her."

"Your mistress, my lord?"

Straff forced himself to remain conscious. As he sat, his vision and balance returned somewhat. One of his door guards was at his side. What was the man's name? Grent.

"Grent," Straff said, trying to sound commanding. "You must bring Amaranta to me. Now!"

The soldier hesitated, then rushed from the room. Straff focused on his breathing. In and out. In and out. Zane was a snake. In and out. In and out. Zane hadn't wanted to use the knife—no, that was expected. In and out. But when had the poison come? Straff had been feeling ill the entire day before.

"My lord?"

Amaranta stood at the doorway. She had been beautiful once, before age had gotten to her—as it got to all of them. Childbirth destroyed a woman. So succulent she had been, with her firm breasts and smooth, unblemished skin. . . .

Your mind is wandering, Straff told himself. Focus.

"I need . . . antidote," Straff forced out, focusing on the Amaranta of the now: the woman in her late twenties, the old—yet still useful—thing that kept him alive in the face of Zane's poisons.

"Of course, my lord," Amaranta said, walking over to his poison cabinet, getting out the necessary ingredients.

Straff settled back, focusing on his breathing. Amaranta must have sensed his urgency, for she hadn't even tried to get him to bed her. He watched her work, getting out her burner and ingredients. He needed . . . to find . . . Zane. . . .

She wasn't doing it the right way.

Straff burned tin. The sudden flash of sensitivity nearly blinded him, even in the shade of his tent, and his aches and shivers became sharp and excruciating. But his mind cleared, as if he'd suddenly bathed in frigid water.

Amaranta was preparing the wrong ingredients. Straff didn't know a great deal about the making of antidotes. He'd been forced to delegate this duty, instead focusing his efforts on learning to recognize the details—the scents, the tastes, the discolorations—of poisons. Yet, he had watched Amaranta prepare her catch-all antidote on numerous occasions. And she was doing it differently this time.

He forced himself out of his chair, keeping tin flared, though it caused his eyes to water. "What are you doing?" he said, walking on unsteady feet toward her.

Amaranta looked up, shocked. The guilt that flashed in her eyes was enough confirmation.

"What are you doing!" Straff bellowed, fear giving him strength as he grabbed her by the shoulders, shaking her. He was weakened, but he was still much stronger than she.

The woman looked down. "Your antidote, my lord . . ."

"You're making it the wrong way!" Straff said.

"I thought, you looked fatigued, so I might add something to help you stay awake."

Straff paused. The words seemed logical, though he was having trouble thinking. Then, looking down at the chagrined woman, he noticed something. His eyes enhanced beyond natural detail, he caught a slight glimpse of a bit of uncovered flesh beneath her bodice.

He reached down and ripped off the side of her dress, exposing her skin. Her left breast—disgusting to him, for it sagged a slight bit—was scarred and cut, as if by a knife. None of the scars were fresh, but even in his addled state, Straff recognized Zane's handiwork.

"You're his lover?" Straff said.

"It's your fault," Amaranta hissed. "You abandoned me, once I aged and bore you a few children. Everyone told me you would, but yet, I hoped . . ."

Straff felt himself growing weak. Dizzy, he rested a hand on the wooden poisons cabinet.

"Yet," Amaranta said, tears on her cheeks. "Why did you have to take Zane from me, too? What did you do, to draw him off? To make him stop coming to me?"

"You let him poison me," Straff said, falling to one knee.

"Fool," Amaranta spat. "He never poisoned you—not a single time. Though, at my request, he often made you think that he had. And then, each time, you ran to me. You suspected everything Zane did—and yet, you never once paused to think what was in the 'antidote' I gave you."

"It made me better," Straff mumbled.

"That's what happens when you're addicted to a drug,

Straff," Amaranta whispered. "When you get it, you feel better. When you don't get it . . . you die."

Straff closed his eyes.

"You're mine now, Straff," she said. "I can make you—"

Straff bellowed, gathering what strength he had and throwing himself at the woman. She cried in surprise as he tackled her, pushing her to the ground.

Then she said nothing, for Straff's hands choked her windpipe. She struggled for a bit, but Straff weighed far more than she did. He'd intended to demand the antidote, to force her to save him, but he wasn't thinking clearly. His vision began to fuzz, his mind dim.

By the time he regained his wits, Amaranta was blue and dead on the ground before him. He wasn't certain how long he'd been strangling her corpse. He rolled off her, toward the open cabinet. On his knees, he reached up for the burner, but his shaking hands toppled it to the side, spilling hot liquid across the floor.

Cursing to himself, he grabbed a flagon of unheated water and began to throw handfuls of herbs into it. He stayed away from the drawers that held the poisons, sticking to those that held antidotes. Yet, there were many crossovers. Some things were poisonous in large doses, but could cure in smaller amounts. Most were addictive. He didn't have time to worry about that; he could feel the weakness in his limbs, and he could barely grab the handfuls of herbs. Bits of brown and red shook from his fingers as he dumped handful after handful into the mixture.

One of these was the herb that she'd gotten him addicted to. Any one of the others might kill him. He wasn't even sure what the odds were.

He drank the concoction anyway, gulping it down between choking gasps for air, then let himself slip into unconsciousness.

I have no doubt that if Alendi reaches the Well of Ascension, he will take the power and then—in the name of the presumed greater good—give it up.

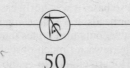

50

"ARE THOSE THE FELLOWS YOU want, Lady Cett?"

Allrianne scanned the valley—and the army it contained—then looked down at the bandit, Hobart. He smiled eagerly—or, well, he *kind* of smiled. Hobart had fewer teeth than he had fingers, and he was missing a couple of those.

Allrianne smiled back from atop her horse. She sat sidesaddle, reins held lightly in her fingers. "Yes, I do believe that it is, Master Hobart."

Hobart looked back at his band of thugs, grinning. Allrianne Rioted them all a bit, reminding them how much they wanted her promised reward. Her father's army spread out before them in the distance. She had wandered for an entire day, traveling west, looking for it. But, she'd been heading in the wrong direction. If she hadn't run afoul of Hobart's helpful little gang, she would have been forced to sleep outside.

And that would have been rather unpleasant.

"Come, Master Hobart," she said, moving her horse forward. "Let's go and meet with my father."

The group followed happily, one of them leading her packhorse. There was a certain charm to simple men, like Hobart's crew. They really only wanted three things: money, food, and sex. And they could usually use the first to get the other two. When she'd first run across this group, she'd blessed her fortune—despite the fact that they had been running down a hillside in ambush, intent on robbing and raping her. Another charm about men like these was that they were rather inexperienced with Allomancy.

She kept a firm hold on their emotions as they rode down toward the camp. She didn't want them reaching any disappointing conclusions—such as "Ransoms are usually bigger than rewards." She couldn't control them completely, of course—she could only influence them. However, with men so base, it was fairly easy to read what was going on in their heads. It was amusing how quickly a little promise of wealth could turn brutes into near gentlemen.

Of course, there wasn't much of a challenge in dealing with men like Hobart, either. No . . . no challenge, as there had been with Breezy. Now, *that* had been fun. And rewarding, too. She doubted she'd ever find a man as aware of his emotions, and as aware of the emotions of others, as Breezy. Getting a man like him—a man so expert in Allomancy, so determined that his age made him inappropriate for her—to love her . . . well, that had been a true accomplishment.

Ah, Breezy, she thought as they passed out of the forest and onto the hillside before the army. *Do any of your friends even understand what a noble man you are?*

They really didn't treat him well enough. Of course, that was to be expected. That was what Breezy wanted. People who underestimated you were easier to manipulate. Yes, Allrianne understood this concept quite well—for there were few things more quickly dismissed than a young, silly girl.

"Halt!" a soldier said, riding up with an honor guard. They had swords drawn. "Step away from her, you!"

Oh, honestly, Allrianne thought, rolling her eyes. She Rioted the group of soldiers, enhancing their sense of calmness. She didn't want any accidents.

"Please, Captain," she said as Hobart and his crew drew weapons, huddling around her uncertainly. "These men have rescued me from the savage wilderness and brought me safely home, at much personal cost and danger."

Hobart nodded firmly, an action undermined just a bit as he wiped his nose on his sleeve. The soldier captain looked over the ash-stained, motley-clothed group of bandits, then frowned.

"See that these men have a good meal, Captain," she said airily, kicking her horse forward. "And give them space for the night. Hobart, I'll send your reward once I meet with my father."

Bandits and soldiers moved in behind her, and Allrianne made sure to Riot them both, enhancing their senses of trust. It was a tough sell for the soldiers, especially as the wind shifted, blowing the full stench of the bandit crew across them. Still, they all reached the camp without incident.

The groups parted, Allrianne giving her horses to an aide and calling for a page to warn her father that she'd returned. She dusted off her riding dress, then strode through camp, smiling pleasantly and looking forward to a bath and the other comforts—such as they were—that the army could provide. However, first there were things she needed to attend to.

Her father liked to spend evenings in his open-sided planning pavilion, and he sat there now, arguing with a messenger. He looked over as Allrianne swished into the pavilion, smiling sweetly at Lords Galivan and Detor, her father's generals.

Cett sat on a high-legged chair so he could get a good view of his table and its maps. "Well, damn it," he said. "You *are* back."

Allrianne smiled, wandering around his planning table, looking at the map. It detailed the supply lines back to the Western Dominance. What she saw was not good.

"Rebellions back home, Father?" she asked.

"And ruffians attacking my supply carts," Cett said. "That boy Venture bribed them, I'm sure of it."

"Yes, he did," Allrianne said. "But, that's all pointless now. Did you miss me?" She made sure to Tug strongly on his sense of devotion.

Cett snorted, pulling at his beard. "Fool of a girl," he said. "I should have left you home."

"So I could have fallen to your enemies when they raised a rebellion?" she asked. "We both know that Lord

Yomen was going to move the moment you pulled your armies out of the dominance."

"And I should have let that damn obligator have you!"

Allrianne gasped. "Father! Yomen would have held me for ransom. You know how terribly I wilt when I'm locked up."

Cett glanced at her, and then—apparently despite himself—he started to chuckle. "You'd've had him feeding you gourmet foods before the day was through. Maybe I *should* have left you behind. Then, at least, I'd have known where you were—rather than worrying where you'd run off to next. You didn't bring that idiot Breeze back with you, did you?"

"Father!" Allrianne said. "Breezy is a good man."

"Good men die quickly in this world, Allrianne," Cett said. "I know—I've killed enough of them."

"Oh, yes," Allrianne said, "you're very wise. And taking an aggressive stance against Luthadel had *such* a positive outcome, didn't it? Chased away with your tail between your legs? You'd be dead now, if dear Vin had as little conscience as you."

"That 'conscience' didn't stop her from killing some three hundred of my men," Cett said.

"She's a very confused young lady," Allrianne said. "Either way, I do feel obliged to remind you that I was right. You should have made an alliance with the Venture boy, instead of threatening him. That means you owe me five new dresses!"

Cett rubbed his forehead. "This isn't a damn game, girl."

"Fashion, Father, is no *game*," Allrianne said firmly. "I can't very well enchant bandit troops into leading me safely home if I look like a street rat, now can I?"

"More bandits, Allrianne?" Cett asked with a sigh. "You know how long it took us to get rid of the last group?"

"Hobart's a wonderful man," Allrianne said testily. "Not to mention well-connected with the local thieving community. Give him some gold and some prostitutes, and you might just be able to talk him into helping you with those brigands that are attacking your supply lines."

Cett paused, glancing at the map. Then he began to pull at

his beard thoughtfully. "Well, you're back," he finally said. "Guess we'll have to take care of you. I suppose you want someone to carry a litter for you as we head home. . . ."

"Actually," Allrianne said, "we're not going back to the dominance. We're returning to Luthadel."

Cett didn't immediately dismiss the comment; he could usually tell when she was being serious. Instead, he simply shook his head. "Luthadel holds nothing for us, Allrianne."

"We can't go back to the dominance, either," Allrianne said. "Our enemies are too strong, and some of them have Allomancers. That's why we had to come here in the first place. We can't leave the area until we have either money or allies."

"There's no money in Luthadel," Cett said. "I believe Venture when he says the atium isn't there."

"I agree," Allrianne said. "I searched that palace well, never found a bit of the stuff. That means we need to leave here with friends, instead of money. Go back, wait for a battle to start, then help whichever side looks like it's going to win. They'll feel indebted to us—they might even decide to let us live."

Cett stood quietly for a moment. "That's not going to help save your friend Breeze, Allrianne. His faction is by far the weakest—even teaming with the Venture boy, I doubt we could beat Straff or those koloss. Not without access to the city walls and plenty of time to prepare. If we go back, it will be to help your Breeze's enemies."

Allrianne shrugged. *You can't help him if you're not there, Father,* she thought. *They're going to lose anyway— if you* are *in the area, then there's a chance you'll end up helping Luthadel.*

A very small chance, Breeze. That's the best I can give you. I'm sorry.

Elend Venture awoke on their third day out of Luthadel, surprised at how rested he could feel after a night spent in a tent out in the wilderness. Of course, part of that might have been the company.

Vin lay curled up beside him in their bedroll, her head resting against his chest. He would have expected her to be a light sleeper, considering how jumpy she was, but she seemed to feel comfortable sleeping beside him. She even seemed to become just a little less anxious when he put his arms around her.

He looked down at her fondly, admiring the form of her face, the slight curl of her black hair. The cut on her cheek was almost invisible now, and she'd already pulled out the stitches. A constant, low burn of pewter gave the body remarkable strength for recovery. She didn't even favor her right arm anymore—despite the cut shoulder—and her weakness from the fight seemed completely gone.

She still hadn't given him much of an explanation regarding that night. She had fought Zane—who had apparently been Elend's half brother—and TenSoon the kandra had left. Yet, neither of those things seemed like they could have caused the distress in her he'd sensed when she'd come to him in his rooms.

He didn't know if he'd ever get the answers he wanted. Yet, he was coming to realize that he could love her even if he didn't completely understand her. He bent down and kissed the top of her head.

She immediately tensed, eyes opening. She sat up, exposing a bare torso, then glanced around their small tent. It was dimly lit with the light of dawn. Finally, she shook her head, looking over at him. "You're a bad influence on me."

"Oh?" he asked, smiling as he rested on one arm.

Vin nodded, running a hand through her hair. "You're making me get used to sleeping at night," she said. "Plus, I don't sleep in my clothing anymore."

"If you did, it would make things a little awkward."

"Yes," she said, "but what if we get attacked during the night? I'd have to fight them naked."

"I wouldn't mind watching that."

She gave him a flat stare, then reached for a shirt.

"You're having a bad influence on me, too, you know," he said as he watched her dress.

She raised an eyebrow.

"You're making me relax," he said. "And letting me stop

worrying. I've been so tied up with things in the city lately that I'd forgotten what it was like to be an impolite recluse. Unfortunately, during our trip, I've had time to read not only one, but all *three* volumes of Troubeld's *Arts of Scholarship*."

Vin snorted, kneeling in the low tent as she pulled her belt tight; then she crawled over to him. "I don't know how you read while riding," she said.

"Oh, it's quite easy—if you aren't afraid of horses."

"I'm not afraid of them," Vin said. "They just don't like me. They know I can outrun them, and that makes them surly."

"Oh, is that it?" Elend asked, smiling, pulling her over to straddle him.

She nodded, then leaned down to kiss him. She ended it after a moment, however, moving to stand. She swatted his hand away as he tried to pull her back down.

"After all the trouble I took to get dressed?" she asked. "Besides, I'm hungry."

He sighed, reclining back as she scampered out of the tent, into the red morning sunlight. He lay for a moment, quietly remarking to himself on his fortune. He still wasn't sure how their relationship had worked out, or even why it made him so happy, but he was more than willing to enjoy the experience.

Eventually, he looked over at his clothing. He had brought only one of his nice uniforms—along with the riding uniform—and he didn't want to wear either too often. He didn't have servants anymore to wash the ash out of his clothing; in fact, despite the tent's double flap, some ash had managed to work its way inside during the night. Now that they were out of the city, there were no workers to sweep the ash away, and it was getting everywhere.

So, he dressed in an outfit far more simple: a pair of riding trousers, not unlike the pants that Vin often wore, with a buttoning gray shirt and a dark jacket. He'd never been forced to ride long distances before—carriages were generally preferred—but Vin and he were taking the trip relatively slowly. They had no real urgency. Straff's scouts hadn't followed them for long, and nobody was expecting them at their destination. They had time to ride leisurely, taking breaks, occasionally walking so that they wouldn't get too sore from riding.

Outside, he found Vin stirring up the morning fire and Spook caring for the horses. The young man had done some extensive traveling, and he knew how to tend horses—something that Elend was embarrassed to have never learned.

Elend joined Vin at the firepit. They sat for a few moments, Vin poking at the coals. She looked pensive.

"What?" Elend asked.

She glanced southward. "I . . ." Then she shook her head. "It's nothing. We're going to need more wood." She glanced to the side, toward where their axe lay beside the tent. The weapon flipped up into the air, shooting toward her blade-first. She stepped to the side, snatching the handle as it passed between her and Elend. Then she stalked over to a fallen tree. She took two swings at it, then easily kicked it down and broke it in two.

"She has a way of making the rest of us feel a little redundant, doesn't she?" Spook asked, stepping up beside Elend.

"At times," Elend said with a smile.

Spook shook his head. "Whatever I see or hear, she can sense better—and she can fight whatever it is that she finds. Every time I come back to Luthadel, I just feel . . . useless."

"Imagine being a regular person," Elend said. "At least you're an Allomancer."

"Maybe," Spook said, the sound of Vin chopping coming from the side. "But people respect you, El. They just dismiss me."

"I don't dismiss you, Spook."

"Oh?" the young man asked. "When's the last time I did anything important for the crew?"

"Three days ago," Elend said. "When you agreed to come with Vin and me. You're not just here to tend horses, Spook—you're here because of your skills as a scout and a Tineye. Do you still think we're being followed?"

Spook paused, then shrugged. "I can't be sure. I think

Straff's scouts turned back, but I keep catching sight of someone back there. I never get a good glimpse of them, though."

"It's the mist spirit," Vin said, walking by and dumping an armload of wood beside the firepit. "It's chasing us."

Spook and Elend shared a look. Then Elend nodded, refusing to act on Spook's uncomfortable stare. "Well, as long as it stays out of our way, it's not a problem, right?"

Vin shrugged. "I hope not. If you see it, though, call for me. The records say it can be dangerous."

"All right," Elend said. "We'll do that. Now, let's decide what to have for breakfast."

Straff woke up. That was his first surprise.

He lay in bed, inside his tent, feeling like someone had picked him up and slammed him against the wall a few times. He groaned, sitting up. His body was free from bruises, but he ached, and his head was pounding. One of the army healers, a young man with a full beard and bulging eyes, sat beside his bed. The man studied Straff for a moment.

"You, my lord, should be dead," the young man said.

"I'm not," Straff said, sitting up. "Give me some tin."

A soldier approached with a metal vial. Straff downed it, then scowled at how dry and sore his throat was. He burned the tin only lightly; it made his wounds feel worse, but he had come to depend on the slight edge the enhanced senses gave him.

"How long?" he asked.

"Better part of three days, my lord," the healer said. "We . . . weren't sure what you'd eaten, or why. We thought about trying to get you to vomit, but it appeared that you'd taken the draught of your own choice, so . . ."

"You did well," Straff said, holding his arm up in front of him. It still shook a bit, and he couldn't make it stop. "Who is in charge of the army?"

"General Janarle," the healer said.

Straff nodded. "Why hasn't he had me killed?"

The healer blinked in surprise, glancing at the soldiers.

"My lord," said Grent the soldier, "who would dare betray you? Any man who tried would end up dead in his tent. General Janarle was *most* worried about your safety."

Of course, Straff realized with shock. *They don't know that Zane is gone. Why . . . if I did die, then everyone assumes that Zane would either take control himself, or get revenge on those he thought responsible.* Straff laughed out loud, shocking those watching over him. Zane had tried to kill him, but had accidentally saved his life by sheer force of reputation.

I beat you, Straff realized. *You're gone, and I'm alive.* That didn't, of course, mean that Zane wouldn't return— but, then again, he might not. Perhaps . . . just maybe . . . Straff was rid of him forever.

"Elend's Mistborn," Straff said suddenly.

"We followed her for a while, my lord," Grent said. "But, they got too far from the army, and Lord Janarle ordered the scouts back. It appears she's making for Terris."

He frowned. "Who else was with her?"

"We think your son Elend escaped as well," the soldier said. "But it could have been a decoy."

Zane did it, Straff thought with shock. *He actually got rid of her.*

Unless it's a trick of some sort. But, then . . .

"The koloss army?" Straff asked.

"There's been a lot of fighting in its ranks lately, sir," Grent said. "The beasts seem more restless."

"Order our army to break camp," Straff said. "Immediately. We're retreating back toward the Northern Dominance."

"My lord?" Grent said with shock. "I think Lord Janarle is planning an assault, waiting only for your word. The city is weak, and their Mistborn is gone."

"We're pulling back," Straff said, smiling. "For a while, at least." *Let's see if this plan of yours works, Zane.*

Sazed sat in a small kitchen alcove, hands on the table before him, a metallic ring glittering on each finger. They were small, for metalminds, but storing up Feruchemical attributes took time. It would take weeks to fill even a ring's worth of metal—and he barely had days. In fact, Sazed was surprised the koloss had waited so long.

Three days. Not much time at all, but he suspected he would need every available edge in the approaching conflict. So far he'd been able to store up a small amount of each attribute. Enough for a boost in an emergency, once his other metalminds ran out.

Clubs hobbled into the kitchen. He seemed a blur to Sazed. Even wearing his spectacles—to help compensate for the vision he was storing in a tinmind—it was difficult for him to see.

"That's it," Clubs said, his voice muffled—another tinmind was taking Sazed's hearing. "They're finally gone."

Sazed paused for a moment, trying to decipher the comment. His thoughts moved as if through a thick, turgid soup, and it took him a moment to understand what Clubs had said.

They're gone. Straff's troops. They've withdrawn. He coughed quietly before replying. "Did he ever respond to any of Lord Penrod's messages?"

"No," Clubs said. "But he did execute the last messenger."

Well, that isn't a very good sign, Sazed thought slowly. Of course, there hadn't been very many good signs over the last few days. The city was on the edge of starvation, and their brief respite of warmth was over. It would snow this evening, if Sazed guessed right. That made him feel even more guilty to be sitting in the kitchen nook, beside a warm hearth, sipping broth as his metalminds sapped his strength, health, senses, and power of thought. He had rarely tried to fill so many at once.

"You don't look so good," Clubs noted, sitting.

Sazed blinked, thinking through the comment. "My . . . goldmind," he said slowly. "It draws my health, storing it up." He glanced at his bowl of broth. "I must eat to maintain my strength," he said, mentally preparing himself to take a sip.

It was an odd process. His thoughts moved so slowly that it took him a moment to decide to eat. Then his body reacted slowly, the arm taking a few seconds to move. Even then, the muscles quivered, their strength sapped away and stored in his pewtermind. Finally, he was able to get a spoonful to his lips and take a quiet sip. It tasted bland; he was filling scent as well, and without it, his sense of taste was severely hampered.

He should probably be lying down—but if he did that, he was liable to sleep. And, while sleeping, he couldn't fill metalminds—or, at least, he could fill only one. A bronzemind, the metal that stored wakefulness, would force him to sleep longer in exchange for letting him go longer without sleep on another occasion.

Sazed sighed, carefully setting down his spoon, then coughing. He'd done his best to help avert the conflict. His best plan had been to send a letter to Lord Penrod, urging him to inform Straff Venture that Vin was gone from the city. He had hoped that Straff would then be willing to make a deal. Apparently, that tactic had been unsuccessful. Nobody had heard from Straff in days.

Their doom approached like the inevitable sunrise. Penrod had allowed three separate groups of townspeople—one of them composed of nobility—to try to flee Luthadel. Straff's soldiers, more wary after Elend's escape, had caught and slaughtered each group. Penrod had even sent a messenger to Lord Jastes Lekal, hoping to strike some deal with the Southern leader, but the messenger had not returned from the koloss camp.

"Well," Clubs said, "at least we kept them off for a few days."

Sazed thought for a moment. "It was simply a delay of the inevitable, I fear."

"Of course it was," Clubs said. "But it was an important delay. Elend and Vin will be almost four days away by now. If the fighting had started too soon, you can bet that little Miss Mistborn would have come back and gotten herself killed trying to save us."

"Ah," Sazed said slowly, forcing himself to reach for another spoonful of broth. The spoon was a dull weight in his numb fingers; his sense of touch, of course, was being siphoned into a tinmind. "How are the city defenses coming?" he asked as he struggled with the spoon.

"Terribly," Clubs said. "Twenty thousand troops may sound like a lot—but try stringing them out through a city this big."

"But the koloss won't have any siege equipment," Sazed said, focused on his spoon. "Or archers."

"Yes," Clubs said. "But we have eight city gates to protect—and any of five are within quick reach of the koloss. None of those gates was built to withstand an attack. And, as it stands, I can barely post a couple thousand guards at each gate, since I really don't know which way the koloss will come first."

"Oh," Sazed said quietly.

"What did you expect, Terrisman?" Clubs asked. "Good news? The koloss are bigger, stronger, and far crazier than we are. And they have an advantage in numbers."

Sazed closed his eyes, quivering spoon held halfway to his lips. He suddenly felt a weakness unrelated to his metalminds. *Why didn't she go with them? Why didn't she escape?*

As Sazed opened his eyes, he saw Clubs waving for a servant to bring him something to eat. The young girl returned with a bowl of soup. Clubs eyed it with dissatisfaction for a moment, but then lifted a knotted hand and began to slurp. He shot a glance at Sazed. "You expecting an apology out of me, Terrisman?" he asked between spoonfuls.

Sazed sat shocked for a moment. "Not at all, Lord Cladent," he finally said.

"Good," Clubs said. "You're a decent enough person. You're just confused."

Sazed sipped his soup, smiling. "That is comforting to hear. I think." He thought for a moment. "Lord Cladent. I have a religion for you."

Clubs frowned. "You don't give up, do you?"

Sazed looked down. It took him a moment to gather together what he'd been thinking about before. "What you said earlier, Lord Cladent. About situational morality. It

made me think of a faith, known as Dadradah. Its practition-
ers spanned many countries and peoples; they believed that
there was only one God, and that there was only one right
way to worship."

Clubs snorted. "I'm really not interested in one of your
dead religions, Terrisman. I think that—"

"They were artists," Sazed said quietly.

Clubs hesitated.

"They thought art drew one closer to God," Sazed said.
"They were most interested in color and hue, and they
were fond of writing poetry describing the colors they saw
in the world around them."

Clubs was silent. "Why preach this religion to me?" he
demanded. "Why not pick one that is blunt, like I am? Or
one that worshipped warfare and soldiers?"

"Because, Lord Cladent," Sazed said. He blinked, recalling memories with effort through his muddled mind.
"That is not you. It is what you must do, but it is not you.
The others forget, I think, that you were a woodworker. An
artist. When we lived in your shop, I often saw you, putting
the finishing touches on pieces your apprentices had
carved. I saw the care you used. That shop was no simple
front for you. You miss it, I know."

Clubs didn't respond.

"You must live as a soldier," Sazed said, pulling something from his sash with a weak hand. "But you can still
dream like an artist. Here. I had this made for you. It is a
symbol of the Dadradah faith. To its people, being an artist
was a higher calling, even, than being a priest."

He set the wooden disk on the table. Then, with effort,
he smiled at Clubs. It had been a long time since he had
preached a religion, and he wasn't certain what had made
him decide to offer this one to Clubs. Perhaps it was to
prove to himself that there was value in them. Perhaps it
was stubbornness, reacting against the things Clubs had
said earlier. Either way, he found satisfaction in the way
that Clubs stared at the simple wooden disk with the
carved picture of a brush on it.

The last time I preached a religion, he thought, *I was in
that village to the south, the one where Marsh found me.*

Whatever happened to him, anyway? Why didn't he return to the city?

"Your woman has been looking for you," Clubs finally said, looking up, leaving the disk on the table.

"*My* woman?" Sazed said. "Why, we are not . . ." He trailed off as Clubs eyed him. The surly general was quite proficient at meaningful looks.

"Very well," Sazed said, sighing. He glanced down at his fingers and the ten glittering rings they bore. Four were tin: sight, hearing, scent, and touch. He continued to fill these; they wouldn't handicap him much. He released his pewtermind, however, as well as his steelmind and his zincmind.

Immediately, strength refilled his body. His muscles stopped sagging, reverting from emaciated to healthy. The fuzz lifted from his mind, allowing him to think clearly, and the thick, swollen slowness evaporated. He stood, invigorated.

"That's fascinating," Clubs mumbled.

Sazed looked down.

"I could see the change," Clubs said. "Your body grew stronger, and your eyes focused. Your arms stopped shaking. I guess you don't want to face that woman without all of your faculties, eh? I don't blame you." Clubs grunted to himself, then continued to eat.

Sazed bid farewell to the man, then strode out of the kitchen. His feet and hands still seemed like nearly unfeeling lumps. Yet, he felt an energy. There was nothing like simple contrast to awaken a man's sense of indomitability.

And there was nothing that could sap that sensation more quickly than the prospect of meeting with the woman he loved. Why had Tindwyl stayed? And, if she was determined not to go back to Terris, why had she avoided him these last few days? Was she mad that he had sent Elend away? Was she disappointed that he insisted on staying to help?

He found her inside Keep Venture's grand ballroom. He paused for a moment, impressed—as always—by the room's unquestionable majesty. He released his sight tinmind for just a moment, removing his spectacles as he looked around the awesome space.

Enormous, rectangular stained-glass windows reached to the ceiling along both walls of the huge room. Standing at the side, Sazed was dwarfed by massive pillars that supported a small gallery that ran beneath the windows on either side of the chamber. Every bit of stone in the room seemed carved—every tile a part of one mosaic or another, every bit of glass colored to sparkle in the early-evening sunlight.

It's been so long . . . he thought. The first time he'd seen this chamber, he had been escorting Vin to her first ball. It was then, while playing the part of Valette Renoux, she had met Elend. Sazed had chastised her for carelessly attracting the attention of so powerful a man.

And now he himself had performed their marriage. He smiled, replacing his spectacles and filling his eyesight tinmind again. *May the Forgotten Gods watch over you, children. Make something of our sacrifice, if you can.*

Tindwyl stood speaking with Dockson and a small group of functionaries at the center of the room. They were crowded around a large table, and as Sazed approached, he could see what was spread atop it.

Marsh's map, he thought. It was an extensive and detailed representation of Luthadel, complete with notations about Ministry activity. Sazed had a visual image of the map, as well as a detailed description of it, in one of his coppperminds—and he had sent a physical copy to the Synod.

Tindwyl and the others had covered the large map with their own notations. Sazed approached slowly, and as soon as Tindwyl saw him, she waved for him to approach.

"Ah, Sazed," Dockson said in a businesslike tone, voice muddled to Sazed's weak ears. "Good. Please, come here."

Sazed stepped up onto the low dance floor, joining them at the table. "Troop placements?" he asked.

"Penrod has taken command of our armies," Dockson said. "And he's put noblemen in charge of all twenty battalions. We're not certain we like that situation."

Sazed looked over the men at the table. They were a group of scribes that Dockson himself had trained—all skaa. *Gods!* Sazed thought. *He can't be planning a rebellion* now *of all times, can he?*

"Don't look so frightened, Sazed," Dockson said. "We're not going to do anything too drastic—Penrod is still letting Clubs organize the city defenses, and he seems to be taking advice from his military commanders. Besides, it's far too late to try something too ambitious."

Dockson almost seemed disappointed.

"However," Dockson said, pointing at the map, "I don't trust these commanders he's put in charge. They don't know anything about warfare—or even about survival. They've spent their lives ordering drinks and throwing parties."

Why do you hate them so? Sazed thought. Ironically, Dockson was the one in the crew who *looked* most like a nobleman. He was more natural in a suit than Breeze, more articulate than Clubs or Spook. Only his insistence on wearing a very unaristocratic half beard made him stand out.

"The nobility may not know warfare," Sazed said, "but they are experienced with command, I think."

"True," Dockson said. "But so are we. That's why I want one of our people near each gate, just in case things go poorly and someone really competent needs to take command."

Dockson pointed at the table, toward one of the gates—Steel Gate. It bore a notation of a thousand men in a defensive formation. "This is your battalion, Sazed. Steel Gate is the farthest the koloss are likely to reach, and so you might not even see any fighting. However, when the battle begins, I want you there with a group of messengers to bring word back to Keep Venture in case your gate gets attacked. We'll set up a command post here in the main ballroom— it's easily accessible with those broad doors, and can accommodate a lot of motion."

And it was a not-so-subtle smack in the face of Elend Venture, and nobility in general, to use such a beautiful chamber as a setting from which to run a war. *No wonder he supported me in sending Elend and Vin away. With them gone, he's gained undisputed control of Kelsier's crew.*

It wasn't a bad thing. Dockson was an organizational genius and a master of quick planning. He did have certain prejudices, however.

"I know you don't like to fight, Saze," Dockson said, leaning down on the table with both hands. "But we need you."

"I think he is preparing for battle, Lord Dockson," Tindwyl said, eyeing Sazed. "Those rings on his fingers give good indication of his intentions."

Sazed glanced across the table at her. "And what is your place in this, Tindwyl?"

"Lord Dockson came to me for advice," Tindwyl said. "He has little experience with warfare himself, and wished to know the things I have studied about the generals of the past."

"Ah," Sazed said. He turned to Dockson, frowning in thought. Eventually, he nodded. "Very well. I will take part in your project—but, I must warn you against divisiveness. Please, tell your men not to break the chain of command unless they absolutely must."

Dockson nodded.

"Now, Lady Tindwyl," Sazed said. "Might we speak for a moment in private?"

She nodded, and they excused themselves, walking under the nearest overhanging gallery. In the shadows, behind one of the pillars, Sazed turned toward Tindwyl. She looked so pristine—so poised, so calm—despite the dire situation. How did she do that?

"You're storing quite a large number of attributes, Sazed," Tindwyl noted, glancing at his fingers again. "Surely you have other metalminds prepared from before?"

"I used all of my wakefulness and speed making my way to Luthadel," Sazed said. "And I have no health stored at all—I used up the last of it overcoming a sickness when I was teaching in the South. I always intended to fill another one, but we've been too busy. I do have some large amount of strength and weight stored, as well as a good selection of tinminds. Still, one can never be *too* well prepared, I think."

"Perhaps," Tindwyl said. She glanced back at the group

around the table. "If it gives us something to do other than think about the inevitable, then preparation has not been wasted, I think."

Sazed felt a chill. "Tindwyl," he said quietly. "Why did you stay? There is no place for you here."

"There is no place for you either, Sazed."

"These are my friends," he said. "I will not leave them."

"Then why did you convince their leaders to leave?"

"To flee and live," Sazed said.

"Survival is not a luxury often afforded to leaders," Tindwyl said. "When they accept the devotion of others, they must accept the responsibility that comes with it. This people will die—but they need not die feeling betrayed."

"They were not—"

"They expect to be saved, Sazed," Tindwyl hissed quietly. "Even those men over there—even *Dockson,* the most practical one in this bunch—think that they'll survive. And do you know why? Because, deep down, they believe that something will save them. Something that saved them before, the only piece of the Survivor they have left. She represents hope to them now. And you sent her away."

"To live, Tindwyl," Sazed repeated. "It would have been a waste to lose Vin and Elend here."

"Hope is never wasted," Tindwyl said, eyes flashing. "I thought you of all people would understand that. You think it was stubbornness that kept me alive all those years in the hands of the Breeders?"

"And is it stubbornness or hope that kept you here, in the city?" he asked.

She looked up at him. "Neither."

Sazed looked at her for a long moment in the shadowed alcove. Planners talked in the ballroom, their voices echoing. Shards of light from the windows reflected off the marble floors, throwing slivers of illumination across the walls. Slowly, awkwardly, Sazed put his arms around Tindwyl. She sighed, letting him hold her.

He released his tinminds and let his senses return in a flood.

Softness from her skin and warmth from her body washed across him as she moved farther into the embrace, resting her head against his chest. The scent of her hair—unperfumed, but clean and crisp—filled his nose, the first thing he'd smelled in three days. With a clumsy hand, Sazed pulled free his spectacles so he could see her clearly. As sounds returned fully to his ears, he could hear Tindwyl breathing beside him.

"Do you know why I love you, Sazed?" she asked quietly.

"I cannot fathom," he answered honestly.

"Because you never give in," she said. "Other men are strong like bricks—firm, unyielding, but if you pound on them long enough, they crack. You . . . you're strong like the wind. Always there, so willing to bend, but never apologetic for the times when you must be firm. I don't think any of your friends understand what a power they had in you."

Had, he thought. *She already thinks of all this in the past tense. And . . . it feels right for her to do so.* "I fear that whatever I have won't be enough to save them," Sazed whispered.

"It was enough to save three of them, though," Tindwyl said. "You were wrong to send them away . . . but maybe you were right, too."

Sazed just closed his eyes and held her, cursing her for staying, yet loving her for it all the same.

At that moment, the wall-top warning drums began to beat.

And so, I have made one final gamble.

51

THE MISTY RED LIGHT OF morning was a thing that should not have existed. Mist died before daylight. Heat made it evaporate; even locking it inside of a closed room made it condense and disappear. It shouldn't have been able to withstand the light of the rising sun.

Yet it did. The farther they'd gotten from Luthadel, the longer the mists lingered in the mornings. The change was slight—they were still only a few days' ride from Luthadel—but Vin knew. She saw the difference. This morning, the mists seemed even stronger than she'd anticipated—they didn't even weaken as the sun came up. They obscured its light.

Mist, she thought. *Deepness.* She was increasingly sure that she was right about it, though she couldn't know for certain. Still, it felt right to her for some reason. The Deepness hadn't been some monster or tyrant, but a force more natural—and therefore more frightening. A creature could be killed. The mists . . . they were far more daunting. The Deepness wouldn't oppress with priests, but use the people's own superstitious terror. It wouldn't slaughter with armies, but with starvation.

How did one fight something larger than a continent? A thing that couldn't feel anger, pain, hope, or mercy?

Yet, it was Vin's task to do just that. She sat quietly on a large boulder beside the night's firepit, her legs up, knees to her chest. Elend still slept; Spook was out scouting.

She didn't question her place any longer. She was either mad or she was the Hero of Ages. It was her task to defeat the mists. *Yet . . .* she thought, frowning. *Shouldn't the thumpings be getting louder, not softer?* The longer they traveled, the weaker the thumpings seemed. Was she too late? Was something happening at the Well to dampen its power? Had someone else already taken it?

We have to keep moving.

Another person in her place might have asked why he had been chosen. Vin had known several men—both in Camon's crew and in Elend's government—who would complain every time they were given an assignment. "Why me?" they would ask. The insecure ones didn't think they were up to the task. The lazy ones wanted out of the work.

Vin didn't consider herself to be either self-assured or self-motivated. Still, she saw no point in asking why. Life had taught her that sometimes things simply happened. Often, there hadn't been any specific reason for Reen to beat her. And, reasons were weak comforts, anyway. The reasons that Kelsier had needed to die were clear to her, but that didn't make her miss him any less.

She had a job to do. The fact that she didn't understand it didn't stop her from acknowledging that she had to try to accomplish it. She simply hoped that she'd know what to do when the time came. Though the thumpings were weaker, they were still there. They drew her forward. To the Well of Ascension.

Behind her, she could feel the lesser vibration of the mist spirit. It never disappeared until the mists themselves did. It had been there all morning, standing just behind her.

"Do you know the secret to this all?" she asked quietly, turning toward the spirit in the reddish mists. "Do you have—"

The Allomantic pulse of the mist spirit was coming from directly inside the tent she shared with Elend.

Vin jumped off the rock, landing on the frosted ground and scrambling to the tent. She threw open the flaps. Elend slept inside, head just barely visible as it poked out of the blankets. Mist filled the small tent, swirling, twisting—and that was odd enough. Mist didn't usually enter tents.

And there, in the middle of the mists, was the spirit. Standing directly above Elend.

It wasn't even really there. It was just an outline in the

mists, a repeating pattern caused by chaotic movements. And yet it was real. She could feel it, and she could see it—see it as it looked up, meeting her gaze with invisible eyes.

Hateful eyes.

It raised an insubstantial arm, and Vin saw something flash. She reacted immediately, whipping out a dagger, bursting into the tent and swinging. Her blow met something tangible in the mist spirit's hand. A metallic sound rang in the calm air, and Vin felt a powerful, numbing chill in her arm. The hairs across her entire body prickled.

And then it disappeared. Fading away, like the ringing of its somehow substantial blade. Vin blinked, then turned to look through the blowing tent flap. The mists outside were gone; day had finally won.

It didn't seem to have many victories remaining.

"Vin?" Elend asked, yawning and stirring.

Vin calmed her breathing. The spirit had gone. The daylight meant safety, for now. *Once, it was the nights that I found safe,* she thought. *Kelsier gave them to me.*

"What's wrong?" Elend asked. How could someone, even a nobleman, be so slow to rise, so unconcerned about the vulnerability he displayed while sleeping?

She sheathed her dagger. *What can I tell him? How can I protect him from something I can barely see?* She needed to think. "It was nothing," she said quietly. "Just me . . . being jumpy again."

Elend rolled over, sighing contentedly. "Is Spook doing his morning scout?"

"Yes."

"Wake me when he gets back."

Vin nodded, but he probably couldn't see her. She knelt, looking at him as the sun rose behind her. She'd given herself to him—not just her body, and not just her heart. She'd abandoned her rationalizations, given away her reservations, all for him. She could no longer afford to think that she wasn't worthy of him, no longer give herself the false comfort of believing they couldn't ever be together.

She'd never trusted anyone this much. Not Kelsier, not

Sazed, not Reen. Elend had everything. That knowledge made her tremble inside. If she lost him, she would lose herself.

I mustn't think about that! she told herself, rising. She left the tent, quietly closing the flaps behind her. In the distance, shadows moved. Spook appeared a moment later.

"Someone's definitely back there," he said quietly. "Not spirits, Vin. Five men, with a camp."

Vin frowned. "Following us?"

"They must be."

Straff's scouts, she thought. "We'll let Elend decide what to do about them."

Spook shrugged, walking over to sit on her rock. "You going to wake him?"

Vin turned back. "Let him sleep a little longer."

Spook shrugged again. He watched as she walked over to the firepit and unwrapped the wood they'd covered the night before, then began to build a fire.

"You've changed, Vin," Spook said.

She continued to work. "Everyone changes," she said. "I'm not a thief anymore, and I have friends to support me."

"I don't mean that," Spook said. "I mean recently. This last week. You're different than you were."

"Different how?"

"I don't know. You don't seem as frightened all the time."

Vin paused. "I've made some decisions. About who I am, and who I will be. About what I want."

She worked quietly for a moment, and finally got a spark to catch. "I'm tired of putting up with foolishness," she finally said. "Other people's foolishness, and my own. I've decided to act, rather than second-guess. Perhaps it's a more immature way of looking at things. But it feels right, for now."

"It's not immature," Spook said.

Vin smiled, looking up at him. Sixteen and hardly grown into his body, he was the same age that she'd been when Kelsier had recruited her. He was squinting against the light, even though the sun was low.

"Lower your tin," Vin said. "No need to keep it on so strong."

Spook shrugged. She could see the uncertainty in him. He wanted so badly to be useful. She knew that feeling.

"What about you, Spook?" she said, turning to gather the breakfast supplies. Broth and mealcakes again. "How have you been lately?"

He shrugged yet again.

I'd almost forgotten what it was like to try and have a conversation with a teenage boy, she thought, smiling.

"Spook . . ." she said, just testing out the name. "What do you think of that nickname, anyway? I remember when everyone called you by your real name." Lestibournes— Vin had tried to spell it once. She'd gotten about five letters in.

"Kelsier gave me my name," Spook said, as if that were reason enough to keep it. And perhaps it was. Vin saw the look in Spook's eyes when he mentioned Kelsier; Clubs might be Spook's uncle, but Kelsier had been the one he looked up to.

Of course, they all had looked up to Kelsier.

"I wish I were powerful, Vin," Spook said quietly, arms folded on his knees as he sat on the rock. "Like you."

"You have your own skills."

"Tin?" Spook asked. "Almost worthless. If I were Mistborn, I could do great things. Be someone important."

"Being important isn't all that wonderful, Spook," Vin said, listening to the thumpings in her head. "Most of the time, it's just annoying."

Spook shook his head. "If I were Mistborn, I could save people—help people, who need it. I could stop people from dying. But . . . I'm just Spook. Weak. A coward."

Vin looked at him, frowning, but his head was bowed, and he wouldn't meet her eyes.

What was that about? she wondered.

Sazed used a bit of strength to help him take the steps three at a time. He burst out of the stairwell just behind Tindwyl, the two of them joining the remaining members of the crew on the wall top. The drums still sounded; each had a different rhythm as it sounded over the city. The mixing beats echoed chaotically from buildings and alleyways.

The northern horizon seemed bare without Straff's army. If only that same emptiness had extended to the northeast, where the koloss camp seemed in turmoil.

"Can anyone make out what's going on?" Breeze asked.

Ham shook his head. "Too far."

"One of my scouts is a Tineye," Clubs said, hobbling over. "He raised the alarm. Said the koloss were fighting."

"My good man," Breeze said, "aren't the foul creatures *always* fighting?"

"More than usual," Clubs said. "Massive brawl."

Sazed felt a swift glimmer of hope. "They're fighting?" he said. "Perhaps they will kill each other!"

Clubs eyed him with one of those looks. "Read one of your books, Terrisman. What do they say about koloss emotions?"

"They only have two," Sazed said. "Boredom and rage. But—"

"This is how they always begin a battle," Tindwyl said quietly. "They start to fight among themselves, enraging more and more of their members, and then . . ."

She trailed off, and Sazed saw it. The dark smudge to the east growing lighter. Dispersing. Resolving into individual members.

Charging the city.

"Bloody hell," Clubs swore, then quickly began to hobble down the steps. "Messengers away!" he bellowed. "Archers to the wall! Secure the river grates! Battalions, form positions! Get ready to fight! Do you want those things breaking in here and getting at your children!"

Chaos followed. Men began to dash in all directions. Soldiers scrambled up the stairwells, clogging the way down, keeping the crew from moving.

It's happening, Sazed thought numbly.

"Once the stairwells are open," Dockson said quietly, "I want each of you to go to your battalion. Tindwyl, you have Tin Gate, in the north by Keep Venture. I might need your advice, but for now, stay with those boys. They'll listen to you—they respect Terrismen. Breeze, you have one of your Soothers in each of battalions four through twelve?"

Breeze nodded. "They aren't much, though. . . ."

"Just have them keep those boys fighting!" Dockson said. "Don't let our men break!"

"A thousand men are far too many for one Soother to handle, my friend," Breeze said.

"Have them do the best they can," Dockson said. "You and Ham take Pewter Gate and Zinc Gate—looks like the koloss are going to hit here first. Clubs should bring in reinforcements."

The two men nodded; then Dockson looked at Sazed. "You know where to go?"

"Yes . . . yes, I think so," Sazed said, gripping the wall. In the air, flakes of ash began to fall from the sky.

"Go, then!" Dockson said as one final squad of archers made its way out of the stairwell.

"My lord Venture!"

Straff turned. With some stimulants, he was able to remain strong enough to stay atop his saddle—though he wouldn't have dared to fight. Of course, he wouldn't have fought anyway. That wasn't his way. One brought armies to do such things.

He turned his animal as the messenger approached. The man puffed, putting hands on knees as he stopped beside Straff's mount, bits of ash swirling on the ground at his feet.

"My lord," the man said. "The koloss army has attacked Luthadel!"

Just as you said, Zane, Straff thought in wonder.

"The koloss, attacking?" Lord Janarle asked, moving his horse up beside Straff's. The handsome lord frowned, then eyed Straff. "You expected this, my lord?"

"Of course," Straff said, smiling.

Janarle looked impressed.

"Pass an order to the men, Janarle," Straff said. "I want this column turned back toward Luthadel."

"We can be there in an hour, my lord!" Janarle said.

"No," Straff said. "Let's take our time. We wouldn't want to overwork our troops, would we?"

Janarle smiled. "Of course not, my lord."

Arrows seemed to have little effect on the koloss.

Sazed stood, transfixed and appalled, atop his gate's watchtower. He wasn't officially in charge of the men, so he didn't have any orders to give. He simply stood with the scouts and messengers, waiting to see if he was needed or not.

That left him plenty of time to watch the horror unfolding. The koloss weren't charging his section of the wall yet, thankfully, and his men stood watching tensely as the creatures barreled toward Tin Gate and Pewter Gate in the distance.

Even far away—the tower letting him see over a section of the city to where Tin Gate lay—Sazed could see the koloss running straight through hailstorms of arrows. Some of the smaller ones appeared to fall dead or wounded, but most just continued to charge. Men murmured on the tower near him.

We aren't ready for this, Sazed thought. *Even with months to plan and anticipate, we aren't ready.*

This is what we get, being ruled over by a god for a thousand years. A thousand years of peace—tyrannical peace, but peace nonetheless. We don't have generals, we have men who know how to order a bath drawn. We don't have tacticians, we have bureaucrats. We don't have warriors, we have boys with sticks.

Even as he watched the oncoming doom, his scholar's mind was analytical. Tapping sight, he could see that many of the distant creatures—especially the larger ones—carried small uprooted trees. They were ready, in their own way, to break into the city. The trees wouldn't be as effective as real battering rams—but then, the city gates weren't built to withstand a real battering in the first place.

Those koloss are smarter than we give them credit for,

he thought. *They can recognize the abstract value of coins, even if they don't have an economy. They can see that they'll need tools to break down our doors, even if they don't know how to make those tools.*

The first koloss wave reached the wall. Men began to toss down rocks and other items. Sazed's own section had similar piles, one just next to the gate arch, beside which he stood. But arrows had almost no effect; what good would a few rocks do? Koloss clumped around the base of the wall, like the water of a dammed-up river. Distant thumps sounded as the creatures began to beat against the gates.

"Battalion sixteen!" a messenger called from below, riding up to Sazed's gate. "Lord Culee!"

"Here!" a man called from the wall top beside Sazed's tower.

"Pewter Gate needs reinforcements immediately! Lord Penrod commands you to bring six companies and follow me!"

Lord Culee began to give the orders. *Six companies . . .* Sazed thought. *Six hundred of our thousand.* Clubs's words from earlier returned to him: Twenty thousand men might seem like a lot, until one saw how thinly they had to be stretched.

The six companies marched away, leaving the courtyard before Sazed's gate disturbingly empty. The four hundred remaining men—three hundred in the courtyard, one hundred on the wall—shuffled quietly.

Sazed closed his eyes and tapped his hearing tinmind. He could hear . . . wood beating on wood. Screams. Human screams. He released the tinmind quickly, then tapped eyesight again, leaning out and looking toward the section of the wall where the battle was being fought. The koloss were throwing back the fallen rocks—and they were far more accurate than the defenders. Sazed jumped as he saw a young soldier's face crushed, his body thrown back off the wall top by the rock's force. Sazed released his tinmind, breathing quickly.

"Be firm, men!" called one of the soldiers on the wall.

He was barely a youth—a nobleman, but he couldn't be more than sixteen. Of course, a lot of the men in the army were that age.

"Stand firm . . ." the young commander repeated. His voice sounded uncertain, and it trailed off as he noticed something in the distance. Sazed turned, following the man's gaze.

The koloss had gotten tired of standing around, piling up at a single gate. They were moving to surround the city, large groups of them breaking up, fording the River Channerel toward other gates.

Gates like Sazed's.

Vin landed directly in the middle of the camp. She tossed a handful of pewter dust into the firepit, then Pushed, blowing coals, soot, and smoke across a pair of surprised guards, who had been fixing breakfast. She reached out and Pulled out the stakes of the three small tents.

All three collapsed. One was unoccupied, but cries came from the other two. The canvas outlined struggling, confused figures—one inside the larger tent, two inside the smaller one.

The guards scrambled back, raising their arms to protect their eyes from the soot and sparks, their hands reaching for swords. Vin raised a fist toward them—and, as they blinked their eyes clear, she let a single coin drop to the ground.

The guards froze, then took their hands off their swords. Vin eyed the tents. The person in charge would be inside the larger one—and he was the man she would need to deal with. Probably one of Straff's captains, though the guards didn't wear Venture heraldry. Perhaps—

Jastes Lekal poked his head out of his tent, cursing as he extricated himself from the canvas. He'd changed much in the two years since Vin had last seen him. However, there had been hints of what the man would become. His thin figure had become spindly; his balding head had fulfilled its promise. Yet, how had his face come to look so haggard . . . so old? He was Elend's age.

"Jastes," Elend said, stepping out of his hiding place in the forest. He walked into the clearing, Spook at his side. "Why are you here?"

Jastes managed to stand as his other two soldiers cut their way out of their tent. He waved them down. "El," he said. "I . . . didn't know where else to go. My scouts said that you were fleeing, and it seemed like a good idea. Wherever you're going, I want to go with you. We can hide there, maybe. We can—"

"Jastes!" Elend snapped, striding forward to stand beside Vin. "Where are your koloss? Did you send them away?"

"I tried," Jastes said, looking down. "They wouldn't go—not once they'd seen Luthadel. And then . . ."

"What?" Elend demanded.

"A fire," Jastes said. "In our . . . supply carts."

Vin frowned.

"Your supply carts?" Elend said. "The carts where you carried your wooden coins?"

"Yes."

"Lord Ruler, man!" Elend said stepping forward. "And you just *left* them there, without leadership, outside our home?"

"They would have killed me, El!" Jastes said. "They were beginning to fight so much, to demand more coins, to demand we attack the city. If I'd stayed, they'd have slaughtered me! They're beasts—beasts that only barely have the shape of man."

"And you left," Elend said. "You abandoned Luthadel to them."

"You abandoned it, too," Jastes said. He walked forward, hands pleading as he approached Elend. "Look, El. I know I was wrong. I thought I could control them. I didn't mean for this to happen!"

Elend fell silent, and Vin could see a hardness growing in his eyes. Not a dangerous hardness, like Kelsier. More of a . . . regal bearing. The sense that he was more than he wanted to be. He stood straight, looking down at the man pleading before him.

"You raised an army of violent monsters and led them in

a tyrannical assault, Jastes," Elend said. "You caused the slaughter of innocent villages. Then, you abandoned that army without leadership or control outside the most popu-lated city in the whole of the Final Empire."

"Forgive me," Jastes said.

Elend looked the man in the eyes. "I forgive you," he said quietly. Then, in one fluid stroke, he drew his sword and sheared Jastes's head from his shoulders. "But my kingdom cannot."

Vin stared, dumbfounded, as the corpse fell to the ground. Jastes's soldiers cried out, drawing their weapons. Elend turned, his face solemn, and raised the point of his bloodied sword toward them. "You think this execution was performed in error?"

The guards paused. "No, my lord," one of them finally said, looking down.

Elend knelt and cleaned his sword on Jastes's cloak. "Considering what he did, this was a better death than he deserved." Elend snapped his sword back into its sheath. "But he was my friend. Bury him. Once you are through, you are welcome to travel with me to Terris, or you may go back to your homes. Choose as you wish." With that, he walked back into the woods.

Vin paused, watching the guards. Solemnly, they moved forward to collect the body. She nodded to Spook, then dashed out into the forest after Elend. She didn't have to go far. She found him sitting on a rock a short distance away, staring at the ground. An ashfall had begun, but most of the flakes got caught in the trees, coating their leaves like black moss.

"Elend?" she asked.

He looked out, staring into the forest. "I'm not sure why I did it, Vin," he said quietly. "Why should I be the one to bring justice? I'm not even king. And yet, it had to be done. I felt it. I feel it still."

She laid a hand on his shoulder.

"He's the first man I've ever killed," Elend said. "He and I had such dreams, once: We'd ally two of the most powerful imperial houses, uniting Luthadel as never be-fore. Ours wasn't to have been a treaty of greed, but a true political alliance intended to help make the city a better place."

He looked up at her. "I think I understand now, Vin, what it is like for you. In a way, we're both knives—both tools. Not for each other, but for this kingdom. This people."

She wrapped her arms around him, holding him, pulling his head to her chest. "I'm sorry," she whispered.

"It had to be done," he said. "The saddest part is, he's right. I abandoned them, too. I should take my own life with this sword."

"You left for a good reason, Elend," Vin said. "You left to protect Luthadel, to make it so Straff wouldn't attack."

"And if the koloss attack before Straff can?"

"Maybe they won't," Vin said. "They don't have a leader—maybe they'll attack Straff's army instead."

"No," Spook's voice said. Vin turned, seeing him approach through the forest, eyes squinting against the light.

That boy burns way too much tin, she thought.

"What do you mean?" Elend asked, turning.

Spook looked down. "They won't attack Straff's army, El. It won't be there anymore."

"What?" Vin asked.

"I . . ." Spook looked away, shame showing in his face.

I'm a coward. His words from earlier returned to her. "You knew," Vin said. "You knew the koloss were going to attack!"

Spook nodded.

"That's ridiculous," Elend said. "You couldn't have known that Jastes would follow us."

"I didn't," Spook said, a lump of ash falling from a tree behind him, bursting before the wind, and fluttering in a hundred different flakes to the ground. "But my uncle figured that Straff would withdraw his army and let the koloss attack the city. That's why Sazed decided to send us away."

Vin felt a sudden chill.

I've found the location of the Well of Ascension, Sazed had said. *To the north. In the Terris Mountains. . . .*

"Clubs told you this?" Elend was saying.

Spook nodded.

"And you didn't tell me?" Elend demanded, standing.

Oh, no. . . .

Spook paused, then shook his head. "You would have wanted to go back! I didn't want to die, El! I'm sorry. I'm a coward." He cringed, glancing at Elend's sword, shying away.

Elend paused, as if realizing he'd been stepping toward the boy. "I'm not going to hurt you, Spook," he said. "I'm just ashamed of you." Spook lowered his eyes, then sank down to the ground, sitting with his back to an aspen.

The thumpings, getting softer. . . .

"Elend," Vin whispered.

He turned.

"Sazed lied. The Well isn't to the north."

"What?"

"It's at Luthadel."

"Vin, that's ridiculous. We'd have found it."

"We didn't," she said firmly, standing, looking south. Focusing, she could feel the thumpings, washing across her. Pulling her.

South.

"The Well can't be to the south," Elend said. "The legends *all* place it north, in the Terris Mountains."

Vin shook her head, confused. "It's there," she said. "I know it is. I don't know how, but it *is* there."

Elend looked at her, then nodded, trusting her instincts.

Oh, Sazed, she thought. *You probably had good intentions, but you may have doomed us all.* If the city fell to the koloss . . .

"How fast can we get back?" Elend asked.

"That depends," she said.

"Go back?" Spook asked, looking up. "El, they're all *dead*. They told me to tell you the truth once you got to Tathingdwen, so you wouldn't kill yourselves climbing the mountains in the winter for nothing. But, when Clubs talked to me, it was also to say goodbye. I could see it in his eyes. He knew he'd never see me again."

Elend paused, and Vin could see a moment of uncertainty

in his eyes. A flash of pain, of terror. She knew those emotions, because they hit her at the same time.

Sazed, Breeze, Ham. . . .

Elend grabbed her arm. "You have to go, Vin," he said. "There might be survivors . . . refugees. They'll need your help."

She nodded, the firmness of his grip—the determination in his voice—giving her strength.

"Spook and I will follow," he said. "It should only take us a couple of days' hard riding. But an Allomancer with pewter can go faster than any horse over long distances."

"I don't want to leave you," she whispered.

"I know."

It was still hard. How could she run off and leave him, when she'd only just rediscovered him? Yet, she could feel the Well of Ascension even more urgently now that she was sure of its location. And if some of her friends *did* survive the attack . . .

Vin gritted her teeth, then opened up her pouch and pulled out the last of her pewter dust. She drank it down with a mouthful of water from her flask. It scratched her throat going down. *It's not much,* she thought. *It won't let me pewter-drag for long.*

"They're all dead . . ." Spook mumbled again.

Vin turned. The pulses thumped demandingly. From the south.

I'm coming.

"Elend," she said. "Please do something for me. Don't sleep during the night, when the mists are out. Travel during the night, if you can, and keep your wits about you. Watch for the mist spirit—I think it may mean you harm."

He frowned, but nodded.

Vin flared pewter, then took off at a run toward the highway.

My pleas, my teachings, my objections, and even my treasons were all ineffectual. Alendi has other counselors now, ones who tell him what he wants to hear.

52

BREEZE DID HIS BEST TO pretend he was *not* in the middle of a war. It didn't work very well.

He sat on his horse at the edge of Zinc Gate's courtyard. Soldiers shuffled and clanked, standing in ranks before the gates, waiting and watching their companions atop the wall.

The gates thumped. Breeze cringed, but continued his Soothing. "Be strong," he whispered. "Fear, uncertainty— I take these away. Death may come through those doors, but you can fight it. You can win. Be strong. . . ."

Brass flared like a bonfire within his stomach. He had long since used up his vials, and had taken to choking down handfuls of brass dust and mouthfuls of water, which he had in a steady supply thanks to Dockson's mounted messengers.

How long can this possibly last? he thought, wiping his brow, continuing to Soothe. Allomancy was, fortunately, very easy on the body; Allomantic power came from within the metals themselves, not from the one who burned them. Yet, Soothing was much more complex than other Allomantic skills, and it demanded constant attention.

"Fear, terror, anxiety . . ." he whispered. "The desire to run or give up. I take these from you. . . ." The speaking wasn't necessary, of course, but it had always been his way—it helped keep him focused.

After a few more minutes of Soothing, he checked his pocket watch, then turned his horse and trotted over to the other side of the courtyard. The gates continued to boom, and Breeze wiped his brow again. He noted, with dissatisfaction, that his handkerchief was nearly too damp to do him any good. It was also beginning to snow. The wetness would make the ash stick to his clothing, and his suit would be absolutely ruined.

The suit will be ruined by your blood, Breeze, he told himself. *The time for silliness is over. This is serious. Far too serious. How did you even end up here?*

He redoubled his efforts, Soothing a new group of soldiers. He was one of the most powerful Allomancers in the Final Empire—especially when it came to emotional Allomancy. He could Soothe hundreds of men at once, assuming they were packed close enough together, and assuming that he was focusing on simple emotions. Even Kelsier hadn't been able to manage those numbers.

Yet, the entire crowd of soldiers was beyond even his ability, and he had to do them in sections. As he began work on the new group, he saw the ones he had left begin to wilt, their anxiety taking over.

When those doors burst, these men are going to scatter.

The gates boomed. Men clustered on the walls, throwing down rocks, shooting arrows, fighting with a frantic lack of discipline. Occasionally, an officer would push his way past them, yelling orders, trying to coordinate their efforts, but Breeze was too far away to tell what they were saying. He could just see the chaos of men moving, screaming, and shooting.

And, of course, he could see the return fire. Rocks zipped into the air from below, some cracking against the ramparts. Breeze tried not to think about what was on the other side of the wall, the thousands of enraged koloss beasts. Occasionally, a soldier would drop. Blood dripped down into the courtyard from several sections of the ramparts.

"Fear, anxiety, terror . . ." Breeze whispered.

Allrianne had escaped. Vin, Elend, and Spook were safe. He had to keep focusing on those successes. *Thank you, Sazed, for making us send them away,* he thought.

Hoofbeats clopped behind him. Breeze continued his Soothing, but turned to see Clubs riding up. The general rode his horse with a hunched-over slouch, eyeing the soldiers with one eye open, the other perpetually squeezed closed in a squint. "They're doing well," he said.

"My dear man," Breeze said. "They're *terrified*. Even the ones beneath my Soothing watch those gates like they were some terrible void waiting to suck them in."

Clubs eyed Breeze. "Feeling poetic today, are we?"

"Impending doom has that effect on me," Breeze said as the gates shook. "Either way, I doubt the men are doing 'well.'"

Clubs grunted. "Men are always nervous before a fight. But, these are good lads. They'll hold."

The gates shook and quivered, splinters appearing at the edges. *Those hinges are straining . . .* Breeze thought.

"Don't suppose you can Soothe those koloss?" Clubs asked. "Make them less ferocious?"

Breeze shook his head. "Soothing those beasts has no effect. I've tried it."

They fell silent again, listening to the booming gates. Eventually, Breeze glanced over at Clubs, who sat, unperturbed, on his horse. "You've been in combat before," Breeze said. "How often?"

"Off and on for the better part of twenty years, when I was younger," Clubs said. "Fighting rebellions in the distant dominances, warring against the nomads out in the barrens. The Lord Ruler was pretty good about keeping those conflicts quiet."

"And . . . how did you do?" Breeze asked. "Were you often victorious?"

"Always," Clubs said.

Breeze smiled slightly.

"Of course," Clubs said, glancing at Breeze, "we were the ones with koloss on our side. Damn hard to kill, those beasts."

Great, Breeze thought.

Vin ran.

She'd only been on one "pewter drag" before—with Kelsier, two years ago. While burning pewter at a steady flare, one could run with incredible speed—like a sprinter in their quickest dash—without ever growing tired.

Yet, the process did something to a body. Pewter kept her moving, but it also bottled up her natural fatigue. The juxtaposition made her mind fuzz, bringing on a trancelike state of exhausted energy. Her soul wanted so badly to rest, yet her body just kept running, and running, and running, following the canal towpath toward the south. Toward Luthadel.

Vin was prepared for the effects of pewter dragging this time, and so she handled them far better. She fought off the trance, keeping her mind focused on her goal, not the repetitive motions of her body. However, that focus led her to discomforting thoughts.

Why am I doing this? she wondered. *Why push myself so hard? Spook said it—Luthadel has to have already fallen. There is no need for urgency.*

And yet, she ran.

She saw images of death in her mind. Ham, Breeze, Dockson, Clubs, and dear, dear Sazed. The first real friends she had ever known. She loved Elend, and part of her blessed the others for sending him away from danger. However, the other piece of her was furious at them for sending her away. That fury guided her.

They let me abandon them. They forced *me to abandon them!*

Kelsier had spent months teaching her how to trust. His last words to her in life had been ones of accusation, and they were words she had never been able to escape. *You still have a lot to learn about friendship, Vin.*

He had gone on to risk his life to get Spook and OreSeur out of danger, fighting off—and eventually killing—a Steel Inquisitor. He had done this despite Vin's protests that the risk was pointless.

She had been wrong.

How dare they! she thought, feeling the tears on her cheeks as she dashed down the canal's highwaylike towpath. Pewter gave her inhuman balance, and the speed—which would have been perilous for anyone else—felt natural to her. She didn't trip, she didn't stumble, but an outside observer would think her pace reckless.

Trees whipped by. She leapt washouts and dips in the land. She ran as she had done only once before, and pushed herself even harder than she had on that day. Before, she had been running simply to keep up with Kelsier. Now she ran for those she loved.

How dare they! she thought again. *How dare they not give me the same chance that Kelsier had! How dare they refuse my protection, refuse to let me help them!*

How dare they die. . . .

Her pewter was running low, and she was only a few hours into her run. True, she had probably covered an entire day's worth of walking in those few hours. Yet, somehow, she knew it wouldn't be enough. They were already dead. She was going to be too late, just as when she'd run years before. Too late to save their army. Too late to save her friends.

Vin continued to run. And she continued to cry.

"How did we get here, Clubs?" Breeze asked quietly, still on the floor of the courtyard, before the booming gate. He sat on his horse, amid a muddy mixture of falling snow and ash. The simple, quiet flutterings of white and black seemed to belie the screaming men, the breaking gate, and the falling rocks.

Clubs looked over at him, frowning. Breeze continued stare up, at the ash and snow. Black and white. Lazy.

"We aren't men of principle," Breeze said quietly. "We're thieves. Cynics. You, a man tired of doing the Lord Ruler's bidding, a man determined to see himself get ahead for once. Me, a man of wavering morals who loves to toy with others, to make their emotions my game. How did we end up here? Standing at the head of an army, fighting an idealist's cause? Men like us shouldn't be leaders."

Clubs watched the men in the courtyard. "Guess we're just idiots," he finally said.

Breeze paused, then noticed that glimmer in Clubs's eyes. That spark of humor, the spark that was hard to recognize unless one knew Clubs very well. It was that spark that told the truth—that showed Clubs to be a man of rare understanding.

Breeze smiled. "I guess we are. Like we said before. It's Kelsier's fault. He turned us into idiots who would stand at the front of a doomed army."

"That bastard," Clubs said.

"Indeed," Breeze said.

Ash and snow continued to fall. Men yelled in alarm.

And the gates burst open.

"The eastern gate has been breached, Master Terrisman!" Dockson's messenger said, puffing slightly as he crouched beside Sazed. They both sat beneath the wall-top battlements, listening to the koloss pound on their own gate. The one that had fallen would be Zinc Gate, the one on the easternmost side of Luthadel.

"Zinc Gate is the most well defended," Sazed said quietly. "They will be able to hold it, I think."

The messenger nodded. Ash blew along the wall top, piling in the cracks and alcoves in the stone, the black flakes adulterated by the occasional bit of bone-white snow.

"Is there anything you wish me to report to Lord Dockson?" the messenger asked.

Sazed paused, glancing along his wall's defenses. He'd climbed down from the watchtower, joining the regular ranks of men. The soldiers had run out of stones, though the archers were still working. He peeked over the side of the wall and saw the koloss corpses piling up. However, he also saw the splintered front of the gate. *It's amazing they can maintain such rage for so long,* he thought, ducking back. The creatures continued to howl and scream, like feral dogs.

He sat back against the wet stone, shivering in the chill wind, his toes growing numb. He tapped his brassmind, drawing out the heat he'd stored therein, and his body suddenly flooded with a pleasant sensation of warmth.

"Tell Lord Dockson that I fear for this gate's defenses,"

Sazed said quietly. "The best men were stolen away to help with the eastern gates, and I have little confidence in our leader. If Lord Dockson could send someone else to be in charge, that would be for the best, I think."

The messenger paused.

"What?" Sazed asked.

"Isn't that why he sent you, Master Terrisman?"

Sazed frowned. "Please tell him I have even less confidence in my own ability to lead . . . or to fight . . . than I do in that of our commander."

The messenger nodded and took off, scrambling down the steps toward his horse. Sazed cringed as a rock hit the wall just above him. Chips flipped over the merlon, scattering to the battlement in front of him. *By the Forgotten Gods . . .* Sazed thought, wringing his hands. *What am I doing here?*

He saw motion on the wall beside him, and turned as the youthful soldier captain—Captain Bedes—moved up to him, careful to keep his head down. Tall, with thick hair that grew down around his eyes, he was spindly even beneath his armor. The young man looked like he should have been dancing at balls, not leading soldiers in battle.

"What did the messenger say?" Bedes asked nervously.

"Zinc Gate has fallen, my lord," Sazed replied.

The young captain paled. "What . . . what should we do?"

"Why ask me, my lord?" Sazed asked. "You are in command."

"Please," the man said, grabbing Sazed's arm. "I don't . . . I . . ."

"My lord," Sazed said sternly, forcing down his own nervousness. "You are a nobleman, are you not?"

"Yes . . ."

"Then you are accustomed to giving orders," Sazed said. "Give them now."

"Which orders?"

"It doesn't matter," Sazed said. "Let the men see that you are in charge."

The young man wavered, then yelped and ducked as a

rock took one of the nearby archers in the shoulder, throwing him back into the courtyard. The men below scrambled out of the way of the corpse, and Sazed noticed something odd. A group of people had gathered at the back of the courtyard. Civilians—skaa—in ash-stained clothing.

"What are they doing here?" Sazed asked. "They should be hiding, not standing here to tempt the koloss once the creatures break through!"

"*Once* they break through?" Captain Bedes asked.

Sazed ignored the man. Civilians he could deal with. He was accustomed to being in charge of a nobleman's servants.

"I will go speak to them," Sazed said.

"Yes . . ." Bedes said. "That sounds like a good idea."

Sazed made his way down the steps, which were growing slick and wet with ashen slush, then approached the group of people. There were even more of them than he had assumed; they extended back into the street a short distance. The hundred or so people stood huddled together, watching the gates through the falling snow, looking cold, and Sazed felt a little guilty for his brassmind's warmth.

Several of the people bowed their heads as Sazed approached.

"Why are you here?" Sazed asked. "Please, you must seek shelter. If your homes are near the courtyard, then go hide near the middle of the city. The koloss are likely to begin pillaging as soon as they finish with the army, so the edges of the city are more dangerous."

None of the people moved.

"Please!" Sazed said. "You *must* go. If you stay, you will die!"

"We are not here to die, Holy First Witness," said an elderly man at the front. "We are here to watch the koloss fall."

"Fall?" Sazed asked.

"The Lady Heir will protect us," said another woman.

"The Lady Heir has left the city!" Sazed said.

"Then we will watch you, Holy First Witness," the man said, leaning with one hand on a young boy's shoulder.

"Holy First Witness?" Sazed said. "Why call me this name?"

"You are the one who brought news of the Lord Ruler's death," the man said. "You gave the Lady Heir the spear she used to slay our lord. You were the witness to her actions."

Sazed shook his head. "That may be true, but I am not worthy of reverence. I'm not a holy man, I'm just a . . ."

"A witness," the old man said. "If the Heir is to join this fight, she will appear near you."

"I . . . am sorry . . ." Sazed said, flushing. *I sent her away. I sent your god to safety.*

The people watched him, their eyes reverent. It was wrong; they should not worship him. He was simply an observer.

Except, he wasn't. He had made himself part of this all. It was as Tindwyl had indirectly warned him. Now that Sazed had participated in events, he had become an object of worship himself.

"You should not look at me like that," Sazed said.

"The Lady Heir says the same thing," the old man said, smiling, breath puffing in the cold air.

"That is different," Sazed said. "She is . . ." He cut off, turning as he heard cries from behind. The archers on the wall were waving in alarm, and young Captain Bedes was rushing over to them. *What is—*

A bestial blue creature suddenly pulled itself up onto the wall, its skin streaked and dripping with scarlet blood. It shoved aside a surprised archer, then grabbed Captain Bedes by the neck and tossed him backward. The boy disappeared, falling to the koloss below. Sazed heard the screams even from a distance. A second koloss pulled itself up onto the wall, then a third. Archers stumbled away in shock, dropping their weapons, some shoving others off the ramparts in their haste.

The koloss are jumping up, Sazed realized. *Enough corpses must have piled below. And yet, to jump so high . . .*

More and more creatures were pulling themselves onto the top of the wall. They were the largest of the monsters, the ones over ten feet in height, but that only made it easier for them to sweep the archers out of their way. Men fell to the courtyard, and the pounding on the gates redoubled.

"Go!" Sazed said, waving at the people behind him. Some of them backed away. Many stood firm.

Sazed turned desperately back toward the gates. The wooden structures began to crack, splinters spraying through the snowy, ash-laden air. The soldiers backed away, postures frightened. Finally, with a snap, the bar broke and the right gate burst open. A howling, bleeding, wild mass of koloss began to scramble across the wet stones.

Soldiers dropped their weapons and fled. Others remained, frozen with terror. Sazed stood at their back, between the horrified soldiers and the mass of skaa.

I am not a warrior, he thought, hands shaking as he stared at the monsters. It had been difficult enough to stay calm inside their camp. Watching them scream—their massive swords out, their skin ripped and bloodied as they fell upon the human soldiers—Sazed felt his courage begin to fail.

But if I don't do something, nobody will.

He tapped pewter.

His muscles grew. He drew deeply upon his pewtermind as he dashed forward, taking more strength than he ever had before. He had spent years storing up strength, rarely finding occasion to use it, and now he tapped that reserve.

His body changed, weak scholar's arms transforming into massive, bulky limbs. His chest widened, bulging, and his muscles grew taut with power. Days spent fragile and frail focused on this single moment. He shoved his way through the ranks of soldiers, pulling his robe over his head as it grew too restrictive, leaving himself wearing only a vestigial loincloth.

The lead koloss turned to find himself facing a creature nearly his own size. Despite its rage, despite its inhumanness, the beast froze, surprise showing in its beady red eyes.

Sazed punched the monster. He hadn't practiced for war, and knew next to nothing about combat. Yet, at that moment, his lack of skill didn't matter. The creature's face folded around his fist, its skull cracking.

Sazed turned on thick legs, looking back at the startled soldiers. *Say something brave!* he told himself.

"Fight!" Sazed bellowed, surprised at the sudden deepness and strength of his voice.

And, startlingly, they did.

Vin fell to her knees, exhausted on the muddy, ash-soaked highway. Her fingers and knees hit the slushy cold, but she didn't care. She simply knelt, wheezing. She couldn't run any farther. Her pewter was gone. Her lungs burned and her legs ached. She wanted to collapse and curl up, coughing.

It's just the pewter drag, she thought forcibly. She'd pushed her body hard, but hadn't had to pay for it until now.

She coughed a moment longer, groaning, then reached a dripping hand into her pocket and pulled out her last two vials. They had a mixture of all eight base metals, plus duralumin. Their pewter would keep her going for a little bit longer. . . .

But not long enough. She was still hours away from Luthadel. Even with pewter, she wouldn't arrive until long after dark. She sighed, replacing her vials, forcing herself to her feet.

What would I do if I arrived? Vin thought. *Why work so hard? Am I that eager to fight again? To slaughter?*

She knew that she wouldn't arrive in time for the battle. In fact, the koloss had probably attacked days ago. Still, this worried her. Her attack on Cett's keep still flashed horrific images in her head. Things she had done. Death she had caused.

And yet, something felt different to her now. She had accepted her place as a knife. But what was a knife, but another tool? It could be used for evil or for good; it could kill, or it could protect.

That point was moot, considering how weak she felt. It was hard to keep her legs from trembling as she flared tin, clearing her head. She stood on the imperial highway, a sodden, pockmarked roadway that looked—in the softly falling snow—to twist onward for eternity. It ran directly beside the imperial canal, which was a snakelike cut in the land, wide but empty, extending beside the highway.

Before, with Elend, this road had seemed bright and new. Now it looked dark and depressing. The Well thumped, its pulsings growing more powerful with each step she took back toward Luthadel. Yet, it wasn't happening fast enough. Not fast enough for her to stop the koloss from taking the city.

Not fast enough for her friends.

I'm sorry . . . she thought, teeth chattering as she pulled her cloak tight, pewter no longer aiding her against the cold. *I'm so sorry that I failed you.*

She saw a line of smoke in the distance. She looked east, then west, but didn't see much. The flat landscape was clouded in ashen snows.

A village, thought her still-numb mind. *One of many in the area.* Luthadel was by far the dominant city of the small dominance, but there were others. Elend hadn't been able to keep the others completely free of banditry, but they had fared far better than towns in other areas of the Final Empire.

Vin stumbled forward, pressing on through the slushy black puddles toward the village. After about fifteen minutes of walking, she turned off the main highway and made her way up a side road to the village. It was small, even by skaa standards. Just a few hovels, along with a couple of nicer structures.

Not a plantation, Vin thought. *This was once a way village—a place for traveling noblemen to stop for the evening.* The small manor—which would have once been run by a minor noble landlord—was dark. Two of the skaa hovels, however, had light shining through the cracks. The gloomy weather must have convinced the people to retire from their labors early.

Vin shivered, walking up to one of the buildings, her tin-enhanced ears picking out sounds of talking inside. She paused, listening. Children laughed, and men spoke with gusto. She smelled what must have been the beginnings of the evening meal—a simple vegetable stew.

Skaa . . . laughing, she thought. A hovel like this one would have been a place of fear and gloom during the days of the Lord Ruler. Happy skaa had been considered under-worked skaa.

We've meant something. It's all meant something.

But was it worth the deaths of her friends? The fall of Luthadel? Without Elend's protection, even this little village would soon be taken by one tyrant or another.

She drank in the sounds of laughter. Kelsier hadn't given up. He had faced the Lord Ruler himself, and his last words had been defiant. Even when his plans had seemed hopeless, his own corpse lying in the street, he had secretly been victorious.

I refuse to give up, she thought, straightening. *I refuse to accept their deaths until I hold their corpses in my arms.*

She raised a hand and pounded on the door. Immediately, the sounds inside stopped. Vin extinguished her tin as the door creaked open. Skaa, especially country skaa, were skittish things. She'd probably have to—

"Oh, you poor thing!" the woman exclaimed, pulling the door open the rest of the way. "Come in out of that snow. What are you doing out there!"

Vin hesitated. The woman was dressed simply, but the clothing was well made to stave off the winter. The firepit in the center of the room glowed with a welcome warmth.

"Child?" the woman asked. Behind, a stocky, bearded man rose to place a hand on the woman's shoulder and study Vin.

"Pewter," Vin said quietly. "I need pewter."

The couple looked at each other, frowning. They probably thought her mind addled. After all, how must she look, hair drenched by the snow, clothing wet and stuck with ash? She only wore simple riding clothing—trousers and a nondescript cloak.

"Why don't you come inside, child?" the man suggested. "Have something to eat. Then we can talk about where you came from. Where are your parents?"

Lord Ruler! Vin thought with annoyance. *I don't look that young, do I?*

She threw a Soothing on the couple, suppressing their

concern and suspicion. Then, she Rioted their willingness to help. She wasn't as good as Breeze, but she wasn't unpracticed, either. The couple immediately relaxed.

"I don't have much time," Vin said. "Pewter."

"The lord had some fine diningware in his home," the man said slowly. "But we traded most of that for clothing and farming equipment. I think there are a couple of goblets left. Master Cled—our elder—has them in the other hovel. . . ."

"That might work," Vin said. *Though the metal probably won't be mixed with Allomantic percentages in mind.* It would probably have too much silver or not enough tin, making the pewter work more weakly than it would otherwise.

The couple frowned, then looked at the others in the hovel.

Vin felt despair crawl back into her chest. What was she thinking? Even if the pewter were of the right alloy, it would take time to shave it and produce enough for her to use in running. Pewter burned relatively quickly. She'd need a lot of it. Preparing it could take almost as much time as simply walking to Luthadel.

She turned, looking south, through the dark, snowy sky. Even with pewter, it would take hours more running. What she really needed was a spikeway—a path marked by spikes driven in the ground that an Allomancer could push against, throwing themselves through the air again and again. On such an organized pathway, she'd once traveled from Fellise to Luthadel—an hour's carriage ride—in under ten minutes.

But there was no spikeway from this village to Luthadel; there weren't even ones along the main canal routes. They were too hard to set up, too specific in their usefulness, to be worth the bother of running them long distances. . . .

Vin turned, causing the skaa couple to jump. Perhaps they'd noticed the daggers in her belt, or perhaps it was the look in her eyes, but they no longer looked quite as friendly as they had before.

"Is that a stable?" Vin said, nodding toward one of the dark buildings.

"Yes," the man said hesitantly. "But we have no horses. Only a couple of goats and cows. Surely you don't want to—"

"Horseshoes," Vin said.

The man frowned.

"I need horseshoes," Vin said. "A lot of them."

"Follow me," the man said, responding to her Soothing. He led her out into the cold afternoon. Others followed behind them, and Vin noticed a couple of men casually carrying cudgels. Perhaps it wasn't just Elend's protection that had allowed these people to remain unmolested.

The stocky man threw his weight against the stable door, pushing it to the side. He pointed to a barrel inside. "They were getting rusty anyway," he said.

Vin walked up to the barrel and took out a horseshoe, testing its weight. Then she tossed it up in front of her and Pushed it with a solid flare of steel. It shot away, arcing far through the air until it splashed into a pool some hundred paces away.

Perfect, she thought.

The skaa men were staring. Vin reached into her pocket and pulled out one of her metal vials, downing its contents and restoring her pewter. She didn't have much of it left by pewter-dragging standards, but she had plenty of steel and iron. Both burned slowly. She could Push and Pull on metals for hours yet.

"Prepare your village," she said, burning pewter, then counting out ten horseshoes. "Luthadel is besieged—it might have fallen already. If you get word that it has, I suggest you take your people and move to Terris. Follow the imperial canal directly to the north."

"Who are you?" the man asked.

"Nobody of consequence."

He paused. "You're *her,* aren't you?"

She didn't need to ask what he meant. She simply dropped a horseshoe to the ground behind her.

"Yes," she said quietly, then Pushed off of the shoe.

Immediately, she shot into the air at an angle. As she began to fall, she dropped another horseshoe. However, she waited until she was near the ground to Push against this one; she needed to keep herself going more forward than up.

She'd done all this before. It wasn't that different from using coins to jump around. The trick was going to be to keep herself moving. As she Pushed against the second horseshoe—propelling herself into the snowy air again—she reached behind herself and Pulled hard on the first horseshoe.

The horseshoe wasn't connected to anything, so it leaped into the air after her, crossing the distance through the sky as Vin dropped a third shoe to the ground. She let go of the first shoe, its momentum carrying it through the air above her head. It fell to the ground as she Pushed against the third shoe and Pulled on the second one, now far behind her.

This is going to be tough, Vin thought, frowning with concentration as she passed over the first shoe and Pushed on it. However, she didn't get the angle right, and she fell too far before Pushing. The horseshoe shot out behind her, and didn't give her enough upward momentum to keep her in the air. She hit the ground hard, but immediately Pulled the shoe to herself and tried again.

The first few tries were slow. The biggest problem was getting the angle down. She had to hit the shoe just right, giving it enough downward force to keep it in place on the ground, but enough forward motion to keep her moving in the right direction. She had to land often that first hour, going back to fetch horseshoes. However, she didn't have time for much experimentation, and her determination insisted that she get the process right.

Eventually, she had three shoes working pretty well; it helped that the ground was wet, and that her weight pressed the horseshoes down in the mud, giving her a stronger anchor to use when Pushing herself forward. Soon she was able to add a fourth shoe. The more frequently she Pushed—the more horseshoes she had to Push against—the faster she would go.

By the time she was an hour out of the village, she added a fifth shoe. The result was a continuous flow of flipping metal chunks. Vin Pulled, then Pushed, then Pulled, then

Pushed, moving with continual single-mindedness, juggling herself through the air.

The ground raced beneath her and horseshoes shot through the air above her. The wind became a roar as she Pushed herself faster and faster, steering her pathway to the south. She was a flurry of metal and motion—as Kelsier had been, near the end, when he had killed the Inquisitor.

Except, her metal wasn't meant to kill, but save. *I might not arrive in time,* she thought, air rushing around her. *But I'm not going to give up halfway.*

I have a young nephew, one Rashek. He hates all of Khlennium with the passion of envious youth. He hates Alendi even more acutely—though the two have never met—for Rashek feels betrayed that one of our oppressors should have been chosen as the Hero of Ages.

53

STRAFF WAS ACTUALLY STARTING TO feel quite well as his army crested the last hill to overlook Luthadel. He'd discreetly tried a few drugs from his cabinet, and he was pretty certain he knew which one Amaranta had given him: Black Frayn. A nasty drug indeed. He'd have to wean himself from it slowly—but, for now, a few swallowed leaves made him stronger and more alert than he'd ever been before. In fact, he felt wonderful.

He was sure the same couldn't be said for those in Luthadel. The koloss pooled around the outer wall, still beating on several of the gates on the north and east sides. Smoke rose from inside the city.

"Our scouts say the creatures have broken through four of

the city gates, my lord," said Lord Janarle. "They breached the eastern gate first, and there met with heavy resistance. The northeastern gate fell next, then the northwestern gate, but the troops at both are holding as well. The main breach happened in the north. The koloss are apparently ravaging from that direction, burning and looting."

Straff nodded. *The northern gate,* he thought. *The one closest to Keep Venture.*

"Do we attack, my lord?" Janarle asked.

"How long ago did the northern gate fall?"

"Perhaps an hour ago, my lord."

Straff shook his head leisurely. "Then, let us wait. The creatures worked quite hard to break into the city—we should at least let them have a little fun before we slaughter them."

"Are you sure, my lord?"

Straff smiled. "Once they lose their bloodlust in a few hours, they'll be tired from all the fighting and calm down. *That* will be the best time to strike. They'll be dispersed through the city and weakened from the resistance. We can take them easily, that way."

Sazed gripped his koloss opponent by the throat, forcing back its snarling, distorted face. The beast's skin was stretched so tightly that it had split down the center of the face, revealing bloody muscles above the teeth, around the nose holes. It breathed with husky rage, spraying droplets of spittle and blood across Sazed with each exhalation.

Strength! Sazed thought, tapping his pewtermind for more power. His body became so massive that he feared splitting his own skin. Fortunately, his metalminds had been built to expand, braces and rings that didn't connect on one side so that they could bend. Still, his bulk was daunting. He probably wouldn't have been able to walk or maneuver with such size—but it didn't matter, for the koloss had already knocked him to the ground. All he needed was some extra power in his grip. The creature clawed him in the arm with one hand, reaching behind with the other, grasping its sword. . . .

Sazed's fingers finally crushed the beast's thick neck.

The creature tried to snarl, but no breath came, and it instead thrashed about in frustration. Sazed forced himself to his feet, then hurled the creature toward its companions. With such unnatural strength, even a body eleven feet tall felt light in his fingers. It smashed into a pile of attacking koloss, forcing them backward.

Sazed stood, gasping. *I'm using my strength up so quickly,* he thought, releasing his pewtermind, his body deflating like a wineskin. He couldn't continue tapping his reserves so much. He'd already used up a good half of his strength—strength that had taken decades to store. He still hadn't used his rings, but he had only a few minutes of each attribute in those. They would wait for an emergency.

And that might be what I'm facing now, he thought with dread. They still held Steel Gate Square. Though koloss had broken through the gate, only a few could pass through at once—and only the most massive seemed able to jump up to the wall.

Sazed's little troop of soldiers was sorely pressed, however. Bodies lay scattered in the courtyard. The skaa faithful at the back had begun pulling the wounded to safety. Sazed could hear them groaning behind him.

Koloss corpses littered the square as well, and despite the carnage, Sazed couldn't help but feel a sense of pride at how much it was costing the creatures to force their way inside this portal. Luthadel was not falling easily. Not at all.

The koloss seemed rebuffed for the moment, and though several skirmishes still continued in the courtyard, a new group of monsters was gathering outside the gate.

Outside the gate, Sazed thought, glancing to the side. The creatures had cared to break open only one of the massive door gates, the right one. There were corpses in the square—dozens, perhaps hundreds—but the koloss themselves had cleared many out of the way of the gate itself so that they could get into the courtyard.

Perhaps . . .

Sazed didn't have time to think. He dashed forward, tapping his pewtermind again, giving himself the strength of five men. He picked up the body of a smaller koloss and threw it out the gate. The creatures outside snarled, scattering. There were still hundreds waiting for the chance to get in, but they tripped over the dead in their haste to get out of the way of his projectile.

Sazed slipped on blood as he grabbed a second body, throwing it to the side. "To me!" he screamed, hoping that there were men who could hear, and who could respond.

The koloss realized what he was doing too late. He kicked another body out of the way, then slammed his body against the open door and tapped his ironmind, drawing forth the weight he had stored within it. Immediately, he became far heavier, and that weight crashed against the gate, slamming it closed.

Koloss rushed at the doorway from the other side. Sazed scrambled up against the gate, pushing corpses out of the way, forcing the massive portal closed all the way. He tapped his ironmind further, draining its precious reserve at an alarming rate. He became so heavy he felt his own weight crushing him to the ground, and only his increased strength managed to keep him on his feet. Frustrated koloss pounded on the gate, but he held. Held them back, hands and chest pressed against the rough wood, toes wedged back against uneven cobbles. With his brassmind, he didn't even feel the cold, though ash, snow, and blood mixed at his feet.

Men cried out. Some died. Others slammed their own weight against the gate, and Sazed spared a glance behind. The rest of his soldiers set up a perimeter, protecting the gate from the koloss inside the city. The men fought bravely, backs to the gate, only Sazed's power keeping the portal from flying open.

And yet, they fought. Sazed cried out in defiance, feet slipping, holding the gate as his soldiers killed the remaining koloss in the courtyard. Then, a group of them rushed in from the side, bearing with them a large length of wood. Sazed didn't know where they'd gotten it, nor did he care, as they slid it into place where the gate bar had been.

His weight ran out, the ironmind empty. *I should have stored more of that, over the years,* he thought with a sigh of exhaustion, sinking down before the closed gate. It had seemed like a lot, until he'd been forced to use it so often, using it to shove away koloss or the like.

I usually just stored up weight as a side effect of making myself lighter. That always seemed the more useful way to use iron.

He released pewter, and felt his body deflating. Fortunately, stretching his body in such a manner didn't leave his skin loose. He went back to his usual self, only bearing a dreadful sense of exhaustion and a faint soreness. The koloss continued to beat on the gate. Sazed opened tired eyes, lying bare-chested in the falling snow and ash. His soldiers stood solemnly before him.

So few, he thought. Barely fifty remained of his original four hundred. The square itself was red—as if painted—with bright koloss blood, and it mixed with the darker human kind. Sickly blue lumps of bodies lay alone or in heaps, interspersed with the twisted and torn pieces that were often all that remained of human bodies once they were hit by the brutal koloss swords.

The thumping continued, like low drums, on the other side of the gate. The beating picked up to a frenzied pace, the gate shaking, as the koloss grew more frustrated. They could probably smell the blood, feel the flesh that had so nearly been theirs.

"That board won't hold for long," one of the soldiers said quietly, a bit of ash floating down in front of his face. "And the hinges are splintering. They're going to get through again."

Sazed stumbled to his feet. "And we will fight again."

"My lord!" a voice said. Sazed turned to see one of Dockson's messengers ride around a pile of corpses. "Lord Dockson says that . . ." He trailed off, noticing for the first time that Sazed's gate was closed. "How . . ." the man began.

"Deliver your message, young man," Sazed said tiredly.

"Lord Dockson says you won't get any reinforcements," the man said, reining in his horse. "Tin Gate has fallen, and—"

"Tin Gate?" Sazed asked. *Tindwyl!* "When?"

"Over an hour ago, my lord."

An hour? he thought with shock. *How long have we been fighting?*

"You have to hold here, my lord!" the young man said, turning and galloping back the way he had come.

Sazed took a step to the east. *Tindwyl.* . . .

The thumping on his gate grew louder, and the board began to crack. The men ran for something else to use to secure the gate, but Sazed could see that the mountings that kept the board in place were beginning to pull apart. Once they went, there would be no way to hold the gate closed.

Sazed closed his eyes, feeling the weight of fatigue, reaching into his pewtermind. It was nearly drained. After it was gone, he'd only have the tiny bit of strength in one of the rings.

Yet, what else could he do?

He heard the board snap, and men yelled.

"Back!" Clubs yelled. "Fall into the city!"

The remnants of their army broke apart, pulling back from Zinc Gate. Breeze watched with horror as more and more koloss spilled into the square, overrunning the few men too weak or too wounded to retreat. The creatures swept forward like a great blue tide, a tide with swords of steel and eyes of red.

In the sky, the sun—only faintly visible behind storm clouds—was a bleeding scar that crept toward the horizon.

"Breeze," Clubs snapped, pulling him back. "Time to go."

Their horses had long since bolted. Breeze stumbled after the general, trying not to listen to the snarling from behind.

"Fall back to the harrying positions!" Clubs called to those men who could hear him. "First squad, shore up inside Keep Lekal! Lord Hammond should be there by now, preparing the defenses! Squad two, with me to Keep Hasting!"

Breeze continued on, his mind as numb as his feet. He'd been virtually useless in the battle. He'd tried to take away the men's fear, but his efforts had seemed so inadequate. Like . . . holding a piece of paper up to the sun to make shade.

Clubs held up a hand, and the squad of two hundred men stopped. Breeze looked around. The street was quiet in the falling ash and snow. Everything seemed . . . dull. The sky was dim, the city's features softened by the blanket of black-speckled snow. It seemed so strange to have fled the horrific scene of scarlet and blue to find the city looking so lazy.

"Damn!" Clubs snapped, pushing Breeze out of the way as a raging group of koloss burst from a side street. Clubs's soldiers fell into a line, but another group of koloss—the creatures that had just burst through the gate—came up behind them.

Breeze stumbled, falling in the snow. *That other group . . . it came from the north! The creatures have infiltrated the city this far already?*

"Clubs!" Breeze said, turning. "We—"

Breeze looked just in time to see a massive koloss sword sheer through Clubs's upraised arm, then continue on to hit the general in the ribs. Clubs grunted, thrown to the side, his sword arm—weapon and all—flying free. He stumbled on his bad leg, and the koloss brought his sword down in a two-handed blow.

The dirty snow finally got some color. A splash of red.

Breeze stared, dumbfounded, at the remains of his friend's corpse. Then the koloss turned toward Breeze, snarling.

The likelihood of his own impending death hit, stirring him as even the cold snow couldn't. Breeze scrambled back, sliding in the snow, instinctively reaching out to try and Soothe the creature. Of course, nothing happened. Breeze tried to get to his feet, and the koloss—along with several others—began to bear down on him. At that moment, however, another troop of soldiers fleeing the gate appeared from a cross street, distracting the koloss.

Breeze did the only thing that seemed natural. He crawled inside a building and hid.

"This is all Kelsier's fault," Dockson muttered, making another notation on his map. According to messengers, Ham had reached Keep Lekal. It wouldn't last long.

The Venture grand hall was a flurry of motion and chaos as panicked scribes ran this way and that, finally realizing that koloss didn't care if a man were skaa, scholar, nobleman, or merchant. The creatures just liked to kill.

"He should have seen this coming," Dockson continued. "He left us with this mess, and then he just assumed that we'd find a way to fix it. Well, I can't hide a city from its enemies—not like I hid a crew. Just because we were excellent thieves doesn't mean we'd be any good at running a kingdom!"

Nobody was listening to him. His messengers had all fled, and his guards fought at the keep gates. Each of the keeps had its own defenses, but Clubs—rightly—had decided to use them only as a fallback option. They weren't designed to repel a large-scale attack, and they were too secluded from each other. Retreating to them only fractured and isolated the human army.

"Our real problem is follow-through," Dockson said, making a final notation at Tin Gate, explaining what had happened there. He looked over the map. He'd never expected Sazed's gate to be the last one to hold.

"Follow-through," he continued. "We assumed we could do a better job than the noblemen, but once we had the power, we put them back in charge. If we'd killed the whole lot, perhaps then we could have started fresh. Of course, that would have meant invading the other dominances—which would have meant sending Vin to take care of the most important, most problematic, noblemen. There would have been a slaughter like the Final Empire had never seen. And, if we'd done that . . ."

He trailed off, looking up as one of the massive, majestic stained-glass windows shattered. The others began to explode as well, broken by thrown rocks. A few large koloss jumped through the holes, landing on the shard-strewn marble floor. Even broken, the windows were beautiful, the spiked glass edges twinkling in the evening light. Through one of them, Dockson could see that the storm was breaking, letting sunlight through.

"If we'd done that," Dockson said quietly, "we'd have been no better than beasts."

Scribes screamed, trying to flee as the koloss began the slaughter. Dockson stood quietly, hearing noise behind—grunts, harsh breathing—as koloss approached through the back hallways. He reached for the sword on his table as men began to die.

He closed his eyes. *You know, Kell,* he thought. *I almost started to believe that they were right, that you were watching over us. That you were some sort of god.*

He opened his eyes and turned, pulling the sword from its sheath. Then he froze, staring at the massive beast approaching from behind. *So big!*

Dockson gritted his teeth, sending a final curse Kelsier's way, then charged, swinging.

The creature caught his weapon in an indifferent hand, ignoring the cut it caused. Then, it brought its own weapon down, and blackness followed.

"My lord," Janarle said. "The city has fallen. Look, you can see it burning. The koloss have penetrated all but one of the four gates under attack, and they run wild in the city. They aren't stopping to pillage—they're just killing. Slaughtering. There aren't many soldiers left to oppose them."

Straff sat quietly, watching Luthadel burn. It seemed . . . a symbol to him. A symbol of justice. He'd fled this city once, leaving it to the skaa vermin inside, and when he'd come back to demand it be returned to him, the people had resisted.

They had been defiant. They had earned this.

"My lord," Janarle said. "The koloss army is weakened enough already. Their numbers are hard to count, but the corpses they left behind indicate that as much as a third of their force has fallen. We can take them!"

"No," Straff said, shaking his head. "Not yet."

"My lord?" Janarle said.

"Let the koloss have the damn city," Straff said quietly. "Let them clear it out and burn the whole thing to the ground. Fires can't hurt our atium—in fact, they'll probably make the metal easier to find."

"I . . ." Janarle seemed shocked. He didn't object further, but his eyes were rebellious.

I'll have to take care of him later, Straff thought. *He'll rise against me if he finds that Zane is gone.*

That didn't matter at the moment. The city had rejected him, and so it would die. He'd build a better one in its place.

One dedicated to Straff, not the Lord Ruler.

"Father!" Allrianne said urgently.

Cett shook his head. He sat on his horse, beside his daughter's horse, on a hill to the west of Luthadel. He could see Straff's army, gathered to the north, watching—as he watched—the death throes of a doomed city.

"We have to help!" Allrianne insisted.

"No," Cett said quietly, shrugging off the effects of her Raging his emotions. He'd grown used to her manipulations long ago. "Our help wouldn't matter now."

"We have to do something!" Allrianne said, pulling his arm.

"No," Cett said more forcefully.

"But you came back!" she said. "Why did we return, if not to help?"

"We will help," Cett said quietly. "We'll help Straff take the city when he wishes, then we'll submit to him and hope he doesn't kill us."

Allrianne paled. "That's it?" she hissed. "That's why we returned, so that you can give our kingdom to that monster?"

"What else did you expect?" Cett demanded. "You know me, Allrianne. You know that this is the choice I have to make."

"I thought I knew you," she snapped. "I thought you were a good man, down deep."

Cett shook his head. "The good men are all dead, Allrianne. They died inside that city."

Sazed fought on. He was no warrior; he didn't have honed instincts or training. He calculated that he should have died hours before. And yet, somehow, he managed to stay alive.

Perhaps it was because the koloss didn't fight with skill, either. They were blunt—like their giant, wedgelike swords —and they simply threw themselves at their opponents with little thought of tactics.

That should have been enough. Yet, Sazed held—and where he held, his few men held with him. The koloss had rage on their side, but Sazed's men could see the weak and elderly standing, waiting, just at the edge of the square. The soldiers knew why they fought. This reminder seemed enough to keep them going, even when they began to be surrounded, the koloss working their way into the edges of the square.

Sazed knew, by now, that no relief was going to come. He'd hoped, perhaps, that Straff would decide to take the city, as Clubs had suggested. But it was too late for that; night was approaching, the sun inching toward the horizon.

The end is finally here, Sazed thought as the man next to him was struck down. Sazed slipped on blood, and the move saved him as the koloss swung over his head.

Perhaps Tindwyl had found a way to safety. Hopefully, Elend would deliver the things he and she had studied. *They were important,* Sazed thought, even if he didn't know why.

Sazed attacked, swinging the sword he'd taken from a koloss. He enhanced his muscles in a final burst as he swung, giving them strength right as the sword met koloss flesh.

He hit. The resistance, the wet sound of impact, the shock up his arm—these were familiar to him now. Bright koloss blood sprayed across him, and another of the monsters fell.

And Sazed's strength was gone.

Pewter tapped clean, the koloss sword was now heavy in his hands. He tried to swing it at the next koloss in line, but the weapon slipped from his weak, numb, tired fingers.

This koloss was a big one. Nearing twelve feet tall, it was the largest of the monsters Sazed had seen. Sazed tried to step away, but he stumbled over the body of a recently killed soldier. As he fell, his men finally broke, the last dozen scattering. They'd held well. Too well. Perhaps if he'd let them retreat . . .

No, Sazed thought, looking up at his death. *I did well, I think. Better than any mere scholar should have been able to.*

He thought about the rings on his fingers. They could, perhaps, give him a little bit of an edge, let him run. Flee. Yet, he couldn't summon the motivation. Why resist? Why had he resisted in the first place? He'd known that they were doomed.

You're wrong about me, Tindwyl, he thought. *I do give up, sometimes. I gave up on this city long ago.*

The koloss loomed over Sazed, who still lay half sprawled in the bloody slush, and raised its sword. Over the creature's shoulder, Sazed could see the red sun hanging just above the top of the wall. He focused on that, rather than on the falling sword. He could see rays of sunlight, like . . . shards of glass in the sky.

The sunlight seemed to sparkle, twinkling, coming for him. As if the sun itself were welcoming him. Reaching down to accept his spirit.

And so, I die. . . .

A twinkling droplet of light sparkled in the beam of sunlight, then hit the koloss directly in the back of the skull. The creature grunted, stiffening, dropping its sword. It collapsed to the side, and Sazed lay, stupefied, on the ground for a moment. Then he looked up at the top of the wall.

A small figure stood silhouetted by the sun. Black before the red light, a cloak flapped gently on her back. Sazed blinked. The bit of sparkling light he'd seen . . . it had been a coin. The koloss before him was dead.

Vin had returned.

She jumped, leaping as only an Allomancer could, to soar in a graceful arc above the square. She landed directly in the midst of the koloss and spun. Coins shot out like angry insects, cutting through blue flesh. The creatures didn't drop as easily as humans would have, but the attack got their attention. The koloss turned away from the fleeing soldiers and defenseless townspeople.

The skaa at the back of the square began to chant. It was a bizarre sound to hear in the middle of a battle. Sazed sat up, ignoring his pains and exhaustion as Vin jumped. The city gate suddenly lurched, its hinges twisting. The koloss had already beaten on it so hard. . . .

The massive wooden portal burst free from the wall, Pulled by Vin. *Such power,* Sazed thought numbly. *She must be Pulling on something behind herself—but, that would mean that poor Vin is being yanked between two weights as heavy as that gate.*

And yet, she did it, lifting the gate door with a heave, Pulling it toward herself. The huge hardwood gate crashed through the koloss ranks, scattering bodies. Vin twisted expertly in the air, Pulling herself to the side, swinging the gate to the side as if it were tethered to her by a chain.

Koloss flew in the air, bones cracking, sprayed like splinters before the enormous weapon. In a single sweep, Vin cleared the entire courtyard.

The gate dropped. Vin landed amid a group of crushed bodies, silently kicking a soldier's war staff up into her hands. The remaining koloss outside the gate paused only briefly, then charged. Vin began to attack swiftly, but precisely. Skulls cracked, koloss falling dead in the slush as they tried to pass her. She spun, sweeping a few of them to the ground, spraying ashen red slush across those running up behind.

I . . . I have to do something, Sazed thought, shaking off his stupefaction. He was still bare-chested, the cold ignored because of his brassmind—which was nearly empty. Vin continued to fight, felling koloss after koloss. *Even her strength won't last forever. She can't save the city.*

Sazed forced himself to his feet, then moved toward the back of the square. He grabbed the old man at the front of the crowd of skaa, shaking the man out of his chanting. "You were right," Sazed said. "She returned."

"Yes, Holy First Witness."

"She will be able to give us some time, I think," Sazed said. "The koloss have broken into the city. We need to gather what people we can and escape."

The old man paused, and for a moment Sazed thought he would object—that he would claim Vin would protect them, would defeat the entire army. Then, thankfully, he nodded.

"We'll run out the northern gate," Sazed said urgently. "That is where the koloss first entered the city, and so it is likely that they have moved on from that area."

I hope, Sazed thought, rushing off to raise the warning. The fallback defensive positions were supposed to be the high noble keeps. Perhaps they would find survivors there.

So, Breeze thought, *it turns out that I'm a coward.*

It was not a surprising revelation. He had always said that it was important for a man to understand himself, and he had always been aware of his selfishness. So, he was not at all shocked to find himself huddling against the flaking bricks of an old skaa home, shutting his ears to the screams just outside.

Where was the proud man now? The careful diplomat, the Soother with his immaculate suits? He was gone, leaving behind this quivering, useless mass. He tried several times to burn brass, to Soothe the men fighting outside. However, he couldn't accomplish this most simple of actions. He couldn't even move.

Unless one counted trembling as movement.

Fascinating, Breeze thought, as if looking at himself from the outside, seeing the pitiful creature in the ripped, bloodied suit. *So this is what happens to me, when the stress gets too strong? It's ironic, in a way. I've spent a lifetime controlling the emotions of others. Now I'm so afraid, I can't even function.*

The fighting continued outside. It was going on an awful long time. Shouldn't those soldiers be dead?

"Breeze?"

He couldn't move to see who it was. *Sounds like Ham. That's funny. He should be dead, too.*

"Lord Ruler!" Ham said, coming into Breeze's view. He wore a bloodied sling on one arm. He fell urgently to Breeze's side. "Breeze, can you hear me?"

"We saw him duck in here, my lord," another voice said.

A soldier? "Took shelter from the fight. We could feel him Soothing us, though. Kept us fighting, even when we should have given up. After Lord Cladent died . . ."

I'm a coward.

Another figure appeared. Sazed, looking concerned. "Breeze," Ham said, kneeling. "My keep fell, and Sazed's gate is down. We haven't heard anything from Dockson in over an hour, and we found Clubs's body. Please. The koloss are destroying the city. We need to know what to do."

Well, don't ask me, Breeze said—or tried to say. He thought it came out as a mumble.

"I can't carry you, Breeze," Ham said. "My arm is nearly useless."

Well, that's all right, Breeze mumbled. *You see, my dear man, I don't think I'm of much use anymore. You should move on. It's quite all right if you just leave me here.*

Ham looked up at Sazed, helpless.

"Hurry, Lord Hammond," Sazed said. "We can have the soldiers carry the wounded. We will make our way to Keep Hasting. Perhaps we can find sanctuary there. Or . . . perhaps the koloss will be distracted enough to let us slip out of the city."

Distracted? Breeze mumbled. *Distracted by the killing of other people, you mean. Well, it is somewhat comforting to know that we're all cowards. Now, if I could just lie here for a little longer, I might be able to fall asleep . . .*

And forget all of this.

Alendi will need guides through the Terris Mountains. I have charged Rashek with making certain that he and his trusted friends are chosen as those guides.

54

VIN'S STAFF BROKE AS SHE slammed it across a koloss face.

Not again, she thought with frustration, spinning and ramming the broken shard into another creature's chest. She turned and came face-to-face with one of the big ones, a good five feet taller than she.

It thrust its sword toward her. Vin jumped, and the sword collided with broken cobblestones beneath her. She shot upward, not needing any coins to carry herself up to eye level with the creature's twisted face.

They always looked surprised. Even after watching her fight dozens of their companions, they seemed shocked to see her dodge their blows. Their minds seemed to equate size with power; a larger koloss always beat a smaller one. A five-foot-tall human should have been no problem for a monster this big.

Vin flared pewter as she smashed her fist into the beast's head. The skull cracked beneath her knuckles, and the beast fell backward as she dropped back to the ground. Yet, as always, there was another to take its place.

She was getting tired. No, she'd *started* the battle tired. She'd pewter-dragged, then used a convoluted personal spikeway to carry herself across an entire dominance. She was exhausted. Only the pewter in her last metal vial was keeping her upright.

I should have asked Sazed for one of his empty pewterminds! she thought. Feruchemical and Allomantic metals were the same. She could have burned that—though it would probably have been a bracer or a bracelet. To large to swallow.

She ducked to the side as another koloss attacked. Coins didn't stop these things, and they all weighed too much for her to Push them away without an anchor. Besides, her steel and iron reserves were extremely low.

She killed koloss after koloss, buying time for Sazed and the people to get a good head start. Something was different this time—different from when she'd killed at Cett's palace. She felt good. It wasn't just because she killed monsters.

It was because she understood her purpose. And she agreed with it. She *could* fight, *could* kill, if it meant defending those who could not defend themselves. Kelsier might have been able to kill for shock or retribution, but that wasn't good enough for Vin.

And she would never let it be again.

That determination fueled her attacks against the koloss. She used a stolen sword to cut off the legs of one, then threw the weapon at another, Pushing on it to impale the koloss in the chest. Then she Pulled on the sword of a fallen soldier, yanking it into her hand. She ducked backward, but nearly stumbled as she stepped on another body.

So tired, she thought.

There were dozens—perhaps even hundreds—of corpses in the courtyard. In fact, a pile was forming beneath her. She climbed it, retreating slightly as the creatures surrounded her again. They crawled over the corpses of their fallen brethren, rage frothing in their blood-drop eyes. Human soldiers would have given up, going to seek easier fights. The koloss, however, seemed to multiply as she fought them, others hearing the sounds of battle and coming to join in.

She swiped, pewter aiding her strength as she cut off an arm from one koloss, then a leg from another, before finally going for the head of a third. She ducked and dodged, jumping, staying out of their reach, killing as many as she could.

But as desperate as her determination—as strong as her newfound resolve to defend—she knew that she couldn't keep fighting, not like this. She was only one person. She couldn't save Luthadel, not alone.

"Lord Penrod!" Sazed yelled, standing at the gates to Keep Hasting. "You *must* listen to me."

There was no response. The soldiers at the top of the short keep wall were quiet, though Sazed could sense their discomfort. They didn't like ignoring him. In the distance, the battle still raged. Koloss screamed in the night. Soon they would find their way to Sazed and Ham's growing band of several thousand, who now huddled quietly outside Keep Hasting's gate.

A haggard messenger approached Sazed. He was the same one that Dockson had been sending to Steel Gate. He'd lost his horse somewhere, and they'd found him with a group of refugees in the Square of the Survivor.

"Lord Terrisman," the messenger said quietly. "I . . . just got back from the command post. Keep Venture has fallen. . . ."

"Lord Dockson?"

The man shook his head. "We found a few wounded scribes hiding outside the keep. They saw him die. The koloss are still in the building, breaking windows, rooting about. . . ."

Sazed turned back, looking over the city. So much smoke billowed in the sky that it seemed the mists had come already. He'd begun filling his scent tinmind to keep the stench away.

The battle for the city might be over, but now the true tragedy would begin. The koloss in the city had finished killing soldiers. Now they would slaughter the people. There were hundreds of thousands of them, and Sazed knew the creatures would gleefully extend the devastation. No looting. Not when there was killing to be done.

More screams sounded in the night. They'd lost. Failed. And now, the city would *truly* fall.

The mists can't be far away, he thought, trying to give himself some hope. *Perhaps that will give us some cover.*

Still, one image stood out to him. Clubs, dead in the

snow. The wooden disk Sazed had given him earlier that same day tied to a loop around his neck.

It hadn't helped.

Sazed turned back to Keep Hasting. "Lord Penrod," he said loudly. "We are going to try and slip out of the city. I would welcome your troops and your leadership. If you stay here, the koloss will attack this keep and kill you."

Silence.

Sazed turned, sighing as Ham—arm still in a sling—joined him. "We have to go, Saze," Ham said quietly.

"You're bloody, Terrisman."

Sazed turned. Ferson Penrod stood on the top of his wall, looking down. He still looked immaculate in his nobleman's suit. He even wore a hat against the snow and ash. Sazed looked down at himself. He still wore only his loincloth. He hadn't had time to worry about clothing, particularly with his brassmind to keep him warm.

"I've never seen a Terrisman fight," Penrod said.

"It is not a common occurrence, my lord," Sazed replied.

Penrod looked up, staring out over the city. "It's falling, Terrisman."

"That is why we must go, my lord," Sazed said.

Penrod shook his head. He still wore Elend's thin crown. "This is my city, Terrisman. I will not abandon it."

"A noble gesture, my lord," Sazed said. "But these with me are your people. Will you abandon them in their flight northward?"

Penrod paused. Then he just shook his head again. "There will be no flight northward, Terrisman. Keep Hasting is among the tallest structures in the city—from it, we can see what the koloss are doing. They will not let you escape."

"They may turn to pillaging," Sazed said. "Perhaps we can get by them and escape."

"No," Penrod said, his voice echoing hauntingly across the snowy streets. "My Tineye claims the creatures have already attacked the people you sent to escape through the northern gate. Now the koloss have turned this way. They're coming for us."

As cries began to echo through the distant streets, coming

closer, Sazed knew that Penrod's words must be true. "Open your gates, Penrod!" Sazed yelled. "Let the refugees in!" *Save their lives for a few more pitiful moments.*

"There is no room," Penrod said. "And there is no time. We are doomed."

"You must let us in!" Sazed screamed.

"It is odd," Penrod said, voice growing softer. "By taking this throne from the Venture boy, I saved his life—and I ended my own. I could not save the city, Terrisman. My only consolation is that I doubt Elend could have done so either."

He turned to go, walking down somewhere beyond the wall.

"Penrod!" Sazed yelled.

He did not reappear. The sun was setting, the mists were appearing, and the koloss were coming.

Vin cut down another koloss, then jumped back, Pushing herself off of a fallen sword. She shot away from the pack, breathing heavily, bleeding from a couple of minor cuts. Her arm was growing numb; one of the creatures had punched her there. She could kill—kill better than anyone she knew. However, she couldn't fight forever.

She landed on a rooftop, then stumbled, falling to kneel in a pile of snow. The koloss called and howled behind her, and she knew they would come, chasing her, hounding her. She'd killed hundreds of them, but what was a few hundred when compared with an army of over twenty thousand?

What did you expect? she thought to herself. *Why keep fighting once you knew Sazed was free? Did you think to stop them all? Kill every koloss in the army?*

Once, she'd stopped Kelsier from rushing an army by himself. He had been a great man, but still just one person. He couldn't have stopped an entire army—no more than she could.

I have to find the Well, she thought with determination, burning bronze, the thumpings—which she'd been ignoring during the battle—becoming loud to her ears.

And yet, that left her with the same problem as before.

She knew it was in the city now; she could feel the thumpings all around her. Yet, they were so powerful, so omnipresent, that she couldn't sense a direction from them.

Besides, what proof did she have that finding the Well would even help? If Sazed had lied about the location—had gone so far as to draw up a fake map—then what else had he lied about? The power might stop the mists, but what good would that do for Luthadel, burning and dying?

She knelt in frustration, pounding the top of the roof with her fists. She had proven too weak. What good was it to return—what good was it to decide to protect—if she couldn't do anything to help?

She knelt for a few moments, breathing in gasps. Finally, she forced herself to her feet and jumped into the air, throwing down a coin. Her metals were nearly gone. She barely had enough steel to carry her through a few jumps. She ended up slowing near Kredik Shaw, the Hill of a Thousand Spires. She caught one of the spikes at the top of the palace, spinning in the night, looking out over the darkening city.

It was burning.

Kredik Shaw itself was silent, quiet, left alone by looters of both races. Yet, all around her, Vin saw light in the darkness. The mists glowed with a haunting light.

It's like . . . like that day two years ago, she thought. *The night of the skaa rebellion.* Except, on that day, the firelight had come from the torches of the rebels as they marched on the palace. This night, a revolution of a different type was occurring. She could hear it. She had her tin burning, and she forced herself to flare it, opening her ears. She heard the screams. The death. The koloss hadn't finished their killing work by destroying the army. Not by far.

They had only just begun.

The koloss are killing them all, she thought, shivering as the fires burned before her. *Elend's people, the ones he left behind because of me. They're dying.*

I am his knife. Their knife. Kelsier trusted me with them. I should be able to do something. . . .

She dropped toward the ground, skidding off an angled rooftop, landing in the palace courtyard. Mists gathered around her. The air was thick. And not just with ash and snow; she could smell death in its breezes, hear screams in its whispers.

Her pewter ran out.

She slumped to the ground, a wave of exhaustion hitting her so hard that everything else seemed inconsequential. She suddenly knew she shouldn't have relied on the pewter so much. Shouldn't have pushed herself so hard. But, it had seemed like the only way.

She felt herself begin to slip into unconsciousness.

But people were screaming. She could hear them—had heard them before. Elend's city . . . Elend's people . . . dying. Her friends were out there somewhere. Friends that Kelsier had trusted her to protect.

She gritted her teeth, shoving aside the exhaustion for a moment longer, struggling up to her feet. She looked through the mists, toward the phantom sounds of terrified people. She began to dash toward them.

She couldn't jump; she was out of steel. She couldn't even run very fast, but as she forced her body to move, it responded better and better, fighting off the dull numbness that she'd earned from relying on pewter so long.

She burst out of an alleyway, skidding in the snow, and found a small group of people running before a koloss raiding party. There were six of the beasts, small ones, but still dangerous. Even as Vin watched, one of the creatures cut down an elderly man, slicing him nearly in two. Another picked up a small girl, slamming her against the side of a building.

Vin dashed forward, past the fleeing skaa, whipping out her daggers. She still felt exhausted, but adrenaline helped her somewhat. She had to keep moving. Keep going. To stop was to die.

Several of the beasts turned toward her, eager to fight. One swung for her, and Vin let herself slide in the slush—slipping closer to him—before cutting the back of his leg. He howled in pain as her knife got caught in his baggy skin. She managed to yank it free as a second creature swung.

I feel so slow! she thought with frustration, barely sliding to her feet before backing away from the creature's reach. His sword sprayed chill water across her, and she jumped forward, planting a dagger in the creature's eye.

Suddenly thankful for the times Ham had made her practice without Allomancy, she caught the side of a building to steady herself in the slush. Then she threw herself forward, shouldering the koloss with the wounded eye—he was clawing at the dagger and yelling—into his companions. The koloss with the young girl turned, shocked, as Vin rammed her other dagger into his back. He didn't drop, but he did let go of the child.

Lord Ruler, these things are tough! she thought, cloak whipping as she grabbed the child and dashed away. *Especially when you're not tough yourself. I need some more metals.*

The girl in Vin's arms cringed as a koloss howl sounded, and Vin spun, flaring her tin to keep herself from falling unconscious from her fatigue. The creatures weren't following, however—they were arguing over a bit of clothing the dead man had been wearing. The howl sounded again, and this time, Vin realized, it had come from another direction.

People began to scream again. Vin looked up, only to find those she'd just rescued facing down an even larger group of koloss.

"No!" Vin said, raising a hand. But, they'd run far while she'd been fighting. She wouldn't even have been able to see them, save for her tin. As it was, she was able to see painfully well as the creatures began to lay into the small group with their thick-bladed swords.

"No!" Vin screamed again, the deaths startling her, shocking her, standing as a reminder of all the deaths she'd been unable to prevent.

"No. No! *No!*"

Pewter, gone. Steel, gone. Iron, gone. She had nothing.

Or . . . she had one thing. Not even pausing to think on what prompted her to use it, she threw a duralumin-enhanced Soothing at the beasts.

It was as if her mind slammed into Something. And then, that Something shattered. Vin skidded to a halt, shocked, child still in her arms as the koloss stopped, frozen in their horrific act of slaughter.

What did I just do? she thought, tracing through her muddled mind, trying to connect why she had reacted as she had. Was it because she had been frustrated?

No. She knew that the Lord Ruler had built the Inquisitors with a weakness: Remove a particular spike from their back, and they'd die. He had also built the kandra with a weakness. The koloss had to have a weakness, too.

TenSoon called the koloss . . . his cousins, she thought.

She stood upright, the dark street suddenly quiet save for the whimpering skaa. The koloss waited, and she could feel herself in their minds. As if they were an extension of her own body, the same thing she had felt when she'd taken control of TenSoon's body.

Cousins indeed. The Lord Ruler had built the koloss with a weakness—the same weakness as the kandra. He *had* given himself a way to keep them in check.

And suddenly she understood how he'd controlled them all those long years.

Sazed stood at the head of his large band of refugees, snow and ash—the two now indistinguishable in the misty darkness—falling around him. Ham sat to one side, looking drowsy. He'd lost too much blood; a man without pewter would have died by now. Someone had given Sazed a cloak, but he had used it to wrap the comatose Breeze. Even though he barely tapped his brassmind for warmth, Sazed himself wasn't cold.

Maybe he was just getting too numb to care.

He held two hands up before him, forming fists, ten rings sparkling against the light of the group's single lantern. Koloss approached from the dark alleyways, their forms huddled shadows in the night.

Sazed's soldiers backed away. There was little hope left in them. Sazed alone stood in the quiet snow, a spindly, bald scholar, nearly naked. He, the one who preached the religions of the fallen. He, who had given up hope at the end. He, who should have had the most faith of all.

Ten rings. A few minutes of power. A few minutes of life.

He waited as the koloss gathered. The beasts grew strangely silent in the night. They stopped approaching. They stood still, a line of dark, moundlike silhouettes in the night.

Why don't they attack! Sazed thought, frustrated.

A child whimpered. Then, the koloss began to move again. Sazed tensed, but the creatures didn't walk forward. They split, and a quiet figure walked through the center of them.

"Lady Vin?" Sazed asked. He still hadn't had a chance to speak with her since she'd saved him at the gate. She looked exhausted.

"Sazed," she said tiredly. "You lied to me about the Well of Ascension."

"Yes, Lady Vin," he said.

"That isn't important now," she said. "Why are you standing naked *outside* of the keep's walls?"

"I . . ." He looked up at the koloss. "Lady Vin, I—"

"Penrod!" Vin shouted suddenly. "Is that you up there?"

The king appeared. He looked as confused as Sazed felt.

"Open your gates!" Vin yelled.

"Are you mad?" Penrod yelled back.

"I'm not sure," Vin said. She turned, and a group of koloss moved forward, walking quietly as if commanded. The largest one picked Vin up, holding her up high, until she was nearly level with the top of the keep's low wall. Several guards atop the wall shied away from her.

"I'm tired, Penrod," Vin said. Sazed had to tap his hearing tinmind to listen in on her words.

"We're all tired, child," Penrod said.

"I'm particularly tired," Vin said. "I'm tired of the games. I'm tired of people dying because of arguments between their leaders. I'm tired of good men being taken advantage of."

Penrod nodded quietly.

"I want you to gather our remaining soldiers," Vin said, turning to look over the city. "How many do you have in there?"

"About two hundred," he said.

Vin nodded. "The city is not lost—the koloss have fought against the soldiers, but haven't had much time to turn on the population yet. I want you to send out your soldiers to find any groups of koloss that are pillaging or killing. Protect the people, but don't attack the koloss if you can help it. Send a messenger for me instead."

Remembering Penrod's bullheadedness earlier, Sazed thought the man might object. He didn't. He just nodded.

"What do we do then?" Penrod asked.

"I'll take care of the koloss," Vin said. "We'll go reclaim Keep Venture first—I'm going to need more metals, and there are plenty stored there. Once the city is secure, I want you and your soldiers to put out those fires. It shouldn't be too hard; there aren't a lot of buildings left that can burn."

"Very well," Penrod said, turning to call out his orders.

Sazed watched in silence as the massive koloss lowered Vin to the ground. It stood quietly, as if it were a monster hewn of stone, and not a breathing, bleeding, living creature.

"Sazed," Vin said softly. He could sense the fatigue in her voice.

"Lady Vin," Sazed said. To the side, Ham finally shook himself out of his stupor, looking up in shock as he noticed Vin and the koloss.

Vin continued to look at Sazed, studying him. Sazed had trouble meeting her eyes. But, she was right. They could talk about his betrayal later. There were other, more important tasks that had to be accomplished. "I realize you probably have work for me to do," Sazed said, breaking the silence. "But, might I instead be excused? There is . . . a task I wish to perform."

"Of course, Sazed," Vin said. "But first, tell me. Do you know if any of the others survived?"

"Clubs and Dockson are dead, my lady," Sazed said. "I have not seen their bodies, but the reports were from reliable sources. You can see that Lord Hammond is here, with us, though he has suffered a very bad wound."

"Breeze?" she asked.

Sazed nodded to the lump that lay huddled beside the wall. "He lives, thankfully. His mind, however, appears to be reacting poorly to the horrors he saw. It could simply be a form of shock. Or . . . it could be something more lasting."

Vin nodded, turning to Ham. "Ham. I need pewter."

He nodded dully, pulling out a vial with his good hand. He tossed it to her. Vin downed it, and immediately her fatigue seemed to lessen. She stood up straighter, her eyes becoming more alert.

That can't be healthy, Sazed thought with worry. *How much of that has she been burning?*

Step more energetic, she turned to walk toward her koloss.

"Lady Vin?" Sazed asked, causing her to turn around. "There is still an army out there."

"Oh, I know," Vin said, turning to take one of the large, wedgelike koloss swords from its owner. It was actually a few inches taller than she was.

"I am well aware of Straff's intentions," she said, hefting the sword up onto her shoulder. Then she turned in to the snow and mist, walking toward Keep Venture, her strange koloss guards tromping after her.

It took Sazed well into the night to complete his self-appointed task. He found corpse after corpse in the frigid night, many of them iced over. The snow had stopped falling, and the wind had picked up, hardening the slush to slick ice. He had to break some of the corpses free to turn them over and inspect their faces.

Without his brassmind to provide heat, he could never have performed his grisly job. Even so, he had found himself some warmer clothing—a simple brown robe and a set of boots. He continued working through the night, the wind swirling flakes of snow and ice around him. He started at the gate, of course. That was where the most corpses were. However, he eventually had to move into alleyways and thoroughfares.

He found her body sometime near morning.

The city had stopped burning. The only light he had was his lantern, but it was enough to reveal the strip of fluttering cloth in a snowbank. At first, Sazed thought it was just another bloodied bandage that had failed in its purpose. Then he saw a glimmer of orange and yellow, and he moved over—he no longer had the strength to rush—and reached into the snow.

Tindwyl's body cracked slightly as he rolled it out. The blood on her side was frozen, of course, and her eyes were iced open. Judging from the direction of her flight, she had been leading her soldiers to Keep Venture.

Oh, Tindwyl, he thought, reaching down to touch her face. It was still soft, but dreadfully cold. After years of being abused by the Breeders, after surviving so much, she had found this. Death in a city where she hadn't belonged, with a man—no, a *half* man—who did not deserve her.

He released his brassmind, and let the night's cold wash over him. He didn't want to feel warm at the moment. His lantern flickered uncertainly, illuminating the street, shadowing the icy corpse. There, in that frozen alley of Luthadel, looking down at the corpse of the woman he loved, Sazed realized something.

He didn't know what to do.

He tried to think of something proper to say—something proper to think—but suddenly, all of his religious knowledge seemed hollow. What was the use in giving her a burial? What was the value in speaking the prayers of a long-dead god? What good was he? The religion of Dadradah hadn't helped Clubs; the Survivor hadn't come to rescue the thousands of soldiers who had died. What was the point?

None of Sazed's knowledge gave him comfort. He accepted the religions he knew—believed in their value—but that didn't give him what he needed. They didn't assure him that Tindwyl's spirit still lived. Instead, they made him question. If so many people believed so many different things, how could any one of them—or, even, anything at all—actually be true?

The skaa called Sazed holy, but at that moment he

realized that he was the most profane of men. He was a creature who knew three hundred religions, yet had faith in none of them.

So, when his tears fell—and nearly began to freeze to his face—they gave him as little comfort as his religions. He moaned, leaning over the frozen corpse.

My life, he thought, *has been a sham.*

Rashek is to try and lead Alendi in the wrong direction, to discourage him, or otherwise foil his quest. Alendi doesn't know that he has been deceived, that we've all been deceived, and he will not listen to me now.

55

STRAFF WOKE IN THE COLD morning and immediately reached for a leaf of Black Frayn. He was beginning to see the benefits of his addiction. It woke him quickly and easily, making his body feel warm despite the early hour. When he might have once taken an hour to get ready, he was up in minutes, dressed, prepared for the day.

And glorious that day would be.

Janarle met him outside his tent, and the two walked through the bustling camp. Straff's boots cracked on half ice, half snow as he made his way to his horse.

"The fires are out, my lord," Janarle explained. "Probably due to the snows. The koloss probably finished their rampaging and took shelter from the cold. Our scouts are afraid to get too close, but they say the city is like a graveyard. Quiet and empty, save for the bodies."

"Maybe they actually killed each other off," Straff said cheerfully, climbing into his saddle, breath puffing in the crisp morning air. Around him, the army was forming up.

Fifty thousand soldiers, eager at the prospect of taking the city. Not only was there plundering to be done, but moving into Luthadel would mean roofs and walls for all of them.

"Perhaps," Janarle said, mounting.

Wouldn't that be convenient, Straff thought with a smile. *All of my enemies dead, the city and its riches mine, and no skaa to worry about.*

"My lord!" someone cried.

Straff looked up. The field between his camp and Luthadel was colored gray and white, the snow stained by ash. And gathering on the other side of that field were koloss.

"Looks like they are alive after all, my lord," Janarle said.

"Indeed," Straff said, frowning. There were still a lot of the creatures. They piled out of the western gate, not attacking immediately, instead gathering in a large body.

"Scout counts say there are fewer of them than there were," Janarle said after a short time. "Perhaps two-thirds their original number, maybe a bit fewer. But, they *are* koloss. . . ."

"But they're abandoning their fortifications," Straff said, smiling, Black Frayn warming his blood, making him feel like he was burning metals. "And they're coming to us. Let them charge. This should be over quickly."

"Yes, my lord," Janarle said, sounding a little less certain. He frowned, then, pointing toward the southern section of the city. "My . . . lord?"

"What now?"

"Soldiers, my lord," Janarle said. "Human ones. Looks to be several thousand of them."

Straff frowned. "They should all be dead!"

The koloss charged. Straff's horse shuffled slightly as the blue monsters ran across the gray field, the human troops falling into more organized ranks behind.

"Archers!" Janarle shouted. "Prepare first volley!"

Perhaps I shouldn't be at the front, Straff thought suddenly. He turned his horse, then noticed something. An arrow suddenly shot from the midst of the charging koloss.

But, koloss didn't use bows. Besides, the monsters were

still far away, and that object was far too big to be an arrow anyway. A rock, perhaps? It seemed larger than . . .

It began to fall down toward Straff's army. Straff stared into the sky, riveted by the strange object. It grew more distinct as it fell. It wasn't an arrow, nor was it a rock.

It was a person—a person with a flapping mistcloak.

"No!" Straff yelled. *She's supposed to be gone!*

Vin screamed down from her duralumin-fueled Steeljump, massive koloss sword light in her hands. She hit Straff directly in the head with the sword, then continued on downward, slamming into the ground, throwing up snow and frozen dirt with the power of her impact.

The horse fell into two pieces, front and back. What remained of the former king slid to the ground with the equine corpse. She looked at the remnants, smiled grimly, and bid Straff farewell.

Elend had, after all, warned him what would happen if he attacked the city.

Straff's generals and attendants stood around her in a stunned circle. Behind her, the koloss army barreled forward, confusion in Straff's ranks making the archer volleys ragged and less effective.

Vin kept a tight hold on her sword, then Pushed outward with a duralumin-enhanced Steelpush. Riders were thrown, their beasts tripped by their shoes, and soldiers sprayed backward from her in a circle of several dozen yards. Men screamed.

She downed another vial, restoring both steel and pewter. Then she jumped up, seeking out generals and other officers to attack. As she moved, her koloss troops hit the front ranks of Straff's army, and the real carnage began.

"What are they doing?" Cett asked, hurriedly throwing on his cloak as he was placed and tied into his saddle.

"Attacking, apparently," said Bahmen, one of his aides. "Look! They're working *with* the koloss."

Cett frowned, doing up his cloak clasp. "A treaty?"

"With koloss?" Bahmen asked.

Cett shrugged. "Who's going to win?"

"No way to tell, my lord," the man said. "Koloss are—"

"What is this!" Allrianne demanded, riding up the snowy incline, accompanied by a couple of abashed guards. Cett had, of course, ordered them to keep her in the camp—but he had also, of course, expected that she'd get past them eventually.

At least I can count on her to be slowed down by getting ready in the morning, he thought with amusement. She wore one of her dresses, immaculately arranged, her hair done. If a building were burning down, Allrianne would still pause to do her makeup before escaping.

"Looks like the battle has begun," Cett said, nodding toward the fighting.

"*Outside* the city?" Allrianne asked, riding up next to him. Then she brightened. "They're attacking Straff's position!"

"Yes," Cett said. "And that leaves the city—"

"We have to help them, Father!"

Cett rolled his eyes. "You know we're going to do nothing of the sort. We'll see who wins. If they're weak enough—which I hope they will be—we'll attack them. I didn't bring all of my forces back with me, but maybe . . ."

He trailed off as he noticed the look in Allrianne's eyes. He opened his mouth to speak, but before he could do so, she kicked her horse into motion.

Her guards cursed, dashing forward—too late—to try and grab her reins. Cett sat, stunned. This was a little insane, even for her. She wouldn't dare . . .

She galloped down the hill toward the battle. Then she paused, as he had expected. She turned, looking back at him.

"If you want to protect me, Father," she yelled, "you'd better charge!"

With that, she turned and started galloping again, her horse throwing up puffs of snow.

Cett didn't move.

"My lord," Bahmen said. "Those forces look almost evenly matched. Fifty thousand men against a force of some twelve thousand koloss and about five thousand men. If we were to add our strength to either side . . ."

Damn fool girl! he thought, watching Allrianne gallop away.

"My lord?" Bahmen asked.

Why did I come to Luthadel in the first place? Was it because I really thought I could take the city? Without Allomancers, with my homeland in revolt? Or, was it because I was looking for something? A confirmation of the stories. A power like I saw on that night, when the Heir almost killed me.

How exactly did they get the koloss to fight with them, anyway?

"Gather our forces!" Cett commanded. "We're marching to the defense of Luthadel. And somebody send riders after that fool daughter of mine!"

Sazed rode quietly, his horse moving slowly in the snow. Ahead of him, the battle raged, but he was far enough behind it to be out of danger. He'd left the city behind, where Luthadel's surviving women and elderly watched from the walls. Vin had saved them from the koloss. The real miracle would be to see if she could save them from the other two armies.

Sazed didn't ride into the fight. His metalminds were mostly empty, and his body was nearly as tired as his mind. He simply brought his horse to a halt, its breath puffing in the cold as he sat alone on the snowy plain.

He didn't know how to deal with Tindwyl's death. He felt . . . hollow. He wished that he could just stop feeling. He wished that he could go back and defend her gate, instead of his own. Why hadn't he gone in search of her when he'd heard of the northern gate's fall? She'd still been alive then. He might have been able to protect her. . . .

Why did he even care anymore? Why bother?

But, the ones who had faith were right, he thought. *Vin came back to defend the city. I lost hope, but they never did.*

He started his horse forward again. The sounds of battle

came in the distance. He tried to focus on anything but Tindwyl, but his thoughts kept returning to things he had studied with her. The facts and stories became more precious, for they were a link to her. A painful link, but one he couldn't bear to discard.

The Hero of Ages was not simply to be a warrior, he thought, still riding slowly toward the battlefield. *He was a person who united others, who brought them together. A leader.*

He knew that Vin thought she was the Hero. But Tindwyl was right: it was too much of a coincidence. And, he wasn't even certain what he believed anymore. If anything.

The Hero of Ages was removed from the Terris people, he thought, watching the koloss attack. *He was not royalty himself, but came to it eventually.*

Sazed pulled his horse up, pausing in the center of the open, empty field. Arrows stuck from the snow around him, and the ground was thoroughly trampled. In the distance, he heard a drum. He turned, watching as an army of men marched over a rise to the west. They flew Cett's banner.

He commanded the forces of the world. Kings rode to his aid.

Cett's forces joined the battle against Straff. There was a crash of metal against metal, bodies grunting, as a new front came under attack. Sazed sat on the field between the city and the armies. Vin's forces were still outnumbered, but as Sazed watched, Straff's army began to pull back. It broke into pieces, its members fighting without direction. Their movements bespoke terror.

She's killing their generals, he thought.

Cett was a clever man. He himself rode to battle, but he stayed near the back of his ranks—his infirmities requiring him to remain tied into his saddle and making it difficult for him to fight. Still, by joining the battle, he ensured that Vin would not turn her koloss on him.

For there was really no doubt in Sazed's mind who would win this conflict. Indeed, before even an hour had passed, Straff's troops began to surrender in large groups.

The sounds of battle died down, and Sazed kicked his horse forward.

Holy First Witness, he thought. *I don't know that I believe that. But, either way, I should be there for what happens next.*

The koloss stopped fighting, standing silently. They parted for Sazed as he rode up through their ranks. Eventually, he found Vin standing, bloodied, her massive koloss sword held on one shoulder. Some koloss pulled a man forward—a lord in rich clothing and a silvery breastplate. They dropped him before Vin.

From behind, Penrod approached with an honor guard, led by a koloss. Nobody spoke. Eventually, the koloss parted again, and this time a suspicious Cett rode forward, surrounded by a large group of soldiers and led by a single koloss.

Cett eyed Vin, then scratched his chin. "Not much of a battle," he said.

"Straff's soldiers were afraid," Vin said. "They're cold, and they have no desire to fight koloss."

"And their leaders?" Cett asked.

"I killed them," Vin said. "Except this one. Your name?"

"Lord Janarle," said Straff's man. His leg appeared broken, and koloss held him by either arm, supporting him.

"Straff is dead," Vin said. "You control this army now."

The nobleman bowed his head. "No, I don't. You do."

Vin nodded. "On your knees," she said.

The koloss dropped Janarle. He grunted in pain, but then bowed forward. "I swear my army to you," he whispered.

"No," Vin said sharply. "Not to me—to the rightful heir of House Venture. He is your lord now."

Janarle paused. "Very well," he said. "Whatever you wish. I swear loyalty to Straff's son, Elend Venture."

The separate groups stood in the cold. Sazed turned as Vin did, looking at Penrod. Vin pointed at the ground. Penrod quietly dismounted, then bowed himself to the ground.

"I swear as well," he said. "I give my loyalty to Elend Venture."

Vin turned to Lord Cett.

"You expect this of me?" the bearded man said, amused.

"Yes," Vin said quietly.

"And if I refuse?" Cett asked.

"Then I'll kill you," Vin said quietly. "You brought armies to attack my city. You threatened my people. I won't slaughter your soldiers, make them pay for what you did, but I *will* kill you, Cett."

Silence. Sazed turned, looking back at the lines of immobile koloss, standing in the bloodied snow.

"That is a threat, you know," Cett said. "Your own Elend would never stand for such a thing."

"He's not here," Vin said.

"And what do you think he'd say?" Cett asked. "He'd tell me not to give in to such a demand—the honorable Elend Venture would never give in simply because someone threatened his life."

"You're not the man that Elend is," Vin said. "And you know it."

Cett paused, then smiled. "No. No, I'm not." He turned to his aides. "Help me down."

Vin watched quietly as the guards undid Cett's legs, then lifted him down to the snowy ground. He bowed. "Very well, then. I swear myself to Elend Venture. He's welcome to my kingdom . . . assuming he can take it back from that damn obligator who now controls it."

Vin nodded, turning to Sazed. "I need your help, Sazed."

"Whatever you command, Mistress," Sazed said quietly.

Vin paused. "Please don't call me that."

"As you wish," Sazed said.

"You're the only one here I trust, Sazed," Vin said, ignoring the three kneeling men. "With Ham wounded and Breeze . . ."

"I will do my best," Sazed said, bowing his head. "What is it you want me to do?"

"Secure Luthadel," Vin said. "Make certain the people are sheltered, and send for supplies from Straff's storehouses. Get these armies situated so that they won't kill each other, then send a squad to fetch Elend. He'll be coming south on the canal highway."

Sazed nodded, and Vin turned to the three kneeling kings. "Sazed is my second. You will obey him as you would Elend or myself."

They each nodded in turn.

"But, where will you be?" Penrod asked, looking up.

Vin sighed, suddenly looking terribly weak. "Sleeping," she said, and dropped her sword. Then she Pushed against it, shooting backward into the sky, toward Luthadel.

He left ruin in his wake, but it was forgotten, Sazed thought, turning to watch her fly. *He created kingdoms, and then destroyed them as he made the world anew.*

We had the wrong gender all along.

THE END OF PART FIVE

PART SIX

WORDS IN STEEL

If Rashek fails to lead Alendi astray, then I have instructed the lad to kill Alendi.

56

HOW CAN VIN STAND THIS? Elend wondered. He could barely see twenty feet in the mists. Trees appeared as apparitions around him as he walked, their branches curling around the road. The mist almost seemed to live: it moved, swirled, and blew in the cold night air. It snatched up his puffs of breath, as if drawing a piece of him into it.

He shivered and kept walking. The snow had melted patchily over the last few days, leaving heaps in shadowed areas. The canal road, thankfully, was mostly clear.

He walked with a pack over his shoulder, carrying only the necessities. At Spook's suggestion, they'd traded their horses at a village several days back. They'd rode the creatures hard the last few days, and it was Spook's estimation that trying to keep them fed—and alive—for the last leg of their trip to Luthadel wouldn't be worth the effort.

Besides, whatever was going to happen at the city had likely already occurred. So Elend walked, alone, in the darkness. Despite the eeriness, he kept his word and traveled only at night. Not only was it Vin's will, but Spook claimed that night was safer. Few travelers braved the mists. Therefore, most bandits didn't bother watching roadways at night.

Spook prowled ahead, his keen senses allowing him to detect danger before Elend blundered into it. *How does that work, anyway?* Elend wondered as he walked. *Tin is supposed to make you see better. But what does it matter how far you can see, if the mists just obscure everything?*

Writers claimed that Allomancy could help a person pierce the mists, somehow. Elend had always wondered what that was like. Of course, he had also wondered what it felt like to feel the strength of pewter, or to fight with atium. Allomancers were uncommon, even among Great Houses. Yet, because of the way Straff had treated him, Elend had always felt guilty that he hadn't been one.

But, I ended up as king eventually, even without Allomancy, he thought, smiling to himself. He'd lost the throne, true. But, while they could take his crown, they could not take away his accomplishments. He'd proved that an Assembly could work. He'd protected the skaa, given them rights, and a taste of freedom they'd never forget. He'd done more than anyone would have expected of him.

Something rustled in the mists.

Elend froze, staring out into the darkness. *Sounds like leaves,* he thought nervously. *Something moving across them? Or . . . just the wind blowing them?*

He decided at that moment that there was nothing more unnerving than staring into the misty darkness, seeing ever-shifting silhouettes. A part of him would rather face down a koloss army than stand alone, at night, in an unknown forest.

"Elend," someone whispered.

Elend spun. He put a hand to his chest as he saw Spook approaching. He thought about chastising the boy for sneaking up on him—but, well, there wasn't really any other way to approach in the mists.

"Did you see something?" Spook asked quietly.

Elend shook his head. "But I think I heard something."

Spook nodded, then darted off into the mists again. Elend stood, uncertain whether he should continue on, or just wait. He didn't have to debate for very long. Spook returned a few moments later.

"Nothing to worry about," Spook said. "Just a mistwraith."

"What?" Elend asked.

"Mistwraith," Spook said. "You know. Big goopy things? Related to kandra? Don't tell me you haven't read about them?"

"I have," Elend said, nervously scanning the darkness. "But, I never thought I'd be out in the mists with one."

Spook shrugged. "It's probably just following our scent, hoping that we'll leave some trash for it to eat. The things are harmless, mostly."

"Mostly?" Elend asked.

"You probably know more about them than I do. Look, I didn't come back here to chat about scavengers. There's light up ahead."

"A village?" Elend asked, thinking back to when they'd come this way before.

Spook shook his head. "Looks like watchfires."

"An army?"

"Maybe. I'm just thinking you should wait behind for a bit. It could be awkward if you wander into a scout post."

"Agreed," Elend said.

Spook nodded, then took off into the mists.

And Elend was alone in the darkness again. He shivered, pulling his cloak close, and eyed the mists in the direction from which he'd heard the mistwraith. Yes, he'd read about them. He knew they were supposed to be harmless. But the thought of something crawling out there—its skeleton made from random sets of bones—watching him . . .

Don't focus on that, Elend told himself.

He turned his attention, instead, to the mists. Vin was right about one thing, at least. They were lingering longer and longer despite the sunrise. Some mornings, they remained a full hour after the sun came up. He could easily imagine the disaster that would befall the land should the mists persist all day. Crops would fail, animals would starve, and civilization would collapse.

Could the Deepness really be something so simple? Elend's own impressions of the Deepness were seated in scholarly tradition. Some writers dismissed the entire thing as a legend—a rumor used by the obligators to enhance their god's aura of divinity. The majority accepted the historical definition of the Deepness—a dark monster that had been slain by the Lord Ruler.

And yet, thinking of it as the mist made some sense. How could a single beast, no matter how dangerous, threaten an entire land? The mists, though . . . they could be destructive. Kill plants. Perhaps even . . . kill people, as Sazed had suggested?

He eyed it shifting around him, playful, deceptive. Yes, he could see it as the Deepness. Its reputation—more frightening than a monster, more dangerous than an army—was one it would deserve. In fact, watching it as he was, he could see it trying to play tricks on his mind. For instance, the mist bank directly in front of him seemed to be forming shapes. Elend smiled as his mind picked out images in the mists. One almost looked like a person standing there, in front of him.

The person stepped forward.

Elend jumped, taking a slight step backward, his foot crunching on a bit of ice-crusted snow. *Don't be silly,* he told himself. *Your mind is playing tricks on you. There's nothing—*

The shape in the mists took another step forward. It was indistinct, almost formless, and yet it seemed real. Random movements in the mists outlined its face, its body, its legs.

"Lord Ruler!" Elend yelped, jumping back. The thing continued to regard him.

I'm going mad, he thought, hands beginning to shake. The mist figure stopped a few feet in front of him and then raised its right arm and pointed.

North. Away from Luthadel.

Elend frowned, glancing in the direction the figure pointed. There was nothing but more empty mists. He turned back toward it, but it stood quietly, arm upraised.

Vin spoke of this thing, he remembered, forcing down his fear. *She tried to tell me about it. And I thought she was making things up!* She was right—just as she'd been right about the mists staying longer in the day, and the possibility of the mists being the Deepness. He was beginning to wonder which of them was the scholar.

The mist figure continued to point.

"What?" Elend asked, his own voice sounding haunting in the silent air.

It stepped forward, arm still raised. Elend put a useless hand to his sword, but held his ground.

"Tell me what you wish of me!" he said forcefully.

The thing pointed again. Elend cocked his head. It certainly didn't seem threatening. In fact, he felt an unnatural feeling of peace coming from it.

Allomancy? he thought. *It's Pulling on my emotions!*

"Elend?" Spook's voice drifted out of the mists.

The figure suddenly dissolved, its form melting into the mists. Spook approached, his face dark and shadowed in the night. "Elend? What were you saying?"

Elend took his hand off his sword, standing upright. He eyed the mists, still not completely convinced that he wasn't seeing things. "Nothing," he said.

Spook glanced back the way he had come. "You should come look at this."

"The army?" Elend asked, frowning.

Spook shook his head. "No. The refugees."

"The Keepers are dead, my lord," the old man said, sitting across from Elend. He didn't have a tent, only a blanket stretched between several poles. "Either dead, or captured."

Another man brought Elend a cup of warm tea, his demeanor servile. Both wore the robes of stewards, and while their eyes bespoke exhaustion, their robes and hands were clean.

Old habits, Elend thought, nodding thankfully and taking a sip of the tea. *Terris's people might have declared themselves independent, but a thousand years of servitude cannot be so easily thrown off.*

The camp was an odd place. Spook said he counted nearly a thousand people in it—a nightmare of a number to care for, feed, and organize in the cold winter. Many were elderly, and the men were mostly stewards: eunuchs bred for genteel service, with no experience in hunting.

"Tell me what happened," Elend said.

The elderly steward nodded, his head shaking. He didn't seem particularly frail—actually, he had that same air of controlled dignity that most stewards exhibited—but his body had a slow, chronic tremble.

"The Synod came out into the open, my lord, once the empire fell." He accepted a cup of his own, but Elend noticed that it was only half full—a precaution that proved wise as the elderly steward's shaking nearly spilled its contents. "They became our rulers. Perhaps it was not wise to reveal themselves so soon."

Not all Terrismen were Feruchemists; in fact, very few were. The Keepers—people like Sazed and Tindwyl—had been forced into hiding long ago by the Lord Ruler. His paranoia that Feruchemical and Allomantic lines might mix—thereby potentially producing a person with his same powers—had led him to try and destroy all Feruchemists.

"I've known Keepers, friend," Elend said softly. "I find it hard to believe that they could have been easily defeated. Who did this?"

"Steel Inquisitors, my lord," the old man said.

Elend shivered. *So that's where they've been.*

"There were dozens of them, my lord," the old man said. "They attacked Tathingdwen with an army of koloss brutes. But, that was just a distraction, I think. Their real goal was the Synod and the Keepers themselves. While our army, such as it was, fought the beasts, the Inquisitors themselves struck at the Keepers."

Lord Ruler... Elend thought, stomach twisting. *So, what do we do with the book Sazed told us to deliver to the Synod? Do we pass it on to these men, or keep it?*

"They took the bodies with them, my lord," the old man said. "Terris is in ruins, and that is why we are going south. You said you know King Venture?"

"I... have met him," Elend said. "He ruled Luthadel, where I am from."

"Will he take us in, do you think?" the old man asked. "We have little hope anymore. Tathingdwen was the Terris capital, but even it wasn't large. We are few, these days—the Lord Ruler saw to that."

"I . . . do not know if Luthadel can help you, friend."

"We can serve well," the old man promised. "We were prideful to declare ourselves free, I think. We struggled to survive even before the Inquisitors attacked. Perhaps they did us a favor by casting us out."

Elend shook his head. "Koloss attacked Luthadel just over a week ago," he said quietly. "I am a refugee myself, Master Steward. For all I know, the city itself has fallen."

The old man fell silent. "Ah, I see," he finally said.

"I'm sorry," Elend said. "I was traveling back to see what happened. Tell me—I traveled this way not long ago. How is it that I missed you in my journey north?"

"We didn't come by the canal route, my lord," the old man said. "We cut across country, straight down, so that we could gather supplies at Suringshath. You . . . have no further word of events at Luthadel, then? There was a senior Keeper in residence there. We were hoping, perhaps, to seek her counsel."

"Lady Tindwyl?" Elend asked.

The old man perked up. "Yes. You know her?"

"She was an attendant at the king's court," Elend said.

"Keeper Tindwyl could be considered our leader now, I think," the old man said. "We aren't certain how many traveling Keepers there are, but she is the only known member of the Synod who was out of the city when we were attacked."

"She was still in Luthadel when I left," Elend said.

"Then she might live still," the old man said. "We can hope, I think. I thank you, traveler, for your information. Please, make yourself comfortable in our camp."

Elend nodded, rising. Spook stood a short distance away, in the mists near a pair of trees. Elend joined him.

The people kept large fires burning in the night, as if to defy the mists. The light did some good in dispelling the mists' power—and yet the light seemed to accentuate them as well, creating three-dimensional shadows that bewildered the eye. Spook leaned against the scraggly tree trunk, looking around at things Elend couldn't see. Elend could hear, however, some of what Spook must be inspecting. Crying children. Coughing men. Shuffling livestock.

"It doesn't look good, does it?" Elend said quietly.

Spook shook his head. "I wish they'd take down all these fires," he muttered. "The light hurts my eyes."

Elend glanced to the side. "They aren't *that* bright."

Spook shrugged. "They're just wasting wood."

"Forgive them their comfort, for now. They'll have little enough of it in the weeks to come." Elend paused, looking over at a passing squad of Terris "soldiers"—a group of men who were obviously stewards. Their posture was excellent, and they walked with a smooth grace, but Elend doubted they knew how to use any weapons beyond a cooking knife.

No, there is no army in Terris to help my people.

"You sent Vin back to gather our allies," Spook said quietly. "To bring them up to meet with us, perhaps to seek refuge in Terris."

"I know," Elend said.

"We can't gather in Terris, though," Spook said. "Not with the Inquisitors up there."

"I know," Elend said again.

Spook was silent for a moment. "The whole world is falling apart, El," he finally said. "Terris, Luthadel . . ."

"Luthadel has *not* been destroyed," Elend said, looking sharply at Spook.

"The koloss—"

"Vin will have found a way to stop them," Elend said. "For all we know, she already found the power at the Well of Ascension. We need to keep going. We can, and will, rebuild whatever was lost. Then we'll worry about helping Terris."

Spook paused, then nodded and smiled. Elend was surprised to see how much his confident words seemed to soothe the boy's concerns. Spook leaned back, eyeing Elend's still steaming cup of tea, and Elend handed it over with a mumble that he didn't like heartroot tea. Spook drank happily.

Elend, however, found matters more troubling than he'd admitted. *The Deepness returning, ghosts in the mist, and Inquisitors making a play for the Terris Dominance. What else have I been ignoring?*

It is a distant hope. Alendi has survived assassins, wars, and catastrophes. And yet, I hope that in the frozen mountains of Terris, he may finally be exposed. I hope for a miracle.

57

"LOOK, WE ALL KNOW WHAT we need to do," Cett said, pounding the table. "We've got our armies here, ready and willing to fight. Now, let's go get my damn country back!"

"The empress gave us no command to do such a thing," Janarle said, sipping his tea, completely unfazed by Cett's lack of decorum. "I, personally, think that we should wait at least until the emperor returns."

Penrod, the oldest of the men in the room, had enough tact to look sympathetic. "I understand that you are concerned for your people, Lord Cett. But we haven't even had a week to rebuild Luthadel. It is far too early to be worrying about expanding our influence. We cannot possibly authorize these preparations."

"Oh, leave off, Penrod," Cett snapped. "You're not in charge of us."

All three men turned to Sazed. He felt very awkward, sitting at the head of the table in Keep Venture's conference chamber. Aides and attendants, including some of Dockson's bureaucrats, stood at the perimeter of the sparse room, but only the three rulers—now kings beneath Elend's imperial rule—sat with Sazed at the table.

"I think that we should not be hasty, Lord Cett," Sazed said.

"This isn't haste," Cett said, pounding the table again. "I just want to order scout and spy reports, so that we can have information we need when we invade!"

"If we *do* invade," Janarle said. "If the emperor decides to recover Fadrex City, it won't happen until this summer, at the very earliest. We have far more pressing concerns. My armies have been away from the Northern Dominance for too long. It is basic political theory that we should stabilize what we have *before* we move into new territory."

"Bah!" Cett said, waving an indifferent hand.

"You may send your scouts, Lord Cett," Sazed said. "But they are to seek information only. They are to engage in no raids, no matter how tempting the opportunity."

Cett shook a bearded head. "*This* is why I never bothered to play political games with the rest of the Final Empire. Nothing gets done because everyone is too busy scheming!"

"There is much to be said for subtlety, Lord Cett," Penrod said. "Patience brings the greater prize."

"Greater prize?" Cett asked. "What did the Central Dominance earn itself by waiting? You waited right up until the moment that your city fell! If you hadn't been the ones with the best Mistborn . . ."

"Best Mistborn, my lord?" Sazed asked quietly. "Did you not see her take command of the koloss? Did you not see her leap across the sky like an arrow in flight? Lady Vin isn't simply the 'best Mistborn.' "

The group fell silent. *I have to keep them focused on her,* Sazed thought. *Without Vin's leadership—without the threat of her power—this coalition would dissolve in three heartbeats.*

He felt so inadequate. He couldn't keep the men ontopic, and he couldn't do much to help them with their various problems. He could just keep reminding them of Vin's power.

The trouble was, he didn't really want to. He was feeling something very odd in himself, feelings he usually didn't have. Disconcern. Apathy. Why did anything that these men talked about matter? Why did anything matter, now that Tindwyl was dead?

He gritted his teeth, trying to force himself to focus.

"Very well," Cett said, waving a hand. "I'll send the scouts. Has that food arrived from Urteau yet, Janarle?"

The younger nobleman grew uncomfortable. "We . . . may have trouble with that, my lord. It seems that an unwholesome element has been rabble-rousing in the city."

"No wonder you want to send troops back to the Northern Dominance!" Cett accused. "You're planning to conquer your kingdom back and leave mine to rot!"

"Urteau is *much* closer than your capital, Cett," Janarle said, turning back to his tea. "It only makes sense to set me up there before we turn our attention westward."

"We will let the empress make that decision," Penrod said. He liked to act the mediator—and by doing so, he made himself seem above the issues. In essence, he put himself in control by putting himself in between the other two.

Not all that different from what Elend tried to do, Sazed thought, *with our armies.* The boy had more of a sense of political strategy than Tindwyl had ever credited him with.

I shouldn't think about her, he told himself, closing his eyes. Yet, it was hard not to. Everything Sazed did, everything he thought, seemed wrong because she was gone. Lights seemed dimmer. Motivations were more difficult to reach. He found that he had trouble even *wanting* to pay attention to the kings, let alone give them direction.

It was foolish, he knew. How long had Tindwyl been back in his life? Only a few months. Long ago, he had resigned himself to the fact that he would never be loved—in general—and that he certainly would never have *her* love. Not only did he lack manhood, but he was a rebel and a dissident—a man well outside of the Terris orthodoxy.

Surely her love for him had been a miracle. Yet, whom did he thank for that blessing, and whom did he curse for stealing her away? He knew of hundreds of gods. He would hate them all, if he thought it would do any good.

For the sake of his own sanity, he forced himself to get distracted by the kings again.

"Listen," Penrod was saying, leaning forward, arms on the tabletop. "I think we're looking at this the wrong way, gentlemen. We shouldn't be squabbling, we should be happy. We are in a very unique position. In the time since the Lord Ruler's empire fell, dozens—perhaps hundreds—of men have tried to set themselves up as kings in various ways. The one thing they shared, however, was that they all lacked stability.

"Well, it appears that *we* are going to be forced to work together. I am starting to see this in a favorable light. I will give my allegiance to the Venture couple—I'll even live with Elend Venture's eccentric views of government—if it means that I'll still be in power ten years from now."

Cett scratched at his beard for a moment, then nodded. "You make a good point, Penrod. Maybe the first good one I've ever heard out of you."

"But we can't continue trying to assume that we know what we are to do," Janarle said. "We need direction. Surviving the next ten years, I suspect, is going to depend heavily on my not ending up dead on the end of that Mistborn girl's knife."

"Indeed," Penrod said, nodding curtly. "Master Terrisman. When can we expect the empress to take command again?"

Once again, all three pairs of eyes turned to Sazed.

I don't really care, Sazed thought, then immediately felt guilty. Vin was his friend. He did care. Even if it was hard to care about anything for him. He looked down in shame. "Lady Vin is suffering greatly from the effects of an extended pewter drag," he said. "She pushed herself very hard this last year, and then ended it by running all the way back to Luthadel. She is in great need of rest. I think we should let her be for a time longer."

The others nodded, and returned to their discussion. Sazed's mind, however, turned to Vin. He'd understated her malady, and he was beginning to worry. A pewter drag drained the body, and he suspected that she'd been forcing herself to stay awake with the metal for months now.

When a Keeper stored up wakefulness, he slept as if in a coma for a time. He could only hope that the effects of such a terrible pewter drag were the same, for Vin hadn't awoken a single time since her return a week before. Perhaps she'd awake soon, like a Keeper who came out of sleep.

Perhaps it would last longer. Her koloss army waited outside the city, controlled—apparently—even though she was unconscious. But for how long? Pewter dragging could kill, if the person had pushed themselves too hard.

What would happen to the city if she never woke up?

Ash was falling. *A lot of ashfalls lately,* Elend thought as he and Spook emerged from the trees and looked out over the Luthadel plain.

"See," Spook said quietly, pointing. "The city gates are broken."

Elend frowned. "But the koloss are camped *outside* the city." Indeed, Straff's army camp was also still there, right where it had been.

"Work crews," Spook said, shading his face against the sunlight to protect his overly sensitive Allomancer's eyes. "Looks like they're burying corpses outside the city."

Elend's frown deepened. *Vin. What happened to her? Is she all right?*

He and Spook had cut across country, taking a cue from the Terrismen, to make certain that they didn't get discovered by patrols from the city. Indeed, this day they'd broken their pattern, traveling a little bit during the day so that they could arrive at Luthadel just before nightfall. The mists would soon be coming, and Elend was fatigued—both from rising early and from walking so long.

More than that, he was tired of not knowing what had happened to Luthadel. "Can you see whose flag is set over the gates?" he asked.

Spook paused, apparently flaring his metals. "Yours," he finally said, surprised.

Elend smiled. *Well, either they managed to save the city somehow, or this is a very elaborate trap to capture me.* "Come on," he said, pointing to a line of refugees who were being allowed back into the city—likely those who had fled before, returning for food now that the danger was past. "We'll mix with those and make our way in."

Sazed sighed quietly, shutting the door to his room. The kings were finished with the day's arguments. Actually, they were starting to get along quite well, considering the fact that they'd all tried to conquer each other just a few weeks before.

Sazed knew he could take no credit for their newfound amiability, however. He had other preoccupations.

I've seen many die, in my days, he thought, walking into the room. *Kelsier. Jadendwyl. Crenda. People I respected. I never wondered what had happened to* their *spirits.*

He set his candle on the table, the fragile light illuminating a few scattered pages, a pile of strange metal nails taken from koloss bodies, and one manuscript. Sazed sat down at the table, fingers brushing the pages, remembering the days spent with Tindwyl, studying.

Maybe this is why Vin put me in charge, he thought. *She knew I'd need something to take my mind off Tindwyl.*

And yet, he was finding more and more that he didn't *want* to take his mind off her. Which was more potent? The pain of memory, or the pain of forgetting? He was a Keeper—it was his life's work to remember. Forgetting, even in the name of personal peace, was not something that appealed to him.

He flipped through the manuscript, smiling fondly in the dark chamber. He'd sent a cleaned-up, rewritten version with Vin and Elend to the north. This, however, was the original. The frantically—almost desperately—scribbled manuscript made by two frightened scholars.

As he fingered the pages, the flickering candlelight revealed Tindwyl's firm, yet beautiful, script. It mixed easily with paragraphs written in Sazed's own, more reserved hand. At times, a page would alternate between their different hands a dozen different times.

He didn't realize that he was crying until he blinked, sending loose a tear, which hit the page. He looked down, stunned as the bit of water caused a swirl in the ink.

"What now, Tindwyl?" he whispered. "Why did we do this? You never believed in the Hero of Ages, and I never believed in anything, it appears. What was the point of all this?"

He reached up and dabbed the tear with his sleeve, preserving the page as best he could. Despite his tiredness, he began to read, selecting a random paragraph. He read to remember. To think of days when he hadn't worried about why they were studying. He had simply been content to do what he enjoyed best, with the person he had come to love most.

We gathered everything we could find on the Hero of Ages and the Deepness, he thought, reading. *But so much of it seems contradictory.*

He flipped through to a particular section, one that Tindwyl had insisted that they include. It contained the several most blatant self-contradictions, as declared by Tindwyl. He read them over, giving them fair consideration for the first time. This was Tindwyl the scholar—a cautious skeptic. He fingered through the passages, reading her script.

The Hero of Ages will be tall of stature, one read. *A man who cannot be ignored by others.*

The power must not be taken, read another. *Of this, we are certain. It must be held, but not used. It must be released.* Tindwyl had found that condition foolish, since other sections talked about the Hero using the power to defeat the Deepness.

All men are selfish, read another. *The Hero is a man who can see the needs of all beyond his own desires.* "If all men are selfish," Tindwyl had asked, "then how can the Hero be selfless, as is said in other passages? And, indeed, how can a humble man be expected to conquer the world?"

Sazed shook his head, smiling. At times, her objections had been very well conceived—but at other times, she had just been struggling to offer another opinion, no matter how much of a stretch it required. He ran his fingers across the page again, but paused on the first paragraph.

Tall of stature, it said. That wouldn't refer to Vin. It hadn't come from the rubbing, but another book. Tindwyl had included it because the rubbing, the more trustworthy source, said he'd be short. Sazed flipped through the book to the complete transcription of Kwaan's iron-plate testimony, searching for the passage.

Alendi's height struck me the first time I saw him, it read. *Here was a man who was small of stature, but who seemed to tower over others, a man who demanded respect.*

Sazed frowned. Before, he'd argued that there was no contradiction, for one passage could be interpreted as referring to the Hero's presence or character, rather than just his physical height. Now, however, Sazed paused, really seeing Tindwyl's objections for the first time.

And something felt wrong to him. He looked back at his book, scanning the contents of the page.

There was a place for me in the lore of the Anticipation, he read. *I thought myself the Holy First Witness, the prophet foretold to discover the Hero of Ages. Renouncing Alendi then would have been to renounce my new position, my acceptance, by the others.*

Sazed's frown deepened. He traced the paragraph. Outside, it was growing dark, and a few trails of mist curled around the shutters, creeping into the room before vanishing.

Holy First Witness, he read again. *How did I miss that? It's the same name the people called me, back at the gates. I didn't recognize it.*

"Sazed."

Sazed jumped, nearly toppling his book to the floor as he turned. Vin stood behind him, a dark shadow in the poorly lit room.

"Lady Vin! You're up!"

"You shouldn't have let me sleep so long," she said.

"We tried to wake you," he said softly. "You were in a coma."

She paused.

"Perhaps it is for the best, Lady Vin," Sazed said. "The fighting is done, and you pushed yourself hard these last few months. It is good for you to get some rest, now that this is over."

She stepped forward, shaking her head, and Sazed could

see that she looked haggard, despite her days of rest. "No, Sazed," she said. "This is not 'over.' Not by far."

"What do you mean?" Sazed asked, growing concerned.

"I can still hear it in my head," Vin said, raising a hand to her forehead. "It's here. In the city."

"The Well of Ascension?" Sazed asked. "But, Lady Vin, I lied about that. Truly and apologetically, I don't even know if there *is* such a thing."

"Do you believe me to be the Hero of Ages?"

Sazed looked away. "A few days ago, on the field outside the city, I felt certain. But . . . lately . . . I don't seem to know what I believe anymore. The prophecies and stories are a jumble of contradictions."

"This isn't about prophecies," Vin said, walking over to his table and looking at his book. "This is about what needs to be done. I can feel it . . . pulling me."

She glanced at the closed window, with the mists curling at the edges. Then, she walked over and threw the shutters open, letting in the cold winter air. Vin stood, closing her eyes and letting the mists wash over her. She wore only a simple shirt and trousers.

"I drew upon it once, Sazed," she said. "Do you know that? Did I tell you? When I fought the Lord Ruler. I drew power from the mists. That's how I defeated him."

Sazed shivered, not just from the cold. From the tone in her voice, and the air of her words. "Lady Vin . . ." he said, but wasn't sure how to continue. Drew upon the mists? What did she mean?

"The Well is here," she repeated, looking out the window, mist curling into the room.

"It can't be, Lady Vin," Sazed said. "All of the reports agree. The Well of Ascension was found in the Terris Mountains."

Vin shook her head. "He changed the world, Sazed."

He paused, frowning. "What?"

"The Lord Ruler," she whispered. "He created the Ashmounts. The records say he made the vast deserts around the empire, that he broke the land in order to preserve it. Why should we assume that things look like they did when he first climbed to the Well? He created mountains. Why couldn't he have flattened them?"

Sazed felt a chill.

"It's what I would do," Vin said. "If I knew the power would return, if I wanted to preserve it. I'd hide the Well. I'd let the legends remain, talking about mountains to the north. Then, I would build my city around the Well so that I could keep an eye on it."

She turned, looking at him. "It's here. The power waits."

Sazed opened his mouth to object, but could find nothing. He had no faith. Who was he to argue with such things? As he paused, he heard voices below, from outside.

Voices? he thought. *At night? In the mists?* Curious, he strained to hear what was being said, but they were too far away. He reached into the bag beside his table. Most of his metalminds were empty; he wore only his copperminds, with their stores of ancient knowledge. Inside the sack, he found a small pouch. It contained the ten rings he had prepared for the siege, but had never used. He pulled it open, took out one of the ten, then tucked the bag into his sash.

With this ring—a tinmind—he could tap hearing. The words below became distinct to him.

"The king! The king has returned!"

Vin leaped out the window.

"I don't fully understand how she does it either, El," Ham said, walking with his arm in a sling.

Elend walked through the city streets, people trailing behind him, speaking in excited tones. The crowd was growing larger and larger as people heard that Elend had returned. Spook eyed them uncertainly, but seemed to be enjoying the attention.

"I was out cold for the last part of the battle," Ham was saying. "Only pewter kept me alive—koloss slaughtered my team, breached the walls of the keep I was defending. I got out, and found Sazed, but my mind was growing muddled by then. I remember falling unconscious outside Keep

Hasting. When I woke up, Vin had already taken the city back. I . . ."

They paused. Vin stood in front of them in the city street. Quiet, dark. In the mists, she almost looked like the spirit Elend had seen earlier.

"Vin?" he asked in the eerie air.

"Elend," she said, rushing forward, into his arms, and the air of mystery was gone. She shivered as she held him. "I'm sorry. I think I did something bad."

"Oh?" he asked. "What is that?"

"I made you emperor."

Elend smiled. "I noticed, and I accept."

"After all you did to make certain the people had a choice?"

Elend shook his head. "I'm beginning to think my opinions were simplistic. Honorable, but . . . incomplete. We'll deal with this. I'm just glad to find that my city is still standing."

Vin smiled. She looked tired.

"Vin?" he asked. "Are you still pewter-dragging?"

"No," she said. "This is something else." She glanced to the side, face thoughtful, as if deciding something.

"Come," she said.

Sazed watched out the window, a second tinmind enhancing his sight. It was indeed Elend below. Sazed smiled, one of the weights on his soul removed. He turned, intending to go and meet the king.

And then he saw something blowing on the floor in front of him. A scrap of paper. He knelt down, picking it up, noticing his own handwriting on it. Its edges were jagged from having been ripped. He frowned, walking over to his table, opening the book to the page with Kwaan's narrative. A piece was missing. The same piece as before, the one that had been ripped free that time with Tindwyl. He'd almost forgotten the strange occurrence with the pages all missing the same sentence.

He'd rewritten this page, from his metalmind, after they'd found the torn sheets. Now the same bit had been torn free, the last sentence. Just to make certain, he put it up next to his book. It fit perfectly. *Alendi must not reach the Well of Ascension,* it read, *for he must not be allowed to take the power for himself.* It was the exact wording Sazed had in his memory, the exact wording of the rubbing.

Why would *Kwaan have worried about this?* he thought, sitting down. *He says he knew Alendi better than anyone else. In fact, he called Alendi an honorable man on several occasions.*

Why would Kwaan be so worried about Alendi taking the power for himself?

Vin walked through the mists. Elend, Ham, and Spook trailed behind her, the crowd dispersed by Elend's order— though some soldiers did stay close to protect Elend.

Vin continued on, feeling the pulsings, the thumpings, the power that shook her very soul. Why couldn't the others feel it?

"Vin?" Elend asked. "Where are we going?"

"Kredik Shaw," she said softly.

"But . . . why?"

She just shook her head. She knew the truth, now. The Well was in the city. With how strong the pulsings were growing, she might have assumed that their direction would be harder to discern. But that wasn't the way it was at all. Now that they were loud and full, she found it easier.

Elend glanced back at the others, and she could sense his concern. Up ahead, Kredik Shaw loomed in the night. Spires, like massive spikes, jutted from the ground in an off-balance pattern, reaching accusingly toward the stars above.

"Vin," Elend said. "The mists are acting . . . strangely."

"I know," she said. "They're guiding me."

"No, actually," Elend said. "They kind of look like they're pulling *away* from you."

Vin shook her head. This felt *right.* How could she explain? Together, they entered the remnants of the Lord Ruler's palace.

The Well was here all along, Vin thought, amused. She

could feel the pulses vibrating through the building. Why hadn't she noticed it before?

The pulses were still too weak, then, she realized. *The Well wasn't full yet. Now it is.* And it called to her.

She followed the same path as before. The path she'd followed with Kelsier, breaking into Kredik Shaw on a doomful night when she had nearly died. The path she'd followed on her own, the night she had come to kill the Lord Ruler. The tight stone corridors opened into the room shaped like an upside-down bowl. Elend's lantern glistened against the fine stonework and murals, mostly in black and gray. The stone shack stood in the center of the room, abandoned, enclosed.

"I think we're finally going to find your atium, Elend," Vin said, smiling.

"What?" Elend said, his voice echoing in the chamber. "Vin, we searched here. We tried everything."

"Not enough, apparently," Vin said, eyeing the small building-within-a-building, but not moving toward it.

This is where I'd put it, she thought. *It makes sense. The Lord Ruler would have wanted to keep the Well close so that when the power returned, he'd be able to take it.*

But I killed him before that could happen.

The booming came from below. They'd torn up sections of the floor, but had stopped when they'd hit solid rock. There had to be a way down. She walked over, searching through the building-within-a-building, but found nothing. She left, passing her confused friends, frustrated.

Then she tried burning her metals. As always, the blue lines shot up around her, pointing to sources of metal. Elend was wearing several, as was Spook, though Ham was clean. Some of the stonework bore metal inlays, and lines pointed to those.

Everything was as expected. There was nothing . . .

Vin frowned, stepping to the side. One of the inlays bore a particularly thick line. Too thick, in fact. She frowned, inspecting the line as it—like the others—pointed from her chest directly at the stone wall. This one seemed to be pointing *beyond* the wall.

What?

She Pulled on it. Nothing happened. So, she Pulled harder, grunting as she was yanked toward the wall. She released the line, glancing about. There were inlays on the floor. Deep ones. Curious, she anchored herself by Pulling on these, then Pulled on the wall again. She thought she felt something budge.

She burned duralumin and Pulled as hard as she could. The explosion of power nearly ripped her apart, but her anchor held, and duralumin-fueled pewter kept her alive. And a section of the wall slid open, stone grinding against stone in the quiet room. Vin gasped, letting go as her metals ran out.

"Lord Ruler!" Spook said. Ham was quicker, however, moving with the speed of pewter and peeking into the opening. Elend stayed at her side, grabbing her arm as she nearly fell.

"I'm fine," Vin said, downing a vial and restoring her metals. The power of the Well thumped around her. It almost seemed to shake the room.

"There are stairs in here," Ham said, poking his head back out.

Vin steadied herself and nodded to Elend, and the two of them followed Ham and Spook through the false section of the wall.

But, I must continue with the sparsest of detail, Kwaan's account read.

> *Space is limited. The other Worldbringers must have thought themselves humble when they came to me, admitting that they had been wrong about Alendi. Even then, I was beginning to doubt my original declaration. But, I was prideful.*
>
> *In the end, my pride may have doomed us all. I had never received much attention from my brethren; they thought that my work and my interests were unsuitable to a Worldbringer. The couldn't see how my studies, which focused on nature instead of religion, benefited the people of the fourteen lands.*

*As the one who found Alendi, however, I became some-
one important. Foremost among the Worldbringers. There
was a place for me in the lore of the Anticipation—I
thought myself the Holy First Witness, the prophet foretold
to discover the Hero of Ages. Renouncing Alendi then
would have been to renounce my new position, my acceptance, by the others.*

And so I did not. But I do so now.

*Let it be known that I, Kwaan, Worldbringer of Terris,
am a fraud. Alendi was never the Hero of Ages. At best, I
have amplified his virtues, creating a hero where there
was none. At worst, I fear that I have corrupted all we
believe.*

Sazed sat at his table, reading from his book.

Something is not right here, he thought. He traced back a
few lines, looking at the words "Holy First Witness" again.
Why did that line keep bothering him?

He sat back, sighing. Even if the prophecies did speak
about the future, they wouldn't be things to follow or use as
guideposts. Tindwyl was right on that count. His own study
had proven them to be unreliable and shadowed.

So what was the problem?

It just doesn't make sense.

But, then again, sometimes religion didn't make literal
sense. Was that the reason, or was that his own bias? His
growing frustration with the teachings he had memorized
and taught, but which had betrayed him in the end?

It came down to the scrap of paper on his desk. The torn
one. *Alendi must not be allowed to reach the Well of Ascension. . . .*

Someone was standing next to his desk.

Sazed gasped, stumbling back, nearly tripping over his
chair. It wasn't actually a person. It was a shadow—
formed, it seemed, from streams of mist. They were very
faint, still trailing through the window that Vin had
opened, but they made a person. Its head seemed turned
toward the table, toward the book. Or . . . perhaps the
scrap of paper.

Sazed felt like running, like scrambling away in fear, but

his scholar's mind dredged something up to fight his terror. *Alendi,* he thought. *The one everyone thought was the Hero of Ages. He said he saw a thing made of mist following him.*

Vin claimed to have seen it as well.

"What . . . do you want?" he asked, trying to remain calm.

The spirit didn't move.

Could it be . . . her? he wondered with shock. Many religions claimed that the dead continued to walk the world, just beyond the view of mortals. But this thing was too short to be Tindwyl. Sazed was sure that he would have recognized her, even in such an amorphous form.

Sazed tried to gauge where it was looking. He reached out a hesitant hand, picking up the scrap of paper.

The spirit raised an arm, pointing toward the center of the city. Sazed frowned.

"I don't understand," he said.

The spirit pointed more insistently.

"Write down for me what you want me to do."

It just pointed.

Sazed stood for a long moment in the room with only one candle, then glanced at the open book. The wind flipped its pages, showing his handwriting, then Tindwyl's, then his again.

Alendi must not be allowed to reach the Well of Ascension. He must not be allowed to take the power for himself.

Perhaps . . . perhaps Kwaan knew something that nobody else had. Could the power corrupt even the best of people? Could that be why he turned against Alendi, trying to stop him?

The mist spirit pointed again.

If the spirit tore free that sentence, perhaps it was trying to tell me something. But . . . Vin wouldn't take the power for herself. She wouldn't destroy, as the Lord Ruler did, would she?

And if she didn't have a choice?

Outside, someone screamed. The yell was of pure terror, and it was soon joined by others. A horrible, echoing set of sounds in a dark night.

There wasn't time to think. Sazed grabbed the candle, spilling wax on the table in his haste, and left the room.

The winding set of stone stairs led downward for quite some time. Vin walked down them, Elend at her side, the thumping sounding loudly in her ears. At the bottom, the stairwell opened into . . .

A vast chamber. Elend held his lantern high, looking down into a huge stone cavern. Spook was already halfway down the stone steps leading to the floor. Ham was following.

"Lord Ruler . . ." Elend whispered, standing at Vin's side. "We'd have never found this without tearing down the entire building!"

"That was probably the idea," Vin said. "Kredik Shaw isn't simply a palace, but a capstone. Built to hide something. *This.* Above, those inlays on the walls hid the cracks of the doorway, and the metal in them obscured the opening mechanism from Allomantic eyes. If I hadn't had a hint . . ."

"Hint?" Elend asked, turning to her.

Vin shook her head, nodding to the steps. The two began down them. Below, she heard Spook's voice ring.

"There's food down here!" he yelled. "Cans and cans of it!"

Indeed, they found rank upon rank of shelves sitting on the cavern floor, meticulously packed as if set aside in preparation for something important. Vin and Elend reached the cavern floor as Ham chased after Spook, calling for him to slow down. Elend made as if to follow, but Vin grabbed his arm. She was burning iron.

"Strong source of metal that way," she said, growing eager.

Elend nodded, and they rushed through the cavern, passing shelf after shelf. *The Lord Ruler must have prepared these,* she thought. *But for what purpose?*

She didn't care at the moment. She didn't really care about the atium either, but Elend's eagerness to find it was too much to ignore. They rushed up to the end of the cavern, where they found the source of the metal line.

A large metal plaque hung on the wall, like the one Sazed had described finding in the Conventical of Seran. Elend was clearly disappointed when they saw it. Vin, however, stepped forward, looking through tin-enhanced eyes to see what it contained.

"A map?" Elend asked. "That's the Final Empire."

Indeed, a map of the empire was carved into the metal. Luthadel was marked at the center. A small circle marked another city nearby.

"Why is Statlin City circled?" Elend asked, frowning.

Vin shook her head. "This isn't what we came for," she said. "There." A tunnel split off from the main cavern. "Come on."

Sazed ran through the streets, not even certain what he was doing. He followed the mist spirit, which was difficult to trace in the night, as his candle had long since puffed out.

People screamed. Their panicked sounds gave him chills, and he itched to go and see what the problem was. Yet the mist spirit was demanding; it paused to catch his attention if it lost him. It could simply be leading him to his death. And yet . . . he felt a trust for it that he could not explain.

Allomancy? he thought. *Pulling on my emotions?*

Before he could consider that further, he stumbled across the first body. It was a skaa man in simple clothing, skin stained with ash. His face was twisted in a grimace of pain, and the ash on the ground was smeared from his thrashings.

Sazed gasped as he pulled to a halt. He knelt, studying the body by the dim light of an open window nearby. This man had not died easily.

It's . . . like the killings I was studying, he thought. *Months ago, in the village to the south. The man there said that the mists had killed his friend. Caused him to fall to the ground and thrash about.*

The spirit appeared in front of Sazed, its posture insistent. Sazed looked up, frowning. "You did this?" he whispered.

The thing shook its head violently, pointing. Kredik Shaw was just ahead. It was the direction Vin and Elend had gone earlier.

Sazed stood. *Vin said she thought the Well was still in the city,* he thought. *The Deepness has come upon us, as its tendrils have been doing in the far reaches of the empire for some time. Killing.*

Something greater than we comprehend is going on.

He still couldn't believe that Vin going to the Well would be dangerous. She had read; she knew Rashek's story. She wouldn't take the power for herself. He was confident. But not completely certain. In fact, he was no longer certain *what* they should do with the Well.

I have to get to her. Stop her, talk to her, prepare her. We can't rush into something like this. If, indeed, they were going to take the power at the Well, they needed to think about it first and decide what the best course was.

The mist spirit continued to point. Sazed stood and ran forward, ignoring the horror of the screams in the night. He approached the doors of the massive palace structure with its spires and spikes, then dashed inside.

The mist spirit remained behind, in the mists that had birthed it. Sazed lit his candle again with a flint, and waited. The mist spirit did not move forward. Still feeling an urgency, Sazed left it behind, continuing into the depths of the Lord Ruler's former home. The stone walls were cold and dark, his candle a wan light.

The Well couldn't be here, he thought. *It's supposed to be in the mountains.*

Yet, so much about that time was vague. He was beginning to doubt that he'd ever understood the things he'd studied.

He quickened his step, shading his candle with his hand, knowing where he needed to go. He'd visited the building-within-a-building, the place where the Lord Ruler had once spent his time. Sazed had studied the place after the empire's fall, chronicling and cataloguing. He stepped into the outer room, and was halfway across it before he noticed the unfamiliar opening in the wall.

A figure stood in doorway, head bowed. Sazed's candlelight reflected the polished marble walls, the silvery in-laid murals, and the spikes in the man's eyes.

"Marsh?" Sazed asked, shocked. "Where have you been?"

"What are you doing, Sazed?" Marsh whispered.

"I'm going to Vin," he said, confused. "She has found the Well, Marsh. We have to get to her, stop her from doing anything with it until we're sure what it does."

Marsh remained silent for a short time. "You should not have come here, Terrisman," he finally said, head still bowed.

"Marsh? What is going on?" Sazed took a step forward, feeling urgent.

"I wish I knew. I wish . . . I wish I understood."

"Understood what?" Sazed asked, voice echoing in the domed room.

Marsh stood silently for a moment. Then he looked up, focusing his sightless spikeheads on Sazed.

"I wish I understood why I have to kill you," he said, then lifted a hand. An Allomantic Push slammed into the metal bracers on Sazed's arms, throwing him backward, crashing him into the hard stone wall.

"I'm sorry," Marsh whispered.

Alendi must not reach the Well of Ascension. . . .

58

"LORD RULER!" ELEND WHISPERED, pausing at the edge of the second cavern.

Vin joined him. They had walked in the passage for some time, leaving the storage cavern far behind, walking through a natural stone tunnel. It had ended here, at a second, slightly smaller cavern that was clogged with a thick, dark smoke. It didn't seep out of the cavern, as it should have, but billowed and churned upon itself.

Vin stepped forward. The smoke didn't choke her, as she expected. There was something oddly welcoming about it. "Come on," she said, walking through it across the cavern floor. "I see light up ahead."

Elend joined her nervously.

Thump. Thump. Thump.

Sazed slammed into the wall. He was no Allomancer; he had no pewter to strengthen his body. As he collapsed to the ground, he felt a sharp pain in his side, and knew he had cracked a rib. Or worse.

Marsh strode forward, faintly illuminated by Sazed's candle, which burned fitfully where Sazed had dropped it.

"Why did you come?" Marsh whispered as Sazed struggled to his knees. "Everything was going so well." He watched with iron eyes as Sazed slowly crawled away. Then Marsh Pushed again, throwing Sazed to the side.

Sazed skidded across the beautiful white floor, crashing into another wall. His arm snapped, cracking, and his vision shuddered.

Through his pain, he saw Marsh stoop down and pick something up. A small pouch. It had fallen from Sazed's sash. It was filled with bits of metal; Marsh obviously thought it was a coin pouch.

"I'm sorry," Marsh said again, then raised a hand and Pushed the bag at Sazed.

The pouch shot across the room and hit Sazed, ripping, the bits of metal inside tearing into Sazed's flesh. He didn't have to look down to know how badly he was injured. Oddly, he could no longer feel his pain—but he could feel the blood, warm, on his stomach and legs.

I'm . . . sorry, too, Sazed thought as the room grew dark, and he fell to his knees. *I've failed . . . though I know not at what. I can't even answer Marsh's question. I don't know why I came here.*

He felt himself dying. It was an odd experience. His mind

was resigned, yet confused, yet frustrated, yet slowly . . . having . . . trouble . . .

Those weren't coins, a voice seemed to whisper.

The thought rattled in his dying mind.

The bag Marsh shot at you. Those weren't coins. They were rings, Sazed. Eight of them. You took out two—eyesight and hearing. You left the other ones where they were.

In the pouch, tucked into your sash.

Sazed collapsed, death coming upon him like a cold shadow. And yet, the thought rang true. Ten rings, embedded into his flesh. Touching him. Weight. Speed of body. Sight. Hearing. Touch. Scent. Strength. Speed of mind. Wakefulness.

And health.

He tapped gold. He didn't have to be wearing the metalmind to use it—he only had to be touching it. His chest stopped burning, and his vision snapped back into focus. His arm straightened, the bones reknitting as he drew upon several days' worth of health in a brief flash of power. He gasped, his mind recovering from its near death, but the goldmind restored a crisp clarity to his thoughts.

The flesh healed around the metal. Sazed stood, pulling the empty bag from where it stuck from his skin, leaving the rings inside of him. He dropped it to the ground, the wound sealing, draining the last of the power from the goldmind. Marsh stopped at the mouth of the doorway, turning in surprise. Sazed's arm still throbbed, probably cracked, and his ribs were bruised. Such a short burst of health could only do so much.

But he was alive.

"You have betrayed us, Marsh," Sazed said. "I did not realize those spikes stole a man's soul, as well as his eyes."

"You cannot fight me," Marsh replied quietly, his voice echoing in the dark room. "You are no warrior."

Sazed smiled, feeling the small metalminds within him give him power. "Neither, I think, are you."

I am involved in something that is far over my head, Elend thought as they passed through the strange, smoke-filled cavern. The floor was rough and uneven, and his lantern seemed dim—as if the swirling black smoke were sucking in the light.

Vin walked confidently. No, determinedly. There was a difference. Whatever was at the end of this cavern, she obviously wanted to discover it.

And . . . what will it be? Elend thought. *The Well of Ascension?*

The Well was a thing of mythology—something spoken of by obligators when they taught about the Lord Ruler. And yet . . . he had followed Vin northward, expecting to find it, hadn't he? Why be so tentative now?

Perhaps because he was finally beginning to accept what was happening. And it worried him. Not because he feared for his life, but because suddenly he didn't understand the world. Armies he could understand, even if he didn't know how to defeat them. But a thing like the Well? A thing of gods, a thing beyond the logic of scholars and philosophers?

That was terrifying.

They finally approached the other side of the smoky cavern. Here, there appeared to be a final chamber, one much smaller than the first two. As they stepped into it, Elend noticed something immediately: this room was man-made. Or, at least, it had the *feel* of something man-made. Stalactites formed pillars through the low-ceilinged room, and they were spaced far too evenly to be random. Yet, at the same time, they looked as if they had grown naturally, and showed no signs of being worked.

The air seemed warmer inside—and, thankfully, they passed out of the smoke as they entered. A low light came from something on the far side of the chamber, though Elend couldn't distinguish the source. It didn't look like torchlight. It was the wrong color, and it shimmered rather than flickered.

Vin wrapped an arm around him, staring toward the back of the chamber, suddenly seeming apprehensive.

"Where is that light coming from?" Elend asked, frowning.

"A pool," Vin said quietly, her eyes far keener than his. "A glowing white pool."

Elend frowned. But, the two of them didn't move. Vin seemed hesitant. "What?" he asked.

She pulled against him. "That's the Well of Ascension. I can *feel* it inside of my head. Beating."

Elend forced a smile, feeling a surreal sense of displacement. "That's what we came for, then."

"What if I don't know what to do?" Vin asked quietly. "What if I take the power, but I don't know how to use it? What if I . . . become like the Lord Ruler?"

Elend looked down at her, arms wrapped around him, and his fear lessened a bit. He loved her. The situation they faced, it couldn't easily fit into his logical world. But Vin had never really needed logic. And he didn't need it either, if he trusted her.

He took her head in his hands, rotating it up to look at him. "Your eyes are beautiful."

She frowned. "What—"

"And," Elend continued, "part of the beauty in them comes from your sincerity. You won't become the Lord Ruler, Vin. You'll know what to do with that power. I trust you."

She smiled hesitantly, then nodded. However, she didn't move forward into the cavern. Instead, she pointed at something over Elend's shoulder. "What's that?"

Elend turned, noticing a ledge on the back wall of the small room. It grew straight out of the rock just beside the doorway they had entered. Vin approached the ledge, and Elend followed behind her, noticing the shards that lay upon it.

"It looks like broken pottery," Elend said. There were several patches of it, and more of it was scattered on the floor beneath the ledge.

Vin picked up a piece, but there didn't seem to be anything distinctive about it. She looked at Elend, who was fishing through the pottery pieces. "Look at this," he said, holding up one that hadn't been broken like the others. It was a disklike piece of fired clay with a single bead of some metal at the center.

"Atium?" she asked.

"It looks like the wrong color," he said, frowning.

"What is it, then?"

"Maybe we'll find the answers over there," Elend said, turning and looking down the rows of pillars toward the light. Vin nodded, and they walked forward.

Marsh immediately tried to Push Sazed away by the metal bracers on his arms. Sazed was ready, however, and he tapped his ring ironmind—drawing forth the weight he had stored within it. His body grew denser, and he felt its weight pulling him down, his fists feeling like balls of iron on the ends of lead arms.

Marsh immediately lurched away, thrown violently backward by his own Push. He slammed into the back wall, a cry of surprise escaping his lips. It echoed in the small, domed room.

Shadows danced in the room as the candle grew weaker. Sazed tapped sight, enhancing his vision, and released iron as he dashed toward the addled Inquisitor. Marsh, however, recovered quickly. He reached out, Pulling an unlit lamp off the wall. It zipped through the air, flying toward Marsh.

Sazed tapped zinc. He felt something like a twisted hybrid of an Allomancer and a Feruchemist, his sources of metal embedded within him. The gold had healed his insides, made him whole, but the rings still remained within his flesh. This was what the Lord Ruler had done, keeping his metalminds inside of him, piercing his flesh so that they would be harder to steal.

That had always seemed morbid to Sazed. Now, he saw how useful it could be. His thoughts sped up, and he quickly saw the trajectory of the lamp. Marsh would be able to use it as a weapon against him. So Sazed tapped steel. Allomancy and Feruchemy had one fundamental difference: Allomancy drew its powers from the metals themselves, and so the amount of power was limited; in Feruchemy, one could compound an attribute many times, drawing out months' worth of power in a few minutes.

Steel stored physical speed. Sazed zipped across the room, air rushing in his ears as he shot past the open doorway. He snatched the lamp out of the air, then tapped iron hard—increasing his weight manyfold—and tapped pewter to give himself massive strength.

Marsh didn't have time to react. He was now Pulling on a lamp held in Sazed's inhumanly strong, inhumanly heavy, hand. Again, Marsh was yanked by his own Allomancy. The Pull threw him across the room, directly toward Sazed.

Sazed turned, slamming the lamp into Marsh's face. The metal bent in his hand, and the force threw Marsh backward. The Inquisitor hit the marble wall, a spray of blood misting in the air. As Marsh slumped to the ground, Sazed could see that he'd driven one of the eye-spikes back into the front of the skull, crushing the bone around the socket.

Sazed returned his weight to normal, then jumped forward, raising his impromptu weapon again. Marsh, however, threw an arm up and Pushed. Sazed skidded back a few feet before he was able to tap the ironmind again, increasing his weight.

Marsh grunted, his Push forcing him back against the wall. It also, however, kept Sazed at bay. Sazed struggled to step forward, but the pressure of Marsh's Push—along with his own bulky, weighed-down body—made walking difficult. The two strained for a moment, Pushing against each other in the darkening light. The room's inlays sparkled, quiet murals watching them, open doorway leading down to the Well just to the side.

"Why, Marsh?" Sazed whispered.

"I don't know," Marsh said, his voice coming out in a growl.

With a flash of power, Sazed released his ironmind and instead tapped steel, increasing his speed again. He dropped the lamp, ducking to the side, moving more quickly than Marsh could track. The lamp was forced backward, but then fell to the ground as Marsh let go of his Push, jumping forward, obviously trying to keep from being trapped against the wall.

But Sazed was faster. He spun, raising a hand to try to pull out Marsh's linchpin spike—the one in between his shoulder blades, pounded down lengthwise into the back. Pulling this one spike would kill an Inquisitor; it was the weakness the Lord Ruler had built into them.

Sazed skidded around Marsh to attack from behind. The spike in Marsh's right eye protruded several extra inches out the back of his skull, and it dribbled blood.

Sazed's steelmind ran out.

The rings had never been intended to last long, and his two extreme bursts had drained this one in seconds. He slowed with a dreadful lurch, but his arm was still raised, and he still had the strength of ten men. He could see the bulge of the linchpin spike underneath Marsh's robe. If he could just—

Marsh spun, then dexterously knocked aside Sazed's hand. He rammed an elbow into Sazed's stomach, then brought a backhand up and crashed it into his face.

Sazed fell backward, and his pewtermind ran out, his strength disappearing. He hit the hard steel ground with a grunt of pain, and rolled.

Marsh loomed in the dark room. The candle flickered.

"You were wrong, Sazed," Marsh said quietly. "Once, I was not a warrior, but that has changed. You spent the last two years teaching, but I spent them killing. Killing so many people. . . ."

Marsh stepped forward, and Sazed coughed, trying to get his bruised body to move. He worried that he'd rebroken his arm. He tapped zinc again, speeding up his thoughts, but that didn't help his body move. He could only watch—more fully aware of his predicament and unable to do a thing to stop it—as Marsh picked up the fallen lamp.

The candle went out.

Yet, Sazed could still see Marsh's face. Blood dripped from the crushed socket, making the man's expression even harder to read. The Inquisitor seemed . . . sorrowful as he raised the lamp in a clawlike grip, intending to smash it down into Sazed's face.

Wait, Sazed thought. *Where is that light coming from?*

A dueling cane smashed against the back of Marsh's head, shattering and throwing up splinters.

Vin and Elend walked up to the pool. Elend knelt quietly beside it, but Vin just stood. Staring at the glittering waters.

They were gathered in a small depression in the rock, and they looked thick—like metal. A silvery white, glowing liquid metal. The Well was only a few feet across, but its power loomed in her mind.

Vin was so enraptured by the beautiful pool, in fact, that she didn't notice the mist spirit until Elend's grip tightened on her arm. She looked up, noticing the spirit standing before them. It seemed to have its head bowed, but as she turned, its shadowy form stood up straighter.

She'd never seen the creature outside of the mist. It still wasn't completely . . . whole. Mist puffed from its body, flowing downward, creating its amorphous form. A persistent pattern.

Vin hissed quietly, pulling out a dagger.

"Wait!" Elend said, standing.

She frowned, shooting him a glance.

"I don't think it's dangerous, Vin," he said, stepping away from her, toward the spirit.

"Elend, no!" she said, but he gently shook her free.

"It visited me while you were gone, Vin," he explained. "It didn't hurt me. It just . . . seemed like it wanted me to know something." He smiled, still wearing his nondescript cloak and traveling clothing, and walked slowly up to the mist spirit. "What is it you want?"

The mist spirit stood immobile for a moment, then it raised its arm. Something flashed, reflecting the pool's light.

"No!" Vin screamed, dashing forward as the spirit slashed across Elend's gut. Elend grunted in pain, then stumbled back.

"Elend!" Vin said, scrambling to Elend's side as he slipped and fell to the ground. The spirit backed away, dripping blood from somewhere within its deceptively incorporeal form. Elend's blood.

Elend lay, shocked, eyes wide. Vin flared pewter and ripped open the front of his jacket, exposing the wound. The spirit had cut deeply into his stomach, slashing the gut open.

"No . . . no . . . no . . ." Vin said, mind growing numb, Elend's blood on her hands.

The wound was very bad. Deadly.

Ham dropped the broken cane, one arm still in a sling. The beefy Thug looked incredibly pleased with himself as he stepped over Marsh's body and reached his good hand toward Sazed.

"Didn't expect to find you here, Saze," the Thug said.

Dazed, Sazed took the hand and climbed to his feet. He stumbled over Marsh's body, somehow distractedly knowing that a simple club to the head wouldn't be enough to kill the creature. Yet Sazed was too addled to care. He picked up his candle, lit it from Ham's lantern, then made his way toward the stairs, forcing himself onward.

He had to keep going. He had to get to Vin.

Vin cradled Elend in her arms, her cloak forming a hasty—and dreadfully inadequate—bandage around his torso.

"I love you," she whispered, tears warm on her cold cheeks. "Elend, I love you. I love you. . . ."

Love wouldn't be enough. He was trembling, eyes staring upward, barely able to focus. He gasped, and blood bubbled in his spittle.

She turned to the side, numbly realizing where she knelt. The pool glowed beside her, just inches from where Elend had fallen. Some of his blood had dribbled into the pool, though it didn't mix with the liquid metal.

I can save him, she realized. *The power of creation rests just inches from my fingers.* This was the place where Rashek had ascended to godhood. The Well of Ascension.

She looked back at Elend, at his dying eyes. He tried to focus on her, but he seemed to be having trouble controlling his muscles. It seemed like . . . he was trying to smile.

Vin rolled up her coat and put it beneath his head. Then, wearing just her trousers and shirt, she walked up to the pool. She could hear it thumping. As if . . . calling to her. Calling for her to join with it.

She stepped onto the pool. It resisted her touch, but her foot began to sink, slowly. She stepped forward, moving into the center of the pool, waiting as she sank. Within seconds, the pool was up to her chest, the glowing liquid all around her.

She took a breath, then leaned her head back, looking up as the pool absorbed her, covering her face.

Sazed stumbled down the stairs, candle held in quivering fingers. Ham was calling after him. He passed a confused Spook on the landing below, and ignored the boy's questions.

However, as he began to make his way down to the cavern floor, he slowed. A small tremor ran through the rock.

Somehow, he knew that he was too late.

The power came upon her suddenly.

She felt the liquid pressing against her, creeping into her body, crawling, forcing its way through the pores and openings in her skin. She opened her mouth to scream, and it rushed in that way too, choking her, gagging her.

With a sudden flare, her earlobe began to hurt. She cried out, pulling her earring free, dropping it into the depths. She pulled off her sash, letting it—and her Allomantic vials—go as well, removing the only metals on her person.

Then she started to burn. She recognized the sensation: it was exactly like the feeling of burning metals in her stomach, except it came from her entire body. Her skin flared, her muscles flamed, and her very bones seemed on fire. She gasped, and realized the metal was gone from her throat.

She was glowing. She felt the power within, as if it were trying to burst back out. It was like the strength she gained by burning pewter, but amazingly more potent. It was a force of incredible capacity. It would have been beyond her ability to understand, but it expanded her mind, forcing her to grow and comprehend what she now possessed.

She could remake the world. She could push back the mists. She could feed millions with the wave of her hand, punish the evil, protect the weak. She was in awe of herself. The cavern was as if translucent around her, and she saw the entire world spreading, a magnificent sphere upon which life could exist only in a small little area at the poles. She could fix that. She could make things better. She could . . .

She could save Elend.

She glanced down and saw him dying. She immediately understood what was wrong with him. She could fix his damaged skin and sliced organs.

You mustn't do it, child.

Vin looked up with shock.

You know what you must do, the Voice said, whispering to her. It sounded aged. Kindly.

"I have to save him!" she cried.

You know what you must do.

And she did know. She saw it happen—she saw, as if in a vision, Rashek when he'd taken the power for himself. She saw the disasters he created.

It was all or nothing—like Allomancy, in a way. If she took the power, she would have to burn it away in a few moments. Remaking things as she pleased, but only for a brief time.

Or . . . she could give it up.

I must defeat the Deepness, the Voice said.

She saw that, too. Outside the palace, in the city, across the land. People in the mists, shaking, falling. Many stayed indoors, thankfully. The traditions of the skaa were still strong within them.

Some were out, however. Those who trusted in Kelsier's words that the mists could not hurt them. But now the mists could. They had changed, bringing death.

This was the Deepness. Mists that killed. Mists that were slowly covering the entire land. The deaths were sporadic; Vin saw many falling dead, but saw others simply falling sick, and still others going about in the mists as if nothing were wrong.

It will get worse, the Voice said quietly. *It will kill and destroy. And, if you try to stop it yourself, you will ruin the world, as Rashek did before you.*

"Elend . . ." she whispered. She turned toward him, bleeding on the floor.

At that moment, she remembered something. Something Sazed had said. *You must love him enough to trust his wishes,* he had told her. *It isn't love unless you learn to respect him—not what you* assume *is best, but what he actually wants. . . .*

She saw Elend weeping. She saw him focusing on her, and she knew what he wanted. He wanted his people to live. He wanted the world to know peace, and the skaa to be free.

He wanted the Deepness to be defeated. The safety of his people meant more to him than his own life. Far more.

You'll know what to do, he'd told her just moments before. *I trust you. . . .*

Vin closed her eyes, and tears rolled down her cheeks. Apparently, gods could cry.

"I love you," she whispered.

She let the power go. She held the capacity to become a deity in her hands, and she gave it away, releasing it to the waiting void. She gave up Elend.

Because she knew that was what he wanted.

The cavern immediately began to shake. Vin cried out as the flaring power within her was ripped away, soaked up greedily by the void. She screamed, her glow fading, then fell into the now empty pool, head knocking against the rocks.

The cavern continued to shake, dust and chips falling from the ceiling. And then, in a moment of surreal clarity, Vin heard a single, distinct sentence ringing in her mind.

I am FREE!

. . . for he must not be allowed to release the thing that is imprisoned there.

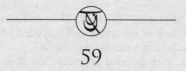

59

VIN LAY, QUIETLY, WEEPING.

The cavern was still, the tempest over. The thing was gone, and the thumping in her mind was finally quiet. She sniffled, arms around Elend, holding him as he gasped his final few breaths. She'd screamed for help, calling for Ham and Spook, but had gotten no response. They were too far away.

She felt cold. Empty. After holding that much power, then having it ripped from her, she felt like she was nothing. And, once Elend died, she would be.

What would be the point? she thought. *Life doesn't mean anything. I've betrayed Elend. I've betrayed the world.*

She wasn't certain what had happened, but somehow she'd made a horrible, horrible mistake. The worst part was, she had tried so hard to do what was right, even if it hurt.

Something loomed above her. She looked up at the mist spirit, but couldn't even really feel rage. She was having trouble feeling anything at the moment.

The spirit raised an arm, pointing.

"It's over," she whispered.

It pointed more demandingly.

"I won't get to them in time," she said. "Besides, I *saw* how bad the cut was. Saw it with the power. There's nothing any of them could do, not even Sazed. So, you should be pleased. You got what you wanted . . ." She trailed off. Why had the spirit stabbed Elend?

To make me heal him, she thought. *To keep me . . . from releasing the power.*

She blinked her eyes. The spirit waved its arm.

Slowly, numbly, she got to her feet. She watched the spirit in a trance as it floated a few steps over and pointed at something on the ground. The room was dark, now that the pool was empty, and was illuminated only by Elend's lantern. She had to flare tin to see what the spirit was pointing at.

A piece of pottery. The disk Elend had taken from the shelf in the back of the room, and had been holding in his hand. It had broken when he'd collapsed.

The mist spirit pointed urgently. Vin approached and bent over, fingers finding the small nugget of metal that had been at the disk's center.

"What is it?" she whispered.

The mist spirit turned and drifted back to Elend. Vin walked up quietly.

He was still alive. He seemed to be getting weaker, and was trembling less. Eerily, as he grew closer to death, he actually seemed a bit more in control. He looked at her as she knelt, and she could see his lips moving.

"Vin . . ." he whispered.

She knelt beside him, looked at the bead of metal, then looked up at the spirit. It stood motionless. She rolled the bead between her fingers, then moved to eat it.

The spirit moved urgently, shaking its hands. Vin paused, and the spirit pointed at Elend.

What? she thought. However, she wasn't really in a state to think. She held the nugget up to Elend. "Elend," she whispered, leaning close. "You must swallow this."

She wasn't certain if he understood her or not, though he did appear to nod. She placed the bit of metal in his mouth. His lips moved, but he started to choke.

I have to get him something to wash it down, she thought. The only thing she had was one of her metal vials. She reached into the empty well, retrieving her earring and her sash. She pulled free a vial, then poured the liquid into his mouth.

Elend continued to cough weakly, but the liquid did its work well, washing down the bead of metal. Vin knelt, feeling so powerless, a depressing contrast to how she had been just moments before. Elend closed his eyes.

Then, oddly, the color seemed to return to his cheeks. Vin knelt, confused, watching him. The look on his face, the way he lay, the color of his skin . . .

She burned bronze, and with shock, felt pulses coming from Elend.

He was burning pewter.

EPILOGUE

TWO WEEKS LATER, A SOLITARY figure arrived at the Conventical of Seran.

Sazed had left Luthadel quietly, troubled by his thoughts and by the loss of Tindwyl. He'd left a note. He couldn't stay in Luthadel. Not at the moment.

The mists still killed. They struck random people who went out at night, with no discernible pattern. Many of the people did not die, but only became sick. Others, the mists murdered. Sazed didn't know what to make of the deaths. He wasn't even certain if he cared. Vin spoke of something terrible she had released at the Well of Ascension. She had expected Sazed to want to study and record her experience.

Instead, he had left.

He made his way through the solemn, steel-plated rooms. He half expected to be confronted by one Inquisitor or another. Perhaps Marsh would try to kill him again. By the time he and Ham had returned from the storage cavern beneath Luthadel, Marsh had vanished again. His work had, apparently, been done. He'd stalled Sazed long enough to keep him from stopping Vin.

Sazed made his way down the steps, through the torture chamber, and finally into the small rock room he'd visited on his first trip to the Conventical, so many weeks before. He dropped his pack to the ground, working it open with tired fingers, then looked up at the large steel plate.

Kwaan's final words stared back at him. Sazed knelt, pulling a carefully tied portfolio from his pack. He undid the string, and then removed his original rubbing, made in this very room months before. He recognized his fingerprints on the thin paper, knew the strokes of the charcoal to be his own. He recognized the smudges he had made.

With growing nervousness, he held the rubbing up and slapped it against the steel plate on the wall.

And the two did not match.

Sazed stepped back, uncertain what to think now that his suspicions had been confirmed. The rubbing slipped limply from his fingers, and his eyes found the sentence at the end of the plate. The last sentence, the one that the mist spirit had ripped free time and time again. The original one on the steel plate was different from the one Sazed had written and studied.

Alendi must not reach the Well of Ascension, Kwaan's ancient words read, *for he must not be allowed to release the thing that is imprisoned there.*

Sazed sat down quietly. *It was all a lie,* he thought numbly. *The religion of the Terris people . . . the thing the Keepers spent millennia searching for, trying to understand, was a lie. The so-called prophecies, the Hero of Ages . . . a fabrication.*

A trick.

What better way for such a creature to gain freedom? Men would die in the name of prophecies. They wanted to believe, to hope. If someone—something—could harness that energy, twist it, what amazing things could be accomplished. . . .

Sazed looked up, reading the words on the wall, reading the second half once again. It contained paragraphs that were different from his rubbing.

Or, rather, his rubbing had been changed somehow. Changed to reflect what the thing had wished Sazed to read. *I write these words in steel,* Kwaan's first words said, *for anything not set in metal cannot be trusted.*

Sazed shook his head. They should have paid attention to that sentence. Everything he had studied after that had, apparently, been a lie. He looked up at the plate, scanning its contents, coming to the final section.

And so, they read, *I come to the focus of my argument. I apologize. Even forcing my words into steel, sitting and scratching in this frozen cave, I am prone to ramble.*

This is the problem. Though I believed in Alendi at first, I later became suspicious. It seemed that he fit the signs, true. But, well, how can I explain this?

Could it be that he fit them too well?

I know your argument. We speak of the Anticipation, of things foretold, of promises made by our greatest prophets of old. Of course the Hero of Ages will fit the prophecies. He will fit them perfectly. That's the idea.

And yet . . . something about all this seems so convenient. It feels almost as if we constructed a hero to fit our prophecies, rather than allowing one to arise naturally. This was the worry I had, the thing that should have given me pause when my brethren came to me, finally willing to believe.

After that, I began to see other problems. Some of you may know of my fabled memory. It is true; I need not a Feruchemist's metalmind to memorize a sheet of words in an instant. And I tell you, call me daft, but the words of the prophecies are changing.

The alterations are slight. Clever, even. A word here, a slight twist there. But the words on the pages are different from the ones in my memory. The other Worldbringers scoff at me, for they have their metalminds to prove to them that the books and prophecies have not changed.

And so, this is the great declaration I must make. There is something—some force—that wants us to believe that the Hero of Ages has come, and that he must travel to the Well of Ascension. Something is making the prophecies change so that they refer to Alendi more perfectly.

And whatever this power is, it can change words within a Feruchemist's metalmind.

The others call me mad. As I have said, that may be true. But must not even a madman rely on his own mind, his own experience, rather than that of others? I know what I have memorized. I know what is now repeated by the other Worldbringers. The two are not the same.

I sense a craftiness behind these changes, a manipulation subtle and brilliant. I have spent the last two years in exile, trying to decipher what the alterations could mean. I have come to only one conclusion. Something has taken control of our religion, something nefarious, something that cannot be trusted. It misleads, and it shadows. It uses Alendi to destroy, leading him along a path of death and sorrow. It is pulling him toward the Well of Ascension, where the millennial power has gathered. I can only guess that it sent the Deepness as a method of making mankind more desperate, of pushing us to do as it wills.

The prophecies have changed. They now tell Alendi that he must give up the power once he takes it. This is not what was once implied by the texts—they were more vague. And yet, the new version seems to make it a moral imperative. The texts now outline a terrible consequence if the Hero of Ages takes the power for himself.

Alendi believes as they do. He is a good man—despite it all, he is a good man. A sacrificing man. In truth, all of his actions—all of the deaths, destructions, and pains that he has caused—have hurt him deeply. All of these things were, in truth, a kind of sacrifice for him. He is accustomed to giving up his own will for the common good, as he sees it.

I have no doubt that if Alendi reaches the Well of Ascension, he will take the power and then—in the name of the presumed greater good—will give it up. Give it away to this same force that has changed the texts. Give it up to this force of destruction that has brought him to war, that has tempted him to kill, that has craftily led him to the north.

This thing wants the power held in the Well, and it has raped our religion's holiest tenets in order to get it.

And so, I have made one final gamble. My pleas, my teachings, my objections, and even my treasons were all ineffectual. Alendi has other counselors now, ones who tell him what he wants to hear.

I have a young nephew, one Rashek. He hates all of Khlennium with the passion of envious youth. He hates Alendi even more acutely—though the two have never met—for Rashek feels betrayed that one of our oppressors should have been chosen as the Hero of Ages.

Alendi will need guides through the Terris Mountains. I have charged Rashek with making certain that he and his trusted friends are chosen as those guides. Rashek is to try and lead Alendi in the wrong direction, to dissuade him, discourage him, or otherwise foil his quest. Alendi doesn't know that he has been deceived, that we've all been deceived, and he will not listen to me now.

If Rashek fails to lead the trek astray, then I have instructed the lad to kill Alendi. It is a distant hope. Alendi has survived assassins, wars, and catastrophes. And yet, I hope that in the frozen mountains of Terris, he may finally be exposed. I hope for a miracle.

Alendi must not reach the Well of Ascension, for he must not be allowed to release the thing that is imprisoned there.

Sazed sat back. It was the final blow, the last strike that killed whatever was left of his faith.

He knew at that moment that he would never believe again.

Vin found Elend standing on the city wall, looking over the city of Luthadel. He wore a white uniform, one of the ones that Tindwyl had made for him. He looked . . . harder than he had just a few weeks before.

"You're awake," she said, moving up beside him.

He nodded. He didn't look at her, but continued to watch the city, with its bustling people. He'd spent quite a bit of time delirious and in bed, despite the healing power of his newfound Allomancy. Even with pewter, the surgeons had been uncertain if he'd survive.

He had. And, like a true Allomancer, he was up and about the first day he was lucid.

"What happened?" he asked.

She shook her head, leaning against the stones of the battlement. She could still hear that terrible, booming voice. *I am FREE. . . .*

"I'm an Allomancer," Elend said.

She nodded.

"Mistborn, apparently," he continued.

"I think . . . we know where they came from, now," Vin said. "The first Allomancers."

"What happened to the power? Ham didn't have a straight answer for me, and all anyone else knows are rumors."

"I set something free," she whispered. "Something that shouldn't have been released; something that led me to the Well. I should never have gone looking for it, Elend."

Elend stood in silence, still regarding the city.

She turned, burying her head in his chest. "It was terrible," she said. "I could feel that. And I set it free."

Finally, Elend wrapped his arms around her. "You did the best you could, Vin," he said. "In fact, you did the right thing. How could you have known that everything you'd been told, trained, and prepared to do was wrong?"

Vin shook her head. "I am worse than the Lord Ruler. In the end, maybe he realized he was being tricked, and knew he had to take the power rather than release it."

"If he'd been a good man, Vin," Elend said, "he wouldn't have done the things he did to this land."

"I may have done far worse," Vin said. "This thing I released . . . the mists killing people, and coming during the day . . . Elend, what are we going to do?"

He looked at her for a moment, then turned back toward the city and its people. "We're going to do what Kelsier taught us, Vin. We're going to survive."

THE END OF BOOK TWO

ARS ARCANUM

1. Metals Quick-Reference Chart

2. Names and Terms

3. Summary of Book One

You can also find extensive annotations of every chapter in the book, along with deleted scenes, a very active blog, and expanded world information at www.brandonsanderson.com.

METALS QUICK-REFERENCE CHART

	METAL	ALLOMANTIC POWER	FERUCHEMICAL POWER
☾	Iron	Pulls on Nearby Sources of Metals	Stores Physical Weight
♄	Steel	Pushes on Nearby Sources of Metal	Stores Physical Speed
☿	Tin	Increases Senses	Stores Senses
♆	Pewter	Increases Physical Abilities	Stores Physical Strength
♃	Brass	Soothes (Dampens) Emotions	Stores Warmth
♀	Zinc	Riots (Enflames) Emotions	Stores Mental Speed
☿	Copper	Hides Allomantic Pulses	Stores Memories
♆	Bronze	Allows One to Hear Allomantic Pulses	Stores Wakefulness

METAL	ALLOMANTIC POWER	FERUCHEMICAL POWER
✦ Atium	See into Other People's Futures	Stores Age
✦ Malatium	See into Other People's Pasts	Unknown
✦ Gold	See into Your Own Past	Stores Health
✦ Electrum	See into Your Own Future	Unknown

NAMES AND TERMS

ALENDI: A man who conquered the world a thousand years ago, before the Lord Ruler's Ascension. Vin found his journal in the Lord Ruler's palace, and thought—at first—that he had become the Lord Ruler. It was later discovered that his servant, Rashek, killed him and took his place. Alendi was a friend and protégé of Kwaan, a Terris scholar who thought that Alendi might be the Hero of Ages.

ALLOMANCY: A mystical hereditary power involving the burning of metals inside the body to gain special abilities.

ALLOMANTIC METALS: There are eight basic Allomantic metals. These come in pairs, comprising a base metal and its alloy. They can also be divided into two groups of four as internal metals (tin, pewter, copper, bronze) and external metals (iron, steel, zinc, brass). It was long assumed that there were only two other Allomantic metals: gold and atium. However, the discovery of alloys for gold and atium has expanded the number of metals to twelve. There have been rumors of other metals, one of which has been discovered. (See also: Aluminum.)

ALLOMANTIC PULSE: The signal given off by an Allomancer who is burning metals. Only someone who is burning bronze can "hear" an Allomantic pulse.

ALLRIANNE: Lord Ashweather Cett's only daughter.

ALUMINUM: A metal Vin was forced to burn in the Lord Ruler's palace. Once known only to the Steel Inquisitors, this metal, when burned, depletes all of an Allomancer's other metal reserves. Its alloy, if it has one, is unknown.

AMARANTA: One of Straff Venture's mistresses. An herbalist.

ANCHOR (ALLOMANTIC): A term used to refer to a piece of metal that an Allomancer Pushes on or Pulls on when burning iron or steel.

ASCENSION (OF THE LORD RULER): The Ascension is the term used to describe what happened to Rashek when he took the power at the Well of Ascension and became the Lord Ruler.

ASHFALLS: Ash falls frequently from the sky in the Final Empire because of the Ashmounts.

ASHMOUNTS: Seven large ash volcanoes that appeared in the Final Empire during the Ascension.

ASHWEATHER: Lord Cett's first name.

ATIUM: A strange metal formerly produced in the Pits of Hathsin. It collected inside of small geodes that formed in crystalline pockets in caves beneath the ground.

BIRCHBANE: A common poison.

BOXING: The slang name for an imperial gold coin. The name comes from the picture on its back of Kredik Shaw, the Lord Ruler's palace—or, the "box" in which he lives.

BREEZE: A Soother on Kelsier's crew, now one of Elend's foremost counselors.

BRONZEPULSE: Another term for an Allomantic pulse.

BURN (ALLOMANCY): An Allomancer utilizing or expending the metals in their stomachs. First, they must swallow a metal, then Allomantically metabolize it inside of them to access its power.

BURNLANDS: The deserts at the edges of the Final Empire.

CAMON: Vin's old crewleader. A harsh man who often beat her, Camon was cast out by Kelsier. The Inquisitors eventually killed him.

CANTON: A suboffice within the Steel Ministry.

CETT: Lord Ashweather Cett is the most prominent king who has managed to gain power in the Western Dominance. His home city is Fadrex.

CHANNEREL: The river that runs through Luthadel.

CLADENT: Clubs's real name.

CLIP (COINAGE): The nickname for an imperial copper coin in the Final Empire. Commonly used by Mistborn and Coinshots for jumping and attacking.

CLUBS: A Smoker on Kelsier's crew, now general of Elend's armies. He once was a skaa carpenter.

COINSHOT: A Misting who can burn steel.

COLLAPSE, THE: The death of the Lord Ruler and the fall of the Final Empire.

COPPERCLOUD: The invisible, obscuring field set up by someone burning copper. If an Allomancer burns metals while within a coppercloud, their Allomantic pulses are hidden from those burning bronze. The term "Coppercloud" is also, sometimes, used to refer to a Smoker (a Misting who can burn copper).

DEEPNESS, THE: The mythological monster or force that threatened the land just before the rise of the Lord Ruler and the Final Empire. The term comes from Terris lore, and the Hero of Ages was the one prophesied to come and eventually defeat the Deepness. The Lord Ruler claims to have defeated it when he Ascended.

DEMOUX, CAPTAIN: Ham's second-in-command, a soldier in Elend's palace guard.

DOCKSON: Kelsier's old right-hand man, informal leader of his crew now that Kelsier is dead. He has no Allomantic powers.

DOMINANCE (FINAL EMPIRE): A province of the Final Empire. Luthadel is in the Central Dominance. The four surrounding dominances are called the Inner Dominances, and include most of the population and culture of the Final Empire. After the Collapse, the Final Empire shattered, and different kings took power, trying to claim leadership of the various dominances, effectively turning each one into a kingdom of its own.

DOX: Dockson's nickname.

ELEND VENTURE: King of the Central Dominance, son of Straff Venture.

EXTINGUISH (ALLOMANTIC): To cease burning an Allomantic metal.

FADREX: A modestly sized, well-fortified city in the Western Dominance. Capital city and home to Ashweather Cett. A main place of stockpile for the Canton of Resource.

FELT: Once one of Straff's spies, the man was (like most of Straff's employees) left behind at the fall of Luthadel. He gave his allegiance to Elend instead.

FINAL EMPIRE: The empire established by the Lord Ruler. The name came from the fact that, being immortal, he felt that it would be the last empire the world ever knew, since it would never fall or end.

FLARE (ALLOMANTIC): To draw a little extra power from an Allomantic metal at the expense of making it burn faster.

GNEORNDIN: Ashweather Cett's only son.

GORADEL: Once a soldier in the Luthadel Garrison, Goradel was guarding the palace when Vin decided to infiltrate and kill the Lord Ruler. Vin convinced him to switch sides, and he later led Elend through the palace to try and rescue her. Now a member of Elend's guard.

HAM: A Thug on Kelsier's crew, now captain of Elend's palace guard.

HAMMOND: Ham's real name.

HATHSIN: See Pits of Hathsin.

HERO OF AGES, THE: The mythological prophesied savior of the Terris people. It was foretold that he would come, take the power at the Well of Ascension, then be selfless enough to give it up in order to save the world from the Deepness. Alendi was thought to be the Hero of Ages, but was killed before he could complete his quest.

INQUISITORS, STEEL: A group of strange creatures, priests who served the Lord Ruler. They have spikes driven completely through their heads—point-first through the eyes— yet continue to live. They were fanatically devoted to him, and were used primarily to hunt out and kill skaa with

Allomantic powers. They have the abilities of a Mistborn, and some others.

IRONEYES: Marsh's nickname in the crew.

IRONPULL: Pulling on a metal when Allomantically burning iron. This Pull exerts a force on the metal item, yanking it directly toward the Allomancer. If the metallic item, known as an anchor, is heavier than the Allomancer, he or she will instead be Pulled toward the metal source.

JANARLE: Straff Venture's second-in-command.

JASTES LEKAL: Heir to the Lekal house title, one of Elend's former friends. He and Elend often talked politics and philosophy together with Telden.

KANDRA: A race of strange creatures who can ingest the dead body of a person, then reproduce that body with their own flesh. They keep the bones of the person they imitate, using them, as kandra themselves have no bones. They serve Contracts with mankind—which must be bought with atium—and are relatives of mistwraiths.

KEEPER (TERRIS): "Keeper" is often used as simply another term for a Feruchemist. The Keepers are actually an organization of Feruchemists dedicated to discovering, then memorizing, all of the knowledge and religions that existed before the Ascension. The Lord Ruler hunted them to near extinction, forcing them to remain hidden.

KELL: Kelsier's nickname.

KELSIER: The most famous thieving crewleader in the Final Empire, Kelsier raised a rebellion of skaa and overthrew the Lord Ruler, but was killed in the process. He was Mistborn, and was Vin's teacher.

KHLENNIUM: An ancient kingdom that existed before the rise of the Final Empire. It was Alendi's homeland.

KLISS: A woman whom Vin knew in the court at Luthadel. She eventually turned out to be an informant for hire.

KOLOSS: A race of bestial warriors created by the Lord Ruler during his Ascension, then used by him to conquer the world.

KREDIK SHAW: The Lord Ruler's palace in Luthadel. It means "the Hill of a Thousand Spires" in the old Terris language.

KWAAN: A Terris scholar before the Ascension. He was a Worldbringer, and was the first to mistakenly think that Alendi was the Hero of Ages. He later changed his mind, betraying his former friend.

LADRIAN: Breeze's real name.

LESTIBOURNES: Spook's real name.

LLAMAS, MISTBORN: Brandon's writing group. Mistborn Llamas burn various kinds of plants to gain super-llaman powers. T-shirts can be found on the Web site.

LORD RULER: The emperor who ruled the Final Empire for a thousand years. He was once named Rashek, and was a Terris servant who was hired by Alendi. He killed Alendi, however, and went to the Well of Ascension in his place, and there took the power and Ascended. He was finally killed by Vin.

LURCHER: A Misting who can burn steel.

LUTHADEL: Capital of the Final Empire, and largest city in the land. Luthadel is known for its textiles, its forges, and its majestic noble keeps.

MALATIUM: The metal discovered by Kelsier, often dubbed the Eleventh Metal. Nobody knows where he found it, or why he thought it could kill the Lord Ruler. It did, however, eventually lead Vin to the clue she needed to defeat the emperor.

MARDRA: Ham's wife. She doesn't like to be involved in his thieving practices, or exposing their children to the danger of his lifestyle, and generally keeps her distance from the members of the crew.

MARE: Kelsier's wife, and a friend of Sazed. Was very active in the skaa rebellion before her death in the Pits of Hathsin.

MARSH: Kelsier's brother. A former leader of the skaa rebellion who infiltrated the Steel Ministry and allowed himself to be made into an Inquisitor in order to help take down the Lord Ruler.

METALMIND: A piece of metal that a Feruchemist uses as a kind of battery, filling it with certain attributes that he or she can later withdraw. Specific metalminds are named after the different metals: tinmind, steelmind, etc.

MIST: The strange, omnipresent fog that falls on the Final Empire every night. Thicker than a regular fog, it swirls and churns about, almost as if it were alive.

MISTBORN: An Allomancer who can burn all of the Allomantic metals.

MISTCLOAK: A garment worn by many Mistborn as a mark of their station. It is constructed from dozens of thick ribbons of cloth that are sewn together at the top, but allowed to spread free from the shoulders down.

MISTING: An Allomancer who can burn only one metal. They are much more common than Mistborn. (Note: In Allomancy, an Allomancer has either one power or all of them. There are no in-betweens with two or three.)

MISTWRAITH: A nonsentient relative of the kandra people. Mistwraiths are globs of boneless flesh that scavenge the land at night, eating bodies they find, then using the skeletons for their own bodies.

NOORDEN: One of the only obligators who chose to stay in Luthadel and serve Elend.

OBLIGATOR: A member of the Lord Ruler's priesthood. Obligators were more than just religious figures, however; they were civil bureaucrats, and even a spy network. A business deal or promise that wasn't witnessed by an obligator was not considered legally or morally binding.

ORESEUR: A kandra employed by Kelsier. He once played the part of Lord Renoux, Vin's uncle. Vin now holds his Contract.

PENROD, FERSON: One of the most prominent noblemen left in Luthadel. A member of Elend's Assembly.

PEWTERARM: Another term for a Thug, a Misting who can burn pewter.

PHILEN: A prominent merchant in Luthadel and a member of Elend's Assembly.

PITS OF HATHSIN, THE: A network of caverns that were once the only place in the Final Empire that produced atium. The Lord Ruler used prisoners to work them. Kelsier destroyed their ability to produce atium shortly before he died.

PULL (ALLOMANTIC): Using Allomancy to Pull on something—either people's emotions with zinc, or metals with iron.

PUSH (ALLOMANTIC): Using Allomancy to Push on something—either people's emotions with brass, or metals with steel.

RASHEK: A Terris packman before the Ascension, Rashek

was hired by Alendi to help him make the trek to the Well of Ascension. Rashek never got along well with Alendi, and eventually killed him. He took the power himself, and became the Lord Ruler.

REEN: Vin's brother, the one who protected her and trained her as a thief. Reen was brutal and unforgiving, but he did save Vin from their insane mother, then protected her during her childhood.

RELEASE (FERUCHEMICAL): When a Feruchemist stops tapping a metalmind, no longer drawing forth its power.

RENOUX, LORD: A nobleman that Kelsier killed, then hired the kandra OreSeur to imitate. Vin played the part of his niece, Valette Renoux.

RIOT (ALLOMANTIC): When an Allomancer burns zinc and Pulls on a person's emotions, enflaming them.

RIOTER (ALLOMANTIC): A Misting who can burn zinc.

SAZE: Sazed's nickname on the crew.

SAZED: A Terris Keeper who joined Kelsier's crew against the wishes of his people, then helped overthrow the Final Empire.

SEEKER (ALLOMANTIC): A Misting who can burn bronze.

SHAN ELARIEL: Elend's former fiancée, a Mistborn whom Vin killed.

SKAA: The peasantry of the Final Empire. They were once of different races and nationalities, but over the thousand-year span of the empire the Lord Ruler worked hard to stamp out any sense of identity in the people, eventually succeeding in creating a single, homogeneous race of slave workers.

SMOKER (ALLOMANTIC): An Allomancer who can burn copper. Also known as a Coppercloud.

SOOTHE (ALLOMANTIC): When an Allomancer burns brass and Pushes on a person's emotions, dampening them.

SOOTHER: A Misting who can burn brass.

SPOOK: A Tineye on Kelsier's crew. The youngest member of the crew, Spook was only fifteen when the Lord Ruler was overthrown. He is Clubs's nephew, and was once known for his use of garbled street slang.

STEEL MINISTRY: The Lord Ruler's priesthood, consisting of a small number of Steel Inquisitors and a larger body of priests called obligators. The Steel Ministry was more than just a religious organization; it was the civic framework of the Final Empire as well.

STRAFF VENTURE: Elend's father, king of the Northern Dominance. He makes his home in Urteau.

SURVIVOR OF HATHSIN: A cognomen of Kelsier, referring to the fact that he is the only known prisoner to ever escape the prison camps at the Pits of Hathsin.

SYNOD (TERRIS): The elite leaders of the Terris Keeper organization.

TAP (FERUCHEMICAL): Drawing power from within a Feruchemist's metalminds. It is parallel to the term "burn" used by Allomancers.

TATHINGDWEN: Capital of the Terris Dominance.

TELDEN: One of Elend's old friends, with whom he would talk politics and philosophy.

TENSOON: Straff Venture's kandra.

TERRIS: The dominance in the far north of the Final Empire. It is the only dominance to retain the name of the kingdom it used to be, perhaps a sign of the Lord Ruler's fondness for his homeland.

THUG (ALLOMANTIC): A Misting who can burn pewter.

TINDWYL: A Terris Keeper and a member of the Synod.

TINEYE: A Misting who can burn tin.

URTEAU: Capital of the Northern Dominance, and seat of House Venture.

VALETTE RENOUX: The alias that Vin used when infiltrating noble society during the days before the Collapse.

WELL OF ASCENSION: A mythological center of power from Terris lore. The Well of Ascension was said to hold a magical reserve of power that could be drawn upon by one who made the trek to visit it at the right time.

WORLDBRINGER: A sect of scholarly Terris Feruchemists before the Ascension. The subsequent Order of Keepers was based on the Worldbringers.

YEDEN: A member of Kelsier's crew and the skaa rebellion. He was killed during the fight against the Lord Ruler.

YOMEN, LORD: An obligator in Urteau who was politically opposed to Cett.

SUMMARY OF BOOK ONE

Mistborn: The Final Empire introduced the land of the Final Empire, ruled over by a powerful immortal known as the Lord Ruler. A thousand years before, the Lord Ruler took the power at the Well of Ascension and supposedly defeated a powerful force or creature known only as the Deepness.

The Lord Ruler conquered the known world and founded the Final Empire. He ruled for a thousand years, stamping out all remnants of the individual kingdoms, cultures, religions, and languages that used to exist in his land. In their place he set up his own system. Certain peoples were dubbed "skaa," a word that meant something akin to "slave" or "peasant." Other peoples were dubbed nobility, and most of these were descendants of those people who had supported the Lord Ruler during his years of conquest. The Lord Ruler had supposedly given them the power of Allomancy in order to gain powerful assassins and warriors who had minds that could think, as opposed to the brutish koloss, and had used them well in conquering and maintaining his empire.

Skaa and nobility were forbidden to interbreed, and the nobility were somehow given the power of Allomancy. During the thousand years of the Lord Ruler's reign, many rebellions occurred among the skaa, but none were successful.

Finally, a half-breed Mistborn known as Kelsier decided to challenge the Lord Ruler. Once the most famous of gentleman thieves in the Final Empire, Kelsier had been known for his daring schemes. Those eventually ended with his capture, however, and he had been sent to the Lord Ruler's death camp at the Pits of Hathsin, the secret source of atium.

It was said that nobody ever escaped the Pits of Hathsin alive—but Kelsier did just that. He gained his powers as a Mistborn during that time, and managed to free himself, earning the title the Survivor of Hathsin. At this point, he turned from his selfish ways and decided to try his most daring plan yet: the overthrow of the Final Empire.

He recruited a team of thieves, mostly half-breed Mistings, to help him achieve his goal. During this time, he also recruited a young half-breed Mistborn girl named Vin. Vin was unaware of her powers, and Kelsier brought her into the crew to train her, theoretically to have someone to whom he could pass his legacy.

Kelsier's crew slowly gathered an underground army of skaa rebels. The crew began to fear that Kelsier was setting himself up to be another Lord Ruler. He sought to make himself a legend among the skaa, becoming almost a religious figure to them. Meanwhile, Vin—who had been raised on the streets by a cruel brother—was growing to trust people for the first time in her life. As this happened, Vin began to believe in Kelsier and his purpose.

During the process of working on their plan, Vin was used as a spy among the nobility, and was trained to infiltrate their balls and parties playing the part of "Valette Renoux," a young noblewoman from the countryside. During the first of these balls, she met Elend Venture, a young, idealistic nobleman. He eventually showed her that not all noblemen were deserving of their poor reputation, and the two became enamored of each other, despite Kelsier's best efforts.

The crew also discovered a journal, apparently written by the Lord Ruler himself during the days before the Ascension. This book painted a different picture of the tyrant; it depicted a melancholy, tired man who was trying his best to protect the people against the Deepness, despite the fact that he didn't really understand it.

In the end, it was revealed that Kelsier's plan had been much more broad than simple use of the army to overthrow the empire. He'd partially spent so much effort on raising troops so that he would have an excuse to spread rumors about himself. He also used it to train his crew in the arts of leadership and persuasion. The true extent of his plan was revealed when he sacrificed his life in a very visible way, making himself a martyr to the skaa and finally convincing them to rise up and overthrow the Lord Ruler.

One of Kelsier's crewmembers—a man who had been playing the part of "Lord Renoux," Valette's uncle— turned out to be a kandra named OreSeur. OreSeur took on Kelsier's form, then went about spreading rumors that Kelsier had returned from the grave, inspiring the skaa. After this, he became Contractually bound to Vin, and was charged with watching over her after Kelsier's death.

Vin was the one who in fact killed the Lord Ruler. She discovered that he wasn't actually a god, or even immortal—he had simply found a way to extend his life and his power by making use of both Allomancy and Feruchemy at the same time. He wasn't the hero from the logbook—but, instead, was that man's servant, a Feruchemist of some great power. Still, he was much stronger in Allomancy than Vin. While she was fighting him, she drew upon the mists somehow, burning them in place of metals. She still doesn't know why or how this happened. With that power—and with the knowledge of his true nature—she was able to defeat and kill him.

The Final Empire was thrown into chaos. Elend Venture took control of Luthadel, the capital, and put Kelsier's crew in prime governmental positions.

One year has passed.

A WORD FROM
BRANDON SANDERSON

If you've enjoyed *The Well of Ascension*—and I certainly hope you have!—you don't have long to wait for the conclusion of Vin and Elend's story. *The Hero of Ages* is set for publication in October. You can find a free sample of it on my Web site at www.brandonsanderson.com.

While you're waiting, I think you might enjoy the work of a colleague of mine, someone I think is doing great things for fantasy and deserves more attention.

Daniel Abraham is one of the field's brightest new talents. His series, The Long Price Quartet, is beautiful. It has everything I love about a good fantasy story: an intriguing magic system, deep and complex characters who deviate from fantasy clichés, and an unexpected plot. Daniel's works are thoughtful, inquiring and—most important—just plain fun to read.

So it is my pleasure and privilege to present to you a chapter from *An Autumn War,* the third book of Daniel's Long Price Quartet. Enjoy!

Brandon Sanderson

Turn the page for a preview

THREE MEN CAME OUT OF the desert. Twenty had gone in.

The setting sun pushed their shadows out behind them, lit their faces a ruddy gold, blinded them. The weariness and pain in their bodies robbed them of speech. On the horizon, something glimmered that was no star, and they moved silently toward it. The farthest tower of Far Galt, the edge of the Empire, beckoned them home from the wastes, and without speaking, each man knew that they would not stop until they stood behind its gates.

The smallest of them shifted the satchel on his back. His gray commander's tunic hung from his flesh as if the cloth itself were exhausted. His mind turned inward, half-dreaming, and the leather straps of the satchel rubbed against his raw shoulder. The burden had killed seventeen of his men, and now it was his to carry as far as the tower that rose up slowly in the violet air of evening. He could not bring himself to think past that.

One of the others stumbled and fell to his knees on wind-paved stones. The commander paused. He would not lose another, not so near the end. And yet he feared bending down, lifting the man up. If he paused, he might never

Copyright © 2008 by Daniel Abraham

move again. Grunting, the other man recovered his feet. The commander nodded once and turned again to the west. A breeze stirred the low, brownish grasses, hissing and hushing. The punishing sun made its exit and left behind twilight and the wide swath of stars hanging overhead, cold candles beyond numbering. The night would bring chill as deadly as the midday heat.

It seemed to the commander that the tower did not so much come closer as grow, plantlike. He endured his weariness and pain, and the structure that had been no larger than his thumb was now the size of his hand. The beacon that had seemed steady flickered now, and tongues of flame leapt and vanished. Slowly, the details of the stonework came clear; the huge carved relief of the Great Tree of Galt. He smiled, the skin of his lip splitting, wetting his mouth with blood.

"We're not going to die," one of the others said. He sounded amazed. The commander didn't respond, and some measureless time later, another voice called for them to stop, to offer their names and the reason that they'd come to this twice-forsaken ass end of the world.

When the commander spoke, his voice was rough, rusting with disuse.

"Go to your High Watchman," he said. "Tell him that Balasar Gice has returned."

Balasar Gice had been in his eleventh year when he first heard the word *andat*. The river that passed through his father's estates had turned green one day, and then red. And then it rose fifteen feet. Balasar had watched in horror as the fields vanished, the cottages, the streets and yards he knew. The whole world, it seemed, had become a sea of foul water with only the tops of trees and the corpses of pigs and cattle and men to the horizon.

His father had moved the family and as many of his best men as would fit to the upper stories of the house. Balasar had begged to take the horse his father had given him up as well. When the gravity of the situation had been explained, he changed his pleas to include the son of the village notary, who had been Balasar's closest friend. He had been refused in that as well. His horses and his playmates were going to drown. His father's concern was for Balasar, for the family; the wider world would have to look after itself.

Even now, decades later, the memory of those six days was fresh as a wound. The bloated bodies of pigs and cattle and people like pale logs floating past the house. The rich, low scent of fouled water. The struggle to sleep when the rushing at the bottom of the stairs seemed like the whisper of something vast and terrible for which he had no name. He could still hear men's voices questioning whether the food would last, whether the water was safe to drink, and whether the flood was natural, a catastrophe of distant rains, or an attack by the Khaiem and their andat.

He had not known then what the word meant, but the syllables had taken on the stench of the dead bodies, the devastation where the village had been, the emptiness and the destruction. It was only much later—after the water had receded, the dead had been mourned, the village rebuilt—that he learned how correct he had been.

Nine generations of fathers had greeted their new children into the world since the God Kings of the East had turned upon each other, his history tutor told him. When the glory that had been the center of all creation fell, its throes had changed the nature of space. The lands that had been great gardens and fields were deserts now, permanently altered by the war. Even as far as Galt and Eddensea, the histories told of weeks of darkness, of failed crops and famine, a sky dancing with flames of green, a sound as if the earth were tearing itself apart. Some people said the stars themselves had changed positions.

But the disasters of the past grew in the telling or faded from memory. No one knew exactly how things had been those many years ago. Perhaps the Emperor had gone mad and loosed his personal god-ghost—what they called andat—against his own people, or against himself. Or there might have been a woman, the wife of a great lord, who had been taken by the Emperor against her will. Or perhaps she'd willed it. Or the thousand factions and minor insults and treacheries that accrue around power had simply followed their usual course.

As a boy, Balasar had listened to the story, drinking in the tales of mystery and glory and dread. And, when his tutor had told him, somber of tone and gray, that there were only two legacies left by the fall of the God Kings—the wastelands that bordered Far Galt and Obar State, and the cities of the Khaiem where men still held the andat like Cooling, Seedless, Stone-Made-Soft—Balasar had understood the implication as clearly as if it had been spoken.

What had happened before could happen again at any time and without warning.

"And that's what brought you?" the High Watchman said. "It's a long walk from a little boy at his lessons to this place."

Balasar smiled again and leaned forward to sip bitter kafe from a rough tin mug. His room was baked brick and close as a cell. A cruel wind hissed outside the thick walls, as it had for the three long, feverish days since he had returned to the world. The small windows had been scrubbed milky by sandstorms. His little wounds were scabbing over, none of them reddened or hot to the touch, though the stripe on his shoulder where the satchel strap had been would doubtless leave a scar.

"It wasn't as romantic as I'd imagined," he said. The High Watchman laughed, and then, remembering the dead, sobered. Balasar shifted the subject. "How long have you been here? And who did you offend to get yourself sent to this . . . lovely place?"

"Eight years. I've been eight years at this post. I didn't much care for the way things got run in Acton. I suppose this was my way of saying so."

"I'm sure Acton felt the loss."

"I'm sure it didn't. But then, I didn't do it for them." Balasar chuckled.

"That *sounds* like wisdom," Balasar said, "but eight years here seems an odd place for wisdom to lead you."

The High Watchman smacked his lips and shrugged.

"It wasn't me going inland," he said. Then, a moment later, "They say there's still andat out there. Haunting the places they used to control."

"There aren't," Balasar said. "There are other things. Things they made or unmade. There's places where the air goes bad on you—one breath's fine, and the next it's like something's crawling into you. There's places where the ground's thin as eggshell and a thousand-foot drop under it. And there are living things too—things they made with the andat, or what happened when the things they made bred. But the ghosts don't stay once their handlers are gone. That isn't what they are."

Balasar took an olive from his plate, sucked away the flesh, and spat back the stone. For a moment, he could hear voices in the wind. The words of men who'd trusted and followed him, even knowing where he would take them. The voices of the dead whose lives he had spent. Coal and Eustin had survived. The others—Little Ott, Bes, Mayarsin, Laran, Kellem, and a dozen more—were bones and memory now. Because of him. He shook his head, clearing it, and the wind was only wind again.

"No offense, General," the High Watchman said, "but there's not enough gold in the world for me to try what you did."

"It was necessary," Balasar said, and his tone ended the conversation.

The journey to the coast was easier than it should have been. Three men, traveling light. The others were an absence measured in the ten days it took to reach Lawton. It had taken sixteen coming from. The arid, empty lands of the East gave way to softly rolling hills. The tough yellow grasses yielded to blue-green almost the color of a cold sea, wavelets dancing on its surface. Farmsteads appeared off the road, windmills with broad blades shifting in the breezes; men and women and children shared the path that led toward the sea. Balasar forced himself to be civil, even gracious. If the world moved the way he hoped, he would never come to this place again, but the world had a habit of surprising him.

When he'd come back from the campaign in the Westlands, he'd thought his career was coming to its victorious end. He might take a place in the Council or at one of the military colleges. He even dared to dream of a quiet estate someplace away from the yellow coal-smoke of the great cities. When the news had come—a historian and engineer in Far Galt had divined a map that might lead to the old libraries—he'd known that rest had been a chimera, a thing for other men but never himself. He'd taken the best of his men, the strongest, smartest, most loyal, and come here. He had lost them here. The ones who had died, and perhaps also the ones who had lived.

Coal and Eustin were both quiet as they traveled, both respectful when they stopped to camp for the night. Without conversation, they had all agreed that the cold night air and hard ground was better than the company of men at an inn or wayhouse. Once in a while, one or the other would attempt to talk or joke or sing, but it always failed. There was a distance in their eyes, a stunned expression that Balasar recognized from boys stumbling over the wreckage of their first battlefield. They were seasoned fighters, Coal and Eustin. He had seen both of them kill men and boys, knew each of them had raped women in the towns they'd sacked, and still, they had left some scrap of innocence in the desert and were moving away from it with every step. Balasar could not say what that loss would do to them, nor would he insult their manhood by bringing it up. He knew, and that alone would have to suffice. They reached the ports of Parrinshall on the first day of autumn.

Half a hundred ships awaited them: great merchant ships built to haul cargo across the vast emptiness of the southern seas, shallow fishing boats that darted out of port and back again, the ornate three-sailed roundboats of Bakta, the antiquated and changeless ships of the east islands. It was nothing to the ports at Kirinton or Lanniston or Saraykeht, but it was enough. Three berths on any of half a dozen of these ships would take them off Far Galt and start them toward home.

"Winter'll be near over afore we see Acton," Coal said, and spat off the dock.

"I imagine it will," Balasar agreed, shifting the satchel against his hip. "If we sail straight through. We could also stay here until spring if we liked. Or stop in Bakta."

"Whatever you like, General," Eustin said.

"Then we'll sail straight through. Find what's setting out and when. I'll be at the harbor master's house."

"Anything the matter, sir?"

"No," Balasar said.

The harbor master's house was a wide building of red brick settled on the edge of the water. Banners of the Great Tree hung from the archway above its wide bronze doors. Balasar announced himself to the secretary and was shown to a private room. He accepted the offer of cool wine and dried figs, asked for and received the tools for writing the report now required of him, and gave orders that he not be disturbed until his men arrived. Then, alone, he opened his satchel and drew forth the books he had recovered, laying them side by side on the desk that looked out over the port. There were four, two bound in thick, peeling leather, another whose covers had been ripped from it, and one encased in metal that appeared to be neither steel nor silver, but something of each. Balasar ran his fingers over the mute volumes, then sat, considering them and the moral paradox they represented.

For these, he had spent the lives of his men. While the path back to Galt was nothing like the risk he had faced in the ruins of the fallen empire, still it was sea travel. There were storms and pirates and plagues. If he wished to be certain that these volumes survived, the right thing would be to transcribe them here in Parrinshall. If he were to die on the journey home, the books, at least, would not be drowned. The knowledge within them would not be lost.

Which was also the argument *against* making copies. He took the larger of the leather-bound volumes and opened it. The writing was in the flowing script of the dead empire, not the simpler chop the Khaiem used for business and trade with foreigners like himself. Balasar frowned as he picked out the symbols his tutor had taught him as a boy.

There are two types of impossibility in the andat: those which cannot be understood, and those whose natures make binding impossible. His translation was rough, but sufficient for his needs. These were the books he'd sought. And so the question remained whether the risk of their loss was greater than the risk posed by their existence. Balasar closed the book and let his head rest in his hands. He knew, of course, what he would do. He had known before he'd sent Eustin and Coal to find a boat for them. Before he'd reached Far Galt in the first place.

It was his awareness of his own pride that made him hesitate. History was full of men whom thought themselves to be the one great soul who power would not corrupt. He did not wish to be among that number, and yet here he sat, holding in his hands the secrets that might remake the shape of the human world. A humble man would have sought counsel from those wiser than himself, or at least feared to wield the power. He did not like what it said of him that giving the books to anyone besides himself seemed as foolish as gambling with their destruction. He would not even have trusted them to Eustin or Coal or any of the men who had died helping him.

He took the paper he'd been given, raised the pen, and began his report and, in a sense, his confession.

Three weeks out, Eustin broke.

The sea surrounded them, empty and immense as the sky. So far south, the water was clear and the air warm even with the slowly failing days. The birds that had followed them from Parrinshall had vanished. The only animal was a three-legged dog the ship's crew had taken on as a mascot. Nor were there women on board. Only the rank, common smell of men and the sea.

The rigging creaked and groaned, unnerving no one but Balasar. He had never loved traveling by water. Campaigning on land was no more comfortable, but at least when the day ended he was able to see that this village was not the one he'd been in the night before, the tree under which he slept looked out over some different hillside. Here, in the vast nothingness of water, they might almost have been standing still. Only the long white plume of their wake gave him a sense of movement, the visible promise that one day the journey would end. He would often sit at the stern, watch that constant trail, and take what solace he could from it. Sometimes he carved blocks of wax with a small, thin knife while his mind wandered and softened in the boredom of inaction.

It should not have surprised him that the isolation had proved corrosive for Eustin and Coal. And yet when one of the sailors rushed up to him that night, pale eyes bulging from his head, Balasar had not guessed the trouble. His man, the one called Eustin, was belowdecks with a knife, the sailor said. He was threatening to kill himself or else the crippled mascot dog, no one was sure which. Normally, they'd all have clubbed him senseless and thrown him over the side, but as he was a paying passage, the General might perhaps want to take a hand. Balasar put down the wax block half-carved into the shape of a fish, tucked his knife in his belt, and nodded as if the request were perfectly common.

The scene in the belly of the ship was calmer than he'd expected. Eustin sat on a bench. He had the dog by a rope looped around the thing's chest and a field dagger in his other hand. Ten sailors were standing in silence either in the room or just outside it, armed with blades and cudgels. Balasar ignored them, taking a low stool and setting it squarely in front of Eustin before he sat.

"General," Eustin said. His voice was low and flat, like a man half-dead from a wound.

"I hear there's some issue with the animal."

"He ate my soup."

One of the sailors coughed meaningfully, and Eustin's eyes narrowed and flickered toward the sound. Balasar spoke again quickly.

"I've seen Coal sneak half a bottle of wine away from you. It hardly seems a killing offense."

"He didn't steal my soup, General. I gave it to him."

"You gave it to him?"

"Yessir."

The room seemed close as a coffin, and hot. If only there weren't so many men around, if the bodies were not so thick, the air not so heavy with their breath, Balasar thought he might have been able to think clearly. He sucked his teeth, struggling to find something wise or useful to say, some way to disarm the situation and bring Eustin back from his madness. In the end, his silence was enough.

"He deserves better, General," Eustin said. "He's broken. He's a sick, broken thing. He shouldn't have to live like that. There ought to be some dignity at least. If there's nothing else, there should at least be some dignity."

The dog whined and craned its neck toward Eustin. Balasar could see distress in the animal's eyes, but not fear. The dog could hear the pain in Eustin's voice, even if the sailors couldn't. The bodies around him were wound tight, ready for violence, all of them except for Eustin. He held the knife weakly. The tension in his body wasn't the hot, loose energy of battle; he was knotted, like a boy tensed against a blow; like a man facing the gallows.

"Leave us alone. All of you," Balasar said.

"Not without Tripod!" one of the sailors said.

Balasar met Eustin's eyes. With a small shock he realized it was the first time he'd truly looked at the man since they'd emerged from the desert. Perhaps he'd been ashamed of what he might see reflected there. And perhaps his shame had some part in this. Eustin was *his* man, and so the pain he bore was Balasar's responsibility. He'd been weak and stupid to shy away from that. And weakness and stupidity always carried a price.

"Let the dog go. There's no call to involve him, or these men," Balasar said. "Sit with me awhile, and if you still need killing, I'll be the one to do it."

Eustin's gaze flickered over his face, searching for something. To see whether it was a ruse, to see whether Balasar would actually kill his own man. When he saw the answer, Eustin's wide shoulders eased. He dropped the rope, freeing the animal. It hopped in a circle, uncertain and confused.

"You have the dog," Balasar said to the sailors without looking at them. "Now go."

They filed out, none of them taking their eyes from Eustin and the knife still in his hand. Balasar waited until they had all left, the low door pulled shut behind them. Distant voices shouted over the creaking timbers, the oil lamp swung gently on its chain. This time, Balasar used the silence intentionally, waiting. At first, Eustin looked at him, anticipation in his eyes. And then his gaze passed into the distance, seeing something beyond the room, beyond them both. And then silently, Eustin wept. Balasar shifted his stool nearer and put his hand on the man's shoulder.

"I keep seeing them, sir."

"I know."

"I've seen a thousand men die one way or the other. But . . . but that was on a field. That was in a fight."

"It isn't the same," Balasar said. "Is that why you wanted those men to throw you in the sea?"

Eustin turned the blade slowly, catching the light. He was still weeping, his face now slack and empty. Balasar wondered which of them he was seeing now, which of their number haunted him in that moment, and he felt the eyes of the dead upon him. They were in the room, invisibly crowding it as the sailors had.

"Can you tell me they died with honor?" Eustin breathed.

"I'm not sure what honor is," Balasar said. "We did what we did because it was needed, and we were the men to do it. The price was too high for us to bear, you and I and Coal. But we aren't finished, so we have to carry it a bit farther. That's all."

"It wasn't needed, General. I'm sorry, but it *wasn't*. We take a few more cities, we gain a few more slaves. Yes, they're the richest cities in the world. I know it. Sacking even one of the cities of the Khaiem would put more gold in the High Council's coffers than a season in the Westlands. But how much do they need to buy Little Ott back from hell?" Eustin asked. "And why shouldn't I go there and get him myself, sir?"

"It's not about gold. I have enough gold of my own to live well and die old. Gold's a tool we use—a tool *I* use—to make men do what must be done."

"And honor?"

"And glory. Tools, all of them. We're men, Eustin. We've no reason to lie to each other."

He had the man's attention now. Eustin was looking only at him, and there was confusion in his eyes—confusion and pain—but the ghosts weren't inside him now.

"Why then, sir? Why are we doing this?"

Balasar sat back. He hadn't said these words before, he

had never explained himself to anyone. Pride again. He was haunted by his pride. The pride that had made him take this on as his task, the work he owed to the world because no one else had the stomach for it.

"The ruins of the Empire were made," he said. "God didn't write it that the world should have something like that in it. Men *created* it. Men with little gods in their sleeves. And men like that still live. The cities of the Khaiem each have one, and they look on them like plow horses. Tools to feed their power and their arrogance. If it suited them, they could turn their andat loose on us. Hold our crops in permanent winter or sink our lands into the sea or whatever else they could devise. They could turn the world itself against us the way you or I might hold a knife. And do you know why they haven't?"

Eustin blinked, unnerved, Balasar thought, by the anger in his voice.

"No, sir."

"Because they haven't yet chosen to. That's all. They might. Or they might turn against each other. They could make everything into wastelands just like those. Acton, Kirinton, Marsh. Every city, every town. It hasn't happened yet because we've been lucky. But someday, one of them *will* grow ambitious or mad. And then all the rest of us are ants on a battlefield, trampled into the mud. That's what I mean when I say this is needed. You and I are seeing that it never happens," he said, and his words made his own blood hot. He was no longer uncertain or touched by shame. Balasar grinned wide and wolfish. If it was pride, then let him be proud. No man could do what he intended without it. "When I've finished, the god-ghosts of the Khaiem will be a story women tell their babes to scare them at night, and nothing more than that. *That's* what Little Ott died for. Not for money or conquest or glory.

"I'm saving the world," Balasar said. "So, now. Say you'd rather drown than help me."

Voted

**#1 Science Fiction Publisher
20 Years in a Row**

by the *Locus* Readers' Poll

———•———

Please join us at the website below
for more information about this
author and other science fiction,
fantasy, and horror selections, and to
sign up for our monthly newsletter!

www.tor-forge.com

BRANDON SANDERSON'S

MISTBORN™

ADVENTURE GAME

LEAP INTO THE ACTION!

Developed with series creator Brandon Sanderson,
the *Mistborn Adventure Game*™ is your passport to experience
the adventure and intrigue firsthand, creating your own hero
and joining a unique crew that may very well change the world.

For more information visit
www.mistbornrpg.com